AUBREY

Nukeville

(Book One)

By
Neil Hannam

Dedication

For my Boys, Louis and Finlay
'Don't stop dreaming'

Chapter 1
03:00 hours, August 1ˢᵗ 2024
Brancaster Woodland, Norfolk Coastline

The double coat was water resistant, perfect for chasing down assailants in a storm; the hunt was on and the scent was getting stronger. Its nose brushed the ground, ignoring pine cones and small twigs, instead it searched for heavy skin particles that may have fallen from the convict during the escape. Betty pulled hard, trying to accelerate up the ridge towards the woodlands that sat proudly on top of the sand bank.

The dynamic canvas of chaos lay directly ahead, as the impressive darkness swallowed the trees. The air felt alive with tension, heavy and humid, charged with heavy rain battering the coast. Suddenly, jagged streaks of lightning tore across the night sky, illuminating the spiralling clouds in stark white and purple tone. Thunder followed, a deep rolling growl miles off shore, resonating in Ross's chest as he advanced up hill, his feet slipping on the muddy surface.

The wind whipped through the woodland, creating a symphony of hissing and howling as the branches swayed. The path was becoming more slippery as the dog, PC Ross Redman and his brother Jack tried to navigate the hill, a small stream of water cascaded down towards Betty who ignored the cold sensation on her paws and dug in as she continued to pull. The German Shepherd was large in comparison to most dogs, standing twenty-four inches tall and weighing seventy pounds, the muscular, well-balanced canine was the perfect tracker.

'Hey Betty, stop pulling so hard…..oh shit!' Ross Redman lost his balance, falling flat on his face and started to slide back down the path, still holding on to the reigns tightly. The dog was being dragged backwards with her handler as she tried stopping herself rolling, jostling from side to side, trying to break free of the reigns. A hand grabbed the young Officers shoulder halting his descent, 'Oi knuckle head, if you ain't got the strength, then blooming give me the mutt;' Jack Redman stood over his younger sibling, bent down and snatched the lead out of his hand. Annoyed, Ross tried to jump up, but lost his footing and slid down the path a few more feet. 'Hey, give me that back you dick!'

A loud whomping noise could be heard overhead as the trees lit up quickly as the NPAS helicopter passed over the canopy, then a deep and consuming blackness resumed, enveloping everything as it quickly flew away to the west. Inside the fuselage, the pilot monitored the horizon and trees below as he followed the shoreline, trying to peer through the heavy rain as it hit the screen. 'Can you see anything? The Co-Pilot stared out the side windows, 'I can't see shit.' A small red indicator flashed on the dashboard followed by a shallow repetitive beep, the Co-Pilot quickly looked down, 'we have thirty minutes,' the Pilot nodded, 'do we have comms yet?' The Co-Pilot shook his head, 'no, comms is still down, bloody weathers playing havoc with the instruments as well, the IRST is still temperamental,' watching the screen flicker.

On the ground, the brothers craned their necks, exhaling mist into the chilly air as they watched the helicopter execute a flawless one-eighty two high above the canopy. The searching blinked out, leave the landscape cloaked in darkness. A faint hum lingered before the chopper vanished into the night. 'Well, I guess we're officially on our own now!' Ross muttered, sinking into the damp ground. The icy water seeped through his cargo trousers, but he barely noticed, his gaze still fixed on the sky. Jack squinted looking up the slope, then glanced at his watch, 'no way that's been two hours already,' his voice was edged with doubt. 'Seventy minutes, tops, but they burned a ton of fuel hovering over those lovebirds in the car park, and it's at least a thirty-minute flight back to the airfield.' The hillside loomed above them, its shadowed contours ominous and indifferent to their plight.

Ross muttered a curse under his breath, thrusting his hand upward towards his brother, silently begging for a pull. But Jack barely glanced at him, instead, he tightened the harness around his wrist, feeling the relentless tug of Betty. 'Heel, you stupid dog!' he shouted, but the dog wasn't slowing. She had her own agenda, dragging him up the muddy path with a single-minded determination.

Gritting his teeth, Ross pushed himself onto one knee, only for the bushes to his left explode in a shower of water. The sudden commotion sent him sprawling back onto his rear, skidding painfully further down the slick hillside. He screamed, his voice swallowed by the pounding rain; for a moment, all he could hear was his own heart hammering in his chest. Then a shadow loomed above. Blinking, Ross wipes his eyes clearing his vision, Sargeant Paul Stewart stood over him, his gloved hand extended like a lifeline. 'Get up lad,' he commanded, his voice was a mixture of exasperation and urgency, 'I've been looking for you two.'

Behind, Jack's laughter echoed over the storm, he was still being hauled uphill by Betty, the dogs tail wagging like she was on the hunt of a lifetime. 'We've lost our eyes in the sky,' Paul said grimly, as he pulled Ross to his feet, his grip like iron. 'For now, it's just us…and the dog.' 'Why didn't you call us on the radio Sarge?' Ross's tone was firm, but Paul barely seemed to notice. The Sargeant's eyes darted around the clearing, scanning the surroundings with an unsettling distraction. Ross opened his mouth to repeat the question when Paul finally turned back, his face tight with unease, 'this area's a dead zone for comms, we've lost contact with the pilot. Commands scrambling to get us some military grade radios, better range, stronger signal.' His words were clipped, almost hurried, as if something unseen demanded his attention.

He started to turn away, then hesitated, fixing Ross with a sharp look, 'you remember the emergency protocol. If we see red flare, we high-tail back to the car park, double time, no exceptions.' Before Ross could respond, Paul was already striding up the path, his voice ringing out over the tension, 'Jack, control that dog will you?...........no, just stay there, we will come to you.…..I said wait for me and your brother.' His words lingered in the crisp air as he disappeared into the shadows ahead.

Ross scanned his surroundings, his eyes straining against the oppressive darkness. The storm didn't just soak the forest, it smothered it, reducing visibility to mere meters. Raindrops lashed against his face as he squinted into the void, the beam of his flashlight swallowed by the dense trees. He pulled out his phone, muttering a curse under his breath. The GPS was still down, 'bloody technology,' he grumbled, shoving it back into his pocket. 'Should've brought a compass;' he'd checked the forecast back in the car park whilst they unloaded from transit, it hadn't been promising then, and it wasn't any better now. They had no maps, no coordinates, nothing but Betty, to guide them through the maze of drenched undergrowth. The unspoken hope hung heavy in the air; that said, she'd catch the convict's scent before the storm erased it entirely.

A while later, the rain continued to hammer the ground like a relentless drumbeat, drowning out every sound. Ross couldn't help but wonder if the Sarge would call it off, retreating to the safety of the car park. A faint hope stirred at the thought, but he doubted it. They'd come too far, and the convict wouldn't wait for better weather. Each step along the slippery path sent water squelching into his boots, the damp cold creeping through socks. He glanced up, spotting Jack striding ahead with Betty, the dogs tail continued wagging as if the storm didn't exist. Ross shivered, his hands stinging with the chill. A curse escaped under his breath as he noticed the mud caked beneath his nails, why hadn't he packed gloves? He tried to scrape the dirt away on his jacket, but the cold and wet made the effort futile. Looking up again, he saw the beam of Jack's torch bouncing erratically through the thick foliage, the light growing dimmer as the distance between them stretched. Ross quickened his pace, unease gnawing at him.

Feeling exposed and uneasy, Ross broke into a cautious jog up the slick hill, his senses on high alert. Every shadow seemed alive, the storm amplifying the tension as he struggled to maintain his footing on the treacherous ground. The rain had turned the slope into a quagmire, and his boots slid underfoot with every step. 'Sarge,' he called out, his voice carrying just enough pierce through the storm. 'You think Command might call off the search?' Paul stopped abruptly, turning to face him. The torch in his hand flared directly into Ross's eyes, forcing him to throw up a hand. 'Hey, I can't see!' Ross protested squinting against the glare.

Paul's face was unreadable, shadowed in the harsh light. His tone was as cold as the rain slicing through the night. 'Look, I know the conditions are crap, but remember, it's just as bad for the maniac out there. The sooner we find him, the sooner we get out of this mess. Got it?' 'Yes, Sarge.' Ross swallowed hard, staring down at his mud caked boots, the chill seeping into his bones. He already knew how the night would end, back at the station, scrubbing the dirt boots and polishing the surface until he could see his own reflection again, the frustration of the search replaying in his mind.

Paul cast a quick glance toward Jack, who stood silhouetted near the ridge's edge, his posture tense as the wind whipped around him. Beside him, Betty sat unnervingly still, her ears perked, and her tongue lolling lazily to one side of her mouth as if the cold air was her only concern. 'Alright,' Paul said, his voice firm but low, 'let's catch up with your brother. Once we're together, keep a two-meter spread. Getting lost out here is bad enough, but getting lost in the dark with a psycho on the loose? Not exactly on my bucket list.' His tone carried a sharp edge, one that left little room for argument. As they fell into step, Ross matched Paul's stride, taking the rare quiet moment to probe for more information. 'So, what's the deal with this guy?' he asked, his voice just loud enough to be heard. The question hung in the air as the two men trudged side by side, the rain drumming a relentless rhythm on their gear.

'Sarge, I've gone over the briefing,' Ross began, his voice edged with hesitation, 'it was…. well, sketchy at best. But there's one thing I just can't wrap my head around.' He glanced at Paul, hoping for a flicker of engagement, but the man's face was a mask – blank, emotionless, unwavering. Ross couldn't help but think he'd have the perfect poker face. But the rain-soaked forest wasn't a casino, and there was no time for games. Shaking off the thought, he pressed on. 'How does an old man escape a Category A prison,' he said, his words picking up speed, 'spend a week dodging towns and villages with barely any supplies, killing random civilians along the way, and then magically show up on the Norfolk coast – a hundred and fifty miles from London.

* * *

The sclera was swollen and streaked with vivid dark crimson veins, as ice blue eyes stared beneath a canopy of rain-soaked matted grey hair. His breath came in ragged, uneven gasps, each one scraping his throat as his pounding heart threatened to burst from his chest. Time had long since turned against him, his skin, once taut and strong, had surrendered its battle with age. The loss of collagen and elastin had left his face and arms resembling sun-weathered leather. Yet, despite the sagging flesh, the muscles beneath remained wiry and unyielding, even as fatigue clawed at his body like a relentless predator. He glanced down at his hand; the grip was steady despite the ache radiating through his arms. Rain washed over him, mingling with the blood that dripped from his fingers, coursing down the slick handle of his Bowie knife. It pooled briefly on the six-inch blade before surrendering to gravity, falling onto the lifeless figure sprawled beneath him.

Inhaling the damp cold air, the Officer held his neck with both hands, trying to prevent the blood from leaving his body through the large laceration across his neck. His white collar started to turn pink, as the blood found its way down on the ground, forming a large crimson puddle next to his shoulders. A dark silhouette stood over him, watching, waiting.

The shouts and barks grew louder, echoing through the storm-drenched forest. They were closing in. He stood frozen, weighing his options, the rain winding down his crooked nose like a cold, mocking reminder of his precarious situation. Closing his eyes, he blocked out the chaotic drum of his heartbeat and listened. The wind hissed through the drenched canopy, shaking the leaves under the relentless downpour. Footsteps splashed through the muck, accompanied by urgent voices, each one sharper, closer. Somewhere beyond the trees, the rhythmic crash of waves against the beach tempted him with fleeting thoughts of escape. But the hunters—three of them—were far too close.

His gaze fell to the body at his feet, lifeless and crumpled. A decision made itself. Kneeling down, he reached out and stroked the dead man's hair, bloodied strands sticking to his fingers like a grotesque memento. Then, with deliberate precision, he drew his blade and pressed it to the corpse's forehead. The steel slid through the skin effortlessly, his practiced hand carving carefully—first one way, then the other. The forest sounds pulsed in his ears: the wind, the rain, the relentless approach of his pursuers. But his focus never wavered. When the task was complete, he wiped the blade clean against his sleeve, smearing the blood into streaks on the dark fabric. Gently, he slid two fingers over the man's eyelids, pressing them shut. The final touch. With a fluid motion, he tucked the knife into the back of his belt and rose, vanishing into the shadows before the shouting voices broke through the trees.

***

"Give it to me, hey, are you even listening?" Jack pressed forward, ignoring his brother's protests. Paul lagged behind, straining his ears against the relentless patter of rain as it drummed on the leaves above. Betty halted suddenly, her nose twitching in the damp, chilled air. Ross, who had been walking beside Jack, stopped as well, eyeing Betty's movements before glancing at his brother. "What's she picking up, eh?" he muttered. Paul joined them, his gaze sharp, scanning the woods behind them. "Keep your eyes peeled, lads. If Betty's onto something, we could be close." With the exception of the beating rain, the forest was eerily quiet as they waited, tense with anticipation, to see which direction the dog would take. The path ahead split in two—left or right—and with the rain washing away any signs, there were no footprints or broken branches to guide them. All they had was Betty's keen nose to choose their way.

Jack gripped Betty's harness tightly with one hand, the beam of his torch slicing through the darkness, casting fleeting shadows over the wet foliage as it swept left and right. The light flickered over every branch, every leaf, but offered no answers. Ross stepped closer, reaching for the harness, but Jack shoved him off with a quick nudge. "Knock it off," he muttered, his tone sharp. Paul moved in, his voice low and tense. "I don't like this. I don't like this one bit." Jack continued to sweep the light ahead, but Ross couldn't hold back, turning to Paul. "Sarge, what do we do?" Paul shot a glance at the young Officer and held up a finger, signalling him to hold tight. He then fished a small radio from his vest, bringing it to his lips with practiced calm. "Tango Eight to Bravo Charlie One, over." His voice crackled through the static. He waited, heart pounding in the silence. "Tango Eight to command, do you read, over?" Nothing.

A long pause. Paul pressed the transmit button again, the only sound their breath and the distant rumble of rain. Finally, he clipped the radio back to his vest with a resigned sigh, lifting his eyes to meet the worried gazes of the brothers. Their faces were a mirror of the fear gnawing at him. Without a word, he fumbled for his phone, checking the signal with frustration. "This is ridiculous," he muttered under his breath, regretting the words the moment they left his lips. But looking up, he saw the uncertainty in Ross and Jack's eyes—he didn't need to say any more. The silence between them said it all.

"Look, lads, there's nothing to fear," Paul said, trying to project calm into the tension-filled air. "It's just an old man, probably lost and exhausted. There's three of us, and another fifty Officers scouring this stretch of the coast. Plus, Halo Two will be return, give us a better chance of finding this guy." But Ross, his nerves beginning to fray, snapped back, "There could be a hundred of us out here, and I'd still put all my money on that madman out there." Paul sighed, frustration bubbling up. Jack stepped forward, "for pity's sake, Sarge, can't we just send this coward back to Command?" Ross's face hardened with rage, his patience finally breaking. Without warning, he spun around, his teeth clenched, and grabbed his brother by the jacket, shoving him hard. "Don't you dare call me a coward," he growled, his anger boiling over, 'fuck you, you're just as scared, don't act like some kind of tough guy.'

Jack yanked Betty back, his hand tightening on the harness as he lunged toward his brother, ready to escalate the confrontation. But Paul was faster, stepping in between them with a forceful presence. Before he could deliver his reprimand, a low growl rumbled from Betty's chest, sending a chill down their spines. In a flash, they all turned towards the path leading to the beach, the hairs on the back of their necks standing on end.

"Focus, lads," Paul commanded, his voice cutting through the tension like a knife. "I want lights scanning left, right, and centre. Jack, keep a tight grip on Betty—let her lead the way, and don't you dare release her until I say so. Understood?" Jack nodded, the urgency of the moment sharpening his focus. He swung his torch forward, its beam slicing through the dark as Betty moved ahead, nose low, instincts on high alert. Paul and Ross flanked him, their torches sweeping the shadows, every step an uneasy step deeper into the unknown.

***

The car park was accessed via a narrow single-track road that veered off from the A149, but today, it was a different story. A temporary barrier now blocked the entrance, and two patrol cars sat parked across it, their flashing blue lights casting an eerie glow in the rain. Four Officers stood vigil, fending off a small group of journalists, ushering them away with an air of quiet authority, as the steady downpour soaked everything in its path.

DCI Stephen Craig emerged from the public toilets, adjusting his trousers with a casual air, his eyes scanning the bustling car park as he navigated between the rows of police vehicles. Officers and emergency staff stood in small clusters, deep in conversation, their voices barely rising above the constant hum of the operation. He skirted around them, his gaze momentarily drifting toward the woodland where a helicopter flew south, its blades cutting through the grey sky, but he paid it no mind.

Approaching the Command trailer, he opened the door and entered, the atmosphere inside a hive of activity. Staff moved swiftly between desks; their faces set with purpose as they worked tirelessly to process information. The DCI made his way to his own desk, a silent presence amidst the chaos. His eyes immediately landed on a black-and-white mugshot pinned to the board in front of him, a striking image that seemed to pulse with meaning. Without missing a beat, he grabbed an envelope marked with the unmistakable "HMP Prison" label from his desk, flicking it open with his fingers. He thumbed through the new paperwork received an hour ago, his mind already working through the details, the weight of the investigation settling over him like a cloak.

"Sergeant Jones, where are we with comms?" The DCI's voice cut through the low hum of the Command trailer; his tone sharp with impatience. The female Officer turned from her desk, her posture stiff as she responded, "Still down, Sir. Engineers are in transit, but their ETA is at least three more hours." The DCI scoffed, glancing at his watch with a grimace. "Bloody hell, that's after sunrise. By then, the convict could be halfway across the North Sea. What is the hold-up?" "Latest reports say there's congestion on the M11."

The DCI's brows furrowed, his frustration mounting. He took a couple of quick strides forward, checking his watch again, as if willing time to speed up. "Congestion? What the hell are you talking about? It's 2 a.m.!" Sargeant Jones, caught off guard, avoided the DCI's gaze, instead focusing on the black-and-white photo pinned to the board over her superior's shoulder. "Apologies, Sir. There are roadworks on the M11. It's down to one lane." Without waiting for a response, she turned back to her desk, shuffling through paperwork with mechanical precision, clearly eager to move past the uncomfortable exchange.

The door of the trailer snapped open, letting in a gust of rain, as Officer Thorman entered, shaking off the water and shrugging out of his hi-vis jacket. He draped it over the back of a chair and glanced around, spotting the veteran DCI across the room. Without missing a beat, the DCI moved quickly across the polythene sheeting that covered the floor, his boots tapping sharply against the surface as he approached Thorman, who was already pouring a steaming cup of coffee into a polystyrene cup.

"Give me a quick rundown, Brian," the DCI said, his voice low but urgent. "What's going on out there?" The atmosphere in the trailer was thick with frustration and fatigue, a reflection of the relentless Norfolk weather that pounded the coastline. Brian took a long, slow sip of his coffee, wincing as it burned his lip, before he gestured for the DCI to follow him to the far end of the trailer, where the space was quieter. "Morale's low," he said, his voice barely rising above the hum of the busy trailer. "It's a bloody mess out there, Sir."

The DCI stood with his arms crossed, his expression unreadable, as he listened intently to Brian's report. The heavy rain outside seemed to echo the weight of the situation. "Well, to be honest, Sir," Brian began, his voice steady but tinged with frustration, "the weather's really complicating things. We've deployed ten Tangos — each with one Officer, one handler, and a Sergeant. Standard protocol, but without comms, our ground teams and air support cannot coordinate. It is like we are operating blind. The rain's washing away any trace of him—no footprints, nothing. It's like he's a ghost. Who the hell is this guy, Sir?" The DCI didn't answer the question, his eyes narrowing as he focused on the operational details. "I see," he said, his voice clipped. "How are you maintaining comms with the ground teams?"

Brian shifted uncomfortably, his face flushing slightly. "To be honest, Sir, we're not. The only option we have right now is Alamo—using a red flare to recall teams back to base. That's it. I can pull them back if you want, and we can just wait for comms to be fixed, but—" The DCI cut him off, his voice hard and decisive. "That's unacceptable, Brian, and you know it. This man is a killer. The longer he's out there, the more bodies we'll find." His gaze locked onto Brian's, every word carrying the weight of urgency.

The DCI looked over Brian's shoulder, his eyes tracking the movements of the Officers in the trailer. Suddenly, the door opened lifted again, and another Officer darted inside, scanning the space before locking eyes with the DCI. Without a word, the Officer hurried over, handing the DCI a folded piece of paper. Taken it, he unfolded the paper with a grimace, his eyes quickly scanning the contents. A bitter laugh escaped him. "Oh, this just gets better and better," he muttered, the frustration clear in his voice.

Brian, who had been holding his breath, couldn't stand the silence any longer. "What's wrong, Sir?" he asked, his voice tight with concern. The DCI didn't answer immediately. Instead, he handed the paper back to the Officer with a slow, deliberate motion as he walked past. "Halo Two needs fuel, we've just lost the initiative," he said, his tone heavy with the weight of the news. The words hung in the air, settling over them like a storm cloud.

***

The oak tree stood thirty feet from the ground, the lobed leaves with pointed ends provided cover from the rain. The deeply grooved thick sturdy trunk felt rugged under his hands as he watched, ten feet below, three Policemen and a dog walked past, arching their torches in unison creating the perfect arch over the woodland.

With the Bowie knife clutched between his teeth, he reached for the nearest branch, ensuring it was thick enough—about a few inches in diameter—and ripped it free from the trunk with a brutal yank. Lightning tore across the sky in a flash of brilliance, illuminating the path ahead as he watched the Officers disappear into the distance, their figures swallowed by the rain and darkness.

He retrieved the knife from his mouth, expertly using the blade to slice away the excess branches and leaves, his movements swift and precise. A sudden bark from the dog cut through the air, sharp and urgent, signalling they were still close. He quickened his work, stripping the branch with his hands before carefully shaping one end into a deadly point. Glancing around, he surveyed the area with a hunter's eye, ensuring he was unseen. From his backpack, he pulled out a small lighter, lighting it briefly before holding the flame to the tip of the spear, using the tree as a shield against the relentless wind.

The dog's barking grew more frantic, a sharp, desperate sound that echoed through the dense underbrush. He watched intently as the bushes ahead rustled violently, a sure sign that they were almost upon the body. Dropping the spear to the ground with a soft thud, he quickly stashed the knife and lighter in his pocket, his movements fluid and instinctive. His eyes darted to the nearest tree branch, his grip tightening around it as he prepared to drop. He glanced down briefly, calculating his next move, then let go. His body dropped, a heartbeat of weightlessness before his hands shot out to grab the next branch eight feet below. The impact rattled through his ribs, but he gritted his teeth, ignoring the searing pain as his muscles absorbed the shock. Without hesitation, he let go again, plummeting downward, each drop faster than the last, his eyes scanning the shadows below for what came next.

In an instant, he hit the ground, the impact barely slowing his momentum. His eyes locked onto the spear, now embedded vertically in the soft mud, and with a swift motion, he seized it from the earth. As soon as the spear touched his palm, he was gone, melting into the undergrowth like a shadow. The dog's frantic barking served as his guide, its echo bouncing off the trees, helping him zero in on their location. With every step, he moved faster, his senses sharp, the sounds of the night swirling around him as he closed in on his target.

Chapter 2
22:20 hours, July 20th 2024
Green Park, London

A lifeless mouse lay sprawled on its side in the middle of the narrow road, its fragile body a grim prize for the pair of quarrelsome crows flapping and screeching around it. The evening air echoed with their grating caws, a discordant symphony reverberating off the stately red brick façades of the Victorian townhouses that lined the street like silent, disapproving witnesses. The rodents' limp form became the centrepiece of a macabre ballet, the crows hopping and lunging in their relentless bid for dominance.

Their ragged beaks tore into the mouse's delicate flesh, each savage peck unveiling a grotesque banquet cloaked in shadow beneath the grade II listed architecture.

The road itself, flanked by cars resting in precisely marked bays, bore the detached sterility of routine urban life. Towering sycamore trees stood sentinel on either side, their naked branches clawing at the dimming sky, casting skeletal patterns across the cobbled sidewalks. Above, the windows of the four-story homes glowed faintly, a patchwork of warmth against the chill of the descending night. Inside, residents sought comfort from the biting cold, their fireplaces roaring to life. Orange embers danced behind iron grates, sending serpentine wisps of smoke spiralling upwards through the grand chimneys, escaping into the sprawling expanse of London's twilight skyline.

Beyond the street, the city pulsed with its own rhythm—a distant hum of traffic, faint echoes of hurried footsteps, and the occasional bark of a restless dog. Yet here, in this quiet enclave, time seemed momentarily stilled by the dark drama playing out below. The crows, undeterred by the creeping frost or the indifferent gaze of passersby, pressed on with their grisly feast. The mouse, reduced now to little more than a tattered relic, became a silent testimony to the primal struggle for survival. Overhead, the first stars pricked through the haze, indifferent to the small, violent theatre unfolding beneath their eternal watch.

Number Seven Curzon Street stood apart from the other grand, Georgian buildings that lined the avenue, its scars telling a tale of resilience. During the Blitz, a relentless bombing campaign had savaged its structure, leaving it battered and roofless while its neighbours remained largely intact. The restoration had been practical, not indulgent—its roof reimagined as a modest studio flat, a stark departure from the opulent family homes that surrounded it. This flat, the only one of its kind in the well-heeled neighbourhood, carried an air of quiet defiance, a testament to the era's ingenuity and the city's ability to adapt under pressure.

Dr. Bill Bonny, a wiry man with an ever-present furrow in his brow, had first arrived in London a decade ago. Freshly graduated and full of ambition, he had sought the buzzing opportunities of the capital, quickly securing work as a junior consultant at one of its prestigious hospitals. The studio, with its proximity to Green Park Underground Station—a brisk five-minute walk-through leafy streets—had been a godsend. Compact and unadorned, it was worlds away from the sprawling apartments occupying the rest of Number Seven. But to Bill, the flat offered precisely what he needed: a functional space that fit within his meagre budget, leaving room for the occasional indulgence in books, records, or a pint at the pub down the road.

Over the years, the flat became his sanctuary, though not without its drawbacks. The walls seemed to hold the whispers of its tumultuous past, faint drafts slipping through aging seals in the windows, and a ceiling that carried ominous cracks like veins running across its surface. Eight years on, the sheen of new beginnings had worn thin. Bill sat on the edge of his narrow bed one dreary evening; his reflection dimly visible in the warped mirror propped against the wall. Papers and medical journals lay strewn across a small desk, abandoned in favour of his mounting introspection.

The air felt heavy, oppressive, as if the very fabric of the room conspired to confine him. His gaze wandered across the crumbling plaster, his imagination turning the imperfections into grotesque shapes that loomed over him like spectres of failure. The weight of his choices—staying here, taking the safe path, enduring the solitude—pressed upon him, squeezing his chest until his breaths grew shallow. The future he had once envisioned with such clarity now seemed murky, obscured by a fog of weariness and routine.

Outside, the sounds of the city drifted in: the faint rumble of a passing bus, the laughter of revellers making their way home, the distant toll of a church bell marking the hour. These noises only deepened his isolation, a cruel reminder of the world carrying on without him. With a sigh, Bill reached for the bedside lamp, his hand brushing against the cold metal base. He paused for a moment, staring into the muted glow that seemed to hold back the encroaching darkness.

Then, with a quiet resolve, he switched it off, plunging the room into shadow. As he lay back, the ceiling's cracks seemed to disappear into the void above him. His thoughts churned, heavy and restless, until exhaustion claimed him. Tomorrow was uncertain, but for now, he would surrender to the darkness, allowing the city's ceaseless hum to lull him into uneasy sleep.

***

06:30 hours, July 21st 2024 - Green Park, London

The following morning unfolded with a quiet majesty. The sun, a molten orb in the east, painted the horizon in strokes of gold and amber, the colours deepening as they spread across the sky. Fluffy clouds, soft as down, blushed with shades of pink and coral, drifting lazily as if unconcerned with the day's demands. The city below began to stir, its waking hum still faint but unmistakable. Inside the modest studio flat, a single ray of sunlight found its way through a narrow gap in the heavy, rugged curtains. It stretched across the room, climbing the walls before settling delicately on Bill's face, coaxing him from the depths of his dream.

He blinked once, twice, the sharpness of the waking world coming into focus. His gaze drifted upward, catching sight of a cobweb swaying gracefully in the soft breeze that slipped through a tiny crack in the window frame. The spider's creation danced with purpose, a fragile yet persistent work of art in the otherwise unremarkable room.

The warmth of the sunlight nudged him fully awake, its golden caress dispelling the lingering fog of sleep. Bill exhaled deeply and swung his legs over the side of the bed, his bare feet meeting the cool floor. He stretched upward, arching his back until he felt the satisfying pull of muscles stiff from the night. A yawn escaped him, unhurried and primal, as his toes flexed against the floorboards. For a moment, he stood there, soaking in the stillness of the early morning, the sounds of the city outside muted by the thick walls. His eyes landed on the microwave clock, its neon digits glowing steadily.

The time stirred something in him, a pang of urgency that banished his lingering tranquillity. With a resigned sigh, Bill weighed his options and swiftly made the decision to forgo breakfast. He shuffled towards the bathroom, his mind already darting ahead to the day's significance. Today wasn't just any day— it was the day.

He hurried through his morning routine, splashing cold water onto his face and smoothing down his unruly hair in front of the small, slightly tarnished mirror. He dressed with care but efficiency, slipping into a crisp white shirt and dark trousers, the uniform of his profession lending him a sense of purpose. The lab awaited, and with it, the culmination of months of meticulous work. Bill knew that arriving early would spare him the ordeal of battling the ever-growing throngs that swarmed London's streets and Underground during the rush hour.

The thought of jostling for space among the hordes was enough to propel him forward with determination. He grabbed his satchel from the chair by the window, double-checking its contents: notes, files, and the packed lunch he had hastily assembled the night before.

Racing down the narrow staircase, Bill took the steps two at a time, his every movement precise and deliberate, as though his mind and body had entered a state of perfect synchronization. The dimly lit stairwell echoed with the dull thuds of his hurried footsteps, the aged wood creaking beneath his weight. His momentum came to a sudden halt as he reached the final step, his hand instinctively bracing against the wall. Carefully, he stepped onto the chequered black-and-white floor tiles of the lobby, the icy chill of the polished surface seeping through his thin soles.

He paused, adjusting his weight, his gaze locking onto the mahogany door to his left. Behind it lay his landlady, Alison Clark—the self-appointed warden of the building and a woman whose sharp tongue and sharper temper had earned her the nickname "the old battle-axe." His heart thudded in his chest as he prayed silently that he might avoid her wrath this morning.

Taking a cautious step forward, Bill crept toward the heavy front door, his movements deliberate to keep the faintest whisper of sound from betraying him. His hand reached out for the brass handle, it's cool metal surface grounding him as he stole a glance over his shoulder. The corridor behind him was silent. For a fleeting moment, he felt the sweet relief of triumph—he was in the clear. He turned the handle, the latch clicking softly as it began to retract. Then came the sound he dreaded: a telltale creak from the mahogany door behind him. The noise sent a shiver down his spine, his stomach knotting as a sharp voice followed.

"Bonny! I want a word with you!"

Bill froze, his hand still on the door, his pulse quickening. Alison Clark's voice carried with it the kind of authority that could stop traffic—or, in this case, him dead in his tracks. For a moment, he debated turning to face her, rehearsing half-hearted excuses in his mind. But his nerves betrayed him. Instead, he opted for escape. Pretending not to hear her, he shoved the door open with one swift motion, its hinges groaning in protest. "Oi, you! Just you wait one goddamn minute!" Alison's slippered feet slapped against the tiles as she emerged into the lobby, hastily pulling her bright pink nightdress together.

She waved a clenched fist, her hair dishevelled and her eyes blazing with indignation. Bill, steadfast in his resolve, stepped over the threshold and onto the pavement outside. The cold morning air bit at his cheeks, but he didn't slow. Behind him, Alison's voice grew louder, fuelled by frustration. "You bloody wait right there, Bonny! I want to speak with you!"

Two pigeons, startled by Bill's sudden appearance, flapped noisily into the air, abandoning the crust of bread they'd been pecking at in the gutter. Without missing a beat, Bill vaulted down the short flight of concrete steps, his shoes crunching against the pavement as he broke into a run. "You owe me two months' rent, you hear me? Two months!" Alison shouted, her Cockney tones slicing through the morning stillness. She stormed out onto the street, planting herself squarely in the middle of the road, hands on her hips as she glared at his retreating figure. Her pink nightdress flapped in the breeze like a banner of war.

Bill didn't dare look back. His strides lengthened as he rounded the corner, his satchel bouncing against his hip. Behind him, Alison's words pursued him like a spectre. "Idiot! I'll be right here when you come crawling back tonight, mark my words!" A loud honk shattered the air as a car swerved to avoid her, its driver gesturing angrily. Alison turned, unperturbed, waving him off with an impatient hand. Stepping back toward the curb, she muttered curses under her breath, her slipper narrowly missing the skeletal remains of a rodent flattened against the asphalt. With a final glance toward the corner where Bill had disappeared, she huffed, shaking her head.

"Bloody useless," she muttered to herself, before retreating to the warmth of the apartment block, her slippers scuffing the ground as she went. The door slammed shut behind her, the building resuming its usual quiet, though the echoes of her tirade seemed to linger in the air.

A few minutes later, Bill found himself standing inside Green Park Underground Station; the damp chill of the northbound platform settling into his bones. He tucked his white shirt back into his trousers, smoothing the creases with deliberate care as he waited for the distant rumble of the next train. Across from him, a giant advertisement loomed: an eight-foot beefeater wielding a pike in one hand and clutching tickets to the London Dungeons in the other.

The oversized figure seemed to glare down from the crumbling station wall, its colours faded by years of grime and neglect. Bill scanned his surroundings, allowing himself a small, satisfied smile. Not only had he managed to evade Mrs. Clark's wrath, but he had also beaten the morning rush. The platform was blissfully empty, save for a few scattered early risers. Soon, the space would transform into a battlefield, as hordes of commuters descended in waves, a relentless tide of suits and skirts that would flood the station, jostling for space like cattle.

He had never understood the logic of the daily grind—the feverish rush to work, the monotonous routine of wake, work, eat, sleep, repeat. Every morning, it was the same: throngs of businessmen and women squeezing onto the packed trains, their faces pinched with irritation as they fought for a scrap of standing room. The memory of being wedged against a stranger's sweaty armpit still made his stomach churn. No, Bill had vowed long ago to avoid such indignities whenever possible, and today he had succeeded.

Looking down, he inspected his polished black shoes, ensuring his toes rested neatly behind the yellow safety line. A small scuff on the heel caught his eye, and he frowned. Lifting his foot, he rubbed the mark vigorously against his trouser leg, his focus narrowing to the rhythmic motion. He was so intent on the task that he didn't notice the figure approaching until a voice rasped from above him. "Got any change, mister?"

Startled, Bill looked up to see a man standing uncomfortably close. His yellowing teeth, crooked and decaying, curved into a grin that was anything but friendly. Long, greasy grey hair framed a weathered face, and the man's tattered shell suit—a relic of the 1980s—was streaked with dirt and old stains. A red-and-white duffel bag hung limply from one shoulder, while his free hand clutched a dented can of cheap beer. The man's bloodshot eyes locked onto Bill's, his voice growing louder and more insistent. "You mutt and jeff! I said, you got any lolly?" "W-what?" Bill stammered, caught off guard by the bizarre slang. The smell of stale alcohol wafted toward him, and he instinctively took a step back. Hoping to avoid any conflict, he turned slightly, signalling his disinterest. Perhaps the man would take the hint and move on. But he didn't. Instead, the man leaned in, his hot, sour breath brushing uncomfortably close to Bill's ear as he let out a belch that reeked of beer and bile. "Let me have a look," he slurred, his grimy fingers darting toward Bill's jacket pocket.

The moment his hand made contact; a surge of anger overrode Bill's initial caution. He shoved the man back forcefully, his voice rising in sharp indignation. "Get your hands off me, you piece of shit! Do you hear me? Crawl back into the gutter where you belong!" The tramp stumbled slightly, his eyes widening in mock surprise. For a moment, the air between them froze, thick with tension. Then, slowly, the man raised both hands in a gesture of exaggerated submission.

"Begging your pardon, me Lord," he said, his tone dripping with sarcasm. He tipped the now-empty beer can toward his lips, shaking it to drain the last, bitter dregs. With a casual flick of his wrist, he launched the can onto the train tracks below, the metallic clang echoing through the station. Bill's heart raced as he watched the man turn on his heel and shuffle away, his gait uneven, his grumbling voice trailing off into the distance.

As the dishevelled man shuffled away toward the southbound platform, his tattered shoes dragging noisily against the ceramic tiles, Bill exhaled deeply. He closed his eyes and silently counted to ten, a ritual to centre himself after any unwelcome encounter. When he opened them, the long curve of the northbound platform stretched out before him, its familiar contours bathed in the sterile light of flickering fluorescent tubes. His gaze drifted to a lone figure standing halfway along the platform.

The man, likely in his late fifties, was dressed in a shabby two-piece suit, the fabric worn thin at the elbows and cuffs. His trousers ended awkwardly above his ankles, revealing a pair of stained white socks, while the stitching on his scuffed leather shoes had given way, leaving one sole flapping precariously with each step. Bill couldn't help but study him. It wasn't a conscious habit, but a natural reflex—people-watching, cataloguing details of their attire and mannerisms. Perhaps it was his mind's way of filling the waiting moments, making a game of the mundane.

His attention shifted downward, catching movement along the concrete edge below the tracks. A tiny mouse darted out from the shadows, weaving expertly around the wooden sleepers as it foraged. Its whiskers twitched as it approached the discarded beer can the tramp had thrown moments before. Tentatively, the mouse sniffed at the liquid pooling at its base, its pink tongue flicking out to taste a droplet. It paused, its tiny body going rigid, as if the bitter tang of the alcohol had momentarily stunned its senses. With a quick shake of its head, the creature turned tail and scurried back into the darkness of the tunnel, its faint squeaks lost beneath the hum of the station.

The tinny crackle of the loudspeaker interrupted Bill's observation, announcing the arrival of the next train in two minutes. The automated voice rattled off a list of stops, ending with a monotonous safety reminder about standing behind the yellow line. As he shifted his weight, a warm gust of air signalled the train's approach, ruffling his cropped black hair and sending a swirl of dust and litter into the air. The fine particles danced in a chaotic mini-cyclone, and Bill instinctively turned his face away from the worst of it.

The screech of brakes grinding against metal filled the air, reverberating off the walls of the concrete tube. It was a sound Bill had grown used to over the years—a grating symphony of modern life. As the train sped past, just a meter from his face, he squinted, trying to gauge if there were any open seats or if he'd need to move further down the platform, closer to the man with the frayed shoes and white socks. Before he could make a decision, the sound of hurried footsteps echoed from the stairwell behind him. Someone was running, their shoes clapping loudly against the hard floor. "Damn it," Bill muttered under his breath, silently urging the train to stop and open its doors before the latecomers reached his spot.

His hopes were dashed as the train slowed at an excruciating pace, the feet behind him drawing closer.

Within seconds, he felt the subtle press of bodies encroaching on his personal space. A quick glance over his shoulder revealed his new companions. An elderly woman, her stooped figure wrapped in a long brown coat, stood directly behind him, her frail frame trembling slightly with the effort of breathing. She began to cough—a raspy, wet sound that sent an unpleasant spray of saliva particles onto the back of Bill's neck. Suppressing a shudder, he reached up to adjust the collar of his trench coat, hoping to shield himself from further contamination. The fabric refused to stay in place, flopping back down onto his shoulders with frustrating inevitability. Cringing, Bill retrieved a tissue from his trouser pocket, dabbing at the wet patch that now lingered on his skin. His stomach churned at the thought of airborne germs settling on him.

If there was one thing Bill hated more than being trapped next to someone's sweaty armpit, it was the invisible assault of microscopic invaders—airborne germs, sneezes, and coughs. He shot the woman a brief glance, her red-rimmed eyes suggesting she was oblivious to the offense, and turned his focus back to the train doors. The hiss of the brakes and the metallic groan of the opening doors drew his attention. Determined not to linger any longer in the confines of the platform, Bill stepped forward, resolute to find a seat and escape the unwelcome press of the morning crowd.

An elderly man stood beside the coughing woman, his wrinkled hand resting gently on her back as he tried to comfort her. "Get off, George, stop fussing," she rasped, batting his hand away. Her tone was sharp, but the edge softened by her obvious fatigue. George stepped back, guilt flickering across his face. "Sorry, love," he murmured, gripping the handle of a large duffel bag slung at his side, the bag's bulging contents betraying its purpose—her clothes, toiletries, and perhaps a few personal items for the hospital stay ahead. George tried again; his voice gentle but tinged with desperation. "Just a few stops on the train, and we'll be at St. Bart's Hospital.

Then you can rest, Joan, while the doctors make you better. How does that sound?" Joan didn't reply, her energy consumed by another fit of violent coughing. Bill turned slightly to observe the pair, noting George's deeply etched worry lines and Joan's pallid complexion. He glanced down at the polished tips of his shoes, his chest tightening with the grim knowledge he carried. They might reach St. Bart's, but Joan would never leave it alive. Within ten days, maybe less, she'd succumb to the aggressive cancer sweeping through the population—a silent assassin, indifferent to age or status. Another life lost, another name added to the mounting statistics of the pandemic.

A short, warm gust swept across his face as the train doors slid open with a hiss, the electronic beeps signalling it was time to board. Bill moved to step inside, placing one foot across the threshold when a broad-shouldered, bald man and his diminutive girlfriend brushed past him. "Oi, bloody wait, will you?" the man barked, barging through the doorway with the entitlement of someone who considered the world his own. Bill quickly stepped back, avoiding eye contact as the man's shoulder clipped him hard, nearly throwing him off balance. The girlfriend chuckled; a grating sound that made Bill grit his teeth. They strode toward the stairs without a backward glance, the man's booming voice fading as they disappeared. Shaking his head, Bill turned and finally boarded the train, the doors hissing shut behind him. He scanned the carriage, but almost every seat was taken. His eyes landed on the elderly couple, George now settled beside Joan, his arm around her shoulders as she continued her laboured breathing. Bill sighed under his breath. Give me a break.

Resigned, he brushed a few stray crumbs off the fabric of the standing cushion by the door and leaned against it. The faint vibration of the train hummed through the padding as it began to move. Across the aisle, a construction worker was slumped in his seat, fast asleep, his mouth wide open. Each exhale escaped with a faint whistle, loud enough to be annoying but not so much as to warrant a reprimand. Nestled protectively in his lap was a plastic lunchbox, topped with a neatly folded copy of the Metro. The bold red text of the front-page headline caught Bill's eye: "Pandemic Cancer Crisis Escalates."

He quickly averted his gaze, unable to stomach the irony of reading about the crisis while surrounded by its victims. His eyes landed on a young girl sitting across from him, no older than six or seven, bundled in a shabby coat with a patch sewn onto the elbow. Beside her was a woman who looked to be in her thirties, her hair pulled back into a messy bun. Bill guessed she was the girl's mother, likely a single parent working multiple jobs to keep a roof over their heads. The girl tugged at her mother's sleeve, her voice small and weak. "Mummy, I don't feel very well. I think I'm going to be sick."

Before the mother could respond, the girl began coughing—deep, wet, rattling bursts that made heads in the carriage turn. Saliva dribbled down her chin, leaving a sticky trail on her coat as her cheeks flushed with exertion. The mother pulled her daughter closer, her voice trembling as she whispered, "Not long now, darling. Let's grab a cab when we get off the train and go straight to the hospital, okay?"

The train rocked gently as it sped through the dark tunnel, the overhead lights flickering faintly. The girl coughed again, but this time it escalated. Tears streamed down her face as she gasped for air, her tiny chest heaving. "Honey, hey, can you hear me?" her mother pleaded, shaking her slightly. Panic tightened her voice. The girl's eyes rolled back, her small body convulsing before slumping into the seat.

"Help! Somebody help!" the mother screamed, her voice cutting through the rising chaos. Passengers surged forward, crowding around the pair as the mother cradled her daughter's limp form. A trickle of blood stained the girl's lips, sticky and vivid against her pale skin. George and Joan watched from their seats, the old man clutching his wife's hand tightly as she coughed into her handkerchief, her eyes glassy with shock.

Bill didn't move. He stared at the commotion, his pulse racing, but his feet felt rooted to the floor. His gaze flicked back to the construction worker's newspaper. The headline seemed to leap off the page, the word pandemic burning into his brain. He swallowed hard, his mouth dry. The train slowed as it approached Piccadilly Circus, the screech of the brakes mingling with the mother's frantic cries. Bill turned away, pressing his forehead against the cool glass divider beside him. The scene played on a loop in his mind—a snapshot of a world unravelling, with no promise of reprieve.

***

One hour later, Bill finally stepped off the train at St. Pancras Station, his usual twenty-minute journey stretched into a gruelling hour by the chaos of the morning. He found himself herded into the flow of passengers moving slowly through the tunnel, a throng of shuffling feet and muffled chatter echoing off the arched concrete walls. The crowd surged like ants in a colony, single-minded and steady, toward the escalator that loomed ahead. The station's lights buzzed overhead, their stark glow casting pale reflections on the polished tiles. Bill kept his eyes fixed downward, focusing on the feet in front of him. A pair of black and gold trainers walked in perfect rhythm with a cluster of scuffed boots and polished oxfords.

He adjusted his grip on his briefcase, the strap biting into his palm. The events of the morning still clung to him like a shadow, the little girl's pale face and the frantic cries of her mother etched into his mind.

"Doctor!" a voice called out, piercing the ambient hum. Bill's shoulders stiffened, but he didn't lift his gaze. He kept moving, hoping to dissolve into the sea of commuters. "Doctor Bonny! Hey, over here!" The voice was louder now, insistent. Bill glanced up, his eyes scanning the tunnel. Near the wall, a young man with dishevelled hair and a red body warmer waved enthusiastically. Jackson. Bill recognized the lab technician immediately but offered no acknowledgment, quickly looking back down. He pretended not to see, his pace steady as he pressed toward the escalator.

Emerging from the station, he inhaled deeply, the crisp morning air biting at his lungs and clearing the stale scent of the train from his nostrils. The towering structure of the Francis Crick Institute loomed across the street, its sleek sandstone façade and towering glass windows glinting in the pale sunlight. The building exuded an air of quiet power, home to over a thousand of the brightest minds in biomedical research. Bill adjusted his coat, his fingers brushing the lapel as he crossed the street toward the entrance. Inside, the atrium was bustling with activity. Scientists in lab coats hurried across the polished floors, clutching folders, tablets, and steaming cups of coffee. The hum of conversation mingled with the distant whir of machinery from the labs above. Bill made his way to the security desk, where the routine began.

He slipped off his trench coat and laid it carefully in a plastic tray alongside his briefcase. The conveyor belt buzzed softly as the tray disappeared into the x-ray machine's housing. A uniformed security guard sat behind the monitor, his eyes scanning the screen intently. Another guard stood by the body scanner; his hand outstretched to guide Bill forward. "Please step through, sir. Arms up and away from your body," the guard instructed, his tone brisk but not unfriendly. Bill complied; his movements mechanical. He avoided eye contact, his unease with authority making his throat tighten. The bright LED panel above the scanner flashed green, and the guard nodded him through. Bill retrieved his belongings from the tray and placed it in the designated rack, his motions deliberate and practiced.

"Please make sure to collect all of your belongings," the guard reminded, though Bill was already slipping his coat back on. It was the same routine every day—unvarying, predictable, and utterly necessary. Security in this building was tight, the protocols rigid and unyielding. No exceptions were made, regardless of rank or title.

As he stepped into the heart of the institute, Bill glanced up at the four blocks of labs arranged around the central atrium. The glass walls revealed glimpses of the work taking place within—scientists hunched over microscopes, the glow of computer screens illuminating their faces. The hum of innovation was palpable, a reminder of the immense responsibility they all carried. Bill's footsteps echoed as he headed toward the elevators. He adjusted his grip on his briefcase, his mind shifting gears. The weight of the morning lingered, but here, within these walls, he could focus. Here, he was not just another passenger on a crowded train or a tenant dodging a landlady—he was Dr. William Bonny, a man with a mission to confront the very thing threatening to unravel humanity.

Removing the lanyard from his neck, Bill swiped the ID card through the reader with practiced precision. The small LED above the chrome button glowed green, and he pressed it firmly, the faint hum of mechanics behind the wall signalling that the lift was on its way. Taking a few steps back, he watched the glowing numbers above the elevator doors as they ticked downward. The polished stainless steel reflected the subdued lighting of the lobby, catching a faint outline of his weary face. The lift arrived with a soft ping, its doors gliding open smoothly. He stepped into the empty cart, the faint scent of disinfectant lingering in the air, and pressed the button marked Sublevel 5. The ride down was always unnervingly quiet, the kind of silence that allowed his mind to wander to the darker corners of his thoughts. Just as the doors began to close, a familiar voice called out. "Doctor! Doctor Bonny, hold the door, please!"

Bill turned his head slightly, catching sight of Scott Barry, his lab coat billowing as he hurriedly gathered his belongings from the security desk. For a brief moment, Bill's hand hovered near the door button, but then a flicker of irritation crossed his face. Instead, he let the doors slide shut, a polite smile still lingering on his lips as he said under his breath, "Sorry, maybe next time." The elevator began its descent, and Bill leaned back against the cool metal wall, letting out a deep sigh. His briefcase rested by his feet, and his coat was slung over one arm. The rhythmic hum of the lift moving downward provided a monotonous backdrop for his thoughts as he watched the numbers on the small panel descend.

Over the last two years, Bill's team had analysed more than one hundred and fifty thousand samples, each one a grim reminder of how aggressive this cancer had become. The disease seemed to evolve with terrifying speed, outpacing treatments and slashing life expectancy by seventy-five percent in those diagnosed. Hospitals across the UK were overwhelmed; emergency wards became makeshift morgues, and patients often arrived too late for any meaningful intervention. The numbers were staggering: one-third of the UK's population gone in less than two years. Despite the tireless efforts of global health agencies, the World Health Organization remained no closer to a solution, their resources stretched thin. The National Health Service, already fragile before the crisis, was now hanging by a thread, understaffed and crumbling under the weight of the epidemic. Bill had once dreamed of a career where his discoveries would save lives, but now, he felt like a man trying to hold back a tsunami with a sandbag.

His team at the Francis Crick Institute had started with twenty of the brightest minds, but as the years dragged on, the pressures mounted, and the results proved elusive, attrition took its toll. Today, only four of the original team remained: Jackson, Tom, Scott and himself. Bill couldn't decide if their perseverance was driven by hope or sheer stubbornness.

Rumours had begun circulating among the scientific community, whispers that had reached Bill through an old university contact now working with MI5. The government, it seemed, was growing impatient with the scientific process and was considering drastic measures. A Special Tactical Scientific Unit—STSU—had reportedly been assembled in secret. Its mission: to combat the epidemic using "unconventional" methods, including direct military intervention to quarantine affected areas and experimental strategies with minimal ethical oversight. There were even murmurs about human testing, though nothing had been confirmed. The notion chilled Bill to his core.

"Is this what it's come to?" he thought, rubbing his temples. He understood the desperation. Every day brought new death tolls, and every failure in the lab felt like a nail in humanity's coffin. But the idea of abandoning the foundational principles of medical science—principles that had guided his entire career—felt like a betrayal. The elevator slowed, a soft vibration running through the floor. Bill straightened, brushing an imaginary speck of lint from his suit. As the doors opened with another quiet ping, the familiar sights of Sublevel 5 greeted him. The corridor was a sterile expanse of white walls and gleaming floors, illuminated by harsh overhead lighting. Glass doors lined the hallway, each leading to a different lab filled with state-of-the-art equipment. Behind those doors, groundbreaking work was conducted daily—though lately, the breakthroughs were few and far between.

Bill made a quick pitstop into the toilet before heading to the lab, passing the frosted glass panels etched with "Cellular Pathogenesis Research Unit." Inside, Jackson was putting on his lab jacket whilst Tom was already at work, his face illuminated by the soft blue glow of computer screens and microscopes. He paused for a moment, observing them. Jackson's youthful enthusiasm contrasted with Tom's more methodical demeanour, the older man meticulously logging data into a spreadsheet. Bill stepped inside, the faint smell of chemicals and sterilizing agents filling his nostrils. He placed his briefcase on the counter, his mind already racing through the day's agenda. There were new samples to analyse, data to cross-reference, and a conference call with international researchers scheduled for the afternoon. But in the back of his mind, the rumours of the STSU loomed large. He couldn't shake the feeling that time was running out—not just for the patients or the population, but for the very ideals he had sworn to uphold.

Chapter 3
23:00 hour, July 25th 2024
Hammersmith, South London

To some, the stench would have been unbearable—a vile cocktail of rotting waste and stagnant water that clawed at the nostrils and twisted the stomach. But to Aubrey, it smelled like freedom. Each breath, no matter how foul, was a reminder of the stark difference between the oppressive walls of imprisonment and the narrow chance of escape this sewer granted him. The dim light filtering through the gaps in the iron manhole cover above was his only guide, a faint beacon that promised the world beyond. Behind him, the inky darkness of the sewer stretched endlessly, the murky water flowing past with a low, ominous gurgle. So far, so good.

Aubrey wiped the sweat from his brow with the back of his hand, smearing grime across his face. His heart pounded in his chest, a wild rhythm that matched the urgency of his movements. He reached for the rusted metal rungs of the ladder embedded in the sewer wall, their surface slick and treacherous. The chill of the metal seeped into his fingers as he gripped tightly, his palms damp with a mix of sweat and the filth of his escape route. One rung at a time, he climbed, the sound of his breath loud in his ears, the rush of adrenaline sharpening every sensation.

When he reached the top, he hesitated, pressing his ear to the cold, damp surface of the manhole cover. Above, the faint hum of the outside world whispered down to him—the distant rumble of an engine, the occasional bark of a dog, and the soft whisper of wind rustling through unseen leaves. Aubrey placed one hand firmly against the underside of the cover and pushed gently. A sliver of light pierced through the gap, and he paused, squinting as his blue eyes scanned the narrow view.

The street above was eerily quiet, bathed in the pale glow of flickering streetlights. Rows of terraced houses lined either side of the narrow road, their brick facades casting long shadows that crept across the pavement. Cars, haphazardly parked, formed a silent convoy along the kerb. Aubrey tilted his head, straining to see further down the road. A faint unease crept over him—he was out of the prison, but not yet free. Freedom would come with distance, with speed, and most importantly, with remaining unseen.

He eased the manhole cover aside, the iron grating against stone with a low groan. The sound seemed deafening to his heightened senses, and he froze, listening for any sign of movement. Nothing. With a final burst of effort, Aubrey pulled himself out of the sewer, the cool night air hitting him like a slap after the oppressive heat and stink below. He replaced the cover carefully, the clang of metal meeting stone reverberating in his ears.

He crouched low, taking one last look in both directions. To the left, the road disappeared into shadow, the streetlights spaced too far apart to offer more than fleeting islands of illumination. To the right, the road bent slightly out of view, the glow of a distant lamp marking the curve. Both directions were empty. Aubrey stood, his muscles tense and ready, and started to run. The asphalt felt rough beneath his prison-issued shoes as he sprinted down Bloemfontein Road. The wind rushed past his face, cool and bracing, carrying with it the scents of wet pavement and distant rain. Behind him, the prison loomed in his memory—a stark, looming shadow that he refused to let catch up to him. His breaths came hard and fast, but he didn't dare slow. Freedom wasn't just ahead of him—it was every step he took away from what lay behind.

The city, which had seemed deceptively calm just moments before, was abruptly jolted from its usual hum by the shrill, ear-piercing wail of an alarm. It echoed through the streets, rattling windows and sending a ripple of tension through the air. Within seconds, the familiar sound of sirens followed, high-pitched and frantic, signalling that the chase had begun in earnest. Aubrey's pulse quickened, his body instinctively reacting to the familiar rush of danger. Now, things were going to get interesting. The police and prison guards were mobilizing, but he had a head start. He had to keep moving.

As he neared the end of the road, Aubrey ducked behind a large, blue wheelie bin, trying to blend into the shadowy corners of the street. He stole a glance to his left, then to his right. A small group of commuters stood at the bus stop, their faces flickering with the faint glow of the streetlight. They didn't seem to notice him, but their presence was a reminder that he couldn't afford to wait too long. Time was slipping away, and the more people who became aware of the situation, the more eyes there were watching for him. He exhaled slowly, doing his best to remain calm. His grey prison tracksuit, once a symbol of his confinement, now served as a camouflage. He hoped it made him look like just another person out for an evening jog. His heart raced as he adjusted his posture, slipping into the most casual, unhurried pace he could muster. Without looking back, he set off, crossing the road with deliberate slowness before disappearing down the next side street, where the shadows seemed to stretch out, welcoming him.

Twenty minutes later, Aubrey stood in the relative safety of Ravenscourt Park. It was a vast stretch of green space, far larger than most parks in the area. The towering trees above him seemed to offer a semblance of protection, and the eerie stillness of the park provided a stark contrast to the frenzy happening just beyond its borders. Aubrey crouched low beneath the trees, his eyes never leaving the road. His pulse quickened again as he saw two police cars race past, their flashing lights cutting through the mist. They were heading south, but he had no way of knowing whether they were searching for him specifically.

Aubrey's instincts told him to stay still, to remain hidden. He crouched further, using the thick bushes to shield his movements, his eyes trained on the scene unfolding before him. Another vehicle pulled up beside the park entrance, and two Officers stepped out. They immediately switched on their torches, their beams slicing through the darkness as they made their way toward the park. One Officer spoke into his radio. "Romeo Xray Five, we are searching the park from the south, over."

Aubrey's mind raced. He had only been free for approximately twenty minutes, and he knew that the authorities would still be scrambling to coordinate a search effort. The prison's resources were limited; they couldn't possibly cover every street and every park within a mile radius in such a short span of time. Time was still on his side, for now. But it wouldn't last.

The Officers continued their search, their footsteps soft but purposeful as they scanned the path ahead, peering into the trees and bushes, their torches sweeping across the undergrowth. Aubrey knew that staying in one place for too long would make him vulnerable, so he decided to move. He hunched his massive frame, trying to make himself as small as possible as he crept across the damp grass, his eyes flicking between the Officers and his surroundings. He made his way swiftly but quietly toward the playground, his breath shallow as he calculated each step. Reaching the low metal fence that bordered the playground, Aubrey didn't hesitate. Without slowing, he leapt over it, his body sailing through the air with surprising agility, despite the weight of his body. He landed lightly on the other side and immediately ducked behind the climbing wall, staying low to avoid being spotted. He listened for any sound of pursuit, but the park remained eerily silent. Still, he couldn't shake the feeling that he was being watched.

In the distance, the sound of sirens grew louder, echoing off the buildings in the streets beyond. Aubrey's stomach tightened. He knew that the closer the sirens got, the more likely it was that someone would spot him. As the wail of the sirens reached its crescendo, he heard a car screech to a halt behind a row of trees. The headlights sliced through the darkness, and Aubrey's heart skipped a beat when he saw the van doors swing open. Four prison guards stepped out; their silhouettes sharp against the light as they quickly moved to take control of the area. Aubrey didn't need to be told that his window of opportunity was quickly closing. He had to move faster, and he had to move now. Without a second thought, he turned and sprinted toward a thick row of bushes at the base of a six-foot stone wall. His legs burned with exertion as he pumped them faster, his arms swinging as he pushed himself harder.

With a burst of energy, he leapt into the air, his hands grabbing the top of the stone wall. He pulled himself up with surprising ease, using his upper body strength to propel his legs over the top. In one fluid motion, he cleared the wall, landing heavily on the other side. The momentum carried him down a steep incline, and as he rolled, the world flashed by in a blur of movement.

The sound of grinding metal grew deafening in his ears, and Aubrey's pulse surged as he realized he had reached the train tracks. A train was barrelling down the tracks toward him, its metal wheels screeching as it raced forward with terrifying speed. Aubrey didn't panic; his mind was clear, his movements controlled. He extended his arms, trying to slow his momentum as he skidded across the grass. The train was only a few feet away, its headlights blinding, and Aubrey could hear the roar of its engine as it came closer.

Just as the train's wheels screamed past his face, he spotted a small metal box lying next to the track. It was just within reach, a potential lifeline in the chaos. With a swift shift of his body, he moved to the right, his left hand coming off the ground as he adjusted his direction. Every muscle in his body was engaged, every nerve alive with the need to survive. The train was mere inches away when Aubrey's feet slammed into the metal box. His heart raced as the massive train roared past, its powerful gust of wind brushing his face. He barely had time to process the near miss before he threw himself onto the ground, lying flat and waiting for the train to pass. It seemed to stretch on forever, the sound of its wheels grinding against the rails deafening in his ears.

When the train finally passed, Aubrey lay still for a moment, his chest rising and falling in deep, rapid breaths. The world was quiet again, the sirens now a distant memory. He didn't waste time catching his breath for too long. The night was still young, and the danger was far from over. Slowly, cautiously, he began to move again, his every step calculated, his every movement a step closer to freedom.

Climbing to his feet, Aubrey felt the ache of his muscles and the sting of scrapes earned during his escape. He stepped carefully over the railway line, the wooden sleepers creaking faintly underfoot. His boots crunched against the gravel as he moved across the tracks, eyes scanning the dark surroundings for any signs of pursuit. The cold air bit at his face, but it was refreshing compared to the suffocating confines of the prison.

Ahead, the steel palisade fence loomed, its spikes adorned with coiled barbed wire glinting faintly in the dim light. Aubrey followed it westward, keeping close to the shadows, his breath fogging in the air. As he approached a bridge, he stopped to survey the area. The brick structure arched over a busy street below, its red facade weathered by years of grime and graffiti. He peered over the edge, calculating the height. The drop wasn't lethal, but even with his powerful frame, a jump like that would almost certainly result in a broken leg—or worse. He clenched his jaw and turned, his sharp eyes scanning the world behind him. The hum of traffic reached his ears, and he could make out the soft glow of headlights moving steadily along the road behind the bridge. He crept closer to the crossroad, noting the southbound traffic slowing as it approached the red light. A queue of vehicles formed—a mix of cars, delivery vans, and at the very end, a red bus. The sight of the bus gave him an idea, but it was risky. Aubrey wasn't one to shy away from risks, not when his freedom depended on them.

He turned back toward the bridge, crouching low against the wall. His heartbeat thudded in his ears as he watched the queue of vehicles begin to shift. A small white car sped away from the light, its engine whining as it accelerated under the bridge. A blue van followed, and then a motorbike, its engine snarling. Aubrey counted down the vehicles, his body tense with anticipation. A green car slowed and turned into a driveway near the bridge, leaving just two vehicles between him and the bus.

Then, the wail of a siren pierced the night. Aubrey's head snapped around. From the corner of his eye, he saw a police car approaching the crossroad at high speed, its flashing lights casting eerie patterns on the nearby buildings. It swerved sharply, tires screeching, and turned onto the road running parallel to the bridge. The sudden appearance of law enforcement made his decision for him. There was no time to second-guess. The next car cleared the bridge, and the bus's rounded roof came into view, its crimson paint illuminated by the streetlights. Aubrey climbed onto the edge of the brickwork and steadied himself. The driver inside the bus was distracted, yawning as he guided the vehicle carefully around a pothole. He didn't notice the shadowy figure above him until it was too late.

Aubrey leapt.

The impact was harder than he anticipated. His weight slammed onto the roof of the bus with a loud thump, causing the driver to jerk the wheel in shock. Aubrey lost his footing and tumbled down the side of the bus, landing heavily on the pavement. His vision spun, but his instincts pushed him to move. Inside the bus, the driver muttered, "What the—" before slamming on the brakes. The passengers, startled by the jarring halt, shouted their protests. "Oi, watch it! Me mam's just banged her head!" one man bellowed, cradling an older woman who scowled in pain.

The driver, ignoring them, jumped out of his seat and opened the doors with a hiss of compressed air. He stepped out cautiously, his eyes scanning the pavement until he saw a figure lying prone on the ground. "Holy shit," he muttered. "Hey! Mate, you alright? I didn't see you…" The driver knelt, reaching out a hand. Aubrey rolled onto his back, his long hair falling across his face. He felt the driver's hand brush his shoulder, and a flash of rage ignited inside him. Before the man could react, Aubrey's hand shot out, wrapping around his throat like a vice.

"Easy, mate! I—gah! I was just—!" the driver choked, his protests fading as Aubrey lifted him off the ground with terrifying ease. The passengers inside the bus froze, too afraid to intervene. The old woman muttered a prayer under her breath while her companion slowly raised his hands, hoping not to draw attention. A commanding voice cut through the chaos. "Hey! Put that man down!"

Aubrey turned his head slowly, his blue eyes narrowing as he spotted a young police Officer standing under the bridge. The Officer's hand rested on his baton, his stance tense but confident. "This is your last warning," the Officer continued. "Let him go, or I will—"

The sentence never finished. With a growl, Aubrey hurled the bus driver toward the vehicle. The man's body crashed through the side window, the glass shattering in a spray of shards. "Shit!" the Officer muttered, reaching for his radio as Aubrey turned and bolted. Aubrey's powerful legs propelled him down the pavement, his broad shoulders cutting through the air. People on the sidewalk jumped aside, some screaming, others simply frozen in shock. The young Officer rushed to the fallen driver, quickly assessing his injuries.

"Xray Zulu One," he said into his radio, his voice taut. "Requesting immediate medical assistance on Rivercourt Road, south of the bridge. Male with head and throat injuries. Suspect heading south toward the river. In pursuit!" The Officer flagged down a nearby couple. "Stay with him until the ambulance arrives!" he barked before sprinting toward his patrol car.

Inside the vehicle, his partner looked up from the dashboard. "What's the commotion?" "It's him," the Officer replied grimly. "The Scrubs escapee." The driver's jaw dropped. "Bloody hell. What's he like?" "Think of a hobo crossed with a bloody strongman. He's dangerous. Let's move!" The car sped into the night, its headlights cutting through the darkness, but as they approached a fork in the road, the Officer's confidence wavered. "Which way?" the driver asked. The Officer hesitated. "I don't know. Wait for backup." The patrol car slowed to a crawl, its occupants scanning the shadows. Somewhere in the darkness, Aubrey was moving— closer to freedom with every step.

✳✳✳

Standing on the muddy embankment of the Thames, Aubrey's chest heaved as he caught his breath. The night was bitterly cold, and the damp air clung to his skin like a second prison uniform. He glanced over his shoulder, his sharp eyes scanning the street above. For now, he was concealed behind a cluster of reeds and debris washed ashore. Two hundred yards up the road, the pursuing Officer had stopped, waiting for reinforcements. Aubrey knew his respite was fleeting.

The river surged westward, its surface churning in the moonlight. The current was stronger than he'd anticipated, a reminder of the river's raw power. Aubrey considered his options. He could swim—his strength and endurance were formidable—but navigating the icy, fast-moving waters while evading detection seemed nearly impossible. London's heart was alive with lights, cameras, and people; staying invisible here would be a monumental challenge. His eyes wandered to a series of barges bobbing near the shore, their silhouettes swaying rhythmically with the current. On the south bank, he spotted a small boathouse. Its wooden exterior looked weathered but intact, a potential hiding spot or, better yet, a chance at securing transport.

Aubrey made his decision. He moved with purpose, careful to keep low, crouching as he approached the nearest barge. The boat's sides were adorned with potted plants, a weathered bicycle frame, and a clutter of other personal items—a haphazard arrangement of someone's floating home. His fingers brushed the cold metal railing as he climbed aboard, careful to avoid making noise. The deck creaked faintly under his weight as his eyes scanned the clutter. His gaze fell on an empty table surrounded by bottles and an open magazine, its pages fluttering in the night breeze. Nothing useful. Frustration welled up until something caught his eye—a terracotta plant pot tucked into a corner. Kneeling, he examined it more closely. The flowers were tied to something—a small piece of hollow wood embedded in the soil.

Curiosity mixed with urgency as Aubrey yanked the flowers free, tossing them onto the deck. He retrieved the hollow stick, turning it over in his hand. A snorkel, crudely fashioned but serviceable. A smirk tugged at the corner of his mouth; someone had been as resourceful as him once. Without wasting another second, he tucked the improvised snorkel into his pocket and climbed back onto the shore. The river's icy embrace hit him like a slap as he waded in, the water rising past his knees, his waist, his chest. He exhaled sharply as the chill reached his core, but he kept moving until the riverbed disappeared beneath his feet.

The current seized him immediately, pulling him downstream. Aubrey kicked hard, his powerful arms slicing through the water as he fought to stay on course. He surfaced briefly, his chest burning from the cold and exertion. Above the roar of the river, he heard the faint wail of sirens and the distant hum of engines. His head whipped around as he spotted a cluster of police cars arriving at the street he had just fled. They wouldn't take long to organize a search.

Taking a deep breath, Aubrey submerged again, his body slicing through the murky water. He moved with calculated strokes, navigating toward the river's centre where he could see the faint shadow of an approaching boat. The low thrum of an engine grew louder, cutting through the night. As Aubrey surfaced again to tread water, he caught sight of the longboat moving steadily downstream. Two figures sat at the bow; their backs turned toward him as they scanned the north bank. Their focus was on the police activity above—a chaotic scene of Officers spreading out and shining torches along the shore.

Timing was everything. Aubrey sank beneath the surface once more, kicking hard toward the boat's shadow. The water pressed against his face as he glided, his eyes barely able to make out the dark hull of the vessel. His lungs burned, but he pushed the discomfort aside, focusing entirely on the task at hand. The shadow grew larger, and soon the longboat passed directly overhead. Aubrey reached out and grabbed hold of a guide rope dangling from its side. His muscles strained as he held on, his body dragged through the water with increasing speed. He clenched the snorkel between his teeth, biting down hard to keep it steady as he adjusted his grip.

The boat surged forward, its speed helping to keep him submerged and hidden. The two men on board, dressed in heavy coats, were engrossed in their conversation, oblivious to the stowaway clinging to the side. They gestured toward the police presence on the north bank, laughing occasionally, their voices muffled by the engine's hum. Aubrey's heart pounded in his chest. His grip on the rope was firm, but the water's relentless pull tested his strength. He shifted his position slightly, his feet finding purchase against the hull as he steadied himself. The river's icy chill seeped deeper into his bones, but he refused to let go.

One hour later, ss the boat carried him farther downstream, Aubrey's mind raced with his next move. The boathouse, houses of parliament, and tower bridge he'd seen earlier was now far behind him, but the riverbanks were becoming less crowded, offering potential for escape. Up ahead, the north bank appeared darker, with fewer lights and fewer prying eyes. The longboat began to slow, its engine humming at a lower pitch. Aubrey risked a glance above the surface, his breath coming in sharp bursts through the snorkel. The men were adjusting course, steering toward a small dock that jutted out from the shore.

Aubrey's mind locked onto the opportunity. As the boat edged closer to the dock, he released the rope and let himself drift in the water for a moment. When he was sure they weren't looking, he kicked hard, swimming silently toward the shadows beneath the dock.

The sound of boots on wood echoed above him as the two men disembarked. Aubrey stayed submerged, his lungs aching as he waited for their footsteps to fade. When he finally surfaced, he found himself in total darkness, concealed beneath the dock's wooden planks. For the first time since his escape began, Aubrey allowed himself a moment to breathe. But it was only a moment.

The hunt was far from over.

Chapter 4
Midnight, July 25th 2024
HMP Wormwood Scrubs, South London

HMP Wormwood Scrubs, was one of London's most iconic and notorious prisons; located in the south west of city, it had become overcrowded and the abuse inflicted by the guards had become common knowledge, however, the Government did not intervene, they simply looked the other way. Constructed in 1875, the Victorian red brick façade, high walls and barbed wire created an intimidating presence and over the years, The Scrubs had housed infamous prisoners, including spies and the Kray twins. Now, DCI Stephen Craig sat in the sparse waiting area outside the Wardens office, his patience wearing thin with every tick of the clock.

Two hours had crawled by since the alarm had sounded: a convict had escaped from Wormwood Scrubs. Not just any convict, either—this was a Category A prisoner, someone so dangerous and high-profile that even the hint of freedom would send shockwaves through the country. Now, the convict could be anywhere. The thought gnawed at him.

His polished brown leather shoe tapped an agitated rhythm on the laminate floor, the hollow sound echoing in the quiet hallway. Outside the high, narrow windows, the dark sky hinted at rain, a dull cold night that mirrored his mood. He stared at the shut door of the Warden's Office, his jaw tightening. Inside, muffled voices rose and fell in heated discussion—an interrogation of sorts. He imagined the Warden was getting his ears thoroughly chewed off by senior officials. A Category A escape wasn't just rare; it was a career-ending failure, and the fallout was only beginning.

The DCI ran a hand through his close-cropped hair, the leather strap of his watch catching the light as he checked the time again. Every second felt like an hour, every minute an eternity. He shifted in his seat, his trench coat bunching awkwardly under him, and glanced at the empty coffee table in front of him. A collection of outdated magazines offered no distraction. Suddenly, a buzz in his pocket snapped him out of his thoughts. His hand darted to his phone. Checking the screen, he saw the familiar name of Detective Louis Paulo flashing up. He pressed the answer button and brought the phone to his ear. "What news?" he barked, his voice taut with anticipation.

On the other end, Louis's voice came through, breathless and urgent. "Sir, we've cordoned off the roads within a two-mile radius of the prison. Officers are stationed at all key intersections, and I've requested NPAS for air support. They're scrambling a chopper now to give us better coverage." There was a pause, heavy with hesitation, before Louis added, "Sir, with all due respect, we need more manpower. The area's too big. If he's got help or planned this well, he's already slipping through the cracks." The DCI exhaled sharply, pinching the bridge of his nose. "I hear you," he said, his voice firm but tired. "I'm working on that. For now, focus on containing the immediate area. Keep your team sharp. I'll see if I can pull strings to get more boots on the ground, but until then, we're flying blind. I might have some intel coming through soon, something that could point us toward where he's likely to go." "Yes, sir," Louis replied, though the strain in his voice was palpable. "We'll keep pushing."

"Good," the DCI said. He ended the call and dropped the phone into his coat pocket, letting out a slow, controlled breath. He had expected chaos the moment the call about the escape came in, but this was turning into a nightmare. His mind raced, replaying what he knew about the fugitive: name, background, associates. Where would he run? Who would help him?

Behind the office door, the voices had grown louder, almost shouting now. He clenched his fists and looked down at his hands. He couldn't wait forever for answers. Time was their enemy now, and the longer this dragged on, the colder the trail would grow. He stood abruptly, pacing to the window and back, trying to shake the creeping frustration building in his chest. As he turned, his gaze caught the flickering light above. It buzzed faintly, its inconsistent hum only adding to the oppressive tension. He thought of Louis and the Officers on the ground, combing the streets and alleys in the growing dark. He thought of the convict—a cold, calculating man who'd managed to slip the grip of one of the most secure prisons in the country. This wasn't some desperate act of impulse; this was orchestrated. And that thought brought a chill to the DCI's core. Straightening his coat, the DCI cast one last look at the door. Whatever awaited him inside, it had better be good. Time wasn't just running out—it was sprinting. And if they didn't catch up soon, the consequences would be catastrophic.

The heavy timber door creaked open, revealing an older man with a weary expression etched into his lined face. He wore a crisp uniform, its buttons dulled by years of service, and his tired eyes locked onto the man sitting opposite. "DCI Craig," he said, nodding briskly. The DCI rose from his seat and extended a hand. "Yes, sir. Thank you for seeing me on such short notice." His tone was polite but firm, betraying the urgency humming beneath the surface. The man, Warden Tony Garraty, gave a small grunt of acknowledgment and stepped aside, gesturing for Craig to follow. The DCI entered the Warden's office, shutting the door with a muted click behind him.

The room was modest in size but exuded an air of solemnity. It felt like stepping back in time. Polished timber panels lined the walls, their rich, dark grain glowing under the amber light of an antique desk lamp. A large oak desk dominated the space, its surface cluttered with neatly stacked files, an old-fashioned blotter, and a black rotary phone. A faint scent of aged leather and pipe smoke lingered in the air. The DCI couldn't help but feel that the room itself was a relic of the 1940s, a stark contrast to the grim modernity of the prison outside.

Warden Garraty gestured toward a chair opposite the desk as he settled into his own. Approaching his sixtieth birthday, Garraty carried the weight of a career spent in the prison system. His face bore the telltale marks of stress: deep crow's feet around his eyes, creases on his brow, and the grey in his closely cropped hair. Working in a prison, even from an administrative position, clearly took its toll. "Mr. Garraty," the DCI began, skipping pleasantries. "I'll keep this brief. We're both aware that every passing minute gives this convict a greater chance to slip further out of reach. I should also make it clear that I'm not here to discuss how he managed to escape." He shot Garraty a pointed look. "I assume that's something you'll be investigating in detail. For now, I need to focus on the convict himself. What do you have for me?"

For a moment, Garraty simply stared at him, his eyes distant as though replaying some grim memory. Then, with a heavy sigh, he lowered his gaze to a thin, green folder sitting in the centre of his desk. He picked it up and held it out. "As you can appreciate, it's going to take us some time to compile a complete report. But for now, this is all I can give you." The DCI accepted the folder with a brief nod of thanks and flipped it open. His eyes scanned the first page quickly, and his expression shifted from curiosity to disbelief in seconds. He looked up sharply. "Is this some kind of joke?" Garraty shook his head, his lips pressed into a grim line. "I'm afraid not."

The DCI's brow furrowed as he glanced back down at the document. It was a standard prisoner profile sheet, the kind he'd seen countless times before. But the details—or lack thereof—were staggering. He turned the A4 sheet over in his hand, searching for clarification, but the reverse was blank. His eyes returned to the text on the front:

HMP WORMWOOD SCRUBS - Prisoner Personal Record
Prison Number: 0301 **Name**: Unknown
Alias: Aubrey Brian Strawberry, aka ABS
Height: 7' 2"
Weight: 198 lbs
Age: Unknown
Address: Unknown
Nationality: Unknown

The DCI read it twice, then a third time, each detail more bizarre than the last. His gaze shot back to Garraty. "This... this can't be real. Everything's unknown? Even his name? And Aubrey Brian Strawberry?" He couldn't keep the incredulity out of his voice. "That sounds like a joke in itself." Garraty leaned back in his chair, folding his hands over his stomach. "Believe me, DCI, I've asked myself the same questions many times since he arrived here. The truth is, this man is a mystery wrapped in a bad sense of humour. No fingerprints match anything in the system. No known affiliations, no prior arrests—nothing. The name, Aubrey Brian Strawberry was given by the Officers transporting the prisoner during intake, and, well, we haven't been able to verify anything else about him."

The DCI frowned, tapping the folder against his thigh as he processed this. "What about his behaviour inside? Did he stand out? Cause trouble? What kind of personality are we dealing with?" Garraty sighed again, reaching for a pack of cigarettes on his desk. "Oh, he stood out, all right. Seven-foot-two, wiry as hell. Quiet, but not in a nervous way. More like he was... observing. Studying. He didn't talk much, come to think of it, he never said anything. He was... unsettling, to say the least." The DCI's stomach turned uneasily.

A towering enigma with no identity, no history, and an unsettling demeanour? This wasn't just a convict; this was a ghost who shouldn't even exist. "Any connections? Did he interact with anyone inside who might help him now that he's out?" "That's the thing, DCI." Garraty exhaled smoke, the haze curling around his lined face. "He kept to himself. Didn't join any of the usual cliques. No visitors. No letters. It's like he was biding his time, waiting for... something."

The DCI closed the folder with a decisive snap, setting it on the desk. "And now that something has arrived." "Looks like it," Garraty muttered. He leaned forward, his eyes hard. "You need to find him, DCI. Fast. There's something about him that doesn't sit right with me. And if he planned this as meticulously as it seems, he's not just running. He's heading somewhere. Or to someone." The DCI's brow furrowed as he read the scant information again, his eyes darting over the page as though a second look might reveal some hidden clue. The absurdity of it all gnawed at him. Pacing the room with restless energy, he glanced occasionally at the Warden, who sat calmly, watching him like a bored teacher observing a student's tantrum. Finally, Garraty checked his watch and cleared his throat. "Is that everything you need, Detective? I'm quite busy, you know."

The sarcasm lit a fuse in the DCI, who stopped mid-stride and whirled around. "You serious, Warden? This is it? You hand me a name that's probably fake, a bunch of blank spaces on a record, and you expect us to track this guy down? For God's sake, we're on the same team here. Can't you give me something to work with?" He slapped the sheet of paper back onto the desk with more force than intended, its corners curling slightly. Frustrated, he made to turn toward the door, but Garraty's voice stopped him in his tracks.

"Aubrey Brian Strawberry," the Warden began, his tone softer, almost reflective, "was brought here in 2023. Normally, when a prisoner arrives, we get a file—a big, fat box of paperwork with everything from their convictions to their medical records. It tells us who they are, why they're here, and what to watch out for. But Aubrey..." He let out a slow whistle through his teeth. "Well, let me tell you what little I know." The DCI paused, intrigued despite himself. Slowly, he returned to his chair, pulling out a small notepad and pen from his jacket pocket. "Go on," he said, giving Garraty a sharp nod.

The Warden leaned forward, lacing his fingers together. "It was spring, 2023. I got a call from a Commissioner at the Department of Corrections. Not a usual occurrence, mind you. This guy tells me they've got a new inmate for us—one they're shipping in under strict orders. Calls him a 'bloody monster,' said the words like he'd seen something he couldn't unsee. Says this fella's serving two life sentences without parole." The DCI's pen froze over his pad. "Two? What for?"

Garraty gave him a look. "They didn't tell me. Not a bloody word. And believe me, I asked. I don't let just anyone into this prison—especially not someone who sounds like they belong in a horror flick. I wanted to know everything: his crimes, his mental state, his history. But the powers that be shut me down, told me it was 'above my clearance.'" His voice dripped with bitterness. "Above my clearance. Imagine that." The DCI scribbled furiously, but his face betrayed his mounting frustration. "And you accepted that? You just... took him in?"

"What else could I do?" Garraty shot back, his voice rising. "This wasn't some petty crook we could refuse. Orders came from the top, and they were crystal clear: Aubrey Brian Strawberry—or ABS, as the other prisoners call him—is not to leave this place alive. That was their only instruction. Keep him here until he dies. But let me tell you, Detective, from the moment he walked in, it felt like we were the ones on his turf, not the other way around." The DCI raised an eyebrow. "What do you mean?"

The Warden chuckled darkly, leaning back in his chair. "He's the kind of man who makes the hair on the back of your neck stand up. Not because he's loud—oh no, he's quiet. Observant. Calculating. And his size..." He gestured to the paper on the desk. "You've seen the stats. When he stepped off the van, every guard in the yard froze. Seven-foot-two, wiry but strong as hell. He looks like a scarecrow, but you can tell there's power under that frame." Garraty's voice trailed off as a knock interrupted him. The door creaked open, and a guard stepped in, holding a manila envelope. "Pardon my intrusion, Warden," the guard said, stepping forward. "Here's the photo you requested for Prisoner 0301. Also, Henry's finished interviewing the guards on shift during the escape. Should I send him up?"

The Warden nodded, taking the envelope and dismissing the guard with a curt, "That'll be all." He handed the envelope to Craig, who opened it swiftly and pulled out a single mugshot. The DCI's eyes narrowed as he studied the photograph. It was a standard prison photo—unforgivingly harsh lighting, plain background—but the man staring back at him was anything but standard. Long, matted grey hair framed a gaunt face, his black beard scruffy and unkempt. His piercing blue eyes seemed to glare through the photograph itself, sharp and unsettling. His skin was deeply tanned and weathered, like someone who'd spent decades under an unforgiving sun.

The DCI exhaled slowly. "This is... helpful." He glanced up at Garraty, his words laced with cautious sarcasm. "At least I know what he looks like now." Garraty ignored the jab, settling back in his chair. Propping his feet on the desk, he let out a sigh and crossed his arms behind his head. "You think this is helpful? Detective, this photo doesn't do him justice. The real thing? He's worse. Much worse." The DCI set the photo down, his pen hovering over his notepad. "Go on," he said again.

The Warden reclined in his chair, his fingers idly drumming on the oak desk as he collected his thoughts. "After his first month here, we noticed he was avoiding the showers. We can't have inmates skipping hygiene, so we decided to intervene. Eight guards dragged him in one day. Big man like that doesn't go quietly, as you'd expect. Once we got him in there, they stripped him down and shoved him under the water." He paused, the memory clearly unpleasant to recount. "There were only a couple of other prisoners in there at the time, thank God, because what happened next..." He sighed. "Before the guards even had time to react, Aubrey had snapped. One man ended up with his nose broken so badly it was nearly flattened. Another? Aubrey bit half his ear clean off, like some kind of animal. A third prisoner left with both arms broken. Took a week in the infirmary to patch him up."

The DCI froze mid-scribble, his pen pressing into the page. Slowly, he looked up, his mouth slightly agape. "Jesus Christ..." he muttered. "And this man is loose? Out there? On the streets?" The Warden leaned back in his chair, folding his arms. "Afraid so. And that's why you need to find him, Detective. Quickly. He's not just dangerous; he's unpredictable. And someone that size, with that temper... Well, it doesn't take much imagination to see what could happen." The DCI rose abruptly, tucking his notepad and pen into his coat pocket. With the mugshot clutched in his hand, he strode toward the door, his pace brisk and determined. As he opened it, he turned back to Garraty, his jaw set in a hard line. "Warden, thank you for your time. We'll get this circulated immediately. A man like him? Prone to violence? He'll leave breadcrumbs, no matter how careful he thinks he's being. It's only a matter of time."

With that, the DCI disappeared through the door, leaving Garraty alone in the dimly lit office. The Warden exhaled heavily, the tension in his shoulders visible as he leaned forward. Reaching for the intercom on his desk, he pressed the button with a calloused finger. "Send up Henry," he said, his voice calm but firm. As the faint buzz of the intercom faded, Garraty leaned back in his chair, staring at the ceiling. His mind lingered on the photograph of Aubrey Brian Strawberry, the piercing blue eyes that seemed to mock him even now. He muttered under his breath, his words barely audible but heavy with meaning. "God help whoever crosses his path."

Chapter 5
01:45 hours, July 26th 2024
Dagenham, East London

Chequers Lane lay under the oppressive shroud of a chilly night, the potholed tarmac stretching like a neglected artery toward the heart of Dagenham. The road's unusual width—a concession to the towering skip lorries and HGVs that roared through by day—now felt ominous in the silence. Shadows spilled across the pavement, cast by dim pools of light from a sparse scattering of streetlamps, their tired bulbs barely illuminating the path alongside industrial units and crumbling docks. Security cameras perched on rusting gates stared blankly at the emptiness, while motion sensor lights occasionally flickered to life, startled by the nocturnal dance of scavengers.

Aubrey crouched in the cover of darkness, his drenched clothes clinging to his lean frame, the steady drip of rainwater from his long, matted hair pooling at his boots. His breath came slow and measured, a predator's calm. Fifty meters ahead, a fox emerged from the shadows, its narrow frame gliding across the cracked road. Aubrey watched intently as the animal made a bee-line for a pile of rubbish festering in a ditch beneath a scraggly bush. Its sharp paws rifled through the refuse, but finding nothing edible, the fox sniffed the damp air and moved on, its sleek body melting into the shadows as it padded toward the docks.

The fox's presence gave Aubrey a strange sense of reassurance. Animals, he'd learned, were often the first to sense danger. As the fox passed under a dimly glowing lamp, its gait briefly faltered. A light affixed to an eight-foot pole in the yard of a skip hire company buzzed to life, its harsh white beam slicing through the gloom. The fox froze, its nose twitching. Then, in a blur of russet fur, it darted sideways, slipping between two bent fence posts and vanishing into the night.

Pleased by the fox's reaction, Aubrey stirred. It was time to move. He stepped lightly along the opposite side of the road, careful to keep the looming buildings between himself and any functional CCTV cameras. He knew many of the cameras were mere deterrents, their cracked lenses and peeling paint speaking to years of disrepair. But some would still work, silently capturing his image for the authorities to scrutinize long after he was gone.

A distant siren keened through the air, piercing the quiet and quickening Aubrey's pulse. He stopped mid-step, scanning the horizon. The city never truly slept. Somewhere, someone was always in trouble. But was this siren meant for him? He couldn't be sure, and uncertainty was dangerous. Every flicker of blue light, every wail of a siren, brought the same chilling question: was he the hunted, or was the city merely catching its breath in the aftermath of another skirmish? He clenched his fists. He couldn't linger. The countryside called to him with promises of open spaces, scarce cameras, and fewer prying eyes. Aubrey had prepared for this moment over years, weaving contingencies into the fabric of his life. The coastline awaited him, its sprawling isolation offering refuge, but first, there was an errand to run—a critical piece of his plan that could not be skipped.

He broke into a jog, his steps splashing through shallow puddles as he navigated the uneven road. The street curved and disappeared beneath the hulking shadow of a flyover—the Thames Gateway. Above him, the arterial road thrummed with the movement of vehicles: the low growl of lorries, the faint hiss of bus brakes, the impatient rumble of commuters. The concrete structure loomed like a monolith, stretching east and west along the path of the Thames, a silent witness to the lifeblood of London.

As Aubrey neared the flyover, the pale orange light of the sodium lamps overhead cast a sickly glow on the wet asphalt. The railway lines of Dagenham Dock station emerged in the distance, their high-voltage cables sagging slightly under the damp weight of the night. Beyond the station lay the promise of sanctuary—Hainault Forest, the M11, and the chance to vanish entirely.

His chest tightened, a knot of anxiety coiling deep in his stomach. Between here and there lay a gauntlet of risk—every step forward was fraught with uncertainty, every shadow potentially hiding a pair of prying eyes. His heart thudded in his chest as he navigated the familiar street, each noise amplified in his ears, each corner a potential threat. The thrill of the escape was tempered with the biting reality that he couldn't afford to be seen, not now. As he trudged along, his gaze shifted to the right, catching sight of a metal recycling container. It was scarred by layers of graffiti—bright splashes of colour and scrawled messages marking the urban decay around him. Piles of discarded glass jars and broken bottles were shoved haphazardly into the dirty cardboard boxes that had been abandoned nearby. This was the kind of place you could disappear into, hidden amongst the forgotten detritus of the city, just another piece of the trash littering the streets.

He approached cautiously, his footsteps muffled on the cracked sidewalk, every sound feeling louder than usual in the eerie stillness of the night. The air was heavy, carrying the faint scent of wet earth mixed with a whiff of something unpleasant—rotting food or stale beer, maybe both. He scanned the area quickly, ensuring the road remained empty before stepping closer to the metal bin. His eyes narrowed as he searched through the cardboard boxes, his fingers brushing over the rough edges of the discarded packaging, the flaps falling open to reveal a mishmash of bottles, cans, and wrappers. Nothing of immediate use, but he wasn't looking for anything pristine, just something useful—something to help with his plan.

His eyes flickered to the side of the bin, and that's when he saw it—tucked between a plastic crate and the rusted metal of the bin was a weathered bag. A quick scan told him everything he needed to know: two empty wine bottles were nestled inside, their clear glass reflecting the dim light from the nearby streetlamp. Perfect, he thought, a quick smile crossing his lips. This was exactly what he needed. Grabbing the bag with a sense of urgency, he placed it carefully on the floor, his fingers brushing against the gritty pavement as he looked up and down the road. All clear—nothing but the quiet hum of the city in the distance. He exhaled slowly, his pulse still quickened, the adrenaline pushing him forward.

With a grim resolve, he eyed the bottles. Their usefulness would be short-lived if they stayed intact—he needed them broken. He shifted his weight, positioning himself over the bag, then pressed the heel of his boot down on one of the bottles. A sharp crack echoed in the still night as the glass shattered beneath his weight. The sound was almost satisfying, a brief moment of release, but he wasn't done yet. He adjusted his stance, bringing his full weight onto the second bottle. This time the glass exploded with a violent hiss, shards of jagged glass scattering across the ground. The pieces glinted briefly in the dim streetlight, a chaotic reflection of his fractured thoughts. Once satisfied with the result, he stepped back, eyeing the remnants.

Carefully, he picked up the bag again, with the bottles destroyed, the risk had been minimized, but the job wasn't finished. He had to keep moving. The station wasn't far, but the closer he got, the greater the risk of crossing paths with someone who might recognize him. The weight of the night still hung heavily on him, but for now, he was still one step ahead. He glanced at up as a lorry thundered down the road above —time was slipping away. He adjusted his hood, pulling it tighter over his face, and plunged forward into the underpass. The sound of his footfalls echoed around him, swallowed by the vast, cold emptiness of the space. He couldn't afford hesitation now. Every step brought him closer to freedom—or to the kind of mistake that would end it all.

The Turkish Kebab shop was still buzzing, the scent of sizzling meat and garlic wafting into the cool night air. Inside, a few stragglers leaned against the counter, their voices a low murmur beneath the hum of the rotating spits. Outside, the street burst to life as the last group of lads staggered out of the nightclub at the end of the road. "Keep it moving lads… that's it… cheers now," growled the huge doorman as he shepherded the group out through the emergency exit. His broad frame filled the doorway like a human barricade. Before closing the door, he leaned out, fixing his steely gaze on the tallest of the bunch. "And next time, bruv, think twice 'bout floggin' your dodgy gear in my club, yeah? You're lucky I don't get the Old Bill involved. Now jog on back to whatever shit tip you crawled out of." The heavy metal door slammed shut with a clang that echoed down the street. The four lads stood in the glow of the kebab shop's neon sign, bursting into drunken laughter.

"Bloody 'ell, bruv," Moses barked, slapping the back of Nick Deane's head. "Can't believe you pulled that crap in there. You tryin' to get us all nicked or what?" Nick grinned sheepishly, rubbing his head. "Relax, Mo, it weren't nothin' serious." Simon and Rene, struggling to stand upright, leaned against each other for support. Their laughter came in hiccupping bursts as their red-rimmed eyes darted around the street. The effects of the weed hadn't quite worn off, leaving their vision blurred and their senses dulled.

Moses, the self-appointed leader of their ragtag crew, turned sharply toward them. His tall, muscular frame cast a shadow over the pair. "And you two muppets, knock it off, yeah? Keep smokin' that trash, and you'll end up brown bread, you dig?" His voice was stern, but there was an undertone of concern. Rene waved a hand dismissively, a crooked grin plastered across his face. "Chill, Mo, we're sound." "Yeah," Simon added, slurring his words. "Just a laugh, innit?"

Their carefree attitude made Moses groan. He ran a hand over his shaved head, muttering under his breath. He didn't have time to lecture them further. Whomp! A sharp backfire cut through the air as a black Golf GTI skidded around the corner, its tires squealing against the pavement. The lads' heads snapped up in unison, their senses momentarily sharpening. The car roared toward them, the bass from its stereo vibrating the windows of the kebab shop. "Ride's here," Moses announced. He grabbed Simon and Rene by their jackets, dragging them to the curb. "Let's move."

The Golf screeched to a halt a few meters away, the driver impatiently honking the horn. Moses glanced over his shoulder at Nick, who was lingering near the kerb. "Yo, Nicky! You sure you don't wanna sponge a lift, bruv?" Nick waved him off, already drawn to the bright glow of the kebab shop. "Nah, I'm starving, mate. Gotta soak up the suds. Catch you lot tomorrow, yeah?" Moses rolled his eyes, muttering something about Nick's priorities as he shoved Simon and Rene into the backseat. The car peeled away with a screech, the horn blaring a cheeky farewell as it disappeared into the night.

Nick pushed open the kebab shop's door, the warmth and smell of grilled meat hitting him like a wave. He barely noticed the man behind the counter shaking his head in disapproval. "Bloody joyriders," the man muttered, his eyes briefly flicking toward the retreating Golf. Without his friends, Nick felt a strange unease creep in, like he'd been stripped of his armour. Vulnerability wasn't something he enjoyed, but hunger had won out over caution. He shuffled to the counter and slapped a ten-pound note on the glass. "Doner kebab, no salad, yeah? Cheers."

The man snatched the note without a word, sliding it into the till. He turned to the rotating spit, expertly carving thin slices of sizzling meat. Nick's eyes darted around the shop. To his right, a small plastic lighter sat forgotten on the counter. His fingers itched. Quick as a flash, he swiped the lighter and stuffed it into his pocket just as the man turned back. "Any sauce with that?" Nick shook his head, grabbing the paper-wrapped kebab as soon as it hit the counter. He didn't wait for a goodbye, stepping back out onto the street with his prize. Behind him, the door swung open with a bang. "Oi! You little shit!" the man shouted, stepping into the road. "Bring back my bloody lighter right now!" Nick didn't look back. With a smug grin, he took a big bite of the kebab and disappeared into the shadows.

Chewing on the last mouthful of greasy doner meat, Nick swallowed it down, feeling the warmth spread through his chest as he walked along the dimly lit road. The station was just up ahead. He pulled his phone from his pocket and checked the time. Ten more minutes, he thought, then the train would be here. Just five stops until he finally headed home, away from the madness of the night. He couldn't wait to be in his own space again. As he finished the last bite, he rolled the crumpled paper bag into a tight ball and tossed it up into the air. With a lazy swing of his foot, he tried to kick it back down to earth, but it missed his shoe by inches and fluttered to the ground. "Bloody hell," he muttered to himself. Shoving his hands into his trouser pockets, he took the lighter he'd swiped earlier and twirled it between his fingers, the metal cool against his skin. His mind wandered for a moment—do I have time?

His curiosity got the best of him. Reaching into his back pocket, he pulled out a cigarette—thick and hand-rolled, its soft black resin studded with furry green cannabis leaves. He slid it between his lips, flicked the lighter, and took a long, deep drag. The smoke filled his lungs and he exhaled slowly, watching the cloud disappear into the night air. The high hit him almost immediately, and a wave of euphoria spread through his body. His limbs felt light, and the world suddenly seemed... better, more vibrant. A smile crept onto his face as happiness overtook him.

He continued his slow stroll toward the station, now beneath the cold concrete bypass that arched overhead. The traffic hummed above, distant and muffled, like a world that had nothing to do with him. That's when he saw him—a man standing on the opposite side of the road. The two of them locked eyes, and for a moment, time seemed to stop. Neither of them moved. Nick's stomach tightened as he watched the stranger, something about him unsettling. He took another pull on the cigarette, the once blissful euphoria now waning, replaced with a creeping feeling of unease. He glanced at the man again, this time more suspiciously, out of the corner of his eye. Something wasn't right. His calm was evaporating. The paranoia was setting in. Slowly, he stopped in his tracks. His breath hitched as he took one step into the road, his heart beginning to race.

"Hey, knock it off," Nick called out, trying to sound tougher than he felt, his voice trembling slightly. "Go on, get the hell out of here..." His words hung in the air, but the man didn't move, just stood there, his gaze unwavering. He was waiting. Nick's hand tightened around the cigarette, the soft embers glowing as he drew another long drag. He was feeling more anxious now. His legs started moving again, but faster this time, a nervous urgency pushing him forward towards the station. He could feel his heart thumping in his chest, and despite his outward bravado, fear gnawed at him from the inside. He looked back over his shoulder. The man hadn't budged.

With his pace quickening, the anxiety turned into frustration. "What you looking at, you fucking piece of shit?" Nick yelled, his voice cracking with rage. "You want some, do ya? Well, come and get it!" But before he could take another step, the stranger surged forward, his feet pounding on the pavement as he jumped into the street. His movement was swift, and Nick's blood ran cold. "Oh shit," he gasped under his breath. The cigarette slipped from his fingers and dropped onto the ground. Panic flooded his veins. Without thinking, he turned and bolted toward the station entrance, his legs pumping furiously as he ran.

He could hear the man's heavy footsteps closing in behind him. His heart raced, and in a split-second decision, he reached into his jacket pocket, pulling out a small plastic sachet of dried green leaves. With a frantic glance over his shoulder, he tossed it toward the man, the packet skimming the air before landing on the ground. "Sorry, mister, it's yours—take it," Nick shouted, his voice hoarse with fear.

He didn't wait to see if the man would pick it up. Without hesitation, he ducked through the station doors and sprinted inside. His breath was ragged, his legs aching from the sudden sprint. His heart thudded in his chest, drowning out the noise of the world around him. He darted past the ticket booth, not bothering to wait in line. In one fluid motion, he jumped over the turnstile and dashed for the platform, his footsteps echoing in the empty hall. As he reached the platform he turned around, he could see the man standing in the darkness, waiting for him, "oh no, his gonna kill me," turning quickly, he lost he footing, falling towards the track just as the train rolled past.

Standing to the side of the entrance, hidden in the shadows, Aubrey's senses were on high alert. The cool air of the station pressed against him, sharp and biting, but his mind was racing far faster than the chill in his bones. The sounds around him felt distorted, the usual hum of the station warped by the weight of what was happening. The train doors hissed open with a pneumatic whine, their sound cutting through the tension in the air. For a brief moment, the world felt unnervingly still, like time had stretched thin, the seconds dragging on for what felt like an eternity.

Then, a scream sliced through the silence.

The sharp, frantic wail of a woman echoed down the platform, followed by a chorus of panicked voices. Someone shouted for help—no, multiple voices now, rising in terror, their fear palpable. Aubrey's heart skipped a beat, his chest tightening. His eyes darted across the station, searching for the source of the chaos, but he couldn't see anything from where he stood. The darkness hid him well, but his instincts screamed that this situation was escalating fast, and he was caught in the middle of it. His thoughts snapped back to focus. Move. Now. His mind raced as he weighed his options. He could feel the weight of the situation settling heavily on his shoulders, a dark weight that urged him to keep moving, to keep his head down, to disappear. The echo of footsteps on the platform grew louder, hurried, frantic. The train was still there, the doors open, but the screams had taken on a new edge. Desperation. Panic.

Aubrey swallowed hard; police sirens were already wailing in the distance. In moments, this place would be crawling with Officers, a swarm of flashing lights. He had to move fast—faster than the inevitable rush of law enforcement that would flood the area in minutes. There was no time to waste. He had planned for this, but the gravity of the situation still hit him like a punch to the gut.

He moved. Quietly, swiftly, like a shadow slipping through the night. His feet barely made a sound against the concrete as he crept along the road toward the far end of the platform. He kept low, using the shadows to his advantage, his back pressed against the cold brickwork. Every sense was heightened now. His mind raced through escape routes, ways to blend in, to disappear into the crowd. He knew the area well enough—there were alleyways behind the station, underpasses, places where he could melt into the night. But he had to be quick. He couldn't afford to hesitate. As he reached the end of the path, his eyes flicked toward the opening in the fence; the exit barrier stood a few meters away and was positioned at the east end of the platform. The police would be here soon. The crowd would scatter, chaos would reign, and in the middle of it all, he needed to vanish.

He jumped over the barrier just as the first police car screeched to a halt outside the main entrance. The flashing lights illuminated the street, casting long, erratic shadows on the pavement. He didn't look back. He couldn't afford to. The station was now a war zone, filled with shouting Officers and frantic civilians. His plan was simple: move. Don't stop. Don't draw attention. He kept his head down as he stepped out on to the platform, a sea of people were being herded towards the booking hall. He ran to the end of the train, jumped down onto the tracks and disappeared into the shadows.

***

Standing on the crowded platform, chaos rippled like a tangible force. Shouts, cries, and a wave of stunned disbelief surged through the mass of people. The air was thick with tension, pierced by the frantic screams of a woman, her voice trembling with shock and horror. She had clearly witnessed the unthinkable—the figure who had jumped. Sergeant Beth Rose's sharp voice cut through the commotion. "We need to contain this crowd until support arrives!" Her tone was commanding but measured, the anchor of authority in a storm of confusion. She quickly issued orders to her team. "Luke, head down there—check if anyone's still inside the train and secure the exit. Tyson, take the booking hall. Get the staff to pull the shutters down!" She scanned the platform, her eyes swiftly evaluating the space. "There's enough room here for now. I'll send the crowd through once the room is secure. After that, get back out here and help clear the platform."

Without hesitation, Officers Luke and Tyson disappeared into the throng, their shoulders brushing against panicked commuters as they moved with purpose. Beth pushed forward, her own movements brisk and deliberate as she headed toward the front of the train. The scene near the cab was no better. The train guard, visibly shaken, stood as a lone barrier between the onlookers and their phones, raising his hands to discourage passengers from filming. The glow of screens illuminated eager faces, each swipe and tap driven by the relentless hunger for social media's fleeting fame. Beth bit back a curse. "Bloody social media."

Just as she reached the guard, someone grabbed her arm. Instinctively, she bristled at the physical contact, her reflexes sharp from years on the job. But as she turned, her irritation melted into surprise. A small elderly woman clung to her sleeve, her fragile frame trembling, tears streaming down her weathered cheeks. Beth softened, crouching slightly to meet her eye-to-eye. She placed a firm but gentle hand on the woman's shoulder, her voice calm and soothing. "Yes, madam, do you need assistance?" The woman sniffled, dabbing her face with a floral handkerchief. In a quavering voice thick with an unfamiliar accent, she stammered, "Es esta la parada para el Palacio de Buckingham?" Beth blinked, momentarily thrown by the question. She glanced around at the chaos engulfing the platform, the thought of Buckingham Palace almost laughably out of place here. Before she could answer, a kindly elderly man appeared beside the woman, his face a mask of both concern and exasperation. "No, dear," he said with a chuckle that seemed almost inappropriate amid the tension. "This is Dagenham. The Queen doesn't live here."

Beth exhaled, a wry smile tugging at the corners of her lips despite herself. For a moment, the absurdity of the exchange cut through the grim reality of the scene, a brief spark of humanity amidst the chaos. Straightening, she patted the elderly woman's hand reassuringly. "Let's get you somewhere safe, madam. The Palace can wait." And with that, she resumed her march down the platform, her mind racing to prioritize the ever-growing list of problems that demanded her attention. The crowd pressed closer, the scene unfolding as a grim testament to the frailty and resilience of human nature in the face of tragedy.

Beth spun on her heel and headed toward the train driver, weaving through the knot of stunned passengers. Her steps were purposeful, boots clicking against the concrete as she dodged outstretched arms and sidestepped oblivious bodies. Reaching the cab, she tapped firmly on the door. The driver, a middle-aged man with wide, bloodshot eyes, cracked it open, his face pale as a ghost. "Excuse me, sir," she began, her voice steady but brisk. "I can take over from here. Do you have a radio in the cab? I need you to contact station staff immediately. We need them out here before this situation spirals out of control." The man nodded mutely, too rattled to argue, and retreated into his cab. Beth caught a glimpse of the train's windshield—still streaked with blood and fragments of tissue. Her stomach turned at the sight, but she steeled herself, unwilling to let the horror of the moment slow her down. The driver turned his back to the gruesome mess, fumbling with the radio handset as he began to speak.

Beth faced the milling crowd, her police training kicking into high gear. She raised her voice, aiming for calm authority over the restless murmur of voices. "Ladies and gentlemen, if I could just have your—" Her words were cut short as a man near the edge of the platform raised his phone, its camera lens pointed at the train. Beth's voice sharpened like a whip. "Hey, buddy—no. Put your phone away right now!" The man hesitated, caught between defiance and embarrassment. She held his gaze until he sheepishly lowered the device. "Thank you," she snapped, then turned back to the crowd. "Sorry, everyone. As I was saying, shortly my colleague will lead you into the booking hall. Please follow him in an orderly fashion. We need to clear this platform as quickly as possible. Thank you for your cooperation."

A hush settled over the platform. Passengers exchanged uneasy glances but stayed rooted in place, waiting for further instructions. Beth allowed herself a quick breath, her eyes scanning the area for any signs of further disturbance. She turned back to the cab. "Any luck?" she called to the driver. He nodded, his voice still trembling as he replied, "Yes... um... apologies. The lads were in the mess room taking a break. They didn't realize what was going on until now." Beth's jaw tightened in irritation. "Great," she replied dryly. "Okay, listen. I need you to stay here until the platform is completely cleared. Do not leave the station or move that train until I have spoken to you again. Understood?"

The driver bobbed his head in agreement, but Beth was already moving, not waiting for a response. She pushed through the throng, her shoulders brushing against passengers who instinctively stepped back, sensing her urgency. As she neared the booking hall, she mentally reviewed the next steps: securing the shutters, coordinating the staff, and controlling the flow of people to prevent any further chaos. The booking hall loomed ahead; its usual hum of activity replaced by the eerie stillness that came in the wake of tragedy. Inside, a cluster of station staff stood huddled, their faces a mix of confusion and fear. Beth tightened her grip on her radio, readying herself for yet another round of orders.

Luke strode purposefully down the platform, the cacophony of the crowd fading behind him with each step. The sharp scent of brake dust and the metallic tang of blood still lingered in the air, clinging to his senses like an unwelcome shadow. He moved alongside the train, its once-pristine carriages now smeared with tragedy, peering into each open doorway. His voice rang out steady and professional, practiced over years of duty. "If anyone is still in here, please leave the train immediately at the nearest available exit and make your way to the front of the train. Thank you."

The repetition felt mechanical now, his tone calm but firm, designed to cut through the shock and confusion he knew passengers might still feel. As he reached the sixth carriage, his pace slowed. The air here felt heavier, quieter. Instead of calling out, he pressed his face briefly to each glass panel, scanning the dim interiors for any lingering figures. Empty rows of seats stared back at him, shadows stretching along the floor as the overhead lights flickered erratically. The static crackle of his radio snapped him out of his focus. "Sergeant Rose here. Luke, any stragglers on your end?" He pressed the button on his handset. "No, Sarge. Train's empty. Proceeding to the exit now. Over."

Letting the radio drop back to his belt, he resumed his walk, his eyes still scanning instinctively for anything out of place. As he neared the end of the train, a glint of colour on the floor caught his eye, barely noticeable in the dim lighting. He crouched, picking up a small, slightly crumpled piece of laminated paper. It was a season ticket for West Ham United, the club colours unmistakable even in the gloom. "Bloody hell," he muttered under his breath, turning it over in his hand. The member's name was printed in neat black lettering, the familiar signs of a dedicated fan. A pang of regret twisted in his chest. "Shame," he murmured, slipping the card into his pocket. He didn't know the name, but it was enough to make the tragedy feel all the more personal. Someone had lost more than their ticket tonight.

Reaching the exit, he leaned against the wall, folding his arms as he surveyed the platform. His breath fogged slightly in the cool night air. Two hours into his shift, and it already felt like a lifetime. The scene was still fresh, but the emotional weight of it was settling in. "Long night ahead," he muttered, half to himself, half to the echo of the empty station. Still, he thought with a grim smirk, beats chasing after low-lives through alleyways and council estates. His radio buzzed faintly again in the background, and he straightened, pulling himself out of his thoughts. There was still work to do, and standing still wouldn't make the night any shorter.

***

Beth stepped into the booking hall, her boots clicking against the polished floor as she surveyed the scene. The space was quieter than she expected, a stark contrast to the chaos on the platform. Tyson stood near the shuttered ticket counter, talking to three railway staff. Spotting her, he excused himself, weaving through the open barrier to meet her halfway. "Sarge," he began, brushing a hand over his short-afro hair, "they've pulled the shutter down, but apparently, it's not fully secured. Something about fire regulations or some other nonsense." He shrugged. "Anyway, the tall one's the Station Supervisor—name's Ted. The other two? Just grunts."

Beth absorbed the information with a quick nod. "Thanks. Right, here's the plan. I'll send those two out onto the platform to start filtering the crowd through into the hall. We need the platform cleared ASAP. Support should be here any minute, but for now, start taking down names and details—station staff, eye-witnesses, anyone involved. Leave the driver for now. I'll deal with him myself when I get back." Tyson raised an eyebrow. "What, where are you headed?" Beth pointed over his shoulder toward a bank of security cameras mounted high on the wall. "Cameras, mate. Let's hope they're working."

With a faint smile, she walked past him toward the three-railway staff by the exit. The tallest of the group straightened as she approached, his uniform crisply pressed despite the tension etched on his face. "You're Ted, right? Station Supervisor?" she asked, her tone brisk but not unkind. Ted nodded. "That's correct. Look, Sergeant, I—" Beth held up a hand, cutting him off. "No need for apologies, not right now. What I need from you is simple. These

64

two," she gestured to the other men, who exchanged uneasy glances, "out on the platform. Have them keep things calm and polite. Politely, Ted. Ask everyone to move into the booking hall. My Commanding Officer's on their way, and I need that platform cleared before they arrive."

The two men muttered between themselves but nodded, heading off toward the platform with a resigned air. Ted stayed put, his brow furrowed. "And what about me, Sergeant?" he asked, voice tinged with both respect and trepidation. Beth turned, pointing toward the cameras on the wall. "You're going to show me the footage from those cameras. They're working, right?" Ted nodded quickly. "Yes, they've been recording all evening." "Good," she replied, her tone sharper now. "Lead the way," she added, giving him a pointed look. As they made their way toward the control room, the muffled wail of sirens reached Beth's ears, growing louder with every second. She exhaled sharply, a small measure of relief flooding through her. Finally. Backup.

The Station Supervisor unlocked the heavy, secure metal door with a metallic click, pushing it open to reveal a small, dimly lit surveillance room. The air inside smelled faintly of stale coffee and old electronics. With a flick of the switch, the lights buzzed to life, casting a harsh white glow over the cramped space. "Screens are over there," he said, gesturing to a desk cluttered with monitors, a battered keyboard, and a single, worn-out chair. "Unfortunately, we only have one chair, so…" Beth stepped in, letting the door swing shut behind her with a soft thud. "That's OK," she replied, her tone brisk but polite. "I'll stand." She crossed her arms, scanning the setup as Ted, the Supervisor, lumbered over to the chair. It squealed loudly under his weight, the sound grating in the small room. He settled in and cracked his knuckles before typing in a password, the monitors flickering to life with grainy images of the station.

Ted cleared his throat, adopting a slightly formal tone. "As you can see, we've got four cameras. Two on the platform—one facing east, the other west—and two in the booking hall." He leaned back slightly, tapping his finger on the desk as if to punctuate his explanation. Beth narrowed her eyes at the screens, deep in thought. "Right," she said after a moment. "Let's check out Camera Two, the one facing east. Rewind it to about ten minutes before the train arrives."

Ted hesitated for a beat, as if savouring the opportunity to show his expertise. "The train came in at 2:07," he said, glancing at his watch as if confirming his memory. "So, that'd be 1:57. Here we go." He clicked on the screen, enlarged the feed for Camera Two, and began scrubbing backward through the footage. The monitor briefly fuzzed with static as the timeline rewound, the images jerking in reverse. "Stop," Beth said sharply. "That's it. Play from there."

Ted hit play, and the video rolled forward in real time. Leaning in, Beth rested her hand on the desk, just inches from Ted's. He could feel her presence keenly, her focus laser-sharp as her head hovered near his, their faces almost touching as they scrutinized the screen. A bead of sweat rolled down his temple, though the room wasn't warm. The seconds ticked by. The platform remained eerily empty. "OK," Beth said finally, her voice taut with impatience. "Fast forward to 2:06." Ted obeyed, clicking the button to speed up the footage. The scene blurred slightly as time accelerated. The train appeared in the distance, growing larger as it approached the station. The platform was still devoid of life. "Looks like our individual must have arrived late," Ted remarked, but Beth shushed him with a curt wave of her hand. The seconds flew past. Then, suddenly, a figure entered the frame.

"There!" Beth said sharply, her hand brushing Ted's aside as she pointed to the screen. Her movements were quick, almost involuntary, and her voice was electric with urgency. "Shit, there he is." Ted's eyes widened as he focused on the man. The figure seemed to emerge out of nowhere, stepping dangerously close to the platform's edge. Their gazes were glued to the screen as the train roared closer. The man swayed. Then, in an instant, he fell backward—just as the train thundered past the camera. "Shit!" the Sargeant exclaimed, her voice cracking. "Didn't see him go under." He turned to Beth, his face pale. "Why the hell would you want to see that, young lady?"

Beth blinked, realizing the implication of her earlier outburst. "No, sorry," she said quickly, her tone defensive but measured. "I didn't mean it like that. What I meant was, the camera angle cuts him off just as the train passes. We can't see what caused him to fall—it's just out of frame. We don't know if he jumped, slipped, or was pushed." Ted sighed heavily, rubbing his temples as he paused the video. He swivelled slightly in his chair to face Beth, his expression a mix of frustration and resignation. "I don't know what you're trying to find here," he said, his voice tinged with impatience. "It's clear as day. The guy just… fell, straight in front of the train. No one else was there, so he wasn't pushed." He leaned back, crossing his arms defensively. "Look, we get all kinds of people hanging around this station. Who's to say this poor guy wasn't just in a bad place? You know… suicide."

Beth stayed quiet for a moment; her gaze unwavering on the frozen image on the screen. She wasn't ready to dismiss this as an open-and-shut case. Finally, she broke the silence, her tone cool and steady. "Play it again. One more time, please." Ted sighed audibly but obliged, hitting play. Together, they watched the train glide into the station, the rhythmic clatter of its wheels almost audible in their minds. The driver's face was visible, a blurred figure looking straight ahead. The platform remained desolate as the train approached the edge of the camera's frame. Then, the man darted into view, his movements abrupt and frantic. The driver appeared to jolt inside the cab just as the man pitched forward, vanishing beneath the onrushing train. Ted slapped his hands on his thighs and turned to Beth, as if to say, "case closed." "See? Nothing. Just an unfortunate accident," he declared, his tone final.

Beth stood abruptly, her chair scraping against the floor. "No, it wasn't," she said firmly. "Rewind it. Five seconds." Ted groaned under his breath but complied, dragging the video timeline back. Again, they watched the moment play out. Ted was beginning to feel a queasy sense of monotony, replaying the man's death over and over, but Beth leaned forward, her eyes narrowing. She jabbed a finger at the screen. "There. Do you see that?" Ted squinted. "See what?"

Beth paused the video, her finger still hovering over the screen. "Look closely. Right there. Our friend isn't just running—he's looking over his shoulder. He's scared. He's running away from someone." Ted blinked, leaning in. "You think someone was chasing him?" His tone had softened, curiosity creeping in despite his earlier resistance. Beth didn't answer. Instead, she reached for the mouse, gently pushing Ted's hand away. Her fingers moved deftly, minimizing Camera Two and pulling up the feeds from the other three cameras. "This one," she said, selecting Camera Four. "Let's see what's in the booking hall."

Ted leaned back, folding his arms. "That's facing the entrance. You really think you'll find something there?" Beth didn't answer, already rewinding the footage. The screen flickered, the grainy video zipping backward until it reached 2:05. She hit pause. For a moment, nothing caught their attention. The entrance appeared empty; the road outside faintly visible. Overhead lights from the station created stark contrasts, casting the upper half of the screen into shadow. "Wait," Beth murmured, her voice low. She pointed to the edge of the frame, where the light met the shadow. "What's that?"

Ted squinted again. To the far left, just where the light faded, a faint outline was visible—shoes, half-hidden in darkness. "I wonder..." Beth whispered, her voice trailing off. Without hesitation, she minimized Camera Four and pulled up Camera Three. The feed shifted to show the booking office. Ted frowned. "What are you even looking for? The booking office closed at ten last night. Nobody's been in or out since." Beth ignored him, her eyes scanning the screen. "Do these cameras have zoom?" she asked, her voice clipped and focused. Ted nodded reluctantly. "Yeah. Hold the left mouse button and use the scroll wheel."

Beth worked quickly, zooming in on the glass window of the booking office. The image became grainier as she adjusted the angle, dragging the screen left and right. She was so absorbed in her task that she barely noticed Ted standing up and heading toward the door. "I've had enough of this," he muttered, his hand on the doorknob. "I'm going to check on the lads." Beth didn't respond. The door clicked shut behind him, leaving her alone with the hum of the monitors and her own steady breathing. She continued scanning the video feed, her fingers methodically dragging and zooming until something on the screen made her freeze.

Her heart skipped a beat as her eyes locked on the reflection in the glass. There, faint but unmistakable, stood a tall man. His long hair and beard were unkempt, and his hollow gaze seemed to pierce through the screen. Her stomach turned as she took in the details of his attire: a grey tracksuit, the kind issued in prison. Beth's breath hitched. She leaned closer, her voice barely a whisper. "Holy shit…"

***

03:02 hours, July 26th 2024 - Hammersmith, London

The searchlights danced relentlessly across the murky river, their beams slicing through the darkness and reflecting off the rippling water, where secrets from decades past lay hidden. On the north and south banks, Officers scoured the terrain, while the steady hum of helicopters filled the air. DCI Craig stood motionless on the muddy shore, his overcoat flapping in the cold night wind. His eyes tracked a police boat zigzagging the current, its engine growling faintly against the noise of the search. The scene was tense, charged with the weight of what—or who—they were hunting.

Behind him, the crunch of footsteps on gravel signalled company. Detective Louis Paulo emerged from the gloom, clutching two steaming cups of tea. Passing one to his superior, Louis gestured to the river. "You really think he swam across?" he asked sceptically. The DCI raised the cup to his lips, only to curse as the hot liquid seared his tongue. "Maybe across to the south bank – waters full of all kinds of shit though. If I were in his shoes, I'd head for the coast. Keep away from major ports and harbours. Maybe commandeer a smaller boat. My guess? South coast. Somewhere quiet." Both men turned their gaze skyward as a helicopter roared overhead, its rotors thundering like a drumbeat of urgency. The spotlight it wielded skimmed the water before circling back westward. The radio crackled, snapping both men back to attention. "Halo Seven to DCI Craig, copy," came the pilot's voice. The DCI pressed the transmit button. "Copy, go ahead." "Sir, we've finished the south bank sweep. No signs of the convict. Returning to base for refuel. Over." The DCI's jaw tightened as he watched the helicopter bank sharply, its lights fading into the distance. Before he could dwell on the setback, another Officer jogged over, holding a slip of paper.

"Update from the prison, Sir. We've spoken to more inmates. Turns out one of them had a run-in with the convict six months back. Bad one. The guy ended up in the infirmary for a month. Broken pelvis, both arms dislocated…" The Officer hesitated, glancing at both men. "And?" Louis pressed. The Officer swallowed. "He also tried to crush the man's skull. Guards intervened before he could finish him off." The DCI exhaled sharply; his breath visible in the chill night air. He watched a duck take off from the water as a police RIB sped by, its wake rippling toward the shore. "Nothing we haven't heard before," he muttered. "Just another violent scumbag. But tell me—how'd he get his hands on a weapon?" The Officer shook his head. "He didn't, Sir. He used his hands."

Louis froze mid-sip, lowering the report in his hand. Before anyone could respond, the DCI's phone rang, its shrill tone slicing through the night. "DCI Craig," he barked. "This is Bravo Charlie One, Sir," came a brisk voice. "Patching through a call from a Sergeant at a train station in Dagenham. She says it's about a fatality." The DCI groaned, irritation flaring. "I'm a bit busy, Command, it's probably a suicide. Get a detective to—" "Apologies, Sir," the voice interrupted. "She insisted it's urgent." The mention of urgency froze the DCI in place – had the convict been hit by a train? He muttered under his breath before hitting the speaker button. "DCI Craig speaking. Go ahead." A woman's voice came through, tentative but firm. "Sir, this is Sergeant Beth Rose. I'm at Dagenham Dock Station. We've had a fatality."

"Is he dead?" the DCI snapped, hoping against hope. A pause. "Well, yes, Sir, it's a fatality. But that's not why I'm calling." The DCI's patience wore thin. "Then make it quick, Sergeant. What's the issue?" Rose took a steadying breath. "Sir, I believe the man you're hunting was in the vicinity at 2:05 a.m. I've reviewed CCTV footage from the platform and booking hall. There's a reflection in the glass—a man fitting the description posted to our station." The DCI exchanged a glance with Louis, muttering a curse. "North," he whispered. "He's heading north." Gripping the phone tighter, the DCI's mind raced. "Sergeant Rose, stay where you are. Detective

Paulo is en route to verify the footage. Lock down the station and position Officers at all access points. I'll dispatch helicopters to sweep the train line in case he's using it to escape. Understand?" "Yes, Sir," she replied.

The DCI ended the call with a decisive click, turning sharply to Louis, who was already striding toward his car. "Leave the car!" he barked after him, his voice slicing through the tension in the air. Louis stopped mid-step, glancing back with a raised brow. "Halo Three will pick you up. Get to the clearing in the park—now. I need confirmation in twenty minutes. Understood?" Louis nodded, his movements quickening into a jog. The fading sound of his footsteps was lost beneath the rush of the restless river as the DCI stared into the darkness. Somewhere out there, Aubrey was slipping further and further from their grasp. Every second that passed brought him closer to the outskirts of London, where the dense network of surveillance cameras gave way to the shadows of the countryside. If he reached those quiet, unmonitored roads, it wouldn't just be a chase—it would be a needle in a haystack.

The DCI's jaw tightened as he keyed his radio. "DCI Craig to Command, copy?" "Copy, DCI." "I need Halo Three on the deck immediately to collect Detective Paulo and take him to Dagenham. Once they're airborne, notify me at once. Additionally, I want all senior staff in the briefing room in five minutes. Tell Sergeant Jones to bring detailed maps of every major road leading in and out of the city. Full coverage. Understood?" "Understood, Sir. over."

The line went silent. The DCI exhaled sharply, the weight of the operation pressing down like a lead blanket. Time was their enemy now, and it wasn't on their side. He pulled his phone from his pocket, scrolling swiftly through the contacts before landing on Detective Mauro Arruda's name. The phone rang twice before Mauro's familiar, crisp voice answered, "Yes, sir?" "Mauro, listen carefully. We're going to need Operations to ramp this up. I need you to push for more manpower." There was a brief pause on the other end, a telltale sign of Mauro piecing it together. "Understood, but how many units are we talking?"

"All available. Aubrey is heading north—or so it seems. I'm expecting visual confirmation from Louis shortly, but we can't afford to sit on our hands. I want roadblocks on every major artery north and northeast of the Thames. If he makes it past our perimeter, he's gone. I know it's a tall order, but we don't have the luxury of time." "Yes, sir," Mauro said firmly. "I'll make it happen." The DCI ended the call, his fingers curling tightly around the phone. The city sprawled before him, a labyrinth of opportunities for escape. Somewhere within that maze, Aubrey was running, his path lined with potential traps for the team. But the DCI wasn't about to let him slip through—not tonight.

The clock was ticking, and the DCI was determined to beat it.

Chapter 6
08:30 hours, 26th July 2024,
Francis Crick, London

The lab doors hissed open with a sterile precision, and Bill stepped into the dimly lit hallway. Almost immediately, a guard rose from his desk, his heavy boots echoing off the polished floor. The man was built like a refrigerator, with a buzz cut and an expression of perpetual suspicion. He held up a hand, signalling Bill to stop. "Sorry, Doctor. You know the drill," the guard said, his voice gruff but professional. Bill reached into his pocket, pulling out his security pass, and held it up for inspection. He stared blankly at the guard, offering no small talk or pleasantries. The guard's eyes flicked between the photo on the ID and Bill's face, scrutinizing every detail with the precision of a forensic examiner. "Looks good," the guard finally said, handing the pass back. "Have a nice day."

Bill gave a slight nod, slipping the card back into his pocket as the guard retreated to his desk. He continued down the corridor, the motion sensors detecting his presence and activating the ceiling lights in synchronized bursts. Each step he took illuminated more of the path ahead, revealing pristine white walls that seemed to stretch endlessly. At the far end of the corridor, a single red metal door stood in stark contrast to the sterile surroundings. A prominent biohazard symbol was painted next to the door's biometric scanner, a silent reminder of the danger that lay beyond.

The corridor always felt longer than it was, a psychological trick of its blank, featureless design. As Bill walked, the soft tap, tap of his shoes against the tiles reverberated in the otherwise silent space. Despite the ominous surroundings, his mood was unusually light.

Whistling a cheerful tune—a habit that earned him the occasional side-eye from his colleagues—he made his way toward the red door. It was the kind of whistling that wasn't so much about happiness but rather a way to fill the silence, to push back the weight of the tomb-like atmosphere.

When he reached the door, he stopped, his hand hovering over the biometric scanner. Placing his thumb on the pad, he watched as a green light swept across the ridges of his print. A soft beep followed, and the heavy locking mechanism clicked open. Bill pushed the door with his shoulder, its weight requiring more effort than it seemed, and stepped inside. He let it swing closed behind him, pausing to ensure the latch engaged fully. The last thing anyone wanted was a compromised seal in this particular lab.

The room beyond the door was a stark contrast to the corridor. This was the heart of the facility, the nerve centre of their research. Rows of sleek, black workstations were lined with cutting-edge equipment—centrifuges, spectrometers, and microscopes that cost more than a small house. Large monitors displayed scrolling data and molecular structures in vivid detail. In the centre of the lab stood an isolation chamber, its reinforced glass walls encasing a sample containment unit bathed in a faint blue light. Bill scanned the room, his gaze landing on Tom, who was hunched over one of the workstations. The man's shoulders were tense, his fingers moving swiftly across a keyboard. His muttered curses were barely audible over the faint hum of the lab's air filtration system. "Morning, Tom," Bill said, his voice breaking the monotony of the room.

Tom didn't look up. "Morning. You're late," he coughed into his hand. Bill frowned slightly but didn't reply. He made his way to the lockers near the far wall, their surfaces gleaming under the overhead lights. He placed his briefcase on the bench and began to unpack, retrieving his lab coat, gloves, and a pair of safety goggles. As he buttoned up his coat, Bill glanced over his shoulder at Tom, who was now peering into a microscope, his brow furrowed in concentration. "What's got you such a cheerful mood?" Bill asked, a touch of sarcasm in his tone. Tom straightened, rubbing the back of his neck. "Another batch of samples from the Midlands came in this morning. Same story. Aggressive proliferation, no response to the new inhibitors." Bill sighed, the upbeat whistle from earlier now a distant memory. "Well, let's hope today's the day we find something new."

Tom gave a noncommittal grunt and returned to his work. Bill turned his attention to his workstation, powering up his computer and pulling up the day's agenda. The screen flickered to life, displaying an array of reports, graphs, and images of cellular structures. The samples they were studying weren't just cases—they were people. Faces he would never meet but whose lives hung in the balance. As the data loaded, Bill's thoughts drifted back to the rumours of the STSU. The idea of militarized science was troubling, but part of him couldn't help but wonder if they were running out of time for ethical considerations. If their lab couldn't crack this, who else could?

"Morning, Doctor," Jackson greeted, stepping into the lab and carefully securing the door behind him. Bill turned to acknowledge him with a curt nod, his attention still focused on the rows of data displayed on his computer screen. "Morning," Bill replied, barely looking up from the glowing screen. He was deep in concentration, scanning through the test results from the previous day. Jackson, undeterred by Bill's distracted response, began unbuttoning his coat and hanging it on one of the designated hooks along the wall. "I'll review last night's test results before our briefing at 0-900," Bill continued, finally glancing at Jackson. "Can you and Tom start preparing today's batch? I want to make sure we're ready to proceed before lunch. Is that clear?" "Yes, of course, Doctor," Jackson replied, but as he turned to leave, he noticed Bill was already deep into the lab, snatching a clipboard off Tom's desk. Jackson shook his head, amused at how quickly his superior always moved. Bill's pace, always brisk and deliberate, left little room for unnecessary chatter.

As Jackson finished changing into his white coveralls, he joined Bill and Tom at the lab's central workstation. Bill, his face tight with concentration, was scanning through pages of data, his fingers tapping the clipboard with a rhythm that betrayed his frustration. "Is everything okay, Sir?" Jackson asked, unsure of the source of Bill's apparent anxiety. "No, Jackson, it's not," Bill muttered, not looking up from the pages. "These figures don't make any sense." He paused, tapping his pen against his cheek in thought. "Are you sure these are from yesterday's tests?" Jackson exchanged a quick glance with Tom, who simply nodded. "Yes, sir," Jackson confirmed. "I ran them first thing this morning, and the unique batch numbers are listed on the left, as you can see. The results on the right match."

Bill didn't respond immediately, his gaze intense as he dissected each line of data. He considered asking Jackson to rerun the tests, but something told him it wasn't a simple case of error. He looked up, locking eyes with Jackson. "So let me get this straight," Bill said slowly, his voice laced with a hint of disbelief. "For my own sanity, let me confirm that we ran 123 tests yesterday, all of which were uploaded to the system and ready for analysis. We're double-checking that the data input was precise and that it matches the result sheets?" "Yes, that's right," Jackson confirmed, though he could sense Bill's growing unease.

Bill's expression didn't change, but he was still troubled by something. "What I'm still struggling to understand," he continued, "is which blood samples were these taken from?" At this, Jackson perked up. "They were taken from X198-YZ," he said, his voice quickening with confidence. "This is the batch that arrived last week. Remember?" Tom, ever the more cautious one, added, "The unmarked crate, Sir." Bill's mind flashed back to the previous week. The blood samples that had arrived under mysterious circumstances—a consignment that hadn't come through the usual channels, instead being cleared by security and making its way directly to their lab without explanation.

"Right," Bill muttered, walking over to the filing cabinet at the far end of the room. Jackson followed, opening the drawer and rifling through the hanging files. With a quiet exclamation of success, Jackson pulled out the folder marked with the sample numbers. "Here we go," he said, walking back to Bill's desk. Bill took the clipboard from Jackson's hands, his eyes scanning the paperwork as he processed the information. The batch—numbers 7986 to 8009—matched the consignment note exactly. He nodded in agreement, but a seed of doubt still lingered in his mind. "Excuse me, sir," Jackson asked hesitantly, his brow furrowed with concern. "Is there a problem?"

Bill didn't respond immediately. Instead, he turned back toward his desk, placing the clipboard down and quickly typing in the batch numbers into his computer. The machine hummed softly as the system ran the figures, comparing them against the existing data. Bill leaned over the desk, his elbows resting on the surface as he stared at the screen, his eyes following the movements of the data with laser-like precision. The cursor hovered over the "Run" button, and with a deliberate click, the computer began to process the figures. Bill held his breath, his fingers drumming against the surface of the desk as the hourglass icon appeared, signalling that the system was working. The seconds stretched into minutes, and Bill's patience was tested to its limits.

The numbers slowly began to populate on the screen, the data shifting and recalculating with eerie precision. Bill's eyes moved rapidly over the results, his gaze narrowing as he studied the figures. Suddenly, he stopped, his hand frozen just above the mouse. The smile that crept across his face was one of both surprise and cautious optimism. "Well, I'll be damned," Bill whispered, his voice low as if he couldn't quite believe what he was seeing. Jackson and Tom exchanged looks of confusion and curiosity as Bill slowly stood up from his desk. His hands were shaking slightly as he grabbed the clipboard again, scanning over the paperwork with renewed interest. The results of sample 8008, buried among the others, seemed to tell a different story—a story they had been waiting for but had not expected so soon.

The data was… promising. Almost too promising.

Bill's grin grew wider, the realization of what he was looking at beginning to sink in. "Bloody hell," he muttered, more to himself than to the others. He turned to Jackson and Tom, his eyes alight with excitement. "I think we may have something here." Jackson's heart skipped a beat, and Tom stood up straight, his eyes wide with anticipation. It wasn't often that Bill's stone-faced demeanour cracked, but when it did, it usually meant they were on the brink of a breakthrough. They had been working on this for years, chasing answers in a world that seemed increasingly reluctant to give them up. And now, just as the situation was growing increasingly dire, they might finally have discovered something that could change everything.

But as Bill scanned the numbers once more, he knew the road ahead would be fraught with obstacles. This discovery—if it was indeed a discovery—would come with its own set of questions, and Bill wasn't ready to raise his hopes just yet. Still, for the first time in a long while, a sense of cautious optimism began to take root. They were onto something. Finally.

Chapter 7
03:27 hours, July 26th 2024,
Beam Parklands Country Park, East London

The mud clung stubbornly to his sweater, its damp chill seeping through the fabric as he lay sprawled on the field at the crest of the hill. From this vantage point, he could watch the intricate dance of vehicles weaving along the motorway below. The M25, notorious for its endless congestion, was eerily subdued at this early hour. Only hulking HGVs lumbered along, their headlights carving pale streaks into the morning gloom as they rumbled east before curving south towards Folkestone and the Channel Tunnel. The hum of their engines was a faint backdrop to the otherwise tranquil stillness.

He shifted slightly, his eyes flicking towards the horizon where the first faint blush of dawn began to chase the night away. Behind him, the city loomed like a shadowed titan, its skyline jagged with ambition. The Shard rose proudly above its neighbours, a crystalline sentinel over the gleaming towers of Canary Wharf. Tiny pinpricks of light traced the heavens above, airplanes drawing invisible lines in the sky as they converged on Heathrow and Gatwick. It was a mesmerizing tableau, one that might have inspired awe if he were not so bone-weary.

To his right, the M11 snaked its way out of the capital like a living thing, its curves and straightaways bathed in the dim glow of scattered streetlights. He watched as cars darted below the M25, vanishing momentarily beneath a bridge only to reappear moments later, speeding north. Each movement was a reminder of the life carrying on as usual—a life from which he was now irreparably severed.

The last twelve hours had been a brutal gauntlet, a punishing blend of physical strain and mental endurance. Every muscle ached, every nerve was stretched taut, but there was no time to rest. He knew the daylight would bring an added layer of danger. In the dark, he could fade into the shadows, but once the sun rose, there would be nowhere to hide. All it would take was one set of curious eyes, one bystander recognizing his face, and the police would close in like hounds on a scent. They would release his prison mugshot soon, no doubt urging the public to assist in his capture. He could almost hear the appeal, the carefully chosen words designed to stir civic duty.

But first, he had to cross the motorway, a feat as dangerous as any he had faced so far. Rising slowly, he brushed at the worst of the mud clinging to his hands and knees, though the effort was futile. Every movement was deliberate, calculated. He couldn't afford mistakes. Edging down the slope, he moved toward the dense hedge that lined the northbound carriageway of the M11. The branches scratched at his hands as he pushed his way through, the smell of damp earth and crushed leaves sharp in the cold air.

He crouched low, scanning the traffic. Timing was everything. A single misstep could spell disaster, but failure was not an option. His plan demanded stealth, precision, and above all, distance. The farther he got from London, the better his odds. Each mile put him closer to freedom, but also deeper into the unknown. As he prepared to make his move, his mind raced. The choices he made in the next few minutes could determine everything. Would he make it unseen, or would this hill, with its perfect view of the capital, become his last?

The bag felt heavier in his hand than it should have, its contents rattling faintly with each step. The sharp klink of glass striking glass was a reminder of the audacity of his plan. It was reckless, yes, but also essential. If he wanted to move forward, if he had any chance of staying ahead, this gambit had to succeed. His heart pounded; the rhythm more intense than the quiet thrum of distant engines.

Reaching the hedge, he crouched low and pressed himself into a small gap, the thorns snagging at his clothes as he wriggled through. Beyond the hedge, a wooden fence stood as the final barrier, its weathered planks creaking softly as he climbed over. Crouching again on the other side, he scanned the road ahead. The M11 stretched out like a silver ribbon, glistening faintly in the headlights of vehicles streaking past in an unending stream of motion. He turned his head right, eyes fixed on the blur of lights sweeping past one after another. Each vehicle's roar seemed louder than the last, a reminder of how fast time was slipping through his fingers. The timing had to be flawless.

Forty minutes passed. Forty tense, agonizing minutes during which he watched the flow of traffic, calculating patterns and waiting for the exact conditions he needed. His muscles ached from staying still, but his focus never wavered. Finally, he saw it: a lorry towing an empty flatbed trailer barrelling down the motorway. He tracked it as it moved into the left lane and signalled to join the M25 eastbound. It was perfect—exactly the disruption he needed to buy a few precious seconds.

He turned his head south, scanning for the next vehicle in line. A single pair of headlights pierced the darkness about a mile away, growing brighter by the second. It was closing fast. The window of opportunity was narrowing. Now or never.

Adrenaline surged as he climbed over the fence and launched himself down the embankment, his feet slipping slightly on the dewy grass. Reaching the edge of the slow lane, he knelt and quickly upended the bag, its contents clinking as they spilled out in a glittering cascade across the asphalt. Shards of broken glass glinted like tiny, jagged stars under the sweeping headlights. The trap was set.

His mind raced through the critical factors that would make or break this gambit:

The car had to be traveling in the slow lane. If the driver changed lanes too soon, the plan would unravel.

The driver needed to stop when they hit the debris. A spare tire and the know-how to replace it were essential.

And most crucially, the driver had to remain on the M11, heading north, once they resumed their journey.

Glancing back toward the oncoming vehicle, he estimated he had maybe twenty seconds—thirty at most—before it reached the glass-strewn section of road. He turned and sprinted back up the hill, his legs burning with the effort. Every step felt like a lifetime as he made for the cover of the hedge. From this vantage point, he could see Junction 8 in the distance, the motorway branching off like veins in a great iron network. Eight hundred yards down the road, the junction loomed—a critical fork where the M11 met the broader web of highways.

Hidden at the top of the hill, he crouched low, breathing hard, his pulse roaring in his ears. This was the moment of truth. He cast one last glance back at the car, its headlights a piercing glare in the darkness. The plan was in motion now, completely beyond his control. All he could do was watch, wait, and hope that fate would favour him just this once. If it didn't—if the driver didn't stop or turned onto the M25 instead of continuing north—everything he'd done, every risk he'd taken, would be for nothing. As the car drew closer to the trap, he tightened his grip on the wooden fence beside him. The outcome was no longer in his hands.

****

The Ford Raptor thundered down the motorway in the middle lane, its oversized frame slicing through the cool night air. Inside, the Didlick twins, Chloe and Laura, were in full concert mode, their voices blending into a spirited, albeit off-key, rendition of Cruel Summer. The truck swerved slightly, veering into the fast lane as Chloe gestured dramatically to an imaginary crowd, then back toward the middle lane as the sisters belted out the song's final chorus.

The energy was electric, fuelled by the afterglow of a sold-out Taylor Swift concert at the O2 Arena. They'd spent two hours trapped in the chaos of the car park, inching forward in agonizing increments, followed by an equally frustrating forty-five minutes navigating the Blackwall Tunnel. Now, as the clock ticked past midnight, they were finally free, barrelling down the open road with the windows cracked just enough to let in the brisk night breeze. The frustrations of the evening had melted away, replaced by adrenaline and music-fuelled euphoria.

As the song ended, Chloe glanced at the speedometer. Her stomach dropped. "Shit, better slow down," she muttered, noticing the needle hovering just below ninety-five miles per hour. Laura let out a dismissive laugh, flipping her long hair over her shoulder. "Why? There's no police out this late. Besides, I've got work in four hours, and I need to get to bed. Hit the gas, love." Chloe shook her head, easing the truck down to a more sensible seventy-five. "Yeah, well, I'd rather not get pulled over, thanks. I loved that song though. Shall we play it again?" Laura grinned, her eyes sparkling with mischief. "Why not? What is this, the seventh time? Hell, let's make it eight!"

As if on cue, Taylor Swift's voice burst through the speakers once more. The sisters swayed their heads in perfect sync, laughing as they crooned along. Chloe let herself get carried away by the rhythm, her eyes fluttering closed briefly with the motion. "Hey, lady, keep the car in the lane, will ya?" Laura barked, nudging Chloe's arm with mock severity. Chloe snapped her eyes open, grinning sheepishly, and corrected the truck's course. Laura turned up the volume, drowning the cab in the pulsating beats of Cruel Summer. They were mid-chorus, screaming along with the iconic line—"Whoa-oh, and it's a cruel summer..."—when Laura's eyes widened in horror.

"WATCH OUT!"

The Raptor's front tires struck the glass before Chloe could process what was happening. Tiny shards shot up beneath the chassis, ricocheting with sharp, metallic pings. The truck jolted violently to the left, veering toward the grass verge. "What the fuck?!" Laura screamed, gripping the door handle. Chloe yanked the wheel in a panicked overcorrection, sending the truck careening toward the central reservation. The rear tires skidded, rubber shredding against the jagged shards littering the road. With a deafening BANG, the rear passenger-side tire burst, sending debris flying into the night.

The Raptor spun wildly, its massive frame twisting across the lanes in a cacophony of screeching metal and smoking rubber. Finally, it came to a shuddering halt on the hard shoulder, facing the correct direction but battered and askew. For a long moment, neither sister moved. Chloe's hands gripped the steering wheel so tightly her knuckles turned white. Her breath came in shallow gasps. "You okay?" she managed, her voice barely above a whisper. Laura turned slowly, her face pale. "What the hell just happened?" Chloe shook her head, exhaling shakily. "Beats me…" Reaching forward, she silenced the radio. The cab descended into eerie quiet, broken only by the ticking sound of the cooling engine.

Minutes passed before they finally unbuckled their seatbelts and stepped out into the cold night. The breeze was sharp against their flushed skin, offering little comfort as they surveyed the damage. The sisters circled the truck, starting at the front and moving cautiously toward the back. "Bloody hell, sis," Laura said, pointing at the shredded rear tire. "Look at that. It's completely wrecked." Chloe ran a hand through her hair, muttering under her breath. Laura started pacing. "Alright, don't panic. We've got a spare, yeah? We just need to swap it out, and we'll be good to go. No harm done." Chloe nodded, pulling open the truck's hatch. "Here it is. Come on, give us a hand."

Together, they wrestled the spare tire onto the grass. The sharp scent of burned rubber lingered in the air as Laura glanced back down the road. Under the harsh glare of the roadside lights, the scattered glass sparkled like diamonds. "Would you look at that?" Laura murmured; her voice tinged with unease. "It looks like someone smashed a chandelier or something." Chloe straightened, wiping her hands on her jeans. "Yeah, or something," she said grimly. As they prepared to fix the tire, a sliver of doubt crept into their thoughts.

"Hey, will you focus? We need to get this changed pronto." Chloe's voice cut through the cool night air, sharp with frustration. She stood with her hands on her hips, her silhouette illuminated by the headlights of the Ford Raptor. Laura, crouching near the shredded wheel, looked up and smirked. "So… you've done this before, I take it?" "Nope," Chloe admitted with a shrug, "but it can't be rocket science."

Stepping back onto the grassy verge, Chloe studied the truck critically. "At least we're on level ground—that's something. Last thing we need is this beast tipping over on us." She turned to check on Laura's progress but stopped when she noticed her sister's distracted gaze. Laura wasn't listening. Her eyes were fixed on the motorway, her expression tense. The shards of glass on the road still sparkled under the lights, but Laura's attention was further down, toward a faint glow in the distance. "Is that… police cars?" she asked, squinting into the dark.

Chloe straightened, following her sister's line of sight. A flicker of blue light danced on the horizon. "Looks like it. Maybe we can flag one down and get some help." Both girls stood, their hands shading their eyes as the flashing lights drew closer. Laura tilted her head, murmuring, "Looks like they've stopped for something… wait, no, they're still coming. They must have just slowed down." Chloe glanced back at the shredded tire, then at the spare lying useless on the ground. She scratched her chin thoughtfully. "You know what? I don't think I can do this. Let's try flagging them down—ladies in distress and all that. Might as well see if chivalry isn't dead."

The two of them moved a few meters away from the truck, stepping cautiously onto the hard shoulder. Chloe nudged Laura with her elbow. "Alright, sis. Start jumping and waving your arms. Give it some drama." Without hesitation, they threw their hands in the air, waving frantically as the first police car sped toward them in the fast lane. The vehicle's blue lights reflected off the tarmac like ripples of water, the Officers inside giving them a quick glance— then accelerating forward. "What the hell!" Chloe snapped, dropping her arms in disbelief.

Laura huffed, her hands on her hips. "Seriously? Unbelievable." She glanced back at the convoy of police cars behind the first. Her face lit up with sudden determination. "Hang on, I've got an idea." Chloe turned just in time to see her sister scrambling onto the back of the truck, hoisting herself up onto the flatbed with surprising agility. "What are you doing?" Chloe demanded, rolling her eyes.

"They have to see us now!" Laura shot back, standing tall and waving both arms above her head like a shipwreck survivor flagging down a passing boat. Chloe snorted but couldn't hide her grin. "Alright, Captain Drama, let's hope your performance gets their attention." More flashing lights appeared in the distance, growing brighter as the convoy of police cars approached. The rumble of engines was now unmistakable, the sound building like a storm. Laura turned her head, frowning as the lead car veered left, leaving the motorway to block the exit to the M25. "What on earth are they doing?" Laura muttered, climbing down from the truck.

The line of police cars began to slow as they neared the stranded vehicle. The convoy moved in perfect formation, lights flashing rhythmically. Chloe and Laura exchanged uneasy glances as the cars manoeuvred around their position with precision, the Officers seemingly more focused on the surrounding area than on the girls themselves. In the lead car, Sergeant Dave Greggs leaned forward, his eyes narrowing as he spotted the Raptor on the shoulder. Picking up his radio, he thumbed the transmit button. "Tango Whisky Four, pull over and check out that vehicle," he ordered, his tone calm but firm. The reply came instantly. "Copy that."

Greggs checked his rear-view mirror, watching as the last vehicle in the convoy glided smoothly past the truck before pulling over in front of it. Inside the Raptor, Chloe and Laura exchanged nervous glances. "What's with the whole convoy for a flat tire?" Chloe whispered. Laura, still staring at the flashing lights, shook her head. "I don't know, but this feels like overkill. Something's going on."

As the last police car came to a stop, a single Officer stepped out, his flashlight cutting through the night as he approached. His hand hovered near his utility belt as he scanned the scene, his expression unreadable. "Evening, ladies," he said, his voice steady but cautious. "Everything alright here?" Chloe opened her mouth to respond, but Laura cut her off, pointing down the road. "We hit something—a bunch of glass. Look down there, it's everywhere. Then the tire blew out, and—"

The Officer held up a hand to silence her, his eyes narrowing as he followed her gesture toward the sparkling debris on the motorway. Turning back to his radio, he spoke quietly but urgently. "Dispatch, confirm location of the target. Possible connection to debris on M11, requesting immediate update."

The sisters exchanged a confused look.

"Target?" Chloe mouthed.

***

The plan had gone off without a hitch—so far. Thirty tense minutes had passed since Aubrey had triggered the first stage of his elaborate escape strategy. From his concealed position behind the hedgerow, he watched the scene unfold with laser focus, his muscles coiled like a predator waiting for the perfect moment to strike. The police Officer had exited his vehicle and approached the stranded pickup truck, where the two girls stood awkwardly by the spare tire. The Officer appeared to be chatting amiably, while the other, gesturing firmly for the girl perched on the back of the truck to climb down.

Aubrey's mind raced as he calculated his next move. By his reckoning, nearly an hour had passed since he'd shattered the glass on the road and retreated into the shadows. Time was slipping away. The first light of dawn was creeping ever closer, and with it, the risk of being spotted increased exponentially. His options were dwindling: either he stayed put and prayed for an opportunity to present itself—a risky gamble—or he doubled back, abandoning the carefully plotted route north in favour of a hastily improvised alternative. Neither option inspired confidence.

He shifted his gaze back to the police vehicles, their flashing lights casting an eerie glow across the empty motorway. The Officers had fortified their position, setting up blockades at the underpass on the northbound M11 and reinforcing the slip road leading to the M25. They weren't just searching for a needle in a haystack; they were determined to burn the whole haystack down if that's what it took to find him. Aubrey clenched his jaw. His only viable path forward was the pickup truck.

His eyes darted back to the girls and the Officer. The situation remained chaotic but manageable. The policeman, still preoccupied with the girls, wasn't paying attention to the broader surroundings. He spoke into his radio, while the girls gestured toward the shredded tire. The Officer nodded, then grabbed a broom from his car and headed over to the loose shards of glass, sweeping them onto the hard shoulder. Seconds stretched into minutes. Each tick of the clock was a fresh jolt to Aubrey's fraying nerves. He couldn't afford to wait much longer. He crouched lower, his fingers pressing into the damp soil as he calculated the precise timing, he'd need to execute his plan.

Movement caught his eye. Up ahead, amber lights flickered in the darkness. A recovery truck had arrived, pulling to a stop in front of the Ford Raptor. The bald man who emerged was dressed in coveralls and a hi-vis vest, his demeanour brisk and professional as he greeted the girls. Aubrey's heartbeat quickened. This new development could complicate things—or provide the opening he desperately needed.

The police were thorough. Too thorough. The Officer began a meticulous search of the Raptor, crawling underneath to inspect the undercarriage before moving to the cab. He rifled through the glove compartment, tossing its contents onto the passenger seat, and then moved to the truck bed, pulling out a toolbox and other gear for inspection. Satisfied there was nothing suspicious, the Officer walked over to the recovery truck and subjected it to the same scrutiny. Meanwhile, the bald man seemed engrossed in conversation with the girls, gesturing to the damaged tire and then pointing toward his truck. He looked relaxed, even cracking a joke that elicited a faint laugh from the sisters. Aubrey noted the exchange with interest. People at ease made mistakes.

As the Officer concluded his search, he spoke into his radio again. His words were indistinct from this distance, but the meaning was clear enough when he gave a thumbs-up to his partner. The Officer waved to the girls, who responded with polite nods before the man climbed back into his patrol car. Within moments, the vehicle roared to life and sped off, joining the blockade under the bridge.

Aubrey exhaled slowly; his breath visible in the cool night air. The scene had changed, but his window of opportunity hadn't closed entirely. The girls and the recovery driver remained by the truck, seemingly engrossed in their conversation. The motorway was quieter now, save for the occasional car being redirected at the roadblocks. He studied the roadblocks intently. Each vehicle that approached was stopped, its driver ordered to exit while Officers and dogs conducted a painstaking search. The process was efficient, almost mechanical, but it wasn't foolproof. Aubrey could see the cracks forming in the operation's rhythm. The Officers were spread thin, their attention divided between the search and maintaining traffic flow.

His gaze snapped back to the pickup truck. The Raptor was still functional despite its damaged tire, and its size and power made it an ideal vehicle for his needs. He watched the girls laughing nervously as the bald man fetched tools from his truck, oblivious to the tension simmering just out of sight. A plan began to form in Aubrey's mind. It was risky—desperate, even—but it was all he had. Timing would be everything. He sank lower into the bush, his muscles tensing as he prepared to make his move.

✳✳✳

The bald Asian man, Ben, scratched the dry skin on the back of his head, visibly uncomfortable. "Look, I'm really sorry, but we don't stock these kinds of tires. The best I can do is tow you to the next service station." Chloe's shoulders slumped as she exchanged a glance with her sister. Laura, clearly fuming, threw up her hands. "This is bullshit! I'm gonna be late for work now. Just great! What's wrong with the spare we've got on the floor?" Ben looked down at the offending tire, rubbing the back of his neck with a sheepish expression. "Uh, yeah… that's a tractor tire. It won't fit your truck. Someone must've swapped it at some point. Happens more often than you'd think." Chloe crossed her arms, glaring at him. "OK, so if that's all you can do, what happens now?"

Ben motioned toward his van. "Look, it's cold out here, and you two look like you're freezing. Go sit in the cab; the heater's on. I'll get your truck hooked up. We'll be rolling in twenty minutes tops." The girls exchanged a glance, muttered a half-hearted "fine," and stomped off toward the warmth of the van, slamming the door behind them. Ben sighed and turned back to the task at hand. He loaded the spare tractor tire into the bed of the pickup, then bent down to retrieve the rubber wheel blocks he'd placed under the truck earlier.

From the shadows, Aubrey crouched low behind the timber fence, his muscles taut as he watched Benny's every move. This was the opportunity he'd been waiting for. The growing queue of cars and lorries behind the police blockade meant time was running out. If he didn't act now, he'd be trapped as more vehicles filled the lanes, making an undetected escape impossible. Aubrey inhaled deeply, steadying his nerves. As Ben turned and walked toward his van to check on the girls, Aubrey launched himself over the fence in one fluid motion. He darted down the embankment, his boots slipping slightly on the dew-soaked grass but regaining balance as he reached the tarmac. The back of the pickup was still open. He slid inside, pressing his body flat and pulling the hatch shut behind him just as Ben came back into view.

Inside the van, Chloe and Laura sat in silence, the warmth of the heater doing little to thaw the tension between them. Laura sat hunched by the window, arms crossed, her foot tapping against the floor as her mind raced. How was she going to explain this mess to her boss? Late wasn't even the word for it now. Chloe, on the other hand, stared straight ahead, watching the sea of taillights stretching into the distance. A sudden bump rocked the van as Ben re-entered, making Chloe jolt in her seat. "Right," he said, his tone chipper, "all set back there. Your truck's secure, and we're good to go." Chloe forced a polite smile. "Thanks for your help. We appreciate it."

Ben gave a friendly nod, then turned the van around, skilfully manoeuvring it into the growing line of vehicles creeping toward the roadblock. Behind them, the Ford Raptor rattled slightly on the tow platform, its weight causing the entire setup to sway as Ben navigated around impatient drivers honking their horns.

Hidden in the truck bed, Aubrey lay perfectly still, his breathing shallow as the vibrations of the tow rattled through his body. He'd pressed himself into the tightest corner of the bed, cloaked in shadow and surrounded by loose tools and debris. The queue of vehicles slowed to a crawl as they approached the police checkpoint.

Aubrey's heartbeat quickened. He listened intently, his ear pressed to the cold metal. Outside, Officers barked instructions to drivers, ordering them to exit their cars and step aside as police dogs sniffed around for any trace of their target.

Inside the cab, Chloe and Laura watched the roadblock with growing unease. Officers flanked the lanes, their expressions tense and focused, while the sound of dogs barking pierced the otherwise still night. "What do you think they're looking for?" Chloe asked, her voice barely above a whisper. Laura, still staring out the window, shook her head. "No idea. Maybe a lost person or something? I don't care—I just want to get home." Ben, unfazed, drummed his fingers on the steering wheel as they inched forward. "Don't worry, ladies. They're just being thorough. Once we're through, I'll drop you at the service station, and you can call your insurance." The girls said nothing, the tension in the van thick enough to cut with a knife.

Back in the truck bed, Aubrey braced himself as the convoy drew closer to the checkpoint. His muscles ached from holding still in the cramped space, but his mind remained sharp, assessing every sound, every vibration. He knew this was the most critical moment of his escape. If the police decided to inspect the towed truck, it would be over. He could already hear the muffled voices of Officers outside, their boots crunching on the gravel-strewn shoulder as they circled the vehicles in line. The van jerked slightly, pulling to a stop. Aubrey's breath hitched. Outside, Ben rolled down his window, greeting the Officer with his usual affable grin. "Evening, Officer. Got a breakdown here, just towing these ladies to the next service station." The Officer peered inside the van, his flashlight sweeping over the girls. Laura squinted against the harsh light, while Chloe forced another polite smile. "Everything alright?" the Officer asked. "Yeah, just a blown tire," Ben replied.

Lying in the cramped darkness of the pickup's boot space, Aubrey fought to stay awake. His body ached, every muscle stiff from the awkward position he'd been in for hours. Sleep tugged at him like an anchor, but he knew it wasn't safe to let his guard down. He strained his ears to listen beyond the hum of the tires, trying to gauge their progress. The vehicle crawled forward, stopping and starting in a sluggish rhythm, the telltale signs of a bottleneck near the roadblock.

Voices drifted closer, muffled but distinct. Aubrey's heart quickened. He couldn't see anything in the pitch-black compartment, couldn't even feel his way around for something he might use as a weapon if he were discovered. He would have to rely on his instincts, on the training that had kept him alive before, and pray he had enough strength left to act if it came to that.

The van moved forward again, inching ahead at what felt like a snail's pace, and then stopped abruptly. Outside, the sound of boots crunching on gravel drew nearer, followed by the low growl of a dog. Aubrey froze, every muscle coiled like a spring. A bark rang out, sharp and commanding, just outside the truck bed. He held his breath as the dog sniffed loudly near the hatch, the sound magnified in the silence. Then came a voice, loud and irritated. "Hey, Ross! Not that one, mate. We've already searched it. … Yeah, and the pickup too. Look, stop wasting time and move on to the next one!"

The dog's handler muttered something unintelligible, and Aubrey felt the vehicle shift as the van rolled forward. Relief flooded through him as the sounds of the checkpoint receded, replaced by the hum of tires on open road. They were moving again, faster now, the tension of the roadblock left behind. For now, his plan had worked.

In the cab, Chloe and Laura were fighting their own battle with exhaustion. The warm air blasting from the heater enveloped them like a blanket, making it harder to resist the pull of sleep. Chloe leaned back against the headrest, her ears still ringing faintly from standing too close to the stage during the concert. She couldn't remember the last time she'd danced so much. Ben broke the silence. "We're almost there. Thornwood Services should be open if you need to use the facilities or grab something to eat. You can call your insurance company and let them know you're at the services. Hopefully, they won't take too long to get someone out to you."

Chloe gave him a small, tired smile. "Thanks for all your help again. We really appreciate it. That's very kind of you." She nudged Laura with her elbow, but her sister barely reacted, continuing to stare out of the window. Laura's jaw was tight, her face drawn with fatigue and frustration, she stared at a sticker of a small clown on the glove compartment.

As they approached the slip road, Ben downshifted, slowing the van as it prepared to exit the motorway. The girls glanced out the windows at the signs glowing in the distance. Chloe perked up, spotting a familiar logo. "Ooo, look, sis, they've got a Starbucks!" Laura barely acknowledged her, keeping her gaze fixed on the road ahead. Her eyes caught a sudden flicker of movement in the side mirror—a shadow dropping from the back of the pickup. She snapped her head toward the window, pressing her face to the glass for a better look, but the van turned sharply into the service area, and her view was blocked.

Chloe noticed her sudden movement and frowned. "Everything alright, sis?" Laura leaned back in her seat, shaking her head as if to clear it. She was too tired to trust what she thought she'd seen, and the adrenaline spike left her feeling even more drained. "Yeah," she muttered, rubbing her temple. "Think I need a coffee."

Outside, Aubrey crouched low, his breaths coming fast as he dashed into the shadows of the service station's car park. The jump from the truck had been risky, but he'd timed it perfectly, landing with barely a sound as the van slowed to make its turn. Keeping to the edges of the lot, he scanned the area quickly. The bright lights of the petrol station bathed everything in harsh fluorescence, leaving few places to hide. He spotted a cluster of parked lorries in a far corner, their engines idling as drivers rested inside. Aubrey moved toward them; his footsteps silent on the damp tarmac.

He needed to disappear before anyone noticed him. His stomach churned with hunger, his throat dry, but he ignored the discomfort. Survival came first. Reaching the lorries, he slipped between two trailers and crouched in the shadows, watching as the van carrying the girls and the pickup came to a stop near the station entrance.

Back in the cab, Ben killed the engine and turned to the girls. "Alright, ladies. You're safe here now. I'll unload your truck, and you can wait inside for your insurance to sort things out, if you wouldn't mind popping out when I'm done, I just need you to sign some paperwork." Chloe stretched, stifling a yawn. "Thanks again, Ben. We owe you one." Laura, still staring out the window, mumbled something under her breath. "What was that?" Chloe asked, raising an eyebrow. "Nothing," Laura snapped, grabbing her purse. "Let's just get that coffee."

They climbed out of the van and headed toward the glowing Starbucks sign, their figures disappearing into the warm, welcoming light of the service station.

Chapter 8
21:52 hours, July 26th 2024
Chickney, Essex

St. Mary's, a timeless flint-rubble church adorned with weathered limestone dressings, stood at the edge of the village like a secret guardian. Tucked away from the bustle of everyday life, it seemed to dissolve into the surrounding countryside, its red-tiled roof just a whisper among the trees. The little building was a perfect sanctuary, a place where time seemed to pause, its charm heightened by its seclusion. Only those who ventured down the narrow, winding country lane might catch a glimpse of it, its spire peeking out as if greeting the heavens.

The Reverend Sharon Daniel had just completed the evening service, her words lingering in the cool, crisp air. Standing on the broad concrete step outside the porch, she clasped her hands in front of her, a warm smile lighting her face as the last of her congregation departed. The small group moved in quiet camaraderie down the gravel path, their torches cutting soft beams through the encroaching darkness. The crunch of footsteps faded into the night as the villagers made their way back, their homes waiting like beacons beyond the rise of the hill. Above, the sky was a pristine canvas, splashed with countless stars that twinkled like diamonds scattered by a careless hand. Sharon glanced upward, catching sight of a plane carving its path across the heavens, its lights a fleeting streak against the dark expanse. It was heading southwest, undoubtedly bound for Stansted Airport. For a moment, Sharon allowed herself to linger, letting the peace of the night settle over her like a gentle shawl. Then, turning with a contented sigh, she pushed open the heavy oak door and stepped into the nave.

The church interior was silent, a vast and hallowed stillness that magnified every sound. Her footsteps echoed softly against the cold, worn quarry tiled floor, each one carrying a faint memory of the hundreds of souls who had tread here before her. The air was tinged with a faint, familiar blend of wax, aged wood, and stone—a scent as ancient as the building itself. The flickering candlelight from the altar played tricks with the shadows, making the empty pews appear like watchful sentinels. At the rear of the church, beyond the Chancel, was a small, weathered wooden door. Its iron handle was polished smooth from years of use, but the hinges creaked and groaned with every movement, a stubborn complaint that Sharon knew all too well. Twisting the handle, she used both hands to coax the door open. It yielded slowly, revealing a snug room that served as her vestry.

She removed her black robe, folding it with care before hanging it neatly on the hook by the wall. The action felt ritualistic, a quiet conclusion to the day's work. Her eyes flicked to the small table where her essentials awaited—a modest rucksack and a helmet. With practiced ease, she slung the bag over her shoulder and tucked the helmet under her arm. Tomorrow was another day, full of its own promises and challenges, but for now, the night was hers.

Moments later, Sharon emerged into the cool night air, her footsteps soft on the gravel path as she walked back toward the gated entrance. She paused briefly to lock the heavy oak door behind her, the metallic clink of the key echoing faintly in the stillness. The gate was only a short distance away, and there, leaning against the weathered post, her bike waited patiently where she had left it, secured with a sturdy chain. The combination lock felt cold and unyielding as she turned the dial, the numbers aligning with quiet clicks. As she worked the lock, she felt it—a subtle stirring behind her. The faintest of sounds, barely louder than the whisper of the breeze. She stilled, the hairs on her arms rising as an instinctive sense of awareness prickled through her. Slowly, she turned her head, glancing over her shoulder toward the church. The tops of the trees began to sway, their dark silhouettes moving in harmony with the soft night wind. For a moment, her imagination toyed with her, and she could have sworn she saw a shadow flicker across the ancient stone walls.

"Just the wind," she murmured under her breath, shaking her head to dispel the notion. Yet, a sliver of unease lingered as she turned back to the task at hand. She was almost finished unlocking her bike when a voice cut through the quiet, startling her. "Good evening, Reverend. You just finished?" Sharon gasped, spinning toward the sound, her heart skipping a beat. A man leaned casually over the gate; his grin illuminated by the faint glow of a nearby lantern. His ginger moustache stretched across his face as he smiled. "Yes…yes, sorry, you startled me," she said with a nervous chuckle, catching her breath. "How are you?"

"Doing well, thank you," he replied, his tone friendly and unhurried. "I was about to head to work but thought I'd swing by, see if everything's still on track for Saturday." The familiarity of his face and voice calmed her. "Oh, Alex! Yes, of course," she said, finally recalling the connection. "The ceremony's set for midday. Just make sure the wedding party is seated fifteen minutes beforehand. Do you have ushers to help manage everything?" Alex nodded confidently. "All sorted. My brothers will handle it." "Perfect." She turned back to her bike, giving the lock one final twist before it clicked open with a satisfying snap. Lifting her helmet, she secured it on her head, tightening the straps with a practiced motion. "Would you mind holding the gate for me? It seems you need to be an octopus these days," she joked, gesturing to the bike as she grasped its handlebars. "Not a problem," Alex said, stepping forward to oblige. He held the gate wide, watching as she manoeuvred the bike through the narrow opening.

"Thank you," Sharon said warmly, standing astride her bike. "Well, young man, I'll see you and your lovely bride on Saturday. Enjoy the rest of your evening." "You too, Reverend," Alex replied, tipping an imaginary hat as she mounted the bike. Sharon flicked on the small handlebar light, its narrow beam cutting through the shadows as she pedalled away into the night. Alex stood by the gate, his gaze following her as the faint hum of her tires faded into the distance.

He lingered for a moment longer, checking his watch. Still early. His shift wouldn't begin for another hour, and the drive to work was barely ten minutes. Turning back to the church, he leaned his arms on the gate, allowing his thoughts to wander. The ancient building looked serene, bathed in moonlight, but it wasn't the stone arches or the stained-glass windows that filled his mind. Instead, he pictured the sanctuary bustling with loved ones, their faces turned expectantly toward the aisle. His heart swelled as he imagined Zoe, radiant and beaming, making her way toward him.

And then there was Eli. A grin broke across Alex's face as he thought of his young son, holding tight to Sox, their spirited dog, who would carry the rings. It was a big responsibility for the boy, and Alex could already picture the laughter as Sox trotted down the aisle with Eli in tow. It would be a memorable moment, a surprise for the guests, and a perfect touch of joy to begin their new chapter. For a few more moments, Alex stood there, soaking in the peacefulness of the scene and the anticipation of the life waiting for him. Then, with a deep breath, he turned away, ready to begin the journey toward the rest of his night—and his future.

Whomp.

The first sound slipped past Alex's consciousness, blending seamlessly into the haze of his daydreams. He had been lost in the thought of Zoe—her smile, her dress, the moment she'd walk down the aisle. A smile had unknowingly crept onto his face as he imagined their son, Eli, holding onto Sox as they plodded dutifully with the rings. Whomp! This time, the noise yanked him from his reverie. His head snapped toward the church instinctively, his eyes scanning its silhouette under the faint glow of the crescent moon. The porch door was firmly shut. The arched windows, glimmering faintly in the moonlight, remained unbroken. Everything appeared untouched. "What the hell?" he muttered to himself, his voice breaking the stillness.

Whomp.

His stomach tightened. Gripping the top of the gate, Alex pushed it open with a low creak, stepping onto the gravel path. Each crunch beneath his boots felt unnaturally loud in the otherwise silent graveyard. The faint silver light from the crescent moon offered just enough illumination for him to pick his way forward. His breath came in shallow puffs, the cool night air brushing his face. The headstones loomed like spectral sentinels; their weathered surfaces dappled with moss. Most were old—older than Alex could recall. The names and dates etched into them had begun to fade, the passing years claiming the legibility of each inscription. Some leaned at odd angles, as though the earth beneath them had grown tired of holding their weight.

Whomp.

The noise was elusive, its source impossible to pinpoint. Alex stopped and turned slowly; his ears straining. For a moment, he considered calling out, but something deep in his gut stopped him. Instead, he resumed walking, veering toward the shadowy side of the church.

Whomp. Whomp!

The sound was louder here, echoing off the ancient stone walls. This side of the grounds was darker, the moon hidden behind the steep pitch of the church roof. The faint glimmer of moonlight vanished, leaving Alex to rely on his hearing. Each step off the gravel brought him onto softer ground, the damp earth sinking slightly beneath his boots. He found himself moving down a narrow row of graves, the stones leaning more noticeably here, their bases encroached upon by gnarled roots and creeping ivy. His heart beat faster as the night seemed to press closer around him. Whomp. The noise grew more rhythmic, as though something was striking the ground with increasing urgency.

Alex froze as his eyes caught the faint outline of a small cross atop a fresh mound of earth. The sight sent a pang through his chest—Tanya Taylor's grave. She'd passed only weeks ago, her life cut tragically short at just four years old. The loss had gutted the village, the air still heavy with grief. Alex swallowed hard, thinking of his son, Eli. A lump formed in his throat as a tear welled in the corner of his eye. He wiped it away briskly, forcing himself to look away from the tiny grave.

Whomp.

The sound snapped his attention back to the present. His eyes shifted toward the rear fence, a weathered boundary where the churchyard gave way to the edge of the woods. He glanced to his left, just barely able to make out the faint shape of the lane and his car sitting in the darkness. Turning right, he continued farther from the church, stepping cautiously between the graves.

His stomach churned as the noise became even more insistent, reverberating through the stillness. Whomp. Whomp. The faint metallic clang that followed made his breath hitch. It was sharper than before, more deliberate, and carried an eerie finality.

Alex stopped abruptly, scanning the area with growing unease. His eyes darted between the faint outlines of gravestones, their crooked shapes casting long, jagged shadows in the pale moonlight. He strained his ears, trying to pick out any additional sounds— footsteps, whispers, anything. Swallowing hard, Alex took a tentative step forward, his boots sinking slightly into the soft earth. A shiver crept up his spine as he neared the fence line, his gaze darting toward the treetops that swayed gently in the breeze. Still, nothing seemed out of place—no movement, no figures lurking in the darkness.

"Hello?" he called out, his voice cracking slightly. The word echoed hollowly, swallowed quickly by the night. There was no response. A sudden snap of a branch nearby sent him spinning toward the sound, his heart pounding in his chest. For the first time, he felt the primal grip of fear settling in, tightening around him. He clenched his fists, trying to ground himself. "Who's there?" he demanded, his voice firmer this time, but the shadows offered no answer.

Alex ran his eyes along the fence once more, squinting against the shadows that seemed to writhe and stretch under the faint moonlight. His gaze landed on a large oak tree in the far corner. At first glance, the tree appeared to press tightly against the fence, its gnarled roots clawing into the soil. But then, as his eyes adjusted, he noticed something unusual—a glimpse of white protruding from behind the trunk. Narrowing his eyes, he realized it was the edge of a small cross, barely visible in the shifting shadows. He hesitated, glancing at his watch. Time was slipping by, and he should already be on his way to work. With a resigned sigh, he began to turn away, but his curiosity clawed at him. He stopped mid-step. The pull was too strong to resist. Quietly, Alex tiptoed toward the tree, his movements slow and deliberate to avoid making noise.

As he approached, the faint vibration of his phone startled him. The device buzzed insistently in his pocket; the glow of its screen faintly visible through the fabric. Alex froze in place, his heart thudding loudly in his chest. He looked up toward the tree, holding his breath and praying he hadn't been noticed. Seconds dragged on like hours. The phone continued to buzz, its insistent hum grating against the silence. Finally, it stopped. Alex exhaled slowly, relief washing over him. Fishing the phone out of his pocket, he glanced at the screen. Missed Call: Zoe. The device buzzed again in his hand; this time accompanied by the soft chime of a message notification. Annoyance flared, but he quickly swiped the notification away and stuffed the phone back into his pocket. Whatever Zoe needed would have to wait. His curiosity was in full command now.

The graveyard had fallen eerily silent. The rhythmic whomp sound had ceased entirely, leaving only the soft rustle of leaves overhead. Alex's disappointment mingled with a vague sense of unease as he crept closer to the oak. His steps grew more confident, and with a quick burst of adrenaline, he closed the last few feet, pressing his back firmly against the tree trunk. The bark was rough against his jacket as he stood still, trying to blend into the night. The oak towered above him, its sprawling branches obscuring what little moonlight remained. A chill ran down his spine as the wind picked up, rattling the leaves directly above his head. He glanced up nervously, noting the clouds beginning to drift across the sky, their edges swallowing the faint glow of the crescent moon.

Darkness closed in. The graveyard seemed to fold in on itself, shadows stretching and multiplying until it felt as though the world had shrunk to the confines of the tree. Alex cursed softly under his breath, then immediately regretted it. "What the fuck," he muttered, realizing how exposed he was. Then, almost instinctively, he whispered a quiet apology to no one in particular, half-hoping the silence would forgive him. Time felt suspended as he stood there, pressed against the tree. Then, a break in the clouds sent a silvery beam of moonlight washing over the graveyard, illuminating the tops of the headstones like tiny beacons. It was now or never.

Pushing off the tree, Alex moved cautiously around its base, his boots brushing against the soft ground. The white cross he had seen earlier came fully into view, stark against the dark bark. It was nestled just behind the trunk, small and weathered, its paint chipped and flaking. And then, directly below it, a six-foot hole yawned in the earth. Alex froze, his stomach tightening as he stared down into the freshly dug grave. "What on earth…" he whispered, the words barely audible as his mind raced. Who had dug this? And why was it here, hidden so far from the rest of the cemetery?

A faint flicker of movement caught his eye, and Alex whipped his head around, scanning the shadows. The graveyard remained empty. The rows of tilted headstones stood silently, their inscriptions worn and unreadable, and the perimeter fence framed the scene like a forgotten painting. Despite the stillness, he couldn't shake the feeling that he was being watched. Shaking off his nerves, Alex reached for his phone, fumbling to unlock it with trembling fingers. Swiping across the screen, he opened the torch app, and the LED beam cut through the darkness, illuminating the hole in stark detail. The grave was neatly dug, its edges clean and precise as though crafted with care. The bottom was shrouded in shadow, the beam of the torch failing to reach its depths. Alex swallowed hard, his breath hitching as the beam of light danced over something metallic glinting near the edge of the hole. He hesitated, every instinct screaming at him to turn back. But his curiosity overpowered his fear, and with a deep breath, he leaned closer, the light quivering as his hand began to tremble.

The beam of the torch illuminated the open grave, its stark light casting eerie shadows over the pile of freshly dug earth that sat neatly to one side. At the bottom of the hole, Alex could make out the outline of a coffin, its wood aged and splintered. It looked as though it had been hastily disturbed. His brow furrowed as his eyes adjusted, picking out a grey shape lying near one end of the coffin, partially buried in the loose soil. Curiosity gnawed at him. He stepped carefully around the edge of the grave; each step deliberates to avoid slipping into the pit. Kneeling down, the cold, damp earth pressed against his knees, sending a chill up his spine. The smell of freshly churned dirt filled his nostrils, mingling with the faint, musty odour rising from the grave itself. Holding the torch steady in one hand, he leaned forward, reaching tentatively into the dark opening.

His fingers brushed against something soft but gritty, its texture unsettlingly familiar. Gripping it, he pulled the object free with a grunt, holding it up to inspect it under the torchlight. "What have we got here?" he murmured, his voice trembling slightly despite his attempt to sound casual. In his hand was a grey sweater, dirty and damp, its fabric stained with a mix of soil and |what looked suspiciously like sweat. The matching trousers clung to it in a tangled mess, as though hastily discarded. Alex's mind raced, unease prickling the back of his neck. Who did these belong to? And why were they down there, buried in a shallow grave alongside what appeared to be a broken coffin?

The phone in his pocket suddenly vibrated, startling him. The torch flickered off as the screen lit up, and a small beep signalled a new message. Groaning in frustration, he set the dirty clothing aside and reached for his phone, his fingers fumbling slightly. He tapped the notification, and a text message appeared: "Hi Alex, just checking if you're still coming to work this evening. Your shift started fifteen minutes ago." "Shit!" he hissed under his breath, glancing at the time displayed on his screen. 10:45 PM. How had the minutes slipped away so quickly? He cursed himself for getting so caught up in the mystery of the grave. His job—his pay check— depended on him being reliable. Turning the torch back on, he quickly checked his surroundings. The grey clothes lay crumpled on the ground where he'd dropped them, the faintly glowing screen of his phone casting long shadows over the disturbed soil. He brushed the dirt off his knees, his hands trembling slightly as he stood up. "This is definitely something for the police," Alex muttered to himself, his voice trying to drown out the creeping dread that coiled in his gut. "Grave robbers, maybe? Not on my watch." He shook his head, already rehearsing what he'd say when he reported the incident after clocking in at work.

As he turned to leave, the sharp crack of a snapping branch echoed above him. He froze mid-step, the sound far too close for comfort. His pulse quickened as he tilted his head upward, the torch beam following his gaze. The first thing he saw was the canopy of the oak tree, its leaves swaying gently in the night breeze. But then, something moved. He squinted, heart pounding, and suddenly two large, gnarled hands burst out of the leaves, their fingers splayed wide like talons. Before Alex could react, the hands shot downward, clamping around his neck with an iron grip. His breath caught as he felt himself being yanked off the ground, his feet leaving the damp earth. The torch clattered to the ground, its beam spinning wildly and casting disorienting patterns over the surrounding headstones.

Alex clawed desperately at the hands constricting his throat, gasping for air as his vision blurred. The pressure around his neck was relentless, his body swinging helplessly as he was hoisted higher into the air. Above him, through his dimming sight, he could just make out a shadowy figure obscured by the thick branches, its face hidden but its presence unmistakably menacing. A guttural, almost inhuman growl rumbled through the darkness, vibrating through Alex's very bones. He kicked wildly, his boots scraping against the tree bark as he struggled to free himself, but the hands held firm. "Let... me... go!" he managed to choke out, his voice rasping against the crushing grip.

Alex's feet flailed desperately, scraping against the rough bark of the tree trunk as his lungs screamed for air. The hands around his neck tightened like a steel vice, their grip merciless. His vision swam as the edges of the world began to blur; his panicked breaths reduced to faint gasps. Above him, he caught glimpses of the figure responsible for his suffering. Long, straggly hair hung in wild strands from the man's head, framing a shadowed face that remained maddeningly out of focus. The man's legs were looped effortlessly over a thick, sturdy branch high above, supporting both his weight and Alex's dangling body with terrifying ease. Alex kicked harder, his boots striking the bark of the oak tree and flinging clumps of loose dirt into the air. He threw wild punches toward the figure's arms, each strike weaker than the last. It was futile. The harder he fought, the tighter the grip became, as though the man were feeding off his struggle. Pain radiated through Alex's neck and chest. His movements slowed, his body growing limp as his strength ebbed away. Desperate, he managed one final, weak punch before his vision dimmed entirely. There was a sharp flick, a nauseating crack reverberating through the air.

Then everything went silent.

The body hit the ground with a sickening thud, crumpled in a lifeless heap at the base of the oak tree. Aubrey landed beside the corpse with a predator's grace, his boots hitting the earth without a sound. The man's body lay twisted at an unnatural angle, his glassy eyes staring vacantly toward the starry sky. Aubrey crouched beside him, inspecting his work with an air of clinical detachment.

The graveyard was still. The only sound came from the faint rustling of leaves overhead as the night wind stirred the oak's branches. Satisfied that no one had witnessed the scene, Aubrey turned his attention to the grave. Dragging the man's body by the ankles, he heaved him unceremoniously into the open pit, letting him fall atop the splintered coffin below. The sound of flesh and bone striking wood echoed faintly, swallowed quickly by the surrounding silence. Straightening up, Aubrey turned toward a small rucksack tucked neatly behind the mound of dirt. He knelt, flipping open the flap and peering inside. The contents glinted faintly in the moonlight as he rifled through them.

First, he pulled out a large black coat, its fabric heavy and lined to shield him from the night's chill. He slid it on with practiced efficiency, adjusting the sleeves so they sat snugly against his wrists. Next, he retrieved a six-inch Bowie knife, its serrated blade catching the faint light. He ran a thumb over the edge, nodding in approval before tucking it into the belt at his waist. Reaching deeper into the rucksack, his hand brushed against a slim glass tube nestled in a side pocket. He pulled it free, holding it up to inspect its contents. The liquid inside remained undisturbed, its surface smooth and unbroken. Satisfied, he carefully secured it back into the bag.

From the main compartment, he retrieved a small folded piece of paper and a lighter, setting them aside momentarily. Finally, his fingers closed around the ghillie suit stored at the bottom of the bag.

He checked it quickly for tears or signs of wear; it would serve its purpose when the time came. Aubrey stood, slinging the rucksack over one shoulder as he surveyed the scene. Everything was as it should be. He grabbed the small shovel he had borrowed earlier in the evening—its blade already caked in soil—and began the task of refilling the grave.

The minutes stretched on as Aubrey methodically shovelled the displaced earth back into the pit, his motions steady and unhurried. Dirt cascaded over the corpse and coffin below, erasing the evidence of his handiwork with each passing moment. When he finally stepped back, wiping a hand across his brow, the graveyard looked undisturbed, save for the faint outline of recently turned soil. As he picked up the rucksack to leave, a faint noise reached his ears, stopping him mid-step. Aubrey turned sharply, his eyes narrowing as he scanned the area. The sound came again, soft but unmistakable—the muffled strains of a ringtone. He froze, the blood draining from his face. His gaze dropped to the grave he had just filled. The sound was coming from beneath the dirt.

Alex's phone.

A low growl of frustration rumbled in Aubrey's throat. He had been careless. A ringing phone would leave breadcrumbs for anyone curious enough to investigate. His mission had no room for such mistakes. Cursing under his breath, he tossed the rucksack to the ground and grabbed the shovel again, plunging it into the fresh soil with renewed vigour. Dirt flew in all directions as he worked quickly, each stroke of the shovel accompanied by the relentless buzz of the phone beneath.

When his shovel finally struck something solid, Aubrey tossed it aside and dropped to his knees. He clawed at the dirt with his bare hands, pulling Alex's limp body back into view. The phone glowed faintly from the man's pocket, its ringtone still playing. Aubrey snatched it out, silencing it with a furious tap of the screen. For a brief moment, he stared at the device, debating whether to keep it or destroy it. Making his decision, he slammed the phone against the nearest headstone, shattering the screen into jagged shards; throwing the broken pieces, into the grave once more.

With the phone dealt with and the grave refilled a second time, Aubrey hoisted the rucksack over his shoulder. He paused, his eyes sweeping over the graveyard one last time. The night was deepening, and time was slipping away. The mission lay ahead. There was still much to do before the sun rose. With a final glance at the silent graveyard, Aubrey melted into the shadows, disappearing into the night.

Chapter 9
22:30 hours, July 26th 2024,
Scotland Yard, London

Marching briskly down the seemingly endless corridor towards the incident room, DCI Stephen Craig adjusted the large brown folder tucked under his arm. His polished shoes clicked sharply against the floor, echoing with every determined step. The dim overhead lights created an oppressive atmosphere, one he had grown accustomed to over the years. As he neared the door, a young Officer straightened to attention. "They're all ready for you, Sir," the Officer said, his tone steady but his eyes betraying curiosity. With a curt nod, the DCI pushed the heavy door open, stepping into the bustling hive of the incident room. The space was cavernous, lit by harsh lights that rendered everyone's faces pale and drawn. At the front, a long table stood as the focal point, where three detectives and his Commanding Officer, were deep in discussion. To the side, six rows of chairs were packed with journalists—reporters and photographers buzzing like restless bees, whispering, and clicking their pens.

The DCI took a deep breath, steadying himself. Though his career had been defined by action and investigation, these public performances left his stomach churning with dread. He loved police work, the relentless pursuit of justice, but this—the facing of the press—was his least favourite part of the job. He strode to the front, his measured steps a façade of calm, and climbed onto the small stage. The air in the room shifted as conversations dwindled to a murmur. Reporters adjusted their seats, cameras aimed in his direction, and all eyes followed his movements with unyielding scrutiny.

Detective Sergeant Harper leaned over, offering a handshake, which the DCI accepted with a brief, tight smile. The other detectives followed suit before they all took their seats at the long table. The DCI placed the folder carefully before him and pulled the microphone stand closer, sparing himself the need to raise his voice. His gaze swept the room, taking in the eager faces before him. Opening the folder with deliberate precision, he removed a single sheet of paper and laid it flat on the table. Clearing his throat, he addressed the room, his voice calm but firm.

"Thank you for joining us. As of twenty-two hundred hours, 25th July 2024, officials at Wormwood Scrubs have confirmed that one of their prisoners has escaped and is currently at large. Police are working closely with the prison authorities to ensure the swift apprehension and detention of the individual." A ripple of interest passed through the reporters. Pens moved frantically, and camera shutters clicked incessantly. The DCI pressed on; his tone unwavering. "At this stage, we have limited information to share. However, I want to assure the public that every resource is being directed toward capturing this convict and ensuring their return to custody."

The room grew still again, the air charged with anticipation. The DCI glanced up briefly, noting the sceptical expressions on some faces. One reporter, a wiry man in the third row, leaned over to whisper something to his colleague. Another, a woman with a sharp bob and a sharper tongue, folded her arms, clearly unimpressed. The Superintendent rose from her seat, commanding the room's attention with a simple gesture. "Thank you, DCI Craig. I'd like to remind everyone that we are at an early stage of this investigation. Please keep your questions concise and relevant." She turned back toward the DCI, nodding for him to continue. He scanned the room, his finger pointing toward a tall man in a dark suit who stood out among the crowd. "Harpeet Singh, The Herald, " the man introduced himself. "DCI Craig, you've told us very little about the escaped convict. Is he dangerous? Should the public be concerned for their safety?" The DCI's fingers brushed the edge of the paper on the desk as he crafted a measured response. "At this stage, we cannot disclose specifics about the convict's profile. However, I can confirm that

Aubrey Brian Strawberry was in the first year of his sentence." The room murmured, but before he could continue, another reporter interrupted, his voice loud and cutting. "That's great, but what was he convicted for?" the man demanded. "There's a world of difference between tax fraud and serial murder. Surely the public deserves to know." The DCI exhaled slowly, fighting the urge to roll his eyes. "I understand your concerns. Unfortunately, the nature of the investigation requires discretion. Rest assured; the safety of the public remains our utmost priority."

Two reporters stood, the taller one fixing a steely glare on his shorter counterpart as the latter hesitated, then grudgingly sank back into his seat. The first reporter, with the air of someone who would not be overshadowed, rose briskly. "Anne-Marie Smith, Times and Citizen," she began, her voice cutting cleanly through the low hum of murmurs in the room. "What can you tell us about the increased police presence along the Thames? Eyewitnesses have claimed to see patrol boats sweeping the waters as far as the docks. Do you think there is a chance the convict managed to commandeer a vessel and is making his way toward the coast?" She delivered her question with measured precision, her pen poised above her notepad, ready to immortalize every word. The room seemed to still for a moment as all eyes turned to the DCI, who adjusted his tie and coughed into his hand—a preamble, perhaps, to buying himself a moment to gather his thoughts.

"Ms. Smith," he began, his tone calm but clipped, "to address your first question, it is standard procedure to intensify patrols in the vicinity of an escape. The Thames is a logical focus for such efforts, given its proximity to the prison and the potential for clues or evidence that might aid our investigation." He paused, letting the weight of his words settle. "As for the suggestion that he could have reached the coast by now—Kent, East Sussex, or beyond—that scenario is highly improbable. The timeline simply doesn't support such a journey. Even with a boat, the odds of navigating the Thames undetected, let alone reaching open waters, are slim to none." Smith tilted her head slightly, her pen scribbling furiously as a flicker of scepticism crossed her face. The other reporters stirred, eager to jump in, but the DCI's gaze swept across the room, silencing them.

Clearly, this was a story with more questions than answers, and Anne-Marie intended to pry out every last one.

A woman in the front row seized her chance, standing abruptly. Her voice carried a note of urgency. "DCI Craig, can you comment on the young man found dead in Dagenham earlier this morning? Is there any connection to Strawberry's escape?" The DCI met her gaze head-on, his tone firm. "I can confirm that the incident in Dagenham is unrelated to the escape of Aubrey Brian Strawberry. We are pursuing both cases with diligence and focus." The room erupted into a cacophony of voices, reporters shouting over each other in an attempt to have their questions heard. Cameras flashed, capturing the DCI's resolute expression as he rose from his chair, gathering his folder.

The press conference was over. The questions would keep coming, but the DCI had delivered what he could—for now. Behind the door, the real work awaited, and for that, he was grateful. The hunt was on.

***

Pushing the door a little harder than intended, the DCI walked past the young Officer, who had quickly stepped swiftly to the side, the momentum almost throwing him off balance. His heart quickened as he caught sight of Superintendent Anna Sheard striding purposefully out of the room following the DCI down the corridor, heels echoing sharply against the laminate flooring. Moments later, the sound of her voice carried back, sharp and commanding. "Wait a minute, Stephen, I need a word." She was moving fast, but her tone left no room for negotiation. The DCI paused, halfway to his office door, before pivoting with a composed smile. "Yes, Ma'am, of course." He masked his apprehension well, the years of discipline shining through, but inside, his mind churned.

Standing at his door, Stephen watched her approach, her expression resolute. The authority she carried in her presence was palpable, but something else flickered there too—something more personal, almost like concern. "Not out here," she said briskly. "Let's take this in your office." He stepped aside, holding the door open for her to enter first, a silent acknowledgment of her rank. As she brushed past, the faint scent of her perfume lingered—a reminder of the many years they had worked together. Whilst the DCI tried to keep his face neutral, his thoughts raced. Had he made a mistake? Had the interview earlier gone awry? What could she possibly want that couldn't wait? Shaking off the unease, he closed the door behind them and gestured toward the chair across from his desk. "Please, take a seat," he offered.

But Anna remained standing, folding her arms tightly across her chest. Her face was set, her eyes narrowed in a way that signalled she was deliberating her words carefully. The DCI braced himself. "Look, Stephen," she began with a sigh. Her tone softened slightly, though her demeanour stayed stern. "I've known you for nearly twenty years. You've worked hard—damn hard—to get to where you are today, and I respect that. But I'm not going to sugarcoat this." The DCI tensed as she let the silence hang in the air for a moment, her words gathering weight. "This assignment is going to be a turning point for you. It will either end in your promotion—or your resignation. Do I make myself clear?" The words hit him like a gut punch, but Stephen managed a stoic nod. He knew Anna wasn't one for dramatics, and if she was framing it this way, the stakes had to be as high as she claimed. "Yes, Ma'am. I understand."

Her eyes softened, but only briefly, before she turned away and walked toward the office window. She parted the blinds with two fingers, her gaze flicking to the busy street below. The DCI could feel the tension rolling off her as she watched the traffic weave through the city, her mind clearly elsewhere. He waited, the silence stretching uncomfortably. She was choosing her next words with even more care, and that only heightened his anxiety. Finally, Anna turned back, her jaw set. "Right," she began. "I'm going to temporarily remove you from CID."

The DCI's mouth opened instinctively, but before he could voice his protest, she held up a hand to silence him. "Don't panic," she said firmly, though her tone held no patience for argument. "Your position will be waiting for you when this is over. But for now, I need you to transfer to the Special Criminal Task Force." The words landed heavily, unfamiliar and unexpected. "SCTF?" he repeated, the confusion evident in his voice. "What's that?"

Anna allowed herself the faintest smile, though it didn't reach her eyes. "The Special Criminal Task Force," she repeated, "is a new initiative we've been developing. Its sole purpose is to track and apprehend high-profile criminals—serial offenders, international fugitives, individuals who are more than just a blip on the radar. And," she added, her voice hardening, "people like our 'friend' currently on the run." Stephen felt his heart rate quicken again. The implications of her words were staggering. High-profile criminals. Serial offenders. International fugitives. His mind raced as he tried to connect the dots.

He nodded slowly, though the weight of what she was saying had yet to fully sink in. "Understood, Ma'am," he said, his voice steady but uncertain. "But who will I be working with? And what's my jurisdiction?" Anna moved back toward the door, signalling the end of the conversation. She turned to point at the map hanging on the office wall. "You'll build your team from CID. Choose whoever you think is best for the job. As for jurisdiction—England, Wales, and Scotland. You'll have access to resources from local police departments nationwide. I expect you to use them wisely." The DCI stared at the map, his mind already turning to names and possibilities. This was bigger than anything he'd handled before, and he knew it.

Anna's voice pulled him back to the moment. "Twenty-four hours have already passed since our fugitive escaped," she said briskly. "I suggest you get moving, DCI Craig. There's no time to waste." "Yes, Ma'am." He watched her leave, the door clicking shut behind her, and for a moment, the office felt oppressively quiet. The DCI let out a slow breath, his thoughts racing. The stakes were higher than he could have ever anticipated, but there was no turning back now.

He glanced at the map again, his resolve hardening. It was time to build a team—and take on the challenge that would either make or break his career.

Chapter 10
06:00 hours, July 27th 2024, Green Park, London

Bill awoke early, the quiet of his apartment offering a momentary sense of peace before the inevitable rush of the day. He had barely slept, his mind spinning with the implications of the data he'd seen the previous day. The discovery from sample 8008 had kept him up, wondering if it could truly be the breakthrough they had been chasing for so long. He had to remind himself that one test wasn't enough—he needed more data, more confirmation. But still, the potential was there, and that thought kept him restless through the night. With a grunt, he swung his legs over the edge of the bed, the coolness of the wooden floor sending a shiver up his spine. He rubbed his face, trying to shake the lingering tiredness, and headed for the bathroom. The boiler in his flat had always been temperamental—one minute it worked fine, the next it was cold enough to freeze a person's bones. He walked to the small vision panel next to the kitchen and peered inside the boiler's compartment. Satisfied to see the pilot light was lit, he turned towards the bathroom, tugging on the string that switched on the light. It flickered briefly before bathing the room in a warm orange glow.

Bill adjusted the temperature on the shower dial, waiting for the water to reach the perfect warmth. Steam began to rise, filling the room with the comforting scent of warm water and cleanliness. He stepped out of his clothes, removing his vest and boxer shorts before stepping under the steady stream. The warmth of the water felt like a balm to his tired body, and for a moment, he simply stood there, letting it pour over his black hair and down his body. His thoughts started to drift as he relished the sensation, the quiet of the apartment settling around him like a protective blanket.

The last twenty-four hours played back in his mind. The world was still drowning in crisis, with thousands dying every day from the mysterious cancer that was sweeping the globe. There were no cures, no answers, and the illness seemed to be advancing faster than anyone could predict. Yet, amidst the despair, something had shifted in his lab. Sample 8008 had been analysed thoroughly, following the same meticulous procedures they always used. The results were clear—no signs of contamination, no errors, no anomalies. It had tested clean, and that in itself was something they hadn't seen in months.

Picking up the shampoo, Bill squeezed the bottle, a steady stream of liquid filling his palm. He worked the shampoo into his scalp, massaging it gently as the warm water continued to cascade over him. The simple act of washing his hair became a moment of respite from the mounting pressure of his work. He tried to calm his racing thoughts, reminding himself that this could be the start of something important. But he knew better than to jump to conclusions—until they could confirm the results with more tests, there was no point in celebrating. His thoughts began to wander as he finished rinsing the shampoo from his hair. Jackson and Tom had received a stern lecture the previous evening. Bill had made it clear that their findings were not to be discussed outside the lab—not until they could run additional tests and ensure the results were reproducible. They couldn't afford to be careless, especially not now. He had emphasized the importance of confidentiality, warning them that the stakes were too high to take any risks.

As he reached for the soap, Bill heard a faint ringing noise from the next room. At first, he didn't pay much attention to it, too absorbed in his own thoughts. But as the sound continued, the irritation grew. He could feel his patience thinning. He had been up late, and the last thing he wanted was a phone call to disrupt his rare moment of calm. "Bloody hell," he muttered under his breath, reluctantly stepping out of the shower. The cold air hit him like a slap in the face as he grabbed a small towel and wrapped it around his waist. He could feel the dampness of the shower water clinging to his skin as he crossed the bathroom floor, leaving small puddles behind him. The linoleum felt cold beneath his bare feet, an unpleasant contrast to the warm water he had just enjoyed.

He made his way to the kitchen, where his phone sat on the countertop, its screen blank. Bill frowned as he reached for it, wondering who would be calling at this hour. The ringing was still echoing faintly from the other room. He unlocked the phone, hoping for some sign of who the call was from, but it remained blank. Confused and a bit annoyed, he set the phone back down. Just as he did, there was a loud crash from outside his window, followed by the rumble of a garbage truck. It made him jump, his heart racing for a moment before he realized it was just the dustbin men collecting the waste from the recycling bins in the street below. He took a deep breath and wiped the remaining droplets of water off his face. His mind, still caught between the excitement of yesterday's breakthrough and the exhaustion of the endless work ahead, fought to focus on something else for a moment. The noise outside had thrown him off track, but it was an unexpected reminder of how strange and chaotic the world had become.

He glanced at the time. It was early—far too early for anyone to be calling. But the ringing had unsettled him, a reminder that no matter how isolated he tried to make himself, the world outside was always knocking at his door, asking for more. He grabbed the phone again and checked it once more, but nothing had changed. The screen remained blank, the silence between the ringing almost suffocating. With a frustrated sigh, he tossed the phone back onto the counter. Bill stood in the middle of his living room, listening intently as the strange ringing continued. His mind, still foggy from the abrupt awakening and the surreal nature of the morning, tried to make sense of the situation.

He scanned the room, searching for the source of the noise, his eyes darting from corner to corner as if the answer might be hidden in plain sight. He closed his eyes for a moment, attempting to block out the sounds of the outside world—the trucks, the distant chatter, the hum of the city—and focused entirely on the ringing. And then, as if a switch had been flipped, the source became clear. It was coming from the front door. His heart rate quickened, a sudden surge of adrenaline cutting through his sleepiness as his mind raced with possibilities. Who would leave a phone at his doorstep? More importantly, why?

Bill moved cautiously across the carpet. He reached the door, his eyes narrowing as he looked down at the doormat. There, tucked into the corner, was a small, unmarked jiffy envelope. No return address, no identifying marks—just plain, simple packaging. The mystery of it seemed to heighten the tension in the air. Holding onto his towel with one hand, he crouched down and reached for it. The end flap of the envelope was strangely undone, the adhesive unsealed. He turned it to its side, his fingers grazing the paper's edge. As he tilted it, something inside shifted and fell, landing with a soft clink into the palm of his outstretched hand. Bill's eyes flicked from the object in his hand to the envelope and back again. It was a small black phone—old, unbranded, the kind of device one might use if they wanted to remain untraceable. The phone continued its incessant ringing, louder now, almost demanding his attention.

For a moment, he hesitated. His mind immediately flashed to MI5, his contact there, and the possibility of getting this to them to check for prints. He was, after all, a man of science, not someone who dealt with clandestine threats or covert operations. But the curiosity gnawed at him, the need to understand, to decipher what was happening. His fingers gripped the phone, the cheap plastic cold and foreign in his hand. With a deep breath, he pressed the green call accept button and placed the phone to his ear. The ringing stopped abruptly, and there was a brief moment of silence before a voice crackled through the receiver.

"Doctor Bonny?"

The voice was clear but distant, unfamiliar, and heavily laced with an accent Bill couldn't quite place. It was neutral enough that it could have been from anywhere in the world. The tone was calm, methodical—there was no trace of urgency or aggression, only a cold precision. Bill's pulse quickened, but he managed to keep his voice steady. "Speaking." "Please listen carefully," the voice continued, smooth and deliberate. "Do not speak. We want you to remember everything you are about to hear. And when we are done, you will remove the SIM card from the phone, then flush it down your toilet. If you agree to comply, press the hash button."

Bill's finger hovered over the hash button, a bead of sweat forming on his brow. His mind spun with questions. Who was this? What was this all about? Why was someone contacting him with such strange, specific instructions? Was it a hoax? Or something far more dangerous? He took the phone away from his ear, contemplating the next step. Should he play along? Should he comply? The voice on the other end of the line was waiting, patient but insistent. It felt almost mechanical, as if the person speaking had rehearsed this moment a thousand times. Bill's mind began to race. Could this be a prank? Maybe someone was toying with him, testing his nerves. But then again, the object left at his door—the phone, the unmarked envelope—none of it felt like an ordinary joke. He thought back to the previous day, to the mysterious sample 8008, to the breakthrough in the lab. Could there be a connection? Was someone trying to silence him? Or, on the other hand, perhaps this was a plea for help, a warning of something larger—something he wasn't yet seeing.

His finger hovered a moment longer, the tension building in his chest. He considered going to MI5, alerting them about this strange communication. But there was something about this moment, about the feeling that the message was urgent, that made him pause. What if this was the key to something even bigger? What if this was the thread that could unravel everything, the answer to the question he hadn't yet dared to ask? He exhaled slowly, his breath catching in his throat as he made his decision. With a sharp movement, he pressed the hash button.

The line went silent for a beat, then the voice returned, softer now, almost as though it were pleased with his decision. "Good. Now listen carefully, Doctor Bonny. What you are about to discover could change everything. We are aware of your work; of the data you've been compiling on the cancer samples. The breakthrough you think you've made—it's not what you believe. The answers you're looking for are in a different place, and you're dangerously close to uncovering something bigger than you realize." Bill's pulse raced. The voice was no longer giving instructions—it was giving a warning. A shiver ran down his spine as the words settled in, sinking in with an unsettling weight. He wanted to ask questions, to demand answers, but he couldn't bring himself to interrupt. The voice seemed to know exactly what it was doing—leading him down a path, step by careful step.

"You've been on the right track," the voice continued, "but there are forces at play here you cannot comprehend. What you think you know—about the cancer, about the samples, about your research— it's only the beginning. You will find more answers in the next 72 hours. We will contact you again. Follow these instructions. Trust no one." He felt a strange chill run through him, and his hand trembled slightly as he squeezed the handset closer to his ear.

"Go to your coat and look inside the pocket," the voice crackled through the phone, urgent and commanding. Bill opened his mouth to protest, to ask for clarification, but then he remembered the earlier instructions. The voice had warned him about the need for compliance, and despite the confusion clouding his mind, he knew he had little time to waste. "Hurry, Doctor, we only have a few minutes, the jacket, now!" the voice insisted, more desperate now. Bill swallowed hard, his breath catching in his throat. Something about the urgency of the tone unsettled him. It was as though there was something he couldn't yet see, a danger lurking just out of reach. With trembling hands, he walked toward the hook on the back of his door, still holding the phone to his ear. His feet felt heavy, like they were sinking into the floor with every step he took. He reached into the first pocket of his coat—nothing. The coat felt heavier, more suffocating than it ever had before, the fabric pressing against his chest as if it too were part of the growing sense of dread.

He reached into the next pocket, his fingers brushing against something small and cold. His heartbeat quickened as his hand closed around it. At first, he couldn't tell what it was—a tiny, clear plastic packet. A part of him wanted to throw it aside, to leave it untouched, but something inside urged him to look closer. Just as his fingers wrapped around the packet, a sharp, sudden pain hit him in the nose. A rush of warmth followed, and Bill instinctively pulled his hand away, feeling liquid dripping down from his nostrils. Blood.

His head spun, the world around him tilting dangerously as he fumbled to understand what was happening. He pressed the back of his hand to his upper lip, desperately trying to stop the bleeding, but the blood flowed faster than he could manage. His vision blurred, and the pounding in his skull intensified with each passing second. "What the fuck is going on?" he muttered weakly, staggering backward. His legs seemed to lose their strength, and he collapsed onto the bed, his body feeling as if it were made of lead. The phone slipped from his hand, bouncing on the duvet before coming to a rest just beside his head. His breath came in shallow gasps as he tried to focus, to make sense of the surreal situation unfolding before him. He looked down at the back of his hand, now stained red as blood seeped between his fingers and dripped down his wrist.

The pounding in his head became almost unbearable. His thoughts were a blur of confusion and panic. Was this a reaction to the cancer strain? Had he been exposed to something that was now making its effects known? His mind raced, but each thought felt more distant than the last. Then the voice came again, calm but insistent: "Doctor, if you can hear me, you have thirty seconds. Take the blue pill out of the bag and swallow it."

Bill's mind was reeling. His body felt foreign to him now, as though it belonged to someone else, some other version of himself. He could barely move. His limbs were heavy, and every inch of his body screamed with exhaustion. He tried to push the fog from his mind, tried to force himself to focus, but the room seemed to spin around him, the walls narrowing and blurring into the distance. Was this it? Was this what he had been warned about? He rolled onto his side, his arms trembling as he struggled to move, but the weight of his own body held him down. His legs were numb, unresponsive, as if the blood had stopped circulating. He reached for the plastic packet with shaking fingers, desperately trying to tear it open. But his hands betrayed him, slipping and failing to grip the edges of the packet. Panic surged through him as he tried to summon the strength to tear it open.

"Hurry, Doctor!" The voice again. Urgent, impatient.

With every ounce of willpower left in him, Bill forced his fingers to grip the edges of the packet, and finally, it tore open. The blue pill lay inside—small, innocuous, yet menacing in its simplicity. The phone felt like it weighed a thousand pounds in his hand, but he pressed it to his ear, the voice still urging him on.

"Swallow it. Now!"

Bill, his head swimming and his body betraying him, placed the pill on his tongue. For a brief moment, he paused. Was this the right choice? Was this what he needed to survive? But he didn't have time to think. With the last vestiges of his strength, he swallowed the pill, feeling it slide down his throat like a cold stone.

As soon as the pill was gone, the room seemed to tilt even more dramatically, his vision going dark around the edges. He could feel the darkness creeping in from all sides, a heavy, suffocating presence that pulled him deeper. His body, finally too weak to resist, gave way to the overwhelming blackness. Bill closed his eyes, but it was too late. His body went limp, the phone slipping from his hand and clattering onto the bed beside him. The darkness closed in, and the last thing he heard was the faint sound of the voice, distant and cold.

"Goodbye, Doctor."

Then, there was nothing.

***

07:00 hours, July 27th 2024,

Francis Crick, St Pancras

The hum of the van's engine was barely audible, a low vibration beneath the tense silence inside. Four men, clad in black tactical uniforms, sat inside the dimly lit, unmarked vehicle parked inconspicuously across from the Francis Crick Institute. Rain pattered lightly against the windshield, beads of water streaking down and distorting the view of the imposing building across the street. The air inside was heavy, the kind of tension that didn't need words to make itself known.

In the back of the van, two soldiers, Sargeant's Josh Pearson and Dean Myers, gripped their MP5 submachine guns tightly, their gloved hands resting just below the trigger guards. They were motionless but hyper-alert, their eyes hidden behind the black visors of their helmets, scanning the dark interior of the van as if waiting for something to leap out of the shadows. In the front seats, Captain Ali Inwood and the Commander Ralph Wardley sat in silence, their gazes fixed on the entrance of the building. The Commander, a man in his mid-forties with a square jaw and streaks of grey running through his brown hair, shifted slightly in his seat, his body taut as a coiled spring. He adjusted his earpiece and glanced at his Captain, a younger Officer whose sharp features betrayed an intensity bordering on impatience.

Through the windshield, they watched as civilians poured out of the nearby underground station. Some moved quickly, shielding themselves with umbrellas or huddling under coats, while others meandered, glancing down at their phones or chatting in small groups. Now and then, a person would break away from the flow, heading toward the building's brightly lit entrance, where uniformed security guards stood at attention.

The Commander checked his watch, the faint glow of the face illuminating his gloved hand. He exhaled slowly, a sound that was both a sigh and a way to steady himself. "Any minute now," he murmured, his voice low but carrying the authority of someone used to being obeyed. "Be alert." The soldiers in the back nodded in unison, a silent acknowledgment of his command. The Captain tapped his fingers against the steering wheel, his jaw tightening. And then, the phone rang. The sound cut through the silence like a blade. The Commander's head snapped toward the dashboard where the phone sat, vibrating slightly with each trill. Reaching over with deliberate precision, he snatched it up and held it to his ear. "Yes," he said, his voice flat, professional.

The reply was immediate, the tone familiar yet detached. "The doctor is contained. Proceed with Phase Two." The line went dead with a soft click before the Commander could reply. Slowly, he lowered the phone, staring at it for a moment as if weighing the weight of those four words. Then, slipping it into the breast pocket of his tactical vest, he turned to the others. "Green light," he said, his voice low but carrying an edge of steel. "Let's go."

The van came alive in an instant. The Captain shifted into gear, the engine's hum rising to a low growl as the vehicle moved forward, pulling into the nearest alley to conceal their approach. In the back, the soldiers checked their weapons, chambering rounds with a metallic click that sounded far louder in the confined space. "Five minutes," the Captain said, glancing at the Commander. "Do we have confirmation on interior security?"

The Commander pulled out a tablet from the dashboard compartment and tapped the screen. A blueprint of the building appeared, overlaid with a heat map showing movement inside. "Minimal," he said, studying the glowing red dots. "Two guards at the front entrance, three patrolling the atrium, and one at the elevators. The rest are stationed on upper floors." He paused, his lips pressing into a thin line. "We'll need to be quick. If they trigger an alarm, we'll have less than ten minutes before reinforcements arrive." "Understood," the Captain replied. His voice was steady, but there was a glint of anticipation in his eyes.

The van came to a halt behind the building, shielded by the shadows of a narrow service alley. The Commander and Captain exited first, their boots crunching softly against the wet pavement. The two soldiers followed, moving with practiced precision as they fanned out behind their superiors. The air outside was cold and damp, the scent of rain mixing with the faint metallic tang of the city. The Commander gestured toward a side door, its keypad glowing faintly in the darkness. "Entry point," he said. "Sierra, cover our six. Delta, you're on the lock."

Sargeant Myers, a wiry figure with a knack for electronics, stepped forward. From his vest, he pulled a small device resembling a smartphone with protruding wires. He connected it to the keypad, the screen lighting up with scrolling lines of code. After a few seconds, the lock beeped softly, the red light above it turning green. "We're in," Delta whispered. The Commander nodded, pushing the door open just enough to peer inside. The corridor beyond was dimly lit, sterile, and eerily quiet. With a quick hand signal, he motioned for the team to move in.

They entered silently, their movements fluid and rehearsed. The soldiers took the lead, their MP5s raised and sweeping the hallway as they advanced. The Commander and Captain followed closely; their footsteps muffled against the polished tile floor. Ahead, the corridor split into two directions. The Commander pointed left, toward the service elevator. He knew the package was being held in a secured lab on Sub Level Five, and the elevator would be the fastest way down. But it was also a potential bottleneck—if they were detected, they'd be trapped. "Clear the route," the Commander whispered. The team pressed on, their senses heightened, every shadow a potential threat. As they reached the elevator, Delta moved forward again, disabling the camera above it with a quick spray of black paint. The Captain pressed the button, and the elevator doors slid open with a soft chime. "Stack up," the Commander ordered. The four of them entered, the soldiers taking positions at the corners while the Captain hit the button for SL5. As the elevator began its ascent, the tension inside was palpable, the hum of the machinery underscoring the rapid thudding of their hearts.

✳✳✳

07:12 hours, July 27th 2024,
Sub Level Five, Francis Crick, St Pancras

Sitting on the freezing ceramic tiles, Tom Harris clung to the toilet seat as if it were an anchor keeping him tethered to the world. His head throbbed mercilessly, but the worst of it was subsiding. In the bowl below, the remnants of his stomach swirled in a grotesque mixture of bile and blood, the stench both nauseating and suffocating. He reached for the handle, flushed, and watched the chaos disappear into the abyss. His throat burned, raw and inflamed from hours of violent retching. He tried to cough, but the pain was excruciating, leaving him gasping for air.

Tom's bloodshot eyes fell on his trembling hand, still clutching the empty syringe. The Serum was gone now, coursing through his veins like a dark promise, but he had no idea what it would do to him. He didn't even care anymore. What choice had he been left with? The cancer was unrelenting, a cruel predator that wouldn't stop until it consumed him completely. It wasn't just about survival—it was about defiance. Roll the dice, or die a statistic.

Two weeks ago, life had seemed routine, predictable even. The headaches were the first sign, sharp and sudden like a warning siren. Then came the dizzy spells and relentless nausea, each wave worse than the last. He had brushed it off as burnout from long hours at the lab. It was easy to dismiss, to convince himself he just needed rest. But the symptoms wouldn't be ignored, and neither could his colleagues. They started noticing his pallor, the tremor in his hands, the way he clutched at his head during meetings. A trip to the local practitioner confirmed his fears—something was wrong. When the hospital called later that evening requesting urgent tests, Tom already knew what they would find. The abnormality in his blood wasn't a question anymore. It was a sentence.

Now, on unsteady legs, Tom pulled himself upright, gripping the cubicle door handle for support. The pain in his skull was easing, but the burning in his throat was relentless. He stumbled to the sink, splashing cold water on his face, the icy shock grounding him. His reflection stared back, a ghost of the man he'd been—a hollow shell of fear and desperation. Grabbing a towel, he dried his face and tossed it into the bin. He took a shaky breath and stepped out of the restroom.

"Freeze."

The voice was cold, the command punctuated by the click of a gun's safety being released. Tom's heart stopped as he raised his hands instinctively, his throat tightening. Inches away, the barrel of a weapon was pointed directly at him. "Who... who are you? What do you want?" Tom stammered, his voice barely above a whisper. Another man stepped forward, ripping the lanyard from around Tom's neck. "Tom Harris. One of the Doctor's lab rats. Let's go." The soldier grabbed Tom's arm, his grip like a vice.

"Wait! I didn't do anything! I swear!" Tom protested, but it was futile. He was dragged down the corridor, his protests swallowed by the overwhelming sense of dread. The doors to the Doctor's office were flung open with a deafening crash. Inside, two of his colleagues, Jackson and Scott, were already on their knees, hands clasped behind their heads. The fear in their eyes mirrored Tom's own as he was shoved down to join them. "Sit," barked the soldier, pushing Tom hard enough to send him sprawling. He scrambled into position, his heart pounding.

The Commander entered, a presence that sucked the air from the room. He surveyed the three men with cold detachment, his hand resting casually on the grip of his sidearm. "Listen carefully," he began, his voice like steel. "We're taking all of your research. You have a choice—come with us and continue your work under Doctor Bonny at a secure facility, or…" He raised the pistol slightly, his meaning clear. Jackson, the senior technician, broke the silence, his voice quavering. "The Doctor's… on board with this?" The Commander nodded once, a thin smile playing at his lips. "Entirely."

There was no hesitation in Jackson's response. "If the Doctor agrees, so do we." Tom's stomach churned as the Commander holstered his weapon. The room felt colder, the air heavier. "Good," the Commander said. "Now, empty your pockets—anything personal, anything that can identify you. Leave it here." Jackson and Scott obeyed immediately, dumping wallets and phones onto the desk. Tom hesitated, his mind racing, but fear propelled him into action. "Sixty seconds," the Commander snapped.

The next few minutes were a blur of orders and movement. Beta and Delta worked efficiently, stripping the room of equipment and data while the technicians gathered research materials. Tom's mind spun as they were herded into a tight formation and led down the corridor, the soldiers' weapons at the ready. At the service lift, Jackson broke the tense silence. "How do you plan to get us out of here unnoticed?" His voice was a whisper, but the desperation was clear. The Commander didn't turn. He touched his earpiece, then spoke over his shoulder. "Chopper's inbound. Two minutes. To the roof."

Tom's breath hitched. Whatever gamble he had made with the Serum, it was now bound to this terrifying new chapter.

✱✱✱

The Merlin helicopter roared through the air, its powerful blades slicing the sky with mechanical precision. Inside, Tom sat by the window, staring out at the endless expanse of clouds drifting lazily overhead. Their tranquil movement was in stark contrast to the chaos inside him. His thoughts were a storm—memories of the lab, the breakthrough they'd stumbled upon, and the sudden, violent intrusion of the military. One minute, he and his colleagues had been on the brink of a miracle; the next, they were prisoners, whisked away to some classified destination.

Across from Tom, Jackson and Scott shifted uncomfortably in their seats, sneaking glances at Beta, the soldier sitting opposite them. His face was hidden behind a tactical mask, an inscrutable wall of fabric and armour that betrayed nothing of the man beneath. The large black bags containing all their research sat ominously on the metal floor between the technicians and the soldiers, their presence a stark reminder of the stakes at play. Sitting directly across from Tom was the Commander, the de facto force controlling their fate. He wore a headset, listening intently to the chatter from the cockpit. Occasionally, he'd murmur a curt acknowledgment, but his body language betrayed nothing of his thoughts. The Commander radiated an unsettling calm, as though this operation was nothing more than routine.

Tom shifted in his seat, coughing lightly into his hand. When he pulled his hand back, his stomach dropped—blood. His fingers trembled as he quickly balled his hand into a fist, hiding the evidence. He glanced up cautiously, only to find the Commander's eyes locked onto him. Even behind the tactical mask, Tom could feel the weight of the man's scrutiny, as if he could see right through him. "Copy that," the Commander said, breaking the silence as he turned to look out the window. Below, the island came into view— a stretch of dense woodland interrupted by an open field. He raised two fingers, signalling the rest of his unit. "Two minutes," he said, his voice clipped and direct. The soldiers moved with practiced efficiency, checking their weapons and adjusting their gear. Jackson and Scott sat up straighter, the tension palpable. Tom kept his eyes down, willing himself to disappear under the Commander's gaze.

As the helicopter began its descent, it banked sharply to one side, giving the technicians a clear view of the ground below. The field was larger than it had seemed from a distance, bordered by trees that swayed violently in the downdraft of the rotor blades. In the centre of the clearing stood a lone vehicle, its paint dull and utilitarian.

Next to it was a figure, standing rigidly, his face obscured by the swirling dust.

The skids touched down with a jarring thud, the chopper rocking slightly as the pilot steadied it. A soldier reached for the side door and slid it open, unleashing a torrent of wind and noise into the cabin. The Commander's voice rose above the chaos, sharp and commanding. "Watch your heads as you get out. Follow Beta to your transport. It's been a pleasure, gentlemen." Scott and Jackson didn't need to be told twice. They grabbed the bags containing their research and leapt from the chopper, ducking low as the rotors continued to spin overhead. Beta gestured for them to follow, leading them toward the waiting vehicle.

Tom started to rise, his muscles stiff from the tension and cold, but before he could move, the Commander's hand shot out, shoving him firmly back into his seat. "Not you," the Commander growled, his voice low and final. He drew his sidearm in one fluid motion, resting it casually on his thigh. "You're staying put." Tom's heart pounded in his chest. He didn't dare argue, his eyes darting between the Commander's mask and the gun. He swallowed hard, his throat dry and raw.

Outside, Sierra and Delta worked quickly, hefting the research bags into the vehicle's trunk. The lone driver, a man with a stern expression and a military demeanour, closed the trunk with a decisive slam. Jackson, standing nearby, frowned as he watched the helicopter. "Hey!" he called out, stepping closer to the soldier. "Why's Tom still on that thing?" The soldier gave a dismissive shrug. "Get your arse in the vehicle," he barked, his tone brooking no argument. Jackson hesitated, glancing back toward the chopper, but the soldier's glare silenced any further questions. With a frustrated sigh, he climbed into the back seat beside Scott, who seemed almost excited by the unfolding drama.

"Where do you think they're taking us?" Scott asked, his voice laced with curiosity as the vehicle started moving. "Classified," the driver said curtly, shifting the car into gear. The tires bit into the uneven ground, kicking up dirt and rocks as they accelerated down a narrow track leading toward the forest.

Meanwhile, back in the helicopter, Tom sat frozen, his mind racing as Beta and Sierra climbed back in, sliding the door shut. The Commander hadn't spoken again, but the weight of his presence was suffocating. The chopper's engines roared as it lifted off once more, the ground falling away beneath them. Tom stared out the window, his thoughts a whirlwind of fear and confusion. What had gone so wrong? The Serum, their miracle discovery, was supposed to save lives. Now, it had thrust them into a shadowy world of secrets and military force. The Commander finally broke the silence. "You're important, Harris," he said, his voice calm but heavy with meaning. "Too important to let wander off into the unknown." Tom didn't respond. What could he say? The words felt more like a threat than reassurance, and the glint of the sidearm resting in the Commander's hand only deepened the pit in his stomach. Whatever lay ahead, he was a prisoner of circumstances far beyond his control.

***

The helicopter cut through the air with a low, relentless hum, the distant roar of the ocean growing louder as the coastline came into view. Below, jagged cliffs jutted out defiantly against the crashing waves, their stark beauty a reminder of nature's indifference to human affairs. Inside the cabin, Tom sat rigidly by the window, his stomach turning as his thoughts spiralled out of control. His head had stopped spinning, but unease gnawed at him, a feeling that something was catastrophically wrong. He glanced at the Commander, seated across from him, locked in a hushed conversation with Beta. Their voices were low, conspiratorial, and laden with an authority that made Tom's skin crawl.

Tom coughed lightly, his throat raw, his body rebelling against itself. He darted a glance at the soldiers surrounding him. Sierra and Delta cradled their guns, their postures deceptively casual, though their eyes were sharp and ever-watchful. His gaze swept the cabin, searching for anything he could use—a weapon, an escape, a plan. His stomach growled audibly, a futile protest from a body that had far greater problems to contend with. He shifted uncomfortably, trying to suppress his growing panic. Then it hit him. A violent coughing fit erupted from his chest, his lungs seizing painfully as blood sprayed from his lips. A warm trickle slid from his nose, running down to his top lip as he struggled to steady his breathing. The metallic tang of blood filled his mouth, and his vision swam.

The soldiers turned in unison, their attention snapping to Tom. Sierra leaned forward, his gloved hand gripping his shoulder firmly. "Get back in your seat. NOW," he barked, his voice sharp and commanding. But Tom's body betrayed him. He fell forward, collapsing onto the cold metal floor. Blood pooled beneath him, glistening darkly against the deck. The Commander rose, his voice calm but urgent as he spoke into his headset. "Divert. Adjust heading along the coastline. We need immediate access to medical support." The helicopter banked sharply, following the jagged cliffs as the pilot acknowledged the order. "Roger that, sir. Two mikes from base."

Tom's hands fumbled weakly against the floor, his breath ragged as Sierra and Delta moved to restrain him. But then their movements stilled as they realized what was in his hand. "Bollocks," Sierra muttered under her breath. Tom's fingers clutched a grenade, his thumb pressing firmly on the strike lever. His trembling hand held it like a lifeline, the only thing giving him control in a situation spiralling out of it. The cabin filled with tension, the air electric as the soldiers froze in place. The Commander raised his hands slightly, his voice calm and steady, though his eyes burned with intensity. "Where do you think you're going, sunshine? You jump out of this bird; you'll be dead before you hit the water."

Tom didn't respond. Tears streamed down his face, his expression a mixture of despair and defiance. He inched toward the cabin door, his body weak but driven by sheer willpower. His breathing was shallow, punctuated by hacking coughs that sprayed more blood across the floor. The Commander's voice softened, adopting a coaxing tone. "Harris, listen to me. We have the best doctors, the best medical care. Whatever's happening to you, we can fix it. You've got to trust me." Tom's tear-filled eyes met the Commander's, but there was no trust left in them—only a desperate resolve. Without a word, he released the pin and dropped the grenade onto the floor. The clink of metal against metal was deafening in the silent cabin. Then, with a final glance at the soldiers, Tom let himself fall backward, disappearing out of the open door.

"Bloody hell!" Sierra lunged forward, grabbing the grenade and hurling it out of the helicopter. It exploded mere feet above the ocean's surface, a fiery plume that sent shockwaves rippling through the water. The helicopter jolted from the force of the blast, the pilot instinctively banking hard to stabilize the aircraft. The Commander surged toward the open door, gripping the frame tightly as he scanned the churning waves below. The ocean swallowed Tom whole, the water roiling violently where he'd plunged.

"Lower us!" the Commander barked into his headset, his calm demeanour cracking for the first time. "I want eyes on him now!" The helicopter descended rapidly, skimming just above the surface as Beta joined the Commander, both men peering intently into the frothy sea. But there was nothing—no sign of movement, no trace of the man who had just fallen from their grasp. The pilot's voice crackled in their earpieces. "Sir, conditions are unstable. We need to return to base." The Commander didn't respond immediately. His eyes remained fixed on the waves, searching for something—anything—that might contradict the obvious. Finally, he straightened, stepping back into the cabin. "He's gone," Beta said quietly, his voice heavy with resignation.

The Commander's jaw tightened beneath his mask. "Not yet," he said coldly. "Nobody disappears without a trace. Get us to the base. I want every resource we've got sweeping this coastline. If he's alive, we'll find him. If not…" He let the thought hang in the air, unfinished but clear. The helicopter climbed once more, leaving the turbulent waters behind. Inside, the tension remained thick, the soldiers exchanging grim glances as they returned to their seats.

✳✳✳

The helicopter's engines roared like a distant storm, its powerful blades slicing through the air as it banked sharply westward, hugging the rugged coastline. From her vantage point on the dunes, the woman squinted against the late afternoon sun, her tousled hair whipping in the salty breeze. The explosion had jolted her awake, its concussive force reverberating through the sand beneath her. Now, as the thin trail of smoke dissipated into the cerulean sky, she watched the Royal Navy chopper hover briefly over the sea, circling with an urgency that betrayed the gravity of whatever they were searching for.

Her sharp eyes followed the scene, taking in every detail: the frenzied motion of the aircraft, the glint of light reflecting off its metallic frame, and the persistent churn of waves below. Something—someone—was out there. She could feel it in her gut, a strange intuition that made her hesitate even as the helicopter banked westward, retreating further down the coastline.

The woman brushed grains of sand from her worn cargo trousers, the gritty sensation grounding her as she slowly rose to her feet. Her muscles protested against the stiffness of her impromptu nap, and she stretched languidly, a yawn escaping her lips. As she moved, she cast a final glance toward the helicopter's retreating form, the roar of its engines fading into the distance.

Whatever had caused the explosion, it wasn't her concern—or so she told herself. Still, the peculiar timing gnawed at her. This stretch of the coastline was remote, rarely disturbed save for the occasional fishing boat or adventurous hiker. Explosions and military helicopters were not part of the usual scenery. She felt a pang of unease as she turned away, her boots sinking slightly into the warm, golden sand. Her steps were measured as she began her walk along the beach, the tide retreating and leaving a slick, glistening expanse of wet sand in its wake. The sun painted the sky in hues of amber and crimson, casting long shadows that stretched toward the dunes. She shoved her hands into her pockets, her fingers brushing against a worn piece of string, an old habit she used to keep her restless hands occupied.

The beach was quiet now, save for the rhythmic crash of waves and the occasional cry of a seagull overhead. Yet, the woman couldn't shake the feeling that something lingered—a presence, a question unanswered. Her sharp instincts, honed over years of solitude and self-reliance, told her that whatever had happened out there wasn't over. She glanced over her shoulder, her gaze sweeping the stretch of dunes and the churning sea beyond. The horizon was empty now, the helicopter gone, leaving only the vast expanse of ocean and the faint scent of salt and smoke hanging in the air. She sighed, shaking her head as if to dismiss her own thoughts, and continued on her way.

Chapter 11
07:15 hours, July 27th 2024, Near Bury St Edmunds, Suffolk

Wiping the sleep from his eyes, Aubrey sat up, the damp ground pressing against him, a familiar discomfort he had grown accustomed to through years of living on the move. He stretched his aching limbs, the cool morning air mingling with the earthy scent of wet leaves and soil. Above him, perched on a low-hanging branch, a sparrow flitted restlessly. It pecked and tugged at a twig, sending tiny flecks of bark fluttering down before taking flight deeper into the woodlands. Its abrupt departure left the space eerily still, save for the faint rustle of leaves overhead.

Sliding a hand into his jacket pocket, Aubrey's fingers brushed the smooth surface of the small tube nestled there. He withdrew it carefully, holding it up to inspect it in the filtered sunlight streaming through the canopy. The liquid inside was as clear as mountain spring water, its transparency deceptive. The plain white label revealed no secrets, save for the cryptic black lettering: "X-75." Turning the tube slowly between his fingers, he caught the sunlight at just the right angle, watching as a tiny rainbow arced momentarily within. The sight was fleeting, but it gave the object an almost magical quality, as though it held far more than the unassuming liquid it appeared to contain.

A sudden rustling to his right shattered his concentration, the sound startlingly close. Aubrey froze, his hand instinctively closing around the tube before tucking it back into the safety of his pocket. Leaning carefully around the massive trunk of the tree at his back, he caught sight of the source. A rabbit, brown and sleek, sniffed the ground a few meters away, its nose twitching as it worked its way along the narrow forest trail. Aubrey's stomach tightened at the sight, a stark reminder of his gnawing hunger. He had been pushing himself relentlessly northward, burning through reserves of energy that even his disciplined body struggled to replenish. Rest and sustenance were no longer luxuries but necessities he could not ignore.

His eyes narrowed, instincts sharpening. The rabbit moved with cautious precision; its small paws soundless on the leaf-strewn ground. Aubrey's fingers found the hilt of his knife, his grip steady and familiar as he drew it silently from its sheath. The blade gleamed faintly in the dappled light; a tool of survival honed to a razor's edge. He glanced skyward; the nearby branches were still, the morning air calm. No wind to throw off his aim. All he needed now was patience. Every muscle in his body was taut as he watched the creature, his breath shallow to avoid detection. Timing was everything. The moment he shifted, the rabbit would sense the danger—nature's perpetual game of predator and prey. Holding the knife delicately by its tip, he balanced its weight between his thumb and forefinger, poised for the throw. The rabbit paused, sitting up on its haunches, ears swivelling as it sniffed the air. Aubrey's heart pounded in anticipation; had it sensed him?

Before he could release the knife, a sudden crash echoed through the forest, the sound shattering the fragile stillness. The rabbit bolted, a blur of brown fur disappearing into the underbrush. Aubrey's blade struck the empty ground milliseconds later, embedding itself into the soft earth with a dull thud. He exhaled sharply, his frustration mingling with the realization that his meal had eluded him. Rising slowly, he retrieved the knife, brushing off the dirt. Whatever had caused the noise was not far. His eyes scanned the woods, instincts prickling. Hunger might not be his only problem today.

✳✳✳

Ten minutes earlier, a blue Toyota SUV hurtled down the narrow country road, its engine growling as it pushed well past the speed limit. Inside, tension simmered. In the passenger seat, Nicola twisted around to check on her daughters, curled up in the back seat, their small bodies bundled in bright pink pyjamas. The girls clung to their teddies, lost in the deep sleep of early childhood, blissfully unaware of the speed at which their father drove. Nicola turned back toward the front, her gaze catching the flicker of the speedometer needle climbing dangerously high. "Christ, Martin," she said sharply, her tone a mix of concern and irritation. "I'd like to arrive in one piece, if it's all the same to you." Her husband, jaw tight and knuckles white on the steering wheel, didn't answer. His focus was singular, locked on the winding road ahead.

The morning was just beginning to break, the pale light of dawn filtering through the trees that flanked either side of the road. The SUV's tires screamed against the tarmac as Martin rounded a bend too fast, the car briefly straying onto the empty oncoming lane before snapping back into position. "If you don't slow down this instant, Martin Ward," Nicola snapped, her voice rising, "I'm going to make you wish you'd never dragged us on this bloody holiday!" The sharpness of her tone seemed to cut through his single-minded determination. He exhaled, easing his foot off the accelerator just slightly. The roar of the engine softened, and for a moment, the cabin was filled with the steady hum of tires on asphalt. He shot her a sidelong glance, a hint of guilt flashing across his face.

"Sorry, love," he murmured, the tension in his voice melting into something softer. "I'm just eager to get there, that's all. You know how it is—we don't have much time before we're back to the grind again." Nicola softened, too, leaning back in her seat, though her hands remained clenched in her lap. She stole a glance at the rearview mirror. The sight of their daughters, their faces serene and angelic in sleep, eased her nerves. Even in chaos, they were her constant source of peace. Martin noticed her expression and, with a small smile, reached over to squeeze her hand. "We'll make this a trip to remember," he said, stealing a quick kiss on her cheek. For a fleeting moment, a sense of calm settled between them.

But the calm was shattered in an instant.

The blare of a horn exploded through the quiet, jolting them both. The sound came from nowhere, sudden, and overwhelming, filling the interior like a siren. Martin's head snapped up, eyes widening as he caught sight of headlights bearing down on them, impossibly close, from the opposite direction. "Shit!" he cursed, yanking the steering wheel to the side. His foot slammed onto the brake, the force throwing Nicola forward against her seatbelt. The girls stirred in the back, but before they could fully awaken, Nicola's scream pierced the air—a sound of raw terror that seemed to stretch time itself. The screech of tires, the metallic crunch of impact, the world spinning—a kaleidoscope of sound and motion swallowed them whole. And then, silence.

The road, moments ago alive with the growl of engines and human voices, lay eerily still. Dust settled slowly in the dawn light. The blue SUV rested at an unnatural angle, its front crumpled like paper, steam hissing from its engine. One of the teddies had fallen to the floor of the car, its button eyes staring blankly ahead, a silent witness to the chaos.

The oak tree's massive trunk jutted forward like a menacing sentinel; its coarse bark now deeply entangled with the mangled front of the vehicle. The once-sleek blue Toyota was a ruin, its bonnet peeled back as if torn apart by claws, exposing the twisted, smoking innards of the engine. Steam and the acrid smell of oil filled the cool morning air, mixing with the faint metallic tang of blood. The airbags had deployed, their once-pristine white fabric now smudged with grime and streaks of red. They had done their job, saving Martin and Nicola from immediate death—but the crash had still left its mark. In the back of the car, chaos reigned. Abby's high-pitched screams sliced through the stillness as she clutched her nose, crimson dripping between her fingers. Beside her, Shannon wailed, the coppery taste of blood in her mouth from a tongue bitten in terror. Their small bodies trembled in their car seats, their wide, tear-filled eyes darting between their unconscious father and their barely-moving mother.

Nicola stirred, her head lolling forward before she lifted it with effort. The world spun, her vision swimming in a haze of white and red. The crumpled airbag lay slack against the dashboard like a deflated balloon, its presence oddly surreal in the midst of destruction. For a moment, she was disoriented, unsure of where she was or how she had gotten there. Then her gaze shifted, landing on Martin. His head rested heavily against the shattered window;

crimson droplets streaked across the cracked glass like a grotesque painting. A gash above his temple trickled blood that painted trails down his ashen face. "Martin…" she murmured, her voice weak, but there was no response. Her chest tightened, panic threatening to overtake her—but then a new sound broke through, piercing and relentless.

The children.

The realization hit her like a bolt, propelling her into action. Adrenaline coursed through her veins, momentarily dulling the throbbing pain radiating from her ribs. She turned her head painfully toward the back seat, squinting through her blurry vision at her daughters' terrified faces. "Shhhhh... hey, girls... shhhhh," she soothed, her voice trembling but steady. "It'll be okay. Mummy's coming. Just hold on." She fumbled for her seatbelt, her fingers shaking as she pressed the release button. The mechanism clicked, and the strap recoiled with a snap. As she twisted her torso to reach for her daughters, a sharp, searing pain stabbed through her ribs, making her gasp. For a moment, she was paralyzed, nausea rising in her throat. But she swallowed it down, gritting her teeth against the pain. The girls needed her.

She reached out to Martin, grabbing his shoulder and giving it a desperate shake. "Martin... hey, Martin... HEY, wake up!" she shouted, her voice rising with urgency. His body shifted slightly, a low groan escaping his lips as his head rolled away from the window. Relief flooded her, though it was tempered by the sight of his dazed, bloodied face. He mumbled something incoherent, his eyes fluttering but not quite focusing. Nicola's own vision was still blurred, but her instincts overrode the fog in her mind. She turned toward the passenger door, gripping the handle with both hands. The door resisted, groaning loudly as she pushed against it with her weight. Metal ground against metal, the sound setting her teeth on edge, but she didn't stop. After what felt like an eternity, the door creaked open wide enough for her to slip through. She stepped out onto the uneven ground, her legs wobbling beneath her.

The cold morning air hit her face like a slap, the fresh smell of earth and bark a sharp contrast to the chaos she had left behind in the car. She leaned heavily on the door for support, her free hand clutching at her aching ribs. Every breath was a struggle, shallow and painful, but she forced herself to stay upright. Her children's cries were still ringing in her ears, spurring her on. Steadying herself, she turned back toward the wreckage. The oak tree loomed large and immovable, its bark smeared with paint from the vehicle and bits of shattered glass sparkling like cruel diamonds on the ground. The SUV was a grotesque, crumpled husk, steam rising from its open hood. For a moment, Nicola felt overwhelmed by the enormity of the scene, but then another sob from Abby pulled her back to the present.

She could not afford to freeze. Her family needed her.

Standing unsteadily, Nicola felt the world tilt and spin, a kaleidoscope of pain and disorientation. Her head throbbed violently, the sensation like a drumbeat threatening to crack her skull. She pressed her hand against her temple, trying to steady herself when suddenly, something brushed her shoulder. Her body jerked instinctively, stumbling backward as her heart leaped into her throat. "Whoa, lady, you OK?"

A man stood before her; his hands raised in a gesture of reassurance. His face was pale, his wide eyes darting over the scene with clear alarm. The worry in his voice carried a panicked edge. "I'm... I'm fine," Nicola managed to croak, though her trembling legs and ragged breathing betrayed her. "Stay right there," the man said, already moving toward the crumpled car. "I'll check on your partner." Nicola staggered sideways, leaning against the wrecked door for support as her vision blurred again. The sharp pain in her head worsened, a splitting ache that pulsed in time with her rapid heartbeat. Over the car's crushed roof, she could just make out the man—a stout figure with a short beard—as he pried at the driver's side door.

"Hey, buddy, you alright?" the man called to Martin through the broken window. Martin's groan was faint but audible, his head still lolling forward. "No... no, wait there... it's OK. Let me help you." The man wrestled the door open with a metallic screech and reached in to support Martin as he tried to climb out. Nicola watched with bated breath, her heart hammering as Martin's disoriented form emerged from the vehicle. His face was a mask of blood, a deep gash stretching across his forehead. The wound oozed sluggishly, the crimson streaks painting his nose and cheek. He stumbled as the man steadied him; his legs weak beneath him. "Martin!" Nicola gasped, her panic rising again. But then the sharp sound of her daughters' cries pierced through the air, cutting through her thoughts like a blade. She turned sharply toward the backseat, where Abby and Shannon's frightened wails grew louder with every passing second. Panic clawed at her chest.

"The girls! The girls are still in the car!" she cried, lunging toward the back door. Her fingers fumbled with the handle, pulling with all her strength, but the door refused to budge. "Martin!" she called desperately. "Hey, over here... the girls... can you get them out? I'll come around!" Martin, still dazed, turned sluggishly toward the back of the car. He grabbed the door handle and pulled hard, but it didn't move. He gritted his teeth, frustration flashing across his bloodied face. "Bloody hell!" he swore, stepping back to glare at the stubborn door.

The bearded man moved beside him. "Here, let me," he offered, motioning Martin to step aside. "Simon... Simon Barker," he added as he wrapped both hands around the handle and pulled with all his strength. His face flushed red with effort, veins bulging in his neck, but the door remained stubbornly shut. "Damn thing's jammed," Simon muttered, stepping back and shaking his hands out. Martin cursed under his breath and looked around, his eyes scanning the ground until they landed on a thick branch, broken off in the crash. He picked it up, testing its weight in his hands as he approached the back window. "Stand back!" he barked, raising the log over his shoulder.

Nicola's voice cut through the air like a whip. "Don't be so fucking stupid! The glass, Martin! The girls are inside! Seriously, think for once!" Her words froze him mid-swing. Martin's jaw clenched, his grip tightening on the log before he let it fall with a frustrated thud. He looked away, chest heaving with restrained anger and desperation.

Across the road, his eyes caught sight of the other vehicle—a black BMW that lay on its side, its crumpled body surrounded by debris. Scattered across the asphalt were boxes, packages, and what appeared to be catering trays, their contents spilled and splattered. Martin squinted, noticing movement further down the road. About fifty meters away, a figure stood between two trees, a stark silhouette against the rising morning light. The man was dressed entirely in black, his posture unnervingly still as he stared at the scattered food at his feet. Something about the way he lingered, detached and unmoving, sent a chill down Martin's spine. He pointed toward the figure, his voice rough as he addressed Simon. "What about him? Think he can help?"

Simon followed his gaze, his brow furrowing at the sight. "Maybe..." he said hesitantly, glancing back at Nicola and the crying children. "I'll go ask. Stay here." As Simon jogged toward the mysterious man, Martin turned back to the car, his mind racing for solutions. His daughters' screams grew fainter, muffled behind the thick, unyielding metal of the vehicle. Nicola leaned heavily against the car, clutching her ribs, her face pale with worry. "Hang in there," Martin murmured, his voice more to himself than anyone else. Time felt like it was slipping away, and he knew they needed to act fast.

Nicola moved slowly around the wrecked car, one hand clutching her ribs as she peered into the backseat. Abby and Shannon had stopped crying, their wide, tear-streaked eyes fixed on their parents outside. Abby pressed her small hands against the glass, her nose scrunched in confusion. "Who's that man, Mommy?" Shannon asked, her voice quivering but curious. Nicola shook her head, glancing toward the hulking figure still shrouded in shadows. She didn't answer but instead looked at Martin, who was leaning against the side of the car, his bloodied face turned toward the road. Martin shrugged, clearly exasperated. "How am I supposed to know? And honestly, I don't care if he's Santa Claus or the Tooth Fairy—just as long as he can get these damn doors open."

Nicola didn't respond, her mind too occupied with worry. Together, they watched Simon close the gap between himself and the stranger. The two men seemed to exchange words, Simon gesturing animatedly toward the wrecked car while the other man stood stiff and silent, like a statue carved from stone. Minutes dragged on, feeling like an eternity, before Simon began jogging back toward them. Behind him, the stranger followed, his strides long and deliberate. As he emerged from the shadows of the trees and into the early morning light, Nicola's eyes widened. "Bloody hell," she muttered, glancing at Martin. "He's huge." A slow grin spread across Martin's face as he took in the man's imposing frame. The stranger towered over Simon, his shoulders broad and his arms thick with muscle that strained against the seams of his black coat. His beard was dense and wild, his expression stern but calm.

"Yeah," Martin said with a hint of amusement. "He looks like he could peel that door back like it's a tin of sardines." The faintest flicker of hope sparked in Nicola's chest, though she wouldn't let herself fully believe it yet. As the man approached, the girls stirred again in the backseat, their fear giving way to curiosity. Shannon's small voice piped up, soft but clear. "Mommy, is that Hagrid?" Nicola blinked, startled, and turned back toward the car. "What was that, sweetie?" Shannon's angelic face peered up through the window, her tear-streaked cheeks now flushed pink. "Hagrid," she repeated earnestly. "You know, Harry Potter's friend?" Abby nodded solemnly beside her sister, her little hands clutching her teddy bear tightly. "He's big like Hagrid." Nicola couldn't help but let out a strained chuckle, the sound sharp with tension. "No, darling, I don't think it's Hagrid. But maybe he's a friend, hmm? Let's hope he's as helpful." The man reached them, standing ten meters away as Simon approached the couple, his expression a mix of apprehension and determination. "Right, I think he's going to help," he said, his voice tinged with uncertainty.

Nicola, still clutching her ribs, followed his gaze to the man standing a fair distance away. The imposing figure stood motionless, his broad shoulders casting a long shadow on the ground. Something about his stillness made her uneasy. "What do you mean, you think?" Martin asked, narrowing his eyes at Simon. His tone was sharp, his patience already stretched thin. Simon hesitated, glancing down at his feet as though embarrassed. "Well... I explained the situation," he began, rubbing the back of his neck nervously. "Told him there are kids stuck in the car, the doors are jammed, and we really need his help." Nicola folded her arms, her voice growing firm. "Yes, and? What did he say?"

Simon sighed, shrugging helplessly. "That's just it—he didn't say anything. He just... nodded. Like, really slowly. Then he followed me back here." Nicola groaned softly, pushing past Simon with a muttered, "Unbelievable." Over her shoulder, she called out to Martin, "Honey, call emergency services. And the police—they'll need to close the road or something." Martin pulled his phone from his pocket, dialling 9-9-9 with shaking fingers. As he waited for the call to connect, he watched Nicola approach the silent giant. She held out her hand in thanks, her face still wary as she spoke to him. Simon stood awkwardly nearby, shifting his weight from foot to foot.

Then, within the span of ten seconds, chaos erupted.

Aubrey, moved with terrifying speed. From under his coat, he withdrew a knife—a long blade glinting in the pale sunlight—and slashed it across Nicola's throat in one fluid motion. A crimson arc sprayed from the wound as Nicola staggered backward, her hands clutching at her neck. She crumpled to the ground in a heap, blood pooling beneath her. Martin froze, the phone slipping from his grasp as a guttural scream tore from his throat. "Nicola!" The girls, wide-eyed and trembling in the backseat, pressed their faces to the window just in time to see their mother collapse. Shannon screamed, but Abby yanked her sister down into the footwell, both girls shaking as they clung to each other.

Aubrey didn't stop. His focus shifted to Simon, who had begun backing away in terror, his hands raised in a feeble attempt to placate the attacker. "Hey, hey, man—just take it easy," Simon stammered, edging toward the car for cover. Aubrey moved like a predator. He lunged, tackling Simon to the ground with a brutal force that echoed in the stillness of the road. Simon struggled, kicking out wildly, but Aubrey was too quick. He dodged a flailing boot, rolling effortlessly to his feet before grabbing Simon's legs and yanking him back down.

Simon cried out, clawing at the asphalt as he tried to crawl away. Aubrey followed with eerie calm, stalking his prey with the grace of a hunting cat. When Simon's strength faltered, Aubrey reached down, seized a handful of his hair, and yanked his head back. The serrated edge of the knife glinted briefly before it sliced across

Simon's throat. A strangled gurgle escaped Simon's lips as his body went limp. Aubrey let him fall to the ground without a second glance. His eyes turned to Martin, who was still kneeling on the road, sobbing incoherently.

"Please," Martin whispered, his voice breaking. "Don't... we haven't done anything... please..." Aubrey's steps were deliberate, each one crunching against the shattered glass littering the ground. He stood over Martin for a moment, his face expressionless. Then, with a single, swift motion, he brought the knife down hard. The blade drove deep into Martin's skull with a sickening crunch. Inside the car, the girls huddled in the footwell, trembling violently. Shannon buried her face against Abby's shoulder, her tears soaking into her sister's shirt. Abby kept her eyes fixed on the window, her breath shallow and rapid.

They heard the crunch of glass under heavy boots, the sound growing fainter as Aubrey walked away. For several moments, silence enveloped the wrecked car, broken only by the distant rustle of leaves in the breeze. Shannon whimpered softly. "Is he gone?" Abby didn't answer, her eyes still fixed on the window above them. She didn't dare move, didn't dare breathe too loudly. Somewhere in the distance, a faint siren wailed, drawing closer.

Minutes crawled by, feeling like hours to the two little girls huddled in the footwell of the car. They clung to each other, their small bodies trembling as they tried to stay as quiet as possible. Shannon whispered, her voice barely audible, "Do you think he'll come back?" Abby squeezed her sister tighter, her own voice shaking. "I don't know... but we have to stay down. Don't let him see us, okay?" Shannon nodded, biting her lip to keep from crying. Her imagination raced with terrifying possibilities. What was that man? He wasn't like anyone she'd ever seen. Monsters lived in fairy tales, but this—this was real. Did he eat little girls? The thought made her shudder, and she buried her face against Abby's shoulder.

Outside, Aubrey moved with methodical purpose. Ignoring the faint cries of the children, he crouched on the asphalt, picking up the scattered remnants of the catering delivery. Pieces of chicken, wedges of cheese, and even crushed pastries disappeared into his jacket pockets. He picked up a drumstick and sank his teeth into it, crunching through the meat with no regard for the dirt and grit that clung to its surface. His powerful jaw worked as he stripped the bone clean, tossing it aside with casual disdain. As he chewed, his eyes scanned the scene, settling on a trail of cake crumbs leading toward the car lying on its side.

A whisper echoed in his mind, sharp and teasing. "Don't leave any breadcrumbs."

He frowned slightly, shaking off the thought. Dropping the last of the food into his pockets, he wiped his mouth with the back of his hand and turned his attention back to the upright vehicle. A flicker of movement caught his eye—a tiny face peeking out through the smudged window. He froze, locking eyes with the child for a split second before she ducked back out of sight. A slow grin spread across his face, cold and predatory. Removing his knife from its sheath, he approached the car with deliberate steps.

Martin's lifeless body lay crumpled near the front of the vehicle, his blood pooling in the cracks of the asphalt. Aubrey crouched beside him, his knife gleaming in the pale light. With precision, he grabbed Martin's shirt and sliced a large strip from the fabric. The ripping sound was sharp and jarring against the stillness of the road. Inside the car, the girls whimpered. The sound of the blade, coupled with the movement outside, sent their imaginations spiralling. "What's he doing?" Shannon whispered; her voice tight with fear. "I don't know," Abby replied, trying to sound braver than she felt. She pressed herself lower into the footwell, keeping her sister close.

Aubrey ignored their muffled whispers, turning his attention to the car's rear panel. He ran a hand along the surface until he found what he was looking for—the fuel compartment. Instead of unscrewing the cap, he drove his knife into the panel, prying it away with a loud screech of metal. The sharp noise made the girls flinch, their hands flying to their ears. The fuel cap exposed, Aubrey gripped the pipe and shoved the torn piece of fabric inside, leaving one end hanging loosely. His movements were calm, almost methodical, as if he'd done this countless times before.

Inside the car, panic was spreading. The girls had begun to cry, their tiny hands patting at the window. "Mommy! Daddy! Wake up!" Shannon shouted, her voice high and desperate. Abby joined in, pounding on the glass as if sheer willpower could revive their parents. Aubrey barely noticed their cries. His focus was elsewhere. Reaching into his jacket, he pulled out a battered lighter, flicking it open to reveal a tiny, wavering flame. He turned his head slightly, ears pricking at a distant sound—a siren wailing faintly in the distance. A shadow of annoyance crossed his face, but he remained undeterred. Holding the lighter steady, he brought it closer to the exposed rag, the flame reflecting in his cold, unblinking eyes.

***

The paramedic's adrenaline surged as she swerved around the final bend, her vehicle's sirens wailing into the stillness of the forest road. Tall trees arched overhead, casting long shadows that seemed to close in around her. Her knuckles whitened on the steering wheel as she glanced at the GPS screen—she was approaching fast.

Then she saw it.

The road ahead was a tableau of destruction. A mangled blue SUV lay smashed against a tree, its bonnet crumpled like paper. Debris was strewn across the tarmac: shards of glass, scattered food, and a trail of dark stains leading ominously toward bodies sprawled across the asphalt. "Bloody hell," she muttered, her pulse quickening as she pressed harder on the accelerator. Grabbing the radio, she barked into it: "Oscar Mike One to base, I've arrived at the scene. RTA involving two vehicles, debris all over the road. Requesting immediate police and additional paramedic support."

Her car screeched to a halt just short of the wreckage, tires kicking up small clouds of dust and gravel. Snatching her bag from the backseat, she bolted toward the nearest body. It was a man— short, bearded, lying in a widening pool of blood. She crouched and pressed two fingers to his neck, searching for a pulse - nothing. "Come on, mate," she whispered, willing him to respond. But when she gently turned him onto his back, her stomach dropped. A deep, jagged wound stretched across his neck; the gash so severe it was clear he hadn't stood a chance. The sight was grim, but she didn't have the luxury of dwelling. She clicked her chest radio again.

"Oscar Mike One to base. One confirmed fatality. Multiple casualties on-site. Requesting Medevac. We're going to need all hands on deck." Her ears caught a faint sound—a small voice, barely audible over the crackle of fire and distant sirens. Children crying. Her heart leapt. She scanned the scene and spotted the source: two little girls, their frightened faces pressed against the rear window of the SUV.

Another body lay further away—a woman sprawled on her side, motionless. The paramedic darted toward her, kneeling to assess for signs of life. Blood seeped from a head wound, matting the woman's hair, but there was still warmth to her skin. The paramedic leaned close, gently shaking her shoulder. "Ma'am? Can you hear me?" No response. The children's cries grew louder, and the paramedic's head snapped up. A man was slumped against the back wheel of the SUV, face down, blood trickling from a gaping wound at the top of his skull. Another fatality? She couldn't tell without closer inspection, but every instinct told her to prioritize the living. The girls' tear-streaked faces haunted her as they peered out from behind the front seats.

She sprinted to the driver's side, flinging open the door. "Hey, darlings," she called gently, crouching down to meet their frightened eyes. "It's okay, I'm here to help. You're safe now." The girls cowered further into the footwell, their small bodies trembling. "Mommy!" one of them wailed, pointing toward the woman outside. The other clutched her sister tightly, tears streaking her cheeks. The paramedic extended her hand, her voice calm and soothing despite the chaos. "Come on, sweethearts. I'll get you out of here. Just take my hand—"

Before the words were fully out, a deafening roar shattered the moment. The SUV erupted in an explosion of fire and smoke; the force so intense it threw the paramedic backward. Heat engulfed the area, licking at her skin and igniting the debris scattered around the scene. For a moment, everything was noise and flame—a violent cacophony that drowned out even the children's screams.

The paramedic hit the ground hard, dazed and gasping for breath. Her ears rang, and the acrid smell of burning fuel stung her nostrils. Staggering to her feet, she shielded her face against the blistering heat and tried to make sense of the carnage. The SUV was engulfed, a roaring inferno consuming everything inside. Flames danced across the road, devouring bits of debris and the three bodies lying on the floor, black smoke spiralled into the sky.

From a tree stump a short distance away, Aubrey watched the scene with unsettling detachment. He popped the last bite of chocolate cake into his mouth, savouring it as though he were enjoying a picnic on a sunny afternoon. The heat of the blaze warmed his face, but he didn't flinch. Instead, he licked his fingers clean, brushing crumbs from his chest with a casual flick of his hand. Sirens grew louder, their urgency cutting through the crackling flames and chaos. Aubrey stood slowly; his expression unreadable as he turned toward the dark cover of the woods. Without a backward glance, he melted into the shadows, the trees swallowing him whole.

The paramedic stumbled forward, choking on the thick smoke as she reached for her radio again. "Base, we have an explosion at the scene—multiple casualties confirmed. I need assistance now. Now!" But even as she spoke, her eyes darted toward the treeline, where the faintest movement caught her attention. A shadow disappeared between the trunks, silent and deliberate.

The monster was gone.

Chapter 12
10:30 hours, July 27th 2024, Green Park, London

Birds chirped peacefully outside the window, a dog barked happily in the distance, and the gentle hum of the electric extractor fan filled the room. The rhythmic sound of water falling into the tray echoed faintly as it cascaded down the plug. It was a quiet morning, one that felt deceptively ordinary, as if nothing out of the ordinary could happen on a day like this. But just as Bill was starting to settle into the stillness of his surroundings, a loud, forceful bang on the door shattered the peace. "I know you're in there! Open this bloody door, you hear me?" The voice was angry, filled with an edge of urgency that cut through the calm like a knife.

Bill's eyes shot open, his body jolting upright in a panic. For a moment, everything was a blur, his senses sluggish as his mind struggled to catch up with reality. The room swam in and out of focus, the edges of the walls warping. His head felt heavy, the remnants of whatever he had swallowed still lingering in his system. The sound of frantic knocking continued, relentless, a rhythmic pounding that seemed to vibrate through the very floor beneath him.

Bang! Bang! Bang!

"Open up now! I'm warning you!" The voice was closer now, more insistent, as if the person on the other side knew exactly what he was doing, knew that he was awake. Bill blinked hard, trying to shake off the grogginess that still clung to him. His hand instinctively went to his forehead, feeling the dried blood, the sticky remnants from earlier. He stared at the red smudge on his fingers, recalling the surreal conversation he had had with the mysterious voice on the phone just hours ago. It all felt like a dream now, a bad dream that was slipping through his fingers, leaving behind nothing but confusion and dread.

Bang! Bang! Bang! Bang! Bang!

"Right, that's it, I can hear you moving around in there! Don't think this door is going to protect you!" The words were sharp, threatening, and full of menace. Bill's mind raced, the fog lifting slowly as the adrenaline kicked in. Mrs. Clark, had been the one knocking. She had been vocal before, but this was different. This was too forceful, too angry. He listened intently as her footsteps retreated, echoing down the stairs as she huffed her way out of the building, no doubt heading down to the street below. The sound of her heavy boots faded into the distance, and then… silence. Still reeling from the shock, Bill stood up, adjusting the towel around his waist. The movement felt mechanical, as if his body wasn't entirely his own. Each step felt like it required more energy than it should. He needed to clear his head, to wash away the remnants of whatever had happened to him, to somehow regain control of his surroundings.

He shuffled into the bathroom, steam still clinging to the air, swirling around in tendrils. Bill squinted through the mist, feeling the oppressive weight of the atmosphere in the small room. He reached for the shower dial, adjusting it with shaky hands. The last few drops of water drained from the showerhead before it fell silent. The sound of running water echoed in his mind, a strange comfort in the midst of the chaos.

Turning to the sink, Bill splashed cold water onto his face, desperately trying to rid himself of the sensation of blood that still clung to his skin. He scrubbed at his hands, his movements jerky, as if he were fighting against something that didn't want to let go. The phone ringing in the next room caught his attention, a sharp interruption that broke the rhythm of his thoughts. The familiar, almost anxious tone of the phone seemed too much to ignore. Reluctantly, Bill turned off the tap, wiped his hands on the towel, and made his way back to the bed. He saw his phone on the side of the bed, the small light blinking on its screen, an indicator of an incoming call. His heart skipped a beat. It had been a while since he'd checked his phone—he hadn't even remembered turning it off. He reached out and picked it up, his thumb instinctively tapping the screen to answer.

"Yes?" His voice was hoarse, but the words came out steady. "Doctor, hey, it's me. Just checking you're alright. Do you know what time it is?" Bill frowned, looking around the room, trying to gauge how much time had passed. He glanced toward the microwave on the counter. The power light was off. It was as though time had stopped completely for a few moments, a strange sensation that left him unsettled. "No, what time is it?" he replied, trying to sound casual, but something inside him was starting to twist with unease. "Oh, okay, well it's 10:30, sir. We have our briefing at midday, and we were unsure what to do about, well, you know, that thing."

Bill's stomach dropped at the mention of the briefing. The "thing." It all clicked into place now—the incident, the strange phone call, the blood, the feeling of being watched. Something was going on, and Bill could sense it, but there were too many unanswered questions. His instincts screamed at him to keep the conversation brief. His phone wasn't secure, and he had no idea who was listening. He had to be careful, had to keep it to the essentials. There was a threat somewhere—he could feel it. "Thank you for your concern, but everything is good," Bill said, trying to mask the tension in his voice. "I will see you shortly." "OK, we have set up the new lab in the prison, however, Tom's gone missing." Bill nodded, his thoughts lay somewhere else, "that's great Jackson thanks."

He ended the call abruptly, silencing the buzzing in his ear. For a moment, the room felt still, and Bill couldn't help but feel a cold shiver run down his spine. He stared at the blank screen of his phone, the silence settling around him like a heavy fog. What had he just stepped into? What was happening to him? Bill exhaled slowly, trying to calm himself, but the nagging feeling that something was terribly wrong wouldn't leave him. He glanced at the door, wondering if Mrs. Clark would return with even more questions or accusations. He had to be ready. Whatever was coming, he couldn't afford to let his guard down. Not now. Not when everything was starting to unravel.

Twenty minutes later, Bill was dressed, his mind still racing with the remnants of the night's events. He grabbed his briefcase and coat from the bed and made his way towards the door, but just as his fingers brushed the handle, his phone began to ring again. The sudden noise startled him, and he glanced back at the bed, where his phone lay silently blinking. A surge of unease flooded him, but he walked over and grabbed it anyway, answering with a sharp intake of breath. Before he could speak, a cold, controlled voice cut through the line.

"Listen carefully. Standing on the other side of the door is your landlady and her son. Wait three minutes, then leave. Make sure you have all personal effects with you—leave nothing behind." The line went dead with a sharp click, leaving only the dial tone in its wake. Bill froze, his heart hammering in his chest. His eyes darted to the door as he listened carefully, trying to discern any sounds. For a moment, nothing but silence filled the room, and then—creak. The faintest of footsteps echoed across the floorboards outside. His grip tightened on the phone. The caller was right. Someone was out there. His mind raced. Who had called him? What was happening? But there was no time to waste. He grabbed a small suitcase from underneath his bed, moving quickly but quietly, like a man already on borrowed time. He stuffed clothes, books, toiletries, anything he could think of, into the case, not bothering to organize it. His thoughts were clouded, moving faster than he could process. All that mattered was getting out.

Checking the time on his phone, Bill tried to steady his breathing, focusing on the seconds ticking away. He stood by the door, straining to listen. The faint sound of shuffling feet. A low breath. A soft thud against the door. Bill's pulse quickened as the noise grew louder—another crash, this time the force of it rattled the door frame. He stepped back instinctively, his stomach dropping. Suddenly, something crimson began to seep underneath the door, dark and slick, soaking into the carpet. Blood. "What the hell…" Bill's voice was a mere whisper, caught between disbelief and terror. He stood frozen for a moment, staring at the growing stain on the floor, before shaking himself out of the daze.

He stepped forward cautiously, his heart racing as he grasped the door handle, turning it just enough to crack the door open. A soft breath caught in his throat as he peered through the gap, waiting for the door to explode outward, for the chaos to erupt. But instead, the silence in the hallway was unsettling, like the calm before the storm. Just as he was about to make his move, the phone rang again, the shrill sound splitting the tension in the air.

"St Pancras, 11:55, platform six. Your pre-paid ticket will be waiting at the booking office. Do not deviate. The train will terminate. Head out of the station to the taxi rank. You will be collected by an unmarked SUV, which will bring you to the rendezvous point. To confirm, press the hash button." His hands trembled slightly as he gripped the suitcase handle tighter, the weight of the situation settling deeper into his bones. He looked down at the screen, his thumb hovering over the hash button, feeling the gravity of the moment. He pressed it, the confirming beep adding a layer of finality to the situation.

Without another thought, Bill shoved the phone into his pocket and stepped out of the room, the suitcase dragging behind him. The hallway was eerily quiet, save for the steady drip of blood that trickled from underneath the door. He took one last glance at the room, making sure he hadn't left anything behind, before moving forward.

The first body he encountered was Mrs. Clark, his landlady. She lay face down on the floor in front of him, her head unnaturally turned to the side, her lifeless eyes wide open in a frozen look of shock. The blood pooled around her, dark and sticky, dripping from a small puncture wound at the centre of her forehead. He swallowed hard, staring at her body as his stomach twisted. It was the kind of death that didn't make sense—quick, efficient, almost surgical. A sickening thought crossed his mind: had this been intended for him? But there was no time to dwell on it.

He took a step forward, his feet brushing against something soft, something yielding. He looked down and saw Tommy Clark, Mrs.

Clark's son, half-lying, half-crumpled at the foot of the stairs. The man's left leg was caught between two spindles, his body twisted in a grotesque angle. Bill didn't recognize the exact cause of death, but he didn't need to. The blood staining the stairs and the twisted position of Tommy's body told him all he needed to know. It was a brutal, vicious end.

Bill didn't linger. He checked the time on his phone once more, hearing the distant echo of sirens outside, but he couldn't afford to be distracted. He descended the stairs quickly, careful to avoid stepping on Tommy's body, moving with a quiet urgency. Each creak of the floorboards underfoot seemed amplified in the silence of the building. His pulse raced as he reached the ground floor, praying none of the other residents were home. He couldn't afford to be caught now. Not with everything on the line.

As he reached the hallway of the building's ground floor, he moved faster, ducking into the shadows near the exit. His breath was shallow, his mind focused solely on one thing: escape. Bill had no idea who was after him or why, but the bloody scene that greeted him told him everything he needed to know. He had to get out. And fast.

***

14.00 hours, July 27th 2024,
Scotland Yard, London

Scratching his head, DCI Craig cast a long, reflective glance over the cluttered desk; his gaze drifted to the cardboard box perched precariously on the chair by the door. The contents of the box—personal effects, old case notes, and a few mementos—felt like fragments of a life he was reluctantly leaving behind. With a resigned sigh, he adjusted his tie, mentally ticking off his checklist. Almost ready. A sharp knock broke his reverie. "Come in," he called, his voice carrying an edge of authority. The door creaked open, revealing Detectives Louis Paulo and Mauro Arruda. They stepped inside, closing the door softly behind them. The two men stood with practiced stillness, arms crossed, their expressions both respectful and resolute. "You both packed and ready?" the DCI asked, his tone neutral but his eyes scanning them with a mixture of pride and apprehension. "Yes, Sir," Mauro answered immediately, his voice steady. "I think I can speak for Louis, too, when I say thank you for this opportunity."

The DCI nodded, his lips pressing into a thin line. He had worked with both men through some of the toughest cases in his career. They were diligent, reliable, and unyieldingly loyal—qualities that had earned them a place in this bold, new endeavour. "As you're aware," he began, his voice measured, "we'll no longer have a fixed base of operations. The SCTF will be entirely mobile. We've been assigned a Command Trailer—state-of-the-art, fully equipped—so we can stay close to the action, wherever that might take us." Louis took a cautious step forward, holding out a neatly folded sheet of paper. "Sir, I've compiled the list you requested."

The DCI accepted it with a quick nod. "Thank you." Turning to Mauro, he said briskly, "Head downstairs and ensure the trailer's ready to roll." Mauro hesitated, then asked, "What's our destination, Sir? In case anyone asks." The DCI scanned the sheet, his brows knitting. "Find us a spot east of the city. The convict was last seen in Dagenham, so we're working on the assumption he's either heading into East Anglia or making his way north. Go." As the door clicked shut behind Mauro, Louis stepped around the desk, joining the DCI as the senior officer scrutinized the paper. "What exactly are you looking for here, Sir?" Louis asked, his tone inquisitive but deferential. The DCI's finger trailed down the list as he muttered, "The trail's gone cold. No sightings since Dagenham. Roadblocks didn't turn up anything, which means we need to start thinking farther afield." Louis leaned in, his brow furrowing. "So you're looking for connections—something tying any of these to the man we're after?"

"Exactly," the DCI confirmed. His finger paused over the first item on the list. "Take this. Mr. Edwards. Found dead in his house in Norwich. No suspicious circumstances—likely natural causes. He was eighty-two. Plus, the distance from Dagenham to Norwich on foot? Unlikely."

Louis nodded, absorbing the details as the DCI moved on. "Then there's this missing persons report—filed last night. Two young women, last seen heading home from London. Our own Sergeant

Greggs spotted their car broken down on the M11. Officers searched the vehicle. Nothing. Probably just teenagers sneaking off. Their parents claim it's not the first time they've taken the father's car without permission, but usually returned home the same day."

The DCI handed the report to Louis, who skimmed it quickly, his own instincts kicking in. "We'd better get moving," the DCI said, straightening. "Traffic's going to be a nightmare, and I want us mobilized within thirty minutes." "Wait, Sir," Louis interrupted, his eyes fixed on a specific entry. "What about this one?" The DCI paused, turning back. "What've you got?" "RTA. Near Bury St. Edmunds." The DCI frowned, considering. "The distance could work, but an RTA? Not likely. The convict's avoiding transport." Louis pressed on. "Yes, Sir, but the paramedic's statement is unusual. Five deaths. Two children in an SUV that exploded. A man and woman with throat wounds. Another man with a puncture wound to the skull." The DCI froze, the details sinking in. He set the box down. "Wait. Start over. When was the RTA reported?"

Louis flipped to the relevant page. "An incomplete call came in at 07:30." The DCI thought aloud, piecing together the timeline as he studied the report in the Detective's hand. "So, say the crash happens around 07:20. Ten minutes later, someone calls for help, but it's cut off. Fifteen minutes later, the paramedic arrives—around 07:45. And the explosion?" "Two minutes after the paramedic got there," Louis confirmed. The DCI's expression darkened. "So, the paramedic arrives to find three adults already dead outside the vehicle, and then the SUV explodes with the children inside?" "Exactly, Sir."

The DCI paced, running his hand through his hair. "Does that sit right with you? Three adults with wounds that don't match the crash? The explosion timed so conveniently after the paramedic's arrival?" Louis shook his head. "No, Sir. Shall I dig deeper?" The DCI grabbed the box again, his jaw set. "Contact Suffolk Constabulary. Get access to every report they have—statements, autopsies, the lot. But tread carefully. The Superintendent's made it clear: no mistakes." With that, he opened the door, the weight of the hunt pressing heavily on his shoulders. This case wasn't just about the convict anymore—it was about uncovering the truth, no matter how deeply buried it was.

Chapter 13
18:27 hours, July 28th 2024,
Two Mile Bottom, Norfolk

The driver flicked his indicator, deftly overtaking the slow-moving tractor that trundled north out of Thetford. Neil Freeman, a seasoned self-employed courier, had been on the road since early morning, his schedule packed with tight deadlines and long drives. He'd just completed a drop-off for a timber frame manufacturer, delivering vital fixings to a construction site. It had been a lucky break; the site had officially closed nearly an hour before he arrived, but fortune smiled upon him when he caught the Site Manager just as he was locking up and securing the fencing. With brisk efficiency, Neil unloaded forty heavy boxes of nails and several cumbersome rolls of polythene sheeting in just under ten minutes. Now, as he sped along the A1066, his van rattled slightly with each bump in the road.

The sun dipped lower in the sky, casting a golden glow over the fields that stretched out on either side of the carriageway. He reached the roundabout and cruised straight over onto the A134, the road stretching ahead like a ribbon of opportunity. The familiar strains of The Bangles' Eternal Flame filled the van, its timeless melody spilling from the speakers mounted in the doors. Neil couldn't resist joining in, his voice cracking slightly as he attempted to match the high notes.

Glancing at the clock on the dashboard, Neil debated whether to head back to the depot to wrap up his day or take a moment for himself. His bladder, full from hours of coffee and water, quickly made the decision for him. He needed a pit stop. His eyes scanned the road for a suitable place, and soon a sign loomed into view:

Thetford Power Station. It seemed a promising spot to pull in for a moment, but as Neil approached the entrance, he caught sight of a stern-faced guard standing by the barrier.

The guard's sharp gaze discouraged any thought of sneaking in for a quick break. Muttering a curse under his breath, Neil kept driving, the discomfort in his bladder making him more determined to find relief. A second sign appeared ahead, this one brown and bearing the words: Two Mile Bottom Picnic Site. A grin tugged at the corners of his mouth. Brown signs meant public spots, and public spots meant a chance to stretch his legs and finally answer nature's call. Accelerating slightly, he made a mental note of how ironic it was that he had just raced against the clock to deliver building materials, and now his most pressing delivery was finding a bathroom.

Easing off the accelerator, Neil let the van slow down as his eyes scanned for the picnic site entrance. The road ahead was quiet, the golden light of late afternoon spilling over the tarmac. To his right, he spotted a small car ducking under a height-restriction barrier, the vehicle's roof just barely clearing the six-foot metal bar. "Shit on it," he muttered, watching the precarious manoeuvre.

Slowing to a crawl, Neil gave the driver a quick flash of his headlights, signalling them to go ahead as they cut across the road. The car darted north, and its silhouetted driver raised a hand in a quick wave of thanks before disappearing around a bend. Glancing into his side mirrors, Neil confirmed the coast was clear behind him. With no other vehicles in sight, he rolled forward at a lazy five miles per hour, scanning for the turnoff. Just as he spotted the narrow dirt entrance, his grin widened—there was a small layby just before it, an ideal spot for his van.

Cranking the wheel, he guided the vehicle into the rough patch of turf. The suspension groaned slightly as the wheels bounced over uneven ground, and Neil's seat gave a jarring thud when he came to a stop. He killed the engine and flung open the door, slamming it shut behind him as he made a beeline for the nearest tree. His fingers fumbled with the button on his trousers as he hurried along, already feeling the sweet relief of the impending moment. With one hand braced against the tree and his gaze fixed warily down the road, Neil let out a long sigh as the pressure in his bladder finally eased. "Another ten minutes and this would've been a bloody disaster," he muttered to himself, chuckling at the thought. It wouldn't have been the first time, either—a memory of a past roadside mishap briefly flickered in his mind before he pushed it aside.

As he zipped up and turned away from the now-damp tree trunk, Neil took a moment to survey the picnic area. Across the gravel parking lot, a small brick building caught his eye. The door was ajar, and the white WC sign above it glinted in the sunlight. He shook his head, laughing bitterly at the irony. "Of course there's a toilet. Bloody typical." Rolling his eyes, he pivoted on his heel and started walking back to the van. His pocket buzzed, the faint vibration startling him out of his thoughts. Fishing out his phone, Neil glanced at the screen and saw Ally's name flash up. A small smile tugged at his lips as he answered.

"Evening," he said warmly, already picturing her voice on the other end. "You had a nice day?" "Yeah, thank you," Ally replied, her tone soft and familiar. "Took the dog for a walk this morning, did a little photo shoot this afternoon, and now I'm settling down with a glass of wine. What about you? What time will you be home? Shall I put something in the oven for you?" Neil leaned against the van, rubbing the back of his neck as he glanced at the waning sunlight. "Sounds like a good day. I've had the usual—early starts, heavy boxes, dodging tractors. I'll probably be home in a couple of hours, if the traffic stays kind. As they chatted, Neil felt a little of the day's tension slip away. Even with the chaos of work and the long hours, moments like these—quick conversations with Ally, her voice grounding him—reminded him why he kept at it.

A sharp snap echoed from the nearby bush, pulling Neil's attention like a hook on a line. He spun around, his heart kicking up a notch as his eyes searched the dense foliage. For a moment, all was still. Then, Ally's voice broke through the tension, tinny and slightly distorted through his phone. "...I said, did you want me to put dinner on?" she repeated, her tone laced with the patient irritation of someone being ignored. Neil hesitated; his mind still half-focused on the sound. "Errr... no, it's okay," he replied, shaking his head as if to clear it. "I picked up a bite when I left Thetford. Just taking a quick ten-minute break." He checked his watch, the second hand sweeping in its endless rhythm. "Should be home soon."

Before Ally could reply, another noise came, this time closer. A rustling. A crunch. Neil stiffened, his muscles locking tight. "What the hell…" he muttered under his breath. "What? What did you say?" Ally's voice rose an octave, her confusion giving way to concern. "Neil, is everything alright?" Sensing the panic building in her voice, he forced a casual chuckle. "Yeah, yeah, I'm good," he lied, the tension in his shoulders betraying him. "Sorry, just… heard something in the bushes. Probably a rabbit or something." His eyes stayed fixed on the spot, unwilling to look away. "Listen, I gotta go. Need to eat something and hit the road. You rest up—and don't you dare start the show without me, alright?" "Okay," she replied reluctantly, her voice uncertain. "Just… be careful, Neil." "Always," he said with a forced grin before ending the call.

He took a deep breath, willing himself to ignore the little voice in his head telling him to stay on guard. He turned back to the van, leaning into the driver's side door to grab the bottle of drink nestled in the cupholder. Uncapping it, he drained the last few dregs, the warm liquid doing little to quench his thirst. His stomach growled audibly as he reached over to the passenger seat and retrieved a brown paper bag. The rich, greasy aroma of the burger inside hit him instantly, making his mouth water. As he unwrapped the foil, a new sound froze him in place. A soft thump. This time, it wasn't the bushes. It was coming from the back of the van. "What the hell now?" he muttered, setting the burger carefully on his seat. His heart beat faster as he stepped out of the van, moving toward the rear. Each crunch of his boots on the gravel seemed deafening in the otherwise still air.

Reaching the end of the vehicle, Neil darted quickly around the corner, his eyes scanning for movement. At first, everything seemed normal. Then he noticed the rear doors—one of them was ajar. His pulse quickened, a bead of sweat slipping down the back of his neck. He stepped forward, gripping the handle of the door firmly before yanking it open with one swift motion. The back of the van was empty. He leaned inside, sweeping his gaze over the neatly stacked contents. Nothing appeared out of place. Still, unease prickled at the edges of his mind as he double-checked the lock, making sure it was secure before slamming the door shut. "Calm down," he muttered to himself, turning back toward the front of the van. As he rounded the corner, his stomach growled again, louder this time, demanding attention. But when he reached the open driver's door, his heart sank.

The paper bag was gone. So was his burger. "For God's sake!" he snapped, frustration boiling over. He spun around, scanning the picnic area. His eyes landed on the small brick toilet building across the gravel lot. The door, which had been ajar when he arrived, was now firmly closed. "Seriously? Pinch my dinner, will you?" he growled under his breath.

Opening the compartment under his seat, Neil rummaged through the collection of tools until his fingers closed around the cold, heavy handle of a metal wrench. He contemplated briefly taking a small knife but shook the idea away. "I'm not a bloody psycho," he muttered. He just wanted to scare whoever thought it was funny to nick his food, not cause real harm. Gripping the wrench tightly, he slammed the van door shut and stormed across the clearing. The gravel crunched with each angry step as he walked towards the brick building, his jaw clenched and his eyes narrowed. Reaching the door, he paused for a moment, listening for any sound from within. His knuckles tightened around the wrench as he prepared to confront whoever—or whatever—had ruined his break.

As Neil approached the toilet block, he glanced nervously around the clearing, his fingers tightening around the wrench in his hand. He knew how he must look—storming toward a public restroom with a weapon-like tool wasn't exactly a good look, and the last thing he needed was someone calling the police. Satisfied that he was alone, he stopped in front of the weathered wooden door. The corroded edges of the old WC sign caught his eye, the chipped paint forming a jagged border around the bold black lettering. Beneath it, the silhouette of a female figure stood stark against the peeling surface.

Neil hesitated. A small voice in the back of his mind reminded him that barging into a women's restroom was a bad idea. It felt wrong, invasive. But then his stomach growled, a low, insistent reminder of the burger thief who had driven him here in the first place. He shook his head, his frustration overriding his hesitation. It's not about the toilet, it's about my food, he thought. Taking a deep breath, he placed his palm against the door and pushed. The hinges let out an agonizing squeal, the sound reverberating like an alarm. Neil winced, freezing in place. So much for stealth. "Hey, who's there?" he called into the dim interior, his voice echoing slightly. Silence answered him.

For a moment, he considered retreating. He turned halfway, his eyes flicking back to his van parked safely in the layby. He thought of Ally, cozy at home with her wine, waiting for him to join her. You're being ridiculous, he told himself. But then his stomach growled again, louder this time, pulling him back. He sighed. "Alright," he muttered to himself, turning back to face the door. Steeling his nerves, he stepped inside. The faint smell of stale urine hit him immediately, making his nose wrinkle. The interior was dim, lit only by a small, grimy skylight above. "Look, I don't want any trouble," he said aloud, his voice firm but slightly strained. "Just give me my food, and I'll leave you alone… alright?"

The room remained eerily silent. His eyes swept the space, taking in the cracked ceramic sinks lined up against the far wall, each streaked with rust and grime. To his left were three cubicles, their green-painted doors closed tight. He crouched slightly, trying to peer beneath them, but the gaps at the bottom were too narrow. Great, he thought. Looks like I'm doing this the hard way. He approached the first cubicle cautiously, his footsteps echoing faintly on the tile floor. Reaching out with his left hand, he gently pushed the door. It creaked open, revealing a grimy toilet with a bowl full of disintegrating paper. Neil grimaced. "Gross," he muttered under his breath, sidestepping to the next door.

This time, he used only two fingers to nudge it open, keeping the wrench firmly in his other hand. The door swung inward slowly, revealing another empty cubicle. A small sigh of relief escaped him, but before he could turn away, something caught his eye. Sitting squarely on the closed lid of the toilet was his burger, still neatly wrapped in its brown paper. "Well, I'll be damned," he said aloud, a mixture of relief and confusion washing over him. He stepped forward and picked it up, turning the package over in his hands as if it might reveal some kind of clue. Why would someone steal it only to leave it here?

As he backed out of the cubicle, his shoulders hit something solid. His breath caught in his throat. He froze, his mind racing. The wall was at least two meters behind him—there shouldn't be anything there. Then he felt it. A warm, steady exhale of air brushed against the back of his neck, teasing the small hairs there. Neil's grip on the wrench tightened as a cold wave of dread swept over him. He wasn't alone.

Neil's instincts took over as he swung the wrench in a blind arc, hoping to connect with something—anything—that would buy him a chance to escape. Instead, the wrench slammed into the cubicle door with a deafening clang, vibrating in his grip. "Shit!" he hissed under his breath, realizing too late the noise only amplified his desperation. The tight space left him no room to manoeuvre. He was trapped. He glanced upward, and his heart froze. Cold blue eyes bore down on him from beneath a mess of matted, greasy grey hair. The man—if you could even call him that—was enormous, his shoulders so broad they nearly filled the cubicle doorway. Neil's stomach twisted with the sickening realization that this brute could tear him apart without breaking a sweat.

Grateful for having already emptied his bowels earlier, Neil stepped back until the porcelain of the toilet pressed against the backs of his legs. With nowhere to go, he raised the wrench above his head like a makeshift club. "Don't come any closer!" he shouted, his voice cracking with panic. "I'm warning you—I know how to use this!" As the words left his mouth, he immediately regretted them. You sound like an idiot, Neil. The man didn't flinch, his icy stare unchanging, almost amused. He remained in the doorway, blocking any hope of escape.

Neil's eyes darted to the flimsy cubicle door, wondering if he could slam it shut and latch it before the man lunged. But one look at the man's size told him it was pointless. This guy could rip the door off its hinges like it was cardboard. "What do you want?" Neil tried again, his voice tinged with a mix of anger and fear. He raised the burger like an offering, still neatly wrapped in its paper. "Take it! Take the bloody burger!" With a frantic motion, he lobbed it at the man's chest. It bounced off with a dull thud before landing on the grimy tile floor.

"WHAT DO YOU WANT!" Neil screamed, his panic spiralling.

The man didn't respond. Instead, he moved with a chilling calmness, reaching into his pocket. When his hand reemerged, Neil's stomach plummeted. A knife. The blade was long and serrated, glinting faintly even in the dim light of the cubicle. The man held it out, the tip angled toward Neil's chest. Neil's breath came in shallow gasps as he pressed himself deeper into the corner, wishing the walls would swallow him whole. He raised the wrench again, but his grip trembled, the weight of the metal suddenly feeling useless against the menace before him. To Neil's horror, the man stepped forward, closing the cubicle door behind him with an eerie finality. The latch clicked softly; the sound almost swallowed by Neil's pounding heart.

***

Moments later, the cubicle door swung open again.

Aubrey emerged, his massive frame filling the doorway. His hands were stained red, but it was what he held that drew the eye. Gripped firmly in one hand was the severed head of the man, the cold brown eyes now lifeless and wide in eternal horror. Blood dripped onto the floor in sluggish rivulets as Aubrey's gaze dropped to the ground. There it was—the burger, still wrapped neatly in its paper. He bent down, his motions unhurried, and picked it up. The head dangled from his other hand like a grotesque trophy. Aubrey straightened; his expression unreadable as he walked toward the exit.

Stepping into the sunlight, the warmth illuminated his blood-streaked face. Aubrey turned to his left, heading toward the open bin near the edge of the picnic area. Without hesitation, he tossed the severed head into the bin. It landed with a sickening clunk, the lifeless eyes staring skyward, frozen in a look of terror. Unwrapping the burger, Aubrey took a bite, chewing slowly as he began to walk away. The faint sound of birdsong returned to the clearing, and the breeze carried the scent of grease and blood. Aubrey disappeared into the treeline, leaving nothing behind but silence—and the faint horror etched into the face of his victim.

Chapter 14
19:30 hours, July 29th 2024,
Thetford Forest, Norfolk

Walking down the stairs in his snug lycra shorts, the rich aroma of stew simmering in the slow cooker wafted up to meet Iain. He paused momentarily, savouring the scent, but Jo Matthews' laughter brought him back to the present. She stood, walked out of the kitchen, a playful smirk on her face as she teased him, her gaze dropping meaningfully. "You know," she said, a twinkle in her eye, "you should try stuffing a pair of socks down there. Save yourself the embarrassment." Iain chuckled, his cheeks colouring just slightly. As he reached the bottom of the stairs, he leaned in to plant a soft kiss on her cheek. "Cheeky," he quipped, delivering a light smack to her backside before stepping past her. Jo laughed again, shaking her head. "Hey, just a short one tonight," she reminded him. "Dinner's on and will be ready for eight. Be home on time, okay?"

Turning to the door, Iain grabbed the latch, pausing to give her his signature mischievous grin. "Alright, boss," he said with a mock salute before stepping outside and closing the door behind him. The early evening air surprised him with its mildness, a gentle warmth lingering as the sun began its slow descent toward the horizon. A golden haze spilled across the silhouetted rooftops, painting the scene with a glow that was both serene and invigorating. It was the kind of evening that begged to be experienced outdoors. Walking his sleek racing bike down the driveway, he couldn't help but glance at the dimly lit windows of his neighbour's houses. Most of them were probably glued to their televisions, letting another evening slip by in a haze of reality shows and reruns. Iain had never understood that kind of passivity. Why sit inside, sedentary, when the open road and a Norfolk sunset beckoned?

The carbon-aero wheels of his bike kissed the asphalt as he mounted it, his movements fluid and practiced. He slipped the gear down, pedalling faster to warm up, feeling the familiar stretch and burn in his hamstrings. As he coasted past, he spotted Sid, one of his neighbours, walking his scruffy terrier along the pavement. "Evening, Sid," Iain called out, his voice light and cheerful. Sid, startled out of his reverie, looked up and grinned. "Evening, you're out again, eh?" "Yeah," Iain replied, glancing briefly at the dog, which had plopped down onto the pavement, panting heavily. "Beautiful sunset tonight." "Sure is," Sid said, turning to admire the sky. "Enjoy your ride!" With a small wave, Iain pushed onward, the wheels of his bike humming against the road. As he approached the end of the street, he slowed, contemplating his route for the evening. To the right lay the town centre—a dreary maze of traffic and streetlights. To the left stretched the promise of open countryside. It wasn't much of a decision.

Standing on the pedals, he leaned forward, pushing harder as his bike surged toward the pastoral expanse that surrounded Lynford. The breeze kissed his face, carrying with it the faint, earthy scent of freshly turned soil. His legs worked rhythmically, muscles firing in harmony, as he left behind the humdrum of suburban life for the boundless beauty of the Norfolk fields. The horizon opened up before him, a patchwork of golden fields and hedgerows, the distant chirp of birds punctuating the air. This was freedom—this was life, and Iain couldn't imagine spending the evening any other way.

✳✳✳

Walking along the narrow, uneven road, Aubrey cast a wary glance ahead, his sharp eyes scanning the landscape for any opening in the dense hedge that bordered the fields. The scent of damp earth and wildflowers hung in the air, a stark contrast to the unease that gnawed at him. He hated being exposed like this, every step on the open path a calculated risk. The thought of unseen eyes tracking his movements from the shadows sent a shiver down his spine, but he pushed the paranoia aside. It wasn't the first time he'd walked such perilous paths, and he doubted it would be the last.

As he trudged on, his mind began to wander, the rhythm of his boots against the gravel lulling him into a contemplative haze. What lay ahead for him, beyond the objective he had set his sights on? The question felt foreign, almost absurd. Aubrey had never allowed himself the luxury of imagining life after the mission; it wasn't the way he operated. A man like him didn't dream of peaceful retirements or idle afternoons spent basking in the sun. He had been conditioned to focus solely on the task at hand, to compartmentalize, to survive. What point was there in weaving fantasies of golden beaches and turquoise waters when the odds were so starkly against him? No point at all, he decided grimly. Planning for a future he might not live to see was a fool's errand.

Still, he couldn't entirely banish the thought. The image of warm sands underfoot and waves lapping at the shore flickered briefly in his mind, a fragile sliver of hope he didn't dare entertain for long. Reality, cold and unyielding, pulled him back like a snapping tether. He knew how this would end—had known since the day he first set out on this journey. Capture, death, or both. The inevitability of it was as much a part of him as his heartbeat. And yet, knowing his fate had not dissuaded him. If anything, it had steeled his resolve.

The road stretched on, each step taking him closer to whatever awaited him beyond the horizon. The hedge loomed to his right, a wall of green that separated him from the field where safety—or perhaps only a better vantage point—might lie. His mind churned with thoughts of his past and the choices that had brought him here, but he shook them off with practiced ease. Regret was another indulgence he couldn't afford. Ahead, the road curved slightly, and Aubrey quickened his pace, his senses on high alert. There was no room for distraction now. The weight of his mission pressed against him like an invisible hand, urging him onward. Whatever his fate, he would meet it head-on, just as he always had.

Turning the corner, he halted abruptly, his pulse quickening as his gaze locked onto a patrol car parked a short distance away. Two Officers sat inside; their heads bowed over something that held their attention. Their faces were lit by the faint glow of a device or paper in the dim interior, and the muted murmur of their conversation was carried on the breeze. For now, they hadn't noticed him. He exhaled slowly, forcing himself to think. Scanning his surroundings, he quickly assessed his options. The thick hedge running parallel to the road offered no passage; its dense, thorny branches were an impenetrable barrier. The road behind him stretched into open terrain, and backtracking would only delay the inevitable—if the Officers resumed their patrol, they'd spot him in seconds. A bead of sweat trickled down his temple as he weighed his choices. He needed to act, and fast.

A flicker of an idea sparked in his mind. If he couldn't disappear, perhaps he could blend in. With a swift motion, he ran his fingers through his hair, smoothing it back in an effort to appear less dishevelled. Pulling his coat tighter around him, he shoved his hands deep into his pockets, the picture of a man lost in thought. His heart thundered in his chest as he forced his feet to move. Every step felt measured, deliberate, the sound of his boots on the gravel deafening in the quiet road. He kept his head tilted downward, feigning nonchalance, while his peripheral vision stayed locked on the Officers. Out of the corner of his eye, he saw one of them pull a large map from the glovebox, spreading it across the dashboard. The other leaned closer, gesturing animatedly, their fingers tracing unseen lines on the paper. Whatever they were discussing, it seemed to absorb them completely.

When he reached the patrol car's bonnet, he allowed himself a momentary pause, his breath hitching as he gauged their attention— or lack thereof. Then, with a swift and silent motion, he dropped to his knees, pressing his body low to the ground. The cool surface of the road bit into his palms as he ducked out of view. Flattening himself against the earth, he strained to catch fragments of their conversation. Their voices were muffled, but distinct enough to make out snippets of irritation and confusion. "Wrong turn," one muttered, his tone clipped. "No, it's supposed to be west from here," the other replied, exasperation edging his voice. "The map says— look—this is the crossroads we passed earlier." "No way. That was east—"

The exchange went on, their debate growing more heated with each passing second. Aubrey's pulse began to settle as he realized their preoccupation might work to his advantage. For now, they were more concerned with navigating the map than scanning their surroundings. He shifted slightly, careful not to make a sound, the gravel beneath him shifting softly. If he could just edge a little farther along the side of the car, maybe he could slip out of their line of sight entirely. But he'd need perfect timing—and nerves of steel. The Officers were still arguing over the map, oblivious to the figure lying next to the car.

Crawling on his belly, Aubrey felt every rough pebble dig into his chest and elbows, but he ignored the discomfort, his focus locked on the vehicle above him. The patrol car's exhaust rattled noisily in its loose bracket, puffing out clouds of sooty smoke that stung his eyes and throat. As he edged closer to the rear wheel, the acrid scent of burned oil clung to the air, and he fought back a cough. He could just make out the muffled voices of the Officers inside, still locked in their heated debate. Then he heard it—a distant rumble growing louder. Another vehicle was approaching. His heart jolted. Without a second thought, Aubrey shifted his weight and rolled underneath the car, sliding into the narrow gap between the undercarriage and the ground. The move was swift but tight, his face mere inches from the grimy frame above. He stayed utterly still, forcing his breath to steady as his ears strained to gauge the situation.

The other patrol car pulled up behind, its engine rumbling to a stop. Aubrey craned his neck as best he could, risking a glance toward the front of the car he was hiding under. He could just make out the Officers shifting in their seats. Calm, he told himself. Stay calm. Instead of panicking, he homed in on the conversation above, the sharp tone of their words cutting through the muffled thrum of engines. "Look, I don't care what you think—it's this way," snapped Sergeant Lorraine Jones, her irritation palpable. PC Dom Loadman, his knuckles white as they gripped the steering wheel, muttered back. "Definitely not, Sarge. I swear we just passed the turning. I'm sure I saw a signpost back there."

There was a pause, the tension thick enough to choke on. Aubrey could imagine the glares exchanged above him as the two Officers processed their disagreement. Then came the telltale creak of seats shifting as both of them turned to look over their shoulders at the approaching patrol car. "Well," Lorraine said with a resigned sigh, "we can't reverse, so get us moving forward." Dom let out a defeated grunt, adjusting his grip on the gear stick. He shoved it into gear and began releasing the handbrake. Aubrey felt the subtle shudder of the car shifting above him. He tensed, bracing himself to stay perfectly still as the vehicle prepared to move. But just as Dom eased his foot off the brake, the crackle of the car radio erupted, startling him. His foot slipped, and the engine sputtered to an abrupt stop. "Bloody hell," Dom cursed under his breath, thumping the steering wheel in frustration.

Lorraine, unfazed, reached for the handset. "Whisky Tango Seven, over," she said, her tone clipped and professional. The response came almost immediately, sharp and authoritative. "This is Whisky Tango One, copy." Their attention was about to be locked firmly on their location. He stilled every muscle, his body pressed tightly against the cold, oil-slicked ground. Lorraine listened waiting for the next communication. "Whisky Tango Seven, what is your location? Over." Dom grabbed the map, fumbling with it as he traced his finger along the winding lines representing the road they were on. Lorraine gave a sharp nod in confirmation. "Sir, we are east of Thetford Forest on an unmarked road," she replied crisply. "Whisky Tango Five is following. Over." The radio crackled once more. "Copy. Over and out."

As silence fell, broken only by Dom's annoyed muttering as he restarted the engine, Aubrey's mind raced. They weren't as lost as he'd hoped. They had a location now, and backup close by. He had to think fast. Lying prone beneath the car wouldn't keep him safe for long, not with two patrol vehicles in play and an alert chain of command. Above him, the engine roared back to life, the car vibrating as Dom prepared to move forward again. Aubrey shifted slightly, muscles taut, his mind already working through his next move. If the car began to move, he'd have only seconds to act. The next steps would determine everything.

Breathing slowly, Aubrey stilled himself, focusing intently on the muffled sounds around him. The crunch of gravel underfoot reached his ears, and his heart skipped a beat. Someone had stepped out of the car behind him. The footsteps were deliberate, unhurried, coming within mere feet of his hidden position. He pressed his body even flatter against the cold ground, hardly daring to breathe. From above, he heard the faint hum of a car window rolling down. A gruff voice broke the tense silence. "What's the hold-up, Sarge?" "Junior here's lost," came the terse reply from Sergeant Lorraine Jones. Her tone dripped with impatience. "He reckons he saw the turning back there. I've checked the map—it's one mile up the road." "Well," the first voice said, tinged with mild irritation, "if it's all the same, can we just get moving, Sarge? I need to get Betty out—she needs a bathroom break."

Aubrey risked a small exhale as he heard the footsteps retreat, the Officer returning to their car. The sound of the engine roaring to life behind him set his nerves alight. He tensed, his thoughts racing. The road was narrow, the cars tightly packed, but it would take only the smallest mistake for his cover to be blown. Timing was everything. If he moved too slowly, he'd be crushed or, worse, discovered.

The car above him shifted. Aubrey pressed his body as low as he could, feeling every rumble as the vehicle began to roll forward. He watched the undercarriage drift past, the floor frame sliding away like a receding tide. Then came the rear wheels, the exhaust, and, finally, a sliver of daylight. His muscles screamed in protest as he prepared to move. The second car was already advancing, the grille closing in fast. With a sudden burst of motion, Aubrey rolled to his left, his hand brushing the back of the first car just as the second vehicle's wheels passed perilously close to his face. The gravel shifted under him, but he stayed perfectly still, his pulse hammering in his ears. Both cars crawled forward at an agonizingly slow pace. Just as he thought he might be in the clear, something in the window of the rear car caught his eye.

A dog.

Its sharp, curious gaze locked onto him instantly. A surge of dread coursed through him as the animal began to bark furiously, its excitement transforming into a frantic dance of motion. It bounced up and down, jumping from side to side in the confined space.

Aubrey froze, his body a taut wire of tension. Had the dog truly seen him? He couldn't be certain. If one of the Officers glanced in a mirror, it would be over. "What's got her knickers in a twist?" muttered PC Jack Redman, his eyes fixed on the tail lights of the car in front. His hands hovered over the wheel, ready to brake if Dom decided to stop abruptly. In the passenger seat, Ross lounged, his focus entirely absorbed by his phone. His thumbs tapped away furiously at the screen. "Maybe she can't wait any longer," he replied absently, not even glancing up. "Little lady's been holding it since our last stop near Thetford."

Jack's patience was wearing thin. The incessant barking grated on his nerves, but it was Ross's indifference that truly pushed him over the edge. For the last hour, his younger brother had done nothing but play Plants vs. Zombies, showing no interest in their mission or the manhunt at hand. With a frustrated growl, Jack reached over and snatched the phone from Ross's hands. "Enough!" he snapped, flinging the device into the back seat. Ross let out an indignant shout, unbuckling his seatbelt to retrieve it. "You jerk! Now I'm probably dead!"

Ignoring the barking dog, Ross twisted in his seat, his arm stretching toward the back. "It's alright, sweetheart," he cooed to the dog without much thought. "Daddy's told your uncle Jack to pull over shortly. Just a few more minutes, princess." His fingers brushed the edge of the phone, but then something caught his eye. His gaze flicked upward, past the bounding dog. In the rear window, a large shape shifted. "Who's that?" Ross said, his voice sharp with alarm. Jack's hands tightened on the wheel, his head snapping toward Ross. "What are you talking about?" But Ross wasn't listening. His eyes remained fixed on the figure beyond the dog, his confusion rapidly morphing into realization. Aubrey's heart plummeted. It was only a matter of seconds before the barking would turn into shouts, and his fragile anonymity would shatter.

Both patrol cars screeched to an abrupt halt, their tires skidding on loose gravel. Aubrey, still crouched low, twisted to glance over his shoulder. His pulse spiked as he spotted a female Officer—Sergeant Jones—throwing her door open and leaping out. She moved with purpose, her sharp eyes scanning the road. Spotting something—perhaps a faint impression in the gravel or a hint of movement—she pointed with authority before snatching the radio from her vest. Her voice, clipped and urgent, carried through the still air. Aubrey didn't wait to hear the details. Adrenaline surged through him as he turned and bolted up the hill to his left, his boots pounding the uneven terrain. Loose soil crumbled beneath his feet, but he didn't falter, his movements fuelled by sheer desperation. Cresting the hill, he dove over the ridge, vanishing into the dense thicket beyond.

In the second patrol car, Jack Redman let out a string of curses, slamming the gearstick into reverse. The car jolted as he hit the gas, the engine roaring angrily. Gravel spat out from beneath the tires as they spun in place for a moment before catching traction. "How the hell did he get past us?" Jack growled; his knuckles white on the wheel. Ross, his younger brother and unwilling passenger, clung to the door handle for dear life. His face was pale, his voice barely above a squeak. "I—I don't know! Just don't hit a tree!" The dog, still in the rear, barked incessantly, its yelps adding to the chaotic symphony inside the car.

Lorraine stood in the middle of the lane, her gaze narrowing as she watched the other patrol car—Whisky Tango Five—jerk and swerve its way backward up the narrow road. The vehicle clipped the verge multiple times, its rear wheels churning up patches of dirt and wild grass. Lorraine scowled. "Idiots," she muttered under her breath before turning to Dom. "Get ready, Dom," she barked, sliding back into the passenger seat and slamming the door shut. Dom didn't need to be told twice. He had already revved the engine, his foot hovering at the bite point, every muscle in his body coiled like a spring. The tension in the car was palpable, the only sound the low, angry growl of the engine.

Lorraine keyed the radio, her voice brisk and commanding. "Whisky Tango Seven, convict sighted on a narrow lane east of Thetford Forest. He's heading toward Santon Downham, approximately one mile south of the village. Whisky Five and Seven are in pursuit. Over." The radio crackled faintly in response, but Lorraine wasn't waiting for acknowledgment. She motioned to Dom with a sharp nod, and he raised his foot off the clutch. The car leaped backward, lurching with unexpected force as Dom expertly accelerated up the lane in reverse, his eyes darting between the rearview mirror and the narrow confines of the road.

At the same time, Aubrey pushed deeper into the thicket on the hillside, his lungs burning with each desperate breath. The terrain was unforgiving, with dense underbrush clawing at his legs and branches whipping at his face. He could still hear the faint roar of the patrol cars below, their engines a menacing reminder that his pursuers were relentless. Reaching a slight clearing, he paused for a split second to orient himself. He knew the area well enough to realize his options were limited. To his left lay an open field—too exposed. To his right, a steep drop-off that led to a dried-out riverbed. Behind him, the unmistakable sounds of engines and shouting voices grew louder. Forward, the forest thickened, offering both concealment and treacherous ground. A decision made in a heartbeat: he darted forward, plunging towards the forest. Above the hum of the engines, he heard Lorraine's voice shouting commands, echoed faintly by Jack in the other car. He knew they'd be on him soon, tracking him like hounds.

Back on the road, Jack finally managed to control his erratic reversing, aligning Whisky Tango Five with the lane. His frustration boiled over as Ross unhelpfully yelled from the passenger seat. "Go faster! He's gonna get away!" Jack glared at him. "Shut it and let me drive!" But even as he snapped, his eyes flicked anxiously to the barking dog in the rear, her agitation growing with every passing moment. "Something's back there!" Ross exclaimed, twisting in his seat to peer into the gloom. "Yeah, it's the dog losing her mind," Jack shot back, trying to ignore the pounding in his chest. "No— something else! I saw it move!" Ross's voice was shrill with panic. Slamming the wheel, Jack muttered a curse. "We're losing him! Hold on!"

✳✳✳

The radio crackled, and the call came through. Detective Louis Paulo's grip tightened on the handset, his heart pounding with the rush of adrenaline. They finally had a breakthrough. The thrill of the chase was coursing through his veins like wildfire. Racing up the

172

B1107 toward Santon Downham, he felt a surge of excitement. This was the part of the job he lived for—the chase, the strategy, the glory. Catching this high-profile fugitive would not only be a significant win for justice but also a golden star on his record, one that could all but guarantee the promotion he had been angling for at year's end. "Whisky Tango Seven, this is Whisky Tango One," he barked into the radio, his voice sharp and controlled. "We're five miles south of Santon Downham. Push the convict southeast of the village. We should intercept in five minutes. Over."

He tossed a quick glance at his driver, PC Dave Marlow, who was focused intently on the road ahead. "This son of a bitch is going down," Louis growled. "Let's box this animal in. Charlotte," he called over his shoulder to the Officer in the back seat, "get Cody ready." In the rear, PC Charlotte Hilliard nodded, her hands steady as she stroked the thick mane of the German Shepherd seated in the boot. Cody sat alert, his sharp eyes reflecting the gleam of the flashing lights outside, his tail wagging slightly in anticipation. Even he seemed to sense the heightened tension in the air, enjoying the thrill of the hunt.

The two patrol cars roared north, their engines howling as they tore through the countryside. The serpentine road twisted ahead of them, hemmed in by tall hedges on either side. The village of Santon Downham loomed in the distance; its faint glow now visible above the horizon. Louis leaned forward in his seat, his eyes narrowing with determination. "Sixty seconds, folks," he announced, his hand hovering over the door handle. His pulse quickened as he mentally rehearsed the takedown, ready to spring into action. The car swerved suddenly to avoid a man wobbling along on a bicycle, and Dave couldn't help but smirk. "Bloody cyclists," he muttered, shaking his head.

The chase grew more chaotic. Up ahead, the dense hedge lining the road glowed eerily in the strobing light of their sirens. They were closing in, but the terrain was becoming treacherous. As they approached a narrow turning, the unexpected happened: Whisky Tango Five, their backup unit, reversed abruptly into the road directly in front of them. The car shot out like a battering ram, leaving Dave barely enough time to react. "Hold on!" Dave shouted, yanking the steering wheel sharply. His foot slammed onto the brake while his other hand yanked the handbrake with a sharp motion. The patrol car skidded violently, tires screeching against the asphalt as it spun sideways. Time seemed to slow as the vehicle slid to a halt, just inches from colliding with the other unit.

Dave's quick thinking saved them from a crash, but the chaos wasn't over. The sharp manoeuvre sent the rear wheels into a grass bank, jarring everyone inside. Charlotte braced herself against the seat, instinctively gripping Cody's harness. In the front, Louis barely noticed the jolt. His eyes were locked on a figure in the distance, heading towards the forest. "There he is!" Louis shouted, throwing open his door before the car had fully stopped. "Out! Out now!" Dave scrambled to unbuckle his seatbelt, but Louis was already on the move. The detective vaulted over the doorframe, his boots hitting the gravel with a crunch. He sprinted toward the convict, shouting into his radio as he ran. "Whisky Tango Five, block the east side! Tango Seven, follow my lead! He's moving into the field!"

Aubrey, was already climbing a weathered wooden fence, his movements quick but desperate. He threw a glance over his shoulder, his face a mask of determination and fear. His foot slipped slightly on the top rail, but he recovered, vaulting over and dropping into the field beyond. Louis reached the fence minutes later, barking orders at the Officers behind him. "Flank him! Dom, take the right! Charlotte, hold Cody for now, wait for my command!" His voice carried authority, cutting through the cacophony of engines and shouts. On the other side of the fence, Aubrey was running full tilt, the field's tall grass slowing his stride. The sunlight offered little cover, casting shadows starkly against the ground.

Behind him, Louis climbed the fence with ease, dropping down and landing heavily in the grass. He sprinted after Aubrey, the thrill of the chase coursing through him like electricity. He could hear the Officers closing in, their shouts growing louder, and the low growl of Cody, restrained but eager. The convict veered toward a darker patch of the field, where the terrain sloped downward into a small wooded area. It was his last chance to disappear, but Louis wasn't about to let him go. With a roar of determination, he shouted into his radio. "Box him in now!

Spotting Detective Louis Paulo sprinting toward the fence in the distance, Lorraine didn't wait to answer. Her instincts kicked in as she bolted to join him. When she reached the fence, she grabbed the top rail, hauling herself up to get a better look. "Bloody hell," she muttered under her breath as her sharp eyes locked onto a shadowy figure darting through the tall grass beyond. Aubrey was moving fast, his silhouette a blur as he closed in on the edge of the forest. "He's heading for the trees!" she yelled. Her voice carried a mix of disbelief and frustration. "Shit, he's moving like a bloody gazelle!"

Turning on her heel, Lorraine shouted back towards the road. "Sergeant Greggs, take Whisky Tango Two and Five! Cut through the east and box him in! I'll take Whisky Tango One and go west!" She gestured sharply to Dom, who was hovering next to her. "You stay here with the vehicles! Radio in for support—give Command our location and the direction he's heading!" Dom nodded, already reaching for his handset as Lorraine sprinted off across the field. Within moments, a flurry of activity overtook the scene. Officers scrambled to their assigned positions, their radios crackling with updates. Engines roared to life, tires spitting gravel as patrol cars sped off in multiple directions. In less than thirty seconds, the chase was in full swing. Detective Louis Paulo, two sergeants, five constables, and two dogs surged into the open field, their boots crunching against the earth. They pushed forward, watching as Aubrey disappeared into the dense forest at the field's edge.

Louis, running at the rear of the pack, kept one hand on his radio and the other on his belt. His breath came in sharp bursts as he spoke into the radio. "Whisky Tango One to Command. Convict has entered the forest. Requesting support units to the north and west in Santon Downham. Over." The response crackled in his earpiece almost immediately. "Command, copy. We have three units heading to Santon Downham. Halo Two is also en-route. ETA thirty minutes." "Halo Two?" Louis muttered, a small grin breaking through the tension. "About damn time we got some air support."

Ahead of him, Ross and Charlotte were leading the pack, their dogs—Betty and Cody—straining against their leashes, noses low to the ground as they picked up Aubrey's scent. The forest loomed closer, its dark silhouette swallowing the fugitive's figure as he disappeared into the underbrush. The Officers didn't slow. If anything, the sight of their quarry vanishing spurred them to move faster. Lorraine, running a few strides ahead of Louis, shouted over her shoulder. "He knows this terrain! He's moving too deliberately for someone who's panicking. Stay sharp—this could be a trap." "Noted," Louis called back, his tone clipped but focused.

The first line of trees came up fast. The Officers didn't hesitate, plunging into the shadows after Aubrey. The air changed immediately, the open field giving way to the dense, humid embrace of the forest. Branches clawed at uniforms, and the crunch of leaves underfoot mingled with the low growls of the dogs as they strained forward. Betty suddenly barked sharply, veering to the left. Ross struggled to keep up, stumbling over a gnarled root. "She's got something!" he yelled, regaining his footing. Louis keyed his radio again. "Whisky Tango One to all units—suspect likely heading northeast, deeper into the forest. Units near Santon, block off exits north and west!"

The trees thickened as the Officers pressed on. Aubrey was somewhere ahead, weaving through the undergrowth with the agility of someone who had prepared for this moment. His breath came in sharp gasps as he darted between trees, his mind racing. He could hear the Officers gaining ground behind him, their shouts punctuated by the barking of dogs. Pausing for a split second, Aubrey looked around, assessing his options. He spotted a fallen log to his right, partially hidden by moss and ferns. Without thinking, he dove toward it, scrambling beneath the natural cover just as the beam of a flashlight swept over the area. He held his breath, willing himself to stay silent as the sound of footsteps grew louder. Above him, the hunt continued, relentless and unforgiving. The Officers were closing in, and Aubrey knew his window of escape was narrowing with every passing second.

***

Aubrey crouched low beneath the forest's dense canopy, his eyes scanning the scene as he counted the Officers and dogs fanning out in the distance. Their shouts echoed faintly through the trees, blending with the rhythmic barking of the dogs straining on their leashes. He estimated he had minutes—if that—before the canines locked onto his trail. Worse still, the low hum of an approaching helicopter made his stomach churn. Air support. His window of opportunity was closing rapidly. His eyes dropped to the ground. He needed a plan, and fast. Searching for any sign of an alternative route, his gaze locked onto a faint horseshoe print pressed into the damp soil. The mark was faint but discernible, leading away into the shadows of the forest. Without hesitation, he began following the trail, scanning for more tracks as he moved. The path meandered, winding deeper into the thicket until it opened into a small clearing. Aubrey hesitated, glancing over his shoulder. The faint sounds of pursuit had grown louder, sharper. The dogs were on his scent now; it was only a matter of time.

Thirty meters ahead, the path narrowed again, leading into a dense corridor of brush. Aubrey's gaze swept the ground. His heart leapt when he spotted what he needed: a muddy puddle glistening in the dim light, and to its side, a pile of horse manure. It was a disgusting but effective solution. He crouched down, scooping thick handfuls of mud and smearing it over his exposed skin—his hands, face, and neck. The cold muck clung to his flesh, dampening the sting of sweat that had begun to drip into his eyes. He gritted his teeth as he grabbed chunks of manure, rubbing the pungent mess into his clothes until his scent was buried beneath layers of filth. Standing again, he tilted his head, closing his eyes to focus on the forest's sounds. The Officers were closer now, the dogs' barks sharper and more urgent. The telltale crunch of boots breaking twigs punctuated the canine cries. Aubrey knew his crude camouflage wouldn't buy him much time, but it might be just enough. He had to keep moving.

Without a backward glance, he turned and sprinted along the narrowing path. Each step felt heavier, the thick mud clinging to his boots and weighing him down. The forest around him seemed darker now, the sun slipping below the horizon and casting long, jagged shadows across the ground. Soon, night would envelop the woods entirely, providing him the cover he needed to truly vanish. But he wasn't there yet. The forest was vast—over eighteen thousand hectares of sprawling pine, heathland, and broadleaves. It was both a blessing and a curse: a perfect maze to disappear into, but nearly impossible to navigate without losing himself entirely. Ahead, a flash of light broke through the tree line—a sign that the forest thinned in that direction. Aubrey quickened his pace, his breath coming in sharp bursts. The gap between the trees opened into another gravel path. He skidded to a halt, scanning his surroundings. The sun's final, orange glow blazed in the distance, breaking through the thick canopy above. For the first time in hours, Aubrey felt a sense of direction.

He turned northward, his eyes locking onto the far side of the path. Aubrey darted forward, his boots crunching against the gravel before plunging back into the dense woods. The air here was cooler, the pine trees taller and thicker, their canopy creating an almost suffocating darkness. But he welcomed it. Every step he took deeper into the forest felt like a step away from the Officers closing in behind him.

Despite the mud caking his body, he could still feel the tension in the air, like a predator sensing its prey. Aubrey knew the police weren't far off. Their strategy would likely be to encircle him, using the terrain to funnel him into a trap. But he also knew the forest better than they did. He'd studied its layout, memorizing the twists and turns, the dead ends and hidden clearings. It wasn't a perfect advantage, but it was something. He pressed onward, the shadows growing thicker as the sun dipped below the horizon. Twilight turned the forest into a labyrinth of silhouettes and shifting light, each tree seeming to lean in closer, their jagged branches clawing at his arms as he pushed forward. Pausing for a moment to catch his breath, Aubrey crouched beneath a dense thicket of brambles, his ears straining. The dogs' barking had grown more distant, and he could no longer hear the distinct crunch of boots on leaves. Either they'd lost his trail, or they were attempting to flank him. He couldn't be sure. His fingers brushed against the forest floor, sifting through the cool earth as he considered his next move.

A faint sound overhead made him freeze—a helicopter's blades slicing through the air. Aubrey glanced up through the trees, the sound growing louder as it swept over the forest canopy. The searchlight would come next, sweeping the woods in broad arcs. He needed to find cover—thick, unassailable cover—and fast. Spotting a dense cluster of low-hanging pines nearby, Aubrey crept toward them, ducking low and disappearing beneath their sprawling branches. His breath came shallow and quiet as he pressed himself flat against the ground, his eyes fixed on the faint glow of the helicopter's light cutting through the treetops. Somewhere above, his hunters were circling, waiting for him to slip.

∗∗∗

The three police cars rolled cautiously into Santon Downham, their engines purring softly against the tranquil backdrop of the village. The narrow streets, lit dimly by old-fashioned lamps, seemed deserted, the usual charm of the quiet community overtaken by the tension of the ongoing hunt. The lead car, a sleek black SUV with the words Police Tactical Unit emblazoned on its side, signalled left and turned onto Mark Lane. Moments later, all three vehicles parked in the modest lot in front of Wico Collectables, their doors opening almost in unison. Twelve Officers, clad in dark tactical gear and armed with flashlights and radios, stepped into the chilly night. Two police dogs barked softly, straining against their leashes as their handlers quieted them with firm commands. Without hesitation, the team slipped around the back of the brick building, entering the open field that stretched towards the edge of the forest. One by one, their flashlights clicked on, slicing through the dark like searchlight beams, their steps purposeful but measured.

Detective Mauro Arruda, a seasoned Officer with sharp features and a no-nonsense demeanour, led the group. He gripped his radio tightly, speaking in clipped tones, "Whisky Tango One, this is Whisky Tango Twelve. We are in position, just south of Santon Downham, heading towards the forest, over." His voice carried an air of authority, but the slight furrow in his brow betrayed the weight of the situation. The radio crackled to life in response. "Whisky Tango One, copy that. Maintain current position. We're one mile south of your location, over." Mauro nodded to himself, glancing back at his team to ensure they were holding formation. The Officers moved with quiet precision, scanning their surroundings with disciplined focus. The dogs, tails wagging and noses low, strained eagerly at their handlers' sides. All eyes were on the looming silhouette of the forest ahead, its tall pines swaying gently in the breeze.

Mauro's gaze drifted upward. Halo Two, the police helicopter, hovered in tight circles above the trees ahead, its searchlight sweeping the canopy and forest floor. Its rhythmic drone filled the air, a mechanical heartbeat in the eerie stillness. Mauro squinted, noting the helicopter's precise position. If Louis Paulo's team was under its beam, then they were close—close enough that the convict was likely caught in the tightening net. The team pressed forward, the forest gradually enveloping them. The tall pines seemed to stand like sentinels, their shadows merging to form an almost impenetrable black wall. The village lights faded behind them, and the quiet became more oppressive. Not even the rustle of wildlife disturbed the night, as though the natural inhabitants of the woods had retreated in the face of the human invasion.

Mauro lifted his radio again. "Whisky Tango One to Halo Two, do you have visual, over?" The response was immediate, but not encouraging. "Negative, Whisky Tango Twelve. Thermal imaging has not picked up anything, over." Mauro frowned, lowering the radio slowly. He heard a murmur behind him as one of the dog handlers spoke. "Sir, shouldn't the chopper have spotted him by now? He couldn't have gotten far in this terrain." Mauro turned sharply to address the man; his voice low but firm. "Stay focused. Eyes on the forest, not the sky." But inwardly, Mauro shared the handler's unease. The helicopter had circled for over twenty minutes without a single heat signature. The convict should have been visible, especially in the dense patch of woods between their location and Louis Paulo's team. There was too much unaccounted-for space in that no-man's-land—enough for a cunning convict to bide his time or set a trap. He brought his radio to his mouth once more. "Whisky Tango One, be advised. We're encountering significant negative space between our current position and yours. Proceed with caution; suspect may be hiding or doubling back, over."

The Officer walking beside him, a younger recruit with wide eyes and a tight grip on his flashlight, whispered nervously, "Do you think he's lying low, sir? Or do you think he's already slipped through?" Mauro didn't respond immediately. Instead, he signalled for the team to spread out, increasing their coverage as they neared the thicker part of the forest. When he finally spoke, his voice was measured but edged with tension. "This guy isn't a rookie. He's planning something. Stay sharp and keep your distance from the trees." The Officers adjusted their formation, the beams of their flashlights slicing through the dense undergrowth. The dogs sniffed furiously at the ground, occasionally letting out low growls that made the hair on Mauro's neck stand on end. The helicopter above adjusted its flight path, its searchlight now sweeping more deliberately, but still finding nothing.

As they neared the point where the forest grew thickest, Mauro raised his hand, signalling the team to stop. The air felt heavier here, the darkness almost tangible. Somewhere in the distance, faint barks from another unit's dogs reached their ears, followed by the sharp commands of Officers. The convict was close—too close. "Alright," Mauro said softly, "let's move in slow. No sudden movements. Stay together and keep comms open. We don't know what we're walking into." The team advanced again, their lights flickering as the forest seemed to close in around them. Each step felt like a gamble, the oppressive silence broken only by the crunch of boots on dry leaves. Mauro's instincts screamed that something wasn't right, but he pushed the thought aside. The hunt was on, and hesitation wasn't an option.

✳✳✳

The pedals churned furiously under Iain's feet, his legs burning as he powered along the forest path. The chain whirred in a frantic rhythm, blurring with speed as he pushed harder, desperation driving every turn. He was already late, and he could practically hear Jo's exasperated voice when he finally got home. Why do you always do this? Her irritation was justified, but guilt wasn't going to get him home faster. He'd made a choice—taking the off-road trail that skirted the forest—and now he was paying for it. The sun was sinking quickly, casting a burnt orange glow across the treetops while shadows crept like predators over the earth. He cursed under his breath, regretting his decision to leave his bike lights at home. The path was treacherous, littered with gnarled roots and jutting rocks that seemed eager to throw him off balance. He gripped the handlebars tightly, feeling every bump and jolt shoot up his arms as the uneven trail challenged his control.

In the distance, the faint but distinct thrum of helicopter blades interrupted the forest's quiet, and Iain glanced up, startled by the sound. Between the shifting shadows of the trees, something moved—just a blur in the dim light, gone as quickly as it appeared. His heart skipped a beat. Was it an animal? A deer, maybe? He shook his head, forcing himself to focus. Get it together, Iain. You're just spooking yourself. But the unease lingered, gnawing at the edges of his thoughts as he pushed on. He tightened his grip on the handlebars and accelerated, the vibrations from the rough terrain ricocheting through the bike frame and into his chest. Ahead, scattered points of light danced across the field that bordered the forest, flickering like fireflies. Flashlights. What the hell are they looking for?

The question barely formed in his mind before his world turned upside down—literally. One moment, he was pedalling furiously, and the next, he was airborne, his bike flipping beneath him as he hurtled toward the ground. He landed with a bone-rattling thud, his back smacking the hard earth and knocking the wind from his lungs. For a moment, he lay there, gasping for breath, his ears ringing and vision blurred. Pain radiated through his ribs and shoulders. What just happened?

Turning his head slowly, Iain spotted the reason for his tumble: a man crouched nearby, his silhouette dark against the fading light. The stranger coughed, one hand braced against the ground as he struggled to rise. "You okay, fella? I'm... I'm really sorry," the man stammered, his voice hoarse. "Didn't see you... honest mistake..." Iain pushed himself up onto his elbows, wincing as his muscles protested. The man straightened to his full height, and Iain felt a cold wave of dread wash over him. The guy was enormous, towering above him with broad shoulders and an imposing presence that made the dim light seem darker. Something about his posture—rigid, coiled—set Iain on edge. The cyclist scrambled to his feet, forcing a nervous chuckle. "No harm done, mate. I'll just grab my bike and get out of your way, yeah?" He bent to pick up the bent frame, his eyes never leaving the stranger.

Then the man turned, and Iain's breath caught in his throat. A blade, long and gleaming, caught the last rays of sunlight, its edge shimmering like liquid fire. The stranger took a step forward, his movements slow but deliberate, the knife held loosely at his side. Panic exploded in Iain's chest. "Hey, whoa—listen, I'm sorry! Whatever this is, I don't want any trouble!" His voice cracked as he swung a leg over the bike frame, fumbling to steady himself. His foot missed the pedal once, twice, and the stranger closed the gap with terrifying speed. "Fuck!" Iain shouted, finally catching the pedal and kicking off, but it was too late. The man lunged, slamming into him with the force of a freight train. The impact sent him careening sideways, his bike smashing into a nearby tree. The front wheel crumpled, and the handlebars twisted grotesquely, trapping Iain beneath the twisted metal.

Disoriented, Iain struggled to free himself, his limbs flailing as the man loomed above him. The knife glinted in his hand, catching every flicker of light as it hovered ominously over Iain's chest. "Wait! Please!" Iain's voice broke, raw with fear. "You don't have to do this! I—I've got money, okay? Take it! Just—just don't—" The man didn't speak. His expression remained cold, unreadable, as he raised the knife high above his head. Iain's pleas dissolved into a strangled cry. "No! Nooo—"

The blade came down in a brutal arc, piercing his chest with devastating force. Pain flared, sharp and consuming, but it lasted only a moment before darkness enveloped him. The world faded, and Iain's last thought was of Jo, waiting at home, oblivious to what had just happened in the shadow of the forest. As the man straightened, wiping the blade on his sleeve, the forest swallowed the silence once more. Somewhere in the distance, the helicopter's rotors continued their rhythmic thrum, unaware of the horror hidden beneath the trees.

***

The dog's sudden halt was sharp, its nose twitching in the crisp, damp air as it sniffed intently, its ears twitching at the slightest sound. The handler, glanced sharply at the Detective. "Did you hear that, Sir?" he asked, his voice low but edged with uncertainty. "Sounded like someone screaming." The Officers behind him exchanged wary glances, the chill of unease settling over them like a heavy fog. They had been closing in on their target for hours, and now, they were treading on dangerous ground. The convict was close—too close, and they all knew it. The forest was dense, the shadows thick, and the slightest mistake could mean disaster. Mauro felt the weight of the fear pressing down on his team, their nerves palpable, their body language betraying their anxiety. He knew the stakes, and he could sense their unease. The last thing he needed now was hesitation. He straightened his posture, drawing in a breath to steady himself before speaking.

"Right, listen up," Mauro's voice cut through the silence, steady but commanding. "Dogs to the front. Close the gap. I want everyone arm's length apart, one single line. We move slowly, methodical. If you see something, no matter how small, you call it, understood?" The Officers nodded, but their expressions were unreadable, their eyes trained ahead on the treeline. It was a silent agreement, a unified understanding that they were walking into the unknown, every step putting them closer to their target—and closer to danger. The dog handlers stepped forward, moving into position on either side of the Detective. The dogs, now alert, growled low in their throats, their bodies tense as they pulled the Officers forward, dragging them towards the dense forest. The growls reverberated through the air, the sound of barely-contained aggression as the dogs sensed the danger ahead. Every Officer's eyes were fixed on the thick tangle of trees and underbrush in front of them, but they couldn't shake the gnawing sense of being watched—hunted.

Mauro's eyes flicked upwards for a moment, his gaze scanning the dimming sky. The helicopter, Halo Two, was still a long way off, its flashing lights distant and fading, too far to provide immediate backup. He considered radioing in for assistance, but he knew better. If he called in Halo Two now, he'd risk giving away their position, and the convict would slip through the cracks. They couldn't afford to lose the initiative. Not now. His fingers tightened around the strap of his radio as he resisted the urge to reach for it. If they called for backup, the time it would take for the helicopter to arrive, the confusion it would cause—it was too much of a risk. The convict, whoever he was, was already ahead of them, hiding somewhere in the labyrinth of trees, and they were running out of time.

We move forward. We stay focused. We close the distance.

Mauro's thoughts were sharp, his mind racing as his boots pressed against the uneven forest floor. He could feel the tension building in the air, could hear the dog's growls growing louder as they drew closer to their prey. Every step was crucial. The dogs, with their finely-tuned instincts, were pulling them forward, but even their heightened senses couldn't guarantee they would catch the convict before he vanished again into the vast, dark forest.

The trees were thick here, their gnarled branches reaching out like twisted fingers, casting deep shadows across the path. The light from the fading sun struggled to break through the dense canopy, leaving everything shrouded in an eerie twilight. The air smelled of damp earth, wet leaves, and the faint scent of pine, but there was something else lingering beneath it all—something foul, something unnatural. Suddenly, one of the dogs gave a sharp bark, its growl escalating. The handler yanked the leash, pulling the dog back slightly as it began to pull in the direction of the scent, its body rigid with tension. The Officer's eyes flicked towards Mauro, who nodded grimly. They had him. At least, they were close.

The team moved faster now; the air thick with the expectation of a confrontation. There were no more words spoken—only the rhythmic sound of boots pressing against the forest floor, the occasional snap of a twig, and the low growls of the dogs. Every Officer's breath was shallow, steadying themselves for what was to come. Then, without warning, the dogs stopped again. This time, it wasn't a sniff. It was a complete, sudden stillness. Mauro's heart skipped a beat. "What is it?" he asked sharply, his voice steady but laced with urgency.

One of the handlers slowly raised his hand, signalling the team to halt. The dogs were sniffing the air again, their bodies still tense, eyes locked ahead into the darkening trees. It was as if the forest itself was holding its breath, waiting for something. Mauro's mind raced. Where was he? He slowly scanned the forest, his hand resting on the grip of his firearm. The trees ahead were dense, and he could see little beyond the thick mass of trunks and underbrush. Somewhere out there, in the shifting shadows, the convict was waiting, his presence just out of reach. The dog gave another low growl, this time more intense, as if it had caught something it wasn't ready to face. Mauro's stomach tightened as the hairs on the back of his neck stood up. Something was wrong. He could feel it deep in his gut.

The dense canopy of trees loomed just ahead, only a hundred meters away now, casting long, eerie shadows across the forest floor. Mauro raised his hand, signalling the team to halt. The air was thick with tension as every Officers paused, muscles taut, eyes fixed on the darkening treeline, every sense on high alert. The time for action was near. "Hold this position," he commanded quietly, his voice cutting through the silence like a knife. "We now wait for Whisky Tango One to spring the trap."

The team stood motionless, a line of anticipation. The only sounds were the soft rustling of leaves in the wind and the distant hum of the helicopter, which circled above the trees like a mechanical hawk. Mauro's mind raced as he thought about their quarry—the convict. He had to be close; the dogs could sense it; the Officers could feel it. This was their moment, but they had to wait, hold the line, and trust the plan. Whisky Tango One, was supposed to move in and box the convict in. Any movement now, any noise, and they'd be ready to spring into action. But as they stood there in the stillness, the unexpected happened.

A shuffle of footsteps from behind broke the concentrated silence. Before any of the Officers could react, an elderly man emerged from the shadows behind, huffing and puffing as he approached the group. He was wearing a faded, weather-beaten jacket, an old pair of wellington boots, and a flat cap perched awkwardly on his grey head. With a hand held up as if to reassure them, he looked at the Officers with a mixture of confusion and mild irritation. "Begging your pardon, Officer," he began, his voice a raspy drawl, "but I thought I'd better let you know someone's broken into my building over there." The words hung in the air, thick with irony. The last thing Mauro needed right now was an old farmer complaining about his broken-down barn. Still, the Detective was good at keeping his composure. His eyes locked on the farmer, his jaw tightening as he processed the new information.

"Err…" Mauro's voice was calm, but his patience was clearly thinning. "Thank you, sir, for bringing this to our attention. As you can appreciate, we have our hands full here at the moment. But as soon as we're done, I'll get one of the lads to pop over and check it out." The elderly man didn't seem to be listening, however. Some of the Officers behind Mauro shifted uneasily, clearly losing interest in the interaction. They returned their focus to the trees, scanning the shadows with growing anxiety. The man wasn't finished. "And what exactly are you doing in my field?" he grumbled, his voice rising with a hint of frustration. "What, you lot planning on trampling all over my crops?" Mauro took a deep breath, forcing his voice to stay level. "We're looking for someone," he replied. "A dangerous individual."

The farmer paused, eyeing them with growing scepticism, before giving a dismissive shake of his head. There was an uncomfortable silence between the two parties. The farmer, clearly annoyed at the interruption to his day, turned away and began walking back towards the village. "Right," Mauro muttered, his gaze quickly returning to the trees. The Officer beside him gave a subtle sigh of relief as the farmer disappeared from view, but there was no time to relax. They had a mission to focus on, and the convict wasn't about to be caught by a distracted team. Turning back to face the dense forest once more, Mauro surveyed the treeline, his eyes narrowing as the last rays of daylight started to fade. The canopy overhead was becoming a patchwork of shadows as dusk began to settle. High above, the helicopter—Halo Two—hovered at the edge of the woods, its lights sweeping across the expanse of trees. They were so close, so close to trapping the convict, but something didn't feel right. The tension in the air had shifted, growing thicker by the second.

The whir of the helicopter's rotors grew louder, but still, the convict was nowhere to be seen. Mauro's hand tightened around his radio, his instincts prickling with the sense that something was about to go wrong. "Whisky Tango One to Whisky Tango Twelve, do you copy?" Mauro said into the radio, his voice steady but firm. "Whisky Tango Twelve, this is Whisky Tango One, copy," came the response from the backup team, their voices tinged with urgency. "We're heading your way, closing the distance." Mauro's eyes darted back to the treeline. There was still no sign of movement, no break in the underbrush to indicate that the convict was there. He was too well-hidden. But then, just as Mauro was about to issue another order, a voice bellowed from behind them.

"This person you're looking for," the voice called out, the words cutting through the silence like a sudden burst of static. "He's not a giant, is he?" Mauro froze, his muscles tensing. The voice was unmistakable—the farmer had returned. "Not a giant?" Mauro repeated, his eyes narrowing. He turned to see the farmer now standing twenty meters away, casually stuffing tobacco into a pipe, as if nothing was happening at all. The Officer beside him shot a nervous glance towards the farmer before looking back at the trees. "Never seen anything like it," the farmer continued nonchalantly, not missing a beat as he fished for his matches. "As tall as a house, and as wide as a bus."

Mauro's stomach dropped. The description was unmistakable—the farmer had just described the convict perfectly. The realization hit him like a hammer, the implications unfolding in an instant. The convict wasn't just some criminal—they were dealing with a man whose size and strength could easily make him nearly impossible to capture. Before anyone could process the information, one of the Officers to Mauro's left suddenly snapped to attention. "Sir, Whisky Tango has arrived," the Officer reported, his voice urgent. "They're heading this way!"

Mauro's heart skipped a beat. He whipped his head around to see the backup team emerging from the field, moving fast in the direction of the trees. The helicopter's spotlight swept across the ground, its beams dancing wildly over the shifting terrain. But there was still no sign of the convict. The woods were empty, shrouded in an impenetrable darkness. "Damn it," Mauro muttered under his breath, frustration boiling over as the team began to move into position. Despite all the planning, all the coordination, they had walked straight into a trap. The convict was gone. And for the first time that night, Mauro felt the unsettling grip of failure closing around him.

✱✱✱

The cool evening air hung heavy over the farm as Detective Louis Paulo and Detective Mauro Arruda stood at the entrance, surveying the scene before them. The farm was smaller than most in the area, nestled between rolling fields that stretched into the distance. Two silos loomed at the back of the property, casting long shadows as the sun began to dip below the horizon. To the right, a battered open cattle shed stood, its rusted walls a testament to years of use. But it was the large building in the centre that drew their attention: a brick structure with a corrugated cement roof, the kind that looked as though it had been there for decades, its purpose shrouded in mystery.

Louis glanced at the farmer, Mr. Giles, who stood beside them, puffing on his pipe, eyes darting between the Detectives as he awaited. "What's in there, Mr. Giles?" Louis asked, pointing towards the building. Mr. Giles flicked the ash from his pipe before answering. "In there's just cows, that's all," he said nonchalantly, though there was an edge to his voice, as if he had nothing to hide, or perhaps, he was hiding something altogether.

Louis exchanged a look with Mauro, sensing there was more to this than the farmer was letting on. The tension in the air was palpable as the Officers lined up with their dogs, the heavy sound of helicopter blades cutting through the night sky. The bird circled the building, its spotlight cutting across the landscape, but the pilot's report wasn't reassuring. Mauro, speaking into his radio, furrowed his brow. "Halo Two is not picking anything up inside the building," he relayed to Louis. Louis, now even more confused, turned back to Mr. Giles. "But you said there are cows in that building. If that's the case, why is Halo Two not picking up anything?" The farmer gave a slow, deliberate roll of his eyes, as though he were speaking to an inexperienced child rather than seasoned detectives. "Yes, I did. And there are cows... dead cows. It's a slaughterhouse, sonny."

A heavy silence fell over the group as the implications of the farmer's words sank in. The two Detectives shared a glance, one of understanding, their silent exchange cutting through the confusion. They now knew the danger was greater than they had thought. The building wasn't just a place of business—it could be hiding something far more sinister. Louis took a deep breath, his eyes scanning the team around him. "Okay, listen up," he said, his voice steady but commanding. "Whisky Tango One, you'll stay at the entrance. I will have command from here on. If you see or hear anything, report it to me first so we can keep communication clear." The Officers shifted uneasily, adjusting their stances as the tension built. Louis continued, his voice louder now, with more conviction. "Whisky Tango Five and Seven, you cover the access points. Nothing comes out of there unless it's in handcuffs. Whisky Tango Two and Twelve, you're with Detective Arruda."

Without waiting for any further questions, Louis turned on his heel, signalling for his team to follow. They moved swiftly into position, all eyes focused on the darkened building ahead. The hum of the helicopter above echoed in the distance, still circling the area, its searchlight flashing intermittently across the farm's sprawling landscape.

Mauro moved forward with his team, his heart pounding in his chest. He could feel the weight of responsibility on his shoulders— he was in command now. With him were Sergeant Lorraine Jones, a no-nonsense officer with a sharp mind and quick instincts; PC Dom Loadman, a seasoned cop with a cool demeanour; and eleven other officers, their faces a mix of determination and anxiety. Two dogs padded silently beside them, their heightened senses alert for any sign of movement. The industrial door loomed before them, massive and imposing. Mauro's radio crackled to life. "Whisky Tango One to Whisky Tango Twelve," came the voice from the entrance team. "Teams are in position. Proceed with breach. Good luck."

Mauro nodded at the sound of the command, his gut tightening with anticipation. His eyes flicked to the Officers around him, each of them bracing for what was to come. His hands, although steady on the grip on his torch, shook ever so slightly. He tried to mask his unease with a thin smile, offering what little reassurance he could to his team. "We've got this," he said quietly, more to himself than anyone else. He raised his hand, signalling the handlers to move in. The dogs' ears perked up, their bodies tensing as they sensed the moment of action approaching. Mauro stepped forward, his heart pounding in his chest as the large industrial door loomed closer. There was no turning back now. They had come this far, and the truth—whatever it was—was just inside that building.

The team began to move. The dogs were the first to slip through the entrance, their handlers leading the way, their steps silent but swift. The Officers followed, eyes scanning every corner, every shadow. The door creaked open with a slow, ominous sound, revealing the darkness within. The musty smell of old hay and blood filled the air, mingling with the faint metallic scent of rust and decay. The silence of the evening was shattered only by the soft scrape of boots on the concrete floor, the growl of the dogs as they sniffed the air, and the distant whirring of the helicopter above. As they ventured deeper into the building, the shadows seemed to grow longer, and the atmosphere became suffocating. Each step felt heavier than the last, as if the very walls of the slaughterhouse were closing in around them. Mauro's mind raced as he signalled for the team to spread out. His radio crackled again, this time with static, and then the voice of Louis came through, cold and direct. "Watch yourselves in there. If anything goes wrong, pull back immediately. We're not risking anyone's life tonight."

The roof loomed high above the concrete floor, suspended securely over the steel framework. The dim interior of the building was almost suffocating, as the farmer had explained that the cows were only slaughtered during daylight hours when the doors could be opened to allow ambient light to filter in. But now, in the eerie quiet of the building, the interior was shrouded in shadows, the only source of illumination the weak beams of the Officers' torches, cutting through the dark like fragile threads of light. As the team moved forward, the air grew heavier, thick with the unmistakable stench of blood.

The pungent odour made their eyes sting as they worked their flashlights over the rows of hanging carcasses. Each body dangled from its hook, its rib cage exposed, flesh raw and pale against the dark backdrop of the room. The only sound was the dull, rhythmic panting of the dogs, and the soft clack of boots against the cold concrete floor. The building felt far too vast and cavernous, as if the darkness inside had swallowed every trace of the convict they were hunting.

Mauro kept his eyes trained ahead as he walked, his breath slow and measured, but his thoughts racing. To his left, Sergeant Lorraine Jones was leading one of the dog handlers, five Officers trailing her. She was methodical in her movements, eyes darting from one hanging carcass to the next, searching for any sign of the fugitive. Behind them, Sergeant Dave Greggs and Fred Brooks led a team down the left side of the room, while Mauro, one of the dog handlers, and two Officers cut through the centre.

The light from their torches illuminated the hanging cows, casting grotesque, elongated shadows across the floor. The air grew colder as they ventured deeper into the room, the smell of death and decay growing stronger with each step. The tension was thick, the weight of anticipation pressing on their chests. They had to find him. He had nowhere to hide—nowhere to go. The walls of the slaughterhouse were solid and unforgiving, and every possible exit was blocked. He was trapped.

But as they moved further, there was still no sign of the man. No movement, no sound—nothing but the eerie silence of the room, broken only by the occasional bark of the dogs. Lorraine's voice cut through the quiet, her tone low and edged with frustration. "Where the hell is he, Sir?" Mauro's thoughts were a tangled mess. He had expected the convict to be hiding in the farthest corner, or perhaps waiting for the opportunity to strike. But as he scanned the rows of hanging carcasses again, doubt crept into his mind. Was it possible they'd missed something?

He pulled out his radio, his fingers brushing against the cold metal. Pressing the button, he spoke in a low, controlled voice. "Whisky Tango One, this is Whisky Tango Twelve. We've almost reached the other side. No sign of the convict. Over." Outside, Detective Louis Paolo was pacing, the frustration evident in his every step. How had they missed him? The man had to be somewhere inside. He couldn't have vanished—there was nowhere for him to escape to. The doors were sealed. The walls were solid. Louis clenched his fists, seething with impatience. This was a puzzle that refused to fit together, and it was driving him mad. Turning to PC's Dave Marlow and Charlotte Hilliard, who were standing beside the road with Farmer Giles, Louis said, "You two stay here. I'm heading down to see what's going on inside."

As he approached the large opening in the building's wall, Louis could see the three teams standing at the entrance. He noticed Mauro, his face set in grim determination, and grabbed him by the arm, pulling him inside. "Where the fuck is he?" Louis' voice was tight, a mix of anger and disbelief. "He can't just vanish into thin air! You're sure you've looked everywhere?"

Mauro nodded, though his own frustration was mounting. "Yes. The building is just one large open space. There are no inner rooms, no hidden doors. We even checked the roof, just in case our convict is suddenly able to climb like Spider-Man." Louis shot him a look, unamused by the attempt at humour, then followed his gaze across the room. His eyes narrowed as they settled on a corner of the building. "What's that over there?"

Mauro followed Louis' gaze, squinting in the dim light. His lips tightened, and he scoffed in irritation. "We checked that already. It's just a pile of innards, guts, and waste. The farmer uses that small space for things he doesn't want to deal with." He paused, then added more bitterly, "We had the dogs sniff around, but it's all just refuse." Louis turned away sharply, unable to mask his rising frustration any longer. He stormed towards the entrance, his footsteps echoing in the cavernous space. "Well, better give the DCI the bad news then," he muttered, his tone dark and heavy with exasperation.

Behind him, the Officers exchanged uneasy glances. They had all heard the tension in Louis' voice, and now they were beginning to wonder if they had been chasing a ghost. The thought of coming up empty handed after all this effort was almost too much to bear. They were closing in, and yet somehow, the convict had slipped through their fingers.

The tension in the air was palpable as Detective Mauro Arruda stared at the blank screen of his radio. The sunset had already stretched on far too long, and the only thing more frustrating than the silence was the uncertainty gnawing at him. "Halo Two, you picking up anything?" he asked again, his voice tight with barely-contained frustration. "No, sir. That's a negative," came the crackling voice from the helicopter team. "We've got heat signatures outside the building, but nothing inside." Mauro's gaze hardened as he processed the information. His team was on high alert, and yet the convict had seemingly vanished into thin air. He could feel Lorraine's eyes on him, the same question weighing on her mind. She stepped forward, her voice low, almost a whisper, but full of anxiety. "Where the hell is he, sir? No way did he get past us. We had every exit covered."

Mauro's mind raced as the question echoed in his thoughts. How had they missed him? He cast a quick glance at the building, then back to his team. His instincts screamed that something was off, but the longer they stood there, the more it seemed like they were chasing a ghost. Without warning, he raised a finger to his lips, signalling for silence. The team froze, eyes locking onto the Detective as he stepped back into the building, his senses heightened. His head tilted slightly, as if listening to something just beyond the grasp of his hearing. His eyes narrowed, scanning the room for any sign of movement. Then, like a bolt of lightning, it hit him. "Shut up all of you," he snapped. "Listen." His voice had dropped to a near whisper, the urgency clear in his tone.

The team fell still, their breath held. And then, faint but unmistakable, they heard it too: the distant sound of running water. Mauro's eyes snapped open, a sudden clarity washing over him. Without wasting another moment, he turned and bolted forward, flashlight in hand, his footsteps echoing against the concrete floor.

The team followed suit, trailing behind him as Lorraine shouted, "You guys with me, the rest of you, cover the exits." The beam of Mauro's flashlight bounced erratically off the hanging carcasses as they moved quickly through the space.

Some of the bodies swung loosely, creating an eerie, unsettling rhythm in the otherwise still room. It was as if the shadows themselves were moving, shifting with a mind of their own. The smell of blood and decay continued to cling to the air, thick and suffocating, but Mauro's focus never wavered. "Over here! Quickly!" Mauro's shout cut through the air, and Lorraine pushed herself harder, her boots slapping against the cold floor, her heart racing.

As they neared the last cow, the flashlight's beam bounced wildly across the space, revealing a small open duct tucked at the back of the room. There, standing in the middle, was Mauro. His face was drawn tight, his eyes fixed on something on the floor beneath him. Lorraine's heart dropped as she followed his gaze. There, in the centre of the floor, was a large hole—roughly four feet wide. The cast iron grate that once covered it had been moved aside, revealing the dark, dank space below. Dry blood caked the edges of the hole, staining the concrete and adding to the thick, oppressive atmosphere.

Without hesitation, Mauro dropped to his knees beside the hole, shining his flashlight down into the darkness. Lorraine approached cautiously, her stomach churning with a sense of dread. Six feet below, she could just make out the faint outline of water flowing sluggishly through a pipe—dark, stagnant, and contaminated. Mauro's face hardened as the realization began to set in. He immediately grabbed his radio, his fingers trembling as he keyed it into the speaker. "Whisky Tango One, can you ask Mr. Giles where the drainage system runs to?" The static crackled in his ear, followed by a long pause that seemed to stretch on forever. Lorraine watched the Detective's face as the colour slowly drained from it, his shoulders sagging as he absorbed the news. The unmistakable weight of the situation settled over him.

"He says the contaminated water runs out a few miles to the treatment plant, west of the village. Why do you ask?" came the response, confused but still professional. Mauro's mind raced as his worst fears were confirmed. He closed his eyes for a moment, the sheer frustration of it all surging through him like a wave. He could feel his heart pounding in his chest as the realization dawned. "We need to get over there quickly," he muttered to himself, his voice low but urgent. "The convict is no longer in the building." Punching the cold flesh of a nearby cow in frustration, Mauro cursed under his breath, a growl of frustration escaping him. He rose to his feet quickly, motioning for the others to follow him. He didn't have time for second thoughts. Every moment they wasted here gave the convict a greater lead. They had to move, and fast. Lorraine nodded sharply, her eyes already scanning the space around her, calculating their next steps. She didn't need to ask any more questions. They knew where they had to go next.

The team rushed out of the building, the urgency of their movements heightening as they made their way towards the exit. The heavy industrial door clanged open, the sound echoing through the stillness of the night. Outside, the night air was crisp, the tension thick in the air as the last few Officers quickly sealed the building behind them.

Minutes later, the large roller shutter door rumbled down, its steel frame meeting the concrete floor with a loud metallic screech. Farmer Giles stood alone off to the side, puffing away at his pipe as he watched the proceedings with a look of quiet detachment. He wasn't involved in their hunt, merely an observer. Inside, the silence was broken only by the faint shifting of the carcasses. The bloodstained entrails, once still, began to move. Aubrey, stirred beneath the weight of the rotten innards, his limbs trembling as he slowly rose to his feet. His eyes, glazed with a mixture of exhaustion and dark determination, flicked toward the exit.

He had waited long enough.

Chapter 15
07:30 hours, July 30th 2024,
English Channel, 10 Miles off the English Coastline

The sea stretched out to the horizon, an ever-changing canvas of deep blue and silver that appeared, then vanished again, as the HMS London's powerful propulsion system cut cleanly through the swelling waves. The Type 26 frigate, a marvel of modern naval engineering, moved with steady precision, its sleek hull slicing eastward at a measured 10 knots. The English coastline, faint and fleeting, hugged the northern horizon like a distant memory, a reminder of home for the sailors aboard.

Onboard the ship, life bustled with the rhythm of duty and camaraderie. With a complement of 185 crew members, including 28 seasoned Royal Marines, the frigate was a hive of disciplined activity. Narrow corridors and tightly arranged compartments left little room for solitude, making privacy a rare commodity. Even the Officers, accustomed to navigating the delicate balance between authority and camaraderie, found it challenging to carve out moments of quiet reflection.

Military Liaison Ralph Wardley had learned this the hard way. His arrival onboard had been marked by the organized chaos of departure, the frigate's crew executing their well-rehearsed roles as the ship pulled away from Portsmouth's historic docks. The HMS London was no ordinary vessel. As one of the Royal Navy's most advanced warships, it boasted state-of-the-art sensors, weapons systems, and stealth capabilities. Its mission was as much about maintaining a visible presence of British power as it was about deterring potential threats. For Ralph, every moment onboard offered a lesson in adaptability, as he strived to understand the complex world of naval operations while carving out a place for himself amid the disciplined hierarchy of the crew.

This was only the second time Ralph Wardley had set foot on a Navy ship, and the contrast to his first experience was stark. That first time, he had been aboard a small, utilitarian patrol boat that had ferried him across the choppy waters to the Isle of Wight for a meeting with an informant. The patrol boat was cramped, almost claustrophobic, and wholly functional, offering little in the way of sophistication or comfort. In comparison, the HMS London felt like an entirely different world—monumental in scale, bristling with advanced technology, and humming with a sense of purpose.

Standing on the deck, Ralph took in the vastness of the vessel. Towering above him, the bridge commanded the best view of the surrounding sea, perched directly over the operations room, the nerve centre of the frigate. Just forward of him, the gleaming five-inch gun stood as a silent sentinel, its imposing barrel angled toward the sky. The weapon looked almost alive; a creature of precision engineering designed to strike at a moment's notice. Toward the stern, the cavernous hangar housed a Merlin helicopter, its rotor blades partially disassembled as a team of engineers swarmed around it. Their tools clinked and echoed in the metal enclosure, the whir of drills and the low murmur of technical jargon filling the air as they worked tirelessly to replace a damaged rotor. The Merlin was a workhorse of the fleet, and every minute of downtime was a dent in the ship's operational readiness.

Ralph wanted to linger, to marvel at the sheer complexity of this floating fortress, but there was no time to admire the intricacies of modern naval warfare. His thoughts were interrupted by the clipped voice of Petty Officer Lee, who was tasked with escorting him to his assigned quarters. "This way, Sir," Lee said crisply, gesturing toward a nearby hatch. "Please mind your head on the bulkhead as we step through the door." Following the Officer's lead, Ralph ducked his head and stepped cautiously through the narrow frame. It was a small reminder that this was a ship designed for function, not comfort. The corridor beyond was narrow, lined with exposed pipes and conduits that ran along the ceiling and walls like veins in a living organism. The metallic scent of the ship, a mix of oil, salt, and steel, was omnipresent, as was the low vibration of the engines rumbling beneath his feet.

As they moved briskly down the passageway, Ralph instinctively pressed himself against the wall to allow two sailors to pass. They moved with the practiced ease of men who knew every inch of this ship, nodding respectfully as they squeezed by. "Thank you, Sir," one of them said, a polite murmur as they hurried on, tools clinking in their hands. Ralph nodded in response, feeling both an outsider and a welcomed guest in this bustling, self-contained world. The passage was a maze, each turn revealing another identical corridor or a steep flight of stairs leading deeper into the heart of the ship. Ralph tried to memorize the route, but the sheer complexity of the vessel's layout left him disoriented. Petty Officer Lee, however, navigated with the confidence of someone who had walked these halls a thousand times before, barely breaking stride as he ducked under low beams and sidestepped protruding fixtures.

The ship was alive with activity. Somewhere nearby, the sharp call of a bosun's whistle signalled a crew assembly, followed by the rhythmic clatter of boots on metal as sailors moved to their stations. The faint hum of distant machinery filled the air, a constant background chorus that reminded Ralph of the ship's dual nature—both a workplace and a weapon of war. For now, it was a workplace, and he was a visitor trying to make sense of it all.

Opening the solid metal door, Ralph stepped into the room and froze. It was spacious by naval standards, immaculately clean, with every surface gleaming under the harsh lights. Against one wall, six cots were neatly arranged in a row, each tucked with military precision. A Petty Officer gestured to the middle one. "You've been allocated Cot Four, Sir. The one in the centre." Ralph's eyes scanned the room, his stomach sinking as he took in the lack of privacy. The air smelled faintly of disinfectant and salt, the latter seeping through the very walls of the ship. He exhaled slowly, trying to maintain his composure. "I'm sorry," he said, his tone clipped but controlled. "This will not do. The orders your Captain received specifically requested a single cabin. Complete privacy."

Petty Officer Lee straightened slightly, his expression blank. Years of service had taught him not to question orders, even ones that seemed impractical or odd. "I see, Sir. My apologies. Please wait here, and I'll speak to the Captain." Without waiting for further comment, Lee turned and disappeared back into the corridor, his boots clanging against the metal floor as he climbed the narrow staircase toward the upper decks. Ralph stood stiffly by the door, gripping the handle of his travel bag and tapping his fingers against the metal frame. The rhythmic hum of the ship's engines vibrated through his soles, a constant reminder of the living machine that surrounded him.

More sailors bustled past in the corridor, their uniforms sharp, their movements purposeful. None paid him any attention, which only heightened his growing frustration. Minutes ticked by with agonizing slowness, the confined space pressing in on him. Ralph paced the room, then stopped by the door, leaning out to glance down the hallway. Where was Lee? Surely it didn't take this long to sort out a simple matter. As the tenth minute passed, Ralph felt his patience evaporating, replaced by a simmering anger. He tightened his grip on his travel bag, his knuckles whitening as he considered marching up to the Captain himself. This was unacceptable. Just as he moved to step into the hallway, a loud alarm pierced the air, its shrill tone reverberating through the metal corridors. Startled, Ralph turned toward the sound, his irritation momentarily giving way to unease.

Before he could react further, the clatter of boots on steel echoed down the hallway. A squad of ten men in camouflage uniforms appeared, moving with military precision, their machine guns held tightly to their chests. Their faces were set with focus and determination as they ran toward him. Ralph instinctively stepped back, pressing himself against the wall as they stormed past in single file, their heavy footfalls shaking the deck beneath him. One by one, they disappeared up the staircase at the far end of the corridor, leaving behind a tense silence. Ralph leaned forward, cautiously peering out into the corridor, his heart still racing from the sudden commotion. Before he could make sense of what had just happened, a familiar figure appeared, nearly colliding with him. It was Petty Officer Lee, his expression calm but slightly apologetic. Ralph took a step back, trying to collect himself as the Officer spoke.

"My apologies, Sir," Lee began, a hint of urgency in his tone. "It seems there was a mishap with your orders. You've been allocated a single cabin, but it's on the lower decks. If you'll follow me, I'll take you there right away." Ralph exhaled sharply, the frustration still bubbling beneath the surface but tempered by the sudden turn of events. "Fine," he said curtly. He slung his bag over his shoulder, casting one last glance at the cramped room behind him. "Lead the way." As they moved down the corridor, the faint sound of shouting from the upper decks reached Ralph's ears. The ship was teeming with activity, and though his annoyance lingered, a flicker of curiosity sparked within him. What had prompted the sudden mobilization of armed men? He shook the thought from his mind, focusing instead on following Lee through the labyrinthine corridors, eager to finally reach his promised privacy—and perhaps, a chance to catch his breath.

Within the hour, Ralph was reassigned to a smaller cabin, tucked away in the quieter, lower decks of the HMS London. The room was a stark contrast to the open cot arrangement he had seen earlier. It was a tight, utilitarian space, the walls painted a bland off-white, with just enough room to turn around without bumping into something. A five-and-a-half-foot bunk occupied one corner; a thin mattress neatly tucked beneath crisp sheets. A small blue curtain, suspended on a thin rail, could be drawn to create a semblance of privacy—a feeble barrier against the constant hum of the ship and the ever-present movement outside. Mounted to the opposite wall was a compact desk, just large enough to hold a small laptop and a few scattered papers. A bolted-down chair, its plastic seat hard and unyielding, completed the setup. Above the desk, a single overhead light cast a sterile glow, illuminating the confined space. Despite its cramped quarters, Ralph found it sufficient. Privacy was a luxury aboard a vessel teeming with personnel, and here, at least, he could focus on his work undisturbed as the frigate continued its steady journey toward Kent.

Sitting down at the desk, Ralph placed his laptop before him and powered it on. The soft whir of the device blended seamlessly with the ship's ambient hum. He flexed his fingers before settling them on the keyboard, his posture tense but purposeful. His work required precision and confidentiality—qualities he had cultivated over years in his field. The screen came to life, its light reflecting faintly on his glasses. After typing a series of credentials into the secure interface, he hit "Enter."

The screen flickered for a moment before an icon appeared: a spinning hourglass, turning slowly, its pixels loading the next step in deliberate increments. Ralph's eyes remained fixed on it; his expression unreadable. Patience had become a practiced skill for him, though the anticipation of what awaited still sent a ripple of unease through his chest. The hourglass disappeared, and the screen went blank. A stark white box blinked into existence in the centre of the display. Ralph's shoulders tensed as he stared at the box. It was an innocuous thing, but he knew better than to underestimate it. This simple digital gateway was his link to the clandestine world he operated within, a world of covert communications, encoded messages, and classified intelligence. Each interaction brought with it the weight of responsibility and risk.

He leaned back slightly, his fingers poised above the keyboard as he waited. The seconds dragged on, each one stretching longer than the last, amplified by the isolation of his surroundings. His mind drifted momentarily, drawn to the faint vibrations of the ship beneath him and the distant sounds of activity—voices echoing in the corridors, the occasional clank of tools against metal. Out here, amidst the cold waters of the Channel, the frigate felt like a small island adrift in a vast and uncaring expanse.

A sharp beep snapped him back to the present. The box on the screen flickered again, and a line of text appeared. It was a single command, terse and direct, written in an unadorned font: "Awaiting Input." Ralph's lips pressed into a thin line as he leaned forward, his fingers resuming their steady dance across the keys as he typed in his Personnel Number and Password. Each stroke was deliberate, the clicks echoing softly in the confined space.

What lay ahead was uncertain. He had boarded the HMS London under strict orders, the details of his mission shrouded in need-to-know secrecy. Whatever he was about to uncover—or initiate—would set the course for the days ahead. As he typed, the screen began to populate with encrypted data streams, cascading like digital rain. Ralph's world had narrowed to the glow of the monitor and the quiet resolve in his chest, even as the frigate carried him closer to the unknown.

Progress?

The cursor blinked expectantly, and Ralph's fingers flew over the keys in response, the clatter of each keystroke punctuating the stillness of the room.

Broadsword in transit… ETA… eleven hundred… establishing contact.

The screen flashed momentarily as the message transmitted. Ralph's gaze flicked to the door. It remained firmly closed; the heavy metal frame reassuringly secure. He exhaled softly and returned his attention to the laptop. The reply came almost instantly.

Copy…

The simplicity of the response made his stomach knot with frustration. He hesitated, biting his bottom lip as his finger hovered over the power button. Part of him wanted to terminate the transmission. Shut it all down, pack up, and wait until they reached Norfolk. But the unanswered questions gnawed at him. Why such vague instructions? Why the urgency cloaked in secrecy?

He straightened his shoulders and typed again.

Objective…

The message lingered on the screen, unresolved. Ralph sat back, his nerves on edge, glancing again at the door. He strained to hear any movement outside, his ears attuned to the faint metallic creaks and hums of the ship. Was his transmission being monitored? Had they logged off already? He drummed his fingers lightly against the desk, trying to suppress his unease.

A sudden clang jolted him, followed by two sharp raps on the door. His pulse quickened. "Mr. Wardley," came the familiar voice of Petty Officer Lee. Ralph composed himself in an instant. "I'm just getting changed," he called out, keeping his voice steady. "What can I do for you?"

There was a brief pause, then Lee's measured response: "Begging your pardon, Sir, but the Captain wanted to provide an update on your ETA. We're sixty minutes from the destination. Merlin One is being fuelled and prepped to take you ashore." Ralph's eyes darted back to the screen as it flickered with a new message.

Recover X-75...

His breath hitched, and his fingers moved quickly, typing with purpose even as he called over his shoulder, "Thank you. I'll just finish getting ready—give me ten minutes." Silence followed, but Ralph could sense Lee lingering just beyond the door. He kept his focus on the laptop, the screen a portal to answers he desperately needed.

And the mark? he typed, the question emerging like a shot in the dark.

The reply came faster than he expected, as if whoever was on the other end had been anticipating the query.

Eliminate. Out.

The words struck with the force of a physical blow, and for a moment, Ralph simply stared at them, the implications settling over him like a weight. He inhaled sharply, then closed the laptop with deliberate care. No more questions. No more doubts. The next phase of his mission was clear.

Sliding the laptop into his travel bag, Ralph stood and pushed the chair neatly beneath the desk. The routine act grounded him, if only slightly. He opened the door, and as he'd expected, Petty Officer Lee was waiting outside, standing at attention with his back against the wall. "All good, Sir?" Lee asked, his tone respectful but curious. "Yes, thank you," Ralph replied, his voice steady, his expression impassive. He gave a curt nod and followed Lee into the corridor, the steady thrum of the ship's engine reverberating through his soles as they walked.

The air in the corridor was sharp with the scent of salt and fuel, mingling with the faint metallic tang of the ship's interior. Ralph's mind raced ahead, dissecting the message and the finality of its instructions. Recover X-75. Eliminate. It was more than an assignment—it was a test, one he could neither afford to fail nor question. As they approached the staircase leading to the upper deck,

Ralph glanced at the Petty Officer. "Merlin One," he said, his voice even. "Everything's ready?" "Yes, Sir," Lee confirmed. "We'll have you ashore on schedule." Ralph nodded, already rehearsing his next moves in his mind. Whatever awaited him in Norfolk—whoever awaited him—was one step closer. The weight of the mission pressed against his chest, but he wore his composure like a shield, his thoughts hidden behind a mask of calm determination.

08:30 hours, July 30th 2024,

Chigwell, London

DCI Craig stepped out of the command trailer, his breath condensing in the chilly morning air. He yawned, a long, unguarded exhalation that left him feeling marginally more awake. With a groan, he raised his arms above his head, stretching until his spine gave a satisfying pop. The movement sent a fleeting warmth through his shoulders. As he lowered his arms, his eyes caught a flock of starlings weaving intricate patterns against the pale dawn sky, their synchronized flight briefly mesmerizing him. "Morning, Sir," came a voice from nearby. The DCI turned to see PCs Thorman and Iqbal standing by one of the squad cars, steaming cups of tea cradled in their hands. The two constables were leaning casually against the vehicle, their uniform jackets undone slightly, a sign of the cold seeping through the layers.

"Morning, gentlemen," the DCI replied, nodding as he approached them. His boots crunched against the frost-tipped gravel, a sound that seemed to punctuate the stillness of the early hour. He took a moment to survey the scene before him. The makeshift command post had been set up in the middle of a small, dismal parking lot. The lot was old and crumbling, its weathered tarmac riddled with cracks and faded white lines that once marked parking bays with precision. Now, they were barely visible, overtaken by creeping weeds and the passage of time. The surrounding area was eerily quiet, bordered by tall trees that loomed like silent sentinels over the forgotten space. A scattering of other police vehicles dotted the lot, their blue and white livery muted under a thin layer of dew.

"Quite the scenic spot for an investigation," the DCI muttered dryly as he joined the two constables. Thorman smirked into his cup. "Picturesque, Sir. Really makes you appreciate urban decay." Iqbal chuckled softly, blowing on his tea to cool it. "At least we've got the park nearby. Makes it feel… less grim." The DCI snorted. The park, with its overgrown grass and leafless trees, wasn't doing much to brighten the mood. A rusty swing set stood in the distance, its chains swaying faintly in the breeze, the ghost of childhood laughter lingering in its creaks. "What's the status?" Brian asked, rubbing his hands together for warmth. "Any updates from the night shift?" "Not much," the DCI replied. "Search teams finished their sweep about an hour ago. No new leads. Forensics are still working on that scene near the slaughter-house, but nothing definitive yet. They're bagging a few more samples, but it's slim pickings."

Iqbal nodded. "We had a couple of local dog walkers stop by, curious about the commotion. Nothing significant, just being nosey." The DCI sighed, his breath escaping in a visible puff. "Figures. The trail's already gone cold. This isn't looking good." He glanced toward the edge of the lot, where a path disappeared into the thick tree line. The trailer door creaked open behind him, and DS Kelly stepped out, a clipboard in one hand and a phone pressed to her ear with the other. Her sharp gaze swept the lot, locking onto the DCI as she approached.

"Morning, Sir," she said briskly, tucking the phone into her jacket pocket. "Just got off with the tech team. They're pulling CCTV from the surrounding areas. It's going to take a bit longer— some of the cameras are older than this parking lot." The DCI gave a short nod. "And the victim's ID? Anything from Missing Persons?" "Still waiting for confirmation," Kelly said, her tone tinged with frustration. "They've narrowed it down to two possibilities based on the preliminary description. Should have something solid within the hour, Lynford is a small town so shouldn't take long to get an answer," turning she stepped back inside the trailer.

"Good," the DCI replied, though his tone betrayed little optimism. He turned back to Thorman and Iqbal. "Finish up your tea and get ready. I want you both good to go in the next thirty minutes. Someone must have seen or heard something. There's no way a body ends up here without leaving a trace." "Yes, Sir," the constables said in unison, already straightening from their relaxed postures. The DCI adjusted his coat as a gust of wind swept through the lot, cutting through him like a blade. As he glanced once more at the bleak surroundings, his jaw tightened. The scene felt heavy with unspoken secrets, the kind that refused to reveal themselves easily. This wasn't just another case—it had the makings of something far darker. He just hoped they'd find answers before the silence of the morning swallowed them whole.

Brian seized the moment to dig for more details, his curiosity bubbling over. "If you don't mind me asking, Sir, what's the latest on how the convict managed to escape?" His voice carried a mix of professional interest and genuine intrigue, the kind of tone that encouraged sharing. DCI Craig considered the question for a beat before stepping closer, leaning against the car alongside the two constables. He folded his arms across his chest, his gaze drifting momentarily to the distant treetops swaying in the breeze.

His expression was tight, his jaw set—a man carrying the weight of a case growing colder by the minute. "Well," the DCI began, his voice heavy, "we lost him Thetford, he had used the woods as cover." Brian and his fellow constable, Iqbal, exchanged quick glances. Brian leaned in slightly, his interest clearly piqued. "And the dogs couldn't track him, Sir?" The DCI shook his head, the frustration evident in his features. "Not a trace. He was smart— damn smart. Probably covered his scent somehow or doubled back to throw them off. By the time we expanded the search grid, it was too late. We scoured the woods for hours. Sent in drones, brought in additional units… nothing."

He shifted his weight, his eyes narrowing as he recounted the next twist. "Then things took a darker turn. A cyclist was found dead near Lynford—off the main road, close to one of those quiet trails people use for birdwatching. Poor sod didn't stand a chance. It was brutal, and from the initial signs, it was clear our man was responsible." Iqbal's brow furrowed, his grip tightening on his mug. "And that's when you tracked him to the slaughterhouse?" The DCI nodded. "Exactly. We got a tip about someone matching his description heading that way. It was a big, decrepit place, barely operational. A couple of the lads swore they saw him slip inside, so we surrounded the building, locked it down. Sent in a search team to sweep every inch of the place."

He paused, his tone darkening. "But it was like he vanished into thin air. No footprints, no signs of a struggle, no blood trail— nothing. Just the eerie sound of those machines humming and the stench of death hanging in the air. We found a few spots that looked like someone might've been hiding, but that was it. Not a bean." Brian frowned; his curiosity now tinged with unease. "Do we think he's still in the area, Sir?" The DCI let out a long sigh, pushing a hand through his hair. "That's the million-pound question, isn't it? He could be holed up somewhere nearby, waiting for the heat to die down.

Or he could've slipped through our fingers entirely, blending in with the morning rush before we even knew it. Either way, this isn't your average runaway convict. He's calculated, resourceful… and dangerous as hell." The constables absorbed the information in silence for a moment, the weight of the situation settling over them. A convict on the loose was one thing; a cold-blooded killer capable of eluding seasoned Officers and slipping through a full-scale search was something else entirely.

"Slippery fish, that one," the DCI said, his voice quieter now but no less resolute. "And it's on us to reel him in before he does any more damage. So, finish your tea, lads. It's going to be a long day, and we've got work to do." He pushed himself off the car, the determination etched into his posture as he glanced back toward the command trailer. The two constables exchanged a final look before quickly downing the last of their drinks, their focus sharpening. Whatever lay ahead, it was clear this wasn't a case they could afford to lose.

From across the parking lot, the sharp voice of an Officer pierced the chilly morning air. "Sir, phone call!" DCI Craig sighed, his brief respite evaporating. He straightened his shoulders, brushing invisible dust off his coat as he muttered, "Excuse me, gents. Break time's over, it seems." Brian and Shaheed nodded, watching their boss stride purposefully across the uneven tarmac toward the trailer.

There was something in the DCI's gait, a stiffness that betrayed the mounting pressure he carried. They exchanged a glance, both silently noting how much this case was weighing on him.

Reaching the trailer, the DCI accepted the phone from the Officer with a curt nod. "Cheers," he said, before turning on his heel and walking toward the edge of the lot. The entrance, framed by a low chain-link fence and shadowed by a pair of scraggly oak trees, offered a semblance of privacy. He stepped to the side, away from the Officers congregating near the command post. He needed space—both physical and mental—to process whatever was coming next. Raising the phone to his ear, his voice was low but authoritative. "This is DCI Craig. To whom am I speaking?"

The reply was formal, clipped, and unexpected. "Military Liaison Ralph Wadley. The DCI's brows furrowed at the introduction. Military? He shifted the phone to his other ear, his mind racing to catch up. What could the military possibly want with a regional police investigation? His instincts prickled, sensing a complication he wasn't ready for. He scanned the lot as if seeking answers in the mundane activity around him. A cluster of Officers chatted near the trailer; their conversation punctuated by occasional laughter. Brian and Shaheed were off to the side, idly kicking a stone back and forth. From the animated gestures and smirks on their faces, it was clear they were revisiting highlights of last night's football match. The normalcy of it all felt almost jarring against the sudden mystery unfolding in his ear.

"Mr. Wadley," the DCI said, his tone cautious but firm, "to what do I owe the pleasure? I wasn't aware the military had an interest in this case." Wadley's voice came through steady, like a man accustomed to cutting through red tape. "DCI Craig, I'll get straight to the point. This isn't a courtesy call. We've been monitoring your investigation closely—specifically, the escapee and subsequent events in Thetford and Lynford. As of this morning, your case has intersected with one of our own operations." The DCI's grip on the phone tightened. "Intersected how, exactly?" Wadley hesitated, just long enough for the DCI to notice. "The individual you're pursuing is not just a convict. He's a former operative". We have reason to believe his escape was not coincidental but orchestrated."

The DCI blinked, stepping closer to the fence as if the proximity to the cold steel would anchor him. "You're telling me this man isn't just a convict but some sort of... military asset gone rogue?" "Precisely," Wadley confirmed. "And before you ask, I can't disclose the specifics of his prior missions or why he was being held in the first place. What I can tell you is this: he's classified as a high-risk individual with extensive survival training. That's why your units struggled in Thetford. He knows how to evade pursuit. He's been trained to vanish." The words hit the DCI like a gut punch. He felt the familiar weight of responsibility press down even harder. "And the cyclist?" he asked, his voice quieter now, the image of the gruesome scene flashing in his mind. "Was that part of his training too?"

"We're still assessing that," Wadley replied evenly. "But yes, it's possible. Desperation can make even the best-trained operatives unpredictable. If he felt cornered, he would've done whatever was necessary to stay ahead of you." The DCI rubbed his temple, trying to process the flood of new information. "And why am I hearing about this now, after the fact?" Wadley's tone remained unflappable. "Because, until this morning, we believed we could handle the situation internally. Clearly, that's no longer the case. We're deploying a joint task force to assist in the search, but until then, I'm here to liaise with you directly." The DCI bristled at the implication that his team was out of its depth, but he held his tongue. There was no room for ego in a situation like this. "Fine," he said after a moment. "But if you're bringing in your own people, I need to know how this changes the operation. My Officers have been running themselves ragged for the last thirty-six hours. If you've got intel, it's time to share it." There was another pause, shorter this time. "Understood."

The line went dead before the DCI could respond. He lowered the phone, staring at the screen for a moment before slipping it into his coat pocket. The weight on his shoulders had grown heavier, the simple chase for a fugitive now entangled with military secrecy and implications far beyond his jurisdiction. As he turned back toward the trailer, his eyes fell on Brian and Shaheed, still laughing over their makeshift football game. For a fleeting moment, he envied their ignorance of the storm about to hit. But it wouldn't last. Soon enough, they'd all be pulled into the vortex. The DCI took a deep breath and started back toward the command post, already dreading the conversation ahead.

Chapter 16
09:26 hours, July 30th 2024,
West Toffs, Norfolk

Knee-deep in murky, foul-smelling water, Aubrey crouched low in the shadowy ditch, his heart pounding like a drum in his chest. He dared not lift his head above the jagged edge of the embankment, where he would be exposed to the open expanse of agricultural fields that stretched endlessly on either side. To his right, barely five meters away, a narrow, weathered road cut through the landscape, its gravel glinting faintly in the sunlight. There was no cover—no dense trees, no abandoned structures, no bushes to conceal him. The ditch was his only sanctuary, a grim refuge that barely offered protection. He prayed they would not stop and search, knowing that even the faintest ripple in the water might give him away.

The distant roar of engines grew louder, an ominous chorus accompanied by the strobe of blue lights bouncing off the fields. The sirens, shrill and unrelenting, pierced the morning, setting every nerve in Aubrey's body on edge. It was a full-blown convoy—a fleet of police cars and vans tearing down the narrow road, their purpose clear and terrifying. The manhunt was in full swing, and he was their prey. Aubrey's breath hitched as he pressed himself lower into the ditch, feeling the chill of the water seep into his clothes. Every second stretched endlessly, the tension suffocating as he strained his ears to track the vehicles. Would they speed past, oblivious to his presence, or would they screech to a halt, spilling Officers into the fields like hounds on a scent? He clutched the muddy walls of the ditch, his fingers trembling as he fought the rising panic. For now, all he could do was wait—and hope.

The noise was deafening, the tyres churning loose stones on the asphalt as loose chippings reigned on top of Aubrey, feeling his exposed skin sting with the impact of the small stones. The cars were accelerating, which was good news, as the last one flew past, he breathed a sigh of relief, once again he had managed to avoid detection, but he knew his luck would sooner or later run out, it was only a matter time. Crawling up the slope towards the road, he peered over the top, suddenly behind him, he heard another car approaching at speed, without turning he let his body slide back down the bank, splashing into the water.

His face pressed against the cold, damp mud, eyes squeezed shut, Aubrey barely dared to breathe as the hum of an approaching car grew louder. The vehicle slowed, gravel crunching beneath its tires, and then came the sound he dreaded: the screech of brakes. His stomach knotted in fear. They had seen him. They must have. Should he run? Or stay frozen and hope for a miracle? Either way, they'd be on him within thirty seconds, and his choices would vanish as swiftly as they'd appeared.

The car door creaked open, the sound sharp and clear in the oppressive stillness. A gruff voice broke through the tension. "Yeah, hang on... I just need to pop over here. Give me a second, will ya?" The door slammed shut, followed by the crunch of boots on gravel. Aubrey's pulse thundered in his ears as he tracked the movements. The Officer—a stocky, short man with close-cropped black hair— rounded the back of the patrol car. His gait was casual, indifferent, as if he was not actively hunting an escape convict but simply stepping away for a momentary reprieve. Unbuttoning his trousers, the Officer moved toward the ditch. Holding his breath, Aubrey's stomach clenched. Stay still, stay invisible. The man stood near the edge of the bank; his gaze fixed on the horizon as he relieved himself. A tractor lumbered across a distant field, dragging a massive trailer and kicking up a thick plume of dust that glittered in the sunlight. The Officer watched it, seemingly mesmerized, whistling a tuneless melody as he finished up.

Behind him, the passenger window of the patrol car slid down with a metallic hum. A second Officer, lanky and irritated, leaned out, poking his head through the gap. "For crying out loud, get a move on! They're leaving us behind!" His tone carried the frustration of a man too accustomed to his partner's antics. "Stick a cork in it, will ya? Nature calls," the first Officer snapped back, his tone laced with annoyance. He buttoned his trousers and turned away from the ditch, heading back toward the car with a deliberate lack of urgency.

For a moment, silence returned, broken only by the soft rustle of the grass and the faint hum of the idling engine. Then came the slam of the car door, and the vehicle roared to life, spitting gravel as it accelerated away, its occupants oblivious to the man submerged just a few feet from where they'd stood. Aubrey emerged from the water with a gasp, his chest heaving as he gulped in fresh air. He looked around frantically, scanning for signs of the Officers. They were gone. Only the faint echo of the car's engine remained, fading into the distance. His entire body was soaked, his clothes clinging to him like a second skin. The cold gnawed at him, sharp and unrelenting.

Grabbing the muddy edge of the bank, Aubrey hauled himself out of the ditch with trembling arms, every movement an effort against his waterlogged limbs. He rolled onto his back, sprawled out in the sun's warmth, letting it seep into his chilled body. For a moment, he allowed himself to relax, closing his eyes and focusing on steadying his breath. His heart, which had been hammering wildly, began to slow. The fields around him were quiet again, save for the distant drone of the tractor. He had bought himself a reprieve, a fleeting window of safety in the relentless pursuit. But he knew it wouldn't last. North. He had to keep moving north. Reopening his eyes, Aubrey stared at the sky for another heartbeat, drawing strength from the sunlight before rolling back to his side and pushing himself to his feet. His journey wasn't over—not yet, closing his eyes he let his mind drift.

04.00 hours, September 6th 1975,

Unknown Location, Scotland

Darkness enveloped him, suffocating and absolute. He struggled to control his nerves, but his body betrayed him—his torso trembled violently as fear and adrenaline coursed through his veins. His breathing came in shallow bursts, muffled by the suffocating linen bag pulled tightly over his head. Above him, the deafening roar of helicopter rotors obliterated all other sounds, drowning out even his own ragged breaths. The vibrations of the machine resonated through the cold metal floor beneath him, a stark reminder of his helplessness.

Moments ago—or was it hours? —he had been asleep in the barracks, surrounded by the familiar warmth and camaraderie of his unit. The world had been peaceful then, filled with the soft snores of his comrades and the muted hum of base life. But that tranquillity had shattered in an instant. Multiple hands, rough and unyielding, had grabbed him, yanking him from his cot with alarming force. He remembered the scratchy texture of the bag as it was shoved over his head, the smell of sweat and fabric filling his nostrils as they blinded him.

At first, confusion had taken hold. His mind had scrambled for explanations. Was this a prank? Chinny, his notorious prankster of a friend, had pulled stunts like this before. But the hands were too rough, their movements too purposeful. Then came the boot. A sharp, brutal kick to his stomach stole the air from his lungs and any fleeting hope of humour from his mind. Pain radiated through his torso as he doubled over, coughing and gasping, his cries of protest drowned out by the chaos.

He fought back instinctively, his training kicking in. His fists swung blindly, his body twisting and thrashing against the grip of his assailants. "Help!" he had yelled, or at least he thought he had. The memory blurred in the haze of panic. No one came. The hands tightened their grip, iron vices around his arms and legs, hauling him like a sack of grain. He felt the cool night air on his skin as he was dragged outside, his boots scraping against rough terrain, offering no purchase.

Then the cold steel of the helicopter's floor met his body with an unforgiving thud. The sharp bite of metal sent a shiver through him, cutting through the haze of fear. Before he could rise, they bound his wrists and ankles with brutal efficiency, the ropes digging into his skin. He thrashed, testing the bonds, but they held firm. The helicopter lurched, the vibrations intensifying as the rotors spun faster, the sudden lift pressing him down against the unforgiving surface. He felt gravity shift as the aircraft climbed higher, taking him further from the safety of his unit, further from answers, and further into uncertainty.

His thoughts raced, wild and fragmented. Who were they? What did they want? He tried to piece it together, but the pain in his stomach and the panic in his chest clouded his mind. Each question he asked himself only deepened his terror. The linen bag was stifling, the air inside warm and stale, amplifying his sense of disorientation. His ears rang with the unrelenting drone of the helicopter, a maddening backdrop to his spiralling thoughts.

Somewhere deep within, a faint ember of defiance flickered. He wouldn't break, not yet. He forced himself to focus on the cold metal beneath him, grounding himself in its harsh reality. His breaths, shallow and uneven, began to slow. He needed to stay calm, conserve his energy. Whatever awaited him, he knew one thing: he had to survive.

They had been flying for an hour—maybe two. Time had lost meaning in the suffocating darkness of the linen bag. His mind spun wildly, lurching from one desperate theory to the next. Each scenario he conjured felt more absurd than the last, yet all of them led back to one conclusion: this must be a test. A cruel, elaborate test designed by his superiors to push him to the brink. That had to be it. Wasn't it? The helicopter's pitch changed suddenly, the deafening rotors slowing as the aircraft began its descent. His body tensed. They were lowering altitude. He could feel it in the subtle shift of pressure, in the weightlessness creeping into his limbs. Something brushed against his leg, making him instinctively pull his knees to his chest. His breathing quickened, his senses straining to make sense of the chaos.

Then, without warning, a loud buzzing noise erupted, cutting through the steady drone of the helicopter. It sent a jolt of fear down his spine. He couldn't see anything, but through the fabric of the bag, he detected a faint red light flashing in the periphery of his vision. The air vibrated with a sharp, mechanical whirring, and before he could brace himself, he felt the cold, hard surface beneath him tilt. His stomach lurched as his body began to slide backward.

Panic clawed at him. His mind screamed questions: How high are we? What's below? He scrabbled at the slick metal floor, desperate for a handhold, his heart pounding as gravity pulled him toward the open void. Suddenly, a firm hand grabbed his shoulder, anchoring him. The warmth of breath near his ear sent a shiver through him as a voice spoke, calm and clipped. "Corporal, you have 24 hours. Good luck... don't get caught."

Before he could process the words, the bindings around his legs were cut with a swift motion, the rope falling away. He barely had time to register the shift in tension before multiple hands seized him. In one fluid, brutal motion, they lifted him and hurled him into the void. The wind roared past his ears as he plummeted through the air, the bag still over his head. The world spun wildly, a chaotic blur of motion and sound. For a fleeting moment, he thought this was the end. So long, life. His body tensed, bracing for impact, bracing for nothingness.

Thump!

The ground hit him like a freight train, knocking the air from his lungs in a violent rush. Pain exploded in his shoulder as it absorbed most of the impact, a sharp, burning ache that spread down his arm. He lay sprawled on the ground, gasping like a fish out of water, his chest heaving as he fought to regain his breath. The linen bag still clung to his head, damp now with sweat and saliva, but he was too dazed to pull it off immediately. Overhead, he heard the helicopter's engines shift again. It circled once, as if ensuring he had landed in one piece, before retreating into the distance. The sound faded into the horizon, leaving behind an eerie, suffocating silence. He was alone.

Finally, he clawed at the bag, ripping it from his head. Moonlight bathed the landscape in pale silver, revealing dense woods and rolling hills. He had no idea where he was. The last thing he remembered was falling asleep in the barracks, safe among his comrades. Now, he was here—wherever here was—with nothing but the clothes on his back and a throbbing shoulder.

One thing was clear: this wasn't just a prank. It wasn't just a drill. Somewhere out there, someone—or something—was coming for him. The rules had been given: he had 24 hours. To survive, to evade, to fight if necessary. He pushed himself upright, ignoring the stabbing pain in his shoulder. His breath steadied, his mind clearing. Whatever this was, whoever had orchestrated it, he wouldn't go down without a fight. He scanned the horizon, his instincts kicking in. If they expected him to crumble, they'd picked the wrong man. Hands still bound; he started to move. The clock had begun, and he intended to make every second count.

Walking backward up the rugged hill, he paused every few steps, scanning the horizon with a sharp, anxious gaze. His heart raced in sync with the pounding of his boots against the uneven earth, but he forced himself to stay alert. The terrain, though breathtaking, was no comfort. It seemed indifferent to his plight, its stark beauty almost mocking his vulnerability. The surrounding hills, their summits chiselled by ancient glaciers and softened by centuries of rain, rose like silent sentinels around him. Steep-sided glens stretched out below, draped in a thick carpet of purple heather that swayed gently in the cool breeze. It was the kind of landscape that belonged in a fairy tale—if not for the fact that he was the hunted protagonist in a grim game.

No buildings, no roads, no trails to guide him. The isolation pressed down on him like a weight. Hundreds of miles from civilisation, with no food, no water, and no tools, he was utterly alone. The soft hum of the breeze and the distant cry of a bird were the only sounds to accompany his thoughts. Yet, despite the tranquillity, he knew better than to trust the peace. Somewhere out there, someone was tracking him. Maybe it was a single person. Maybe an entire team. He couldn't afford to find out the hard way.

Turning, he faced the slope ahead and decided to climb toward the ridge. The higher elevation would give him a vantage point to survey the surrounding terrain, possibly providing a clue about which direction he should head. His every movement was deliberate, his body tense with focus. As he stepped over the springy heather, his eyes flicked downward. He scanned the ground carefully, searching for a sharp rock or a jagged stone—something, anything, to help him. His hands were still bound, a thin plastic cable tie cutting into the skin of his wrists. The pain was tolerable for now, but the longer it stayed, the deeper the grooves it carved. Worse, it rendered him defenceless. He knew he had to release his hands soon. But the rocky surface beneath the heather offered no immediate solution. No sharp edges, no loose shards, nothing he could use to saw through the binding.

Frustration bubbled up in his chest, but he forced it down. Focus. Looking at his wrists, he studied the cable tie. The plastic was thick and industrial-strength, but it wasn't invincible. He clenched his hands, testing the resistance, feeling the material bite into his skin as he moved. Then, with determination hardening his jaw, he formed two large fists, brought his hands together, and tensed every muscle in his arms. With a sharp motion, he yanked his wrists apart, throwing all his strength into the movement. At first, nothing happened. The plastic stretched slightly but held firm. He gritted his teeth, his breath coming in short bursts, and tried again. This time, there was a faint snap—the sweetest sound he'd heard in hours. The cable tie broke under the force, falling uselessly to the ground.

He froze for a moment, staring down at his reddened wrists in disbelief. A slow wave of relief washed over him, but he knew better than to linger in it. He flexed his hands, letting blood flow freely into his fingers again. They tingled painfully, but he ignored it. His freedom was worth the discomfort. Now that his hands were unbound, his confidence grew. He crouched low, grabbing a small stick from the heather-covered ground and whittling it against a jagged rock he finally found nestled beneath the vegetation. It wasn't much—a crude tool at best—but it would serve as a weapon if needed. Standing again, he adjusted his footing and began the climb toward the ridge, moving faster now.

The wind picked up slightly, rustling the heather more insistently. His senses sharpened; every sound amplified in the quiet expanse. He glanced over his shoulder every few steps, expecting to see movement in the glens below, shadows that shouldn't be there. But so far, there was nothing. When he finally reached the ridge, the view was both awe-inspiring and daunting. The land stretched out in all directions, a sea of hills and glens, untouched and wild. The ridge offered no clear answers—no smoke trails, no distant buildings, no signs of civilisation. But he spotted a faint glimmer far to the west, perhaps a reflection off water. A lake? A river? Water meant survival, and survival was all that mattered now.

He crouched low, taking a moment to catch his breath. The clock was ticking, and he had no idea who—or what—was coming for him. But with his hands free and his next destination in mind, the spark of determination inside him flared. They had dropped him into this wilderness thinking it would break him, but they were wrong. He was still here, and he wasn't about to make it easy for them. Setting off he started heading west, keeping his eyes moving, watching.

An hour later, Aubrey found himself descending from the ridgeline into a wide, sprawling valley. The landscape shifted as he moved lower—the sharp, barren peaks gave way to gentler slopes, where patches of green began to dominate the sea of purple heather. Below, a narrow river meandered through the valley floor, its clear waters glinting in the sunlight as it wound its way south. The sound of the river reached him faintly, a soothing murmur that contrasted with his parched throat and dry, cracked lips. Thirst clawed at him with every step. He quickened his pace, eager to reach the water. But as he crept closer to the riverbank, his attention snapped to movement on the far side of the valley. A flash of colour—a dull green—caught his eye. Aubrey froze, dropping to a crouch, his heart pounding. Squinting against the sunlight, he saw the outline of a truck moving slowly along a dusty road, partially obscured by a thin treeline. Its khaki green body blended with the surroundings, but it was unmistakable—a military vehicle. His stomach twisted.

He scanned the area, following the truck's path as it rolled toward a stone bridge spanning the river. Taking a cautious step forward, he froze again as the situation grew more complicated. The green truck wasn't alone. Trailing behind it were two sleek black Range Rovers, their windows tinted and paint gleaming unnervingly in the sunlight. Panic surged. Without thinking, Aubrey dove sideways, throwing himself into the heather and flattening his body against the uneven ground. The wiry stems of the plants scratched his face and arms as he settled into place, keeping as low as possible. From his vantage point high on the slope, he was confident they hadn't spotted him—at least, he hoped they hadn't. He adjusted his breathing, forcing himself to slow down and keep quiet.

The convoy worked its way closer, the truck bouncing slightly over the uneven dirt road. Aubrey kept his eyes locked on it, barely daring to blink. The vehicles reached the bridge and stopped suddenly, their engines idling with a low, menacing growl. A figure stepped out of the lead Range Rover. The man moved with a deliberate precision, his uniform marking him as an Officer. He was tall and broad-shouldered, wearing army-issue camouflage that looked freshly pressed. His boots crunched against the gravel as he approached the edge of the bridge, stopping in front of the truck. Aubrey's heart sank as he saw the man raise a pair of binoculars, tilting them upward toward the ridgeline.

The lenses glinted in the sunlight, scanning the hills in slow, methodical arcs. Aubrey's pulse thundered in his ears as the binoculars paused, seemingly pointed directly at him. No, no, no... He forced himself to stay still, his body pressed so close to the earth that he could feel the cool dampness of the soil seeping into his clothes. The Officer stood motionless; binoculars fixed on the spot where Aubrey was hiding. Every instinct screamed at him to move, to crawl further down the slope or make a break for the dense cover of the valley below. But he knew better. The soldier was watching intently, likely anticipating that very reaction. If Aubrey moved, it would all be over.

Instead, he stayed put, fighting the urge to flinch as a bee buzzed dangerously close to his ear. He focused on his breathing, counting each inhale and exhale, trying to stay calm. His hands dug into the earth, grounding himself, as he continued to watch the Officer. Minutes passed like hours. Finally, the soldier lowered the binoculars, his gaze lingering on the hills for a moment longer before turning away. He said something to the driver of the truck, gesturing toward the road ahead. Aubrey couldn't hear the words, but the tone was sharp and commanding. The Officer climbed back into the Range Rover, and after a tense moment, the convoy started moving again, the vehicles rolling across the bridge and disappearing behind the treeline.

Aubrey remained frozen in place, not daring to move until the growl of the engines faded into silence. Only then did he let out a shaky breath, his body relaxing slightly. His heart still pounded, but relief mixed with the adrenaline. He had narrowly avoided detection—for now. Pushing himself deeper into the heather, he stayed low, watching the road to ensure no one doubled back. The Officer's sharp, methodical behaviour unsettled him. This wasn't a random patrol—they were looking for him, and they were well-organized. Aubrey knew he couldn't stay in the open for long. The valley might offer water and temporary cover, but it was also a trap, its open spaces leaving him vulnerable.

He would need to move carefully, and quickly, if he wanted to stay ahead of them. Taking a final glance at the bridge and road below, he began crawling down the slope, his mind racing with plans for his next move. The hunt was far from over, and to make matters worse, that sun had started rise in the east.

As he reached the bottom of the slope, Aubrey instinctively stayed low, his movements deliberate and cautious. He scanned his surroundings, first to the left, then to the right. The valley was eerily still, save for the soft murmur of the stream winding its way through the landscape. No sign of the convoy, no silhouettes moving against the backdrop of the hills, and no sounds beyond the natural chorus of birdsong and rustling leaves. Satisfied that he was alone, he crept toward the stream, each step crunching softly on the loose gravel. When he reached the water's edge, he dropped to his knees, his body protesting after the long trek downhill. He leaned forward, scooping the cool, clear water into his hands and bringing it to his parched lips. The liquid was icy against his tongue, a sharp relief that cut through the dryness in his throat. He drank deeply, the tension in his chest easing with each gulp. The cold water stung his cracked lips, but he didn't care.

Wiping his mouth with the back of his hand, Aubrey tilted his head back and looked skyward. The sun, once blazing high and unrelenting, now ducked behind a large white cloud, casting a long shadow over the valley. The sudden coolness made his skin prickle. Above him, a bird of prey soared in graceful arcs, its sharp eyes trained on the lone figure kneeling by the stream. Aubrey couldn't help but smile at the sight, the sheer freedom of the creature a stark contrast to his own predicament. But the smile didn't last. Rising from his knees, he forced himself upright, shaking the lingering fatigue from his limbs. He couldn't stay here. The water had been a welcome reprieve, but the open valley left him exposed. He glanced back at the way he had come, the bridge now little more than a dot in the distance. Then, turning his back to it, he began walking along the dirt road, heading in the opposite direction the military convoy had travelled.

Four hours later, Aubrey found himself standing beneath a row of ancient sycamore trees. Their towering trunks stretched skyward, their dense canopies forming a natural guardrail along the road. The air here was cooler, shaded by the trees, and carried the faint scent of damp earth and leaves. He leaned against one of the trunks for a moment, grateful for the chance to rest his aching legs. Looking out across the valley, he took in the vast expanse before him. The road stretched endlessly, winding through the hills and glens until it seemed to vanish into the horizon. It was tempting to stay on this path—it was flat, direct, and easier on his tired body. But it was also dangerous. If the convoy had backup—or if anyone else was searching for him—they would expect him to follow the road.

Turning his gaze to the left, he studied the towering peak of the next hill. Its steep incline promised a gruelling climb, but the elevation would give him an advantage. From up there, he could see for miles, giving him time to react if anyone approached. He weighed his options, his brow furrowed. The road offered speed and comfort, but the hill offered safety. Aubrey glanced over his shoulder one last time, back toward the bridge, now almost lost to memory. The decision made itself. He couldn't afford to play it safe. Climbing the hill would buy him time if anyone found his trail.

Tightening his jaw, he left the road behind and started the ascent. Each step felt heavier than the last, the loose rocks and uneven ground threatening to throw him off balance. The sun climbed in the sky, casting the hill in long shadows. Above him, the bird of prey he'd seen earlier was still circling, as if it had taken an interest in his struggle. As he climbed, his thoughts turned inward. He tried to recall every detail of the night before, every face in the barracks, every fleeting moment that could explain how he'd ended up here. But the answers remained elusive, and the uncertainty gnawed at him.

Reaching a plateau halfway up the hill, he paused to catch his breath, wiping sweat from his brow with the back of his hand. The valley stretched out below him, a patchwork of greens and purples fading into the distance. It was beautiful, but he couldn't let himself admire it for long. He had to keep moving. Resting his hands on his knees for a moment, he glanced upward at the summit, still a daunting climb away. With a deep breath, Aubrey pushed on, determined to reach the ridge before nightfall. He knew one thing for certain: the higher ground would give him an edge, and right now, every edge mattered.

As Aubrey reached the top of the ridge, he cursed under his breath. Hill after hill stretched out in every direction, an unbroken sea of jagged peaks and rolling crests. It was endless, desolate, and utterly demoralizing. He squatted down, his knees trembling from the climb, and placed his hands on his thighs, trying to catch his breath. The cool wind bit at his sweat-soaked face as he exhaled sharply. He was in trouble, deep trouble, with no clear way out. Suddenly, a sound cut through the wind, sharp and unmistakable. Bark! He froze, his pulse quickening as his eyes darted across the horizon. Bark! Bark! The noise repeated, sharper and closer this time. A jolt of adrenaline coursed through him as his brain snapped to attention. Dogs. His eyes scanned the ridgeline frantically, searching for the source of the sound, but it seemed to echo from everywhere and nowhere.

Dropping to his stomach, he crawled back to the edge of the hill, peering cautiously over the lip. His stomach dropped. They had found him. A platoon of soldiers was methodically making their way up the slope he had just climbed. Their formation was tight and practiced, the glint of their weapons visible even from this distance. But it wasn't the soldiers that terrified him. It was the two massive black dogs bounding ahead, their sleek bodies moving with feral determination. Off their leashes, they barked in unison, their sharp yelps cutting through the air as they homed in on his scent.

Panic overtook him. Without a second thought, Aubrey turned and bolted, his boots slipping slightly on the loose gravel as he sprinted along the ridge. He pumped his arms furiously, willing his aching legs to keep moving. Each step felt heavier than the last, but he pushed through the burning in his thighs. His mind raced, scanning the terrain ahead for something—anything—that could offer cover. But there was nothing. He was exposed, a lone figure running across the crest of the world. A glance over his shoulder confirmed his worst fears. The dogs had reached the top of the hill, their powerful legs propelling them faster than he could hope to run. Their barks grew louder, more frenzied, as they closed the gap, saliva flying from their open jaws. Behind them, the soldiers were still climbing, their pace deliberate but relentless.

Aubrey forced his eyes forward, his chest heaving as he sprinted along the ridge. Up ahead, the ground dipped sharply, offering a glimmer of hope. But as he drew closer, hope turned to dread. The slope didn't lead to a path—it ended abruptly at a sheer cliff face. Jagged rocks jutted out like broken teeth, looming over a glittering lake far below. He skidded to a halt, his boots sending loose stones tumbling into the abyss. Heart hammering, he turned to face his pursuers. The dogs were only fifty meters away now, their muscular bodies moving with terrifying speed. He could see the whites of their eyes and the foam dripping from their snarling mouths. Behind them, the soldiers crested the ridge, rifles raised as they spotted their quarry.

There was no time to think. Surrender? He doubted they'd take him back to his unit unscathed. And those dogs—he didn't fancy his chances against them in a fight. The cliff offered the only escape, however impossible it seemed. Taking a deep breath, Aubrey took two big steps backward, bracing himself. The wind whipped at his face as he fixed his gaze on the edge ahead. This is madness. But madness was better than capture. Without another thought, he sprinted forward, his legs propelling him off the rocky ledge and into the open air. The world dropped away beneath him. For a split second, he was weightless, the wind roaring in his ears as the ground fell away. High above, the dogs skidded to a stop at the cliff's edge, their barks replaced by confused growls as they peered after him.

Aubrey twisted midair, catching a brief glimpse of the soldiers lining up at the precipice, their dark silhouettes stark against the bright sky. Then the water rushed up to meet him.

Thwump! The impact knocked the breath from his lungs as his body hit the lake like a hammer. He plunged deep into the icy depths, the shock of the cold jolting his senses. Bubbles erupted around him, obscuring his vision as the lake swallowed him whole. His ears popped painfully from the pressure, and he instinctively spread his arms and legs to stop his descent. The cold gripped him, numbing his limbs as he forced his eyes open, the murky water surrounding him in every direction. He knew the soldiers were watching. To them, he was either dead or dying. They'd expect his body to float to the surface, limp and lifeless. But Aubrey wasn't giving them that satisfaction. Fighting the urge to kick upward for air, he stayed submerged, his lungs screaming for oxygen. He clawed at the water, moving sideways, deeper into the shadows cast by the towering cliffs. His mind screamed at him to rise, to breathe, but he ignored it, calculating every second. If he surfaced too soon, he'd be an easy target. If he stayed too long, he'd drown. It was a razor-thin line, and he was walking it blind.

Finally, when his chest felt ready to explode, Aubrey let himself rise slowly, his body straining against the effort. He broke the surface with a silent gasp, sucking in air as quietly as he could. The cliff's shadow shielded him from view, and he craned his neck to see the ridge above. The soldiers were still there, scanning the water. One of them pointed, shouting orders. Aubrey sank back beneath the surface, swimming toward the shoreline. His muscles burned, and his thoughts were a blur of panic and determination. He didn't know where he'd go next, but one thing was certain: the chase was far from over.

Aubrey dragged his weary body out of the frigid water, the icy chill still clinging to his muscles. The sharp stones lining the bank bit into his hands and knees, but he barely noticed, his mind racing. He collapsed onto the ground beside a large limestone rock near a thicket of tangled bushes, his chest heaving as he tried to catch his breath. For a moment, he just sat there, staring up at the cliff face he had just plummeted from. White, fluffy clouds drifted lazily above the jagged edge, indifferent to the chaos below. The soldiers had vanished—at least for now—but he knew better than to assume they were gone for good.

Instead of panicking, Aubrey forced himself to think, his soldier's instincts kicking in. If he were in the Officer's boots, leading a manhunt like this, how would he track down one man in an expanse of wilderness that stretched endlessly in every direction? The answer was obvious—use the sky. A helicopter or drone could scan miles of terrain in minutes, saving precious time. Yet, as he scanned the heavens, he had not seen or heard a single aircraft. That detail gnawed at him, a puzzle piece that didn't quite fit. Were they underestimating him? Or was this part of some larger plan he couldn't yet see?

Shifting slightly, Aubrey frowned as he felt the wet squelch of water pooling inside his boot. It was a discomfort he couldn't afford to ignore. Reaching down, he began tugging at the laces to loosen them. But as he pulled the tongue aside, something caught his eye— a small, unfamiliar object embedded just beneath it. Frowning, he pinched it between two fingers and pulled it free. It was smooth to the touch, a black metallic disc no larger than a coin, and perfectly camouflaged against the fabric of his boot. His stomach dropped as realization struck him like a punch to the gut. A tracking device. Standing abruptly and scanning his surroundings. The implications hit him in rapid succession. They knew he was here. Dead or alive, they would come. And not just to confirm their suspicions—they would come in force. The water had bought him a few precious moments, but if he didn't act fast, he'd be cornered.

Instinctively, Aubrey moved to throw the device into the lake, his arm pulling back. But then he hesitated. Think. Tossing the tracker into the water might buy him some time, but it would also confirm to his hunters exactly where he had been. And what if it was more than a simple tracker? Could they trace its signal even as it sunk to the lakebed? He couldn't risk it. Instead, he slid the disc into his pocket and crouched low, tying his boot back up with quick, precise movements. His heart pounded as he glanced around the edge of the lake. A decision had to be made. Sitting still meant death. He scanned the shoreline, his eyes landing on a patch of dense woodland about two hundred meters away. The trees were thick, their overlapping branches creating a canopy that could offer him cover—at least for a while.

Bending low to stay out of sight, Aubrey began to move, following the curve of the lake. The squelching of his boots was maddeningly loud to his ears, every step a reminder of how exposed he was. His soaked clothes clung to his skin, the weight slowing him down as he moved. He tried to stay close to the water's edge, where the reeds and tall grasses might help obscure him from any observers.

Halfway to the woods, he paused, crouching behind a large boulder. He craned his neck to look back toward the cliff. The ridge was still clear of movement, but that wouldn't last. His pursuers would figure out soon enough that he hadn't drowned. And when they did, they'd come after him with renewed ferocity. Reaching into his pocket, Aubrey pulled out the tracker again, turning it over in his hand. It was maddeningly simple, just a smooth, black circle, yet it felt heavier than it should—a symbol of the noose tightening around him. He needed to use it to his advantage. An idea began to form. If he could create a diversion—something to mislead them or buy himself more time—he might stand a chance.

An hour later, Aubrey sat hidden inside a dense thicket, his back pressed against the rough bark of a large tree. The woodland provided sufficient cover for the time being, offering a small oasis of shelter amidst the vast, rugged terrain. He closed his eyes for a moment, his chest rising and falling as he took deep, controlled breaths. This was it—the trap was set, and all he had to do now was wait. In the distance, faint but unmistakable, the sound of barking dogs reached his ears. The beasts were getting closer again, their shrill barks echoing through the trees. Aubrey knew they would be followed by soldiers, their movements methodical and relentless. But for the moment, he was hidden, and he needed to stay calm, focused.

Ahead, in a small clearing, he could see his trap: a loose loop made of his boot lace hanging just six inches off the ground, suspended from a small, crooked branch. Beneath it, a carefully laid-out buffet—fragments of dried wild grass and reeds from the lake

—sat invitingly just a few inches from the noose. It had taken him almost half an hour to gather the bits and pieces, each item placed carefully in hopes of luring the creature he needed.

A rustle from the right caught his attention. He stilled, not daring to move a muscle. Two small ears appeared from the undergrowth, followed by a twitching nose, and then, the bright, curious eyes of a rabbit. The creature sniffed the air, clearly alert, yet unaware of the danger lying in wait. Aubrey's breath caught in his throat as the rabbit's head slowly emerged from the bushes, its nose twitching, searching for any sign of threat. He remained completely still, praying that the wind would remain on his side and that the rabbit wouldn't pick up his scent. His muscles ached; the tension unbearable as the small animal edged closer to the trap. Every tiny movement seemed amplified in the thick silence of the woods. The rabbit took a step forward, cautiously sniffing the ground near the food. Aubrey's heart began to race. This is it—he thought, willing himself to stay calm.

Suddenly, the rabbit paused. Its ears twitched. Then, without warning, it turned and darted back into the underbrush. Aubrey cursed under his breath, his frustration bubbling up, but he didn't move. The dogs were getting closer now, and he desperately hoped that the rabbit hadn't sensed the threat. Silence followed, and the tension in the air seemed to stretch for an eternity.

Just as Aubrey began to think he might have lost his chance, the rabbit reappeared from the opposite side of the trap. His heart skipped a beat as the small creature hesitated at the edge of the clearing, eyes wide and wary. Slowly, it inched forward, drawn to the food laid before it. It sniffed cautiously, its small body trembling ever so slightly with each step. Aubrey's body tensed like a coiled spring. The moment was at hand. Without making a sound, he surged forward. The trap was set. Before the rabbit could reach the loop, he thrust his arm out, his fingers closing around the animal's body with surprising speed. The bushes opposite him erupted in motion as the rabbit tried to escape. Its tiny body squirmed and kicked, but Aubrey held it firm, his grip unyielding.

In one swift motion, Aubrey bent down and grabbed the rabbit by its body, lifting it off the ground. He was careful not to harm it too much, though the creature kicked furiously, its legs flailing in a panic. He held its head in both hands, keeping his fingers well away from the sharp, anterior incisors. The rabbit's struggles were relentless, but Aubrey had no time to hesitate. He needed to be quick. With a precise movement, he reached into his pocket and withdrew the small black disc—the tracker he had found earlier, now his only hope. He held the rabbit's mouth open, using his fingers to keep its jaws from snapping shut. For a moment, the creature stilled, its wide eyes locked onto his. Aubrey's pulse quickened, but his movements remained steady. He gently dropped the tracker down the rabbit's throat, watching it disappear. Then, without wasting a second, he slammed the rabbit's mouth shut, forcing the small creature to swallow.

The rabbit's body spasmed immediately, its legs kicking out wildly as it tried to escape. It fought with all its might, but Aubrey's grip was too strong. His muscles strained as he held it down, his focus unshaken. He had no choice but to wait for the tracker to do its job. Once he was certain the tracker had settled into place, he removed the loop from the rabbit's neck and set the creature down on the ground. It bolted into the underbrush without a second thought, disappearing into the woods like a shadow. As the last of the rabbit's movement faded from his sight, Aubrey stood up, his heart hammering in his chest. The barking was growing louder, much closer now. He didn't have time to tie his boot or retrieve the discarded lace. The soldiers would be near the edge of the woods by now, and the dogs would be on his scent. There was no more time to waste.

Without a moment's hesitation, he turned and ran, his boots pounding against the soft earth beneath him. The wind rushed in his ears as he pushed forward, every muscle in his body protesting, but he had no choice. His only hope was that the tracker would mislead the soldiers, give them a false trail, long enough for him to get a head start. As he sprinted through the dense forest, the sound of the dogs' barking grew fainter, but he knew better than to think he was free. The hunt was far from over, but for now, he had one small victory—and a fleeting chance to disappear into the wilderness once again.

Twenty-three hours and fifty-six minutes later, they found him. Hidden away under the sagging metal beams of an abandoned bridge, he lay curled up against the bitter night air, exhaustion having finally overtaken him. The rustling of boots on gravel barely registered before a dull, sharp thud erupted against his forehead. His eyes fluttered open just in time to catch the flash of a weapon's muzzle before it struck him again, driving him into darkness. The bridge, his last desperate refuge, loomed thirty miles north of the designated drop-off zone, a distance he had covered in sheer panic, moving like a hunted animal. He had hoped the isolation would buy him time—time to plan, time to breathe—but hope had long since been replaced by raw survival instinct. Now, as the fog of unconsciousness threatened to claim him, he realized how badly he had miscalculated.

When he woke, his nightmare hadn't ended; it had only evolved into something far worse. Cold steel bit into his wrists, binding him to an upright post. A dim, flickering light cast eerie shadows across a barren room, and the low murmur of voices outside the door told him he wasn't alone. Blood trickled down his forehead, pooling warm and sticky over his brow. His heart raced as he realized: they hadn't come to kill him. Not yet. He had something they wanted, and they intended to take it—piece by agonizing piece, if necessary.

✳✳✳

10.00 hours, January 3rd 2018,
St Pancras, London

The carriage swayed rhythmically as it hurtled down the line from Euston, the faint hum of the train mingling with the murmur of passengers. Aubrey leaned back against the cool glass of the window, his gaze flitting over the sea of commuters. Most were absorbed in the glow of their phone screens, scrolling endlessly through social media feeds, hunting for the latest morsels of gossip or outrage. He pitied them—these small lives tethered to fleeting digital distractions, oblivious to the world outside their narrow lenses.

Dressed in dark blue jeans, scuffed boots, and a long black coat that hung just so over his lean frame, Aubrey looked like any other traveller escaping the chill of the winter morning. His woolly hat was pulled low over his ears, completing the disguise. To anyone watching, he was just another city-goer blending into the crowd, perhaps heading to St. Pancras to catch the Eurostar or indulging in the festive buzz of the holiday season. But unlike the others, Aubrey was here with purpose, his sharp eyes darting over the faces around him, cataloguing movements, habits, and potential threats. The driver's voice crackled through the intercom, shattering the monotony: "Next station is St Pancras. Change here for Eurostar trains to Europe, Thameslink Trains, Victoria, Piccadilly, Circle, District, Hammersmith and City lines."

The announcement jolted the carriage to life. Half the passengers stood abruptly, a coordinated chaos of bags slung over shoulders, hands gripping poles, and feet shuffling toward the doors. The faint whoosh of the station's air caught up with them as the train barrelled into the platform. Through the glass, Aubrey saw the blur of the bustling platform, every bit as crowded as the carriage. It was a sea of winter coats, scarves, and hats, a tangle of movement under the fluorescent lights. He had counted on the crowd; it was both his shield and his battlefield.

St. Pancras was a hive of activity, and in the swarm of holiday travellers, he could slip unnoticed—or so he hoped. The plan had been laid meticulously, but plans had a way of unravelling, especially when the stakes were this high. As the train slowed to a stop, Aubrey shifted, ready to follow the flow of bodies pouring onto the platform. His eyes narrowed, scanning the edges of the crowd, searching for anything—anyone—that didn't belong. The moment stretched as he exhaled slowly, feeling the familiar, icy calm settle over him. St Pancras awaited, and with it, the next move in a game where one misstep could mean the end.

The doors slid open with a hiss, and Aubrey stepped out, keeping his head low and his pace casual. A family bustled ahead of him, the parents shepherding two children who could barely contain their excitement. The little boy darted a few steps ahead, only to be reeled back by a sharp, but not unkind, "Hey mister, —you don't want to get lost!" Aubrey stayed in their shadow, letting the noise of their chatter mask his own presence as they moved toward the escalators.

He merged into the crowd, the rhythmic click of footsteps echoing off the tiled walls. On the opposite side, a chaotic surge of commuters and tourists descended the escalator, their hurried strides almost a tumble as they raced to catch a departing train. Some muttered curses under their breath; others clutched their tickets tightly, their eyes flicking between their phones and the flickering digital boards announcing destinations and delays.

Aubrey remained calm, blending seamlessly with the flow. When he reached the top, a biting chill hit him like a slap. The warmth of the underground was abruptly replaced by a blast of arctic air that felt sharp enough to cut. He paused for a moment, tucking his chin deeper into his scarf as he stuffed his hands into his coat pockets. The air outside carried the unmistakable sting of a snowstorm, the kind that seeped through layers and gnawed at bare skin.

Pulling out his ticket with one hand, Aubrey stepped toward the turnstiles. He handed the slip of paper to the guard without a word, nodding curtly as it was scanned and returned. The barrier beeped and swung open, and he moved through quickly, avoiding eye contact. Ahead, the exit beckoned—tall glass doors vibrating slightly in the forceful wind outside. Pushing the door open, he was met with a scene straight out of a Christmas card—if Christmas cards included the bitter sting of frostbite. A pristine blanket of snow covered the streets, muffling the usual city din. People trudged past, heads bowed, hands clutched tightly around scarves and coats as they braved the gale-force winds. The blizzard painted everything in shades of white and grey, flakes whipping through the air like frozen needles.

Aubrey ignored the elements, his boots crunching audibly as they sank deep into the powder. His breath came out in short, visible puffs, but he didn't slow. He crossed the road without so much as a glance for oncoming traffic, the sparse vehicles moving sluggishly through the icy conditions. His gaze lifted briefly, watching the fat, lazy snowflakes swirl down from the sky like silent messengers of winter's wrath. Ahead loomed his destination. The building was a hulking mass of red brick, standing stark and defiant against the snow-covered streets. To the casual observer, its design reflected a marriage of local history and urban functionality—a nod to the area's architectural past. But to Aubrey, it was nothing more than a brick-and-mortar cage. A box that promised no escape.

He stood at the curb for a moment, his eyes narrowing as he studied the façade. It was imposing, yes, but it didn't intimidate him. The real threat lay within. Taking a final breath of icy air, Aubrey adjusted his scarf, squared his shoulders, and marched forward, his boots leaving deep impressions in the snow that quickly began to fill with the storm's unrelenting assault.

The large glass entrance radiated a soft, inviting glow, a stark contrast to the icy storm raging outside. As Aubrey approached, his sharp eyes caught every detail: the security cameras positioned at strategic angles, their lenses sweeping in silent vigilance, and the floodlights discreetly embedded in the architecture, casting a warm but calculated light across the entrance. The building wasn't just imposing—it was impenetrable, a fortress disguised as a modern office.

The door slid open with a smooth hiss, and a wave of warm air enveloped him, a welcome reprieve from the bitter cold. He stepped inside, pausing briefly to scrape the slush from his boots on the textured mat. The lobby was a stark contrast to the storm outside, every detail designed for precision and efficiency. The floors gleamed with a mirror-like polish, and the faint scent of pine hung in the air, likely from the oversized Christmas wreath mounted above the entrance. Ahead, a sleek black granite reception desk commanded the room. Behind it sat a young woman, perfectly composed and impeccably dressed in a tailored navy blazer. Her long black hair was styled into a flawless bob that curved neatly at her shoulders, framing her face with practiced elegance. She glanced up as he approached, her professional demeanour softening into a polite smile.

"Good morning, Sir, welcome to Francis Crick. How can I assist you today?" she asked, her voice warm but with the distinct neutrality of someone who repeated the phrase a dozen times a day. Aubrey removed his woollen hat, shaking it lightly as clumps of melting snow tumbled onto the granite surface, forming tiny, glistening puddles. He ignored her brief glance at the mess, reaching into the inner pocket of his coat with deliberate slowness. His hand emerged holding a small, yellow post-it, slightly crumpled at the edges. Without a word, he slid it across the desk to her. The receptionist hesitated, her smile faltering for the briefest moment as she picked up the note. She turned it over, her brow furrowing as her eyes scanned the scribbled message. Whatever it said was enough to make her sit up a little straighter. Her carefully maintained mask of politeness returned, but now it carried a subtle edge of alertness.

"Thank you," she said, folding the note neatly before tucking it under the edge of her keyboard. "Would you mind waiting just over there?" She gestured gracefully toward a seating area, her manicured nails pointing toward a corner where a large fern stood proudly in an oversized ceramic pot. The plant, lush and vibrant, seemed almost out of place amidst the sleek, minimalist décor of the lobby. Nearby, a pair of leather armchairs flanked a low glass table stacked with glossy magazines. "Someone will be down shortly," she added, her tone neutral but firm.

Aubrey nodded once, his expression unreadable, and turned toward the indicated spot. As he walked away, he could feel her eyes on him for a moment longer than necessary, as though trying to piece together the man who had handed her a simple post-it yet carried himself like he belonged to neither the cold outside nor the warmth within. He lowered himself into one of the armchairs, his movements fluid and deliberate, his attention never straying far from the reception desk. The hum of hidden machinery and faint murmur of voices behind closed doors filled the air, but the space around him was empty. Aubrey leaned back, feigning relaxation, but his senses were alert. He studied the layout, noting every exit, every camera, every detail of the environment around him. Time stretched as he waited.

Ten minutes passed, stretching into an eternity as Aubrey remained seated, his posture relaxed but his mind razor-sharp. The faint tick of a distant clock punctuated the silence, blending with the muted hum of the building's heating system. Finally, soft footsteps approached from behind. "Excuse me," a voice said, smooth but faintly unsure. "Would you please come this way?" Aubrey rose smoothly, turning to face the speaker. The man was younger than he expected—mid-to-late twenties, with a slim build and a clean-cut appearance that screamed "junior staff." Standing about five foot ten, he radiated nervous energy, a subtle twitch of his hand revealing that he was no seasoned professional. This wasn't the man Aubrey had come to see.

The man began walking briskly, leading him toward a corner where an unmarked elevator waited. Aubrey followed, his heavy boots echoing faintly on the polished floor. The elevator had no visible buttons or markings, just a sleek black panel embedded in the wall. The young man reached into his pocket and retrieved a blank white card. It gleamed under the sterile overhead light as he swiped it across the pad. The device emitted a soft beep, and the elevator doors slid open with a whisper, revealing a small, featureless interior. "This way, if you please," the man said, stepping inside. Aubrey followed, his towering frame filling most of the cramped space. The younger man realized his mistake almost immediately as Aubrey's imposing presence consumed the lift. He shifted uncomfortably, the tight quarters leaving him little room to breathe, let alone manoeuvre. The faint scent of snow and leather clung to Aubrey, and the weight of his silence was palpable.

The doors slid shut, and the elevator began its descent. The younger man, clearly eager to fill the oppressive quiet, offered a nervous smile. "Name's Harris. Tom Harris. Pleasure to meet you...?" He trailed off expectantly, glancing at Aubrey for a response. Aubrey didn't acknowledge him, his eyes fixed forward, his expression unreadable. The tension in the air thickened as Harris fidgeted with the card in his hand, his earlier confidence dissolving under the weight of Aubrey's indifference.

The elevator came to a halt with a soft ping, and the doors slid open to reveal a stark and uninviting space. Aubrey stepped out first, his boots crunching faintly on the rough concrete floor. The room stretched ahead like a tomb—a vast, hollow expanse of battleship-grey concrete that absorbed light and sound alike. The ceiling, walls, and floor were bare, devoid of any markings, insignias, or decoration. It was a place built for utility, not comfort—a space designed to erase individuality. Tom edged past Aubrey; his footsteps hesitant as if the room itself unnerved him. He gestured down a long corridor that disappeared into shadow. "This way, please... it's not far now."

Aubrey followed without a word, his footsteps heavy and deliberate. He could feel the tension radiating off Tom, the man's shoulder twitching slightly with each step as though he expected something—or someone—to emerge from the shadows. As they moved deeper into the concrete maze, Aubrey's eyes darted discreetly, cataloguing the space. No cameras were visible, no signs or directions marked the way. It was deliberate, this blank, oppressive design. A place meant to strip away identity, leaving only compliance and silence in its wake.

The corridor stretched ahead like the mouth of a cavernous black hole; its end shrouded in darkness. Aubrey's boots thudded against the concrete floor as he walked, the sound swallowed by the oppressive silence. Then, with a faint click, small sensor lights embedded in the walls flickered to life, illuminating just enough to guide their path. Behind them, as soon as they moved out of range, the lights snapped off again, plunging the passage behind them into shadow. Clever, Aubrey thought. No clues, no hints. Just enough to lead you forward while hiding what lies behind.

Tom turned his head slightly, offering a strained smile over his shoulder. His voice echoed faintly in the empty space as he spoke. "We're now on Sub Level Five. As you can appreciate, this is a restricted area. We don't get many visitors down here." He chuckled nervously at his own comment, his laughter trailing off into an awkward silence when Aubrey didn't react. The taller man's stoic expression remained fixed; his piercing blue eyes focused straight ahead. "Anyway," Tom continued, clearing his throat. "Here we are." He came to an abrupt stop in front of a heavy, windowless red steel door. The edges were perfectly flush with the surrounding wall, giving no indication of what lay beyond. Tom extended a hand toward it, his smile faltering as he avoided making direct eye contact. "Please, do go in. He's waiting for you."

Without waiting for a response, Tom turned on his heel and retreated down the corridor, disappearing into the darkness. The flickering sensor lights followed him in reverse, one by one extinguishing his figure until Aubrey was alone. Aubrey reached for the steel handle, his gloved hand gripping it firmly. The door creaked faintly as it swung open, revealing a room bathed in clinical brightness. The stark white light was almost blinding after the dim corridor, and as he stepped inside, the door closed behind him with a loud, echoing clang.

His sharp gaze swept the room. Everything was meticulously arranged, every surface spotless. Glass partitions divided the space, reflecting the overhead lights. Polished metal counters gleamed like mirrors, and plastic stools sat perfectly aligned beneath them. Shelves filled with binders, test tubes, and rows of labelled vials lined one wall, while computers and medical equipment occupied the other. Even the filing cabinets were devoid of a single smudge, their handles catching the light like the facets of a jewel. The sterile, calculated order of the place set Aubrey's nerves on edge.

At the far end of the room, a man stood motionless, his back turned to the entrance. His focus was fixed entirely on the clipboard he held, its surface illuminated by the cold, fluorescent light overhead. The pristine white of his lab coat gleamed, spotless and uncreased, as though it had been plucked straight from its packaging moments ago. His hair was impeccably neat, every strand in place, with just a faint dusting of silver streaking his temples—a testament to his years, perhaps, but not his demeanour, which radiated an almost military precision. The man's posture was stiff, a spine of iron, and when he finally turned, it was with the deliberation of someone accustomed to command. His sharp, appraising eyes locked onto Aubrey's, scrutinizing him with an intensity that felt more surgical than human. A polite but calculated smile tugged at his lips, its warmth purely cosmetic, as though practiced for occasions like this. He moved forward with measured steps, halting just shy of invading Aubrey's personal space, and extended a hand in greeting.

"Welcome, Major," he said, his voice low and meticulously controlled, each syllable clipped and deliberate. "I'm Doctor Bill Bonny." His gaze flickered over Aubrey briefly, a subtle assessment of the towering figure before him. "I understand you've been assigned to assist with a new project." Without waiting for a response, Bonny turned on his heel and strode toward a nearby desk, his movements efficient and devoid of hesitation. The faint click of his polished shoes echoed against the sterile walls as he retrieved a sealed envelope. With an air of detached precision, he slid a single sheet of paper from within and scanned its contents, his brow furrowing slightly in thought. "This facility," he began, his tone shifting to something colder, "is a biomedical research centre. Cutting-edge work, as I'm sure you're aware." He looked up, his eyes narrowing as they fixed on Aubrey again. "However, as you can appreciate, funding these days is a delicate matter. Running an operation like this—it costs the government a considerable amount of money. And with the recent elections... let's just say our future is uncertain." His words hung in the air, a faint undercurrent of resentment threading through them.

Aubrey stood motionless, his face a mask of stoic indifference, offering no indication of what he thought or felt. He simply listened. Bonny's lips pressed into a thin line as he continued. "When your Commanding Officer, General Gray, extended his... rather generous offer, I'll admit we were surprised. We're not in the habit of turning away resources, Major, especially in these times." He began to pace, the paper still in his hand, though his attention was wholly on Aubrey now. "But let me be perfectly clear." He stopped abruptly, standing mere inches away from Aubrey, his chin tilted upward to meet the Major's piercing blue eyes. The tension in the air was palpable as Bonny's voice dropped, steel lacing every word. "This project—Project X-75—if I catch even a hint that this is some sort of biological weapon, I won't hesitate. I'll shut it down immediately. Do you understand me, Major?" Bonny's eyes searched Aubrey's face, waiting, daring him to flinch, to reveal something—anything. But Aubrey remained silent, his presence unyielding, like a mountain weathering a storm.

Chapter 17
14:05 hours, July 30th 2024, West Toffs, Norfolk

Aubrey's boots crunched over the dirt track, each step deliberate, his breath shallow and quick. The dry, dusty earth beneath his feet seemed to groan with every movement, as though it, too, was aware of the danger that trailed close behind him. The sun hung high in the sky, relentless and burning, casting a warm golden light across the landscape. Its rays slanted through the leaves of the trees that lined the path, painting intricate patterns of light and shadow on the ground. The shadows shifted with the breeze, fluid and ever-changing, like ghostly figures moving just out of sight.

A few clouds drifted lazily in the sky, their edges tinged with the softest pinks and blues, unaware—or perhaps indifferent—to the storm that raged within Aubrey's chest. He could feel the sweat beading at the back of his neck, the weight of the sun pressing down on him. It should have been a peaceful scene—serene, even—but to Aubrey, every element of the landscape was a reminder of the peril that pursued him. He could feel eyes on him. Not literal eyes—those were further down the path—but the sensation was real. Like a hunter's gaze lingering, waiting for its prey to make the smallest of mistakes. Aubrey's instincts screamed at him to stay alert, to move carefully, to leave no trace. He knew he was being hunted.

The wind whispered in his ears, but the sound of his own heartbeat drowned it out. His breath came in shallow gasps, quick and ragged, though he forced himself to remain as silent as the shadow he had become. Every step, every movement counted. He was keenly aware of the rhythm of his body—the slight rustle of his clothes, the faintest scuff of his boots against the track, the quick glances he threw over his shoulder. One wrong move, one moment of hesitation, and he could be detected. He scanned the trees around him, his eyes darting between the dappled patches of sunlight and the darkened pockets of shade where an enemy might hide.

He avoided the bright open areas where the sunlight hit hardest, knowing that he would be an easy target. The shadows offered him cover, but only if he moved carefully, deliberately, like a predator on the prowl. Aubrey's mind raced with calculations, running scenarios of escape through his thoughts—each one flawed, each one a potential risk.

The sound of birds calling in the distance was deafening in its silence, the only other noise to break the tension in the air. Aubrey kept moving, his posture rigid, his body coiled like a spring ready to snap. It was the kind of heightened awareness that only came when survival was at stake. The path ahead seemed to stretch on forever, yet it felt as if time itself had slowed, stretching each moment into eternity. A distant noise made his heart skip a beat—the faintest rustle of a branch snapping underfoot. He froze mid-step, holding his breath, his body taut with readiness. But the sound didn't come again. His muscles relaxed ever so slightly, though his vigilance never wavered. The feeling that someone—or something—was still close behind him clung to him like a second skin.

In the distance, Aubrey spotted the small figure of a boy, his legs pumping furiously as he pedalled a beat-up bike down the winding road. The child's laughter rang out in the open air, a sound full of innocence, as he zipped along without a care, unaware of the dark presence trailing him. Aubrey's heart clenched at the carefree joy in the boy's voice, a stark contrast to the tension that coiled in his own chest. He paused, crouching low behind the thick trunks of the trees, his breath shallow. Every muscle in his body was taut, his senses stretched tight like a bowstring, ready to snap. The boy's voice echoed through the air, each note full of freedom and life, oblivious to the threat lurking just behind him. Aubrey kept his distance, the rustling of leaves underfoot barely noticeable as he shifted his weight. His gaze never left the boy, his eyes narrowing as he gauged the child's every movement.

Aubrey's grip tightened on the hilt of his knife, the cold steel comforting in his hand. He was no stranger to stalking. No stranger to being hunted, either. But something about the boy's innocent joy made him hesitate. For just a moment, his pulse quickened, not from fear, but something darker—a deep, gnawing reminder of what he had lost and what he was forced to become.

He pushed the thought aside, focusing on the task at hand. Stay focused, he told himself. The boy's laughter echoed again, louder this time, as the child pedalled harder, the wheels of the bike spinning faster. Aubrey followed, a shadow on the outskirts of the scene, his steps deliberate, his body moving with an eerie calmness. He couldn't afford to let his guard down. Not now. Not when he was so close. The farmhouse was just ahead, and if he could stay out of sight for a few more moments, he could slip into the shadows and find somewhere to hide until the dark sky returned.

The boy swerved suddenly; veering left down a narrow path that Aubrey had not noticed before. It was an old dirt lane, overgrown with weeds and barely visible under the thick canopy of trees. The path was a natural divider between the open road and the property, a space that offered the boy some cover. Aubrey hesitated for a split second. It was a risk to follow so closely—there was nowhere to hide now, no trees to shelter behind—but he was too close to turn back. He had come too far. With barely a second's pause, he moved quickly, his pace quickening as he darted from tree to tree, keeping to the shadows. He moved like a phantom, the trees his only refuge. The boy didn't notice him. He was too busy navigating the narrow path, his focus entirely on the way ahead. Aubrey's eyes were fixed on the boy, calculating the distance, watching his every move. The gap between them was closing.

As they neared the farmhouse, Aubrey saw the front gate come into view, the old wrought-iron structure rusted with age. He had to be careful now—he was within range of the house. The boy reached the gate and slowed, coming to a stop. Aubrey crouched low behind a thick hedge, his chest tight, waiting. Just as the boy nudged the gate open and began to pedal through, a woman's voice called out from inside the house, sharp and commanding, though tinged with warmth. "Jack Orchard, come in for dinner!"

The voice carried through the open air, unmistakable in its affection, yet firm, like a mother's call that brooked no argument. Aubrey's heart skipped a beat as he watched the boy turn his head in response, the sound of his mother's voice still lingering in the air. Jack turned and pedalled toward the house, the door opening before him. Aubrey kept still, not daring to move. He could see the child's small figure vanish through the door, the creak of the old wooden frame echoing softly as it closed behind him. The house was quiet again, the outside world still for the briefest of moments. Aubrey's eyes locked on the shut door. His pulse raced. Now, he thought. Now's my chance.

He knew his time was short. If the boy's mother saw him, if anyone in the house caught sight of him, it would all be over. Everything he had worked for, everything he had endured, would unravel in an instant. The boy had vanished inside, but the house was still a fortress. He had to get closer. He needed to see the layout of the building, to figure out the best place to lay low. But he couldn't risk the mother hearing him. Aubrey knew that if he was detected here, even for a moment, his chances of escape would dwindle to nothing. He would have to move quickly, with precision.

The breeze picked up slightly, rustling the trees, but Aubrey remained motionless, waiting for the right moment. The warmth of the sun on his back was a stark contrast to the coldness that gripped his gut. The house loomed ahead, its peeling white paint and crooked shutters standing in stark contrast to the peaceful serenity it presented. It looked like the perfect home—a family tucked inside, safe and secure. But Aubrey knew better. There was no safety here. There never had been. Aubrey shifted his weight, the dirt crunching softly beneath him. He would wait. A few moments longer. Time was on his side—for now. But once the night fell, there would be no more shadows to hide in. He had to act fast. No mistakes.

With a quick glance around to make sure no one was watching, Aubrey slipped silently into the woods that surrounded the farmhouse, his movements swift and fluid as he melted into the dense thicket. The tall trees and thick underbrush offered him a sense of security, a temporary sanctuary. The rustling leaves above his head masked any sound he might make, and the tang of damp earth filled his nostrils as he carefully navigated through the undergrowth. His footsteps were light, barely a whisper on the forest floor, but his mind was sharp, alert to every shift of the wind, every crack of a twig underfoot. He knew how quickly danger could come. The large barn came into view at the far end of the property, standing tall against the pale sky. It was an old structure, its timbers weathered by time, but it had an undeniable presence.

Aubrey paused for a moment, his eyes narrowing as he assessed his surroundings. The barn seemed like the perfect place to wait. It was far enough from the house to remain unseen, but close enough to keep an eye on the family. He needed somewhere to retreat to until darkness fell—until the night cloaked him once again and made him invisible. The idea of being lost in the shadows was comforting, a familiar feeling. The stillness of the woods pressed in around him, thick and heavy. Silence reigned, but in that silence, there was an underlying tension. Aubrey could feel it deep in his bones. It was the quiet before a storm, the calm that made his senses buzz with anticipation. His breath slowed as he crouched, watching the farmhouse, watching for any movement, any sign that he had been detected. But the house remained peaceful, the windows dark and uninviting, the quiet hum of life within just out of reach.

After a few moments of observation, Aubrey made his move. He crouched low and moved with careful deliberation around the side of the house, keeping to the shadows. The barn loomed closer now, but as he passed a window, his eyes caught a glimpse of movement inside. Through the glass, he could see the boy and his mother. They were setting the dinner table together, the soft glow of the fading afternoon sun casting a warm, golden light on their figures. The boy's laughter echoed faintly from within, a sound so innocent and carefree that it made Aubrey's heart clench with something he couldn't quite place. A longing, perhaps. A yearning for a life that had long since slipped from his grasp. A normal life. A family. It seemed so distant now, something he could never return to. He didn't belong in that world anymore. He couldn't. But as he watched them, a part of him wondered what it might have been like to stay hidden away, to live without the shadow of violence hanging over him. Aubrey quickly tore his eyes away from the window. The last thing he needed was to get distracted, to let his emotions cloud his focus.

The heavy barn door creaking as he entered. The smell of dust, old hay, and aged wood filled the air—familiar, yet unsettling. The barn had a certain emptiness to it, as though it had been forgotten, left behind in the rush of time. Aubrey's muscles ached from the constant tension, but he didn't let himself rest for long. Not yet. He found a quiet corner, hidden from view, and sank down to sit on the cool, hard ground. His back pressed against the barn's wooden walls, and he exhaled slowly, trying to push the weight of his thoughts aside. His body was exhausted from the constant vigilance, but his mind refused to settle. His grip on the knife in his hand tightened, the cold steel a constant reminder of his purpose.

The barn was quiet, save for the occasional sound of small feet scurrying across the floor. The barn rats were always the first to seek shelter, always the first to return after the sun had gone down. Aubrey tensed. The scurrying grew louder, closer. He froze, his hand stilling over the knife's handle. His instincts, honed over years of survival, took over as he scanned the shadows for any movement. The rustling stopped for a moment, and then—a quick flicker of movement. Aubrey's eyes narrowed as he saw the rat dart across the floor, its small body sleek and fast, its beady eyes gleaming in the dim light. The creature was bold, hungry, moving with a purpose. Aubrey's reflexes were sharper than most—too sharp. Before he could even think, his knife was in his hand, and in one smooth motion, he drove it into the rat's side.

The creature squealed, its small body thrashing violently as it tried to escape, but Aubrey's grip on the knife was firm. He twisted the blade, silencing the rat with a final, swift movement. The barn fell back into stillness as the rat's body went limp. Aubrey wiped the blade clean on his sleeve, his eyes flicking to the small carcass at his feet. He hadn't planned on the kill, hadn't expected it, but survival was a way of life now, and that meant making use of everything, no matter how small. Aubrey hesitated for a moment, the warmth of the fresh kill in his hand. The raw meat. He hadn't eaten since the morning, and his stomach twisted with hunger. He looked at the rat again, his mind already pushing past the thought of disgust. It was survival. Nothing more. Nothing less.

He knelt down, his hands steady as he began to peel back the skin, exposing the pale, tender flesh beneath. His fingers worked quickly, efficiently, years of experience guiding his hands. He didn't think about what he was doing. He just did. The taste of raw meat was familiar to him, an old companion he had learned to accept. Aubrey took a bite, the tough flesh filling his mouth, gritty and gamey. It wasn't much, but it would keep him going for now. Survival was never about comfort. It was about getting by, moment by moment, doing whatever it took to stay alive.

The rat's body in his hands was a reminder of what he had become. What he had been forced to become. He closed his eyes for just a moment, his grip tightening on the creature, and then, with a sharp breath, he focused again. He couldn't afford to get lost in these thoughts. Not now. Not when there was still so much to do. The night was coming. And with it, the shadows would once again swallow him whole.

Suddenly, the barn door creaked open, the sound sharp in the otherwise quiet stillness of the evening. Aubrey froze, every muscle in his body locking into place. The knife remained gripped tightly in one hand, the cold metal cool against his palm. In his other hand, he clutched the still-warm rat, its lifeless form a grim reminder of his survival. His breath caught in his throat as the figure in the doorway became clear.

A small boy, no older than seven or eight, stood in the doorway, his eyes wide with innocent curiosity. The fading sunlight framed his small form, casting long shadows behind him. He looked nothing like Aubrey, not in the way that mattered. The boy's face was open, unguarded, and full of the kind of wonder that Aubrey hadn't seen in a long time. The boy's gaze darted around the barn, taking in the dimness, the strange, unsettling quiet of it all. "Have you seen my dad?" the boy asked, his voice high-pitched and laced with concern. Aubrey's heart skipped a beat at question.

Aubrey's grip on the rat tightened involuntarily. The boy's innocent question hit him harder than he expected. He could hear the plea in the child's voice, the worry that came with the absence of a beloved pet. For a split second, Aubrey's mind drifted. He thought of a time long ago, a time before everything had unravelled, before survival had become his sole purpose. But that life was gone now, lost to the years and the choices he had made.

He shook his head slowly. The boy's brow furrowed slightly, a mix of confusion and concern washing over his face. Aubrey remained still, the rat still clutched in his hand, his other fingers curled around the knife's hilt, ready. Always ready. Then, from behind the boy, the sound of a man's voice rang out sharply, slicing through the silence. "Jack! Get away from there!" The boy flinched at the sound of the shout, his wide eyes snapping toward the voice, then back to the barn. Aubrey didn't wait. His instincts kicked in. He backed into the deeper shadows of the barn, his body melting into the darkness, his breath slow and steady. The knife remained clenched in his hand, though his grip loosened slightly. He knew the man would be there soon.

The boy hesitated for a moment, looking back toward the barn as if sensing something was wrong, but then he turned and began to run, his small legs moving quickly across the grass. The thudding of his footsteps was heavy in the quiet, a sound that would surely draw attention. "Dad, there's a man in the barn!" the boy yelled, his voice full of fear and urgency. Aubrey's heart pounded in his chest, a steady thrum of adrenaline that spurred him to move silently, retreating deeper into the shadows, into the farthest corner of the barn. He crouched low, his muscles tense, waiting for the inevitable confrontation. He could hear the boy's footsteps fade as he ran toward the house, but now, it was the man's voice that cut through the air. "Get inside with your mother, Jack!" The man's tone was commanding, no room for disobedience, and Aubrey could hear the panic laced in his voice, the fear for his son evident.

The boy's small feet pounded across the yard, racing toward the house. Aubrey's eyes tracked him, watching as the boy reached the front door. Julie, the boy's mother, was waiting there, her figure a silhouette in the doorway. As the boy reached her, she ushered him inside quickly, slamming the door shut with a finality that echoed in the stillness of the yard. The sound seemed louder than it should have been, and Aubrey's heart rate quickened, his senses heightened. His chance to slip away was slipping by with each passing second. A few moments of silence passed, and then the man's voice rose again, this time louder, more urgent. Aubrey could hear the unmistakable click of a rifle being readied, and then the unmistakable growl of a command. "Get out here!" Andrew shouted, his voice laced with anger and fear. Aubrey's muscles tensed further, and he shifted slightly, trying to keep himself hidden in the deep shadows of the barn. His eyes darted toward the door, measuring his options. The man was right outside, the rifle aimed directly at the barn. Aubrey could feel the weight of it, the barrel pointing in his direction, even though the man hadn't yet seen him.

Andrew's voice rang out again, the final words carried with an almost desperate force. "I've got a gun!" Aubrey's pulse surged in his throat, the cold metal of his knife suddenly a poor match for the rifle that was poised to strike. The man was serious—he wasn't going to back down. Aubrey's mind raced, calculating, assessing. He had a decision to make, and he needed to make it fast. The barn door was wide enough that it allowed a sliver of light to pierce through the darkness, but it was also a trap. He couldn't stay here for long, not with the man right outside, gun in hand. His escape routes were limited, but his reflexes were sharp. He could hear the man's footsteps, the crunch of boots on the dry earth as Andrew took his position. The tension in the air was thick, suffocating. Aubrey knew one thing for certain: He wasn't going down without a fight. The shadows in the barn were his only allies now. Time was running out. The door was already beginning to swing open again. Aubrey needed to act. Fast.

Aubrey moved with a speed fuelled by instinct, his pulse racing as the weight of the situation pressed down on him. Without a second thought, he threw his body forward, bursting through one of the barn's old wooden panels. The impact was deafening, a splintering crack that echoed across the yard, sending chunks of rotting wood flying in all directions. For a split second, the world seemed to pause. But then came the sharp report of a rifle—a sudden, violent BANG—followed by the acrid scent of gunpowder and the smoke that billowed from the barrel. The force of the bullet slammed into the barn, sending sharp splintered fragments of wood flying in all direction. Aubrey staggered, his body jerking with the shock of the hit. Blood began to seep from the wound, dark and warm, staining his top, but there was no time to stop.

He gritted his teeth, feeling the searing pain spread through his shoulder, but he didn't falter. The sound of the rifle echoing in his ears only pushed him forward. He sprinted, his feet pounding against the ground, each stride an act of defiance against the agony tearing through his body. His heart hammered in his chest, the rhythm frantic, but steady. The sound of the man's voice erupted behind him in fury, calling for him to stop, but Aubrey didn't look back. There was no time to reason, no room for hesitation. He had to get away— he had to keep moving.

Gunshots followed in quick succession, each blast ringing out like a death knell. One bullet whizzed past him; the sharp whistle of its passage so close that Aubrey could feel the rush of air against his skin. The splintering of wood echoed in his ears, his mind flashing with images of the barn's walls breaking apart. Another bullet narrowly missed him, the sting of near impact making him wince. Pain flared in his shoulder as blood seeped down his arm, but he pushed the sensation aside. The urgency to escape swallowed everything else.

Aubrey's legs burned with exhaustion, but he didn't slow down. The barn loomed behind him, and he needed to put as much distance between himself and the man with the rifle as possible. Every instinct in his body screamed to keep running, to keep moving, until he was lost in the cover of the trees. The sound of the man's heavy footsteps echoed behind him, growing louder as the man chased after him, but Aubrey didn't let it break his focus. He wasn't done yet. As he rounded the corner of the barn, Aubrey stumbled slightly, his footing momentarily unsteady. He gritted his teeth, his breath ragged, but he kept moving. His escape was so close, the woods just ahead, offering the cover he so desperately needed. His vision blurred for a moment as pain coursed through his shoulder, but he forced his legs to keep going, to push past the weakness threatening to overtake him. He was almost there.

Behind him, the man's footfalls grew closer, the sound of boots striking the ground heavy with determination. Aubrey could hear the man's breath, sharp and desperate as he closed in. But Aubrey was already rounding the corner of the barn, weaving through the shadows as his body carried him towards the trees. Every instinct in his body told him to keep running, to get deeper into the cover of the forest where he would be harder to track. He could already hear the wind rustling the leaves, the forest welcoming him like an old friend, ready to hide him from pursuit. The man was still coming. Aubrey could feel it. The moment of confrontation was almost upon him. He could hear the rifle's stock hitting the man's shoulder as he moved, the sound of breathing quickening, the pace of pursuit relentless. Aubrey's heart raced faster, but he didn't slow. He couldn't.

The man rounded the corner of the barn, his breath coming in shallow gasps. For a moment, he froze, his eyes scanning the barn's weathered walls, tracing the bloodstains on the rotting wood. Aubrey's trail was clear now—red droplets marking his path like a grim breadcrumb trail leading deeper into the woods. The man stepped forward, raising his rifle again, his eyes darting across the ground as he searched for any sign of movement, any sign of where Aubrey had gone.

The man's gaze shifted from the blood trail to the dark, open space where the woods began. He took a cautious step forward, his rifle still raised, but there was no movement, no hint of where Aubrey had disappeared. The woods were thick with shadows, the evening light just starting to fade, and all the man could see now was the dense thicket stretching out before him. Aubrey had been here, and there was no doubt that he had bled. But now… now, the only trace of him was the faint, disappearing trail of crimson that wound deeper into the woods.

The man's frustration was palpable. His fingers tightened around the rifle, his gaze narrowing as he scanned the area once more. He could still feel the urgency, the need to finish what had started, but Aubrey was already lost. His presence had melted into the forest, swallowed by the thick undergrowth and the encroaching night. The man raised his gun one final time, the tip of the barrel trembling slightly, but Aubrey was gone.

With one last glance at the bloodstains, the man let out a frustrated, bitter curse. He could feel the adrenaline still pumping in his veins, but it wasn't enough to push him further into the woods. He was too late. Aubrey had already vanished into the shadows, a ghost in the night. The man stood there for a moment, the rifle in his hands heavy and useless, the echoes of his pursuit fading into the thickening dark. Aubrey had escaped. For now. As then walked back to the farmhouse, he shouted at Julie who watching out of the window with little Jack, "better call the police honey."

Chapter 18
20:59 hours, July 30th 2024,
Great Palgrave, Norfolk

The black jumper clung to him, damp and heavy, as he sat on the edge of the bath. His movements were deliberate but strained, each small gesture sending a flicker of pain through his torso. With a grimace, he tugged one arm free of the sleeve, then the other, wincing as the coarse fabric brushed against the wound just below his shoulder blade. The gash was small, barely the size of a penny, but the blood told another story. It streaked across his chest in vivid, angry lines, mingling with the grey hairs and pale, weathered skin, painting a grotesque mosaic of red and white.

He reached behind awkwardly, his fingers probing the tender flesh at the back of his shoulder. The pain flared, sharp and electric, but he ignored it. Bringing his hand back in front of his face, he scrutinized his fingertips—clean. Whatever had pierced him was still lodged deep inside. The thought gnawed at him. Infection was a certainty if he didn't act soon. His jaw clenched as he weighed his next steps. Pushing himself upright, he steadied against the sink for a moment, his breathing shallow but steadying. He glanced at his reflection in the tarnished bathroom mirror. The sight stopped him. He hardly recognized the man staring back. The sagging lines of his face, the haggard eyes ringed with exhaustion, the streak of blood that had dried like war paint on his cheek—he looked like someone battling a ghost only he could see.

The moment passed, and he forced himself to move. Opening the cabinet above the sink, he scanned the shelves with impatient eyes. Toothpaste. Cotton buds. A toothbrush, no, two. Soap, still in its pristine box. A bottle of shampoo that hadn't been touched in weeks. His gaze landed on a small white box tucked at the back. He grabbed it, the cardboard scraping roughly against his skin as he fumbled to check the label: Naproxen.

He tore the box open with his teeth, spitting out a shred of cardboard, his movements swift and mechanical. Four tablets tumbled into his palm. Without hesitation, he tossed them into his mouth and bent over, drinking straight from the faucet. The icy water jolted his senses, cutting through the fog of his growing panic. He swallowed, his throat burning slightly, and straightened up. For a moment, he stood still, the sound of the dripping tap filling the silence. He placed both hands on the sink, gripping tightly, and exhaled through his nose. He wasn't done yet—not by a long shot. Whatever had struck him was still inside, and getting it out wasn't just a necessity. It was survival.

Wiping the droplets of water from his beard with a quick swipe of his forearm, he reached for the small, battered box of table salt perched on the edge of the bath. The cardboard was soft and worn from moisture, and the top flap gave way with a single tug. He tipped the box experimentally, a few coarse granules spilling into his palm. It would do.

Bracing himself, he turned to the mirror again, his reflection a grim partner in the task ahead. With his uninjured arm, he reached back awkwardly, his fingers fumbling to find the torn skin just below his shoulder blade. The pain flared instantly, a bright stab that made him hiss through clenched teeth, but he didn't stop. His fingers dug into the surrounding skin, pressing hard as he worked to force the embedded shard out. The muscles in his arm trembled with the effort.

He shifted slightly, craning his neck to catch the progress in the mirror. A flicker of relief mingled with revulsion as he saw it—the tip of the splinter, a dark, jagged sliver of timber, pushing its way stubbornly through his torn flesh. Blood beaded around it, the sight both fascinating and grotesque. With a final press, he forced the shard free, and it dropped to the floor with a faint tick. He stared at it briefly—tiny, inconsequential-looking, but the cause of so much agony—before shaking it from his mind. Turning back to the box of salt, he tilted it again, this time letting the granules spill freely into his palm, creating a small mound. They sparkled in the dim light like shards of crushed ice, innocent in appearance but about to serve a brutal purpose. Without hesitation, he slapped the handful of salt directly onto the open wound.

The effect was instantaneous. A shockwave of searing pain surged through him, sharp enough to take his breath away. His muscles locked, and his vision blurred for a moment, but he didn't flinch. Didn't make a sound. Instead, he bore down, his grip on the edge of the sink tightening until his knuckles turned white. The salt burned like fire, digging into the exposed tissue, purging whatever filth might have lingered in the wound. He let it sit, counting under his breath, each second an eternity.

When he finally straightened, his chest was heaving, sweat slicking his brow and neck. Blood mixed with the salt on his shoulder, a messy concoction of grit and crimson, but it didn't matter. The wound was clean now—or at least clean enough. He glanced at the shard of wood on the floor one more time, as if daring it to mock him, before reaching for a towel to press against his shoulder. The pain was still there, gnawing and persistent, but it was a pain he could work with. A pain that meant he was still alive.

He sat in silence, the soft hum of the bathroom fan blending with the faint drip of the faucet, a rhythm so subtle it might have gone unnoticed if not for the stillness. The air smelled faintly of soap and rust, a dampness clinging to the walls that seemed to amplify the quiet. As he leaned back against the cold tiles, the weight of the moment pressed on him, but so did something else—something less immediate but far more profound. The ambience of the small, cramped bathroom tugged at a memory he hadn't visited in years, one so deeply buried it startled him with its sudden clarity.

It was the night he broke out of the prison.

The details came back to him in fragmented flashes at first, like staring through the shifting haze of a dream. The clang of the metal gates, the relentless rhythm of boots against concrete, the biting cold of the night air as he slipped through the final gap in the perimeter fence. He could still feel the raw scrape of barbed wire against his hands, the burn of adrenaline surging through his veins as the blaring alarms faded into the distance.

In the silence of the bathroom, his mind began piecing it together, step by step. How he had moved with a singular focus, using every ounce of cunning and instinct to stay ahead of the search teams. How he had slipped into the shadows of the dense woods that stretched for miles, trusting the cover of darkness to shield him from the floodlights and dogs. He remembered the hunger gnawing at his stomach, the unrelenting ache in his legs as he pushed forward, night after night. The world outside those prison walls was vast and ruthless, but he had survived by becoming something smaller, less noticeable—a ghost slipping between the cracks of a society too large to notice him.

He calculated his current position carefully, retracing the mental map he'd drawn during those frantic early days. Forty miles. He was less than forty miles from the coastline now. That realization hit him with a strange mixture of relief and unease. It wasn't the distance itself—it was the weight of how far he'd come. To be this close to his goal after all this time felt surreal, almost fragile, like speaking it aloud might shatter the delicate balance he'd been walking. Getting here had been nothing short of a miracle. No transport, no money, no technology—he had avoided every modern convenience, not out of principle but necessity. Each was a tether, a traceable thread back to him, and that couldn't be allowed. His success had relied on simplicity, on the discipline to trust his own two feet and the knowledge he carried in his head. Every decision had been deliberate: which roads to avoid, which towns to skirt, which streams to follow when water was scarce. The discipline was brutal, but it was the only way. He couldn't afford to leave a single breadcrumb for those who hunted him.

He thought of the coastline, the vast expanse of water that would greet him, its horizon a promise of freedom. It had felt impossibly distant when he first escaped, little more than a whisper of hope to keep him moving forward. But now, it was tangible. The thought brought a faint, almost imperceptible curl to his lips. Not a smile— something smaller, something earned. The distant memory faded, slipping back into the recesses of his mind as the present reasserted itself. The bathroom seemed smaller now, more stifling, the dripping faucet a reminder that he couldn't stay here long. He had miles to cover, a plan to finish. But as he stood and steadied himself, the memory of that first night clung to him like a shield—a reminder of what he was capable of, and how much he had already endured to get here.

Since intercepting X-75 in Cockfosters, Aubrey had become a ghost. The Grey Man and his network of operatives were relentless, but he'd managed to stay ahead of them, slipping through the cracks by keeping a low profile and sticking to a simple rule: trust no one, leave no trail. Jobs that paid cash were his lifeline. They weren't glamorous—odd jobs on construction sites, even unloading crates at the docks when the foreman wasn't asking questions—but they were enough to keep him moving. Each day was a careful balancing act of blending in and staying invisible.

The night of the mission replayed in his mind like a film on an endless loop. The X-75—the "tube," as he'd come to call it—was smaller than he'd imagined, no bigger than a flashlight, and deceptively plain. Its appearance belied its value. Nations would kill for it; corporations would start wars over it. Aubrey had known the moment it was in his hands that it was both his salvation and his curse.

He'd taken the tube directly to the underground station. Riding the train to the outskirts of London, he had found a graveyard, he'd packed the tube into a bag alongside a few other essentials. There, under cover of night, he buried it in the soft earth beneath a neglected headstone, marked only by a dead vine curling over its face. If anyone came for him—and Aubrey knew they would—it was better to meet them empty-handed. If caught with the tube, his fate was sealed: torture, interrogation, and ultimately, execution. Without it, they might let him die quickly. Or, if luck held, they'd find nothing and be left with questions he would never answer.

A week passed in a blur of exhaustion and vigilance. Aubrey scraped by on odd jobs, earning just enough to eat and keep a roof over his head. The construction site job had been the easiest so far, though "easy" was relative. Compared to his mission and the desperate hours that followed, moving bricks and mixing mortar was nothing. His size and rugged appearance ensured the other labourers gave him a wide berth. Nobody wanted to tangle with the quiet, pale man who kept to himself. That suited Aubrey fine; he had no interest in forging connections that might unravel under scrutiny.

The day he was arrested caught him completely off guard. Fevered and weakened, he'd taken refuge in a derelict building on the outskirts of the city. The cold concrete floor was unyielding, but he'd scavenged enough cardboard and old newspapers to create a crude bed. His body betrayed him as sickness took hold, his usually sharp instincts dulled by fever dreams and the ache of infection spreading through his wound. He drifted in and out of consciousness, the chill of the room blending with the heat burning under his skin. It was there, amidst the wreckage of his fragile sanctuary, that they found him. Not Bonny's men, nor the authorities—at least, not at first. Instead, it was three middle-aged urban explorers, the kind who revelled in the decay of forgotten places. At first, they thought he was a tramp, another unfortunate soul swallowed by the city's indifference. They might have left him there had it not been for the blood.

One of them spotted the stains on his shirt and the dried streaks on his arms. Alarm bells went off. They hesitated for a moment, whispering among themselves, but concern—or perhaps curiosity— overrode caution. After a few prods failed to rouse him, one of them made the call. The police arrived within minutes, dragging Aubrey from his fevered haze into the harsh reality of flashing lights and cold steel cuffs. As he was hauled into the back of a squad car, his mind raced through possibilities. They had no idea who he was— not yet. But once they started asking questions, the tenuous anonymity he'd clung to would unravel. And then, inevitably, the Grey Man would find him. Aubrey's fevered brain latched onto one thought: he had to escape, and he had to do it fast.

Three days later, Aubrey awoke in a hospital bed, disoriented and weak. The spotlights overhead buzzed faintly, their cold glare making the white room feel sterile and hostile. His wrists ached, and when he tried to move, he realized why: heavy steel handcuffs bit into his skin, chaining him to the bed. He blinked hard, his head throbbing, as the fragmented memories of his fevered arrest flooded back.

A plain-clothed Officer sat in a chair beside him, leaning forward with a notepad balanced on his knee. The man was middle-aged, with thinning hair and a gut that strained against his cheap shirt. His badge hung loosely around his neck, the only indication he was law enforcement. Aubrey barely heard the first few words as the man began to speak, his tone measured but insistent. It wasn't until the name "Clapham Common" cut through the fog in his brain that Aubrey's senses sharpened. "Five bodies in total," the detective said, sliding glossy photos across the tray table in front of him. "One by the canal, four scattered across Clapham Common. Each one mutilated. Care to explain?"

Aubrey's eyes flicked to the photos against his will. The images were brutal. Torn flesh, twisted limbs, lifeless eyes staring at nothing. He didn't flinch, didn't let his expression betray even a flicker of recognition, though the implications hit him like a hammer. Someone had been busy framing him, and whoever it was had gone to great lengths to make sure he'd take the fall. He shifted his gaze to the Officer, not bothering to respond. Silence was his best weapon now. Anything he said could be twisted and used against him. The detective frowned, leaning closer. "Come on, we know you're involved. The witnesses might be sparse, but the evidence isn't. Blood on your clothes matches one of the victims. You've got priors, don't you? What is it? Assault? And now this. It's not looking good, mate."

Aubrey tuned him out. His attention drifted to the room around him. Two armed guards stood stationed on one side of the door, their hands resting on the grips of their holstered pistols. Through the small window in the door, he caught a glimpse of four more Officers patrolling the hallway beyond. His eyes dropped to his body, scanning his restraints. Both wrists cuffed to the rails of the bed, and his ankles secured just as tightly. He was trapped, completely at their mercy.

Two weeks later, the gavel fell, and Aubrey's fate was sealed. The trial had been swift, the outcome inevitable. Despite his refusal to cooperate, the prosecution painted him as a monster—a cold-blooded killer who had eluded capture for too long. The judge handed down four life sentences without the possibility of parole. Wormwood Scrubs would be his new home, and barring a miracle, he would never leave it.

The prison guards wasted no time branding him a threat. His physicality alone set him apart from the general population, and rumours about the gruesome crimes followed him inside the walls like a shadow. Solitary confinement was deemed the safest option— for both him and the other inmates. The cell was small, barely enough space to stretch out, but Aubrey had no intention of wallowing in despair.

The first days in solitary were gruelling. The silence was oppressive, and the walls seemed to close in on him, but he refused to let it break him. Instead, he embraced the isolation, turning inward. His body had grown weak from illness and neglect, but that could be fixed. Every morning, he began his ritual: sets of push-ups, sit-ups, squats, and planks. At first, his muscles screamed in protest, but each day the pain dulled, replaced by a growing sense of power. Soon, he was doing over a thousand push-ups and sit-ups daily, his body transforming into a weapon. The rhythm of his exercises became a meditation, sharpening his mind even as it strengthened his body.

The physical preparation was only the first step. As his strength returned, Aubrey began to think beyond the cell. He replayed every detail of his arrest, his transfer, and the layout of the prison itself, committing it all to memory. He listened to the guards as they made their rounds, noting the patterns of their footsteps, the clink of keys, the moments of silence that hinted at gaps in their patrols. Escape wasn't just a possibility—it was an inevitability. The guards had underestimated him, assuming the walls of solitary could hold him indefinitely. They didn't realize they were giving him time, and time was all he needed.

Aubrey's hands, now calloused and strong, clenched into fists as he stared at the ceiling of his cell. He had been framed, abandoned, and locked away, but he wasn't broken. The guards and the system might think his life was over, but they didn't understand who they were dealing with.

Escape wasn't just the next step. It was his salvation—and his revenge.

***

The car jolted violently as it struck another pothole, tossing its four passengers unceremoniously in their seats. The vehicle's shocks groaned in protest, a sound lost amid the collective mutters and sharp expletives from within. "Bloody hell, Shaheed, watch where you're bloody driving!" barked PC Brian Thorman, his voice tinged with irritation as he braced himself against the dashboard. Behind the wheel, PC Shaheed Iqbal tightened his grip on the steering wheel, his knuckles whitening as he fought to steady the car on the treacherous road. His brow furrowed, and he leaned so far forward that his chin nearly touched the leather-wrapped wheel. "Sorry, mate," he shot back, his tone clipped with concentration. "Hard to focus on this goat track without veering into one of these damn ditches. You want a smoother ride? You're welcome to walk."

Thorman gave him a withering glare out of the corner of his eye but said nothing more, shifting his attention to the endless expanse of country road ahead. The rain-slicked surface gleamed under the hazy moonlight, riddled with dips, cracks, and potholes deep enough to swallow a wheel. Flanking the narrow path on either side were ditches overgrown with reeds and weeds, their dark waters glinting menacingly in the light of the high beams. It was a route designed to fray nerves, and it was doing its job spectacularly.

In the back seat, Sergeant Dave Greggs grunted as his head nearly collided with the window again. "Shaheed, if you hit another one of those, I swear I'm going to sue the council for whiplash," he muttered, gripping the door handle above him with one hand and planting his other firmly on the seat to steady himself. His tone was light, but his face betrayed exhaustion. A twelve-hour shift followed by an unexpected midnight run out to the middle of nowhere was not his idea of a good time. Beside him, DCI Craig sat stiffly, phone pressed to his ear as he tried to maintain a semblance of privacy in the cramped quarters of the car. His voice was low, a near-whisper that barely carried over the sound of the engine and the occasional groans of protest from Greggs. "Yeah," the DCI murmured into the receiver, his tone soft, almost uncharacteristically tender. "I'll be back soon. Love you too."

The call ended as the DCI pocketed the phone with a sigh, his sharp eyes flicking briefly to the rearview mirror to catch Shaheed's reflection. He caught the younger Officer's curious glance and raised an eyebrow in silent warning. Shaheed quickly returned his gaze to the road. Greggs, ever the observant one despite his fatigue, smirked faintly. "Sweet nothings, sir?" he teased, adjusting his grip on the handle as the car hit another small bump. The DCI shot him a sidelong glance, his expression unreadable. "Just ensuring someone knows I'm not dead yet," he replied dryly, brushing imaginary lint from his neatly pressed coat. "Well, give it time," Thorman muttered from the front.

The car rattled on, each passenger settling into their respective discomforts. Outside, the countryside was cloaked in shadow, the occasional silhouette of a tree or the ghostly outline of an abandoned barn flashing by in the headlights. It was the kind of road that felt like it went on forever, looping endlessly into the night. "How much farther?" Greggs asked, breaking the uneasy silence that had fallen over the car. "Couple more miles," Shaheed replied, glancing briefly at the sat-nav mounted to the dashboard. "Assuming this thing's even accurate out here. Signal's dodgy as hell." "Great," Thorman grumbled. "Just what we need. Lost in the middle of nowhere with the world's most aggressive suspension system." "Better lost than ambushed," the DCI said pointedly, his voice cutting through the banter with a quiet authority that immediately silenced the others. The mention of an ambush wasn't lost on anyone. They were heading to a farmstead linked to a string of grisly murders—a place far enough from civilization to make reinforcements a pipe dream.

Shaheed broke the silence after a moment. "Well, if we're lucky, the bloke's as knackered as we are and surrenders without a fight." The DCI didn't respond, his gaze fixed out the window, his mind already running through scenarios. Beside him, Greggs adjusted himself, the leather creaking faintly in the confined space. Thorman sighed heavily, pulling out a packet of mints and popping one into his mouth with a grimace. "Hope for the best, prepare for the worst," the DCI said finally, his tone a quiet admonition. "Classic optimist,"

Greggs quipped, though his smile didn't quite reach his eyes. The car hit another bump, and the entire vehicle shuddered. Shaheed swore under his breath, tightening his grip on the wheel as he guided the car back onto the narrow strip of road. Up ahead, a pair of headlights appeared on the horizon, cutting through the darkness. "Looks like we're not the only ones out here," Thorman muttered.

The shrill ringtone cut through the quiet tension in the car, making everyone flinch. The DCI snatched up the phone, pressing it to his ear with a sense of urgency. "DCI Craig speaking," he said sharply, his voice carrying the no-nonsense tone of someone used to barking orders. He listened for a moment, his expression hardening. "Yes, that's correct... No... Tell them I want the Command Trailer relocated immediately." In the driver's seat, Shaheed glanced in the rearview mirror, his curiosity barely concealed, but he kept his eyes mostly on the twisting, pothole-riddled road ahead. Sergeant Dave Greggs, sitting in the back, turned his head slightly, angling his ear toward the DCI's low voice without making it obvious. The DCI noticed but didn't care; this wasn't a conversation that could be entirely hidden.

"There's no point having our support staff a hundred miles away," the DCI continued, his tone clipped. "Yes, East Anglia. That's where he was last seen... No, I'll make the decision once I have all the facts. Give me an hour." He terminated the call with a sharp press of his thumb, letting the phone drop into the inner pocket of his jacket. For a moment, he simply stared out the window, the rhythmic thrum of the tires on the rough road filling the silence. He sighed heavily, the weight of his thoughts evident in the set of his shoulders. He didn't need to turn around to know the others in the car were waiting, their unspoken questions hanging thick in the air. Finally, he broke the silence. "Right, lads," he began, his voice steady but laced with an edge that made the others sit up straighter. "As you've probably guessed, I've just instructed Bravo Charlie One to relocate and join us. There's no sense in having our team miles away from the action."

He paused, his jaw tightening as his gaze drifted back out the window. "Problem is..." He trailed off, leaving the sentence unfinished, his reflection in the glass as still as a statue. Greggs, never one for patience, frowned. "Problem is what, sir?" he prodded, his tone carefully neutral but tinged with frustration. The DCI didn't respond immediately. Instead, he let his silence draw out, the tension in the car thickening with every passing second. Finally, he spoke again, his voice quieter, almost reflective.

"Problem is," he said, turning his gaze toward Greggs and Thorman, "this man—if you can even call him that—isn't playing by the same rules we are. Every move we've made, he's been three steps ahead. Every lead we've chased, he's burned to ash. And now, he's right here, in our backyard." Shaheed let out a low whistle, his knuckles tightening around the steering wheel. "You think he knows we're coming?" The DCI nodded grimly. "I don't just think it. I know it. And he'll be ready. The question is whether we are."

The car fell silent again, the mood inside shifting from tense to grim. Outside, the countryside rolled by in shadowy shapes, the rain-soaked fields stretching endlessly toward the horizon. Greggs finally broke the silence, his voice heavy. "If he knows we're coming, Sir, what's the play? Do we wait for backup or go in hard?" The DCI's lips pressed into a thin line, his mind already weighing the options. "We'll assess when we get there," he said firmly. "This isn't a man you corner lightly. If we push too hard, he'll vanish again—or worse." Thorman, who had been uncharacteristically quiet, finally spoke up. "Or worse?"

The DCI's gaze met his, cold and unyielding. "Or worse, he'll start stacking more bodies." The car rattled over another bump, the vehicle lurching as if in agreement. No one spoke after that, each of them retreating into their thoughts. The only sounds were the low hum of the engine as they closed the distance to what promised to be a deadly confrontation.

Ten minutes later, Shaheed glanced down at the dashboard, the soft glow of the fuel gauge catching his attention. "Uh, excuse me, sir," he said hesitantly, breaking the thick silence in the car. "Sorry to interrupt, but we're down to a quarter tank. Might need to top up at the next station if that's alright." He flicked his eyes to the rearview mirror, catching the DCI's sharp gaze. After a moment's consideration, the DCI gave a curt nod. "Do it." Shaheed refocused on the road, his hands tightening on the wheel. As the beams of the headlights cut through the night, a structure began to take shape on the horizon—a squat, unassuming building perched alone on the edge of the fields. Its illuminated sign flickered faintly in the distance, and as they drew closer, one by one, the lights inside winked out.

"Odd," Shaheed murmured, narrowing his eyes.

The building loomed larger as they approached. The sign hanging above the door read 'Carol's Slap-Up Grill' in bright, bold letters. Shaheed noticed a woman stepping out of the entrance, her figure silhouetted in the dim light spilling from within. She paused for a moment, then turned to pull the door shut behind her, locking it with deliberate care. "Pull in here, Officer," the DCI ordered suddenly, his voice cutting through the quiet. "Here, sir?" Shaheed asked, glancing at the diner and the now-dark windows. "That's right," the DCI replied, a hint of impatience creeping into his tone. As if on cue, his stomach let out an audible growl, and he shifted in his seat as though embarrassed. "Might as well grab something to eat while we're stopped. Wait a moment."

Before anyone could respond, the DCI opened the door and stepped out, his shoes crunching on the gravel parking lot as he approached the woman. She turned at the sound, her keys jingling faintly in her hand. "Sorry, sir," she called, her voice polite but firm. "We're closed for the night. Doors open again at seven in the morning." The DCI held up a hand, his expression calm but insistent. "I'm afraid this isn't just a casual visit," he said, showing her his identification and gesturing back toward the car where the three other Officers were watching from inside. "We're on an official assignment and could really use some hospitality. Perhaps just a quick meal to keep us going?" The woman hesitated, her gaze darting from the DCI to the vehicle. There was a flicker of reluctance in her expression, but after a moment, she sighed and nodded. "Alright," she said, slipping the key back into the lock. "But just a quick one. I've got to be up early." She pushed the door open and stepped back inside, flipping a switch to reignite the lights. The DCI turned to the car, raising a hand to beckon the others. "Looks like dinner's back on the menu," he called.

As the lights buzzed back to life, the warm, slightly greasy ambiance of the diner was revealed—a checkerboard floor scuffed from years of use, faded vinyl booths lining the walls, and a counter adorned with chrome trim that had long since lost its shine. The faint smell of fried food hung in the air, as though the scent had become part of the place itself. The three men climbed out of the car, their boots crunching against the gravel as they made their way inside. They found the DCI already seated in a corner booth, spreading out a weathered map across the table. His expression was unreadable, his focus on the creased paper in front of him as he smoothed it flat with the edge of his hand.

Sergeant Dave Greggs took a step toward the booth, then paused. Glancing over his shoulder at Shaheed and Brian, he gave a quick jerk of his chin. "Go sit at the bar, will you lads? I need a word with the boss in private." "No problem, Sarge," Brian Thorman replied casually, slapping Shaheed lightly on the shoulder. "Come on, rookie. Let's let the grown-ups have their chat." Shaheed grumbled under his breath but followed Brian toward the bar without protest. The counter was clean, though the faded menus behind it spoke of a place that hadn't changed in decades. He perched on one of the stools, its cracked leather cushion squeaking slightly under his weight. Brian took the seat next to him, glancing around the diner with a raised brow.

"Place has got a... vibe," Brian muttered, his eyes drifting toward an old jukebox in the corner. It was silent, but the selection of dusty song titles suggested it hadn't been updated since the '80s. "Yeah," Shaheed replied, his tone dry. "The vibe is 'last stop before nowhere.'" They both chuckled quietly, though their eyes kept darting to the back, where the woman who had let them in had disappeared. Shaheed's fingers tapped against the counter impatiently. "Think she's actually going to serve us something, or is this just for show?" Brian shrugged, leaning back slightly. "Could go either way. She didn't seem thrilled to have company, did she?"

Meanwhile, at the booth, Greggs slid into the seat opposite the DCI, his broad frame making the table feel smaller than it already was. He folded his arms, his expression serious. "Sir," Greggs began, his voice low. "What's the plan? You've got that look—the one you get when you're not telling us everything." The DCI glanced up from the map, his lips twitching in the faintest semblance of a smile. "Do I? Thought I left that back in the car." "Yeah, well, it followed you in," Greggs shot back. "So, what's the deal? What are we walking into?"

The DCI leaned back slightly, his fingers drumming against the table. His eyes scanned the room briefly before returning to the map. "This is our best shot," he said finally. "Intel puts our guy in this region, and the trail's getting cold. Bravo Charlie One's moving into position, but we need to establish a base here before anything else. Greggs frowned, glancing at the map. "You're saying this is home base? Carol's Slap Up Grill?" "For now," the DCI said, folding the map and tucking it back into his pocket. "It's not ideal, but neither is the situation. We need to make the most of what we've got."

Greggs shook his head slightly but didn't argue. Instead, he leaned back in his seat, his gaze drifting toward the bar where Brian and Shaheed were still waiting. "Speaking of what we've got, what about those two? Rookie seems a bit green for this." The DCI's expression darkened slightly, and his voice lowered. "Green or not, we need boots on the ground. We don't have the luxury of picking and choosing right now." Before Greggs could respond, the woman reappeared from the back, her expression a mix of reluctance and resignation. She held a steaming pot of coffee in one hand and a tray of mismatched mugs in the other. "Hope you like caffeine," she said, her tone flat as she approached the bar. Brian gave her a winning smile. "Coffee's a start, love. Got any biscuits to go with it?" She shot him a look that could curdle milk. "You're lucky you're getting this." As she poured, the DCI watched her from the corner of his eye, his mind already working through the next steps. The tension in the room was palpable, but he knew this was just the calm before the storm.

The DCI ran his fingers absently over the creases of the map spread across the table, his brow furrowed in deep concentration. Sergeant Dave Greggs studied his superior for a moment before speaking. "What's really on your mind, sir?" Dave's tone was softer than usual, laced with genuine concern. "I've known you for nearly twenty years, and I've never seen you this distant. As my mum used to say, 'a problem shared is a problem halved'... or something like that."

The DCI looked up, startled from his thoughts. For a moment, his face betrayed a flicker of weariness before it softened into a faint smile. "Sorry, Sargeant. Just been a long few days, that's all." The two men sat in silence for a beat, the quiet hum of the diner's lights filling the void. Outside a muffled rhythm that seemed to echo the weight of the moment. Greggs leaned back slightly, watching the DCI with the unspoken understanding that only years of camaraderie could bring. Their silence was interrupted as the woman returned; her small pink puffer jacket swapped for an even smaller pink apron that barely covered her floral blouse. She approached the table, her notepad and pen ready, though the weariness in her eyes suggested she'd rather be anywhere else. "So," she said briskly, "what can I get you both?"

Dave reached for the menu, flipping it open with a theatrical flourish. He scanned it quickly, his eyes darting over the sparse options. "Tell you what, sweetheart," he said with a warm, almost cheeky grin. "It's late, and you probably want to get home, so why don't you rustle us up a bacon sarnie each? Nice and simple. And…" He glanced over his shoulder toward the bar, where Shaheed and Brian were chatting quietly. "Get Shaheed over there something vegetable-based—he's a vegetarian." The woman raised a sceptical brow, her pen hovering above the pad. "Vegetarian, huh? In a place like this?" Dave chuckled, holding up his hands in mock defence. "Hey, don't shoot the messenger. He's the one that's picky, not me."

Shaking her head with a bemused smile, she tucked the notepad and pen back into her apron. "Alright, bacon for you three, and I'll see what I can dig up for Mr. Rabbit Food over there. Might be a salad if he's lucky." With that, she disappeared into the kitchen, the faint clatter of pans and the hiss of a stovetop coming to life breaking the stillness.

The DCI exhaled slowly, his fingers resuming their idle tracing over the map. Greggs leaned forward slightly; his voice low but firm. "Look, boss, I get that you've got a lot riding on this. But whatever it is you're carrying—whatever's got you staring at that map like it's a bloody Ouija board—you don't have to do it alone.

You know that, right?" The DCI looked up again, meeting Greggs's steady gaze. His lips twitched in something that might've been another smile, but it didn't quite reach his eyes.

Waiting until the diner door swung shut behind the waitress, the DCI leaned forward, lowering his voice as he spread the map wider across the table. He tapped a spot marked with a small circle, just east of a patch of woodland. "Right," he began, his tone brisk but laced with tension. "We know the convict was last seen here, at this farm in West Tofts. The farmer reported catching him trying to break into the barn just after lunctime. Said he managed to get off a shot as the man ran, possibly hit him, but..." the DCI let the sentence hang, his scepticism clear. "Forensics are scouring the area where he was spotted, but you know them—it'll probably take days before anything useful comes back from the lab. We don't have that kind of time."

Sergeant Dave Greggs rubbed his chin thoughtfully, his other hand drifting to his mouth as he started to gnaw on a fingernail, a habit the DCI knew well from years of working together. Dave's eyes scanned the map, and he finally spoke, his voice deliberate and calm. "I think we've got to assume this convict's still on foot," Dave said, spitting the sliver of nail into his palm and flicking it away with practiced ease. "He's avoiding transport, sticking to back roads and less populated areas. Smart move for someone trying to disappear. Means he's not just dangerous, but sharp."

The DCI nodded grimly. "That's exactly what I'm worried about. He's not your average convict. This guy's been trained, and he knows how to stay off the radar. If the farmer's shot didn't hit anything vital—and honestly, I wouldn't bet on it—then he's still a serious threat. To anyone and everyone in his path." Dave frowned, leaning closer to the map. His finger traced a route through the countryside, following a series of dotted lines that marked hiking trails and minor roads. "Alright, so let's say he's moving north, deeper into the rural areas. He's got no transport and no known accomplices. If he's injured, he's going to need a safe spot to patch himself up. That means farms, abandoned buildings, maybe even campsites. Anything off-grid."

The DCI tapped the edge of the table with his pen, a quick rhythm that mirrored his own racing thoughts. "Agreed. But he's also got to eat. The farmer said he hadn't noticed any supplies missing from store. He's not just surviving out there; he's planning. That tells me he's in it for the long haul." Dave grunted, his lips pressing into a thin line. "Great. So, we're dealing with someone who's not just desperate, but disciplined. That complicates things." "It does," the DCI admitted. "And that's why we need to get ahead of him, predict his next move. Bravo Charlie One will be joining us by morning, but until then, it's just us. We can't afford to sit on our hands while this guy stays one step ahead."

Dave smirked faintly, though there was no humour in it. "No pressure, then." The DCI's expression darkened, and he leaned back in his seat, his gaze fixed on the map as though willing it to give up its secrets. "None at all." A moment of silence passed between them, punctuated by the faint clatter of pans from the kitchen. Finally, Dave spoke again, his voice low. "Sir, I don't like saying this, but... what if he's not just trying to disappear? What if he's working toward something—an endgame? You think there's a chance he's got a bigger plan?"

The DCI's jaw tightened, and he glanced up, meeting Dave's eyes with a look that spoke volumes. "That's exactly what keeps me up at night." Before either of them could say more, the sound of sizzling bacon filled the air, followed by the waitress's voice calling from the kitchen. "Sandwiches'll be ready in a jiffy, lads!" Dave leaned back in his seat, exhaling heavily. "Guess we'll have to chew on this while we chew on that." The DCI gave a faint nod, but his thoughts were clearly elsewhere. As the smell of frying bacon wafted through the diner, the map between them felt like the key to a puzzle that was growing more complex with every passing minute.

The DCI's tone sharpened, his words deliberate and measured. "There are plenty of areas in the UK that fit the profile—a convict looking for rural cover and easy escape routes—but the closest to London, and the most plausible, is East Anglia. Wouldn't you agree?" Dave Greggs nodded, leaning forward to study the map. "Yes, sir. It's also got a lot of agricultural land. Plenty of open fields, woodlands, and farm roads he could use to stay hidden and avoid detection." "Exactly, Sergeant," the DCI replied, his finger hovering over a marked location on the map. "Take a look here—West Tofts. His last confirmed sighting. It's almost in the heart of Norfolk. If he's trying to make it to the coastline within the next few days, he has two realistic options. He could head north toward Hunstanton, or east to Caister-on-Sea. Both routes provide enough cover, minimal surveillance, and access to supplies if he's smart."

Dave's eyes followed the DCI's finger as it traced the potential paths on the map, but then he shifted his focus, pointing to the southern edge of London. "Let's backtrack. Start at the beginning and see if we can piece together his movements. The night of the 25th—he escapes Wormwood Scrubs. We believe he moved along the Thames, staying low and out of sight, before slipping out of the city centre entirely. Somehow, he avoided every surveillance net we had in place." The DCI paused, looking up to ensure Dave was following. The Sergeant nodded; his brow furrowed. "I'm with you so far, sir."

The DCI continued, his voice growing more intense. "The first confirmed sighting was in Dagenham, after midnight. We don't have the exact time, but eyewitness accounts place it between one and two a.m. That's where he claimed his first victim." Dave's jaw tightened, a shadow passing over his face as he processed the words. "The young lad, thought it was suicide," he muttered, his tone low. "Perhaps," the DCI said grimly, his gaze steady. "The footage from the stations CCTV has been cleaned up and we have a positive ID on the convict. What are the chances of him being in the same location at the same time someone just happens to jump in front of a train. It doesn't add up." Dave let out a slow breath, shaking his head. "Poor bloke. Wrong place, wrong time." The DCI's eyes flicked back to the map, his expression hardening. "From there, we've only had sporadic sightings, and most of them have been unconfirmed. But there's a pattern emerging, Dave. He's sticking to areas with low population density, avoiding major roads and public spaces. That tells us he's methodical, thinking several steps ahead. It's not just survival—it's strategy."

The kitchen door swung open with a creak, and the woman, carrying four plates with expert balance on her arm, weaved her way past the bar. Her small pink apron now swapped for a larger, faded one that matched the industrial kitchen vibe. The aroma of sizzling bacon and grilled bread filled the air, a comfort in the otherwise tense silence. She made her way toward the booth where the DCI and Sergeant Dave were seated first, gently placing two steaming plates in front of them. The smell of the crispy bacon was nearly intoxicating, and both men paused for a moment, eyes drawn to the food in front of them. The DCI gave a curt nod to Dave to begin. "Thanks," Dave mumbled, his hands already reaching for his sandwich, his stomach growling in protest.

Before either man could speak, the woman turned and headed over to the bar, where Brian and Shaheed sat. Brian immediately snatched the sandwich up, sinking his teeth into the bread with no hesitation, but Shaheed froze, his eyes locked on his plate in disbelief. The thick, glossy slice of lettuce, the tomato, and a suspiciously green blob he could only guess was avocado, all piled into what he could only describe as a sad excuse for a vegetarian sandwich. His gaze flicked to Brian, who was blissfully munching away, clearly unaware of the 'vegetarian surprise' before Shaheed. He sighed heavily, pushing the sandwich aside.

The DCI's voice broke the momentary silence as he glanced up from his plate, his mind clearly elsewhere. "Two days later, on the 28th, around 7:30 AM, the convict is reported to have killed a family near Bury St. Edmunds. Again, we're waiting on forensics to confirm, but the knife wounds alone tell me we're dealing with the same man." His finger traced a line on the map, his eyes darkening. Dave swallowed the last bite of his sandwich, chewing vigorously, not really tasting the food, his thoughts on the conversation at hand. A smear of grease ran down his chin, which he wiped away absently.

As the DCI continued, his finger moved northward on the map, tapping another location. "On the same day, 11 hours later, a courier is murdered—stab wounds again and decapitated, this time in a layby near Two Mile Bottom." The DCI paused, taking a small bite of his sandwich, the food barely registering as he chewed, his mind running through the details. "The next day, on the 29th, at around 7:30 AM, Officers spotted a man matching the convict's description near Thetford Woods. Paulo and Louis led teams as they chased him, but unfortunately, they lost him near Lynford."

The atmosphere in the diner seemed to thicken with every word. The usual hum of activity—the clink of cutlery, the distant sizzle from the kitchen—was drowned out by the weight of what the DCI was saying. The pace of the man they were hunting was relentless. He was brutal and fast, and it seemed like he was always two steps ahead of them. Dave sat back in his seat, the remnants of his sandwich now a forgotten afterthought, his mind racing. "Lynford Woods, huh?" Dave muttered, half to himself. "He's got to be using the woods for cover, maybe planning to head further north. Could be trying to get out of the country."

The DCI shot him a sharp glance. "Exactly. He's moving methodically, picking his spots carefully. If he's trying to head north, we need to hit these areas harder—start pushing outwards from the woods and close in on any potential exits. He's not just running, Dave. He's calculating." The DCI's eyes flicked back to the map as if waiting for it to give him answers, but the quiet hum of the diner seemed to mock his frustration. Another cold bite of his sandwich, another line on the map, and another life taken by the man they were hunting.

For a moment, no one spoke. The weight of the situation hung in the air, punctuated only by the sound of Shaheed's reluctant fork scraping against his plate. The DCI's mind was elsewhere, his finger still tracing lines across the map, plotting their next move. They were playing a game with a criminal who was too smart, too fast— and they were losing. "We're running out of time," the DCI finally said, his voice low but firm. "This guy's got a head start, and we need to cut him off before he disappears completely." Dave wiped his mouth with the back of his hand, the gravity of the situation sinking in. He nodded without saying another word, his thoughts already on the next steps. They had to catch him.

Taking a deep breath, the DCI leaned back in his booth, eyes locked on the map spread across the table. "Right," he said, his voice steady but tinged with the weight of what they were up against, "this afternoon, possibly as late as 3 PM, the farmer chased the convict off his property in West Toffs, and that's the last confirmed sighting." His gaze swept over the map, fingers trailing over the terrain. "If we look at the route so far, we can make some educated guesses, but it's all speculation without hard intel." Meanwhile, Dave had polished off both slices of bacon, his attention wandering. The last plate in front of him, still untouched, taunted him. Without even looking up, the DCI slid his own plate across the table, the half-eaten sandwich almost teasing. "Thanks, Sir," Dave muttered, grabbing it with a satisfied grin. It wasn't just food now—it was a small, unspoken victory in the face of what had been a brutal stretch of work.

The DCI wasn't finished. He wiped his mouth with a napkin and leaned forward, his tone sharpening, "Now, if we trace a line from the breakout all the way up to the last known sighting, it is clear our convict is heading north-east. We're looking at the possibility of him heading east instead, but right now, we can only deal the cards we've been given." He paused for a moment, looking Dave squarely in the eyes. "Thank you, Sergeant. You've been extremely helpful." Dave stared at his boss, confused, trying to figure out where the conversation had gone. He was still processing the last few words when the DCI stood abruptly, picked up his phone, and stepped outside. "DCI Craig here. Send the Command Trailer towards Hunstanton. I'll confirm the exact location of Bravo Charlie One when you're close."

As the DCI disappeared outside, Dave remained in the booth, the plate of half-eaten food still in front of him. He chewed slowly, processing the DCI's words. Something was off. The shift in mood was subtle, but it was there. The case had reached a critical juncture, and now the DCI was making moves—real moves. There was no time to waste. Meanwhile, at the bar, Shaheed had been watching Brian wolf down his own sandwich, occasionally glancing over at his colleague, who was still frowning at his plate. Brian raised an eyebrow, his expression a mix of curiosity and concern. "You not hungry, fella?" he asked, his voice laced with a hint of amusement.

***

The night was heavy with silence as he walked alone, the soft crunch of sand beneath his boots a quiet companion to the rhythmic crashing of waves against the shore. The sun hung low, a hazy warmth spilling over his face, and the smell of salt air mixed with the earthiness of the damp sand. Ahead of him, a small crab darted across the beach, its tiny legs skittering frantically as it disappeared into the safety of a nearby rock. His footsteps left an imprint in the wet sand, faint but undeniable. He was finally safe—far from the chaos he'd once known.

The sound of the ocean was a balm, soothing his frayed nerves. Each wave that crashed against the shore felt like a cleansing, each gust of wind carrying away the weight of his past. His mind wandered, momentarily freed from the shackles of memory. As he walked, his eyes caught sight of a small puddle of sea water that reflected the fading light. Kneeling beside it, he carefully pushed aside the seaweed that clung to the edges, his fingers brushing the cool surface. He watched the ripples spread, small circles expanding outward before they faded into nothing. Time seemed to slow.

Leaning forward, he caught a glimpse of himself in the water. His reflection was distorted, the lines of his face jagged and uneven—just like the path he'd walked to get here. His forehead, marked by deep furrows, told the story of a life lived in conflict. His once-dark hair was now a tangle of wiry grey, and his piercing blue eyes, sharp and unsettling, stared back at him from beneath thick brows. He stared for a moment longer, something creeping up his throat—a feeling he couldn't quite place. And then, as if from the depths of his very soul, he began to smile.

The smile, however, quickly faded into something far darker. Blood dripped between his teeth, thick and red, staining his lips as his hands trembled. Looking down, he saw that his palms were slick with something warm, the blood dripping through his fingers in slow, thick streams. Panic surged through him, and he jerked his gaze to the left. The beach was no longer empty. An old man, dressed in tattered prison garb, lay sprawled out in a pool of blood. His lifeless blue eyes stared back at him, vacant and empty. Huge bite marks marred the man's torso, the flesh torn open as if something far more monstrous than a mere human had ravaged him. Before he could process the horror, there was a deafening crash that shattered the eerie silence.

CRASH!

Aubrey shot upright in bed, heart hammering in his chest. His eyes snapped open, searching the dimly lit room around him. The familiar sight of the Georgian six-panel door, still closed, brought little comfort. His breathing came in quick, shallow gasps as he turned his head towards the window. The curtains, heavy and drawn, blocked out the world beyond. He was safe here, for now. But the lingering shadows of the nightmare clung to him.

His muscles ached as he swung his legs over the side of the bed and stood, his feet meeting the cold wooden floor. He moved quietly, deliberately, as though any noise might betray him. He approached the window, instinctively positioning himself out of sight, ensuring his shadow wouldn't give him away. His hand reached for the fabric of the curtain, and with a slight tug, he pulled it back just enough to peer through the gap. The view outside was still, too still. The narrow country lane stretched on, empty, as far as the eye could see. Beyond that, the fields were a patchwork of dark greens and browns under the fading moonlight. A cold breeze stirred the leaves. Below, a metal bin had tipped over, its contents spilled across the lawn. Amidst the rubbish, a small tabby cat sat calmly, licking its paw, unaware of the tension that gripped the man watching it.

Aubrey stood motionless, his mind still reeling from the remnants of his dream, the unsettling image of the dead man on the beach lingering in his thoughts. He let out a slow breath, the weight of the past crashing back into his chest. With a deliberate, almost mechanical motion, he let the curtain fall back into place, obscuring the view. His eyes swept across the room, taking in the simple furnishings, the old wooden chair by the corner, the faded rug on the floor. It was a far cry from the chaos he had left behind. But even here, even in this quiet corner of the world, he couldn't escape the darkness that had followed him.

The tablets had dulled the persistent ache in his shoulder, but he knew better than to rely on any kind of relief. Over the years, he had trained himself to ignore the discomfort, to shut it off like a switch, focusing only on the mission. Nothing else mattered. Pain was just a distraction—one he no longer allowed to get in the way.

His eyes skimmed the small, dimly lit room, settling on the antique dressing table beneath the window. A few brushes and an old makeup box sat on top, but they weren't his concern. Some would have been tempted to sift through the drawers, seeking hidden secrets or forgotten trinkets. But not him. He had no interest in the trivialities of this life. He wasn't here for anything personal, just to reach the target. He bent down, his movements deliberate and efficient, tying his boots with a practiced ease. Double knots, as always—because he couldn't afford the time to stop and retie them in the middle of the job. Standing up, he grabbed his jacket from the bedpost, the fabric cool against his fingertips.

As he moved towards the door, he pressed his palm against the smooth, soft wood, his ear instinctively pressed against the surface. The faint, rhythmic ticking of an old grandfather clock echoed down the hall, each tick a reminder that time was always slipping away. With a swift motion, he opened the door just enough to slip through, leaving the gap narrow and unobtrusive. He eased himself into the hallway, his senses on high alert, every creak of the floorboards amplified in the silence. He passed the bathroom—its stained sink a stark contrast to the otherwise tidy surroundings. Salt granules were scattered across the ceramic surface, mingling with small droplets of blood. His gaze didn't linger. The sight wasn't important, not now.

His footsteps were soft but purposeful as he approached the landing. At the top of the stairs, he paused, listening to the faint sound of his breath, making sure the house was still, that there were no signs of movement from below. He placed his foot carefully on the top step, feeling the old wood beneath him. His eyes flickered to the right, and there, in the open doorway of another bedroom, he saw them. An elderly couple, sitting up in bed. They stared back at him, their faces pale and frozen in a look of quiet horror. Blood, now thick and congealing, clung to their necks, the lacerations across their throats still fresh, but not deep enough to kill quickly. They had been alive when he had started, and now they were simply... there, lingering. Not worth another thought. Not worth another second of his time.

Without flinching, he turned and continued his descent, moving quickly, efficiently, as he reached the bottom of the stairs. His eyes flicked up to the clock on the wall, the time staring back at him with cold precision: 1:03 AM. He had always preferred traveling at night. The darkness provided natural camouflage, a cloak of anonymity that had allowed him to get this far without detection. The world was asleep, and so was the vigilance of those who might have stood in his way. It was always easier under the cover of night, the shadows swallowing him whole as he moved toward his goal.

The rest of the world could sleep, but not him. Not now. Not until the job was done.

Reaching the bottom of the stairs, he froze. The sudden flash of blue light painted the hallway with an eerie, pulsing glow. His heart skipped a beat, and for the briefest moment, the weight of the situation pressed against him like a vice. He didn't need to see the flashing lights to know what they meant—he had been found. There was no mistaking it. His mind raced as his eyes flicked up to the small glass panel above the door. The silhouette of a police car outside was unmistakable.

Damn it.

His first instinct was to bolt, to flee, but the house felt like a maze, and the walls were closing in. He couldn't risk it. Not yet. His escape route was compromised, at least for now. He had to wait. Wait for the right moment. His pulse quickened, but he forced himself to focus, to think.

Without wasting another second, he sprinted into the kitchen, the floorboards creaking under his weight. He dove for cover beneath the worktop, his back pressing against the cold parquet flooring. It offered no comfort—just the rough, splintered texture against his skin, the faint scent of polish still lingering in the air. His chest tightened as he pressed himself flat, listening for any sound of footsteps or movement. Every breath was shallow. His entire body was tense, a coiled spring waiting for release.

He poked his head out from behind the corner of the green cupboard doors, the soft creak of the wood making him wince. He could see the bay window in the lounge, the heavy curtains drawn tightly across it. But it didn't matter. He knew someone was out there. The faint, rhythmic beam of a torch swept across the garden like a predator hunting its prey, illuminating the path just outside. The light flickered, darting back and forth, searching. It felt like the glow was inches from his face, though he knew it was still some distance away.

They're not looking for me yet... but they will be soon.

He felt a bead of sweat trickle down his temple, but he didn't dare wipe it away. Every movement, every sound had to be calculated. The darkness was his ally, but that blue light was a reminder of just how fragile his position was. The Officer with the torch outside was thorough. He knew the drill: checking the perimeter, sweeping the yard. If he made a sound, a single wrong move, he would be caught. The silence seemed to stretch on forever, a deafening stillness broken only by the occasional faint sound of the Officer's footfalls outside. His eyes darted across the room. The kitchen, with its mismatched tiles and cluttered countertops, felt more like a trap than a safe haven now. The familiar environment that had once felt mundane was suddenly a gauntlet of possibilities, each one leading to either his capture or his escape.

He waited, barely breathing, barely moving. His mind was working overtime, calculating, analyzing. His escape had been a well-thought-out plan, but it had all been based on perfect timing—timing that now seemed as elusive as ever. The Officer outside was getting closer. He could see the faint shadow through the curtains as the beam of light danced across the glass. Every second that passed felt like a small eternity. The Officer's torchlight swept across the bay window again. The beam lingered for a moment longer, and for a terrifying second, it seemed to hesitate as if sensing something, as if it knew someone was inside. Then, just as quickly as it had come, the light moved on, disappearing into the shadows of the garden.

He exhaled, not realizing he had been holding his breath. The Officer was moving farther away, his search continuing, but the danger wasn't over. It had only just begun. The blue light outside still blinked through the glass, casting long, ghostly shadows along the hallway. Every minute that passed brought him closer to a decision—either stay hidden or make a break for it. Neither choice felt safe, but one was more likely to get him out of this nightmare than the other. As the Officer's footsteps faded into the distance, he took a long, slow breath. He had one shot at this, one shot to slip away into the night. He could still hear the faint hum of the police car's engine outside, idling in the dark. He had no more time to waste.

"Look, Mr. Alten, please, just go back inside," Officer Martin said, his voice soft but firm. "My colleague and I will let you know if we find anything, alright?" The old man, hunched over with years of weathered skin and shaky hands, nodded slowly. His frail fingers grasped the door, ready to close it. But just as it was about to shut completely, he left a small gap, his keen, prying eyes peeking through. Officer Martin couldn't help but sigh inwardly. Bloody nosey neighbour, he thought. The man had always been a little too interested in things that weren't his business.

Behind him, Officer Daniels crouched down by the side window, inspecting the scattered debris. "Looks like something knocked over the trash cans," he muttered, squinting at the mess. "Probably a fox or some other animal." He nudged a few discarded boxes and empty cans with the toe of his boot, sending them rolling lazily across the cobbled path. "This is pointless," Daniels added, straightening up. "There's nothing here. I'm heading back to the car." Martin gave a short nod, watching as Daniels made his way toward the gate, hands stuffed in his pockets, clearly ready to call it a night. He turned back to glance at the old man, whose eyes were still fixed on them from behind the door crack.

"Don't you think we should check the back? Just in case?" Martin asked, watching the shadows cast by the flickering streetlight stretch across the driveway. He wasn't entirely convinced by the story of a fox and an overturned trash can. Something felt off. Daniels, already halfway across the yard, shook his head without even slowing down. "No need," he said dismissively. "It's just an animal. You can go tell Mr. Nosey it was nothing and let him go back to sleep. Trust me, nothing's happening here." Martin hesitated. He wasn't sure why, but a gnawing sense of unease lingered in the back of his mind. He looked once more at the cottage, the lights dimly flickering inside, and the strange, quiet stillness of the neighbourhood pressing in like a fog. But Daniels was already opening the patrol car door, and with a resigned grunt, he made his way up the path toward the neighbour's cottage to deliver the news.

As he approached Mr. Alten's door, the old man's eyes flickered to meet his. He was still standing there, peering through the small crack in the door, eyes wide and expectant. "What can I do for you, Officer?" Mr. Alten asked, his voice low and raspy, like it always was, but there was an unmistakable edge of anxiety in it now. Martin somewhat confused by the strange question, took a deep breath, his training kicking in. "There's no need to worry, Mr. Alten. It was just some animal, knocked over the trash cans. Nothing to concern yourself with." The old man didn't respond immediately. He just stood there, staring at Martin for a long moment, his lips pressing into a tight line. Something about his gaze was... unsettling. Like he was waiting for something else to be said, something more.

Martin shifted on his feet, feeling an odd tension in the air. "Everything's fine," he repeated, trying to sound reassuring. "You can go back inside now. Get some rest, alright?" But Mr. Alten didn't move. He just kept staring, his eyes narrowing slightly, then glancing over Martin's shoulder, past the gate, into the dark shadows of the yard. "Are you sure?" the old man finally asked, his voice quiet, almost too quiet. "Because something doesn't feel right. There's something off about this place tonight... and that... thing in the trash... It wasn't just a fox, was it?" Martin felt a chill creep up his spine. The hair on the back of his neck prickled, and he had to fight the sudden urge to glance over his shoulder, as if something— someone—was watching him from the darkness. Before he could respond, he heard a faint rustling sound coming from behind the cottage, near the treeline at the back of the property. Martin's gaze snapped toward it, and his hand instinctively went to the radio at his belt. "What the hell..." he muttered, his heart racing now.

The wind had picked up, but the rustling didn't sound like branches swaying in the breeze. It sounded... deliberate. Almost like something—or someone—was moving out there, just beyond the shadows. Martin's eyes flicked back to Mr. Alten. The old man's expression had shifted. He wasn't staring at Martin anymore; he was looking beyond him, into the yard. "I told you," Mr. Alten murmured, almost to himself. "Something isn't right. You should've checked the back, Officer." The words hung in the air, heavy with something unspoken. A second later, a loud crash echoed from the back of the house, followed by a low, guttural growl. It came from the same direction as the rustling. Martin's heart skipped a beat as adrenaline surged through his veins. This was no fox, it was cat, "bloody hell," gracefully walking out from underneath a rose bush as it headed up the path away from the cottage.

Inside the old cottage, Aubrey leaned against the cupboard doors, his breath steady as he processed the chaos that had unfolded in the last few hours. The police were closing in—he could feel it. The pressure was mounting, and it was only a matter of time before they were right on his tail. His mind raced, calculating his next steps, weighing his options. Stay calm. Stay smart. He couldn't afford any mistakes. The last few days had been messy, but effective. Bodies were his trail markers now—an eerie calling card, but one that would slow them down. Upstairs, two more bodies awaited discovery. He glanced at the small kitchen, a slight tremor of frustration in his chest. It wasn't ideal, but he had learned to make do with what he had. The microwave hummed softly on the counter, and the old cream Aga cooker beneath the chimney was like something out of a bygone era, but it would do. He had no choice but to improvise.

Rising from his crouch, he moved to the cupboard. He didn't need to be subtle; at this point, it was all about speed. He yanked open one door, then the next, pulling items from their places in a frenzied blur. He knew he didn't have much time. A quick scan of the shelves, his eyes darting from jar to jar, and he found it: a long, flat cardboard box tucked between mismatched plates. His fingers tore it open, and he pulled out a roll of heavy-duty aluminium foil. Outside he heard the patrol car rev its engine, as it sped off down the road. In the haze of urgency, his hands moved with practiced efficiency. The foil came off in a few quick, sharp pulls. He grabbed a mug from the counter, its chipped handle cold under his fingers, and moulded the foil around it, smoothing the edges until it fit snugly inside. He had done this before—knew exactly how long it would take, how much pressure it would create. He wasn't new to this. He had learned the science of survival long ago.

With a glance at the door, he moved toward the microwave, slipping the foil-wrapped mug inside. His fingers flew over the keypad as he punched in the settings—five minutes, max power. The microwave hummed to life, the rotating plate slowly spinning the mug as a low buzz filled the room. Aubrey's focus didn't waver, he reached behind the aga cooker and grabbed the gas pipe, ripping it from the wall, the air hisses as the gas filled the air. He'd built a lot of things with his hands over the years, but this? This was a distraction, an opportunity to escape. He didn't need an escape plan; he needed the chaos.

Walking to the back door, Aubrey paused, his gaze flicking over his shoulder as a faint crackle of electricity buzzed from the microwave. Sparks—small and bright—began to flare from inside the mug, bouncing off the interior metal as the tension built. Just a few more minutes. He could feel the air thickening with anticipation. Reaching the back door, he threw it open, stepping out into the damp night. He had always loved the stillness of the fields at night, the crisp bite of cold air, and the way the land seemed to swallow sound. It was the perfect cover for someone like him. He glanced back one last time, his eyes narrowing on the house as the microwave's whirr turned into a sharper, more violent hiss. The ground beneath him seemed to tremble, just for a second, as if it too knew what was coming.

The explosion came in a violent rush—a deafening roar that shook the earth beneath him. The cottage, his brief sanctuary, erupted in a brilliant flash of light, and for a split second, everything was bathed in the glow of flames. The shockwave rippled outward, sending debris scattering like confetti, and the sound rolled through the air like thunder. Aubrey felt the heat on his face, even from across the field, but it didn't matter. He was already moving. His legs were a blur as he sprinted, his feet pounding against the wet ground, heading north. This time, there would be no breadcrumbs. No trace left behind. The police would have nothing to follow except the wreckage of a burned-out house. No witnesses. No clues.

Just the memory of an explosion, and a man who had learned how to disappear.

Chapter 19
03:15 hours, July 31st 2024,
One Mile North of Fiddlers Green, Norfolk

The night wrapped Aubrey in a blanket of serenity as he strode along the grassy embankment, the cool, dew-kissed blades brushing against his boots. To his right, dense bushes marked the boundary between the open field and the winding road, their shadows dancing under the pale starlight. A narrow, five-foot ditch carved its way alongside the foliage, a gurgling stream weaving through it like a silvery thread. The gentle murmur of the water soothed him, blending harmoniously with the rustling leaves. He paused for a moment, tilting his head to admire the canopy of stars sprawling endlessly above, their pinprick glimmers swallowing the vast, dark expanse of sky.

The distant rumble of lorries punctuated the stillness, their headlights briefly cutting swaths of light through the underbrush as they thundered south along the Attleborough Bypass. They were bound for Folkestone and the towering freight ships waiting to carry their cargo across the channel. Aubrey, undeterred, pressed on, his pace steady and purposeful. Each step brought him closer to the coast, the salt-laden air already faintly tugging at his senses, a silent promise of the sea that lay just ahead.

Ahead, the silhouette of agricultural buildings loomed against the horizon, their stark shapes outlined by a scattering of security lights casting an eerie glow over the scene. The absence of nearby houses or cottages gave the area an air of desolation, a forgotten pocket of farmland where no one would be watching from a cozy window. Aubrey's gut told him the place was locked tight, its owners likely deep in sleep miles away.

The lights themselves posed little threat; deep pockets of shadow clung to the edges of the compound, offering enough concealment to keep him hidden—for now. From his vantage point, he strained to spot any signs of surveillance: swivelling security cameras, the faint flicker of infrared, or even the shadowy movements of guard dogs prowling the perimeter. So far, nothing moved but the wind through the hedgerows.

But a new challenge loomed just ahead. The hedge lining his path abruptly ended about fifty meters from the buildings, leaving an open stretch of field exposed to the compound's lights. His stomach tensed at the thought. With no cover left, he'd have to sprint the gap, trusting there weren't any motion sensors lurking in the darkness—or worse, an unexpected floodlight waiting to blaze down on him like a thief caught in the act.

Crouched low beside the hedge, Aubrey held his breath, his eyes meticulously scanning the compound for any telltale signs of security—cameras, wires, or even the flash of movement from a guard dog. The silence seemed to thrum in his ears, broken only by the distant rustle of leaves.

The courtyard was a mix of practicality and repurposed ambition. Three buildings dominated the space, their brick bases reinforced with weathered metal cladding. The corrugated asbestos-cement roofs, though old, looked rugged, as if they'd seen decades of harsh weather without complaint. These were likely former agricultural structures, their utilitarian bones sold off and refurbished to house offices or storage for local businesses. On the southern side of the compound, a small pond shimmered faintly in the security lights—an almost charming feature, likely added to placate wildlife regulations rather than by choice.

Aubrey's gaze shifted to the fourth building near the entrance. It stood apart with its solid brick-and-concrete construction, lending an air of permanence and strength. Above its door, a sign read *Attleborough Boxing Club*, its bold lettering contrasting sharply with the more industrial vibe of its surroundings. That building would almost certainly be alarmed—he'd need to steer clear of it.

Then, his eyes locked onto something smaller but potentially more intriguing. A squat storage shed sat tucked in the corner, its utilitarian design less polished than the rest. Metal bars crisscrossed its tiny windows, while a hefty steel roller shutter dominated its front, secured by a robust padlock. If anything important was hidden here, it was likely inside that shed.

His attention sharpened as he noticed a narrow footpath trailing from the courtyard. The path snaked around the side of the shed and disappeared behind it, its destination hidden in shadow. Could it lead to a back door—or perhaps an alternative point of entry? The possibilities sent a flicker of anticipation through him. For now, he stayed rooted, waiting for any sign of movement before he dared to make his next move.

Glancing back over his shoulder, Aubrey scanned the road one last time. The route was clear. Without hesitation, he launched himself forward, his boots pounding the ground as he sprinted toward the small building. His arms pumped like pistons, propelling his muscular frame across the open field with explosive speed. In less than ten seconds, he closed the fifty-meter gap, throwing himself against the cold brick wall and vanishing into the shadows.

Breathing hard, he pressed his back against the rough surface, his chest heaving as he willed his form to melt into the darkness. Kneeling low, he closed his eyes and let his senses stretch outward. The faint caress of a breeze stirred the tall grass ahead, its whisper blending with the distant hum of lorries rumbling onto the bypass. Otherwise, the forecourt lay silent, undisturbed. A dull ache throbbed in his knees as he shifted his weight. His legs burned from the sprint, but it was a familiar discomfort, one he had long since learned to master. Pain was a tool, a sharpened edge that kept him moving forward, fuelling his relentless drive toward the coast. As his heartbeat steadied, he opened his eyes, the shadowed terrain before him beckoning him onward.

With his back pressed firmly against the wall, Aubrey crept sideways, his boots brushing lightly against the ground as he edged toward the building's corner. His eyes flicked constantly between the road and his immediate surroundings; his body taut with focus. Reaching the edge, he paused, taking a slow, deliberate breath to steady himself before leaning forward just enough to peek around the corner.

The large building opposite came into view, illuminated by the pale glow of a security light mounted high on the wall. The glare revealed an alarm box perched above the entrance but, to his relief, no cameras scanning the area. He quickly calculated the distance between the two structures, his mind racing. If he stayed close to the wall and on the narrow path, the motion sensors shouldn't detect him. He exhaled sharply and moved, stepping quickly but precisely, his body a shadow flitting across the forecourt.

Rounding the back of the building, Aubrey's sharp eyes caught the outline of a wooden door. It stood unassuming in the gloom, its weathered planks secured by a small padlock threaded through a galvanized steel clasp. The absence of a handle suggested no casual entry was intended here. He crouched low, pressing an ear to the rough surface. Silence. No faint hum of machinery, no muffled voices, no creaking floorboards—just the empty stillness of a building seemingly at rest. His heartbeat slowed slightly, but his mind stayed alert. Whatever lay beyond the door was a mystery for now, but his gut told him it was important.

Aubrey gripped the padlock with both hands, his fingers tightening like a vice around the cold steel. Bracing his boot against the door for leverage, he wrenched backward with all his strength. The clasp groaned in protest, bending under the pressure. One by one, the screws gave way with sharp, metallic pops, each sound echoing faintly in the night. As the final screw tore free, the door creaked open, releasing a gust of air thick with the earthy stench of dirt and manure. He grimaced but stepped inside without hesitation.

The interior was cloaked in shadow, the dim light from outside barely stretching past the doorway. His sharp gaze swept the room, taking stock. The space was stark and utilitarian, its rough wooden beams and concrete floor giving away its origins as a storage shed. Dust motes swirled lazily in the faint light, settling on scattered piles of old tools and sacks of feed. But one detail stood out immediately—there was no second exit. The only way in or out was the door he'd just forced open.

His instincts prickled at the vulnerability. Trapped wasn't a word Aubrey liked, and the thought of being cornered here set his nerves jangling. But exhaustion weighed heavy on him, pulling at his limbs like lead chains. Every muscle screamed for rest, his vision blurring slightly as fatigue clawed at his focus. He clenched his fists, trying to shake off the haze. This place wasn't ideal, but it would have to do. The final leg of his journey loomed ahead, and he'd need every ounce of strength to finish it. For now, he crouched low against the far wall, keeping one ear tuned to the faint creak of the wind outside, ready for anything.

Scanning the dimly lit room, Aubrey's eyes landed on a haphazard stack of polythene bags piled against one wall, their glossy surfaces catching the faint light seeping through the doorway. In the centre of the space sat a battered sit-on lawn mower, its paint chipped and scuffed from years of use. Beside it lay a couple of empty plastic fuel containers, their lids loosely screwed on, and a crumpled dust sheet draped over a rusted metal frame. Curious, Aubrey crouched and grabbed the dust sheet, shaking it loose. A dense plume of dust erupted, swirling like a miniature storm in the stale air. He recoiled instinctively, stepping back as the particles floated lazily around him, catching in his throat and nose. Waving the air clear, he turned his attention back to the room, scanning for a suitable spot to rest.

Near the far corner, tucked between a dented filing cabinet and a collapsed cardboard box, he spotted a wooden bench about five feet long. It wasn't exactly plush, but it would do. Crossing the room, he brushed off the bench with his hand, dislodging a few stubborn cobwebs before easing himself down. His body immediately protested—he was too tall, his legs dangling awkwardly over the edge. With a tired sigh, he angled himself sideways, letting his legs drape over the armrest. Pulling the dusty sheet over his body, he settled in, ignoring its rough texture and musty smell. The makeshift cocoon offered little comfort, but exhaustion was a merciless master. He closed his eyes, letting the room's quiet stillness wrap around him, and within moments, he was sinking into the restless embrace of sleep, the hum of distant lorries on the bypass a faint lullaby in the background.

✳✳✳

"Hey, time to pack it in—we've got work in a few hours," Trevor muttered, glancing at Steve, who was sprawled lazily on his cool box, engrossed in a dog-eared Playboy magazine. Steve's feet rested atop the box as if he hadn't a care in the world, his eyes skimming over the glossy pages. "Come on, another hour, mate," Steve groaned, barely looking up. "I haven't had a bite all night." With a theatrical sigh, Trevor rose from his small folding stool, stretching dramatically. His arms reached toward the starry sky as he let out an exaggerated yawn, his back cracking audibly.

"Start packing up," Trevor grumbled, shaking his head. "We've got to drop this lot off at the lock-up before I clock in. Don't make me late again." Steve rolled his eyes but tossed the magazine aside with a reluctant grunt. The glossy cover landed face-up on the ground, a topless woman frozen mid-smile, her sultry gaze now aimed at the grass. "You're no fun," Steve grumbled as he began dismantling his fishing rod.

"Can't believe you read that crap," Trevor said with a smirk, nudging the magazine with the toe of his boot. "What's Julie think about it?" Steve chuckled; his grin as sly as the Cheshire Cat's. "Firstly, I don't read, mate—I look. And secondly," he paused for effect, "she bought me them for my birthday." "No way," Trevor barked out a laugh, his eyebrows shooting up. "You're full of it." "Swear down," Steve replied, his grin widening. "Said it'd spice things up in the bedroom. Kinky little minx, my Julie." He winked, tossing his packed rod into its case with a flourish. Trevor shook his head, half-amused, half-resigned. "You're one lucky sod," he muttered, gathering his gear. "Now let's move before you start flipping through the centrefolds again."

Moments later, the two of them had efficiently packed away their gear: four fishing rods, two nets, a tangle of floats, and the remnants of bait. With a flick of Steve's wrist, the maggots were unceremoniously dumped into the pond, a wriggling feast for the fish that had eluded them all night. Grabbing their chairs and backpacks, they trudged toward the pick-up truck waiting in the layby, its silhouette barely visible under the faint glow of the stars.

"What's on your agenda today, mate?" Steve asked, shifting the weight of his chair onto his shoulder as they walked.

Trevor fumbled with his gear, trying to balance it in one arm while fishing around in his jacket pocket for the truck keys. "Busy one," he grunted. "Heading to Norwich first—got a load of manure to drop off for a customer. Then I'm swinging by Hunstanton on the way back to pick up the wife's birthday cake." "Nice one," Steve said with a grin, his pace unhurried despite the load. "How's everything looking for the surprise party tomorrow?"

The truck lights flashed once as Trevor finally found the key, unlocking it with a click. He moved to the back, flipping down the tailgate with a practiced motion and opening the boot. "I think we're good," he said, loading his gear into the truck bed. "Nobody's dropped out, and—more importantly—nobody's let the cat out of the bag." "Good sign," Steve chuckled, hoisting his own gear into the truck. "Julie would kill you if this went south." "Don't I know it," Trevor muttered, wiping his hands on his jeans. He smirked at Steve as he slammed the tailgate shut. "So, if you even think about screwing this up, mate, remember—I know where you live." Steve laughed, throwing up his hands in mock surrender. "Relax, Trevor, your secret's safe with me. Now let's get moving before the wives think we've caught more beer than fish."

"Whoa—bloody hell, mate! I didn't see that before. Is *that* yours?" Steve stopped in his tracks, his jaw slack as he pointed toward the back of the truck. Trevor followed his friend's gaze, glancing over his shoulder. "Yeah," he replied nonchalantly, nodding toward the object Steve was gawking at. It was a sleek shotgun, secured snugly in a hard case propped in the corner of the boot. Steve let out a laugh, shaking his head in disbelief. "You're kidding me, right? What's that doing in here?" "Had it in the truck since the other day," Trevor replied, tossing his gear into the bed with a dull thud. "Ever since they announced that bloke escaped from that prison in London."

Steve burst out laughing, clutching his side for added dramatic effect. "Oh, come off it, Trev! That's a bit much, isn't it? Let me break it down for you. One: the prison's miles away. Two: odds are, the guy's making for an airport or port, not some random Norfolk backroad. And three: even if he did fancy a detour, you really think he'd risk running into Elmer Fudd here and his trusty shotgun?" Trevor ignored the sarcasm, his face impassive as he reached for the cabin door. "Laugh it up, wise arse. You'll change your tune if he shows up while we're out here in the middle of nowhere." Steve snorted, shaking his head as he loaded the last of their gear. "Mate, if he's daft enough to come this way, I'm more worried about his luck than ours." He slapped the side of the truck. "Right, we all set?" Trevor didn't answer. Instead, he muttered over his shoulder, "Shut the boot when you're done. I'll get the heater going before we freeze to death out here."

Steve chuckled, slamming the tailgate shut with a loud clunk. "Bloody survivalist," he mumbled under his breath, climbing into the passenger seat. "Next thing, you'll be stockpiling cans of baked beans and barbed wire." Trevor smirked faintly as the truck roared to life, the warmth from the heater already beginning to fill the cabin. "You joke now, Steve," he said dryly, shifting into gear. "But when the bloke's knocking on your door, don't come crying to me."

The engine hummed to life, its low growl vibrating through the cab as Trevor cranked the heater. A gust of cool air hit his face, and he grimaced, waiting for it to warm up. His eyes flicked to the rear-view mirror, catching a glimpse of Steve slamming the boot shut with a satisfying thud. Trevor shifted in his seat, idly watching the house to his left. A faint bathroom light flickered on in one of the upstairs windows, casting a brief shadow across the glass before it vanished just as quickly. He smirked to himself, thinking how quiet everything seemed this time of night.

The passenger door swung open with a creak, and Steve practically leaped into the truck, slamming it shut behind him with a force that rattled the whole cab. "Bloody hell, mate," Steve grumbled, glancing around. "Feels like it's warmer out there than in here." Trevor barely spared him a glance, his fingers tightening around the steering wheel as he shifted into drive. The truck lurched forward with a quiet growl, his foot tapping the accelerator. "You know, you're always welcome to walk home," he muttered, his voice flat.

Steve raised an eyebrow but said nothing, sensing the edge in his friend's tone. Trevor was worn thin, his eyes a little too sharp, his shoulders a little too stiff. Steve could tell he just wanted to be done with the night, the drive, everything. So, rather than engage, Steve bit his lip, staring out of the window as the dark countryside blurred past. The only sound was the hum of the engine and the soft rustle of the wind against the truck. For a moment, the silence between them stretched on, thick and unspoken.

The Ford pick-up tore down the narrow country road, its engine roaring as it left the row of terraced houses behind, swallowed up by the dark expanse of the countryside. The headlights cut through the misty night, illuminating the overgrown hedgerows that seemed to close in around them. Trevor glanced at his friend, a flash of guilt creeping into his chest. With a sigh, he decided to break the silence. "You watching the game this weekend?" Steve didn't respond immediately. His gaze was fixed on the blur of the roadside hedge, his mind clearly elsewhere as the truck's tires hummed over the asphalt. After a moment, he finally spoke, his voice distant. "Probably. Hopefully, the Tractor Boys can grab three points against City... try and avoid relegation." He exhaled slowly, almost like he was resigning himself to the inevitable.

Trevor chuckled, his grip on the wheel tightening slightly. He glanced at Steve before checking the rear-view mirror. The road behind them vanished into an impenetrable blackness, swallowed by the night. "Yeah, well, if they don't, I think it's game over for them this season." Steve turned his head with a wry grin, watching as the glow of the headlights faded into nothing. "You know it, mate. But hey, maybe they'll surprise us."

"Here we go," Trevor muttered, his voice tinged with something that could've been relief. He swung the wheel sharply, the truck descending into the familiar courtyard with a smooth ease that spoke of countless trips. The gravel crunched beneath the tires as he slowed down, casting his eyes around the buildings. The place looked deserted, at least for now.

"Looks like we can unload and get out of here before Jeremy shows up," Trevor said, his tone darkening. He shot a glance at Steve, the corners of his mouth twitching. "Bloody guy's like a bad smell. You can't get rid of him. Just waits for you to show up, then drives that bloody tractor in like he's on some sort of mission. Nosey git." Steve snorted in agreement, leaning back in his seat. "Yeah, he's always got some new gossip or a stupid story. I swear he knows everything before the news does."

Trevor threw the truck in park and killed the engine, the stillness of the night descending over them. "Alright, let's unload, then get out before he starts with his nonsense. You ready?" Steve just grinned. "Born ready, mate." The two of them exchanged a look, knowing full well that whatever the night held, it was about to get a little bit more... interesting. Steve was out of the passenger seat before the engine had even fully turned off. "I'll run inside and get the door open," he called over his shoulder, already moving with purpose toward the building.

Trevor nodded, shifting into reverse and aligning the back of the truck perfectly in front of the building. He glanced in the side mirror and waited. Seconds stretched into minutes, the stillness of the night pressing in around him. The door remained stubbornly shut. He flicked a glance at the clock on the dashboard, then muttered under his breath, "This side of Christmas, mate, for fuck's sake." Frustrated, Trevor turned off the ignition and slammed the door harder than he meant to. The sound echoed through the courtyard. He jogged to the back of the truck, flipping open the tailgate with a solid clunk. He reached inside, grabbing his bag and fishing rod, his movements automatic.

Just as he was about to head back to the cab, Steve came racing around the corner, his feet pounding on the gravel. "Shhh...!" he hissed, skidding to a stop next to Trevor, his eyes wide with alarm. "I think we have an intruder... someone's snapped the lock on the back door!" Trevor froze, a mix of exhaustion and confusion fogging his mind. He blinked a few times, then shook his head. "Wait, what? Did you actually see anyone inside, or are you just imagining things again, Sherlock?"

Steve held up a mangled padlock and the broken clasp in his hand, his face twisted into a sarcastic grin. "I told you so," he muttered, the smirk never leaving his lips. Trevor's eyes locked on the broken lock, and for a brief moment, everything seemed to slow.

His tired brain clicked into gear as the weight of Steve's words hit him. "Shit," he muttered, glancing around the dark courtyard. "Someone's been here." His pulse quickened. The peaceful quiet they'd expected had just cracked wide open.

Steve took a step toward the corner of the building, expecting Trevor to follow close behind. But as he reached the edge, he paused and turned back, his breath catching in his throat. Trevor was emerging from the boot, his hands steady as he methodically loaded a shotgun. The metallic click of the shells sliding into place echoed through the still air. Steve's eyes widened, and he couldn't help but mutter under his breath, "You've got to be shitting me."

Without missing a beat, Trevor strolled past him, the shotgun now firmly locked and loaded, bringing it up to rest on his shoulder with a practiced motion. "Follow me, mate," Trevor said coolly, as if this was just another late-night checkup. "Let's check it out." Steve's heart skipped a beat, his nerves jacking up as he instinctively reached out to grab Trevor's arm. But in a split second, Trevor turned, the barrel of the shotgun swinging toward Steve's face with terrifying precision. "Whoooa, bloody hell, mate!" Steve yelped, his hands instinctively raising in defence as he stepped back. "Watch where you're pointing that thing!"

Trevor's eyes narrowed, frustration seeping into his voice. "What do you want, Steve?" He lowered the barrel slightly, but the tension in the air didn't lift. Steve, still shaken, fumbled in his pocket, retrieving his phone with a quick swipe. He didn't hesitate. "I'm calling the police," he said, his voice steady despite the nerves crawling up his spine. "We don't know who's in there."

Trevor paused, his fingers tightening around the shotgun as he took a slow breath. He didn't say anything at first, just stood there, staring at the darkened building. The decision hung in the air like a thick fog. After a long moment, he nodded once, sharply. "Alright," he muttered, as if the weight of the situation had just hit him. They waited in silence, the distant sounds of the night filling the space around them, the only movement the faint glow of Steve's phone screen. The adrenaline buzzed in Trevor's veins, his instincts telling him to move, but the moment of uncertainty stretched on, thick and suffocating.

Five minutes passed, and the silence between them grew heavier with every tick of the clock. Trevor's impatience was palpable, the tension in his posture as he paced back and forth along the path. His boots cracked against the gravel with each step, his eyes darting between the darkened building and the surrounding landscape. His mind raced through possibilities, none of them good. Meanwhile, Steve had wandered out into the field, staying out of sight, giving the situation the space it needed—or the space he thought it needed. When Steve finally returned, he slid his phone back into his pocket with a look of frustration. "They're sending a car. Should be here in a few minutes, but don't hold your breath." His tone was flat, laced with that subtle disbelief that came from dealing with a situation where time seemed to slow down and nothing seemed to matter.

Trevor glanced at him, then slowly brought his shotgun up onto his hip, holding it with one hand as he struck a ridiculous pose, imitating Rambo with a smirk playing at the corners of his mouth. "We gonna do this or what?" he asked, his voice low and full of mock bravado, but the gleam in his eyes told a different story. He was ready. Steve barely acknowledged the joke, his eyes fixed on the horizon, straining to see any signs of flashing blue lights. He squinted into the darkness, hoping for a miracle—some kind of reassurance that the cavalry was on the way. But there was nothing but the cold, empty road.

"Yeah, okay," Steve muttered, his tone resigned but determined. "You lead the way." Trevor's gaze hardened. With one last glance toward the quiet road, he turned and started toward the building, his boots cutting through the night. The sense of anticipation was almost unbearable, every step taking him closer to the unknown.

Keeping close to the wall, Trevor's fingers tightened around the shotgun's grip, the metal cold against his palms. His eyes were locked down the sight as he moved, his focus razor-sharp, scanning every shadow, every corner. Each step was calculated, measured. When he reached the end of the wall, he made a subtle gesture with his hand, signalling for Steve to advance. Steve frowned from behind, his voice laced with frustration. "Knock it off, mate. You're not playing Call of Duty."

Trevor didn't even acknowledge him, his attention completely on the task at hand. He moved swiftly around the corner, his boots barely making a sound against the ground. There, in the low light, he saw it—a wooden door slightly ajar. His heart rate spiked, but his expression remained calm, controlled. He lowered his voice, speaking over his shoulder. "Grab the door. When I say go, swing it open, then follow me in." Steve moved up behind him, his hand wrapping around the door's handle. He looked toward Trevor, his forehead slick with sweat, nerves fraying at the edges. "I'm ready."

"Now," Trevor whispered.

As Steve pushed on the door, his hand slipped on the old wood, sending a screeching groan through the hinges. Trevor's eyes snapped wide, his body tensing at the sound. "Bloody idiot," he hissed. "Quick, open it!" With a grunt of frustration, Steve grabbed the door with both hands, yanking it open. In one smooth motion, Trevor stepped over the small threshold, his weapon sweeping the room like a predator stalking its prey. His gaze flicked over the room in an instant—walls, ceiling, floor, a lone lawnmower, and rows of polythene bags stacked along the wall. Empty. Silent. Nothing.

But then, he caught it. His breath caught in his throat as his eyes zeroed in on the far corner. The chair. The dust sheet. The unmistakable lump beneath it. His whisper was low, filled with barely-contained excitement. "Got the son of a bitch, Stevo. Over there."

Steve followed close behind, sticking to Trevor like a shadow. His voice was hushed but filled with disbelief. "Fucker's asleep. Like taking candy from a baby." The words were barely out of his mouth when Trevor moved forward, gun still at the ready, eyes locked on the figure beneath the dust sheet. The tension in the air thickened with every step.

They closed in, the silence of the room thick with tension. Trevor could hear his friend's breath, shallow and uneven, rising with every step they took. He wanted to tell Steve to keep it down, but the words stayed lodged in his throat. They were only a meter away now, too close to risk waking whoever was under the sheet. The slightest noise could send everything into chaos.

Steve suddenly tapped him on the shoulder, a subtle but urgent motion. Trevor's eyes darted to the end of the dust sheet. A pair of large feet, exposed at the bottom, sticking out from the cover like a careless mistake. His heart skipped a beat. Trevor shifted the weight of the shotgun, lowering it so the barrel was aimed at the figure's head. His finger hovered on the trigger, tension building in his muscles, his breath steady but his pulse racing. He reached forward, fingers curling around the dusty fabric of the cover, his movements deliberate, almost reverent in the quiet.

As his hand gripped the sheet, he glanced back over his shoulder. Steve's face was tight with focus, but there was a glint of something else in his eyes—something that might have been a smile, or just a flicker of reassurance. Trevor's pulse thudded in his ears. He was close. Too close. They were about to make their move. With a final, quiet breath, Trevor gave a slight nod to Steve, and in one swift motion, yanked the sheet away, ready for whatever would come next.

The Vauxhall Astra tore down the street, its engine growling as it tore past a row of quiet houses. The wheels hummed along the asphalt, pushing seventy-five miles per hour as the skilled driver darted from side to side, narrowly avoiding the looming potholes. The faint glow of blue lights reflected off the pavement ahead, signalling their destination. "ETA in thirty seconds," PC Chen Wong called out, flashing a grin at the driver. "Better start slowing down there, Lewis Hamilton!" Raj flashed a cocky grin back, the adrenaline pumping as he barrelled toward the entrance. "Hold on!" he called, slamming his foot onto the brake, yanking up the handbrake with precision. The Astra screeched, tires squealing as it slid sideways into the entrance, blocking the narrow gap with expert precision. The engine cut out with a soft thud, and Raj swung open the door with a flourish. "And don't forget to tip your driver," he quipped as he clapped his hands on the roof.

Chen, ever the professional, was already out the other side, her sharp eyes scanning the area. The buildings loomed silently around them, but her focus immediately shifted to the lone pickup truck parked next to the roller shutter door. Raj, now standing next to her, peered across the forecourt, his gaze scanning the surroundings. "Buildings look secure," he muttered, hands on his hips. "Probably just a prank call, can't see the guy who reported this." Chen did not answer immediately, her instincts still on edge. Without a word, she started forward, her boots crunching on the gravel as she made her way toward the centre of the forecourt, ready for whatever came next.

The area was unnervingly quiet, the kind of silence that made the hairs on the back of your neck stand up. The small spotlights flickered intermittently, casting long shadows across the concrete forecourt. Each building stood still, unmoving, as though waiting for something. Everything seemed secure — all the doors were locked, and there was no sign of forced entry. The usual signs of a break-in were absent. High up on the walls of the larger buildings, alarm panels blinked steadily, their green lights casting a soft glow in the darkness. Chen Wong surveyed the scene with practiced precision, her gaze scanning the perimeter. "Alarm systems are still functional," she noted, her voice cool and professional. She turned to Raj, whose impatience was starting to show. "Looks like we're going to have to look around a bit. You take the Boxing Club; I'll check out these buildings here."

Raj grumbled in frustration as he opened the back door, grabbing his hi-vis jacket and torch. The moment he slammed the door behind him, his annoyance was palpable. "This is a waste of time," he muttered under his breath, tugging on the jacket with a grunt as he headed toward the building next to the entrance. His movements were exaggerated, as though eager to show his displeasure with the whole situation. When he reached the building, he glanced up at the sign above the door and a smirk crossed his face. With a sudden burst of energy, he started bouncing on his toes, throwing jabs into the air like a boxer preparing for a fight. He could not resist; it was just too easy to imagine himself as the next big champ. "Come on, Rock, show 'em what you've got!" Raj taunted himself, pumping his arms in time with the imaginary punches. His eyes were fixed on the building's entrance, but his mind was elsewhere, dancing in the ring with an invisible opponent.

Meanwhile, Chen was already moving toward the first building, her every step deliberate and focused. She was a study in calm professionalism as she approached the structure, eyes flicking over the windows and doors with expert care. No signs of tampering. She stopped at the door, her hand hovering near the window as she examined the small details — no broken glass, no pry marks on the frame. Satisfied, she cupped her hands around her eyes, peering through the small glass window in the door. The room inside was stark, with two desks positioned in the centre, each topped with a computer, a pile of paperwork and a small cardboard box. A few scattered papers lay on the desks, but there was no sign of any recent activity, no one sitting at the computers, no movement at all. The room was as empty as the street outside.

Chen sighed softly, her breath fogging the glass momentarily. "Nothing here," she muttered to herself, stepping away from the window and turning toward the next building. Her instincts were still on high alert, but there was a growing sense of frustration, too. Whoever had made the call was good at covering their tracks.

Back at the Boxing Club, Raj was still lost in his own world of shadowboxing, his fists flying with a rhythmic intensity. He was a blur of movement, his mind clearly elsewhere, imagining himself in the ring. He finally approached the front door, still swinging his arms, throwing a few last punches before stopping abruptly. Something caught his eye — a small poster plastered inside the front window. It was faded but still visible: "Pilates Classes every Wednesday." Raj's brow furrowed as he leaned closer to the window, intrigued by the photo of a smiling woman in gym gear. He stared at the model in the poster for a moment longer than necessary, his eyes lingering on her toned frame before he finally snapped back to reality. With a shake of his head, he redirected his attention back inside the building.

The interior was dark and still. There were no lights on, no movement, but the posters on the wall suggested it had once been a place of activity. A few empty gym mats lay scattered across the floor, gathering dust. He knocked softly on the door, just in case, and waited, but no response came.

"Great," Raj muttered, pushing away from the door. "Another dead end." He glanced back at Chen, who was already moving toward the next building, and he sighed. "This is getting ridiculous."

***

With a deep, steadying breath, he pulled back the sheet, revealing the still figure beneath. The room felt colder, heavier, as if the very air was thick with the weight of what was about to happen. His fingers tightened around the cold metal of the weapon, the weight of it both comforting and terrifying. Slowly, deliberately, he pressed the barrel forward, his finger hovering above the trigger, ready to end it. But in that heartbeat, everything changed.

Like a flash of lightning, a hand shot out from under the sheet, fast and unearthly, gripping the barrel of the gun with a force that jolted him back. The world seemed to stop as his breath caught in his throat, eyes wide with shock. For a split second, it felt as if time itself had frozen—he could not move, could not think. The hand had a death grip on the weapon, and the fear that coursed through his veins was palpable.

He was no longer in control.

Without thinking, Trevor's finger pressed down on the trigger. A surge of adrenaline clouded his mind, and he squeezed hard, his pulse hammering in his ears. But in that split second, something went horribly wrong.

The barrel, pushed off course by the man's sudden movement, jerked away from the intended target. Trevor did not even register the shift until it was too late. The muzzle now faced directly at him. The world seemed to slow, the breath in his chest frozen as the gun roared to life.

A blinding flash of light exploded from the barrel, searing through his vision, followed by an earth-shattering boom that reverberated in his skull. The shockwave hit him like a punch, his body rocked backward, his mind unable to process what had just happened. The air was thick with smoke, the acrid scent of gunpowder lingering as the sound of the blast still echoed in his ears.

And then, everything was still.

Steve watched in frozen horror as his friend crumpled to the floor in a bloody heap, the sound of bones hitting the ground drowned out by the ringing in his ears. His gaze locked on the gun, now just a few feet away, the cold metal gleaming like a silent promise of power. His hand twitched toward it, the instinct to fight rising in him. But then, the world shifted—his heartbeat pounding in his throat, the hairs on his neck standing on end. His instincts screamed louder than his fear. The gun, the fight—it all felt too slow, too late. Without thinking, he pivoted, every muscle urging him to run, to survive. And so, he did, as the echo of his footsteps raced ahead of the terror closing in behind him.

Outside, Chen froze, the world momentarily deafened by the thunderous noise that ricocheted off the small building next to the pickup. Her pulse quickened, heart hammering in her chest as the sound reverberated, leaving an ominous ringing in her ears. She snapped her head toward the Boxing Club, her breath catching in her throat—then, relief washed over her as Raj emerged from the shadows, looking every bit the calm in the storm. Without hesitation, she turned and sprinted back to the car, only to slam into a cold wall of panic when she realized the door was locked. "Shit!" She cursed under her breath, her gaze flicking desperately to Raj, who was jogging toward her, his movements steady but too slow for her frenzied mind. "Bloody hurry up, will ya?" she shouted, barely able to keep the desperation out of her voice. Raj pushed into a faster sprint, the sound of his feet pounding against the pavement bringing a fleeting sense of hope.

The car's alarm clicked open just as he reached her, his fingers swiping across the remote. Chen flung the door open, almost tumbling inside, grabbing the radio. "Whisky Lima Five to Base, copy," she spoke quickly, voice tight with the adrenaline surging through her. She barely had time to register Raj leaning casually against the car roof, his posture at odds with the tension in the air. "What the hell was that noise, man?" he asked, his voice steady but laced with confusion. "Sounded like someone's blown a tire."

Chen didn't even glance at him, her focus entirely on the screen in front of her, her throat tight with a mix of fear and urgency. "Base to Whisky Lima Five, copy," came the crackling response, cutting through the static. She sucked in a breath, fighting to keep her voice even. The sound of the pickup, still ringing in her ears, would not let her shake the unease gnawing at her.

"Whisky Lima Five to Base, we're at Attelborough Business Park, North of Fiddlers Green, off Deopham Road," she spat out, her words sharp and urgent. "Gunshot heard; casualties unknown. Request immediate backup." She hit the transmission button hard, the weight of what they might be walking into settling heavily on her shoulders. The night felt colder. The air thicker. Something had gone horribly wrong, and they were right in the middle of it.

***

Aubrey rose slowly from beneath the sheet, tossing it aside like an afterthought. His eyes locked onto the man, hand on the door looking at his friend on the floor—easy prey. The room hung thick with tension, and Aubrey could almost taste it in the air. He watched with a detached curiosity as a small puddle formed around the man's ankle, a wet patch blooming on his trousers. Tears streaked down the man's face, but it was the terror in his eyes that caught Aubrey's attention most of all. With deliberate slowness, Aubrey slid his hand beneath his jacket, fingers brushing the cold steel of his weapon, the anticipation rising with every passing second.

Steve, paralyzed with fear, stood frozen, his body betraying him. His legs felt as if they were cemented to the floor. Panic swirled in his chest, and his mind screamed for him to move, to escape. His eyes darted to the door—slightly ajar, only a few feet away. A flicker of hope surged through him, but before he could take a step, the air seemed to thicken.

Whomp!

The sudden, searing pain exploded in his throat, a brutal strike that took his breath away. His body lurched forward, the world tilting wildly as his vision blurred. For a moment, the pain was all-consuming. Then, just as quickly, the world tilted violently, and the room spun into a dizzying chaos. As he crumpled, his head slammed against the doorstep with a sickening crack. Darkness rushed in, cold and relentless, swallowing him whole.

Aubrey rolled his shoulders, the muscles cracking in protest, and let out a deep, weary yawn. The exhaustion weighed heavily on him, but he knew better than to give in to it. Time wasn't a luxury he could afford. Sooner or later, someone would come looking for the bodies, and he didn't plan to be around when they did.

There was no point in covering his tracks—he wasn't in the business of leaving a clean scene. With deliberate steps, he walked over the lifeless body, its empty eyes staring up at him like an accusation. He wedged the door open with a swift nudge, the groan of the hinges filling the quiet room as he glanced up towards the sky. The silence hung thick, but only for a moment.

He wasn't looking for perfection; just a head start. Bending down he grabbed the knife, pulling the blade from the neck then wiping the blood covered blade on the man's hoodie. Closing the door carefully, he tucked the knife back into his belt and headed for the shadows.

*****

Chen climbed back out of the car, her eyes fixed on the building ahead, the tension in her chest tightening with every passing second. The air felt thick with uncertainty. "We going to check it out?" Raj asked, his impatience bubbling just below the surface. Chen didn't even glance his way as she assessed the situation, her tone sharp and calm. "Stay right there," she commanded, her eyes never leaving the building. "We don't know who's inside. Could be one man, could be more... there might even be hostages. We wait for backup."

Raj huffed, frustration clear in his posture as he took a few strides forward before stopping. With a muttered curse, he swung his boot at the hubcap, the metallic clang echoing in the quiet street. "This is bullshit. They could make a run for it—vanish without a trace." He paused, his mind racing. "Hold the phone... hey, you think it could be that fruitcake from the capital? You know, that escaped convict?"

Chen's stomach tightened. She stole a glance down the road, but there were no flashing blue lights on the horizon—no sign of backup. Her gaze flickered to Raj, who was now pacing, tapping his fingers nervously on his thigh. She had to keep him in check, had to manage his frustration before it spiralled. His ego was a beast, one she knew how to handle, but that didn't mean it was easy. For now, though, she had no choice but to play along. "Let's not get ahead of ourselves," she said, her voice steady, but her pulse quickening at the thought of what might be waiting inside that building.

Minutes passed in tense silence, the only sound the steady hum of the distant rustle of the wind. The brick building stood ominously still, nothing stirring inside. Chen leaned into the car, her fingers brushing the radio, ready to check in with base. But as she lifted it, something caught her eye. A flash of movement through the corner of her vision.

She froze.

Raj. He was sprinting toward the pickup, his legs pumping in desperation. Chen's heart skipped a beat as she watched in disbelief as he reached the car, panting and wild-eyed. Without hesitation, he waved her over, gesturing for her to follow, to back him up. "What the hell are you doing, you fool?!" Chen's voice was sharp, biting with the mix of anger and disbelief. Ignoring her, Raj's eyes were locked on the building, oblivious to the chaos he was about to stir. He was already committed.

With a frustrated growl, Chen threw slammed the door, her senses suddenly on high alert. The unmistakable sound of sirens grew louder, cutting through the thick night air. She looked up, eyes widening as a fleet of patrol cars came screaming down the road, their lights flashing like a warning beacon. Here we go. Her stomach twisted with concern. Raj was too close to the action, too exposed. He could get caught in the line of fire.

Without another thought, she bolted across the forecourt, her boots pounding against the pavement. She reached the pickup just as Raj ducked behind it, still too caught up in his own mission to notice the approaching danger. "What the hell do you think you're doing?" Chen hissed, her voice low and furious as she pressed herself against the side of the truck. Raj glanced at her, eyes blazing with something wild and reckless. "We can't just wait. Something's going down, and we need to move now." His voice was firm, but Chen could hear the edge of panic beneath his words. She shook her head, heart hammering. "You're gonna get yourself killed, Raj." The sirens were getting closer, the sound deafening now, and the rush of adrenaline made everything feel like it was happening in slow motion.

The shriek of tires filled the air as a convoy of police cars skidded to a halt, their brakes screaming against the pavement. Engines roared and doors slammed open, one after another, officers spilling out like a wave of black and blue. Some managed to wedge their cruisers into tight spaces alongside the forecourt's existing chaos; others abandoned their vehicles in the middle of the street, blue and red lights painting frantic patterns on the walls.

Raj and Chen stood frozen for a moment, watching as a commanding officer emerged from his car, voice slicing through the noise with barks of authority. He jabbed his finger toward the building, directing teams into action, the tension sharp enough to cut through steel. Chen turned to say something to Raj—only to find herself alone. "You idiot," she hissed under her breath, her heart kicking against her ribs. Her instincts screamed to wait, to let the backup do their job, but this was Raj. Her partner. Her friend. She couldn't let him go in alone.

Muttering a string of curses, Chen ducked low and crept toward the pickup truck nearby, her eyes scanning the shadows for movement. She inched along the truck's side, sticking close to its battered frame, every nerve on edge. As she passed a massive roller shutter door, she paused, her back pressed to the cool metal. A faint sound—a scrape of a shoe? —came from somewhere ahead. Holding her breath, she rounded the corner. There, at the far end of the building, Raj was already in position, his silhouette tense but focused. He hadn't noticed her yet. Chen let out a low sigh of relief and moved to join him, her hand instinctively touching the brickwork. Whatever was coming, they were in it together now.

Chen sprinted along the rough brick wall; her breath tight in her chest. She caught up to Raj, tapping his shoulder to announce herself. He didn't even glance back, his eyes locked on the task ahead. "All clear. Let's go," he muttered, his voice low but steady. They moved cautiously around the back of the building, the faint creak of a door ahead pulling their attention. The wooden door was ajar, swinging lazily on its hinges like it was daring them to step inside. "Hold your horses, cowboy," Chen snapped, holding out a hand to stop him. Her fingers grazed the small radio on her vest as she raised it to her mouth.

"Whisky Lima Five, copy," she said, her voice crisp. A moment later, a deep voice crackled through the static. "Whisky Lima Seven, copy. Where are you and PC Patel? Over." Chen winced. She knew they'd gone off the script, way off. Protocol screamed in her head like a siren, but it was too late to backpedal now. She shot Raj a pointed look before thumbing the radio again. "Whisky Lima Five is positioned at the rear of the small storage building, adjacent to the pick-up," she said smoothly. "Gunshot heard. We've secured the rear to prevent escape. Over." The lie came out clean, but her pulse pounded in her ears as she waited for the response.

"Whisky Lima Seven copies," the voice finally replied. "Sending two units for backup. Do not breach until support arrives. Copy." Chen exhaled a shaky breath, closing her eyes briefly. "Copy that. Out." As the radio fell silent, she grabbed Raj by the collar, yanking him back with surprising force. "You move before backup gets here," she growled, her voice barely a whisper but heavy with steel, "and I'll kill you myself."

Raj arched an eyebrow, his lips twitching into a wry, almost defiant smirk, but he didn't move. The air between them crackled with unspoken words, the kind only partners could understand—a cocktail of trust, frustration, and the raw edge of danger.

Inside the building, a faint sound carried through the stale air— a scrape, a shuffle, maybe footsteps. It was hard to tell, but it was enough to put every nerve in Chen's body on high alert. Her fingers tightened around Raj's collar, nails digging into the fabric as if sheer force could anchor him in place. Her pulse thudded in her ears, matching the electric silence that had fallen around them. The faint sway of the open door creaked again, amplifying the tension. Raj's smirk faded as his eyes flicked toward the building's darkened interior, his body tensing.

The seconds stretched impossibly long, each one ticking closer to chaos. Chen swallowed hard, her breath slow and deliberate as she whispered, her voice razor-sharp. "Whatever happens, we do this my way. Got it?" Raj nodded once, his expression shifting into grim determination. They both knew the storm was coming—it was just a question of when.

***

Kneeling in the frigid water, he watched through the veil of reeds as four more Officers rounded the building, their dark uniforms sharp against the flickering blue lights. The cold bit into his skin, numbing the ache in his joints, but he welcomed it—it was better than the fire of exhaustion that threatened to drag him under. He took a slow, measured breath before sinking his nose back beneath the water, only his eyes and the tips of his hair breaking the surface. The pond smelled of earth and decay, the faint tang of algae clinging to his nostrils. He ignored it, focusing instead on the rhythmic ripples created by his own movement.

When he had first crawled into the pond, desperate for cover, he had disturbed a pair of ducks nestled in a tangle of reeds. They had quacked in startled indignation, their wings flapping briefly before they slipped silently into the water. Thankfully, they paddled to the opposite bank without drawing attention, leaving him alone in the muck. Now, fully-submerged and shivering, he pressed himself tighter into the muddy bottom, trying to make his body as small as possible. His fingers dug into the silt, and his knees sank deeper, the cold water soaking through to his bones. He plucked at a cluster of lily pads and carefully arranged them over his head, letting the green leaves and pale blooms provide a semblance of camouflage.

Through the gaps in the vegetation, he tracked the movements of the police. They moved with precision, their radios crackling faintly as they coordinated. Two Officers were stationed near the front, while the others circled around the sides, closing in on his former hiding spot. He felt a grim flicker of satisfaction—he'd slipped out just in time. But satisfaction wouldn't get him out of this alive.

His mind raced as he studied their patterns, looking for a weak spot, an opening. The pond was shallow and offered no escape on its own. He would have to make a break for it eventually. But where?

The bushes loomed beyond the perimeter, its shadowed branches promising safety if he could just reach them. He stayed perfectly still as one Officer drew closer, his flashlight slicing through the darkness. The beam skimmed across the water, illuminating the rippling surface mere feet from where he knelt. His breath caught. A single wrong move—a shift, a splash, even the faintest ripple— and it would all be over.

The Officer lingered for a moment, then turned away, his attention drawn by a shout from the far side of the building. He exhaled slowly, silently, willing his heart to slow. Not yet, he told himself, gripping a waterlogged root for balance. The time wasn't right. But soon. He just needed one chance, one fleeting second of chaos, to disappear for good.

The additional Officers clustered at the back of the building now, joining the first pair in their frantic charge inside. From his position in the pond, he smirked, imagining their confusion as they stormed through the empty structure. He would have relished the moment, lingering just long enough to savour their frustration, but he couldn't afford the indulgence. His target was still out there, the mission unfinished. Focus was paramount.

Turning his attention to the entrance, his sharp gaze caught the gleam of flashlight beams cutting through the night. Another group of Officers was advancing, weaving methodically between the buildings. His pulse quickened. The clock was ticking—he had minutes, maybe less, before someone spotted the pond again and raised the alarm. Slowly, deliberately, he shifted in the water, careful not to break the surface too abruptly. The ripples he created drifted outward, subtle enough to pass as natural. His muscles burned from the cold and the strain of staying still, but he forced himself to remain calm. Panic was the enemy now.

He scanned the area, his eyes darting from shadow to shadow. The hedge to the east loomed dark and low, offering partial concealment, but it was too thin to stop a determined search. Beyond it lay the ditch, a five-foot depression cloaked in dense overgrowth. It wasn't much, but it was his only option. He suppressed a sigh and began to move. Sliding inch by inch toward the bank, his body cut through the water in agonizingly slow motion. Every movement was calculated, every muscle held in check to avoid a betraying splash. The mud beneath his hands was slick, sucking at his fingers as he crawled toward the edge.

At the bank, he paused, listening. The murmur of voices grew louder, punctuated by the crunch of boots on gravel. His jaw tightened as a flashlight's beam danced too close for comfort, illuminating the reeds just a few feet away. He pressed himself lower, half-covered by muck and lily pads, until the light swung away. Then, with the patience of a predator, he pulled himself onto the bank, the cold night air biting into his soaked skin. He crouched low, his movements fluid, and began to creep toward the hedge. Each step was deliberate, his weight distributed carefully to avoid the telltale rustle of grass.

As he reached the hedge, he glanced back at the pond one last time. The Officers were spreading out now, their flashlights sweeping wide arcs. It wouldn't be long before they found his hiding place. But by then, he planned to be long gone. Sinking into the shadows of the hedge, he slipped toward the ditch, every nerve on edge as he prepared for his next move. The mission wasn't just alive—it was his, and he wasn't about to let it slip away.

Chapter 20
21:27 hours, 6th April 2020,
St Pancras, London

The station thrummed with an energy that defied the late hour, a river of commuters surging down the stairs to the underground platform. Their hurried footsteps echoed like the relentless march of ants, each with a purpose, each desperate to reach home before the cycle began anew the next day. Overhead, the large metal lamps buzzed softly, casting a sterile glow that barely masked the undercurrent of tension weaving through the crowd. Two police officers patrolled with an unhurried authority, their MP5 semi-automatic carbines cradled in practiced arms. The weight of their holstered Glock 17 sidearms gave their strides a subtle swagger, as if to remind anyone watching that they were prepared for far more than fare evasion. Their sharp eyes scanned the platform, landing on a brewing altercation near the ticket barriers.

A wiry teenager was the centre of attention, his arms flailing as he argued with an exasperated staff member. His words spilled out in rapid bursts, a defence of his forgotten ticket and a plea to avoid the dreaded fine. His voice, cracking between bravado and panic, grew louder as another staffer joined in, then another, their orange vests converging like predators circling wounded prey. The boy's appearance did little to help his case. A baggy hoodie hung from his frame; his baseball cap tilted at an insolent angle. His jeans sagged so low that the top of his boxers—and a regrettable glimpse of his rear—were on full display. The Officers paused at a safe distance, their eyes narrowing as they watched the lad's frustration boil over. The crowd's collective hum quieted, heads turning, some spectators shuffling closer, curious to see if the situation would escalate.

For a moment, time seemed to hold its breath, the air thick with the possibility of chaos. Then, one of the Officers tilted his head toward his partner, the faintest smirk tugging at the corner of his mouth, as if to say, here we go again.

"The twenty-one thirty to Peterborough has been cancelled. Please see screens on Platform A for further updates. Thameslink would like to apologise for any inconvenience this may cause," droned the tannoy, its robotic politeness failing to mask the collective groan it triggered. Among the travellers, a few froze mid-stride, their frustration flaring to life as they processed the announcement. Like iron filings drawn to a magnet, they veered toward the knot of staff still entangled with the teenage boy near the ticket barriers.

Voices rose, sharp and accusatory, as three men and a woman, their tailored suits marking them as accustomed to better service, joined the fray. The lad at the centre of it all smirked, the epitome of insolence, as the newly disgruntled commuters turned their wrath on the overwhelmed employees. It was an orchestra of annoyance until the arrival of the two-armed officers. Their slow, deliberate approach brought an instant shift. Aggression melted into stammered civility; the suited quartet suddenly far more interested in smoothing wrinkles from their impeccable outfits than pressing their grievances. From the sidelines, the boy snorted, a derisive laugh bubbling up that seemed to say cowards. But the Officers paid him no mind; their presence alone had done the job.

Meanwhile, the station's double glass doors hissed open, admitting a group of women bustling in from the chill outside. Their laughter and chatter faltered as their eyes settled on the shadowed figure leaning against one of the metal pillars. Dressed in black from head to toe, his bearded face partially obscured by the dim light, he seemed carved from the darkness itself. He didn't move, didn't even acknowledge their presence, his focus locked instead on the building across the street, its windows glowing faintly against the night. Their whispers turned venomous; insults barely audible above the ambient noise. He caught every word, his lips curling in a ghost of a smile as they walked on toward the taxi ramp.

Pathetic little gnats, Aubrey thought, momentarily indulging the fantasy of snapping their necks like brittle twigs. The thought amused him, but only for a moment. He had bigger plans tonight, and they didn't involve distractions. His eyes narrowed, his hands slipping into his pockets as he resumed his silent surveillance, tension coiling in him like a predator biding its time.

The Francis Crick Institute loomed across from St Pancras Station, a gleaming testament to modern science and ambition. Completed in 2016, the building's sleek, futuristic design belied the labyrinthine complexity within. Home to one of Europe's largest biomedical laboratories, it housed over 1,500 scientists working on the frontiers of human biology. Beneath its glass and steel exterior, several sublevels sprawled underground—a secretive hive of cutting-edge research and tightly controlled access.

For Aubrey, the building had been an obsession for three months. He had memorized its rhythms, its vulnerabilities, its secrets—or at least, as many as he could uncover. Tonight, the pieces were finally in place. Standing in the shadows, his sharp gaze darted to his wristwatch. Twenty-one thirty.

Right on schedule.

Through the revolving doors stepped Doctor Bill Bonny, the man of the hour. Dressed in a tailored trench coat, his black briefcase swung lightly at his side, its nondescript appearance doing little to betray its importance. Behind him, a security guard at the reception desk gave a perfunctory wave, but Bonny didn't bother acknowledging it. His eyes were fixed ahead as he descended the steps and turned toward St Pancras Station. Aubrey watched, unmoving, his pulse steady, his patience a tightly wound spring. The moment felt electric, alive with possibility. Bill Bonny was oblivious to the hunter in the shadows, the figure whose long months of preparation were about to converge on this precise point in time. Whatever the contents of that briefcase, whatever secrets Bonny carried—tonight, they would change hands.

Lurking in the shadows, Aubrey tracked Bill's every move, his presence as imperceptible as the whisper of the night. Bill stepped off the curb, his trench coat billowing behind him, oblivious to the white delivery van barrelling down the street. Tires screeched as the driver swerved, the van fishtailing slightly before coming to a halt inch from disaster. "Watch it, you bloody idiot!" the driver bellowed, leaning out of his window and gesturing furiously. Bill, unperturbed, didn't so much as flinch. His focus remained locked on St Pancras Station as if nothing else in the world mattered.

The shadowed observer smirked. Good. Keep moving, Doctor. You've got my full attention.

Bill's hand gripped the briefcase tighter, his knuckles pale against the leather as he quickened his stride. He reached into his jacket pocket and retrieved a ticket, his movements methodical, calculated. Aubrey's sharp eyes followed every gesture, noting the Doctor's increasingly hurried pace as he passed through the station's bustling main hall. Ignoring the chaotic flow of people, Bill beelined toward a distant staircase. The escalators loomed nearby, their metallic hum inviting him to an easier descent, but he spurned them. The stairs offered more control, more speed. His coat flared as he bounded down, weaving through the slow-moving commuters like a wolf among sheep. He cast a brief glance to his left, his expression disdainful. Amateurs, he seemed to think, his lips curling faintly. He didn't need to consult the overhead signs or the Underground map plastered on the walls. Every step he took was purposeful, every turn guided by a deep familiarity with the station's layout. The man in the shadows remained close but unseen, slipping between columns and blending into the surging crowd. Bill had no idea how carefully his path was being mirrored—or how close he was to walking into a trap of his own making.

The escalators stretched ahead of Bill, their metallic steps humming with motion. A man and woman were stalled near the entrance, wrestling a mountain of mismatched luggage. The woman jabbed at her watch, shouting in a language Bill didn't recognize, her tone sharp enough to cut glass. Without missing a beat, he ghosted past them, weaving through the growing throng like smoke through cracks. The right-hand side of the escalator was packed with commuters, each step occupied by someone glued to their phone or staring blankly ahead. Bill moved quickly, his pace unwavering, taking the stairs two at a time until he reached the bottom.

Leaping off the last step before it sank into the floor, he bolted toward the nearest tunnel on the left. A bottleneck awaited him: a cluster of schoolchildren shepherded by harried teachers who seemed barely in control of the chaos. The children chattered endlessly, their excited voices bouncing off the tiled walls. "Did you see the dinosaur skeleton?" one asked, eyes wide. Another held up a small plastic trinket. "This keychain is way better than your magnet!" came the inevitable rebuttal. Bill clenched his teeth, his grip tightening on the briefcase. He searched for an opening, a gap he could slip through to escape this maddening blockade. But the group was an impenetrable wall of brightly coloured backpacks and outstretched arms. For five long minutes, he trudged along behind them, forced to endure an argument between two girls over who had the superior fridge magnet—and an impassioned debate about whether a goldfish could outlive a tyrannosaurus rex.

Finally, the group veered off toward the Victoria Line. Bill sighed in relief. Down a nearby staircase, he heard the faint rumble of an approaching train. He glanced at the sign but couldn't decipher whether it was heading east or west. No time to think. He sprinted up the stairs, vaulted over the last few steps, and darted toward the platform just as the train's doors began to close. With a final burst of speed, he dove through the narrowing gap, landing unceremoniously on the floor of the carriage. Heads turned briefly, then returned to phones, books, or blank gazes. Only an elderly couple sitting opposite seemed interested, their eyes fixed on him with a mix of amusement and suspicion. Bill straightened himself, brushing at the scuffs on his trousers as he grabbed the overhead handle for balance. The carriage was crammed, bodies pressing against him like sardines in a tin. The air was thick, a noxious blend of sweat, stale cologne, and faint traces of cheap perfume.

The train rattled forward, the overhead lights flickering occasionally as it barrelled through the tunnels. A recorded voice chimed in, calm and monotone. "This is Caledonian Road. Please exit the train to your right." The brakes squealed as the train slowed, jerking to a stop. Bill adjusted his grip on the briefcase and scanned the platform ahead, his mind already racing to the next move.

At the far end of the carriage, obscured by the press of bodies, Aubrey watched. The cacophony of the train—the grind of metal on metal, the hum of motion, the murmur of conversations—faded to a distant drone in his mind. His focus was absolute, his piercing blue eyes fixed on one target: Doctor Bill Bonny. Through the veil of his long, greying hair, he observed every movement, every twitch of the man's hand as it rested protectively on the black briefcase.

The carriage was a living, breathing organism, but as the tube sped further from central London, it began to shed its passengers like moulting skin. With every stop, the crowd thinned, and the Aubrey's cover began to dissolve. He adjusted his stance, shifting subtly to blend in with the few remaining commuters. Bill, however, was no fool. His sharp eyes swept the carriage, lingering on each face, each posture, his mind working to categorize the threat level of every remaining passenger. Aubrey smirked inwardly. Good. Stay alert, Doctor. Let your paranoia keep you sharp—it'll make it all the sweeter when I strike.

The tension in the air thickened with every passing minute. The train surged through dimly lit tunnels, rocking gently as it pushed toward its final destination. At last, the driver's voice crackled over the intercom. "This train will be terminating at the next station. All passengers must change here." The announcement jolted the carriage into brief activity. A few scattered passengers stirred, gathering bags and adjusting coats, preparing to disembark. Aubrey remained still, his gaze locked on Bill, who now stood clutching the briefcase with both hands. The Doctor's shoulders were tense, his jaw set, as though bracing for what came next.

The man in the shadows allowed himself a fleeting smile. Game on.

The train screeched to a halt, its brakes whining as the sign for Cockfosters blurred past the window. Bill caught the station name in his peripheral vision, his sharp eyes betraying no reaction. As the tube settled, he moved toward the door, positioning himself near the elderly couple and a heavily tattooed man whose face was a canvas of ink. The doors hissed open, and Bill wasted no time stepping onto the platform, his movements smooth and deliberate. Without hesitation, he turned right, heading for the station exit.

Twenty meters behind, the bearded man slipped from the train, his boots barely making a sound against the platform tiles. His blue eyes scanned over the heads of the dispersing commuters, tracking Bill like a predator shadowing its prey. The crowd bobbed and jostled as they funnelled toward the stairs at the far end of the platform. Aubrey spotted the tube driver ahead, climbing out of his cab, his fluorescent vest glowing under the station's harsh lights. Bill, moving at a brisk pace, led the pack toward the stairs, his trench coat trailing behind him.

Aubrey didn't push. He didn't need to. He knew where Bill was heading. But he couldn't afford to lose visual contact. His heartbeat quickened as the gap between them grew, Bill's head now lost among the shifting bodies. Then, a break in the flow of commuters—just enough space for him to slip through. A narrow opening hugged the tiled wall, and he moved quickly, seizing the opportunity. He hugged the wall as it curved, ducking slightly to avoid the low-hanging tiles. His shoulders brushed the cold surface, the faint scent of disinfectant mixing with the station's stale air. By the time he reached the foot of the stairs, his quarry was already halfway up, the briefcase still clutched in his hand.

Aubrey's jaw tightened as he quickened his pace, the faint creak of his leather boots drowned out by the cacophony of shuffling feet and the distant announcement echoing over the PA system. He looked up. Bill was at the top of the stairs, his figure framed by the bright lights of the ticket hall.

And then he vanished.

Aubrey froze, his gaze snapping from left to right, searching the tide of commuters spilling into the open space above. His pulse hammered in his ears as he took the stairs two at a time, the distance between him and his target suddenly an abyss. Whatever Bill had planned, the game had just shifted. A flicker of unease crept into Aubrey's focus as he began pushing his way through the knot of people struggling up the steep stairs. Most commuters barely registered him until he loomed too close to ignore. One or two opened their mouths to protest but quickly reconsidered when they caught sight of his towering frame, his long, scraggly grey hair, and the grime etched into his skin. There was something feral about him, a primal edge that kept their complaints lodged in their throats.

His boots thudded against the concrete, carrying him swiftly to the top step. His eyes scanned the ticket hall with precision. Crowds queued at the barriers, each person impatiently feeding tickets or cards into the machines, eager to escape into the night. Amid the bustling throng, Bill was easy to spot. He was already beyond the barriers, standing just outside the station's main entrance, his sharp posture betraying tension as he lingered. Aubrey halted. Why isn't he leaving? He hovered near the edge of the barrier area, blending into the shadows cast by a flickering overhead light. His instincts whispered caution, and he hung back, watching.

Outside, Bill shifted on his feet, then reached into his pocket and retrieved a phone. Holding it to his ear, he stepped away from the station entrance, choosing a shadowy nook between two overflowing wheelie bins. His head swivelled, scanning his surroundings before he answered.

"Status."

The word was clipped, businesslike. He turned slightly, angling his body so the casual observer wouldn't overhear. Aubrey edged closer; his bulk concealed by a cluster of commuters fumbling with their tickets. He strained to catch the conversation, his sharp eyes locked on Bill's lips when the voice on the other end of the line wasn't audible. "Almost at the drop-off point," Bill continued, his voice low but clear enough to carry in the quiet corner he'd chosen. "Should be there in a few minutes."

He paused, listening. Whatever the response, it was quick, and it made Bill glance down nervously at the black briefcase. His fingers tightened on the handle. "And what is the status of the package?" The disembodied voice was faint but discernible now, each syllable biting and authoritative. Bill's eyes darted left and right, his paranoia palpable even from a distance. He lowered the phone briefly, casting a furtive glance at the briefcase as though to reassure himself of its presence. Then, with a curt nod, he returned to the call.

"The package is one hundred percent effective," he said, his voice steadier this time. "Good. Now proceed to the drop-off point." There was a faint click as the line went dead. Bill slipped the phone back into his pocket, his expression hardening into something unreadable. He adjusted his grip on the briefcase and took a deep breath before stepping out from between the bins, merging back into the flow of pedestrians outside the station. From his position in the shadows, Aubrey exhaled slowly. Effective. The word hung in his mind like smoke. Whatever was in that briefcase wasn't just important—it was dangerous. His target was on the move again, and the hunt was about to enter its next phase.

Stepping through the barrier, Aubrey emerged into the cool night air of Cockfosters Road. His gaze swept to the right, honing in on Bill's retreating figure as the Doctor strode purposefully down Chalk Lane, the briefcase swinging at his side. The streetlights bathed the road in a soft amber glow, their light reflecting off the polished surfaces of parked cars. One by one, Aubrey's sharp eyes scanned the vehicles, noting their emptiness before shifting his attention back to Bill.

Slowly, deliberately, he moved away from the station entrance, his boots crunching softly against the pavement. His eyes darted left as Bill reached the end of Chalk Lane, pausing briefly before disappearing around the bend. The hunter's jaw tightened. He needed to close the gap. Up ahead, a traffic light switched to green, and the murmur of idling engines gave way to the hum of vehicles accelerating. A red double-decker bus roared down the road, its headlights piercing the darkness. Timing his move with precision, Aubrey lunged into the street, his boots slapping against the asphalt as he darted across, narrowly missing the bus. The driver blared the horn, a harsh reprimand swallowed by the night, but the man didn't so much as glance back.

He slipped into Chalk Lane, his long strides devouring the distance. Keeping to the shadows, he avoided the pools of light spilling from the streetlamps, his figure a dark blur against the road's edge. His breathing was steady, his focus razor-sharp as the hunt continued. The faint creak of a door reached his ears, a subtle sound against the quiet. He froze, pressing himself against the shadow of a parked SUV as a woman stepped out of her house. "Goodbye, Susie. Give the boys a kiss from me!" she called over her shoulder, her voice light and cheerful as she descended the steps.

Aubrey held his breath, his frame tucked low beneath the vehicle. The woman turned right, heading toward Caledonian Road, her red heels clicking rhythmically on the pavement. Her figure was silhouetted against the soft glow of the streetlights, her steps brisk. From his hidden vantage point, Aubrey watched the sway of her small carrier bag, its contents rustling faintly as it swung back and forth, inches from his face. He remained motionless, a silent predator lying in wait, his eyes tracking her until she disappeared into the distance.

The lane fell silent again, the faint echo of her heels fading into nothingness. Slowly, Aubrey slid out from under the SUV, his muscles coiled like a spring. Rising to his full height, he glanced down the road, his sharp gaze locking onto the bend where Bill had vanished moments earlier. He resumed his pursuit, his boots moving soundlessly against the pavement as he melted back into the shadows.

Bill slowed his pace, casting a cautious glance over his shoulder. The road behind him was dimly lit, with only the occasional streetlamp offering a halo of amber light. Most of the houses were dark, their curtains drawn tight, creating an eerie stillness. The darkness provided excellent cover, but he wasn't one to rely on chance. Satisfied for the moment, he turned his focus forward. Fifty meters ahead, the jagged lines of a broken metal fence came into view, marking the path toward his destination. Beyond it loomed the faint silhouette of the Cricket Pavilion. His timing was perfect. Without breaking stride, Bill veered onto the narrow path, pushing open the rusted iron gate with a faint creak that echoed in the silence. He moved quickly, his trench coat rustling faintly as he approached the pavilion. With one last look over his shoulder, he unlocked the wooden door and disappeared inside.

Across the street, Aubrey knelt behind the hood of a parked BMW, his body a hulking shadow against the sleek metallic surface. His breath fogged faintly in the cool night air as he tracked Bill's every move. The briefcase had vanished with him behind that door, and now the hunter's sharp eyes scanned the road in both directions, ensuring they were alone. His instincts whispered that someone else might be watching, and he trusted his instincts like a wolf trusts its nose. Sixty seconds crawled by; each one measured in the pounding rhythm of his pulse. Then, the door swung open again. Bill stepped out empty handed, pausing on the threshold as his gaze swept the street. His eyes lingered in the direction of the BMW, narrowing slightly as though sensing something wasn't right.

Aubrey ducked lower, folding his broad frame tightly against the car's grille. His heart hammered in his chest as he silently cursed his size, praying the shadows would conceal him. The seconds dragged on, each one stretching his nerves taut like piano wire. Had he been spotted? He counted to thirty, muscles coiled and ready to spring. Slowly, he inched his head up until his eyes cleared the edge of the bonnet. Bill stood by the door; his face unreadable. Then, with a subtle nod, he locked the pavilion door and began walking briskly back through the gate.

Waiting, Aubrey straining his ears to follow the sound of Bill's footsteps as they faded into the night. Once he was confident the target was out of earshot, he exhaled a quiet sigh of relief and stood. His chance had come. He darted across the road, moving with surprising speed and agility for a man of his size. The gate was just ahead now, the pavilion behind it silent and foreboding. His focus was razor-sharp, every step calculated—until he collided, hard, with an unexpected figure.

The impact sent a woman flying backward, her startled cry piercing the quiet. She landed on the concrete with a dull thud, her shopping bag scattering its contents—a loaf of bread, a carton of milk, and a tin of beans rolling across the pavement. "Bloody hell!" she shouted, struggling to sit up as she clutched her elbow. Aubrey froze for a split second, his mind racing. His cover was blown, and the sound would surely draw attention. He glanced over his shoulder once more, a fleeting look at the middle-aged woman sprawled on the pavement. Her breath came in short, pained bursts as she rubbed the back of her head, her words spilling out between clenched teeth. "What the fuck, man!"

She winced, eyes squeezed shut, fighting against the throbbing pain. Her fingers touched the back of her skull, pulling away with a grimace as she found the warm, sticky blood. She stared at her hand, her brow furrowed in disbelief. "You idiot... now look what you've—"

Before she could finish, Aubrey moved with practiced precision, punching her in the face. In one swift motion, he slung her limp body over his shoulder. She was light, but the pain in her head kept her still, unconscious before she even realized what had happened. He didn't care about the mess, the blood, or the damage—he had a job to do. Without a second thought, he rounded the back of the pavilion, where the shadows swallowed him whole. The area was pitch black; the faint hum of distant traffic barely audible. He dropped the woman onto the ground, her body falling with a dull thud into the overgrown bushes. Removing his knife from his belt he placed the blade against her throat and cut.

Turning back, he studied the fire exit door. The sign "Fire Exit Keep Clear" was nailed haphazardly to the wood, the faded white paint barely legible in the darkness. His eyes scanned the lock, assessing the vulnerability in the rusted mechanism. There was no need for finesse; force would be his ally here. He stepped back, sizing up the door, then drove his boot into the centre with brutal precision. The sound of the lock snapping was like music to his ears. The door swung open on its hinges with a dull creak, the sound echoing in the stillness.

He stepped inside, moving quickly, blending into the shadows of the building's interior. There was no room for hesitation. The plan was in motion, and nothing—not even a random encounter with a woman—was going to derail it.

Chapter 21
01:02 hours, 1ˢᵗ August 2024,
Bravo Charlie One, Brancaster, Norfolk Coastline

Another police van screeched into the car park, its blue lights slicing through the dark like jagged lightning, their glow flickering off the surrounding trees. Tires squealed as it skidded to a halt beside the weathered brick building. The side door burst open with a metallic clunk, and three officers spilled onto the tarmac, urgency radiating from every movement. "I'll grab Betty," one called over his shoulder, already moving toward the back of the van. Jack and Paul watched as the youngest officer of the group rounded the vehicle, his steps brisk. With a swift pull, he opened the rear doors, and a wiry German Shepherd bounded out, tail wagging with barely contained energy.

"Good girl—no, hold up... okay, got it," he muttered, wrangling the dog's eager frame into her harness. He led her back toward the others, her alert eyes darting between the shifting shadows of the scene. "Where's the Sarge gone?" he asked, tightening his grip on the lead as the dog sniffed at the air. Jack, tugging at his stab vest and clipping his radio into place, nodded toward a cluster of vehicles at the far end of the lot. "Command trailer. DCI's in there briefing the other sergeants." The faint hum of activity carried on the night air—low voices, hurried footsteps, and the occasional crackle of radios. The tension was palpable, the kind that made every moment feel heavier.

Jack leaned into the van, fishing out his jacket from the back seat. He shook it out and slid one arm into a sleeve. "Why're you putting that on? It's mild," Ross said, leaning casually against the doorframe, arms crossed. Jack didn't bother to look up as he shoved his other arm through, the fabric rustling in protest. He tugged the zipper all the way to the top, only to pause with a muttered groan. The radio was tucked underneath. With a sharp exhale, he yanked the zipper back down and fumbled the radio into place. "You check the forecast, genius?" he shot back, finally settling the jacket and zipping it up again. "Storm's coming. Rolling in from the northeast."

Ross scoffed but didn't reply, absently smoothing the crease in his sleeve. Jack, noticing the quiet, grinned and took a step closer. Before Ross could react, Jack reached out and grabbed a handful of his brother's hair, giving it a rough tousle. "Looks like we're about to get drenched, little man," he teased, flashing a lopsided grin. Ross twisted away, smoothing his hair back into its perfect side part. He levelled a glare at Jack that was more bark than bite. "Don't call me that." Jack laughed, a deep chuckle that lingered as he turned back toward the growing commotion in the car park. "Whatever you say, little man."

Two Officers strolled past with another dog trotting dutifully at their side, its ears perked and tail swaying with each step. One of them tipped his head in greeting. "Evening, lads." Jack returned the nod. "Hey, chaps. Any news on what's going on in there?" The Officers stopped, their dog immediately sitting, alert and patient. One scratched his chin and shook his head. "Not much. DCI's been hammering out a briefing for over an hour. Word is the convict's hit a dead end, bloody fortunate they found those two chaps in that storage unit. Might've finally boxed this arsehole in."

Jack reached down and gave Betty a reassuring pat as she stared at the other dog, her tail flicking with interest. With a mischievous grin, he leaned closer to her, lowering his voice. "Don't get any ideas, young lady. He's too old for you." Betty barked, a sharp, playful yip that cut through the quiet car park and drew chuckles from the group. One of the Officers stepped forward, extending a hand. "PC Pete Pheby. I'm with Tango Three," he said, gripping Jack's hand in a firm shake before nodding to his partner. "This here's Shaheed. He's stuck on guard duty at Bravo Charlie One. Lucky bastard." Shaheed smirked, adjusting the strap of his utility belt. "Yeah, 'lucky.' Means I get to miss all the action. You lot be careful out there."

Leaning in slightly, he dropped his voice to a conspiratorial tone. "This guy you're after? He's the real deal. No bluffing, no hesitation. If you find yourself toe-to-toe with him and you're alone? Best advice I can give—turn and run. You catch me?" Jack and Ross exchanged a glance, the weight of the words settling between them. Jack gave a slow nod. "We hear you." With that, the Officers straightened up, tugging their dog back into formation. As they strolled off, the tension in the air seemed to thicken, each man silently weighing the risks of the hunt ahead.

As the two Officers and their dog disappeared into the shadows, Betty suddenly stood up, her ears twitching, body tense as her sharp eyes fixed on someone approaching from behind. "You two, what's your call sign?" The voice was crisp, authoritative, and distinctly female. Jack and Ross turned to see a young sergeant striding toward them with purpose. Her no-nonsense posture was offset by the gleam of curiosity in her eyes. "Hurry it along, lads," she added, her gaze shifting between them.

Jack stepped forward, recovering quickly from the surprise. "Evening, Sarge. It's Tango Eight. We're just waiting for Sergeant Stewart to finish up in the briefing." The sergeant's expression softened just slightly as she moved closer, crouching down in front of Betty. "Cute dog," she remarked, her fingers brushing over the canine's sleek fur. "What's her name?" Ross jumped in before Jack could open his mouth. "Betty, Sarge. She's twenty months, fresh out of training." As Ross spoke, Lorraine kept her focus on Betty, nodding faintly. Her hand moved with practiced ease, scratching behind the dog's ears, and Betty leaned into the attention. Not to be outdone, Jack stepped forward, the slightest smirk tugging at his lips.

"Yeah, but don't let her age fool you, Sarge," he added with a hint of bravado. "This dog doesn't take any crap from anyone." The words hung awkwardly in the air, and the flush of red crept up Jack's cheeks as he realized he'd overstepped. Before he could stumble through an apology, Lorraine stood abruptly, her sharp movements cutting off his words. "Cute," she said simply, her tone neutral. The Sergeant's briefing wrapped up thirty minutes ago," Lorraine said, her tone steady but tinged with something heavier. "If Paul's still in there, he's probably having a one-on-one with the DCI." She paused, her eyes narrowing slightly as if replaying the details of the briefing in her mind. She saw the map spread across the table, the positions marked for each Tango team, the grim faces of the Officers as the DCI outlined the convict's history. Her stomach tightened. She didn't need a crystal ball to predict it—there would be casualties tonight.

"You boys take care of yourselves out there, alright?" she said firmly, her voice betraying none of her unease. Jack and Ross nodded in unison as Lorraine turned sharply and disappeared between two parked patrol cars, her silhouette melting into the dim light. "What on earth was all that about?" Jack muttered, his eyes lingering on the space where she'd vanished, half-hoping she'd reappear with some kind of explanation. Ross chuckled, nudging him with his elbow. "Think she's just looking out for us, that's all."

Jack raised an eyebrow, unconvinced, but before he could respond, Ross smirked and launched into an exaggerated impression, puffing out his chest and lowering his voice. "This dog doesn't take shit from anyone!" Jack groaned, rubbing a hand over his face, but the corner of his mouth twitched. The impression was just ridiculous enough to chip away at his irritation. For a moment, there was an awkward silence, the kind that teeters on the edge of a smirk or a scowl. And then, as if on cue, both brothers burst into laughter, the sound echoing off the parked vehicles.

Betty, not wanting to be left out, barked sharply, wagging her tail as if she were in on the joke. Jack bent down, scratching her behind the ears. "Traitor," he said with mock seriousness, but his grin lingered. Ross clapped him on the back. "Let's hope Lorraine's wrong about tonight. We've got enough to deal with without you trying to impress every Sarge that strolls by." Jack rolled his eyes, but as the laughter faded, the weight of Lorraine's warning settled over them like a low-hanging storm cloud.

***

The hum of conversations and the occasional crackle of radios filled the air as Paul made his way through the trailer. The narrow space was alive with controlled chaos—Officers pouring over documents, maps taped to walls, and whiteboards covered in hastily scrawled notes. He passed a couple of sergeants, exchanging curt nods as he headed toward the back. At the far end, the DCI was leaning over a table with a young female officer, pointing at a map spread out between them. She nodded attentively, her brow furrowed as she absorbed the instructions. Paul slowed his steps, observing the scene briefly before a voice pulled his attention. "Hey, Paul! Long time no see."

He turned, finding himself face-to-face with Dave, an old friend whose grin was as wide as ever. "Dave! How've you been? How's the wife, the kids?" "All good, thanks," Dave replied, clasping his hand warmly. "And you? How's your mum? Haven't seen her in years. She still cooking up those legendary Sunday roasts?" Paul laughed, the sound cutting through the tension of the room. "Yeah, when she gets the chance. These days, though, she's busy volunteering at a charity shop. Bless her." Dave's grin softened into something more genuine, and he clapped a hand on Paul's shoulder. "That's brilliant, mate. She always had a heart of gold."

For a moment, the din of the trailer seemed to fade, replaced by the quiet familiarity of their exchange. But Dave straightened, his tone shifting back to business. "Look, I've gotta dash. I'm coordinating operations tonight, and the lads need to be prepped. It's gonna be a long one—not helped by that bloody storm heading our way." Paul nodded, his own shoulders squaring as the gravity of the night returned. "Stay safe out there, Dave." "You too, mate," Dave said, already turning on his heel and disappearing into the bustling corridor.

Paul lingered a second longer, his gaze drifting back to the DCI and the Officer at the map. The storm wasn't just in the skies. It was brewing here too, and everyone knew it.

Paul strode toward the DCI, who sat hunched over his desk, his thumbs pressing into his temples as if trying to rub away the weight of the night. The air in the room was heavy with tension, the faint rumble of voices and distant radio chatter serving as a constant backdrop. "Excuse me, Sir," Paul said, his tone crisp. "Sergeant Stewart, Tango Eight, reporting in." The DCI looked up; his eyes sharp despite the weariness etched into his face. "Apologies for skipping the pleasantries, Sergeant," he said briskly. "But we've got a lot of ground to cover tonight, and, as usual, I've been sent half the men I requested."

Paul held his stance, offering no comment. He knew better than to wade into the politics that plagued every operation. It wasn't his place, and the DCI's mood made it clear that tonight wasn't the time. Instead, he waited, silent and steady, his hands clasped behind his back. The DCI leaned forward, clasping his hands on the desk as if bracing himself. "Right. Tango Eight, correct?" Paul gave a sharp nod. "Yes, Sir." "Good." The DCI's gaze flicked to a clipboard before returning to Paul. "Have you been allocated a dog and handler?" Another nod. "Yes, Sir. We're good to go."

The DCI leaned back slightly, his eyes narrowing as if scrutinizing Paul's readiness. "Good," he said after a beat. "You'll need them. We're expecting this guy to go to ground before dawn, and I'll be damned if we lose him in this storm." Paul nodded again; his jaw tight. He didn't need to say it—the determination in his stance spoke for itself. The DCI paused, exhaling sharply as he picked up the map sprawled across his desk. It was a mess of red arrows, yellow post-it notes, and hastily scrawled annotations. His finger hovered over the eastern quadrant. "We've got three Tangos operating out east," he said, his voice clipped. "Which means I'm sending you with Tango Two and Tango Three to cover the west."

He placed the map back on the desk and spun it with a precise flick of his wrist so it faced Paul properly. Leaning over, he tapped a spot marked by a faint circle in the car park just south of the beach. "This is where we are now—Bravo Charlie One. The strategy is simple: box the convict in to the north of our position. Teams are pushing east and west, tightening the net as they close in on the beach. Ideally, we force him to surrender on the sand." Paul studied the map, his eyes tracing the paths the DCI was outlining. But something didn't sit right. The DCI continued, tapping another area further north. "Now, there's a possibility he'll double back, but with our coverage, he'd have a hard time breaking through."

The DCI's words hung in the air, but Paul's brow furrowed as his gaze returned to the southern edge of the map. His fingers absently scratched the back of his head. "Begging your pardon, Sir," he ventured, "but what's stopping him from heading south? Straight through us, directly toward Bravo Charlie One?" The question landed like a small ripple disturbing the surface of an otherwise still pond. The DCI's hand froze mid-point, his expression unreadable for a beat. Then, he straightened, folding his arms over his chest. The DCI pushed his chair back with a sharp scrape, rising with deliberate purpose. His eyes locked onto Paul; his expression resolute.

"Because, Sergeant," he said, his voice edged with authority, "I've got four more Tangos waiting here, ready to pounce. It's a double bluff, plain and simple." He leaned forward slightly, resting his hands on the desk as he continued. "The way I see it, this guy's been running rings around us for a week. But now? Now we've got the chance to end this. So, let's give him two choices: he either surrenders on the beach or runs straight back into the trap we've set here." The conviction in his words was unshakable, and Paul felt the weight of the strategy settle over him like a storm cloud—precise, calculated, and inevitable.

Without waiting for a response, the DCI turned sharply on his heel, striding toward another desk where two officers were locked in a heated debate over a glowing computer screen. As he approached, he threw a final instruction over his shoulder. "Report to Tango Two! Sergeant Mark Green has seniority and will be taking the lead."The briskness of his tone left no room for argument, and Paul snapped into action, turning to leave. Behind him, the DCI's voice carried on, a sharp bark cutting through the chatter of the room as he joined the argument at the computer desk. Paul adjusted his gear as he stepped out into the night, the storm-laden wind whipping against his face. The DCI's words replayed in his mind; their strategy razor-sharp yet unpredictable. He only hoped the convict would take the bait.

∗∗∗

The branch creaked ominously under his weight as he shifted, adjusting his ghillie suit then pulling back the cluster of leaves for a clearer view. Perched high above the ground, the convict scanned the chaos unfolding below. About a hundred yards south, the car

327

park was a hive of activity. Police vehicles crisscrossed the lot, their lights flashing in disorienting patterns. Officers moved quickly, some barking commands, others wrangling eager canines straining against their leashes.

Aubrey let out a low breath, steadying himself as the wind began to pick up. His strong arm cradled the swaying trunk, the rough bark biting into his palm. The air smelled of damp earth and oncoming rain, the first cool droplets splattering onto the back of his neck. Above, the sky churned, dark clouds gathering like an unspoken warning. His eyes locked onto a cluster of silhouettes near a large white trailer, their outlines sharp against the glow of vehicle headlights. Twenty, maybe twenty-five Officers, all preparing for something big. He watched as handlers adjusted their dogs' harnesses, their low growls and barks audible even at this distance. The hunt had begun, and he was the prize. Then he spotted it—just a glimmer at first, a small white light on the distant horizon over Titchwell. His jaw tightened as he tracked its movement, the light cutting through the dark like a predator's gaze. It was heading toward them, fast. A helicopter. Aubrey's lips twisted into a faint smile. Things were about to get interesting.

The chopper banked left at first, its speed decreasing as it closed in. He watched intently as the machine's powerful spotlight ignited, a piercing beam slicing through the night. The blinding white light swept the ground below the fuselage in wide arcs, illuminating the forested area and the open car park like a stage. He pressed his body tighter against the tree, the adrenaline coursing through him now. The odds were stacking against him, but he wasn't out yet. The wind howled louder, the tree swaying precariously under his weight. This was no longer just a game of hide-and-seek—it was survival.

The sharp bark of one of the dogs pierced the tense stillness, its voice cutting through the night like a blade. Nearby, another Officer yanked his dog back, the leash snapping taut as the animal strained forward, its hackles raised. The sudden movement caused the group of Officers to shift, splitting into two distinct teams. Aubrey's eyes flicked over them, counting quickly—ten Officers and three dogs on each side. One team was heading straight towards him, while the other veered west.

His pulse quickened, a primal awareness creeping over him as the Officers approached the perimeter fence. Small flashlights flickered to life, their beams dancing across the foliage in sharp, erratic angles, illuminating the underbrush with fleeting moments of harsh light. He stayed as still as possible, barely breathing, watching as they moved with precise, practiced coordination.

The first team—those moving directly toward him—reached the access gate, where two policemen stood guard, their eyes scanning the darkness. Aubrey tensed, anticipating them to move north, onto the path directly below him, the route that would bring them closest. But they didn't. To his surprise, they turned left, taking a narrow trail that wound east, pulling further away from his position and, more importantly, from the dense cover of trees that concealed him.

His mind raced. What are they up to?

He quickly shifted his gaze back toward the car park, his eyes narrowing as the second team reached the opposite gate. Their flashlights ignited in unison, sweeping the area with calculated precision, following the path west. The realization hit him like a punch to the gut. They were circling. They were setting up a trap. A cold smile tugged at the corners of his mouth. He knew exactly what they were trying to do now. The tactic was obvious—force him into a corner, box him in from both sides. The second team would close in from the west, while the first team would push him east. They were trying to herd him, to narrow his options until he had nowhere to run.

Clever, he thought, eyes darting between the two teams as they moved into position. But transparent. They wanted him to make a mistake, to panic and run. They didn't know who they were dealing with. They could try to trap him all they wanted, but he had played this game before. His fingers clenched around the rough bark of the tree. It was time to move.

Bring it on.

*** *

The wind began to howl, whipping through the trees with increasing ferocity, sending low branches swaying and scraping along the narrow pathway. The air was thick with tension as the Officers pressed forward, their footsteps steady but quick.

Sergeant Green led the charge, positioned at the front with Tango Two, his eyes scanning the darkness with sharp precision. At his side, PC Kwarcinski, handler to the lead dog, had his gaze trained ahead as well, directing the rest of the team westward toward the first target point—the small car park north of Titchwell. The large group moved as one, silent but for the occasional shuffle of boots against earth and the low growls of the dogs in harness, their noses twitching as they caught the scent of something—or someone.

Behind Tango Two, Tango Eight followed closely, with Jack and Ross in the midst of the formation. Betty, the young German Shepherd, was trotting at their side, her alert eyes scanning the landscape. Tango Three, bringing up the rear, completed the formation, keeping watch as the Officers made their way through the dense undergrowth.

For a moment, it felt almost normal. Jack and Ross walked in step, flanked by so many Officers, their faces a blend of concentration and camaraderie. The woodlands loomed to their left, dark and silent except for the occasional rustle of leaves in the growing wind, while to their right, the expansive grass plains stretched out, pale under the pale glow of the moonlight. It could've been any group of mates heading home after a night out at the pub—comfortable, familiar, unbothered. Except, of course, for the fact that there was a dangerous, unhinged convict somewhere out there, lurking in the shadows, armed with a large knife, ready to take on anyone who dared get too close.

The normalcy of the moment was shattered by the weight of that truth, a reminder of the fine line they were walking, of the danger hanging over them like a storm cloud. The crackling tension in the air grew palpable as the wind picked up again, howling through the trees, the sense of anticipation rising with every step they took. And in the distance, just beyond the car park, the night seemed to hold its breath.

At the rear of the formation, Sergeant Finlay Charles and PC Charlotte Hilliard kept their focus sharp, their eyes flicking from shadow to shadow, making sure they weren't being tailed. The wind rustled through the trees, but there was something about the night that felt heavier—like the calm before the storm. Charlotte glances sideways at Finlay; her voice low but urgent. "Hey, Sarge," she said, breaking the silence, "any chance we can swap with Tango Eight? I'd feel better being in the middle. You know, in case anything goes sideways." Finlay gave a small nod and smiled. "Aye, man, I'm with you. Let's keep pace with Pete and Katie, no gaps. We're a team."

With a subtle shift in rhythm, they both jogged forward, closing the distance between them and their handler, and his dog, Katie. Their pace matched that of the others, the sound of boots on the ground syncing in time. Meanwhile, PC Pete Pheby had his attention elsewhere. He hadn't noticed that the rest of the team had fallen back. Instead, he was chatting with Ross, showing off his dog Katie to him. "Yeah, Katie's ten now," Pete said with a grin, "you could say she's a vet." Ross glanced at the dog, her ears perked, her eyes alert, but looked back at Pete, his expression confused. "Oh right, I would've said she's only four or five. She looks pretty young. You been her handler long, mate?"

Pete, completely oblivious to the fact that Ross had completely missed the joke, lifted his chin, clearly proud of his partner. "She's been with me since she was six months old. Pretty much raised her myself. You could say she's part of the family." He paused for a beat, his gaze lingering on the two dogs walking side by side, tails wagging in rhythm as they followed Tango Two. "It's funny, you know. They tell you not to get too attached to your dog, but how can you not? She's been through thick and thin with me. You don't just forget about that."

Ross let the words hang in the air as they walked in silence, the intensity of the night creeping back in. His eyes shifted from Katie, who trotted at Pete's side, to Betty, who was keeping pace with them—focused, poised. He'd never thought of it that way. To Pete, Katie was more than a working dog; she was a partner. A friend. The wind picked up again, and a sense of urgency settled over them. The calm was only an illusion; the hunt was still on.

Suddenly, the entire group came to a halt. Ahead, Sergeant Green had raised his hand in a sharp, silent signal, commanding everyone to freeze. The dogs, trained to sense the shift in their handlers' movements, paused instantly, their alert eyes scanning the surroundings for any sign of danger. The only sound now was the wind whipping through the trees and the occasional rustle of leaves underfoot. Ross leaned forward, his voice barely above a whisper as he edged closer to Sergeant Stewart, a few meters ahead. "Hey, Sarge, what's going on? What's the crack?"

His brother shot him a glare, a hard look that silenced Ross before he could finish his sentence. Through clenched teeth, Sergeant Stewart growled under his breath, "Shut the fuck up, you dick." Ross flushed, feeling the heat rise in his cheeks. He hadn't meant to make things awkward, but the tension in the air had his nerves on edge. He looked quickly toward Pete, hoping for some kind of reassurance. Pete, sensing his discomfort, gave a small nod. "It's all right," Pete said quietly, keeping his voice low so only Ross could hear. "Probably nothing. Just stay close to your dog, and keep your eyes peeled. Wait for Tango Two to make the next move."

Ross nodded, feeling a little better, but the nervous energy still buzzed through him. He adjusted Betty's harness, his fingers tight around the leash. The stillness felt too thick, too unnatural. His gaze wandered to the dark expanse of trees to his left. He squinted, trying to make out anything moving, but the shadows played tricks on him. For a moment, it could have just been the wind—branches swaying in the gusts. But then something shifted. Something bigger, darker. A figure moving just outside the edge of the trees. It wasn't the wind. It was too deliberate, too purposeful.

Ross's heart skipped a beat, and his breath caught in his throat. He held perfectly still, his instincts screaming that the hunt was no longer a matter of strategy—it had just become personal. "What the hell is that?" The words cut through the stillness of the moment, sharp and out of place. Immediately, every head turned toward Ross. The weight of the group's gaze made his stomach twist. His eyes darted ahead, and there, striding toward him with purpose, was Sergeant Green. The man's movements were swift, his large frame cutting through the dark like a predator on the hunt. As he closed the gap, his face was mere inches from Ross's, his eyes hard and unreadable. "What'd you see, kid?" Green's voice was low, like the growl of a bear, deep and authoritative.

Ross felt a flush creep up his neck, the heat of embarrassment mixing with the adrenaline still pumping through him. He shifted uncomfortably, trying to explain. "Sorry, Sarge. I thought I saw something moving in the bushes, but it was probably just a rabbit or something." Sergeant Green's expression didn't soften. His massive form loomed over Ross, the width of his shoulders intimidating enough to make Ross feel like he was standing beneath a giant. "No damage done," Green said gruffly, his voice like gravel. "But listen up. If you see something suspect, you raise it with your Sergeant first. Let him assess it. Don't go shouting it out like you're auditioning for a role in Norfolk's Next Top Detective."

He shook his head, as though amused by the rookie's nervousness. With a final stern look, Green turned swiftly, his large frame blocking the narrow path as he tried to move past the group. His eyes briefly flicked over Jack and Paul, taking them in with a single, sharp glance. The kind of look that made you feel like you were being judged, even if you weren't the one being spoken to. Ross stood frozen; the tension still thick in the air as Green moved on. His heart was still hammering, but the sting of embarrassment was quickly replaced with a renewed sense of caution. He'd been called out—and he wasn't likely to make the same mistake again. He glanced over at Jack, trying to shake off the awkwardness. The weight of the moment hung in the air, and he couldn't shake the feeling that they were all being watched, not just by their Sarge, but by something far more dangerous lurking in the shadows.

Nobody said a word to Ross as the group silently resumed their march, following Tango Two up ahead. He could feel the weight of their silence like a physical thing pressing down on him. Every step felt heavier as the echoes of laughter—laughter that was almost certainly at his expense—seemed to hang in the air. He tried to ignore it, but the sting lingered. For the next two hundred meters, the path twisted through dense woods, the only sound the crunch of boots on the earth beneath them and the faint rustling of trees in the growing wind. The tension in the air was palpable. They were no longer just a group of Officers patrolling; they were a team hunting something dangerous.

As the path began to fork, the silence broke, but only for a moment. PC Dimmock, standing a towering six feet tall with a build as imposing as Sergeant Green's, stepped up behind him, his heavy boots thudding against the ground. His voice cut through the quiet. "Which way, Sarge?" Looking at them from behind, you might think Mark Green and Paul Dimmock were a pair of heavyweight tag-team wrestlers, their sheer bulk and presence demanding attention. Sergeant Green pulled out a small map from his jacket, a flashlight flicking on the laminated surface as he traced their route. His voice was calm but commanding. "We need to keep west. Can't head north yet—only when we hit the car park. That's when we make our move."

Just as he finished speaking, the low hum of a helicopter became deafening as Halo Two soared overhead, cutting through the sky like a metallic bird of prey. The trees swayed violently in the gusts from its rotors, the sound almost making the ground vibrate beneath their feet. Paul flinched, his hand instinctively going to his ear, as if the noise had physically rattled him. "Bloody hell," he muttered, his voice barely audible over the roar of the helicopter.

As they began to move again, the radio clipped at Sergeant Green's belt crackled to life, a burst of static hissing through the air. Everyone froze, instinctively checking their positions, their nerves on edge. Green's face hardened as he grabbed the radio, his voice calm and controlled. But for a second, Ross could see the brief flash of something darker in the Sergeant's eyes—he knew that whatever came through that static would either make or break the operation.

Sergeant Green pulled the small radio handset from his jacket, his fingers brushing the cold metal as he pressed it to his lips. His voice was steady, professional. "Tango Two to Halo Two, over." He waited, eyes scanning the path ahead, but the response never came. Silence.

Frustrated, he adjusted his grip on the radio and pressed the transmit button again, but before he could speak, a burst of static erupted, loud and jarring. "Two... to Tan... west... lights... from south..." The fragmented transmission barely made any sense, and the words were lost in the static. Green looked around, brows furrowed, as the crackling on the radio continued. He glanced at his team, then back at Tango Eight, whose expression mirrored his own confusion. "Hey, Sargeant Stewart, see if you can get Halo Two to repeat. I'm getting interference," Green muttered.

Paul, ever diligent, nodded and grabbed his own radio. "Tango Eight to Halo Two, please repeat communication, over." The words hung in the air as the team held their breath, waiting. The radio hissed again—another eruption of white noise. But this time, no garbled message followed. Just more silence. The crackling was deafening, like a distant thunderstorm brewing in the background. Mark and Paul exchanged a look, a silent understanding passing between them. Something was off. Without wasting time, Sergeant Green turned toward the rear of the line. He wasn't surprised to see Sergeant Finlay already reaching for his own radio, a slight tension in his movements. "Tango Three to Bravo Charlie One, copy," Finlay's voice was low, steady—almost too calm. He waited for a response, but there was nothing. The radio sat in the air, suspended in silence, as the crackling continued—louder now, almost alive with menace.

The rest of the team had stopped in their tracks, sensing the shift in the air, a subtle but undeniable tension. Every eye was on Green, waiting for a sign, a command, anything. The woods around them seemed to hold its breath. Something wasn't right. Something was blocking them—an unseen force, or worse, a warning. Sergeant Green knew the storm wasn't just in the air. It was coming from somewhere else. And this was just the beginning.

"Shit," Mark muttered under his breath, eyes narrowing as the crackling static filled the air. "Looks like comms are down. Let's move to the rendezvous point—maybe this treeline's messing with the signal. Should be clearer once we get out in the open." With a sharp turn on his heel, he signalled Joe and Paul to take point, and the rest of the team fell into line behind them, the air thick with anticipation. The silence between them felt heavy now—no chatter, no radio buzz. Just the sound of boots crunching on the forest floor and the wind whipping through the trees.

In the middle of the formation, Jack couldn't help but glance at his brother, his mouth pulling into a wry grin despite the tension hanging in the air. "Well, this just gets better and better, bruv," he muttered, his voice low but tinged with dark humour. Ross shot him a look, lips pressed tight, trying to hide the nervous edge in his eyes. "Yeah, if by 'better' you mean we're walking blind into who-knows-what, then sure. I'm thrilled."

They pushed forward, the woods growing denser, shadows shifting between the trees. Every snap of a twig underfoot felt like it could be a warning, every gust of wind felt like it carried something more than just cold. Something was off, and the lack of comms only amplified the unease. The further they moved into the forest, the more the world seemed to close in around them, like the trees themselves were waiting for something to happen. They were entering the unknown—and every step felt like a countdown.

Chapter 22
01:45 hours, 1ˢᵗ August 2024,
Nukeville Island, Off the Coast of Norfolk

Wiping a dribble of milk from his chin, Rich Garner tossed his head back, draining the last remnants from the carton with a dramatic flourish. Without a second thought, he hurled it across the kitchen, watching in slow motion as it ricocheted off the wall, defying gravity just long enough to land with a satisfying thud into the open bin bag. "That's a goal!" he shouted, arms flung wide in triumph. He sprinted in a victorious circle, his feet tapping out an imaginary victory dance on the tiles. As his laughter echoed through the empty room, he skidded to a halt. The kitchen stood still, quiet. His hands fell, the weight of the moment sinking in. Alone. There was no crowd, no one to share the glory with. He sighed, glancing around at the silent walls. The only applause was the distant hum of the refrigerator.

For most of his life, waking up before the first light cracked open the sky had been second nature. As the rest of Nukeville slumbered, he was already stepping into the cold, quiet streets, the only one alive in a city that still dreamed. There was something deeply satisfying about it—an odd sense of sovereignty in his solitude. The streets, empty and silent, seemed to bow before him. He would stroll, hands in pockets, his mind wandering to grander fantasies: a castle on a hill, overlooking his kingdom, watching over loyal subjects labouring below on the cobbled streets. In these moments, he was the King of Nukeville, ruler of a world untouched by the rush of daylight.

But then, the unmistakable stench of fish, clinging to his worn clothes, would drag him back to reality—his kingdom was small, his throne was a rickety chair by the docks, and his subjects were not so much loyal as they were indifferent. Still, the early mornings, with their quiet solitude, were his alone. He might not have a crown, but in those moments, it felt enough. He grabbed the black bag, giving it a quick spin before tying a tight knot at the top. The contents were surprisingly light—though, considering he lived alone, it was no wonder. His waste, like his life, was minimal compared to his cluttered, bustling neighbours. With a small sigh, he walked toward the door, keys jangling in his hand. He slipped them into his jeans pocket and reached up to grab his waterproof jacket from the hook. The sleeves slid over his arms effortlessly, a familiar motion.

The door creaked open, and he stepped into the cool night air. The town was eerily still, as if holding its breath. Tiny rodents darted through the shadows, their scurrying footsteps barely a whisper against the silence. He smiled to himself—no one cared about them, least of all him. In the distance, an owl hooted softly, perched somewhere high, its sharp eyes no doubt tracking the little creatures weaving in and out of the trash cans. He could almost feel the tension in the night air, like a predator waiting to pounce, and for a moment, he wondered if the owl was watching him too.

The door clicked shut behind him with a satisfying snap, the latch securing with a gentle tug that felt like a quiet promise. He paused for a moment, casting a glance over his two-bedroom house, making sure everything was locked and in place. It was a small ritual, but one that gave him a sense of comfort. A smile tugged at the corners of his mouth. The crime rate here was a perfect zero, and had been for five years running. It was a place where safety was woven into the very fabric of daily life.

He could leave his front door wide open, his personal belongings scattered out on the street, and when he returned hours later, everything would be exactly as he'd left it—unchanged, untouched, and undisturbed. This island was more than just a place to live; it was his home, and the people who shared it with him felt like an extension of himself. There was an unspoken trust here, one that did not need to be earned, because it simply was. In a world full of chaos, Nukeville stood as a quiet sanctuary, where the peace was not just an absence of crime, but a presence of something much deeper—a collective, unshakable bond.

He glanced left, then right—the street was eerily still. Most of the houses lining the road stood silent, their curtains drawn tight, trapping the darkness inside like secrets. The only break in the night's stillness came from the soft glow of three streetlights spaced evenly along the path, their dull yellow light casting long shadows on the empty pavement. Beyond them, a faint, comforting glow shone through a window—little Sofia's nightlight, a soft beacon in the quiet.

Jo Barrett had moved to the island nearly two years ago, pregnant, and alone, with her teenage twins, Conner and Elliot, in tow. Her husband, Ben, was thousands of miles away, caught up in a distant war, fighting the Taliban in Afghanistan. Life had been tough for her, but the island's close-knit community had embraced her. Rich had been there from the start, always willing to lend a hand—whether fixing the boys' bikes or taking care of the general upkeep of the little property they now called home. In such a small community, everyone helped each other, like family, without a second thought. Life, in its own way, was good. Simple, peaceful, with a rhythm that felt unbreakable. But as Rich stood there, taking in the familiar scene, a quiet unease lingered. It was the kind of peace that could be easily shattered, though none of them ever spoke of it—this perfect island, with its secrets buried just beneath the surface, waiting for the night to spill them out.

He headed south, the road stretching out in front of him like an old, familiar friend. His hands were buried deep in his pockets, the cool evening air brushing against his face, but it wasn't cold enough to warrant shedding his jacket just yet. He'd wait until he was on the boat, cutting through the waves on his way out to sea. The thought of it brought a slight smile to his lips—there was something about the ocean at night that made everything feel a little more alive, a little more promising. He was not sure what it was, but after the last four days of disappointing trips, he was cautiously optimistic. The waters between the Norfolk Coast and the island were typically teeming with fish—so much so that his nets should have been bursting. But nature, as it often did, had a way of laughing in his face. The last few excursions had yielded little more than a bucket of cod, sole, and a couple of stubborn skate, not nearly enough to make a decent haul.

But today… today felt different. There was a lightness to his step, a subtle skip that betrayed the quiet confidence bubbling inside him. He did not know why, but he had a good feeling about today—a gut instinct he could not shake. Maybe the sea was just waiting to give back, to make up for the past few days of emptiness. Or maybe it was just hope, that stubborn thing that always made him try once more, even when everything else said to quit. But whatever it was, as the boat loomed closer in the distance, he was ready. Today would be the day.

Lisa Degnan moved from table to table in the dimly lit White Hart, her footsteps quiet against the creaky floorboards. Her arms were tired from a long shift, but she kept moving, collecting empty glasses and half-finished drinks that littered the tables. It was a typical evening in Nukeville—small town, small choices. The locals didn't have much to do but stay home, hoping for a signal on their TV that rarely came through, or head down to the pub for a drink, a little chat, and the latest gossip. Life was simple here, but tonight, it felt particularly slow.

She pulled the cloth from her back pocket and swiped it across the table, the fabric soft and familiar in her hands. Crumbs from a discarded crisp packet fell away, and she scooped them into her palm, tossing them into an empty pint glass with a sigh. The pub was nearly empty now, the last of the evening crowd lingering, reluctant to go home to their quiet, predictable lives. "Hey, guys, last orders were hours ago," she called out, her voice carrying over the low murmur of the room. "It's kicking out time."

She glanced up and spotted Harry Norton and Deborah Smith sitting near the fireplace. The fire had long since died, leaving only charred remnants of timber and a bed of ash in the hearth. Harry was nursing his drink, eyes glazed, lost in thought, while Deborah absentmindedly twisted her glass between her fingers. The pair didn't seem in any rush to leave, as if they were waiting for something—anything—to break the stillness of the night. But nothing ever really happened in Nukeville. Not unless you counted the subtle drama of who was talking to whom, or who was avoiding whose gaze. Lisa gave them a nod, but they didn't seem to notice. Her shift was almost over, and as she surveyed the room, a deep sense of familiarity washed over her. Another evening, another quiet night at the White Hart. Still, she could not help but wonder—what would it take to shake things up around here?

The middle-aged man kicked back his stool, preparing to stand, but the room had other plans. The floor seemed to lurch beneath him, spinning like a carousel, and with a staggered step backward, he came dangerously close to collapsing. His balance faltered, but the rough, cool wall behind him caught him just in time, saving him from a graceless heap on the floor. He leaned against the lath and plaster, eyes wide, his face flushed with the disorienting dizziness of too many drinks. Lisa stood at the bar, arms crossed, watching the spectacle unfold. Deborah, a good ten years older than Harry, followed suit. She rose to her feet with exaggerated care, holding her empty glass aloft as if it were some sort of trophy. She brought it to her lips and took a long, dramatic sip of the imaginary wine, giggling uncontrollably as a loud burp escaped her. "Classy," Lisa muttered under her breath.

"Christ, you guys," Lisa called out, her voice tinged with frustration. "If you don't make your way outta here in the next few minutes, I'm gonna lose my license!" She pushed herself off the bar and walked over to the heavy oak door, pulling it open with a satisfying creak, then stood there, arms folded, waiting with a mix of concern and exasperation. The street outside was dark, quiet, but she could almost hear the clock ticking down—every minute that passed was another closer to closing time. Harry and Deborah barely noticed.

The night had been dragging on, and it was clear the only thing keeping them here was the warmth of the pub and the stubbornness of their own stubbornness. Lisa sighed, but her eyes softened. They were her regulars. They always showed up late, drank too much, and rarely left on time. But she couldn't help feeling a strange affection for them—their predictability was a comforting part of the rhythm of this place. Still, tonight, the door swung wide, the cool air beckoning them out into the night. "Well?" she said, raising an eyebrow, "You planning to help me save this place or what?"

Lisa leaned against the bar, her eyes following the couple as they staggered towards the door, arms wrapped around each other for support. They navigated the maze of tables and chairs with the kind of clumsy grace that only comes from too many drinks and too little coordination. Each step was a delicate dance—bumping into chairs, tripping over stools, and laughing all the while. One stool, propped upside down on top of a table, was knocked to the floor with a loud clatter. "It's alright, I'll get it in a minute, just keep coming this way… no, not that way… over here… follow the sound of my voice," she called out, a mix of exasperation and amusement in her voice.

Deborah was still laughing, but Lisa's eyes lingered on her blouse. Red blotches from spilled wine had dried in strange, abstract patterns across her chest, a map of the evening's chaos. It made Lisa wonder how anyone could not feel the self-awareness of wearing something so clearly stained, but Deborah didn't seem to care. She was too busy focusing on keeping her balance as Harry, half-leaning on her, stumbled toward the door. As they neared the exit, Harry tried to speak, his words slurring together, the hiccup in the middle making his attempt at gratitude all the more comical. "Sfanx fror a... hiccup... a... ruddy good... evening..."

Lisa smiled politely, nodding as if she hadn't heard his slurred attempt at a thank-you. She wasn't sure if he'd even intended to say it, but she wasn't in the mood to correct him. "Take care, you two," she muttered, eager to usher them out. Her smile faded as she turned back toward the bar. There were still plenty of empty glasses to clear, the smell of spilled beer lingering in the air, and a barrel that needed changing before she could lock up and call it a night. The pub wasn't quite as empty as she'd hoped. She glanced over the tables, mentally ticking off the things she still needed to do. It was always the same—closing time was never really the end of the work.

Lisa felt a moment of quiet relief. Still, she couldn't shake the thought of how the night had gone—same old faces, same old routines. She only wished something would happen around here to shake it up a little. Maybe then she wouldn't feel like she was just going through the motions, night after night. A few years ago, Lisa would have called Deborah and Harry a taxi, no question. But that was before things changed, before the island's small-town charm had settled in a little too comfortably. With only six miles of land stretching across the whole place, no one bothered to offer taxi services—everything was within walking distance, even if it felt a little farther after a few too many drinks.

Lisa felt the familiar pang of reluctant responsibility. She was about to close the door when Harry lurched again, clutching Deborah as they both stumbled down the road. She hesitated, one hand still on the door, ear pressed against the oak, listening for the sounds of their footsteps fading into the distance. The guilt hit her like a cold wave, making her stomach churn. She always felt it— this odd tug of concern, even when it wasn't her job to babysit grown adults.

After a long minute, she finally slid the bolt into place, the sound echoing in the quiet. She turned back into the pub, the air inside heavy with the remnants of the night. The tables were cluttered, glasses half-full and scattered across the bar like forgotten promises. The clock above the fireplace blinked 2:30 AM. If she was lucky, she'd have the bar cleared, the barrel changed, and the place ready to reopen. That would give her a solid five hours of sleep before she had to do it all over again—another round of cleaning, serving, and small-town life. It was a grind, sure, but it was all she knew. And as much as she longed for a change, she couldn't help but feel a strange sense of loyalty to the rhythm of it all, even if it left her exhausted, empty, and counting down the hours.

✳✳✳

Rich's boot swung out, his foot making contact with a small stone lying in the middle of the path. With a satisfying crack, it skidded across the concrete slabs, bouncing once before coming to a rest in a bush between two houses. He smirked, feeling a little thrill from the unexpected game. But as his gaze lifted, he caught the faint sound of voices ahead. It wasn't the usual street chatter, though— something about the conversation was off. The words didn't make any sense, slurring together like a puzzle with missing pieces. As he walked south, the voices grew clearer, distorted by the confusion of the night's aftermath. Two shadows stepped into the dim light, barely able to hold each other up. The man's arm was draped around the woman's waist, offering her the kind of support that only a night of heavy drinking could bring.

"Good morning, you two," Rich called out with a wry smile, his voice carrying a hint of amusement. Deborah and Harry stopped in their tracks, swaying in unison, their eyes struggling to focus on him. They blinked, trying to make sense of the scene—Rich Garner, standing in front of them, but there seemed to be three of him. Or maybe four, in their blurry minds. Harry, ever the inquisitive one, poked his finger toward the Rich on the right, trying to prod him into reality. His finger, of course, met nothing but air. His brow furrowed in confusion, but the attempt only made him more unsteady. "You both OK? Need a hand getting home?" Rich asked, genuine concern creeping into his voice, though it was hard to suppress the amusement.

Deborah giggled, her words tumbling out in a jumble. "No, young jam... hiccup... we... are perflexy... amramble... hiccup... of getting... ourselves, innit!" She grinned, proud of herself for getting that much out without falling over. Rich stared at her blankly, trying to piece together the bizarre sentence. "Well, I can see that," he replied, his tone a mix of disbelief and dry humour. He glanced over his shoulder, mentally calculating the distance between where they stood and their house. How far had they walked from The White Hart? They weren't exactly in a state to make it all the way back without help. But the couple stood there, swaying, waiting for further instructions as though Rich were their guiding force through this haze of drunkenness.

"Seeeewwww... hiccup... what's gonna be doin... hiccup... Officer?" Harry slurred, blinking as though waiting for Rich to give the orders. Rich let out a low chuckle, shaking his head as he looked at the pair of them, trying to hold it together but failing miserably. He should've just kept walking, let them figure it out. But instead, he felt a strange sense of responsibility for the two of them, despite their embarrassing state. "Alright," he said, glancing down the street, "let's get you two home, before you get lost,' yeah?" Deborah and Harry nodded vigorously, as if they understood exactly what he meant—though the idea of 'home' seemed as elusive as the ground beneath their feet.

A few moments later, Rich had led Deborah and Harry a few doors down from their own home, the couple swaying like two poorly balanced trees in a storm. He gave them an exaggerated smile, one that felt more like a mask than anything genuine. "Well, looks like you two are good now," he said, his voice light, though his patience was running thin. He turned, pointing as if they were tourists lost in a foreign city. "Just a few more paces and—" he gestured dramatically, "—your front doors right there. See it? The yellow door! No. That's not yours……next one" He waited for a response, but none came. Deborah was too busy giggling, Harry too focused on trying to stay upright. Without another word, Rich stepped into the road, carefully navigating around them like a seasoned dancer avoiding missteps. He didn't want to break their rhythm; they didn't need to change course, not when they were this close to home.

It was a ritual now, the dance they did three times a week. Every time Rich left for work in the morning, he ran into the couple stumbling from The White Hart, always in this state. He could set his watch by it—same time, same foggy expression, same uncoordinated shuffle. The island was small, so it was hard to avoid the familiar faces, but Rich had to admit, this routine with Deborah and Harry had become oddly predictable. It was as if their drunken path had become an extension of his own—one he couldn't quite escape, even if he wanted to. And though he sometimes found himself annoyed by the same scene replaying over and over, there was a strange kind of comfort in it, like the island's pulse beating at a steady, predictable rhythm. "Right, you two take care," Rich said, giving a final glance as he turned to leave. The yellow door was still there, gleaming in the dim light, waiting for them. He didn't stick around to see them stumble inside; he knew they would. They always did.

As Rich reached the end of the road, he stopped for a moment, eyes scanning the familiar scene before him. The school loomed in the distance; its silhouette barely visible in the dim morning light. To his right, his friend's house sat in total darkness, a void of any signs of life. Rich squinted, half-hoping for a flicker of movement in the windows, some sign that Andrew was already awake and on his way. But there was nothing—just the cold, lifeless quiet of the early morning. He glanced down both paths that split off the road. Empty. No sign of anyone—no dog walkers, no early risers, not even the distant hum of a car engine. The island felt frozen, still, like the whole world was holding its breath. Frustration bubbled up in Rich's chest.

"Bloody hell, Andrew," he muttered under his breath, turning sharply and walking away from the quiet road. "You better not be late again!" His footsteps quickened as he made his way toward the harbour, the salty breeze tugging at his jacket, a reminder that time was ticking. The harbour was always his destination, but today, it felt farther than usual, the weight of anticipation adding an urgency to his stride. If Andrew wasn't there on time, it would throw the whole day off, and Rich didn't have time for that today. The sea was waiting for no one—not even Andrew.

As Rich walked down the familiar slope toward the quay, his boots crunching on the gravel path towards the boathouse, he let his gaze wander across the water. There, bobbing gently in the morning light, was Daisy, his trusted boat, rocking in time with the rhythm of the waves. He smiled softly, calling out to her as if she could hear him. "Morning, Princess," he muttered, the words a comforting routine. She was his steady companion on the sea, even when the world seemed uncertain.

But before he could head down to the boat and set sail, there was the matter of the boathouse. He needed to complete the daily log. It was a small but important task, a ritual he had followed for years. The log book had been introduced twelve years ago after a tragedy that still haunted the island. A young fisherman—one of their own— had left the dock for a routine fishing trip, but a thick fog had rolled in so suddenly that it swallowed his boat whole. By the time he tried to turn back, the fog had disoriented him. No one ever saw him again. They never found his body, and the circumstances surrounding his disappearance gave birth to endless rumours. Some believed he had been lost to the sea, swallowed whole by the fog. Others said he had turned his back on the island, slipped away to start a new life on the mainland. But the truth remained a ghost, forever tethered to the island's history.

Rich let out a long breath as he neared the boathouse, the familiar building standing like a silent guardian at the edge of the quay. He quickly glanced over his shoulder, but as usual, there was no sign of Andrew Moss. "Damn you, man," Rich muttered under his breath. It was not the first time his friend had been late. It seemed like it was happening more often these days—sometimes Rich wondered if Andrew had grown tired of the life they led, or if he was just losing his edge.

The door to the boathouse was always left unlocked. It was an unspoken rule, meant for emergencies. Inside, the shelves were stocked with everything a fisherman could possibly need to survive if things went wrong out on the water: a thick woollen blanket, a first aid kit, a flare gun, a defibrillator, and a rubber float that could save a life in the worst of conditions. Rich had seen it all before, but it never hurt to take a quick glance at the supplies.

He walked past the wooden shelves, filled with nets, buckets, and the odd tool or two used to maintain the quay during the harsh winter months. The boathouse was like a time capsule of island life, each item a reminder of the routines they followed year after year. He moved toward the small desk at the far end of the room, a simple wooden thing that had seen better days. Rich clicked on the desk lamp, the faint buzz of electricity flickering to life. He thumbed through the pages of the logbook, his fingers moving with familiarity. The pages were starting to yellow with age, the handwriting on the entries sometimes a little faded but always legible. As he reached the next blank space, he paused, reflecting on the most recent entries. His own scrawl filled the last five pages. "Guess nobody likes leaving the island," he muttered to himself, a wry smile tugging at his lips.

It was a fact that had become painfully clear over the years. Most of the islanders did not leave—could not leave. It was not just the weather or the sea that kept them here; it was something deeper, something woven into the very fabric of their lives. The island was more than just a place—it was home. For some, it was the only home they knew.

Rich finished the entry, his pen hovering over the page for a moment longer than necessary. The water outside the boathouse was still. It always was this time of morning—like the world was holding its breath before the chaos of the day began. Rich shook himself from the momentary trance and closed the logbook, sliding it into its rightful place on the shelf.

He stepped back into the morning light, took a deep breath of the salty air, and glanced once more toward Daisy. She was waiting for him, rocking gently against the quay, as if she too was ready to take on whatever the sea had in store for the day.

The day was just beginning, but already, Rich felt the pull of the water in his chest. The island had a way of doing that—reminding you that life here moved at its own pace, unaffected by the worries and chaos of the world beyond the horizon. But something was different today. There was a quiet hum of anticipation in the air, a feeling that something—something big—was just beyond the edge of the sea, waiting to be discovered. Rich couldn't shake the feeling as he walked back toward the quay. Whatever it was, he knew it was coming, and it was coming fast.

Chapter 23
02:00 hours, 1ˢᵗ August 2024,
Bravo Charlie One, Brancaster, Norfolk Coastline

PC 9420 stepped out of the van into the relentless rain, his steel-toed boots hitting the wet pavement with a satisfying thud. The dull gleam of the floodlights reflected off the polished leather as a broad grin broke across his face. At last, something exciting. After a year of trudging through the sleepy streets of Hunstanton, collaring petty thieves and breaking up squabbles outside chip shops, tonight was different—tonight had a pulse. "Oi, Andy! Don't forget this," the driver called, leaning out the window and thrusting a torch in his direction.

"You're not gonna see a damn thing out there without it. Got the rest of your kit sorted?" Andy nodded, a little too quickly, clutching the torch like it was a lifeline. He replayed the memory of double and triple-checking his gear earlier at the station. His bag had been packed and repacked so many times he was sure he could have done it blindfolded.

"Good," the driver said, his tone softening but his eyes serious. "Listen, this isn't some two-bit pickpocket you're dealing with. Stick with your team, don't go wandering off, and keep your head straight. How're you feeling?" Andy tilted his face up to meet the driver's gaze, his grin widening. "Excited." The older man paused, studying Andy's expression.

His own attempt at a smile was tight, like a parent watching their kid ride off without training wheels for the first time. "Right. Well, just... think before you act, yeah? I'm grabbing a quick piss and heading back to the station. I'll swing by around lunchtime to collect you and your team. Try not to get yourself killed before then." For the first time, the mundane rhythm of his life had cracked open, letting in the thrill of the unknown.

"Thanks," Andy muttered, his gaze darting around as he tried to make sense of the chaos unfolding around him. The rain drummed relentlessly on the sea of vehicles and equipment, while shouts and orders cut through the damp night air. His boots squelched in the mud as he shifted his weight uneasily. "You know where to go?" the driver asked, his tone calm but watchful, as though sizing up the rookie's ability to handle the storm of activity. Andy hesitated, fumbling for an answer. "Uh... not exactly. The brief said to relieve Tango Three, but it's... well, it's a mess here. No one seems to be in charge—or at least, I've no clue who my CO is."

The driver chuckled, shaking his head as if he'd heard it all before. One hand rested on the steering wheel, the other hovered over the gear stick. "Yeah, welcome to the fun, kid. Might wanna start over there." He jabbed a finger towards the Command trailer, its canvas flapping under the weight of the wind. The glow of light inside cast shifting silhouettes on the damp fabric. "If nothing else, they'll tell you who to bother next. Now, move it, sunshine. I've got to squeeze this beast into a parking spot before someone yells at me."

Andy stepped back as the van's window rolled up with a mechanical whir. The engine growled as the driver swung the vehicle expertly into a narrow gap between two mud-splattered Land Rovers. Andy stood there for a moment, torch in hand, feeling like a small cog in a much bigger, more chaotic machine. The Command trailer loomed ahead, and with a deep breath, he started trudging toward it, rain trickling down his collar. "Hey, you!" a booming voice cut through the rain, sharp and commanding. Andy froze mid-step, turning to see a figure a few meters away, silhouetted against the glare of headlights. The voice came again, louder this time. "Yes, you! What's your assignment, lad?" Andy scrambled for the words, his pulse quickening as the details of his briefing swirled chaotically in his mind. "Err... uh, I think... Tango Three. Yes, Sarge! Tango Three!" he shouted, the words tumbling out as he straightened his posture.

Before he could catch his breath, his attention was pulled to a scene nearby. Two Officers and a soggy-looking German Shepherd stood chatting beside a mud-splattered car. The dog's ears perked up as one of the men turned, revealing himself to be a hulking figure in short sleeves and a stab vest. His thick arms crossed as he gave Andy a faintly amused glance before turning to respond to the voice. "Spence!" the shout came again, this time with a hint of impatience. Sergeant Dave Greggs stood nearby; his brow furrowed as he waved toward the group. "What unit are you with? This lad's here to relieve Tango Three. That you?" Spence cocked his head, his smile tugging into something more wry as he stepped away from the car. "We're Six," he said, his voice casual as he nodded toward his colleagues. "Three's, uh…" He trailed off, scratching his chin as if the answer were buried somewhere deep in the folds of his memory. His eyes darted back to Greggs, squinting through the downpour. "Hold on, Sarge, let me think…"

The seconds dragged as they stood there, rainwater pooling around their boots and rivulets streaming down their jackets. Andy shifted awkwardly, unsure whether to speak or stay silent, while Greggs sighed heavily, hands planted on his hips. Somewhere in the distance, the bark of a static from a radio and the muffled thrum of engines added to the cacophony. Finally, Spence snapped his fingers, a spark of realization lighting his face. "Yeah, they're over by the east gate, I think. Someone should've flagged that by now."

"It's Finlay, that's it," Spence said, a self-satisfied grin spreading across his face. "But you just missed him. He headed off a few minutes ago with Pete and his dog." He made a show of turning to leave, clearly pleased with his answer, but stopped mid-step as Dave cleared his throat loudly. "And which way did they go?" Dave asked, his tone sharp as he beckoned Andy to step closer. Spence rolled his eyes but obligingly closed the distance between them, sparing everyone from having to yell over the rain and chaos. With exaggerated sarcasm, Spence jabbed a finger toward the edge of the car park, where the trees loomed dark and foreboding. "That way. Into the woods." He paused, scratching the back of his neck as though recalling a minor detail. "One of 'em hopped in the last transit van back to the station, though. So good luck finding the rest."

Dave's jaw tightened, but before he could respond, Spence clapped his hands together. "Now, if you don't mind, me and the lads here are taking a well-earned break. Four hours out there, Sarge. Four. My feet are chafing like nobody's business." He spun on his heel, not waiting for permission to leave, and strode off toward the toilet block. The other two Officers, their conversation picking up right where it had left off, followed in his wake, the German Shepherd trotting faithfully beside them. Andy glanced at Dave, who exhaled a long, frustrated sigh. "Right, rookie," Dave muttered, already stepping toward the Command trailer. "Looks like we're chasing ghosts tonight."

With a practiced motion, Dave unclipped his radio from his vest and pressed the transmit button, his voice steady and authoritative. "Brave Charlie One to Tango Three, copy." He released the button, waiting as the static crackled ominously in response. A brief pause, then he tried again, his tone firmer. "Tango Three, this is Sergeant 6432 at Bravo Charlien One. Do you copy? Over."

Silence. Only the hiss of dead air answered him.

Dave's frown deepened as he turned to Andy, his expression a mix of frustration and disbelief. "Looks like we've got ourselves a problem, son. Your team's gone and left without you. One man short. That's a breach of protocol." His voice dropped, edged with annoyance. "I need to report this immediately. Stay here. Don't move." Before Andy could respond, Dave spun on his heel and jogged off toward the Command trailer, his boots splashing through puddles as rain slicked his jacket. Andy watched him disappear beneath the flapping canvas, then glanced around, his sense of isolation creeping in with the cold.

He checked his watch, the second-hand ticking in deliberate defiance of the chaos around him. His gaze wandered to the toilet block where Spence and his colleagues lingered. One Officer lit a cigarette beneath the weak shelter of the overhang while another fiddled with his gear. Their dog, blissfully oblivious to protocol and drama, seized the moment to lift its leg against a nearby bin, marking its territory with the nonchalance of someone who had already decided they were in charge. Andy shifted on his feet, gripping his torch tightly. The rain kept falling, and the air felt heavier with every passing second.

Checking his watch again, Andy felt impatience clawing at him. Butterflies churned in his stomach, a strange mix of nerves and excitement. The chaos around him only fuelled the adrenaline: the relentless strobe of blue lights, Officers rushing about with purpose he couldn't quite decipher, and beyond it all, the dark, sprawling woods. Somewhere out there was a convict on the run. His first real manhunt. What wasn't there to be excited about?

He glanced toward the Command trailer, chewing his lip. His team was already out there. How long had it been since they'd left? Minutes? Longer? Maybe they were just waiting by the tree line, just out of sight. He tightened his grip on the torch in his hand, the urge to act bubbling up. "Stuff it," he muttered under his breath. Reaching behind to pull his cap from where it was tucked into his cargo trousers, he jammed it onto his head. With a quick look around, he lowered his gaze and stepped off, moving with purpose toward the woods. His pace quickened, the rain pelting his cap and rolling down his jacket. He barely spared a glance back, silently praying Sergeant Greggs wouldn't spot him before he could disappear into the shadows. Andy's pulse raced as he neared the entrance to the woods, heart pounding at the thrill of taking the first step into the unknown.

Spence strolled out of the toilet block, drying his hands on a crumpled paper towel. "You lot set?" he called, tossing the soggy towel into an overflowing bin. The other two Officers nodded, one tugging their dog away from a pile of discarded beer cans as it sniffed enthusiastically. "Good," Spence said, stretching his arms above his head with a groan. "Let's grab a bite and figure out where our ride's parked. I'm dying for a brew and some shut—" His words faltered as his attention snagged on something across the car park. Between the rain-slicked rows of cars and motorcycles, a lone figure moved with intent.

The young Officer.

Spence squinted, watching as Andy made a direct line for the woods, his cap pulled low, his shoulders hunched like he was trying not to draw attention. "Isn't that…?" one of the Officers started, but Spence cut him off with a smirk. "Yep. That's Three's rookie. Looks like they waited for him by the tree line. Poor sod doesn't have a clue what he's about to wander into." They shared a brief chuckle, the rain dripping from the brims of their caps, before turning back toward the break area. The cold and damp didn't bother them much anymore; their clothes had already plastered to their skin hours ago. They trudged away, the dog trotting obediently at their side, leaving the rookie to his own fate.

***

Slowing his steps, Andy crept between the last two vehicles, the rain dripping steadily off his cap. His eyes locked onto two Officers stationed near the east gate entrance to the woods. "Damn," he muttered under his breath, ducking lower behind a car bonnet. The pair stood casually, chatting and laughing as if the storm and chaos around them were nothing more than background noise. Just five feet behind them, tantalizingly close, was the gate—the gateway to the woods and the action he so desperately craved.

Andy glanced at his watch, the ticking hands doing nothing to calm his nerves. He tilted his head, staring up at the hill that rose toward the dense, shadowy treeline. The woods loomed ominously, their twisted branches clawing at the storm-filled sky like a warning. Menacing? Sure. But also, irresistible. A spark of fantasy ignited in his mind. He could see it now: racing through the woods, his torch slicing through the darkness as he closed in on the convict. Then, the climactic moment—the convict making a last-ditch run for the beach, desperate to board a waiting boat. Andy would dive in, tackling him to the sand, a hero in the spotlight. The papers would run his photo, "Rookie Officer Brings Convict to Justice." The headlines practically wrote themselves.

"Excuse me, son."

The voice snapped him out of his daydream like a bucket of cold water. Andy blinked, startled, and looked up toward the gate. One of the Officers was staring directly at him, a raised brow and a knowing smirk cutting through the rain.

Standing upright, Andy stepped forward cautiously, his expression a mix of innocence and mild panic. "Who, me?" he asked, pointing at his chest. One of the Officers broke away from the gate, a lopsided grin on his face. "Yeah, you. What're you doing skulking around over there?" Andy opened his mouth to respond, but the words came out in a garbled mess of half-formed excuses. The Officer chuckled, holding up a hand to stop him. "Relax, lad. No harm done. Actually, you're just in time to do me a favour. I need a quick pit stop. Can you keep Fred here company while I'm gone? Won't take but a minute."

Andy blinked, unsure if this twist of fate was a stroke of luck or an inconvenience. He glanced over his shoulder toward the Command trailer, but Sergeant Greggs still hadn't reappeared. The rain fell harder, soaking into his collar. "Yeah, sure, no problem," he said at last, jogging over to the gate. The other Officer was waiting, hand extended. "Name's Fred," he said with a firm shake, his grip enveloping Andy's smaller hand like a vice. Andy barely had time to nod before Shaheed turned on his heel and ambled toward the building, waving casually over his shoulder. "Don't let anything happen while I'm gone," he called out, his voice light and teasing. Andy glanced toward the woods, his heart quickening. Alone with the gate—and the path to adventure—he felt the moment stretching before him like an unspoken dare.

The silence between them felt heavier than the rain, broken only by the soft rustle of leaves in the distance. Andy shifted uneasily, his eyes flicking to the other man, who stood with his hands stuffed into his pockets, whistling a jaunty tune. The melody nagged at Andy's memory until he blurted out, "I know that tune… wait, is that Lady Gaga?" Fred stopped mid-whistle, his lips quirking into a grin. "Three points to you, rookie. Now it's your turn."

Andy blinked, caught off guard. "My turn?" "Yeah," Fred said, leaning back casually against the gate. "Your turn. Let's hear it. Whistle something." Andy hesitated, glancing toward the woods as if they might swallow him whole. "I, uh... I really can't," he said, trying to sound apologetic.

Fred's laugh rang out, loud enough to startle a nearby crow from its perch. "What, don't tell me you can't whistle?" Andy shook his head, feigning reluctance. The truth was, he could whistle—exceptionally well, in fact. Piercingly loud and in perfect pitch, a talent that had once won him a bet in school. But the last thing he wanted was to get roped into Fred's ridiculous game. He needed a distraction, something to shift the focus away from himself. Fred, clearly amused, shrugged and started whistling again, the tune slipping seamlessly back into Lady Gaga. Andy forced a smile, his mind racing for an escape plan as the seconds ticked by.

The silence stretched between them once more, thick and uncomfortable. Fred's eyes darted toward the toilets, his impatience palpable as he waited for his colleague to return and resume their pointless game. The seconds dragged by, the only sound the soft patter of rain against the asphalt. Then, to Andy's surprise, Fred started walking away, heading along the fence line with a casual swagger. "Excuse me, Sir, where are you going?" Andy asked, his voice tinged with confusion.

Fred whipped around; his gaze sharp. "Firstly, don't call me 'Sir'. We're the same rank, mate," he snapped, his tone cutting through the air. "Secondly, there's a blind spot just up ahead. I'm sneaking a quick fag. You stay here and keep an eye on the woods. If anyone's coming, shout." Andy didn't respond. He simply turned his back, ignoring Fred's half-hearted request. As Fred disappeared into the shadows, Andy's eyes locked on the trees ahead. A quiet smile tugged at his lips. Alone now, he felt the weight of the moment shift—no longer a passive observer, but a participant in something bigger. The convict was out there, and the thrill of it suddenly felt like something tangible, just waiting for him to seize.

***

Standing next to the Operations Desk, Dave's frustration was palpable. He slammed a hand down on the counter, his voice rising. "What do you mean, the whole system's down?" The young female Officer at the desk didn't even look up from her screen, her fingers flying across the keyboard as she typed furiously. "Yes, comms are down. Been out for the last twenty minutes. The DCI's working on it, but I've been told it's going to take a while to fix." Dave's jaw tightened, and he let out a sharp exhale, rolling his eyes dramatically. "Great. Just what we needed. How the hell are we supposed to keep track of our teams out in the woods if we can't communicate?"

He ran a hand through his hair, pacing in frustration. "And another thing. I've got a rookie in the car park, supposed to be relieving someone from Tango Three. Do you know if they're still on base, or have they gone into the woods? If they're out there and the team's short-handed... we're looking at a serious breach of protocol. This could turn into a big problem, fast." The Officer paused, finally glancing up at him, her expression unreadable. Dave could see the gears turning behind her eyes.

The young woman continued typing, her fingers dancing over the keys, before suddenly halting. She looked up from her screen, pushing her black-rimmed glasses further down her nose, her gaze locking onto Dave's with a calculated calm. "As you're aware, all Tangos are supposed to have three personnel plus one canine, at all times," she stated, her voice cool but firm. Dave's blood simmered beneath his skin, but he forced himself to stay composed, his voice clipped. "That's right. And as I've just informed you, Tango Three is one man down. Sergeant Finlay and Pete are off-base, and as far as I know, they've entered the woods." His words hung in the air, sharp and unrelenting.

The woman stared at him for a long moment, her expression unreadable. Dave's patience thinned, but he softened his tone, trying to rein in his frustration. "Is there anyone else I can speak with?" "Look, PC... Andy," he faltered, a fleeting moment of doubt washing over him. Had he even caught the rookie's last name? The uncertainty gnawed at him, but he pushed forward, his eyes never leaving the woman's face. "Andy? Andy who?" The woman's voice was sharp, pulling Dave from his frustration, and a wave of heat rushed to his cheeks. The exhaustion was starting to catch up with him, making his words stumble. "I—sorry, I didn't get his surname. But there's a young Officer in the car park, waiting to join Tango Three. What do you want me to do with him?"

The female Officer didn't react immediately. Instead, she picked up a steaming cup of tea, savouring the warmth as she took a slow sip. Then, with a soft clink, she set the mug back down on the table and pushed her chair back. With a casual grace, she moved across the trailer, her shoes squeaking against the polythene sheeting on the floor as she approached another desk tucked against the wall.

She bent down, speaking in a low voice to the Officer sitting there. Dave could barely make out the words, but the tone was all business. After a moment, she stood upright again, walking back toward her desk with an air of finality. "Please ask PC... Andy, to come to the trailer," she said, her voice cool. "We'll assign him to other duties for now, until this matter is resolved." With a smile that didn't quite reach her eyes, she sat back down, fingers already poised over the keys, and began typing. She didn't notice Dave turn abruptly, striding quickly toward the door of the trailer. As the door swished closed behind him, the tension that had been building in his chest finally began to ease. He didn't have time to wait for anyone's permission. He had work to do.

The sharp bite of the cold air hit Dave's face, and he was momentarily stunned by how warm the trailer had felt in comparison. His breath came out in a misty puff as he scanned the car park, his eyes searching for the spot where Andy had been standing. But now, the area was eerily empty. His gaze flicked toward the food trailer, and for a fleeting moment, he considered grabbing a quick bite—maybe a hot sandwich to stave off the chill. But just as his stomach rumbled, he spotted Spence and the rest of his team casually strolling toward a van, a cloud of conversation hanging around them like smoke.

Without thinking, Dave broke into a sprint, his boots slapping against the tarmac as he closed the distance. He called out to Sergeant Spence just as the big man was about to step into the vehicle. Spence paused, eyes rolling with a mix of exasperation and amusement, before he turned with a heavy sigh. He hopped back out onto the pavement with a grunt, his boots thudding against the concrete. "You lads mount up," he barked at the rest of his team, "This won't take a minute." His tone was a little less than thrilled, but Dave could see the shift in his posture—the gears in Spence's mind already grinding into action.

Spence walked toward Dave, his stride heavy with exhaustion, his face drawn tight from the hours of relentless work. "Look, David," he said, voice thick with fatigue, "me and the lads are beat. We've been running on fumes for God knows how long. The DCI's got us pulling double shifts now. We really need some rest. So, make this quick." Dave nodded, trying to catch his breath, his chest heaving with the sudden burst of activity. He wiped a hand across his face, squinting into the cold. "Where's Andy... the young lad I was with earlier?"

Spence snorted, a sharp laugh that held no humour. "How the hell should I know? I'm not his babysitter. Last time I saw him, he was standing over there, right where I left you. Now, if you don't mind, I'm going to get some shut-eye. We're back in a couple of hours." With that, Spence turned on his heel, his bulk swinging toward the van. He climbed in with a grunt, pulling the door shut behind him with a decisive slam, leaving Dave standing alone in the cold, the van's engine humming softly as the tension in the air thickened.

Dave's eyes darted across the bustling car park, scanning the chaotic scene with growing frustration. The floodlights cast harsh, glaring beams across the space, leaving patches of shadow that seemed to swallow up any movement. Where the hell is he? The young Officer could be hiding anywhere in those dark corners. His gaze shifted toward the toilet block. There, he spotted Shaheed in the midst of a conversation with another Officer, standing far too relaxed for his liking. Without thinking, Dave broke into a fast stride, closing the distance in seconds, and tapped the officer sharply on the shoulder. "Hey, what the hell are you doing off your post?" Dave's voice cut through the air, a mix of irritation and authority.

Shaheed spun around, his face draining of colour. "Apologies, Sir," he stammered, his voice trembling. "Nature called. I've been holding it for the last hour, and I just couldn't wait any longer." Dave's frustration flared as he grabbed the man's arm, tugging him away from his conversation with the other Officer. "That's not an excuse. You know the rules. Two people are supposed to be guarding that entrance at all times."

Shaheed quickly recovered, plastering a smile on his face as he tried to deflect. "It's OK, Sir. I've got cover," he said, pointing towards the gate. Dave's eyes followed the direction of Shaheed's finger, landing on Fred, alone, hopping from foot to foot. The man looked anything but confident, nervously scanning his surroundings, his posture rigid with concern. Dave's irritation deepened. "Cover?" he muttered under his breath. This wasn't how things were supposed to be done.

***

As Andy glanced over his shoulder, the flickering lights of the car park bled through the trees, casting long shadows across the ground. He could just make out Sergeant Greggs, his voice sharp, barking orders at the two Officers stationed by the entrance. The realization hit him—there was no turning back now. He had crossed the point of no return. With a deep breath, he reached for his belt, his fingers brushing the cold metal of his flashlight. He clicked it on, and a narrow beam of light sliced through the inky darkness, illuminating the twisted shapes of branches and the distant silhouettes of trees. He scanned the shadows, squinting into the abyss, the faintest rustle making his heart skip a beat.

Suddenly, a deafening crack of thunder rolled through the air, shaking the ground beneath his boots. The sound jolted him, and he stumbled forward, his pulse quickening as he stepped cautiously onto the narrow path ahead. Each step felt heavier than the last, the weight of the storm, and the growing tension, pressing in on him as he ventured deeper into the woods.

The dark woodland loomed around Andy, its shadows deep and foreboding, but there was something exhilarating about it. It was a world away from the monotony of checking tyre treads, and the adrenaline of the unknown felt far more alive. As the rain began to pour harder, he tilted his head back, letting the cool droplets slap against his face. He closed his eyes for a moment, savouring the sharp chill that washed over him, feeling the tension in his shoulders ease. Then, out of the corner of his eye, something moved. A rustle, barely audible above the storm, snapped him out of his momentary respite. His gaze shot to the bushes to his left, but the dense undergrowth was impenetrable. His heart skipped a beat. What was that? Panic gripped him for a second, until his fingers instinctively reached for his flashlight. With a quick twist, the beam cut through the darkness, sweeping over the area—nothing.

His breath came out in a shaky exhale. Fear had a way of distorting reality, especially when it was this dark. Rather than retreating to the car park where he'd most likely be chewed out and sent back to the station, Andy gripped his torch tighter and pointed it ahead, toward the winding path that led uphill. With a reluctant but determined step, he pushed forward, the wet earth squelching underfoot, the light from his torch carving a narrow path into the encroaching gloom. The path narrowed, choked with dense, overgrown bushes that seemed to reach out with greedy fingers. Each step was a careful manoeuvre, but it was nearly impossible to avoid the sharp scrape of branches against his legs. With a sudden jolt, one of his trouser legs snagged on a thick stem, and he winced as he tried to free himself. The relentless thorns dug into his skin, sending a sting up his leg. He cursed, the frustration mingling with the sharp pain.

A moment later, a vicious prick sliced across his finger. The sudden warmth of blood trickled down his hand, the sting sharp and immediate. He sucked in a breath, instinctively pressing his finger to his mouth, his tongue brushing against the small wound. The taste of copper filled his mouth as he winced, trying to steady his breath. The darkness around him seemed to close in, the quiet hum of the woods amplified by the rapid thudding of his heartbeat. He spit out a few choice words, but his focus remained on the throbbing pain in his finger as he gingerly sucked at the wound, desperate for any distraction from the growing tension in the air.

Twenty minutes later, Andy stood atop the grassy bank, the path stretching ahead like a dark vein through the dense woods. The distant crash of ocean waves breaking on the shore reached his ears, pulling him into a memory of his training days. He could almost smell the salty air and feel the cold bite of the water as he and ten other recruits took turns dragging a lifeless dummy from the sea.

The day had been gruelling—rescuing the mannequin was one thing, but spending ten frustrating minutes clearing sand from its rubbery mouth under the unblinking gaze of his instructor? That was almost enough to get him booted from the Norfolk Constabulary. Kissing a half-torso for CPR practice wasn't the proudest moment of his life, but it made for a story he'd laugh at later.

A sharp hoot shattered his thoughts, jerking him back to the present. He glanced around, spotting the outline of an owl perched on a nearby branch, its silhouette ghostly in the dim light. A sudden rustle above made him flinch, a shiver racing down his spine as his eyes darted upward. For a brief second, he braced himself—but the bird flapped its wings and took flight, disappearing into the night. Andy exhaled, laughing at his own nerves. "Spooked me, didn't you, stupid bird," he muttered, his voice low and amused. Shaking his head, he turned his attention back to the path, but the eerie quiet of the woods seemed to press in closer, as though mocking his attempt at humour.

Spinning around at the sudden sound behind him, Andy's movement was met with a razor-sharp sting across his neck. The pain was instant and searing, but shock overtook him before he could process it fully. His instinct was to scream, but no sound came, only a choked rasp as his throat tightened. His flashlight slipped from his grasp, tumbling to the ground, casting wild, flickering arcs of light over the grass. His hands flew to his neck, warm liquid spilling over his fingers and soaking into his vest—blood. His blood.

He staggered, gasping for air that wouldn't come. His vision blurred, and his knees wobbled, but his eyes caught something in the torch's weak glow: a pair of muddy boots, planted firmly in the grass. Frozen. Unmoving. His panicked mind screamed for help. With trembling fingers, he reached out toward the shadowy figure, hoping, praying for mercy. Instead, the figure sprang into action. The gleam of a blade sliced through the air with horrifying precision. Andy barely registered the pain as three of his fingers were severed in one fluid motion. He watched, stunned, as the digits spun like broken twigs, glistening briefly in the torchlight before disappearing into the wet grass.

His body reacted before his mind could. Panic took over, and he tried to swallow, but his throat felt foreign, distant, like it didn't belong to him anymore. He clasped the wound with his remaining hand and turned, desperate to flee. His boots slipped on the muddy ground, sending him careening headfirst into a tree with a sickening thud. The world tilted violently, the torchlight now a distant blur, as darkness began to claw at the edges of his vision.

Dazed and sprawled on the wet ground, Andy blinked up at the fractured canopy of trees above. Rain streaked through the gaps, falling in silvery threads that blurred his vision further. A shadowy figure loomed above him, its edges distorted and unreal, like a spectre summoned by the storm. Andy's chest heaved as he tried to draw in air, but each breath felt shallower than the last, a rasping fight against the suffocating darkness creeping in. He considered lifting his hand, a feeble plea for mercy, but the dull throb of his mutilated fingers held him back. Instead, he lay motionless, his blood mixing with the rain-soaked earth beneath him. Help, his lips shaped the word silently, his voice long since stolen by the slash to his throat. His gaze fixed on the figure, watching as it crouched down, its face still obscured in shadow.

The man's hair, long and wild, brushed against Andy's clammy skin, sending an involuntary shiver down his battered frame. For a fleeting moment, Andy thought—Maybe he's checking if I'm alive. But then he felt the cold press of a blade, deliberate and cruel, slicing into him with mechanical precision. The pain was sharp and immediate, but his fading consciousness dulled its edge, leaving only the horrifying realization: this was not a rescue. The rain mingled with his blood, pooling around him as his vision spiralled inward, the stranger's faceless silhouette becoming the last thing he'd ever see.

Chapter 24
02:17 hours, 1ˢᵗ August 2024,
A149, West of Brancaster, Norfolk Coastline

Tapping his debit card against the reader, Jack Maskell waited with feigned patience, his eyes darting to the attendant who was half-lost in the ritual of stacking cigarette packs onto the shelf. The man's hand paused mid-air as the machine beeped, spitting out a receipt like it was eager to move on. He reached to hand it over, but Jack was already on the move—striding down the aisle with a quiet determination, his footsteps muffled against the linoleum floor as he zeroed in on the exit, leaving the receipt and the moment behind him.

Natalia Wallace sat slouched in the driver's seat of the battered Ford Fiesta, furiously tapping at her phone in a losing battle to log into her Facebook account. A glance at the no-service icon at the top of the screen made her groan in frustration. With a resigned huff, she tossed the phone into her handbag, the clink of metal zippers cutting through the quiet. The sudden yank of the car door startled her, and she jumped. "You absolute shit!" she snapped, clutching her chest. Jack slid in beside her, grinning as he slammed the door shut. "What'd you say?" he teased, raising an eyebrow. She punched him lightly on the arm, her glare melting into a smirk. "You made me jump, idiot. So, we good?" Jack jammed the key into the ignition, giving her a cheeky wink as the engine coughed to life. With a playful rev, he pulled off the forecourt, the car rattling slightly as they disappeared into the hum of the road ahead.

As they sped away from the petrol station, the dull hum of the Fiesta's engine underscored Jack's glance toward Natalia. Her profile caught the soft glow of the streetlights, and for a fleeting moment, he forgot the road ahead. "You know what?" he said, a grin tugging at his lips. "Have I told you how much I love you lately?" She turned to him, her eyes dancing with mischief. "Yeah? If you loved me that much, we wouldn't be stuck in this tin can on wheels. You'd have whisked me off to a fancy hotel by now—someplace glam." Jack chuckled, but it was the kind of laugh that masked a pang of guilt.

Four years with Natalia had flipped his world upside down; he was utterly hooked on her. But love wasn't paying the bills, and his track record with jobs was about as reliable as the Fiesta's rattling gearbox. "Sorry, babe," Jack said with a sheepish grin. "I'd love to splash out on somewhere… you know, glam. But money's tight right now. I'm still hunting for another job. Until then, it's just me, collecting glasses at the Dog and Badger, waiting for something better to roll around."

The Fiesta rattled along the dimly lit A149, the sparse streetlights casting long shadows over the road. As they entered Titchwell, Jack eased off the accelerator. "You know," he said, chuckling, "I must've driven through this village a dozen times, and I still manage to miss the bloody turning." He glanced over at Natalia, but her gaze was fixed on the window, her reflection ghosting across the dark glass as houses blurred by. "You good over there? Hey!" He nudged her leg, and she turned to him slowly, her expression soft but distant. "Yeah," she said, offering a faint smile. "I'm alright. Just… thinking, that's all."

Hoping to lighten the mood, Jack reached for the radio dial, but the car erupted in a deafening burst of static that shattered the silence. The noise jolted him, and the Fiesta veered dangerously toward the kerb. "Whoa! Watch it!" Natalia shrieked, clutching the door handle as the car wobbled across to the other side of the road before Jack wrestled it back under control. His knuckles whitened on the wheel. "Would you mind?" she snapped, leaning forward to kill the static with a twist of the dial. The silence that followed felt heavier than before.

Natalia sighed; her voice low. "Maybe it's time we just headed home, yeah?" Jack checked the dashboard clock and grinned, trying to shake off the tension. "Probably a good call. But how are you sneaking in? Doesn't your dad start work in, like, an hour? Won't he catch you?" She shook her head with a sly smile. "Not a chance. He rolls out of bed twenty minutes before he leaves, and I left the back porch unlocked. No worries." Jack smirked, the tension easing as he focused back on the road. "You're a real pro at this, huh?"

Slowing to a crawl at twenty miles per hour, Jack's grip on the wheel tightened as the car snaked around a bend, the headlights barely cutting through the encroaching darkness. He scanned for a spot to turn around, relief flashing across his face when he spotted a narrow road to the left. With a sharp flick of the indicator, he cranked the wheel, the Fiesta groaning as it eased onto the side lane.

"I thought you were just going to reverse out of here," Natalia muttered, her tone edging toward impatience. Jack leaned forward, his face just inches from the wheel, his eyes locked on the rain-slicked lane ahead. The first drops of rain turned into a sudden torrent, hammering the windscreen. He fumbled for the wipers, their rhythmic swiping barely keeping up as water smeared across the glass. "Storm's hitting hard. Can't see a damn thing," he muttered.

Natalia shifted uneasily, folding her arms tightly across her chest. "This is bad, Jack. Can't you just back up to the main road? I don't like this—where the hell is this even taking us?" The car's tyres crunched over loose gravel as the narrow road disappeared into the shadows ahead, the storm's fury intensifying by the second. They drove on intense silence, the car creeping forward as the tyres splashed through puddles that filled the jagged potholes. Each bump rattled the Fiesta, its headlights barely carving a path through the suffocating darkness. A sudden flash of lightning split the sky, illuminating the jagged thunderclouds looming above like a warning.

"Jack, I'm serious," Natalia's voice broke through, sharp with fear. "Stop the car and go back the way we came." He gripped the wheel tighter, the strain showing in his clenched jaw. Truth be told, her fear mirrored his own. The shadows seemed alive, swallowing what little light his headlights offered, and the rain hammered relentlessly against the windscreen, each drop a drumbeat of dread. "There's nowhere to turn around," he said, his voice low but wavering. "We have to keep going. There's gotta be a spot up ahead where we can flip around. We're close to the beach—I can feel it." The storm offered no reassurance, only the growl of thunder in the distance and the unsettling sense that they were driving deeper into the unknown.

Natalia turned her head, glancing over her shoulder, and her breath caught. The trees and bushes lining the road were bathed in an unnatural crimson glow, casting long, twisted shadows that gave the path an unsettling, otherworldly feel. She snapped her gaze back to the front, heart racing, when a flicker of light appeared on the horizon. Before she could even blink, it vanished into the storm-dark sky. "What was that?" Her voice was tight, a mix of curiosity and unease.

Jack, still focused on the road, barely glanced at her. "What was what? What did you see?" Natalia leaned forward, her eyes scanning the window with a nervous intensity. Jack tried to steal a glance at her, but his attention remained mostly on the darkened lane. "I thought I saw a light… or something," she murmured, her voice tinged with uncertainty. Jack dismissed it quickly, trying to keep his own unease in check. "Probably just a fishing trawler. We're close to the beach now. Nothing to worry about." But even as he said it, a twinge of doubt gnawed at him, the echo of the flicker lingering in his mind like a warning he couldn't shake.

A few minutes passed, and the narrow lane began to open up. The car rolled past a weathered barrier next to a signpost. Jack's headlights flashed across it for a split second, and he squinted to read the text. His stomach dropped. "Shit. This is the car park for the RSPB Centre. The cameras are gonna pick up my number plate." Natalia blinked in confusion, chewing on her lip. "What the hell are you talking about? Why the hell is that a concern? If it were me, I'd be more worried about getting me home—Dad's getting up in forty minutes. If he finds out I'm not home, you can kiss goodbye to next weekend."

Jack slowed the car, his thoughts racing. The tyres bumped over a speed hump as they rolled into the car park. "If someone checks the footage, they'll see my number plate, know the time, and then we're toast." She erupted into laughter, not bothering to hide her amusement. "Christ, seriously? Knock it off. You need to stop binge-watching those spy shows. No one's gonna check the footage, and no one is definitely interested in you and this rust bucket." Jack couldn't help but chuckle, but the nagging worry still gnawed at the back of his mind as the rain continued to pour down.

Jack slammed on the brakes, the car jerking to a halt. His heart was pounding as he opened his mouth to speak, but before he could utter a word, movement caught his eye—something shifting in the shadows across the car park. The headlights sliced through the dark, briefly illuminating a figure before it vanished into the blackness. His grip tightened on the steering wheel, his pulse racing. His breath caught as his eyes bulged in disbelief. "What the fuck was that?"

There was no answer. Natalia had curled up, her knees pulled tight to her chest, her face pale, the usual spark in her eyes replaced by something cold and distant. She was shaken, visibly rattled by what they'd just seen. "Maybe it was just a fox, or a dog," Jack muttered, trying to convince himself more than her. But when he glanced at her, he saw the tears welling up in her eyes.

Her voice was quiet, barely a whisper. "Last time I checked, foxes and dogs don't run on two legs… and they sure as hell aren't six feet tall." The words hung in the air, heavy and unsettling, as the night around them seemed to grow even darker. The silence was shattered by a sudden crack of thunder, a deep rumble that seemed to shake the very air around them. Both of them sat motionless, eyes glued to the dark windows, waiting, scanning for any flicker of movement in the shadows. Though they were safely locked inside the car, the oppressive atmosphere made it feel like they were exposed, vulnerable.

An idea crept into Jack's mind. He reached for the small dial next to the steering wheel and, with a twist, turned off the headlights. The world outside the car plunged into darkness, save for the distant flicker of lightning. Natalia let out a shrill scream, her fist landing repeatedly on his arm. "Turn them back on! Now!" Jack quickly complied; his hands raised in a gesture of surrender. "Sorry, sweetheart. It's a night vision thing. You turn off the lights, your eyes adjust, and you can see better… I think." She punched him again, her face twisted in frustration as she gritted her teeth. "Next time you want to play boy scout, leave me the hell at home."

The rain hammered the bonnet, each drop amplifying the tension that hung in the air. Jack's mind raced, his grip tightening on the steering wheel. To turn the car around, he'd have to drive forward—right to the spot where that shadow had appeared and vanished, as if mocking them. His heart hammered in his chest, the fear creeping in, but his pride refused to let it show. He forced a calm smile, his voice steadier than he felt. "Look, chances are it's just the dark playing tricks on us. It's late, you're tired, I'm tired—how about we just swing this car around and get out of here? What do you say?"

He didn't wait for an answer. His foot lifted from the brake, the car creeping forward as he slipped it into first gear. The engine sputtered to life, but the air inside the car felt heavy with anticipation. He focused on the road ahead, his heart pounding louder than the rain as they moved toward the spot where that shadow had disappeared, uncertainty gnawing at the edges of his calm exterior. Without warning, the car was suddenly flooded with blinding light, as if the world had been flipped on its head. It pierced through the windows, dazzling and disorienting, forcing both of them to shield their eyes from the onslaught. "What the hell?" Jack's voice cracked, a hint of panic creeping in.

Confused and shaken, Natalia fumbled across the seat, her fingers desperately reaching for his hand, her touch trembling with fear. "I can't see anything." Jack felt her hand brush against his, and in that instant, reality slammed back into place. He wasn't alone. She was terrified— they were terrified. He grasped her hand tightly, the warmth of her touch grounding him. "It's OK, sweetie," he murmured, his voice soft but steady, as he ran his thumb gently along the side of her palm. "It's OK... I'm here. I'm not going to let anything happen to you, I promise." He could feel her pulse racing, just like his, but he didn't let go. In that moment, the words were all he had to offer, but somehow, they felt like enough.

A whirlwind of scenarios played out in Jack's mind, each one darker than the last, until finally, the horrifying realization hit him like a punch to the gut. His face drained of colour; his body frozen in terror. The bile rose in his throat, and he swallowed hard, his voice barely a whisper. "Shit." The sound snapped Natalia out of her dazed trance. She turned to look at him, barely able to make out his pale, stricken face in the dim light. "What's wrong?" Her voice was trembling, unable to read the panic twisting his features. Jack's breath came in short, ragged gasps as he struggled to make sense of the nightmare unfolding. "I've worked it out... I know what this is... Oh my God, shit, shit, shit!" His words rushed out, panic seeping into every syllable.

Instinctively, Natalia reached for his arm, no longer angry but desperate. She squeezed it hard, her fingers digging into his flesh. "Tell me, Jack. What's wrong? You're scaring me." His voice cracked with fear, his words barely coherent. "Bloody... aliens... UFOs... This is an abduction." Before he could even process what he had just said, the window beside him exploded in a shower of glass. The sharp shards cut across his face as he screamed in shock and pain.

Natalia froze, her heart hammering in her chest as a large, black arms reached through the shattered window. It snaked past Jack, who continued to scream, unbuckling his seatbelt with terrifying speed. The arm yanked him from his seat, dragging him out of the window. The ground rushed up to meet Jack as he hit it hard, the cold puddle soaking into his jeans. His eyes slammed shut, his entire body shaking in fear as he curled up, arms shielding his head, waiting for the final blow. But it never came. "It's alright," a calm voice said. "It's just a couple of kids, damn it. Hey, can you hear me? Stop screaming, you're OK. It's safe... now, remove your arms... that's it, easy now... look up at me..."

Jack hesitated, his arms trembling as he slowly lowered them, his palms sinking into the cold, wet ground. When he opened his eyes, they stung from the wetness, but he managed to squint through the blur. "What's going on? Who are you?" A voice close by answered, steady and reassuring. "You're safe. Don't worry. My name's Mark. I'm a Police Officer. What the hell are you two doing out here? Do you know what time it is?" Still disoriented, Jack reached up, taking the Officer's hand and pulling himself to his feet. His clothes were soaked, his legs stiff from the cold, and he glanced at the wreckage of the car—the window shattered, glass scattered across the seat and footwell. Anger flared inside him as he pointed to the mess. "What do you mean? Look at me! Look at that!" He gestured to the wreckage. "Who's going to pay for this? You?" Mark glanced over at the damaged car, then back at Jack with an unreadable expression. "No harm done. I'll arrange for a tow. Don't worry about the car."

Before Jack could respond, another Officer approached, and Mark turned to him, speaking quietly. When he turned back to face Jack, the tone had changed, firm but professional. "We'll get it towed to town. A car's on the way for you." Jack's mind raced, still trying to process what had just happened, but it was hard to focus with everything swirling around him. As he stood there, Natalia suddenly appeared beside him, her hand gripping his arm, her eyes wide with fear. They both turned towards the sky. Halo Two hovered above the northern edge of the car park, its searchlight sweeping the darkened landscape below. "What are they looking for?" Natalia asked, her voice barely above a whisper. Before Jack could answer, Mark was already on the move, striding towards three Officers and a dog.

"What Tango are you?" Mark asked as he reached them. The Sergeant stepped forward. "We're eight. Where do you want us?" Mark glanced around, assessing the situation. "The suspect was last seen heading west. I've got three Tango's already coming in from Thornham Point. You guys head east, back towards Brancaster Beach." He retrieved a small map from his vest, unfurling it with practiced precision. "We're here. Work your way up this way, then skirt inland past the main car park and head toward the beach. We'll try to box this guy in once and for all."

Paul, one of the Officers, nodded and turned to his team. "Right, lads, let's go. Come on, Betty, lead the way." As they moved out, the sound of distant voices and the whir of the helicopter filled the air, and Jack and Natalia were left in stunned silence, the weight of the moment settling around them like a thick fog.

Chapter 25
03:27 hours, 1st August 2024,
Brancaster Woodland, Norfolk Coastline

Sniffing the air with increasing fervour, Betty yanked harder on the leash, nearly pulling Ross off balance. "Having trouble keeping up, little brother?" Ross teased, his grin cutting through the dimly lit woods. "Cut the chatter, both of you," Paul snapped, his voice low but commanding. "Stay sharp. The convict could be just ahead. Keep those torches steady—we can't afford to lose visibility out here." He shot a quick glance at Ross and Jack before tightening his grip on his own flashlight. His throat tightened briefly, but not with fear—pride surged through him like a quiet, steady current.

After nearly three decades in the Norfolk Constabulary, Paul had seen his share of Officers come and go. Some retired, others succumbed to the job's dangers, and a few simply chose another path. Yet here he was, watching these young men—raw, eager, and full of promise—dedicate themselves to a career that wasn't just a job, but a way to protect and serve their community. It stirred something deep in him: a belief that, despite everything, the future still had good hands to steer it.

The path began to narrow, the thick vegetation clawing at their uniforms as Jack led the group, Betty's nose glued to the ground. Behind him, Ross and Paul tightened their formation, their flashlights slicing through the oppressive darkness ahead. The air felt heavier with each step, the stillness amplifying every crunch of leaves underfoot. Ross wiped a sheen of cold sweat from his brow, his nerves betraying him despite his best efforts to appear calm. "Sarge," Ross ventured, his voice thin, "have you ever done anything like this before?" Paul glanced at him, sensing the younger Officer's unease. Instead of addressing the question directly, he smirked. "What, taking a stroll through the woods? Loads of times. Though, usually, I've got my wife with me—not two clowns tripping over themselves." Jack stifled a chuckle, the sound coming out as a snort, and Ross couldn't help but grin. The humour cut through his tension like a blade, and for a moment, the oppressive weight lifted.

"Funny, Sarge, but seriously," Ross pressed, his smile fading into curiosity. "Have you ever been part of something this big? The resources, the manpower—it's like something out of a movie." Paul paused, turning slightly, his face a shadowy mix of amusement and focus. "A movie, huh? Let's hope this story has the ending we're all aiming for," he said cryptically before pressing on, his words leaving Ross wondering just how much the Sarge had really seen— and how much he wasn't saying.

They approached a fork in the path and came to a halt, their breaths forming faint clouds in the cool night air. Betty lowered her head, sniffing the ground with intent before lifting her nose to the air. Suddenly, she darted toward a nearby tree, tail wagging in a frenzy of excitement. Jack stepped forward; his voice laced with anticipation. "Hold on, lads—she's onto something."

Tango Eight approached cautiously, stopping a meter from the dog. They stood in silence, the beam of their torches fixed on Betty as she investigated the base of the tree. Ross broke the tension. "What do you think she's found?" Jack glanced over his shoulder at his brother, a mischievous glint in his eyes. "Probably a severed head." The blood drained from Ross's face, and his mouth hung open in horror. Before Jack could push the joke further, Paul spun to face him, so close their noses almost touched. "I said knock it off with the horseplay," he growled through clenched teeth, his voice low but sharp.

"Or I'll march you back to Bravo Charlie One myself. You copy?"

Before Jack could respond, Ross cut in, his voice a mix of panic and relief. "Wait—look at her! She's doing something." All eyes turned back to Betty as she paced back and forth near the tree, her nose alternating between the bark, the mud, and the grass. Her movements grew more deliberate, almost methodical, before she finally stopped and squatted on the ground. The group froze, torn between confusion and disappointment. Ross broke the silence with a dry chuckle. "Well, lads, looks like she found... nature calling."

"You have got to be kidding me. Seriously, Betty?" Jack groaned, throwing his hands up as the others erupted into laughter. The tension shattered like glass, replaced by a fleeting, welcome moment of normality. They let the chuckles linger, savouring the brief reprieve. Betty, blissfully unaware of her comedic timing, finished her business and trotted down the right-hand path with an eager wag of her tail. "Hang on, girl! Wait for us!" Jack called, stepping forward with Ross close behind.

A throat cleared behind them, pointed and deliberate. Both men turned to see Paul standing stiffly, a small black bag dangling from his middle finger like a scolding parent's accessory. "Gentlemen," he said dryly, "aren't you forgetting something? Or do you plan on breaking the law tonight?" Jack smirked and turned to his brother, the gleam of trouble sparking in his eye. "Well, Ross, go on then. Make yourself useful. Pick it up." Ross opened his mouth to protest, but Paul was faster. "Actually," he interrupted, stepping forward with mock authority, "as the dog handler, you have the responsibility. So why don't you handle it, Jack?"

Jack's smirk faltered as Ross took Betty's harness with glee. "Your turn, big brother," Ross said, folding his arms. Grumbling, Jack snatched the bag from Paul's outstretched hand and crouched down, muttering under his breath. "Welcome to the glamorous life of the Norfolk Constabulary," Paul quipped, his tone rich with amusement as the group resumed their pursuit.

A few moments later, the now-full bag swung lazily from Jack's belt as he caught up with Paul and Ross. The trio pressed on, their torches carving paths through the thickening darkness as they moved east toward the beach. Jack glanced at his watch, frowning at the time. "Another ninety minutes until our shift ends, Sarge. What do you say we turn around now? Might as well start heading back." Paul slowed to a stop, placing a firm hand on Ross's shoulder to halt him as well. He checked his own watch, the faint glow reflecting off his face. "Let's not call it quits just yet. The sun will be up in a few hours. I say we push another hundred feet up this path, see if Betty can find us some evidence. Be nice to go home with something to show for our trouble."

Ross glanced at the bag on Jack's hip, a smirk creeping across his face as he opened his mouth for a quip. But his brother's icy glare silenced him before he could get a word out. Swallowing his grin, Ross turned instead to follow Betty, who was already sniffing eagerly along the trail. Jack muttered under his breath, adjusting the offending bag at his side as they trudged forward. The humour had waned, replaced by a quiet hope that the dog's keen nose might yet turn their night around.

***

Katie stretched luxuriously across the backseat, her wet mane glistening under the car's interior light. She let out a soft, contented sigh as Pete's tattooed hand stroked her fur. She basked in the attention, her tail giving a half-hearted thump against the seat as Pete cooed at her. Outside the car, Pete glanced toward his commanding Officer. "Sarge, how much longer are we waiting? It's been thirty minutes. We're supposed to be in the woods by now, didn't Sargeant Green say we are supposed to meet him and the rest on the beach," he grumbled, his tone teetering on irritation as he continued to pamper the dog. Finlay took a few steps forward, his eyes scanning the poorly lit car park. He squinted at every figure, his frustration growing with every empty moment. "This is a bloody shower of shit," he muttered, rubbing the back of his neck. "No organisation, no coordination. Christ, it wouldn't surprise me if the convict waltzed straight through here, waving as he passed. And who'd notice? No one, that's who."

Pete smirked but didn't respond, his focus shifting between the dog and his CO. Finlay let out a sharp breath, his frustration mounting as he scanned the car park one more time. The pair exchanged glances, both hoping—praying—to spot the replacement Officer stumbling toward them like a lost sheep. But the longer they waited, the more it felt like the night was slipping further from their control. Finlay's eyes darted across the car park, lingering on the dimly lit toilet block before trailing along the perimeter fence. His gaze stopped at the sight of a man near the East Entrance Gate, shouting animatedly at two Officers. The man's arms flailed wildly, his entire body bouncing with anger. "Looks like Big Dave's tearing someone a new one," Pete muttered, still scratching behind Katie's ears as he nodded toward the scene.

Finlay squinted, his expression sharpening as he turned toward the gate. "Shit," he said under his breath, "things are kicking off." Without another word, Finlay stepped away from the vehicle, his long strides purposeful and direct. A sharp whistle cut through the night air, and Katie sprang off the backseat, landing with a thud before padding to his side. Pete jogged after them, his earlier nonchalance replaced with an edge of urgency. As they approached, the shouting grew louder, the words incoherent but laced with venom. Finlay's posture stiffened, readying himself for whatever mess waited ahead. As they neared the gate, three Officers emerged from the toilet block, chatting casually amongst themselves. One of them, Dale, raised a hand in greeting. "Hey, Fin! What time are you knocking off?" he called out. Finlay glanced at his watch without breaking stride. "Got another four hours. I'll catch you back at the station," he replied briskly, his focus already shifting back to the scene ahead. The three men gave quick nods and disappeared into the shadows of the car park.

Meanwhile, Tango Three picked up their pace, their boots crunching against the gravel as they closed in on the gate. Through the dim light, they spotted Dave, his broad frame pivoting as though ready to storm off toward the trailer nearby. "Hey, Dave! Over here!" Finlay shouted, raising a hand to get his attention. Pete gave a quick wave for good measure. Dave froze mid-step, his shoulders stiffening as he turned to face them. His mouth fell open slightly, his expression caught between relief and disbelief as the two Officers and their alert canine strode toward him. Whatever storm had been brewing seemed to pause, just for a moment, as Dave waited for them to arrive.

Still fuming from the dressing-down he'd just endured, Shaheed glanced over his shoulder and spotted Sergeant Greggs talking to

Finlay and Pete near the gate. His mood shifted instantly, a spark of excitement lighting his eyes as he jabbed Fred in the arm. "Hey, look—it's Tango Three!" Shaheed said, practically bouncing on the balls of his feet. Fred, who had been half-turned toward the woods, followed Shaheed's gaze. His face lit up with surprise and vindication. "Holy shit! You know, I knew they hadn't left base. I just knew it." He smirked, leaning closer to Shaheed as if sharing a secret. "Bet someone's eating their words now, eh? Bloody busybody." Shaheed chuckled, his laughter bubbling up despite the earlier tension. "Yeah, bet he's choking on them," he said, stealing a glance at Dave, who was visibly bristling.

Dave, sharp as ever, felt the weight of their stares and snapped his head around to face the two guards. His eyes narrowed with the authority of a man who had run out of patience. "You two—turn around right now and watch those woods," he barked, jabbing a finger toward the dark tree line. "If I catch you gawking again, I'll have a report on my desk within the hour. You copy?" Both guards swallowed hard, their earlier mirth vanishing like smoke in the night air. "Yes, Sarge," they muttered in unison, spinning back toward the black void of the woods. The laughter was gone now, replaced by the chilling reminder of what might be lurking in the shadows ahead.

"What the hell are you two still doing here?" Dave's voice came out more sharply than he'd intended, his confusion quickly giving way to embarrassment. He rubbed his face, feeling the heat of his own frustration. "I was told you'd left the base and headed into the woods." Finlay and Pete exchanged a look, their eyebrows raised in silent communication. Pete was the first to speak, his voice flat with disbelief. "Err… no, mate, we've got back a while ago – escorted the couple we found in the car park. Now we are waiting for relief. Diggs went back to the station hours ago. You know the rules, three to each Tango and all that."

Pete bent down, gently patting the dog as she lay quietly at his feet, her eyes following Dave's every movement. Finlay stood tall, his expression unreadable, though his eyes narrowed slightly. "Has our relief actually shown up? You're the Duty Officer, right?" Dave nodded slowly, his gaze flicking to the dog, then back to the two officers. "Yeah, I'm Duty… but we've got a serious fucking problem. It seems your guy decided to wander off into the woods alone. And now, we can't find him."

Finlay paused at the trailer door, his hand resting on the canvas as he turned to Pete. "You and Katie wait out here," he said quietly, his voice carrying the weight of years on the job. As Pete gave a quick nod and took his position with the dog, Finlay stepped inside. His record was spotless after seven years on the beat, but this latest mess threatened to unravel everything he'd built.

Inside, the DCI was already waiting, arms folded, a hardened look in his eyes. He gave a curt nod as Finlay and Dave entered. "Better let me handle this, son," the Officer grunted, his voice low and gravelly. "This is a shitshow, and the DCI's got no patience for anyone's excuses. I'll keep it straight—no beating around the bush. That work for you?" Finlay gave a tight, resigned nod, the weight of the situation sinking in. With a glance at Dave, he fell in line behind the older Officer, both men walking through the dimly lit room past cluttered desks and scattered paperwork. Every step felt heavier, each one pulling him deeper into the storm.

They lingered just out of sight, waiting for DCI Craig to finish his call. The low hum of frustration in his voice was unmistakable, the words he spat into the receiver sharp and clipped. It was clear the conversation had something to do with the comms—or maybe Halo Two—but either way, the DCI's patience had already worn thin. The tension in the room thickened, the air heavy with the promise of bad news. When the phone hit the desk with a deafening slam, the handset bounced once, nearly splintering on impact. The DCI sank into his chair, his hands tugging roughly through his hair as a long, exasperated breath escaped his lungs. Out of the corner of his eye, he caught sight of the two Officers by the drink's cooler, shifting uncomfortably.

With a quick flick of his gaze, he acknowledged them, his tone flat but cutting. "Yes, lads? What can I do for you?" Before Dave could even open his mouth, a young female officer stepped forward, her presence sharp and purposeful. She was followed by a man whose black camouflage jacket and cargo trousers screamed military precision. The gun strapped to his hip glinted under the harsh overhead lights, a silent threat hanging in the air.

"Pardon me, Sir. This is Commander Wardley, from…" The tall man paused, his brow furrowing as he glanced at the DCI, awaiting a response. "Sorry, where did you say you were from?" Wardley stepped forward, extending his hand, his posture rigid and formal. The DCI didn't flinch. "Oh, I didn't mention where I'm from, and frankly, it's not relevant, however, we did briefly chat a while ago, if you remember" Wardley replied, his voice a bit sharper than intended. The DCI took the commander's hand, gripping it firmly before quickly sinking back into his chair. His eyes flicked over his cluttered desk, then he grabbed a handful of papers and shuffled them into a pile, feigning orderliness.

From the corner of his mouth, Ralph's lips twitched into a smile, a glint of amusement in his eyes. "Right, well, Sir, I've been dispatched to assist you in apprehending Prisoner Zero-Three-Zero-One. Parliaments in a panic—this manhunt's turning into a media circus, and if you'll pardon my language, it's making the boys in blue look like they couldn't find their own arse with both hands." The DCI shot up from behind his desk, his chair scraping loudly against the floor. His hand hovered in the air, ready to retort, but before he could speak, Wardley pressed on, his words cutting through the air like a sharpened blade.

"This whole operation—if you can even call this a bloody operation," Ralph waved a dismissive hand around the cramped trailer, the edges of his voice edged with contempt, "is a complete shamble. No coordination, no structure. You're fumbling about in the dark, and frankly, it's embarrassing." He let the words hang in the air, his gaze locked on the DCI, daring him to argue. "Now, unless I've misread my intel, you've got ten Tangos out there—three Officers and a dog—tracking Zero-One-Three-Zero? This is a massive mistake. This man kills for sport, not out of necessity. Splitting your forces into smaller units is like handing him the keys to a slaughterhouse."

The room went deathly quiet. Sergeant Greggs, Finlay, and the young female Officer stood frozen, their eyes flicking between the DCI and Ralph, waiting for the storm to break. The DCI, though, didn't move, his jaw tightening with every word. His gaze shot a brief glance at his officers before he levelled an icy, sarcastic stare at Ralph. "Please," the DCI sneered, "do tell me what you suggest, Commander." Ralph's expression hardened as he leaned forward, planting his large hands firmly on either side of the desk. The force of his presence felt almost physical, like a weight pressing down on the DCI's chest. He glared, unblinking, his voice low and venomous. "I suggest you put in a request for a shitload of body bags."

***

Ross's voice trembled with worry as he called for Betty, his eyes scanning the thick underbrush. But the harness was caught on a fallen tree, and the stubborn dog had decided to crawl underneath, wedging herself in so tightly that there was no way to follow without dropping the lead. "Bloody hell, bruv," Jack cursed under his breath, stepping up beside his brother. He craned his neck, trying to catch a glimpse of Betty. He could just make out the flicker of her tail wagging frantically, the rest of her body hidden as she burrowed deeper into a thicket of ferns.

"She's stuck," Ross muttered, frustration creeping into his voice. "Do me a favour—can you hold this?" He handed Jack the harness, and with a grunt, he prepared to crawl over the fallen tree. "I'll climb over, hold on to her, then you can let go, and I'll pull her through." Just then, Paul appeared from behind another tree, adjusting his flies with a sheepish grin. "Sorry, lads," he said with a grimace, "think that last brews finally made its way through my bowels." He winced as he shifted uncomfortably, then continued, "Let's get Betty sorted, turn back, and head to base. Hot meal, cold beer—sound good?" Ross and Jack exchanged a glance, their spirits lifting at the thought of a warm meal and the comfort of home. With a shared nod, they moved with renewed purpose, the promise of a cold pint and their dog's safety driving them forward.

Betty barked sharply, her head briefly emerging from the ferns before disappearing back into the underbrush. She was agitated, digging frantically with her paws, her tail twitching erratically. Jack furrowed his brow, confusion mounting as he tried to peer over the fallen trunk, but couldn't see what had her so worked up. Ross, already moving into action, passed him the harness. "What's eating her?" Jack muttered, his eyes scanning the ground. Ross gave a knowing smile as he climbed up onto the trunk, his boots scraping against the bark. "Probably found a treat or something. You know how she loves her food." With a grunt, Ross swung his leg up, using the fallen tree as leverage, and landed neatly next to Betty. "What you got, girl? Wait there, let's get you loose first."

He grasped her collar firmly, giving her a quick reassuring squeeze, and turned to nod at Jack. "Ready?" Jack crouched down, reaching underneath the tree, where the harness was snagged on a stubborn little stump. "Hang on... It's caught, won't be a sec," he muttered, tugging at the strap. His fingers fumbled for a better grip. "Damn it." Concerned, he glanced over his shoulder. "Hey, Sarge, you're keeping an eye out, right?" Before he could even finish the sentence, Paul's torch beam swung directly into his face, blinding him for a moment. "Quit your bloody bickering. Of course I'm watching," Paul snapped, his voice tight with irritation. "Now get that damn dog out of there, sharpish. My bowels are about to explode!"

With a sharp tug, the harness was freed and Ross grabbed it from Jack's hands, "There you go, princess," he muttered as he passed it underneath, "you're free now. Let's see what tasty little treats you've found." He bent low, reaching into the ferns, his fingers brushing through the thick greenery as he searched for her face. His hands found her muzzle, then gently pried her mouth open. Something was wedged between her teeth.

"She's found something," Ross muttered, his voice low. "Feels like... what the hell?" His eyes widened as his fingers closed around a cold, foreign object. Jack and Paul stepped forward; their curiosity piqued. They placed their hands on the fallen tree, leaning in to see what Ross had uncovered. "What? Come on, man, don't leave us hanging!" Jack teased; his tone impatient. "Sarge here's about to burst, we need answers." Paul shot him a hard look, his patience thinning. "Watch it, mate. We've got a job to do." But he couldn't hide the tension in his voice, his eyes flicking nervously toward the woods.

Ross's fingers wrapped around the end of the object, but as he tugged, he could feel the warm, slimy trail of saliva dripping over his hand. "Right, Betty, release..." he commanded, but the dog stubbornly clung to her prize, her teeth digging deeper. His voice hardened. "Release. Now!" The mutt held on; her eyes locked on Ross as she finally budged. With a frustrated sigh, Ross slowly stood, wiping the back of his hand across his trousers. "Yuk… that's disgusting," he muttered, grimacing as he tried to shake off the sticky mess.

Betty, unbothered by her owner's irritation, plopped herself down, sitting with a determined gaze fixed squarely on Ross. Her paw came up, a silent plea for the treat she had so diligently hoarded. Paul, growing impatient but curious, shouted from behind, "What you got, son?" Ross, still wiping his hand with little success, glanced over at Paul with a glint of mischief in his eyes. He grinned and, without warning, flung the object into the air. "Here—catch!"

Jack snatched the object from the air, a grin spreading across his face. "Yeah, baby! Still got it, what a catch." He held it up triumphantly, but Paul's smile faded as his eyes fell to Jack's palm. His expression shifted from amusement to horror. "Oh, shit…" In Jack's hand, nestled like an unwanted gift, was a bloody, severed ring finger. Small, jagged bite marks exposed raw flesh beneath the skin, the gruesome detail sending a chill through the air.

"Guys…" The word left Ross's lips in a strangled whisper, but it died before it could be fully formed. Jack and Paul stared at the mangled finger in shock, his mind struggling to process the sight. His body froze, then jolted—realization hit him like a freight train. He yelped, the finger slipping from his palm and bouncing off the fallen tree bark before coming to a grim halt between two small branches. A stunned silence followed as Jack fumbled for words, his voice breaking with disbelief. "Whose… whose is that? I… I mean…what the fuck?" Paul didn't answer. He didn't need to. His eyes remained fixed on the finger, his face pale, his body tense. There were no words of comfort—no reassurance. Just the grim weight of what they had found, hanging heavy between them.

"Hey, guys, you listening?" Ross's voice broke through the tense silence, pulling their attention. They both looked up, eyes widening as he casually tossed something into the air. "There's two more here." Without warning, Ross threw them high, and this time,

Jack hesitated, his instincts kicking in. He pulled back, letting the objects hit Paul's vest before bouncing off the tree with a soft thud.

The three of them crowded around, their breath quickening. Paul's torch flickered as he examined the objects in his hands. "Looks fresh," he murmured, his voice tight. "I think this happened recently." The words hung in the air, unsettling. Their pulse quickened, hearts racing as they swung their torches in every direction, the beams of light cutting through the oppressive darkness like fragile threads. But the more they searched, the more the shadows seemed to close in, twisting their surroundings into an even darker, more sinister landscape. Fear gripped them with icy fingers—no matter how much the light pushed back the night, it offered no comfort, only the sickening realization that they were not alone.

Paul's fingers hovered over the radio, his voice barely a whisper as he stopped to speak into the receiver. "Boys, I don't think we're alone. Eyes up. Torches up. If Betty even gives the slightest whimper, we form a tight cluster—back-to-back, understood?" The brothers exchanged a quick, uneasy glance before nodding. Ross's grip tightened around the harness, his fingers slipping slightly as he adjusted his torch. "Tango Eight to Bravo Charlie One, copy," he said, his voice steady, but his eyes darting nervously across the dark woods. The beam of his light flicked over the trees by the path, trying to make sense of their surroundings. The silence felt too heavy, too suffocating.

Suddenly, panic clawed at him. "Tango Eight to Bravo Charlie One, is anybody reading? Over." The words hung in the air, unanswered, thickening the unease that already had them on edge. Jack's voice cut through the tension, sharp and laced with frustration. "This is pointless. Hey, Sarge, why don't we just make a run for it? What did you say, this guys over sixty? Hell, even my snail-paced brother here could outrun a pensioner." He smirked, but the humour didn't reach his eyes. They all knew the stakes were far higher than any joke could cover. Sergeant Paul Stewart's mind hit a full-blown panic. His heart raced as a hot, clammy sensation spread through him, his bowels betraying him in a surge of terror. Warm liquid filled his underwear, and the humiliation hit him like a physical blow, but he couldn't focus on that—he couldn't afford to. The brothers, still scanning the shadows, were oblivious to the stench that now clung to their CO.

Then, out of nowhere, Betty erupted in a vicious bark, her body rigid with tension. All three Officers snapped their attention toward the sound. Their eyes widened as they realized the direction of her gaze—straight toward the path that led back to base. Paul's mind scrambled, the urgency of the moment cutting through his shame. He locked eyes with the brothers, his voice hoarse. "Run."

Before he could even finish, Ross was shouting, "Go, Betty! Follow!" He barely had time to brace himself before the dog yanked on the harness with full force, nearly sending Ross sprawling onto the ground. With a growl, Betty surged ahead, her instincts driving her as she charged through the thick underbrush, cutting through the trees like a freight train. Then, just as quickly, she veered off-course, darting in the opposite direction, straight toward the beach. The Officers exchanged panicked glances, but there was no time to question. They had to move—fast.

Tango Eight tore through the underbrush, their legs burning with effort as they stole quick, frantic glances over their shoulders and to the sides. Their chests heaved with each breath, the weight of panic pushing them forward. Adrenaline surged through their veins, propelling them another two hundred feet—until Betty, at the front, suddenly skidded to a halt.

The three Officers piled into one another, stumbling to a stop. At the rear, Paul whipped his head around, his torch beam slicing through the darkness as he scanned the path behind them. "Why have we stopped?" he gasped, his voice edged with fear. Jack, breathless, tried to peer around his younger brother, his instincts kicking in as Ross dropped to his knees, a grim look crossing his face. "Oh no…"

Before anyone could react, Ross's stomach lurched, and he violently emptied the contents of his gut onto the muddy path. The sound was sickening, the smell unbearable as the splatter echoed in the quiet. Betty, sensing something was wrong, pulled away from her handler, her body tense as she whimpered, her ears flattened in concern. Jack crouched next to Ross; eyes wide with horror. "Hey, Sarge… you better take a look at this." His voice was tight, his mind racing—something was off, and they all knew it.

Leaning over Jack and Ross, Paul's gaze dropped to the ground, and his stomach lurched. In the murky light, something large and wet lay in a pool of blood and mud. He quickly flashed his torch across it—and froze. His breath caught in his throat as the beam revealed what they'd all feared. Someone's intestines, grotesquely spilling out onto the path. "Mother of God…" he whispered, his voice shaking. The air grew heavy with the stench of blood and rot. Betty, still alert, let out a sharp bark—this time not pulling back. Instead, her eyes darted ahead, her body tense, ears straining. She seemed to be staring at something further down the path, something unseen by the Officers but unmistakably drawing her attention.

Ross, his face pale but resolute, slowly rose to his feet. His boots sank into the mud as he took a tentative step forward, parting an overgrown branch with a quiet rustle. He didn't need to say it, but his voice was grim when he finally did. "I think we've found who this belongs to."

Struggling to stay steady on his feet, Paul's breath came in sharp bursts as he followed Jack through the thick underbrush. His muscles screamed with exhaustion, but he pushed forward, the weight of the moment dragging him down with every step. When they finally reached the small opening in the brush, they both froze. Before them, sprawled in a grotesque pool of blood, was a young Officer. His body was pale, face obscured by the grim scene unfolding before them. His eyes were closed, but the image seared into their minds—two bloody, perfect circles pressed into the Officer's eyelids, as if someone had carved them into his face. The sight was haunting, unnatural. The smell of iron and death clung to the air.

Jack's gut tightened as he took a step forward, pushing past Ross and Betty, who stood still, sensing the gravity of the moment. His hand gripped the torch with white-knuckled intensity as he shone the beam over the body, the light dancing across the blood-soaked uniform. Every inch of the Officer's figure seemed to scream tragedy—the tattered edges of his uniform, the unnatural angle of his limbs. "Anyone recognize him?" Jack's voice was barely a whisper, but it broke the silence that had settled around them. His words hung in the air, unanswered. Paul, his own face hard and set, said nothing. Ross remained still, the weight of the discovery sinking in like a lead balloon. Even Betty, ever alert, was unusually quiet.

Jack's throat tightened as he slowly turned the beam of his torch over the Officer's body again, lingering on the bloodstains that were still fresh, still seeping. "Must be one of the new lads," he muttered, more to himself than to anyone else. His voice cracked slightly, the weight of uncertainty and dread creeping into his words. The unease that had plagued them all since the moment they set foot in these woods only deepened, and they knew that whatever was happening here—whatever had happened to this Officer—was far from over.

They stood in the uneasy quiet, the sense of dread growing stronger by the second, their minds racing to make sense of the horror before them. Each Officer was lost in their thoughts, staring at the young man who, just hours before, had been just another face in the squad. And now… now he was just another casualty in this nightmare that had spiralled far beyond anything they could have imagined. Paul and Ross stood in tense silence as Jack crouched over the lifeless body, the beam from his torch cutting through the dark, casting long shadows on the Officer's still form. Jack's gaze flicked over the man's body; each detail more horrifying than the last. "Looks like the laceration to his neck was done with a sharp blade," he muttered, his voice strained. "And... yeah, look here," he pointed toward the Officer's hand, where three fingers had been gruesomely severed. "His missing three little piggies." The words hung in the air, a macabre attempt at dark humour in the face of horror.

Paul's eyes snapped to Jack, his voice a low growl of frustration and dread. "This is no time for jokes, you imbecile," he barked, his patience evaporating. "Do you have any idea how serious this is? We're getting farther and farther from Bravo Charlie One, heading towards the beach like sitting ducks. Meanwhile, we've got a maniac on our tail, hunting us down like animals." His fists clenched, jaw tight with anger and fear. "So, show some damn respect and get your arse up off the ground. There's nothing we can do for him now." Jack's smile faltered as Paul's words hit home, the gravity of their situation sinking in like a stone.

Jack and Paul stood motionless, their eyes locked on the corpse in front of them, each one processing the horror in their own way. The silence between them was suffocating until Jack broke it, his voice tight with frustration. "Well, we can't just leave the poor bastard here, can we? Call it in." The words hung in the air, but Paul's response was sharp, dripping with sarcasm. "Oh, sure, and what should we use to call it in? A pigeon, maybe?" His gaze swept the area, as if searching for a solution in the darkness. "Oh, wait— looks like we're all out of pigeons, genius!"

Jack's jaw tightened, his temper flaring as Paul's mocking tone stung. With a swift motion, he clenched his fists, his arm rising instinctively, ready to strike his commanding Officer. But before he could act on his anger, something caught his eye. "Wait—what's that down there?" he snapped, his attention shifting. Both men turned to follow his gaze. Ross was crouched beside the body, his hand hovering over the officer's forehead. "Looks like some kind of writing," he muttered, his voice filled with confusion.

"X... X... seven, and... I think that's a five." Jack and Paul stepped closer, their eyes narrowing as they tried to make sense of the cryptic markings. The atmosphere shifted from tense to unnerving. "What the hell is that?" Paul breathed, his words barely a whisper. The strange symbols on the officer's skin were like a chilling riddle—one they couldn't yet solve.

A snap of a twig cut through the air, the sound sharp and unmistakable. Betty's ears perked instantly, her nose twitching as she locked onto the new noise. Before anyone could react, the dog's body stiffened, her hackles raised. In an instant, she barked, her jaws snapping in the direction of the sound with a ferocity that sent a chill down the men's spines. Without warning, she lunged forward, darting between two thick bushes with a force that wrenched the harness from Ross's grip. His fingers clawed at the air as Betty vanished into the darkness, her barking now frantic and wild. The three men stood frozen, momentarily paralyzed by the suddenness of it all, their minds racing.

They turned toward the sound of Betty's diminishing barks, the noise growing fainter with each passing second. The distance between them and the dog seemed to stretch, amplifying the silence in its wake. Time felt suspended as the three Officers exchanged glances, uncertainty hanging thick in the air. Should they follow? Or were they better off waiting for Betty to return? Each man was caught in a battle between fear and instinct, unsure if pursuing the dog would lead them into the jaws of whatever was lurking out there in the dark.

"I've had enough of this bullshit," Ross muttered under his breath, his anger boiling over. Without another word, he bolted into the trees, disappearing into the dense underbrush, chasing after Betty. "Hey, you idiot! Are you insane? Get back here!" Jack shouted, his voice cracking with panic. He took a step forward, but his feet felt like they were made of stone, the weight of his fear keeping him rooted in place. His heart raced, adrenaline surging as he fought the urge to run after his reckless brother.

Minutes dragged by in excruciating silence, the air thick with tension. Both men stood motionless, eyes scanning the darkness, waiting, their breath shallow and rapid. Paul's senses were on high alert, every rustle in the bushes making him jump. Suddenly, a sharp rustle shattered the quiet, and Ross's voice broke through the night air, frantic and broken. "I... I can't find her... help me!" Before Jack could process the words, he was moving, his body instinctively reacting. He charged toward his brother, slamming him against the nearest tree, his hands gripping Ross's jacket, his teeth bared in fury. "Don't you ever pull a stunt like that again, you hear me? You could've been killed!" Jack's voice was a low growl, filled with a mix of fear, anger, and relief that his brother was still standing.

Silence.

Ross pulled his hands off Jack's shoulders, gently pushing him back, his voice quiet but sincere. "I'm sorry, alright?" Jack's expression remained hard, frustration boiling in his chest. He wanted his brother to understand just how bad things were, how quickly everything had spiralled out of control. But before he could say anything, Ross's gaze shifted, his face suddenly tight with worry. "Where's the Sarge?" A chill ran through both of them as they stepped forward, feeling more exposed by the second. The dim glow of their torches cast long shadows as they swept through the clearing, their footsteps muffled in the dense undergrowth. "Where the hell is he?" Jack muttered; his voice tight.

Ross's eyes darted around, the beam of his flashlight trembling in the dark. "Maybe he made a run for it," Jack suggested, his words coming out more as an attempt to calm himself than a serious theory. But Ross wasn't buying it. He continued to move his torch across the ground, then froze. Something caught his eye—a glint in the dirt. He crouched down, heart pounding. "Tell me something, bruv," he said, his voice low and tense, "If you were gonna make a run for it... would you leave your torch behind?" The question hung in the air, the silence swallowing up the sound of their breathing. It was the kind of thing you never expected to question... unless things were worse than they'd ever imagined.

The stillness of the night was suffocating. Every muscle in their bodies tensed as they strained to hear even the faintest sound—any sign that the convict might slip up and reveal his position. But there was nothing. The forest was eerily quiet, the usual rustling of leaves and distant animal calls swallowed by an unnatural silence. Even the rain, which had been pouring relentlessly, had abruptly stopped. Ross's breath caught in his throat as he exchanged a look with Jack, silently begging for a plan. "What do we do now?" Ross's voice was barely a whisper, his gaze fixed on his older brother, searching for reassurance. Jack stood motionless, his thoughts racing. The sharp scent of the ocean was growing stronger, and he could hear the distant crash of waves against the shore. "We're close to the beach," he muttered to himself. His eyes narrowed as the pieces of the puzzle clicked into place. "Remember what that Officer said? Three Tangos coming in from the west. So.." He swallowed hard, the weight of the decision settling over him like a heavy fog.

He turned to his brother, determination hardening his features. "We make a run for it—NOW. We head for the beach and hope to God we're not too late." His voice was raw, the fear palpable, but there was no time to hesitate. The clock was ticking, and the only thing that mattered now was getting to the beach before they were cornered. Jack instinctively let Ross take the lead, his older brother's instincts sharper in these moments of high tension. Ross's steady pace matched the urgency of the situation, but Jack was more alert than ever, eyes darting back and forth to watch for any sign of movement. His senses were stretched thin, listening for the slightest sound of footsteps or a shift in the underbrush. Every crack of a branch, every rustle in the leaves made his heart race.

The forest seemed to close in around them as they ran, their boots sinking into the soft earth with every stride. Jack focused on the rhythm of his breathing, steady but laboured, and the rhythmic thud of his boots against the path. Branches reached out like skeletal hands, scraping at their arms and faces as they tore their way through the dense foliage. He could hear the sound of his brother's boots ahead, the slight swish of branches, the occasional grunt of effort as Ross pushed them out of the way. "Almost there, bruv!" Ross's voice called back, laced with relief but still tense. "Just over the ridge now!"

Jack pushed forward, a surge of adrenaline giving him the strength to continue. The path ahead narrowed, the dense underbrush starting to recede as the trees grew sparser. The ridge wasn't far now, maybe another twenty feet or so. They were close to the beach, close to safety—or so Jack thought. He risked a quick glance over his shoulder, his heart pounding in his chest, expecting to see nothing but the dense darkness of the forest behind them. But all he saw was blackness. The shadows seemed to swallow everything, leaving nothing visible. That unsettling quiet pressed in again—the kind of silence that made his skin crawl. Jack's eyes darted back to Ross, who was focused on the way ahead, determined. But as he turned back around, the unexpected happened in an instant.

The crack of a large branch echoed through the night, and before Jack could even register the danger, it whipped across his face with brutal force. He felt a sharp, stinging pain across his cheek and nose, the impact of the branch pushing him off balance. His feet slipped out from under him, and the ground seemed to give way as he fell backward, crashing into a thick clump of underbrush. His breath left him in a rush, and for a moment, he couldn't hear anything but the ringing in his ears.

Dazed, he struggled to get his bearings, limbs tangled in the foliage, his hands scraping against rough bark. His vision swam for a second as he fought to clear his head. Was it the convict? Had he been ambushed? Panic surged in his chest, but he shoved it down—he couldn't afford to be paralyzed by fear now. The sound of leaves rustling urgently around him brought him back to the present, and he quickly scrambled to his knees, heart racing.

"Jack?!" Ross's voice rang out up ahead, a mixture of panic and concern, but Jack could hear him scrambling to get back to him. "I'm good," Jack grunted, pushing himself up and pulling branches away from his legs. He wiped his face, trying to clear the blood from his mouth and eyes, and wiped his hand on his shirt. Everything was happening so fast. He didn't have time to think—only to react. Jake muttered a string of curses under his breath as he fought to untangle his limbs from the vicious thorns that clung to him like an unseen enemy. The sharp, biting pricks of the branches felt like daggers, but he had no time to waste. Through gritted teeth, he finally broke free, just in time to watch his brother, Ross, disappear around a sharp bend in the path. "God damn you, Ross," Jake hissed, his voice thick with frustration.

Panic gnawed at his insides as the silence of the forest pressed down on him, every second stretching into eternity. His pulse thundered in his ears as he scrambled to his feet, fumbling for his torch. He flicked it on, scanning the path behind him, but it was clear—empty. He turned on his heel, pushing himself forward, but his legs felt like lead, the weight of his own fear pulling at him. Each step was a battle, his breath coming in ragged bursts as his heart hammered in his chest, threatening to escape his ribcage. His feet sank into the muck with each stride, the wet earth sucking at his boots, and every corner felt like a potential trap. As he tore through the underbrush, his eyes darted frantically from side to side, scanning the dark shadows of the trees, praying he wasn't walking into something worse. The familiar sting of dread clawed at the back of his mind.

He turned the corner of the thicket, barely avoiding a face-first encounter with a low branch, and skidded into a small clearing. His breath caught in his throat as he paused, suddenly feeling the full weight of the darkness pressing around him. The air was thick and still, broken only by the sound of his own panting. "Hey, Ross! You out there?" His voice cracked the stillness, but the only answer was the distant sound of wind rustling through the leaves, cold and indifferent. He took another step, his boots crunching through the damp undergrowth, and called again, louder this time, "Where did you go?"

But there was nothing. No response, no movement. Just the oppressive silence of the woods, stretching out in every direction. Jake's stomach churned. This wasn't right. Where had Ross gone? The knot in his gut tightened. Something wasn't adding up, and every instinct told him to turn back. But turning back wasn't an option, not with the convict still out there—and not with the way the darkness seemed to be closing in. "Ross?" he muttered again, quieter this time, his voice trembling. His fingers tightened around the torch, his pulse quickening as the weight of the unknown pressed down on him. Something was wrong, and he had to find his brother before whatever was lurking out there found them first.

****

Twenty minutes had passed in strained silence. The young female Officer had quietly returned to her desk, her every move deliberate and measured, while Dave and Finlay stood across the room, their eyes locked on the newcomer. The air in the cramped trailer felt heavy, thick with unspoken questions and simmering tension. Finally, breaking the quiet, the DCI leaned forward, his voice tinged with scepticism. "So let me get this straight. The military sends you, one man, to find a ruthless killer? Seriously? Is this some kind of joke? Who are you really? C'mon, put your cards on the table." His words hung in the air, sharp and cutting.

The DCI's posture stiffened as he folded his arms, his eyes narrowing as he awaited a response. Ralph stood his ground, unfazed by the challenge. For a long moment, the room was thick with anticipation. The man, still calm despite the mounting tension, exhaled sharply. "Look, maybe we've gotten off on the wrong foot," he said, his voice even, controlled. "At the end of the day, I'm here for one reason and one reason only: to find and capture our convict.

Just like you. So, let's stop playing games and focus on what needs to be done." The words seemed to settle over the room like a quiet storm, and for a long second, no one moved.

DCI Craig considered the man's response, his mind churning over what had just been said. Reluctantly, he nodded, the gesture a silent acknowledgment of the truth behind those words. They were all here for the same purpose. With a sharp exhale, he uncrossed his arms, the tension in his shoulders easing ever so slightly. "Alright," he said finally, the words coming out slower than he intended. "We'll move on." The atmosphere shifted, a quiet agreement passing between them as they turned their attention back to the task at hand. The battle was far from over, but for the first time that night, the storm of hostility had subsided, if only for a moment.

A heavy silence fell over the room, stretching out like the calm before a storm. Ralph's eyes never left the DCI, watching for any sign of movement as he waited. The two Officers standing stiffly to the side were a silent presence, their unease palpable. Ralph's gaze flicked to them before turning back to the table. "Perhaps you should deal with these two first," he suggested, his voice smooth but laced with authority. "Then we can get down to business."

With that, he casually moved to the other side of the desk, his every step calculated, eyes still on Stephen, waiting for a response. The DCI gave a subtle nod, signalling to the two men to step forward. The air seemed to thicken as they hesitated for a brief moment before Finlay nervously removed his hat, cradling it under his arm. He exchanged a glance with Dave, who stood beside him, before both men took a collective step forward. "Sir," Dave began, his voice wavering slightly, "it has come to light—recently, I might add—that one of our Officers decided to take matters into his own hands and entered the woodlands alone."

Before the DCI could interject, Ralph was already moving, cutting the air between them with a quick stride. "Tell me..." He stopped abruptly, his eyes meeting Stephen's with a cold intensity. The words seemed to freeze for a moment, the tension thick. Ralph took a breath, his expression unreadable, before starting again. "And don't hold back. I want every detail. No matter how insignificant it might seem." Finlay swallowed, his palms sweating as he glanced at Dave once more as he continued to recount the ill-fated events. The room was still, each word he spoke hanging in the air, heavy with consequence. The moment of truth had arrived, and everything was about to shift.

Five minutes later, the DCI had assembled a small but determined team of Officers: Finlay, Pete, and Katie, along with several others, all moving in tight formation. They marched through the dimly lit car park, the sound of their boots echoing off the pavement. Ralph trailed closely behind, his eyes scanning the perimeter as they approached the treeline. The weight of the task ahead hung heavy in the air, thick with tension.

At the edge of the woods, the DCI came to a halt. He pivoted sharply, his commanding presence silencing the murmurs of the Officers behind him. With a steady, focused gaze, he addressed the group, his voice cutting through the chill of the evening air. "Listen up!" he barked. "We've got a young Officer missing. PC Letting has gone off the grid, and we're not leaving here without him. Commander Wadley has made it clear—splitting up is off the table. So, here's the plan: our call sign is Tango Romeo. We move in formation, two-meter spread at all times. I want eyes up, ears open. We keep the dogs out front where we can see them—those mutts are the first line of defence. I'm not sugarcoating this, people—this is a killer we're up against. A killer who doesn't care.

"Good," he nodded, his expression hardening. "Now, let's go find PC Letting." With that, the team moved forward, a unified front, as the shadows of the woods closed in around them. The hunt had begun, and there would be no turning back. Katie surged ahead, her steps quick and determined, with Pete right behind her. As they reached the centre of the formation, DCI Craig called out, his voice sharp and authoritative, "Alright, lads, spread out! Two meters, remember—keep those torches sweeping every angle. If anyone sees anything, I mean anything, call it out. We don't miss a thing, got it?" The Officers nodded in unison, their faces grim as they trailed the dog and its handler up the hill. They moved with purpose, eyes scanning the darkness that seemed to stretch forever.

Silence fell over the group, broken only by the crunch of their boots against the damp underbrush. The rain had eased, but the cold and the weight of the moment hung heavy. Every footstep felt like it was dragging them deeper into the unknown. Losing one of their own—the thought gnawed at them. In the DCI's mind, a thousand grim scenarios played out. The one he clung to was the hope that Andy wasn't gone—just lost in the dark, wandering somewhere, waiting to be found.

Ralph fell into step beside him, closing the gap with measured strides. His voice broke the quiet, laced with an edge of something like amusement. "Little birdie tells me your comms are down. Is that true?" The DCI's jaw tightened, but he kept his gaze straight ahead, refusing to respond to the other man's presence. He nodded once, barely acknowledging the question. "Yeah, that's right. Anything else you want to know, or are you just here to stir the pot?" There was a flicker of amusement in Ralph's eyes, but he didn't speak. Instead, he let out a soft, almost imperceptible chuckle—one that didn't reach his lips. The DCI could feel the sharpness of the silent laughter behind him, an invisible blade aimed at the back of his head. It only spurred him forward, his mind locked onto the task ahead.

The hill loomed higher; the darkness thicker. The weight of the night pressed down on them, but Stephen kept moving. They were going to find Andy—or they were going to find something that could lead them to him. Either way, they weren't leaving without answers.

Ahead, Katie trotted with purpose, her nose working overtime, sniffing every scent on the damp air. Pete had only been her handler for a long time, they'd formed an unbreakable bond. She was his partner, his protector, and they'd come to trust each other implicitly. As they moved through the underbrush, Pete's voice broke through the quiet, soft and playful, "Hey, baby girl, slow down up there— daddies got something in his shoe." Katie, her ears twitching at the sound of her handler's voice, slowed for a moment, but only slightly, her instincts driving her forward. Pete's heart swelled with affection for the dog, but he couldn't help chuckling at himself.

From behind, Finlay's voice cut through the quiet like a blade, sharp and mocking, "Still talking trash to that dog, huh? Christ, what did they tell you? Don't get too close—show them who's boss, or when the moment comes, they might not be in the right frame of mind to protect you." Finlay had slipped up next to Pete, almost unnoticed, choosing to walk beside the dog rather than with the rest of the team. His words were casual, but there was an undercurrent of seriousness, the kind that only came from years of experience in the field.

Pete shot him a side-eyed glance, irritated by the unsolicited advice, but before he could respond, the night around them seemed to press in closer. The air felt heavier now, as if the dark was alive with unseen eyes. Katie paused for a moment, her ears flicking back, and Pete's smile faded, replaced by a sharp focus. The moment had shifted, the tension thickening like fog, and he knew—whatever was out there, they were getting closer to it. Finlay noticed the change in the air too. His posture straightened, his hand tightening instinctively around his torch. "Keep your head on a swivel," he muttered under his breath, a rare moment of seriousness overtaking his usual easy-going demeanour. They weren't just walking through the woods anymore; they were entering something far darker.

As they crested the ridge, they watched Katie, work her nose intently, picking up every scent in the air. Ten meters ahead of the long line of Officers, she moved with purpose, her paws barely making a sound as she glided through the underbrush. The air felt charged, like the woods themselves were alive, holding secrets just beyond the reach of their flashlights. The torches flickered over trees, branches, and leaves, casting eerie shadows on the ground, but there was no sign of their missing rookie. Nothing.

Finlay's boots crunched softly on the path as he caught up to Pete. The night was thick with tension, the silence of the woods pressing in around them. "I tell you, Fin," Pete muttered, breaking the silence, "if we find this rookie dead, I'm done. I can't take it. This whole thing's been a damn shitshow. And you know what's worse? They'll start asking questions. Everyone's gonna want someone to blame, and I don't want to be standing there when it's time to point fingers."

They pushed forward, the words lingering in the air, mixing with the tension in their chests. Finlay slowed his pace, glancing at Pete. He didn't need to say much; Pete's frustration was obvious, the weight of the situation crushing him. After a long moment, Finlay spoke, his tone quieter, but heavy with agreement. "You know what, I agree. Someone's head's gonna roll for this, and it's usually a Sargeant. Mr. 'My Shit Smells Like Roses' won't take the rap, though," he added with a half-smirk, stealing a quick glance over his shoulder at the DCI, who was methodically sweeping his torch across the dark woods. Pete shot him a sidelong glance, his frustration mixing with a bitter laugh. "Yeah, you're probably right. They'll toss him under the bus to save their own skin."

The woods around them seemed to grow darker, the uncertainty hanging like a thick fog. They both knew the truth—they were heading into dangerous territory. The deeper they went, the less they knew about what they'd find, and the more they feared what they might not be able to control. Each step felt heavier than the last, the ground beneath them shifting with the weight of the situation, and the only certainty now was that something was waiting. But whether that something would be a body or a killer remained to be seen.

Finlay stepped forward, closing the distance again between himself and Pete, his voice dropping to a low murmur. He cast a quick, cautious glance over his shoulder, making sure the others weren't within earshot. The last thing they needed was for this conversation to get carried back to the rest of the team. "And another thing," he said, his tone edged with unease. He tapped the radio on his vest, the metal clicking against his fingers. "These radios— strange, right? They were fine when we got here, no issues. But now? Now they're just useless accessories."

His eyes flicked nervously toward the dense woods, his instincts on high alert. With a sharp motion, he shone his torch over a massive oak tree, the light bouncing off its gnarled bark, before quickly snapping it back to the centre, focusing on Pete's face. "Something's off," Finlay muttered, his voice barely above a whisper. The quiet of the woods pressed in on them, thick with tension. "We've been in the field enough to know when things don't add up. And right now? This whole situation feels like it's been rigged from the start."

* * *

Engulfed by the suffocating darkness, Jack's senses sharpened, every sound amplified, every rustle of leaves or snap of a twig sending his heart racing. His mind screamed for some kind of reassurance, a familiar voice or a sign that he wasn't completely alone in this terrifying silence. He wanted to shout, to break the stillness, but a sharp, primal instinct held him back. The last thing he needed was to give away his position.

He stood in the clearing, his breath shallow, eyes darting from one shadow to the next. Across the way, the path stretched out into the gloom, more open than the dense thicket behind him. The beam of his torch swept over the landscape, revealing the contours of the woodland, the uneven ground and sparse clusters of trees. The slight illumination brought a momentary sense of relief—at least there weren't too many places for someone to hide.

But that comfort was fleeting. The forest felt like a waiting trap, the shadows watching, patient. Jack's grip tightened on the torch, his knuckles white, as he tried to steady his racing thoughts. He couldn't help but feel the weight of the silence pressing down on him, like the woods were holding their breath, waiting for something to happen.

Instead of running headlong into the unknown, Jack forced himself to slow down, his footsteps soft and deliberate as he crossed the clearing, heading toward the distant path. His heart pounded in his chest, but he fought to steady his breath. In the far-off distance, the faint sound of a siren pierced the silence, a distant promise that reinforcements were on their way—help was coming. For the first time in hours, Jack allowed himself to imagine the possibility of escape, of getting out of this nightmare with his brother by his side.

He reached out and touched a nearby tree, the rough texture of the bark grounding him, the coldness of the surface sending a shiver up his arm. Counting to three in his head, he pressed his back against the trunk and slowly peered around it, shining his torch into the shadowy expanse. He expected to see something—anything—that would ease his nerves, maybe even a familiar face. Instead, his torch beam landed on something entirely unexpected.

A dog.

Sitting perfectly still, panting quietly, her eyes reflecting the light. Jack froze. The dog looked familiar, Betty. His breath caught in his throat. "Hey, girl, what are you doing here?" he whispered, crouching down to stroke her head, the soft fur brushing against his hand. The dog didn't respond as expected. There were no signs of distress, no fear in her posture. Her fur was clean, no injuries, nothing to suggest she had been through the chaos. But there was something unsettling about the way she avoided his gaze. Her eyes, once looking up at him, seemed to wander off into the darkness. Confusion gripped him as he shone the torch more carefully over the dog. That's when he noticed the harness, tethered to a nearby branch. His breath hitched. "Did Ross do this?" he murmured to himself, his mind racing as he pieced together the situation. Why would Ross leave the dog here? Was he close?

Jack cupped the dog's head gently in his hands, lifting her face toward his, trying to lock eyes with her, searching for some kind of answer. But the dog pulled away, her attention fixated elsewhere. Her ears twitched, and for a split second, Jack thought he saw a flicker of unease in her eyes. Something wasn't right. He had to find Ross—now.

A sudden, bone-chilling cold washed over Jack, his body going rigid as beads of sweat formed along his brow, despite the freezing night air. He felt a wave of nausea clawing up his throat, the taste of bile sharp and sour. His chest tightened, every breath feeling like it could be his last. He tried to swallow, but it was as though the air had turned to lead in his lungs. His pulse thudded in his ears as he squeezed his eyes shut, hoping that when he opened them again, the nightmare would be gone.

But when he did—the beam of the torch swept upward—it was there.

His brother, Ross. His body was pinned to the trunk of a tree, an unnatural, gruesome sight. A spear-like object impaled through him, the point jutting grotesquely from his chest. Jack's heart lurched as he saw the vacant, glassy stare in Ross's lifeless eyes, the terror frozen in the moment of his death. It was as if time had stopped, trapping his brother in that final, unblinking gaze.

The world spun around Jack, his legs giving way beneath him as his knees buckled, the earth suddenly feeling unsteady, as if everything was slipping away from him. He stumbled back, leaning against something solid, the rough bark digging into his skin as he stared, unable to tear his eyes from his brother's mutilated form. A wave of heat rushed to his face, and he could taste the salt of his own tears before they even fell. His chest heaved, but his throat felt like it was closing in on him, choking him, the scream he wanted to let loose caught deep inside.

His entire body trembled, but his mind was clouded, numb. He wanted to scream. He wanted to rush forward, to hold his brother, to do something. But his limbs wouldn't move. His body was paralyzed in a moment of pure, unrelenting horror. And then, through the haze of shock and grief, he realized: He wasn't alone. Slowly, his gaze lifted from the scene in front of him, and that's when he saw it—the eyes.

Blue. Cold. Unfathomably calm.

A figure emerged from the darkness, standing only a few feet away, watching him. Watching his pain. His face remained impassive, like a predator surveying its prey. And Jack's blood ran cold as he realized who stood before him. This was the moment. The person who had turned his world into this nightmare.

The psychopath.

Chapter 26
04:00 Hours, 1ˢᵗ August 2024,
Brancaster Woodland, Norfolk Coastline

His long, rain-slick hair clung to his face, veiling his intensity as the knife worked relentlessly in his grasp. Each serrated drag through flesh and bone was deliberate, a grim orchestra of grating steel and snapping sinew. With one final, wet crunch, the severed head came free, its weight hanging limp in his hands. The Officer's dead eyes stared past him, empty and accusing, their hollow gaze blending with the damp mist rising from the forest floor.

Above, the night sky began to shift—clouds unravelling to reveal constellations glittering like shards of broken glass on velvet. The horizon smouldered with the first light of dawn, casting the bloodied scene in a surreal, golden-red haze. He froze, listening. The baying of hounds and shouts of men pressed nearer, their urgency bleeding into the crisp morning air. Three hundred yards, maybe four. Close enough to feel the primal heat of pursuit. His gaze lingered on the heavens as if searching for answers in the stars before snapping back to reality. The head dangled from his grip, a grim trophy. He couldn't stay here. Not with time slipping away and death closing in from all directions.

He set the head down gently, almost reverently, its lifeless features catching the faint, flickering light of the rising dawn. With measured steps, he moved to a towering oak, its ancient branches clawing skyward. The wind whispered through the leaves, a subtle symphony that seemed almost mocking in its serenity. His sharp eyes scanned the branches, calculating. Finding one sturdy but worn, he grasped it firmly with both hands, his muscles corded with tension as he pulled downward. The branch resisted with a groan, then gave way with a sharp, satisfying snap. The splintered end glinted like a crude spear as he turned back toward the grisly trophy resting in the dirt.

The man knelt briefly, scooping up the head with an almost practiced efficiency. The wind swirled again, carrying the earthy scent of the forest and the faint, metallic tang of blood. As he rose, the oak's broken branch clutched in one hand and the head dangling from the other, he stood like a savage figure of vengeance, framed against the glowing horizon.

He crouched low, plunging his hands into a shallow puddle that had gathered in a hollow of the muddy earth. The icy water bit at his skin, mixing with the blood and grime as he scrubbed it away in harsh, deliberate motions. Murky rivulets of red and brown swirled and cascaded over his fingers, staining the earth beneath with ghostly streaks. Satisfied, he wiped his hands dry on his trousers, the fabric soaking up the chill like a graveyard shroud. Standing, he cast a glance toward the shadows ahead—an opening between two dense bushes, beckoning like the maw of some dark beast.

The barking of dogs shattered the stillness, closer now. Two hundred yards? No, less. One fifty, at most. A sharp grin split his face, feral and full of defiance. Without hesitation, he slipped into the waiting darkness, the shadows swallowing him whole as the first pale rays of dawn struggled to pierce the dense canopy above.

***

"Hey, cutie pie... HEY! Slow down, will ya?" Pete's voice cracked through the stillness, his boots slogging clumsily through the tangled ferns. The dense undergrowth seemed determined to trap him, every step a battle against wiry stems that lashed at his legs. Ahead, Katie darted effortlessly, weaving through the leafy maze as though the forest itself had bent to her will. Behind him, Finlay's gruff voice rose over the crackle of snapping twigs. "I'm telling you, this better be worth it. What kind of idiot wanders off alone out here, knowing there's a psycho loose?"

Pete cast a quick glance over his shoulder, catching a glimpse of Finlay stumbling after him. The harness in Pete's hands jerked violently, yanking him forward. He barely managed to tighten his grip before Katie's strength could send him sprawling. "Do me a favour!" he panted, the strain clear in his voice. "I'm struggling to hold on here. Take my torch—shine it dead ahead, would ya? If I let go, I'll be eating dirt." Finlay grumbled something unintelligible but lunged forward, snatching the flashlight from Pete's outstretched hand. Raising it high above his head, the beam pierced the darkness, illuminating the path in front of the eager dog. The forest came alive in stark relief: twisted roots and glistening leaves shimmered in the light, the shadows writhing like restless spirits.

As they pressed on, Pete's breath came in short bursts, the tension winding tighter with every step. Katie's nose was down, pulling harder now, her instincts honed on something just out of sight. Finlay's torchlight caught a flash of movement ahead—a blur low to the ground. Pete's stomach churned, but he tightened his grip, muttering under his breath, "this sucks!" The dogs' bark cut through the night, sharp and urgent, as if to answer him.

"What was the lad's name again?" Pete's voice was steady, his focus split between the bounding dog in front and the dim, shadowy forest around them. His eyes darted left and right, scanning for any flicker of movement. "Errr… Letting, I think that's what the DCI said," Finlay replied, his tone laced with skepticism. "Do you know him?" There was a pause, Pete's brow furrowing as he racked his brain. "Hang on… yeah, well, no. Not entirely. But I do remember a young lad…" He trailed off, his face tightening in thought. Suddenly, his fingers snapped with a soft pop before he hurriedly clamped them back on the harness as the dog gave another tug. "Alf—no, Andrew. Andy! That's it. Small lad, if I recall. Seemed pleasant enough. Polite, y'know? But way too eager. Like, trying-too-hard eager."

Finlay raised an eyebrow, glancing sideways as Pete continued. "We were in the mess hall when he came in. Full uniform, polished boots, the works. Problem was, most of us were in civvies, just unwinding after a shift. He stood out like a sore thumb. First thing, he starts badgering Greenie and his crew—you know, big bloke from Tango Two?" "Greenie? Yeah, I know him," Finlay muttered, a faint smirk tugging at his lips. "Well, Greenie wasn't having any of it. Kid kept asking questions, rapid-fire, like he was interrogating them. You could see the lads were getting fed up, but instead of telling him to shove off, Greenie decides to have a laugh. Told the kid he could join Tango Two since they were heading out on some 'special assignment.'"

Pete chuckled at the memory, a brief spark of amusement lighting his face. "You should've seen him. Little Andy's eyes lit up like a kid on Christmas morning. He was bouncing off the bloody walls, practically vibrating. Of course, the 'special assignment' was just a supply run to the arse-end of nowhere, but I swear, he probably thought he was about to save the world." Finlay let out a dry laugh, shaking his head. "Figures. Sounds like the kind of lad who'd go wandering off into the woods and get himself in a mess." Pete's grin faded, his attention snapping back to the dog as its nose dipped closer to the ground. "Yeah, well… let's just hope he hasn't bounced his way into something we can't pull him out of."

"Ouch!" Finlay hissed, jerking his hand back sharply. Pete spun around, his eyes narrowing as he spotted Finlay plucking a thorn from his finger, a thin bead of blood welling up. "What now?" Pete muttered; his frustration barely masked. Finlay stuck his finger in his mouth, wincing theatrically. "Just a thorn. Don't stop on my account—carry on, mate," he mumbled around the digit. Pete rolled his eyes but turned back, focusing on Katie as she bounded ahead, her enthusiasm undampened by the gruelling terrain. Moments later, the dense forest began to thin, and they stepped into a small clearing. The change was abrupt, like surfacing from deep water. Katie halted mid-step, shaking herself vigorously, spraying droplets of water and bits of debris in every direction. "Ah, come on, Katie!" Pete growled, shielding his face as a fine mist peppered him and the nearest leaves.

Emerging behind him, Finlay let out a breathy laugh. "Thank God that's over. I swear, I was about ten seconds away from turning around and leaving you to it." He brushed his hands down his jacket, ridding it of dirt and stray leaves. "Guess we'd better wait for the rest of the crew." They stood in the centre of the clearing, the stillness a stark contrast to the chaos of their trek. The moonlight broke through the thinning clouds, bathing the clearing in an eerie silver glow. The distant rustling and muffled curses from Tango Romeo grew louder as the rest of the team fought their way through the stubborn undergrowth. Finlay folded his arms, glancing sidelong at Pete. "Alright, mate. You've got my attention now. Please, do continue…" Pete smirked but didn't respond, his gaze fixed on the far edge of the clearing, where Katie had stilled completely, her ears pricked and nose twitching.

"Where was I? Oh, yeah," Pete said, a mischievous grin tugging at his lips. "So, Greenie and his boys left the mess to gear up. Meanwhile, Andy—this kid, I swear—was practically bouncing off the walls. He's skipping down the corridor like he's just been handed the keys to Buckingham Palace." Finlay groaned, rolling his eyes. "For pity's sake, get on with it." Pete laughed, glancing at Katie, who was now sitting on the grass, head tilted as if she were hanging on every word. "Alright, alright. So, Andy finally makes it out to the vehicle stock. Tango Two's already there, standing around like they've been waiting for hours. And of course, they've got Barney with them—great dog, by the way."

"Pete," Finlay interrupted, his patience clearly thinning. "Right, right, here's the good bit," Pete said, unable to suppress his smirk. "Greenie tells his lads to head around the front of the transit van, right? Meanwhile, he's hanging back at the rear, waiting for Andy to catch up. And when the poor sod finally shows up, Greenie— playing it cool as ice—sticks out his hand like some squadron leader welcoming a rookie to the team. Shakes the kid's hand and everything, dead serious." Finlay raised a sceptical eyebrow. "Let me guess—Andy was eating it up?" "Like a dog with a bone," Pete confirmed, chuckling. "The kid's grinning ear to ear, probably thinking he's just been knighted or something. Later, Greenie swore the lad was so excited he had a hard-on. And you know what? I wouldn't be surprised if he did."

Finlay snorted, shaking his head. "Christ, no wonder he's out here alone, getting us into this mess. Sounds like he was born to be bait." Pete laughed again, shaking his head. "Poor Andy. Too eager for his own good. But hey, makes for a cracking story, doesn't it?" Katie's ears twitched, and her focus suddenly snapped to the treeline, breaking the moment. Both men followed her gaze, their laughter fading as the tension of the forest returned.

"I digress," Pete said with a grin, though Finlay had already checked out, rolling his eyes before turning his attention to the clearing. His torch beam swept across the perimeter, scanning the trees as his interest in the story faded. Unfazed, Pete carried on, his voice animated as he broke into a laugh. "So, here's the kicker. Greenie tells the lad there's no room up front, right? Real straight-faced, too. Says, 'You'll have to ride in the back.' And, of course, the kid doesn't think twice. Just nods and climbs in."

Finlay's torch paused for a moment, and he cast a glance back, curiosity creeping in despite himself. "Well, it's a bloody dog unit, isn't it?" Pete continued, his shoulders shaking with laughter. "So, Andy's back there with the crates, chew toys, and God knows what else. Greenie tells him to hold tight and slams the door shut behind him. And get this—two hours, Finlay. Two whole hours that twit sat in there! Didn't even think to call on his radio. Just sat there in the dark like a lost puppy." By now, Pete was practically doubled over, and his infectious laughter pulled Finlay in despite his better judgment. He tried to suppress it, but the ridiculousness of the story got the better of him. "Two hours?" Finlay sputtered. "Jesus Christ, did he think he was on some secret mission?"

Pete wiped his eyes, nodding. "Probably thought he was guarding the crown jewels back there. Greenie said when they finally opened the door, the poor lad was sitting on a crate, wide-eyed and clutching a bloody lead like it was the Holy Grail. He even saluted!" That sent Finlay over the edge, his laughter echoing through the clearing. Even Katie seemed amused, her tail wagging as she looked between the two men. "Bloody hell, Pete," Finlay said, catching his breath. "No wonder that kid's gotten himself into trouble. He's got the survival instincts of a goldfish." Pete snorted. "Let's just hope he hasn't gotten himself chewed up by something nastier than a police dog." His tone grew quieter, the humour fading as they both glanced toward the treeline. Something about the stillness felt... off.

Twenty yards back, DCI Craig pushed through the stubborn ferns, their wiry branches clawing at his trousers with every step.

The beam of his torch swept left and right, cutting through the oppressive darkness, as the officers behind him did the same, their lights dancing like restless fireflies. Every snapped twig and rustle of leaves set his nerves on edge as they combed the forest floor for any clue that the missing Officer had come this way. Up ahead, the faint sound of laughter reached his ears. He squinted, spotting the faint outlines of Tango Three in the clearing. Their easy demeanour grated against the tension twisting in his gut. "Bloody idiots," he muttered under his breath, quickening his pace. The missing Officer's life could be on the line, and they were having a laugh.

As he trudged forward, the DCI stole a glance upward. The tangled canopy had finally parted, revealing a sky glittering with stars. His lips curled into a brief, fleeting smile. At least the weather was cooperating for once. The rain had cleared, and the heavens above offered a stark contrast to the chaos below—a quiet reminder that order still existed somewhere in the universe. Stephen's focus snapped back to the path ahead. The stars might guide sailors and poets, but out here, they wouldn't find his missing Officer. That was on him. And with every step, the weight of that responsibility pressed harder on his shoulders.

A few feet behind the group, Commander Wadley moved with deliberate purpose, his boots crunching softly against the damp undergrowth. His hand hovered over his sidearm for a moment before unbuttoning the holster. The faint snap echoed in the still air as he drew the Glock 19, the black metal glinting faintly in the torchlight. In one smooth motion, he ejected the magazine, his sharp eyes scanning the staggered row of brass-tipped rounds. Full. Satisfied, he slammed it back into the grip with a crisp snap, the sound reverberating like a distant warning shot. Wadley slid the Glock back into its holster, but left the flap unsecured, the tension humming in his body like a coiled spring.

His gaze flickered around the perimeter, the dim glow of his team's torches dancing erratically across the trees. They were too absorbed in their search, their heads low as they scanned the undergrowth, oblivious to his quiet preparation. Wadley's jaw tightened. Something about this stretch of woods felt wrong, like the trees themselves were holding their breath. Fingers brushing the edge of his holster, he exhaled slowly and stepped forward, his eyes narrowing as he followed the group, ready for whatever shadows might emerge from the trees.

The laughter died in an instant as Finlay's eyes caught the DCI approaching. The DCI's face was a storm cloud—dark, unforgiving, and about to break. The tension in the air shifted like a tightening noose. Finlay nudged Pete sharply, the grin slipping from his face like a mask. In a flash, he was standing at attention, the easy camaraderie between them evaporating under the DCI's piercing gaze. "You two clowns," DCI Craig's voice cracked through the silence, cold and heavy with authority. "You're this close to having my boot shoved up your arse. Do you have any idea how serious this is? PC Letting—one of our own—is out here. Lost. Possibly injured. And you two idiots are laughing like it's some bloody school camping trip!"

The words hit hard, slicing through the air with a sharpness that stung their pride. Finlay's mouth went dry, and Pete stiffened, the weight of the DCI's glare pressing down on them. The humour drained from their faces as they processed the full gravity of the situation. Their heads dropped in silent submission, each of them swallowing down the rising guilt. As the rest of Tango Romeo pushed through the undergrowth and into the clearing, the tension hung thick. But they were grateful for the shift in the DCI's focus. His attention finally left them, moving to the task at hand. The DCI's sharp eyes scanned the darkness, already calculating the next steps in the search. In that moment, the air felt different. The banter, the jokes—they were gone, replaced by a quiet urgency. Whatever lay ahead in the night, there would be no more laughter. The hunt had begun.

The DCI pivoted to face the group, his eyes sweeping over each Officer with an intensity that made the air between them tighten. With a quick gesture, he ushered them in closer, lowering his voice so it didn't carry across the clearing. No need to alert anything—or anyone—that didn't need to know. Ralph stepped in next to him, his posture stiff, his hand hovering near his holster, fingers brushing the flap that hadn't been properly secured. A subtle movement, but enough to tell Stephen his mind was already calculating potential risks, the unspoken tension between them thickening.

"Alright, lads, nothing yet," the DCI said, checking his watch, the soft glow of the face barely visible in the dark. "We've got thirty minutes until sunrise—visibility will improve, but let's not get complacent." He glanced around, his tone sharpening as he continued, "Let me remind you, our primary objective is to find PC Letting. Nothing else matters until that's done." A brief silence followed. Ralph's jaw tightened as he shot a sideways glance at the DCI, the unease in his frown betraying his thoughts. The DCI's gaze never wavered, his voice cutting through the tension like a blade.

"If the convict is spotted, you report it to me. Immediately. Do not engage. You take no action until I make the call. We move as one unit, understood?" Each Officer nodded, the weight of the DCI's command settling over them. The unspoken truth was clear: this wasn't a standard search. Not anymore. They all turned, eyes locking with the two Officers and their dog, who stood alert, poised like hunters, waiting for the next signal. The air felt thick with anticipation, and Stephen took a step forward. The ground beneath them seemed to hum with the same urgency. Ralph let out a quiet sigh, the sound barely audible in the stillness. A moment passed before he met The DCI's gaze, his thoughts momentarily laid bare. Then, with a curt nod, he adjusted his stance, and the hunt resumed.

"Has the dog picked up anything?" the DCI asked, his eyes darting from Katie, who stood motionless, to Pete. "No, Sir," came the response, clipped and flat. The group stood in tense silence, the only sound the faint rustling of the wind through the trees. The DCI rubbed his chin thoughtfully with his gloved hand, his gaze distant, searching the darkness for some sign, some thread to follow. It was clear—he had no idea which direction to go next.

From the back of the group, Ralph's voice broke the quiet, steady but laced with something sharper. "Begging your pardon, Sir, but may I make an observation?" The DCI snapped around, eager for any direction, and gave a quick nod. "Go ahead, Commander." Ralph stepped forward, his gaze scanning the dense forest around them, his voice steady but deliberate. "Well, if I were lost in these woods, and it was dark, I'd use my senses. Sight isn't much use with this kind of visibility. No, I'd rely on hearing." A hush fell over the group. Even Katie, the dog, seemed to sense the shift. Two Officers shut their eyes, trying to block out the sound of their own breathing, to clear their minds. The DCI stiffened; his curiosity piqued.

Ralph's eyes flicked over the faces of his colleagues. "Tell me," he asked, his voice barely a whisper, "what can you hear?" The group stood still, listening, their breaths almost synchronized. For a moment, the forest seemed to hold its breath as well. The DCI furrowed his brow, his mind straining to pick out anything from the chorus of crickets, the soft rustling of leaves. Everything felt distant, muffled. Then, it hit him—faint but unmistakable. His eyes widened slightly as his breath caught. He turned to Ralph, his voice low but urgent. "The sea..." Ralph nodded slowly, a slight smile tugging at the corner of his lips. "Exactly. We're not as deep in these woods as we thought. The sea's close. The wind's carrying it." The DCI's mind began to click into place, a shift in his thinking that made everything feel sharper. The sea. They weren't just searching the woods; they were hunting along a coastal line. The sound, subtle yet undeniable, was their guide. He turned to the group, his voice now filled with a new edge of determination. "Alright, we've got a lead. Let's move. Keep your senses sharp. The coast is our next target."

Without missing a beat, DCI Craig sprang into action, his commands sharp and clear. "Dog handler, Sergeant, take the lead. Find a route to the beach." He turned to the rest of Tango Romeo, his eyes burning with focus. "Move out. Now." The team fell into motion, the urgency of the situation settling over them like a thick fog. As they advanced, Katie suddenly shot forward, her leash snapping taut as she bounded ahead, her powerful legs eating up the ground. Pete was yanked along behind her, caught off guard by the sudden surge of speed. "Wait a minute!" Pete grunted, his feet struggling to keep pace. He dug his heels in, pulling back on the harness with a firm tug. "Heel, Kathryn!"

The dog paused, her body still trembling with energy as she sniffed the air, nostrils flaring, searching for a scent. The group slowed, watching in silence as Katie dropped her head, her intense focus unwavering. The path ahead was narrow, hemmed in by dense vegetation on either side. The air felt heavy, almost claustrophobic, as the team was forced to move in a tight single file, the ferns and shrubs scraping at their gear with every step. The forest seemed to close in around them, each rustle of leaves echoing like a warning.

Pete gave Katie a quiet pat, a silent reassurance. His eyes darted from the dog to the trail ahead, his mind racing through the possibilities. The tension in the air was palpable, like the calm before a storm. "Stay sharp," he muttered to himself, pulling his jacket tighter against the chill that seemed to be creeping into the woods. Every step felt like they were walking deeper into a world that wasn't quite their own—a world where the only thing more unpredictable than the terrain was whatever they were hunting for.

The woodland stirred with life as the first rays of sunlight pierced the horizon, slowly banishing the lingering darkness from the sky. The forest, once draped in shadows, seemed to inhale deeply, stretching as the light began to touch the trees and bushes, casting long, shifting silhouettes. A chorus of small birds began to sing, their morning songs piercing the quiet air. Tango Romeo pressed forward, their boots crunching softly beneath them as they made their way along the narrow path, their torches now redundant in the growing light. Suddenly, Katie stopped dead in her tracks, her body tense as she lifted her snout, nostrils flaring. "What you got, girl?" Finlay's voice broke the silence, his tone low but expectant. He was close behind, trying to peer past Pete to see what had caught the dog's attention.

Pete squinted into the stillness ahead, his eyes scanning the woods. "I don't see anything," he muttered, his hand instinctively tightening on the leash. His pulse quickened as the air seemed to hold its breath, the quiet unnerving in its stillness. "Nothing," Pete confirmed, his gaze darting nervously through the trees. "Alright, let's keep moving." Katie, still on high alert, tugged fiercely at the leash, her muscles coiled as if ready to charge. But Pete, his face set with determination, yanked back firmly on the harness. "Easy, princess," he muttered, his voice a soothing command. "Easy. Let's take things slow." Katie's body quivered, her instincts urging her forward, but Pete's grip was steady. The dog hesitated for a moment, her sharp eyes flickering toward him in silent understanding. Then, with a low whine, she settled slightly, her pace now more controlled, but still full of intent.

The group continued on, the uneasy feeling in the air hanging over them like a thick fog. Every step felt heavier, each rustle in the underbrush a reminder that they were no longer just moving through the woods. They were being watched.

The team moved in a steady rhythm, their boots crunching softly on the undergrowth as they passed a massive oak tree, its twisted branches gnarled against the early light. They rounded the corner, the narrow path winding ahead, with the rest of the unit following closely behind. Ralph, always cautious, kept his position at the rear, his eyes flicking nervously over his shoulder every few seconds, scanning the dark corners of the forest for any sign of movement. Suddenly, to his right, a flash of bright light flickered in the distance—a brief, sharp burst that cut through the trees. Then it was gone. A moment of quiet before the light flickered again, followed by another, and then another, the pattern repeating like a coded message, each flash sharper, more urgent than the last. Eight times the light flashed, cutting through the dense canopy, before it vanished entirely, leaving only the silence of the woods in its wake.

Ralph's heart raced as he glanced ahead, hoping nobody had detected the light. The others were focused, their attention on the trail in front of them, oblivious to the signal he'd just seen. He tightened his grip on the strap of his holster, instinctively hovering his hand near his weapon. His eyes narrowed, but there was no time to dwell on it now. The Officer in front of him, a massive figure, suddenly halted without warning, his bulk blocking the path. Ralph strained to see past the man's broad shoulders, his neck craning as he tried to make out the cause of the sudden stop. There was something in the air, an unspoken tension that had gripped the group.

Whispering, Ralph tapped the Officer on the shoulder, his voice barely audible over the distant rustling of the leaves. "What's the problem?" The Officer turned slightly, his face a mix of concentration and unease. Ralph could see the edge in his eyes. Whatever had stopped them, it wasn't something that could be ignored. Something wasn't right. And Ralph had a feeling they weren't alone anymore.

PC Dimmock turned his head just enough to glance at Ralph, his eyes still fixed ahead. "Not sure, Sir," he murmured, his voice low but tense. "Looks like the dogs onto something. DCI signalled us to halt, but—" He paused, narrowing his eyes as the movement ahead caught his attention. "Nope, we're moving again." Before Ralph could ask for clarification, the group was already on the move. The rhythm of their steps resumed, boots crunching through the damp underbrush. But then, in an instant, the massive Officer in front of Ralph miscalculated his step, and with a loud splash, he plunged his foot into a puddle hidden beneath the ferns. The freezing water surged up, soaking the bottom half of his trousers in a sudden, icy shock. The Officer cursed softly under his breath but didn't miss a beat. He wiped the splashed water off his legs, grimacing, but kept moving forward, ignoring the biting cold creeping up his calves. The rest of the team barely glanced back, intent on the path ahead. Ralph, however, couldn't help but watch for a moment, the sound of water sloshing around his boots like a fleeting echo.

Shaking off the distraction, he forced his focus forward. There was something more pressing than wet pants now. The air had shifted, the tension thickened as they moved deeper into the woods, every step more deliberate, as if the forest itself was watching them—waiting. Ralph's grip on his holster tightened involuntarily as his senses flared, instinctively alert to the growing unease gnawing at him. He couldn't shake the feeling that they were no longer the hunters.

Katie's barking was frantic, the sound echoing through the trees as she dashed in circles ahead. Pete's heart pounded in his chest as he glanced over his shoulder to Finlay, urgency in his voice. "Quickly, close in!" Without waiting for a response, Pete bolted forward, the weight of his steps adding to the tension in the air. Finlay was right on his heels, the sound of their boots pounding the soft ground matching the frantic rhythm of the dog's barks. They broke through the thick underbrush and into a small clearing, their feet skidding on the slick, muddy surface. Katie was on edge, her hackles raised, and her growl deepened as she circled a prone figure lying motionless on the ground. Pete froze, the sight ahead locking his breath in his chest.

The body was still, sprawled unnaturally across the ground. Pete's stomach lurched as his eyes quickly swept over the figure, searching for signs of life, but finding none. Katie growled louder; her restraint snapped by the scent of blood. Pete's grip on her harness tightened instinctively, his words stuck in his throat as he struggled to process what he was seeing. Finlay's voice broke through the haze of confusion, his hand landing reassuringly on Pete's shoulder. "Hey, bud, pull her back. This is a crime scene. We need to step back and wait for the others." Reluctantly, Pete obeyed, his gaze lingering on the body before he turned, pulling Katie away, her growls softening but still tense. They retreated to the edge of the path, standing in the shadow of the trees, the weight of the moment sinking in. Silence stretched between them until the distant crunch of footsteps signalled the approach of the DCI and the rest of Tango Romeo.

The Officers filed in, their heads bowed, their faces grim as they took in the scene before them. The DCI, eyes flicking to the body, didn't need to say a word. The unmistakable sense of dread filled the air. He stepped forward into the clearing, his voice barely above a whisper, "Oh no…" The horror of the discovery settled in like a dark cloud, and the group braced themselves for what was to come.

The DCI turned sharply to face the rest of the unit, his expression hardening as he raised a hand, signalling them to halt. The tension in the air was palpable, and the men instinctively fell quiet, waiting for his command. Without a word, he gestured to the nearest Officer, a young man whose face had already begun to drain of colour. The reality of what lay ahead had yet to sink in, but the DCI needed him focused—this wasn't the time for hesitation. "Look, son," the DCI's voice was low but firm, cutting through the heavy silence. "We've found PC Letting. It's not good news." The Officer stiffened, a slight tremor in his posture, but he remained silent, his eyes never leaving the DCI. His gaze was unwavering, locked with the man's as he spoke with authority. "I need you to take the rest of Tango Romeo back down this track. There's a path heading east—I think it loops around and re-joins further up. We need to move, now."

The Officer nodded slowly, but Stephen could see the weight of the words hanging heavily on his shoulders. The shock was still there, but Stephen saw a flicker of understanding in his eyes—he knew the mission wasn't over. Not yet. "Son," The DCI continued, his tone softening but not by much, "there will be time for grieving. But for now, focus. Get Tango Romeo to the rendezvous point. I'll stay here to make a note of the location, then head to the beach. We need to get the body out, and I'll need a Halo to lift it."

The Officer stood straighter, his jaw setting with quiet resolve. He nodded, wordlessly turning to signal to the rest of the unit. As he did, the DCI caught the looks of confusion that flickered across their faces. Some men were still struggling to process the loss, but they knew better than to argue. This was a job, and they were professionals. Before the officer could step away, the DCI's eyes flicked over to PC Paul Dimmock, who was lingering at the edge of the group. The DCI's gaze was sharp, his expression unreadable as he motioned for Dimmock to approach. The subtle shift in the air was all it took for the officer to move, closing the distance between them. The DCI's voice was low as Paul came to stand beside him. "Stay sharp, we've still got work to do."

Ralph swallowed hard, his throat tightening as the weight of the moment settled over him. This was the part of the job he dreaded— the stark, unforgiving sight of one of his own comrades fallen, the grim reality that no amount of training could ever truly prepare him for. His boots crunched softly on the underbrush as he followed Paul, the big man's shoulders hunched in resignation, his face shadowed with grief. As they neared the clearing, the scene before them struck like a punch to the gut. Young Andy was lying on his back, his eyes vacant and wide in a lifeless stare. The ground around him was soaked in dry, dark blood, the stain creeping outward, stark against the earth. The deep, jagged laceration across his neck was unmistakable. "Holy shit," Ralph muttered under his breath, his voice hollow, as they both stood frozen in place.

The DCI was the first to snap out of the momentary shock. He moved swiftly, a sharpness in his steps that cut through the heaviness of the clearing. "Finlay, Pete," he commanded, his tone cutting through the silence. "Secure a perimeter." Without hesitation, they moved to carry out their orders, the sense of urgency rising like a wave crashing down on them.

The DCI took a moment, his eyes narrowing as he surveyed the body of Andy, the surrounding area, the thick vegetation that threatened to swallow them whole. He exhaled sharply, the weight of responsibility heavy on his chest. Then, he turned to face Ralph and Paul, his posture rigid, his voice steady but laced with an undercurrent of something darker. "Well, I wasn't expecting this outcome," he said, his eyes locking with Paul's, as though reading the man's grief like a book. "Paul, isn't it?" The big man nodded slowly; his lips pressed into a thin line. His face was a mask of controlled pain, but the anguish was there, raw and untamed behind his eyes. The DCI didn't flinch; he knew what this was. "Good," he said, his voice firm, almost mechanical. "I'll need you to guard the path behind you. The others will take the coastal route. The vegetation's thick, but if the convict approaches, we'll see him coming with enough warning."

Without another word, Paul turned, his broad shoulders hunched in a way that spoke volumes. He didn't look back as he walked the path, his heavy boots pounding against the earth, each step a reminder of the cold reality they now faced. As he positioned himself, legs apart, hands clasped in front of him like a soldier on guard, a lone tear slipped down his weathered cheek, the first sign of the grief he had fought to hold back. He wiped it away quickly, but the vulnerability lingered—fleeting, but unmistakable. In this moment, as the silence settled thick around them, Paul stood alone, guarding more than just the path; he was guarding what was left of his own shattered resolve.

"Commander, will you join me, please?" The DCI's voice broke the silence, sharp and steady. Ralph nodded without a word, his boots crunching softly against the underbrush as he followed the DCI toward the body. Every step felt heavier than the last, as if the weight of what they were about to face pressed harder with each movement. As they approached the lifeless form of PC Letting, their eyes immediately went to the scene, scanning it with a practiced intensity, taking in every single detail. The air was thick with the scent of blood and damp earth, the early morning light struggling to cut through the dense canopy above them. Time seemed to slow, each second stretching longer as they both observed the grim tableau.

After a few moments, the DCI broke the silence, his voice low but steady. "It's clear," he said, his gaze fixed on the body. "PC Letting was murdered here. Looks like he wasn't moved—he's exactly where he fell. The laceration to his neck... that was the fatal blow. Whoever did this knew exactly what they were doing." Ralph's eyes moved over the body, mirroring the DCI's observations. He noted the feet, the legs, the torso—each element of the body telling its own silent story. But it was his hands that caught his attention. He crouched lower, his gaze narrowing on the man's right hand. "Wait," the DCI muttered, his own focus sharpening. "Look here. He's missing three fingers from his right hand." Ralph's jaw tightened, a flicker of understanding flashing across his face. He had already drawn the same conclusion. The absence of those fingers wasn't just an oddity—it was a message. He met the DCI's eyes, and they exchanged a silent understanding. This was no random act of violence. The cruelty of the act was calculated, deliberate. Ralph took a slow breath, his fingers brushing the hilt of his weapon, but he didn't move. They both stood there, locked in the reality of the moment, the weight of the situation pressing down on them with unbearable clarity.

Kneeling carefully, the DCI's movements were deliberate, each step taken with the utmost precision to avoid disturbing the scene. His gaze fell upon the deep, jagged wound at the base of PC Letting's neck, the blood long since dried but still stark against the pale skin. "Deep cut... likely from a serrated knife," he muttered under his breath, his mind already running through the possibilities. The brutality of the wound was clear—this wasn't a crime of passion. This was methodical. Cold.

As he studied the rest of the young man's body, his eyes traced the contours of Letting's face, noting the fine, almost boyish features that contrasted sharply with the violent death he had met. The Officer couldn't have been more than nineteen or twenty, barely out of his teens. A small scar on his right cheek caught the DCI's eye, likely the remnants of a childhood illness—chickenpox, perhaps—

but the faint mark felt trivial against the gravity of the scene. Then, the DCI's eyes shifted, drawn to the closed eyelids. He leaned in closer, brow furrowing in confusion. "What's this?" His voice softened as he examined the detail more closely, as if speaking aloud might somehow bring clarity. His gaze flicked from one eye to the other, then back again. "Looks like the convict closed Andrew's eyes... after death. No prints on the lids... must be wearing gloves."

He pulled back slightly, his mind working to piece the information together. The act of closing the eyes, a small gesture of postmortem care—or perhaps, something more sinister. The lack of fingerprints suggested someone with a methodical approach, someone who thought of every detail, even in the heat of violence. The DCI glanced over his shoulder, expecting to catch Ralph's eye, but instead, he found his colleague distracted, his focus not on the body but somewhere else entirely. The DCI frowned slightly, sensing something off. "Ralph?" he called softly, but his voice only seemed to bounce back from the trees, unanswered. Ralph's distraction was palpable—his posture stiff, his eyes flicking back and forth, but not toward the scene, not toward the details The DCI had just uncovered. There was something unsettling in the way Ralph stood, as if the weight of the discovery had already pressed down on him in a way it hadn't yet reached him.

"Excuse me, Commander. Everything alright?" Stephen's voice cut through the tense atmosphere, his eyes never leaving the body. Unfazed, Ralph turned towards him, his face unreadable. "I was listening. Please, continue." The DCI nodded but couldn't shake the feeling that something was off. His gaze stayed fixed on PC Letting's body as he studied every detail, mentally cataloguing the scene. But before he could gather his next thought, Ralph spoke again, his tone more insistent this time. "Actually, Stephen," Ralph said, his voice low but firm, "I think it's best we back off. There's a possibility we're standing on evidence." The DCI raised an eyebrow, but after a beat, he stood, acknowledging the Commander's concern. "Yeah, I suppose you're right," he muttered, stepping back. As he moved away, he glanced once more at the young Officer's lifeless form, his mind still racing through the growing list of questions.

Before either man could say another word, Katie's sharp barking sliced through the silence. Both Ralph and the DCI spun around in unison, instinctively shifting into a defensive stance. Ahead, Pete was struggling to keep control of the dog, the tension in the air palpable as the animal pulled at her harness. "She's got something, Sir!" Pete shouted; his voice tight with urgency. "Movement! Up ahead, twelve o'clock!" The DCI's heart skipped a beat as Pete yanked Katie back, his grip firm on the leash. Without missing a beat, Pete unclipped the harness, his voice booming with authority. "Go get him, girl!" Katie, her eyes locked on the path ahead, surged forward, pulling with all her might, her instincts taking over as she darted into the underbrush. The air thickened with anticipation, the hunt now well and truly on. The quiet of the clearing was replaced with the frantic pulse of adrenaline as the team braced for whatever came next.

The German Shepherd, her muscles rippling with each powerful stride, tore down the path, her sharp barks echoing through the trees with primal fury. Every instinct in her was honed on the chase, the thrill of the hunt guiding her movements as she disappeared into the dense undergrowth. The tension in the air was thick as the team stood frozen for a moment, watching her vanish into the woods. Finlay gripped Pete's shoulder tightly, his breath shallow, eyes darting between the DCI and the path ahead. The DCI's gaze was sharp as he processed the scene before him. His mind raced—PC Letting's lifeless body lay in front of them, a stark reminder of the danger lurking in the shadows. His thoughts shifted rapidly, calculating the next move. He glanced at Ralph, whose expression was unreadable, offering no reassurance, no direction. The silence was deafening.

Then, the DCI's eyes flicked to the two Officers waiting in the clearing. He didn't need to speak; a single nod from him conveyed the urgency of the moment. The hunt was on. "Pete, Finlay, go!" the DCI barked, his voice cutting through the tension like a blade. Without hesitation, the two Officers sprinted down the path, their feet pounding against the wet earth as they followed the dog's trail. As they took off, Ralph's hand shot out, catching the DCI by the arm. "Go with them," Ralph said, his voice steady but with an edge of something—perhaps recognition of the weight the DCI carried in this moment. "It's OK. We'll stay here with the body. PC Dimmock and I have it covered."

The DCI hesitated for a second, the gravity of the situation pressing down on him. His eyes met Ralph's, and for a brief moment, the two men shared an unspoken understanding. He nodded; his mind now locked into one singular focus: catching the convict before more blood was spilled. With a swift turn, the DCI took off after Pete and Finlay, his heart racing in sync with the pounding of his boots. Behind him, Ralph and PC Dimmock stood still, guarding the lifeless body of their comrade, their eyes scanning the woods for any sign of the danger that had taken one of their own.

* * *

The storm had finally passed, but its aftermath lingered. The sky was still streaked with dark, heavy clouds, their edges glowing faintly in the dying light, as though reluctant to leave. The rain had ceased, but the wind had picked up, howling across the beach and whipping up the sea into a frenzy. Ten-foot waves thundered against the shore, their white caps crashing with a deafening roar. The once-proud SS Vina, a relic of a tragic shipwreck from 1944, now lay half-submerged in the sand, its rotting hull battered by decades of salt and neglect. Only the jagged stern remained visible above the surf, an eerie monument to time's relentless march.

The coastline of Norfolk stretched for ninety miles, a rugged mosaic of beauty and desolation. Here, the land met the sea with stark contrast—tidal salt marshes gave way to towering cliffs, while vast, empty beaches sprawled in between. The air smelled of salt and brine, sharp and invigorating. Brancaster Beach, unlike most other shores in the UK, boasted unusually clear, cool blue water that sparkled beneath the shifting clouds, a rare jewel along the coastline. Its pristine beauty drew crowds in the summer, but today, with the storm's fury behind it, the beach stood empty, save for the relentless crash of waves and the haunting silhouette of the shipwreck. The silence between the wind and sea was almost deafening in its isolation.

The first light of dawn began to stretch across the sky, casting a golden glow that flickered like a promise as the sun slowly rose above the horizon. Its red-tinted rays cut through the storm clouds, infusing the atmosphere with a warmth that seemed to push back the lingering chill of the night. The air was fresh, tinged with the salt of the sea and the earthiness of the damp ground.

In the quiet, a lone figure moved steadily along the path. Agnes, with her silver hair pulled neatly under a worn scarf, walked briskly toward Titchwell, her silhouette etched against the growing light. She relished these early morning walks, the solitude, the peace—moments when the world still felt untouched, before it awoke to the noise and clutter of civilization. For her, there was something sacred in the way the darkness melted away, the first light creeping across the earth like an old friend returning. It was the one time of day when the world felt like it truly belonged to her—a calm refuge between the night's dreams and the day's demands.

Her small ankle boots crunched softly as they pressed into the damp sand, each step leaving a fleeting imprint that the rising tide would soon erase. The rhythmic sound of her footsteps, mingled with the distant crash of the waves, seemed to deepen the quiet of the morning. The wind, cool and biting, tugged at her, sending strands of her silvery-grey hair swirling across her face. She instinctively raised a hand to push it back, but it was no use. With a resigned sigh, she slipped her hands into the warm, familiar pockets of her raincoat. The soft rustle of the fabric, coupled with the comforting warmth that seeped into her fingers, brought a sense of solace she hadn't known she needed.

For a moment, Agnes simply stood still, letting the wind whip around her. The ocean's salty tang mixed with the earthy scent of the wet sand, grounding her in this timeless space between sea and sky. As her hands settled into the coat's pockets, a smile tugged at the corners of her lips. Her mind drifted, carried away by the whispers of a distant memory—perhaps it was of a long-forgotten conversation with a friend, or an afternoon spent in the garden with her children when they were still small. The memories were like fragments, but sweet all the same, warm in the way only time can make them.

The serenity of the moment was briefly interrupted by the low hum of an approaching helicopter. At first, it seemed far off, a faint buzzing that grew louder as it neared. She tilted her head toward the sound, squinting against the wind as she tried to make out its shape. It wasn't the usual sound she heard out here. The occasional fisherman's boat, or perhaps a distant gull, yes—but a helicopter? That was something new. Her brow furrowed slightly, a trace of curiosity flickering in her chest. The whirring grew louder, closer now, breaking the natural harmony of the shoreline as it cut through the air like an urgent whisper.

Agnes paused for a moment, her thoughts pulling back from the memory that had briefly taken hold of her. She glanced up, watching the helicopter draw nearer. It moved in tight circles, almost as if searching for something, its shadow briefly dancing across the sand below. She shivered, not from the cold, but from an odd feeling that settled over her. The air seemed thicker now, the wind less friendly, as though the world itself was bracing for something.

The thought quickly passed as she pulled her coat tighter around her, her fingers curling deeper into the pockets, and took another slow step forward, her boots sinking slightly into the soft sand. The helicopter was soon out of sight, but its hum still hung in the air, an odd reminder that the world was still spinning around her. It was time to keep moving—there were memories to be savoured and moments to be cherished before the day truly began.

The thick branches of the dense undergrowth seemed to reach out like twisted fingers, clawing at the three Officers as they pushed through the tangled path. The air was thick with the smell of damp earth and the wet scent of the forest, but the dog—Katie—was undeterred; they found her sitting in the middle of the path. Attaching the harness, she pulled relentlessly, her sharp barks slicing through the stillness of the woods, urging her handler forward. Pete stumbled over a root, barely keeping his balance as the dog surged ahead, her energy seemingly boundless.

"Bloody hell, Katie! Will you slow it down a little?" Pete panted, trying to catch his breath. "My little legs can't keep up this pace much longer!" Finlay, ever the efficient one, grabbed the harness from his struggling friend, a smirk crossing his face. "Let me take her, mate. You hang back with the DCI. I think he's flagging already," he said, glancing back with a raised eyebrow.

They both shot a quick look behind them. The DCI had stopped, leaning heavily against a tree for support, one hand gripping the rough bark as he bent over, coughing violently. His breath came in short, desperate bursts as he hacked up the remnants of last night's dinner, his face a grimace of discomfort. A few hacking coughs later, he wiped his chin with the back of his gloved hand and looked up, spotting the two men still pushing forward.

"Gotta lay off the biscuits," the DCI muttered, his voice hoarse, a wry grin tugging at the corner of his mouth despite the struggle. With a grunt, he straightened himself, pushing off the tree trunk with a slight stagger before starting to jog again. His breath came more evenly now, but his legs felt like lead as he picked up the pace, eyes focused ahead on the path that wound toward the beach.

"Right, enough of that," he said under his breath, mentally shaking off the discomfort. "Let's catch up." He was already falling behind as the others surged ahead, their figures darting through the foliage, determined to stay on the scent. The dog's relentless barking continued to echo through the trees, a sharp reminder that whatever was ahead, they weren't alone.

The DCI's eyes darted left and right as he ran, every rustle in the undergrowth making his pulse quicken. His mind remained focused, scanning the shadows for any hint of movement. His boots splashed through the muddy path, the chill rain soaking through his jacket as he pushed forward. The search for poor old Andy Letting had distracted him, consumed him even, but now, as the wind howled through the trees and the rain pelted down in sheets, the true nature of his mission hit him hard. He was no longer under the comforting weight of his Command trailer, surrounded by familiar faces, Officers, and support staff ready to react at a moment's notice. Out here, it was just him and a handful of Officers fumbling their way through the night, with nothing but the dark woods closing in around them.

The only thing standing between him and the terror of the unknown was two bumbling Officers and a disobedient dog pulling them along, its incessant barking like a cruel reminder of how out of control this whole thing had become. His hand found his trouser pocket, fingers brushing over the packet of Juicy Fruit gum that had become a strange talisman of comfort amidst the chaos. It bounced with every step, a small reminder that in this madness, there were still little things to hold onto.

The night was slowly giving way to the first faint streaks of dawn, and for that, the DCI was thankful. The cover of darkness, the convict's greatest ally, would soon be gone. The rain would still make the forest treacherous, but the shadows would recede. The convict, however skilled at hiding, would soon have no such luxury. It would be easier to spot him in the growing light. A part of the DCI was already looking ahead, his mind envisioning the moment when they'd catch him. It was only a matter of time. They couldn't keep running forever.

Up ahead, the sudden silence hit the DCI like a punch to the gut. The dog's incessant barking had finally stopped, and for a moment, he thought perhaps the handler had managed to rein her in. But the stillness now felt ominous, unnatural. He skidded to a halt as a sharp voice sliced through the quiet, "Is this the right place, Sir?" It was Sergeant Finlay, his tone heavy with uncertainty. As the DCI rounded the next bend, he could see the two Officers clearly: Pete was crouched down, gently stroking Katie's fur, his face softening as the dog nuzzled his hand. Finlay, however, was more alert, his gaze sweeping the area as though expecting something to jump out from the shadows.

They both turned at the sound of the DCI's footsteps, waiting for him to answer. Finlay's voice came again, but this time tinged with an edge of doubt, "Sir, is this the right location?" The DCI's eyes narrowed as he walked forward, scanning the ground carefully. He knelt briefly to inspect the dirt beneath his boots, his mind ticking. His gaze traced the path they had just come down, noticing the subtle change in the terrain.

The path ahead split—forming a T-junction. He stood for a moment, studying the two options before him. To the left, the path grew brighter, bathed in the first light of the day, leading east toward the distant sound of crashing waves and the cold, unforgiving coastline. That was the route to the beach, the open expanse where they would have more room to manoeuvre, but where the convict could easily be cornered.

To the right, the path disappeared into a darker, more oppressive stretch of woodland, thick with tangled underbrush and the stillness of the shadows. It led deeper into the unknown, further away from the safety of the coastline but offering far more cover for someone trying to evade capture. Stephen stood still for a long moment; the tension thick in the air as his mind raced. He glanced back at the Officers, reading their faces. They were all waiting on him to make a decision, but the weight of it pressed down on him like a vice. Every option had its risks.

Feeling a sense of satisfaction, the DCI cast a brief glance at the two Officers before gesturing to the left, "We need to head that way, but this is our rendezvous point. Tango Romeo should be coming up from down there shortly." He checked his watch, his eyes flicking to the second hand as it ticked steadily forward, the passing seconds amplifying the tension in the air. Pete, oblivious to the seriousness of the situation, leaned down to Katie with a grin, speaking softly to the dog as he made silly faces and kissed her cheek. The sound of his playful affection echoed through the quiet woods. Finlay, on the other hand, couldn't help but wince, his eyes rolling as he nudged his friend with his knee. "Hey, knock it off, dip-shit."

Pete straightened up at the sound of Finlay's voice, his face turning sheepish. Just as he was about to respond, his gaze caught sight of the DCI pacing back and forth, his figure cutting through the misty morning light. Pete froze for a moment, quickly glancing back at Finlay. "Sorry, mate. I just lose myself sometimes, you know?" The sergeant couldn't help but half-smile, shaking his head with a wink. "Yeah, I know." His expression softened, the tension in his shoulders easing for a moment, as if the brief distraction from the task at hand had momentarily lightened the mood.

They both stood there, silent now, each lost in their own thoughts, the weight of their roles heavy on their minds. The forest stretched out before them, still and watchful. As the minutes passed, their attention remained fixed on the path, waiting for the rest of their unit to arrive. Every rustle in the undergrowth, every footstep in the distance made them tense, as they stood vigilant, ready for whatever would come next. The tension in the air was palpable—waiting, watching, and wondering what lay ahead.

Katie's ears shot up, her posture suddenly rigid as she froze, her nose twitching. The three Officers didn't react immediately, but when the dog swiftly rose onto her hind legs, growling low and steady, the tension in the air thickened. "What now?" Pete muttered under his breath, his fingers tightening instinctively around the leather of Katie's harness. The once sturdy material had begun to show signs of wear—threads fraying, the leather thinning with use.

Finlay and the DCI instinctively moved in beside him, their gazes fixed down the path, scanning for any sign of movement. Finlay's voice broke the silence first, his tone uncertain but hopeful, "Maybe Tango Romeo's ahead of us, Sir?" The DCI's sharp eyes flicked back down the empty trail, his mind working quickly, piecing together the situation. "Yeah, possibly," he agreed, though there was a flicker of doubt in his voice.

He stepped forward, his boots crunching softly on the damp earth. "Let's go check it out." Without hesitation, they began to move, slipping into the steady rhythm of a search that was anything but routine. Katie, sensing the shift, tried to surge ahead, her growls intensifying. But Pete, with a practiced hand, pulled back on her harness, keeping her within a few feet of him. "Easy, girl," he murmured, his voice a low whisper, more for himself than for the dog. Katie's energy was palpable, her body straining with anticipation, but Pete's grip was firm, steady—he wouldn't let her rush ahead.

As they advanced, the thick woodland loomed around them, shadows stretching long in the fading light. Every crack of a branch, every shift in the underbrush set their nerves on edge. The air was heavy with the scent of wet earth and the occasional, distant cry of a bird. But none of that mattered. All that mattered now was the path ahead, the creeping sense that something—or someone—was waiting just beyond their sight.

The three men moved cautiously, their boots crunching on the damp earth as they advanced through the thickening trees. Fifty meters later, they emerged into another clearing, larger and more open than the last. A massive oak tree loomed to the left, its twisted branches reaching high into the sky, casting long shadows over the smaller trees and tall grasses that dotted the area. Katie, still on high alert, suddenly broke the stillness with a sharp, unexpected bark, sending the three men jumping back in surprise. Pete spun around, his eyes darting across the open space, but he saw nothing. "Will you button it, Katie? There's nothing there," he muttered, irritation creeping into his voice. But Katie didn't stop. Her barking grew more frantic, her body tense, ears pricked forward. Pete opened his mouth to speak again when, without warning, the DCI's hand shot out and grabbed his arm, pulling him into silence. "That's not your dog barking, son," his voice low but firm, the tension in his tone unmistakable.

The words hung in the air as they stood frozen, listening. Katie, now calm, sat on the ground, her tail wagging lazily, her tongue hanging out to the side. Something wasn't right. Finlay, ever the attentive one, leaned in, his eyes narrowing as he listened carefully. The sound of barking still echoed faintly, but it wasn't Katie. It was coming from somewhere deeper in the clearing. "Sounds like it could be one of ours," Finlay said, his voice barely above a whisper as he pointed toward the large oak tree. "It's coming from over there." The three men shared a look, the unspoken tension rising. The woods around them felt eerily quiet, the birdsong from earlier silenced, as if nature itself had paused to listen. Katie, sensing the change in the air, let out a soft growl, her body tense once again. They moved together towards the oak tree, the distant sound of barking pulling them further into the heart of the clearing. Every step they took seemed to make the air feel heavier, the trees closing in around them.

The DCI's eyes narrowed as he turned to Pete, his voice low but decisive. "Best if Sergeant Charles and I check this out. You hang back with the dog, keep an eye on the rear. Make sure no one's sneaking up on us from behind." Pete gave a quick nod, his focus already shifting as he turned away from the group, positioning himself near the path, watching the shadows carefully. He gripped Katie's leash tighter, sensing the tension in the air.

Finlay, already tense and alert, caught the DCI's signal. Without a word, the DCI gestured to him to move left while he would take the right. They would close in on the tree from different angles, flanking whoever—or whatever—was hiding behind it. Finlay took a breath, feeling his heart pound against his ribs as he adjusted his grip on his torch. Every muscle in his body coiled, ready for action. He glanced sideways just in time to see the DCI slip behind the massive oak tree. Stepping forward cautiously, Finlay inhaled deeply, then exhaled slow—one, two, three. With a burst of energy, he leaped around the opposite side, timing his move with precision. And just as he did, the DCI appeared from the other side, both men catching each other's gaze for a split second. They froze.

At their feet, in the shadows cast by the tree's gnarled branches, was an unexpected sight. A dog—sat perfectly still, its harness tightly secured, yet there was no sign of its handler. The tension in the air thickened. Finlay squatted, instinctively reaching toward the dog, but the animal remained motionless, its eyes flicking between the men. Its presence, and the fact that it was tethered so carefully, sent a chill down his spine.

The DCI crouched beside him, his gaze flicking from the dog to the clearing around them, scanning for any signs of danger. "This is... strange," he muttered, his voice barely audible. "Someone's been here recently. But where the hell is the handler?" The two men exchanged a brief, knowing look—this was no accident, no simple lost dog. Something bigger was at play. The silence was broken only by the soft rustling of leaves, the air growing colder as if nature itself was holding its breath. They stood, waiting for the next move in a game they hadn't fully understood yet.

Finlay took a cautious step forward, his hand outstretched, moving deliberately to reassure the dog. He kept his movements slow, measured—his voice low and calm as he spoke softly to the animal. The dog sniffed the air before leaning forward and gently licking the tips of his gloved fingers, a soft, almost welcoming gesture. Finlay allowed himself a slight smile, his hand moving to stroke the dog's head, the familiar warmth of its fur offering a brief moment of peace amidst the chaos. But then, something cold and unexpected dripped onto his sleeve, a dampness spreading across the fabric. Startled, Finlay froze, his fingers brushing over the wet patch instinctively. The DCI, sensing something was off, sharply signalled for him to stop. "Hold it, Finlay."

The DCI's sharp gaze flicked toward the wet mark on Finlay's arm, a dark, sticky substance now clinging to his sleeve. The DCI removed one of his gloves with deliberate precision, his eyes narrowing as he touched the spot. His fingers lingered, rubbing the fluid between them, the crimson stain becoming more apparent with each passing second. The blood was fresh. "What the hell..." the DCI muttered, his voice thick with disbelief. His eyes, now focused intently on the stain, slowly travelled upward, his expression darkening as he took in the scene before him.

Finlay, his face draining of colour, took an unsteady step backward, his breath catching in his throat. "Mother of God..." he whispered, his voice faltering with horror. The DCI remained frozen in place, his eyes slowly lifting from the ground to the tree above. His mouth went dry, and a chill crept up his spine as he saw it. There, suspended by the branches in a grotesque and unnatural way, was the source of the blood—the body. Twisted and lifeless, it hung there like a macabre ornament, draped in shadows, eyes wide open in a stare that seemed to pierce through the night. The sight was enough to paralyze even the seasoned Officers, their minds struggling to process the gruesome discovery. The dog, now eerily silent, sat stiffly at their feet, its eyes locked on the body above as though it, too, understood the gravity of the situation.

"Get back," the DCI ordered, his voice hoarse but commanding, snapping Finlay out of his trance. He gestured sharply for him to retreat, even as his gaze remained glued to the body in the tree, the sickening reality of their discovery sinking in. The woods felt suddenly suffocating, the air thick with tension. The only sound was the soft rustle of leaves and the rhythmic beating of their hearts, the uneasy calm before the storm of questions, theories, and dread that would soon follow.

The sharp edge of fear in his friend's voice hit Pete like a slap in the face. Instantly, he and Katie bolted into action, the dog's paws slapping against the damp earth as they raced toward the commotion. They circled the base of the tree, looking for anything out of the ordinary. At first, there was nothing—just the same grim scene they had already seen, with Finlay and the DCI performing what could only be described as an Oscar-worthy portrayal of shock. But then, Pete's gaze shifted, and his breath caught in his throat. Sitting motionless next to the tree was another dog—older than Katie, its fur matted with the remnants of what could only be described as a sickening display. Pete's heart raced as he followed the gaze of his colleagues, his eyes rising slowly up the tree. Then the horror hit him like a ton of bricks.

"Shit... shit... shit." The words barely escaped his lips, his mind struggling to process the gruesome reality before him. Six feet off the ground, wedged between two branches, was an Officer's lifeless body, impaled through the chest by what appeared to be a spear. The grotesque arrangement of limbs and the unnatural angle of the body made it clear that the man had been placed there—deliberately and with brutal force. For what felt like an eternity, the three men simply stood there, unable to look away from the nightmare that lay before them. Katie and the other dog, sensing something was wrong, began to bark furiously, but their frantic yelps felt hollow, swallowed by the raw terror that hung thick in the air.

The DCI, his voice hoarse and broken, was the first to speak, though his words seemed to hang uselessly in the air. "Who... who could do something like this?" he muttered, the weight of the scene almost too much to bear. He stepped closer to the body, his eyes scanning it, but the horror kept his thoughts scattered. "The strength... the sheer power it must've taken to get a man that high up... I... I've never seen anything like this in my day..." As he spoke, a prickling sensation crept along the back of his neck. He paused, suddenly aware of something watching him, something just outside the reach of his senses. His head turned slowly, the hairs on the back of his neck standing on end.

And that's when it hit him—he gasped, his breath catching in his throat, his legs collapsing beneath him as the world around him seemed to collapse into nightmare. He fell to his knees, his heart pounding, a cold sweat breaking out across his forehead. Behind him, Finlay and Pete whirled around, following the DCI's horrified gaze. The sight before them made their blood run cold. There, impaled on a large stick, was another Officer's head. The eyes were wide and glazed, rolled back into the skull, the pupils barely visible. But it was the mouth—the grotesque, unnatural gape of it—that sent a bone-chilling fear through their entire bodies. The expression frozen on the Officer's face was one of pure terror, and the way his mouth hung open, contorted in eternal horror, felt like a silent scream trapped in time.

For a moment, none of them could move. The enormity of what they were witnessing, the sheer savagery of the scene, was enough to paralyze them. Every instinct screamed to run, to get as far away from this madness as possible, but they were rooted to the spot, trapped by the horror of it all. And yet, through the silence that followed, the sound of the dogs' barking still filled the air, their frantic cries a strange contrast to the oppressive stillness that had taken over the clearing. It was as though the very forest itself was holding its breath, waiting for something even worse to unfold.

***

Caribbean blue eyes scanned the vast stretch of golden sand before him, the shoreline curving endlessly in both directions. The soft dunes of grass whispered in the wind, a natural camouflage, offering the perfect cover as he assessed his surroundings with military precision. The rhythmic pounding of the waves against the beach filled the air, their intensity mirroring the storm that had raged within him over the last twelve hours. He knew he had faced worse, much worse. But this—this was just another test, another hurdle he would have to leap if he was going to complete his plan.

He shifted slightly, blending deeper into the grasses, his focus narrowing as movement caught his eye. A lone figure emerged, a silhouette against the fiery orange hues of the rising sun, walking along the beach with a careless ease. The person was oblivious to the chaos that had unfolded in the hours prior, walking as though the world had not just turned upside down. His fingers brushed the cold, worn handle of his bowie knife, the metal familiar in his grip, its weight a comforting presence. He considered the options. The woods to the south were a potential escape route—a dark, tangled mess of trees and undergrowth where he could easily slip past the police line and move inland. But the beach... the wide, open expanse of sand? It presented a dilemma.

The figure ahead wasn't a threat. He could tell that much. There was no sign of urgency in their movement, no tension in their posture. But it was the space between them, the vast, empty sand stretching out like an ocean of vulnerability, that made him hesitate. There would be no cover here, no shadows to melt into. If he made a move now, he would be exposed, an easy target in the open, with nowhere to hide.

The sea churned with a violent energy, but it offered no sanctuary. Only the cold expanse of sand, an unforgiving wasteland, stood between him and freedom. The choice seemed clear: risk the beach and potentially be spotted, or slip back into the safety of the woods, weaving through the trees where danger lurked in every shadow but provided the concealment he desperately needed. The wind whipped at his face, and for a moment, the world seemed to hold its breath. Time was running out. The question was no longer about whether he could outsmart the police—it was about how long he could keep up the charade before the walls closed in.

He closed his eyes, shutting out the harsh sunlight, the biting wind, the salt on his lips, and the constant crash of waves against the shore. For a moment, everything faded away, and he allowed himself to sink into the stillness. His mind emptied, a blank canvas awaiting direction. Then, a voice, steady and commanding, broke through the silence: "Risk is just part of the game. Without risk, there can be no reward..."

The words echoed in his skull, familiar yet cold. He opened his eyes, exhaling slowly, the weight of the decision settling deep within him. There was no turning back now. The world around him snapped into focus, and he could feel the tension in the air, like the calm before a storm. With a single sigh, he pushed himself up from the sand, crouching low, his movements smooth and deliberate as he began to move forward.

His eyes locked on the figure approaching, her outline growing clearer with each passing second. A woman. She seemed to be walking aimlessly, unaware of the danger closing in on her, but his instincts told him to be wary. She was older than most he encountered—possibly seventy-three, maybe seventy-four—but still agile, her posture straight and confident. At only five feet two inches, she was shorter than most, but her walk had an assuredness to it. Her hands were stuffed deep into her pockets, and though there was no immediate sign of a weapon, he knew better than to underestimate anyone, especially in his line of work.

His cracked lips tingled, dry and yearning for moisture, but he didn't take his eyes off her. His fingers brushed the cool, comforting metal of the bowie knife hidden at his back. He could feel its weight, the familiar grip, and he knew it was only a matter of time before their paths crossed. She didn't know it yet, but her fate was sealed the moment she stepped onto this beach. A grin curled on his lips, sharp and calculating. He would not be the one to shy away from the inevitable. Whatever this woman was doing here, it didn't matter. She had become part of his world now—whether she liked it or not.

His heart raced with a mix of excitement and calm anticipation. This was the moment he'd been waiting for, the point where risk and reward met head-on. He moved silently, the sand barely giving under his feet, his body low to the ground, watching, waiting. And when their eyes met, as they inevitably would, he would be ready.

***

Sergeant Lorraine Jones led Tango Romeo down the narrow, winding path, the crunch of their boots the only sound cutting through the stillness. The unit moved with tense precision, eyes scanning the dense underbrush and the shadowed corners of the woods, but there was an unspoken heaviness in the air. The atmosphere felt thick, like the calm before a storm, and the silence among them was palpable, suffocating even.

Something had happened at the clearing —something that had rattled even the seasoned DCI. Lorraine could sense it in the way the commanding officer's eyes flickered uneasily, the quick, sharp movements of his hands as he motioned them to halt. The unease was contagious, spreading through the unit like a quiet wave of dread. The DCI's attempts to keep them from entering the area only made their suspicions grow. Something had gone terribly wrong, and they all knew what it likely meant: the Officer they had been searching for, the rookie, was dead.

The thought of a fallen comrade was always a bitter pill to swallow, but the loss of someone so new to the force, so young, made it worse. They had all been rookies once—wide-eyed, full of determination, eager to prove themselves—but this wasn't supposed to be the reality. No one was ever prepared for this kind of outcome, especially not when it was a life still fresh, untainted by the harshness of the job. A rookie with dreams, with hopes of making it through to become one of them. To know that one of their own had fallen in the line of duty, and so soon into their career, was a wound that would be felt long after the mission was over.

The weight of the loss pressed on them, but they couldn't afford to dwell on it—not yet. They had a job to do. The clearing ahead held secrets, and it was clear that whatever had unfolded there was something they were going to have to face. But as they drew closer, each step felt like a countdown to a moment they would all wish they could forget.

The faint, soothing sound of running water drifted through the air, drawing the team's attention as they crested a short ridge. Below, a small stream trickled lazily under a rickety wooden bridge. On any other day, the peaceful scene would have been the perfect backdrop for a quick photo or a moment of quiet reflection. But today, there was no time for appreciation. The weight of the mission hung over them, pressing down hard. They weren't here for scenic views or snapshots. They were here to end this—once and for all.

Lorraine waved the team forward, the urgency in his motion pushing them onward. She navigated the steep bank carefully, the loose gravel beneath her boots sending small rocks skittering down the slope. One by one, the rest of the unit followed, their footing unsteady as they scrambled down the incline. The stream's soft murmur seemed almost mocking in its tranquillity. "Right, lads, sixty seconds," Lorraine barked, her voice cutting through the quiet. "Catch your breath, then we're going up that hill." She pointed toward the towering bank on the far side of the stream, the incline steep and unforgiving. A few of the men groaned, their legs sore and stiff from the relentless pace. They leaned against the bridge, massaging sore joints and stretching aching backs, the kind of exhaustion that sank deep into their bones. It was the kind of tired that made every step feel like an eternity.

Lorraine was already moving before they could even think about resting. "Come on, lads, up and over," she called, pushing herself across the wooden bridge with a determined stride. "Boss is waiting at the top. Let's not keep him waiting." One by one, they followed, the rhythm of their boots slapping against the bridge echoing in the stillness of the woods. It was only as they neared the base of the hill that the faintest rustling sound caught the attention of the man at the back. But none of them noticed it—none of them took a second look. They were too tired, too focused on the climb ahead, too consumed by the singular goal to worry about anything else. Not the dark shadow beneath the bridge. Not the headless body lying still in the brush.

With a grunt, Lorraine reached the top of the hill and stopped, wiping the sweat from her brow with the back of her sleeve. She glanced back over her shoulder, watching as the rest of his men struggled toward the summit. The groans of her men echoed in the air as they followed, each step harder than the last. "Come on, lads, nearly there," she said, her voice a little softer this time, but still carrying that edge of command. "Just a few meters. We've got this." The men looked up, eyes weary, expressions heavy with the realization that their journey was far from over. The sighs that followed were almost universal, a collective release of frustration and exhaustion. Lorraine took two more long strides, reaching the top with a small, triumphant breath. She glanced around, quickly assessing the terrain. It was good news. The land flattened out ahead, and the path stretched onward toward a small clearing just thirty meters away.

But that sense of relief was short-lived. As they moved into the clearing, the uneasy feeling in the pit of Lorraine's stomach told her something wasn't right. They had reached the final stretch, but the real challenge still lay ahead. And there was no telling what awaited them in the dark woods beyond.

Lorraine checked her watch, her mind calculating the minutes as they ticked by. She had left the DCI nearly twenty minutes ago, but the distance felt much longer. Her eyes scanned the ridge, his breath quickening as the first of the unit began to appear at the top, one by one, their tired figures breaking through the thick trees. "Right, that's it!" she called out, her voice tight with urgency. "As soon as you're clear, head this way—fast as you can, please!" She didn't wait for a response. Turning sharply, she began moving down the path, her legs pushing her forward with a pace she hoped would match the rising tension in his chest. The DCI was under immense pressure, and Lorraine wasn't about to make the mistake of being late. The rendezvous point was critical—every second mattered.

The dense woods seemed to press in on him as she walked, but she refused to slow. The heavy silence was unnerving. She had long since stopped telling her men to stay quiet. The convict was still out there, somewhere in the shadows. Each crack of a branch, each shuffle of feet, made the air feel thick with danger. Yet the weight of that knowledge didn't stop them. They had a job to do. Finally, she reached the small clearing he had planned to meet the DCI at. Her feet scraped the dirt as he stood there, waiting. The Officers behind him appeared, trudging wearily along the path, their faces a mix of exhaustion and frustration.

Lorraine scanned the area, her eyes darting from side to side, searching for any sign of the DCI or the team. There was nothing. Just an empty space. The only movement came from a small sparrow, tugging at the soil with its beak, oblivious to the tension that hung in the air. "Where is he?" The voice came from behind him, thick with impatience. Lorraine's jaw tightened, but she didn't answer immediately. Instead, she looked around again, her heart pounding. There was no sign of anyone, not a single trace of the team.

"Not sure," she muttered, her eyes scanning the trees in every direction. "Maybe they're still at the other clearing." Before she could say more, the same Officer who had spoken earlier scoffed. "Or maybe they've already gone without us. This is pointless."

Lorraine bit back her frustration, her fingers tightening around the strap of her gear. She didn't have time for doubts, not now. Her eyes flickered to the path ahead, her mind calculating possible routes, but still no signs of the DCI. The team was in disarray, scattered across the woods, and the rendezvous was slipping further out of reach. They were running out of time.

"Stay focused," Lorraine snapped, the command sharp in the tense air. "We can't afford to fall apart now. We need to find the DCI and regroup, and we need to do it fast." The Officers fell silent, their eyes now scanning the trees, the weight of the mission settling heavily on their shoulders. Something felt wrong. The air was thick with the expectation of a confrontation, but the clearing was still eerily quiet, save for the rustle of the wind in the leaves. Lorraine swallowed hard, her pulse racing. Every instinct told her to move forward, to push past the unease and find their missing leader. But as she glanced back toward the darkening woods, a knot formed in his gut, a gnawing feeling that the worst was still to come.

Lorraine spun on her heel, the Officer standing so close that their noses almost brushed. Her heart hammered in her chest as she locked eyes with the man, her frustration bubbling over. Through clenched teeth, she kept her voice low, hoping the others wouldn't overhear. "Look, do you think this is easy for any of us? Take a goddamn look around! We're all scared out of our minds," Lorraine hissed, her gaze scanning the silent woods. "I'm tired. You're tired. We're all tired. But stop and think for a second—how do you think the DCI's feeling, huh? What kind of pressure is that man under? This lunatic's out there, slicing people up, and it's on us to find him. If you don't like it, then piss off back to Bravo Charlie One. Understood?"

The words hung in the air, sharp and heavy. The rest of the team stood frozen, their faces a mixture of shock and disbelief. Lorraine's chest tightened with immediate regret. She had lost control—she had let the stress of the situation get the better of her. As their CO, he was supposed to keep them focused, steady, but all that pressure, the fear, the uncertainty, it had boiled over. The silence stretched on, the weight of his words settling on the team. Lorraine's eyes dropped to the ground, trying to collect himself. She closed his eyes, focusing on her breathing, hoping to ground herself in the chaos.

Then, it came. A scream—sharp and gut-wrenching—cut through the stillness of the forest.

The moment shattered. Lorraine's head snapped up, her heartbeat pounding in her ears. Another scream followed, distant but unmistakable. The blood drained from her face as the sound of terror echoed through the trees. "What the hell?" Lorraine whispered under her breath; her voice barely audible. The moment stretched into a long beat of silence, but this time, it was different. This silence was filled with a dread so palpable it made the air thick.

The team didn't move at first. They stood, still processing the scream, as if waiting for the world to make sense of it. But Lorraine knew. This was no random scream. The fear that rippled through his gut told him everything he needed to know. "Go!" Lorraine barked, her voice snapping back into command mode, adrenaline coursing through her. "Get moving—NOW!" The Officers quickly snapped to attention, instinctively following their CO's lead. Lorraine's mind raced as her boots hit the ground, moving toward the scream. He could hear it again—closer this time, a shrill, desperate cry for help. "Stay close!" Lorraine shouted, barely recognizing the tightness in her voice.

But something was wrong. The scream had changed. It had turned into something darker, something that made his skin crawl. The sounds of the forest around him grew louder—more chaotic— as if the trees themselves were reacting to the horror unfolding just ahead. And still, no one dared to speak. They just moved—faster, harder—driven by the primal instinct that this was no ordinary call for help. It was a warning. A warning that they were getting closer to something far worse than they had ever imagined.

***

The scream sliced through the air, sending a cold shiver down DCI Craig's spine. The sound echoed in the trees, haunting, desperate—like something out of a nightmare. Stephen stood frozen, eyes locked with the other Officers, a silent exchange of unspoken fear and understanding. The dogs, alert as ever, were on edge, their ears twitching like radar dishes, trying to locate the source of the scream. Katie's head tilted to the side, her keen senses straining to pinpoint the sound.

Pete opened his mouth to speak, but the DCI held up a finger, silencing him. His focus narrowed as his heart pounded, adrenaline surging through his veins. Another scream, this one closer, sharper, and it only deepened the growing dread in his gut. Stephen's mind raced. The body... the head... the dogs... everything was a blur for a moment, a surreal snapshot of terror. This was no longer just about the convict—they were about to be caught in the heart of something much worse.

"Right, Pete!" the DCI barked, his voice sharp and commanding. "Take that dog, Wait for Sargeant Jones" he pointed at the new mutt by Pete's side, its wide eyes scanning the area nervously. "Finlay, grab your dog and follow me. Double time." The Officers exchanged quick glances as they swapped harnesses, the urgency of the moment apparent in their swift, practiced movements. The DCI turned back to Pete; his expression grim but determined. "I don't need to warn you the convict is still at large, but we're walking into the unknown. Remain vigilant. Don't approach unless you have to. The dog will hopefully keep him at bay, but we can't be sure."

Unconvinced but ready, Pete gave a sharp nod. The DCI didn't wait for further confirmation. He took off down the path at a pace that left little room for hesitation. Katie and Finlay followed closely behind, their footsteps a steady rhythm of urgency. "Hey, Fin, look after her, please!" Pete called after them, his voice filled with a mix of concern and command. He stood there for a moment, watching as the others disappeared down the darkening trail. The new dog sat by his side, looking up at him with wide, innocent eyes. Pete bent down slowly, taking hold of the dog's collar, the cool metal brushing his fingers. He searched for the ID tag, flipping it over in his hand, feeling the weight of the moment settle in. "Hello, Betty," he muttered, the name sounding strange, like a lifeline in a storm. Betty looked back at him, her gaze unblinking, her stance alert. There was no time to waste. He could hear the crunch of leaves as the others moved ahead, the sound growing fainter. Pete's grip tightened on Betty's collar as the sense of isolation began to settle in. They were out here now—alone, exposed, and closer to the danger than any of them had anticipated.

With a quick glance over his shoulder, Finlay continued forward, the weight of the unknown pulling at him. "Come on, girl," he murmured, his voice barely a whisper. "Let's find him before it's too late." The forest seemed to close in around them as the path wound tighter, the air thick with the smell of damp earth and the sound of their boots crunching on the forest floor. The dogs led the way, noses to the ground, ears alert. But in the back of Pete's mind, the scream still echoed—a reminder that this was only just beginning.

The DCI's legs burned with each stride, his muscles screaming in protest, but the woman's cries in the distance kept him moving, each desperate scream a reminder of what was at stake. His mind was exhausted, pushing back against the physical pain, but the weight of all the death he'd witnessed in the past hour hung over him like a dark cloud. The thought that it could all end here, that they might finally have a chance to stop the madness, drove him forward. He had to end this. Now. Glancing back, he shouted, "Sargeant, take the lead!" Without hesitation, Katie surged ahead, her paws pounding the ground with primal speed. Finlay, slightly behind, was giving it everything he had to keep up, but Katie's sheer drive kept her in front. The DCI pushed on, though his breath was ragged, the pain in his muscles creeping into every movement.

The path twisted ahead, narrowing between thick trees, then opened up, and for a moment, the air felt different. Less dense. They were nearing the edge of the woods, and the thought of stopping— to catch their breath, to regain some semblance of control—was almost a relief. But not yet. As they reached the base of some wooden steps, the sound of the wind blowing through tall grass up ahead gave the DCI a momentary distraction. The handrails of the stairs creaked under the strain of his hand as he grabbed for balance, the rhythmic sound of his boots on the weathered wood echoing in his ears.

Katie was already two steps up, eager to continue. Finlay pulled back on the leash, the dog's energy electrifying as it sensed the tension in the air. "Heel, Katie. Heel…" Finlay muttered, but his words faltered as he peered over the ridge. The DCI caught up, out of breath, eyes searching for what had halted his sergeant's pace. "What's wrong, Sargeant?" Finlay's voice was steady but his eyes betraying the tension in his frame. "Sir, once we crest this bank, it's most likely that we're face to face with the convict. I just need to know what your plan is. He's already taken out three Officers in the last hour. We need to be prepared."

The DCI's stomach twisted. He could hear the woman's scream again, carried by the wind. He stepped forward, trying to ignore the cold dread creeping up his spine. "Look, son," the DCI said, breathing hard, his chest heaving. "I don't have time for plans. There's a woman out there who needs help, and that's all I care about right now. Let's get over this ridge and see what's going on. Our training will kick in, don't worry. We're gonna take this bastard down, one way or another." Finlay met his eyes, a mixture of respect and wariness in his gaze. He nodded once, a half-smile playing at the corners of his mouth. "Copy that, sir."

Without another word, Finlay turned and sprinted up the wooden steps, his boots striking with precision, each step a beat in the rhythm of urgency. Katie, a blur of muscle and instinct, surged forward, the leash pulled taut as she ran ahead, driven by the smell and sound of the convict just over the ridge. Her fur bristled, her body coiled like a spring, ready to pounce. The DCI's heart raced as he followed, his legs screaming, but the scream in the distance cut through his thoughts—closer this time, more frantic. "Hurry, Finlay! Hurry!" the DCI urged; his voice low but filled with raw urgency. They crested the ridge together, and the world seemed to pause for a heartbeat. The wind swept through the long grass, but everything else was still. Silent. Waiting. The air thick with anticipation, the hunt was finally upon them.

As they reached the top of the ridge, a violent gust of wind whipped sand into their faces, stinging their skin like a thousand tiny needles. Instinctively, they raised their arms to shield themselves, but the gusts were relentless, the sand swirling like an angry storm cloud. Katie, undeterred by the wind, barked furiously, her ears flattened against her head, eyes scanning the horizon. But even she seemed confused by the shifting sands. The sun had just broken the horizon, casting an orange glow across the beach, its light reflecting off the sand in a blinding haze that made it nearly impossible to see. The glare felt like a trap, pushing the men to squint and shield their eyes further.

Shouting over the wind, the DCI leaned toward Finlay, his face twisted in frustration. "I can't see a damn thing. We need to get down to the beach—maybe the wind's not as strong at ground level. Let's move!" Finlay nodded without hesitation, barking an order to Katie as he ushered the dog forward, eyes narrowed against the wind. The DCI followed closely, his boots slipping on the wooden steps as he grasped the metal railing tightly, his muscles straining against the elements.

Katie leapt down the last few steps onto the beach, barking wildly as she pulled hard on the leash, eager to charge ahead. But Finlay, struggling to maintain his balance, felt the dog's sudden force throw him off-kilter. "Bloody heel, Katie! Stop yanking!" he growled, trying to regain control of the dog and his footing. His arms were growing heavy, the leash burning through his hands as Katie dragged him forward. In a flash, the DCI was there, hands on Finlay's shoulders, hoisting him back onto his feet. "I got you. Come on, let's go. The wind's dropping."

With one final tug, Finlay regained his balance, and together, they made their way down the final steps, the wind now a sharp whisper in the distance. As they reached the beach, the raw energy of the ocean stretched before them, waves crashing rhythmically against the shore. But as they scanned the beach, the vast expanse of sand seemed unnervingly empty. No sign of the woman. No sign of the convict. Finlay squinted into the distance; his brow furrowed with concern. "Where are they?" he muttered, voice tinged with confusion and worry. "This isn't right." He scanned the horizon again, but the beach was still as far as the eye could see, with only the waves as company. The DCI's gut twisted. Something felt off, like they were missing a piece of the puzzle. The woman's screams had been so close, but now? Nothing. It was as if the very air had swallowed them whole.

The leather soles of their boots seemed to sink deeper into the sand with every step, as though gravity itself had turned against them. Each stride felt like walking through thick, cloying water—heavy, suffocating. They continued towards the sea, eyes scanning left and right, searching for anything that would break the oppressive silence. The dog had stopped barking, and more alarmingly, there were no more screams—only an eerie stillness.

In the distance, the DCI could hear the familiar sound of a helicopter rotor, low and powerful. Without turning around, he muttered, "I think Halo Two's back in the air." Finlay didn't respond, his focus still fixed on Katie's leash, his thoughts lingering on the haunting image of Pete running from the carnage in the woods. He prayed his friend was safe. "Hopefully, they'll head this way, Sir." The DCI's voice broke the silence, but it was strained. He gave a short, bitter laugh. "Nice thought, but with comms down, no one knows we're here. The pilot will follow protocol, head west, stick to the original route."

The silence that followed felt heavier than the weight of their gear. With each step, the sense of unease grew, crawling like ants beneath their skin. A thousand scenarios played out in the DCI's mind, but they all ended the same way—him, lying on his back, his blood mixing with the sand. "This guy's a ghost," Finlay muttered, trying to break the tension. "Seriously, Sir. He pops in, strikes like a phantom, and then vanishes without a trace. No signs, no evidence… it's bloody amazing, really." The DCI stopped in his tracks, eyes narrowing as he turned toward the horizon. "Don't forget who we're after," he said, his voice cold. "This isn't some elusive genius. This is a monster. A criminal who's taken far too many innocent lives, including ours. Good people who didn't deserve this."

They stood in silence, looking out towards the sea, the rhythmic sound of the waves crashing against the shore the only thing keeping them grounded in the moment. Finlay, trying to lighten the mood, broke the stillness. "You know, Sir, any other day, I'd say this view's a bloody pleasure. The sunrise, the warm glow on the horizon, it's a real spectacle." The DCI smiled, but it didn't quite reach his eyes. "Yeah," he agreed. "Under different circumstances, I'd happily sit here, deck chair, a beer in hand, and…" He trailed off as his gaze snapped forward, eyes locking onto something buried in the sand. "Wait," the DCI said urgently, rushing forward. "Look—she's under the sand, there!"

Finlay, startled, jerked Katie's leash, the dog whining in confusion as it was dragged away from its peaceful resting spot. Squinting, Finlay scanned the beach, trying to make sense of the DCI's frantic pointing. Then, his heart skipped a beat. Amid the smooth expanse of sand, half-submerged and eerily still, a single, bloodied hand jutted out from the ground, its fingers twisted unnaturally, frozen in place like a grim warning. A sickening realization hit him as the hand seemed to stand upright, almost reaching out to them. "Jesus," Finlay breathed, a cold shiver crawling up his spine. "What the hell is going on here?"

As they reached the spot, they leaped into action, digging frantically. Katie used her paws to shovel sand between her hind legs, creating a small mound behind her. Each frantic movement brought them closer to whatever was buried beneath the grains. With every passing second, the weight of the moment sank deeper into their bones. Then, the hand rolled over, revealing its gruesome state. "Sweet Jesus," Finlay gasped, choking on the bile that rose in his throat. He spun away, spitting violently, his stomach revolting at the sight. The DCI froze, eyes locked on the severed wrist. The blood was still flowing, a dark, red stream seeping into the sand.

Before either could react further, the ground ten meters behind them stirred. Something—someone—shifted beneath the sand. Slowly, a man rose, his body emerging from the earth like some nightmarish apparition. Sand cascaded from his clothes and hair, each movement sending waves of dirt falling like a waterfall. He rotated his shoulders, the sound of cracking bones filling the silence.

Katie, now agitated, lunged forward, barking with a primal ferocity. Without hesitation, she bolted toward the figure, her speed a blur. Both Officers turned just in time to see the man, now fully standing, effortlessly catching the dog mid-air by the throat. The man's attire—a ghillie suit—seemed to swallow the light, blending him seamlessly into the landscape. His right hand held a six-inch bowie knife, the blade gleaming red with fresh blood.

The Officers stood frozen, fear striking their hearts. But then, as if on instinct, Finlay realized the dog was doomed. Before he could shout a warning, Katie was airborne, jaws snapping, trying to tear at the man's arm. But with lightning reflexes, the man squeezed tighter, holding her in a death grip. Katie's sharp teeth were useless against his unyielding hold. The DCI watched in stunned silence as the convict, with cold precision, placed the knife into the back of his belt. Using both hands, he pulled Katie's face closer to his, their eyes meeting for a brief moment. The dog's frantic thrashing stilled, and an eerie silence settled over the scene. The convict whispered something inaudible, his expression unreadable.

Finlay, heart racing, opened his eyes, dreading the worst. He expected to see Katie's lifeless body crumpled at the man's feet, but instead, to his disbelief, the dog went limp in the man's grasp. The convict gently placed her back on the sand, patting her head as though she were a pet. Katie, surprisingly unharmed, wagged her tail and turned back toward the woods without a second glance at the Officers. "Well, I'll be damned," Finlay muttered, watching in disbelief as the dog ran off into the distance, leaving the two men behind.

The convict, however, was far from finished. He turned his gaze toward the two men, his eyes sharp and calculating. With deliberate slowness, he reached for the knife once more, pulling it free from his belt. Without a word, he began walking toward them. Finlay's instincts kicked in, and he took a step back, heart pounding in his chest. "Sir, we gotta go... come on, man, we gotta move!" But the DCI stood still, eyes locked on the approaching figure. The tension in the air was palpable.

"Sir!" Finlay shouted, desperation creeping into his voice. "This way!" But the DCI, rooted in place by an unshakable resolve, seemed to ignore him. The convict was closing in, and the air around them hummed with an almost tangible menace. Grabbing his CO's arm with a vice-like grip, Finlay yanked the DCI back, his heart hammering in his chest. The convict kept advancing, a relentless predator, closing the gap between them with every step. The air felt thick with tension as they looked around, searching for a way out. There was nowhere to hide. In the distance, the unmistakable hum of the helicopter was growing louder, spinning in a wide arc before heading toward the sea.

"You see that, Sargeant?" the DCI muttered; his voice tight. "We just keep this piece of shit occupied for a couple more minutes, and we'll have him in cuffs." He forced a tense smile, trying to hide his nerves. Finlay swallowed, his eyes flicking nervously to the man closing in. "Somehow, I don't think our friend here wants to sit down and chat." He kept inching backward, but the convict didn't slow down. The noise of the sea behind them grew louder, the spray from the crashing waves hitting the back of their necks, cold and sharp. Without looking back, the DCI spoke through gritted teeth.

"Dammit, I reckon another twenty feet and we'll be treading water." Finlay's pulse raced, his mind racing to calculate their dwindling options. The helicopter was nearly upon them, but there was still no sign the convict was slowing down. The DCI's eyes flicked toward the sky; his face grim. "Sixty seconds, give or take." Finlay's gaze was locked on the glint of the knife, blood already staining the steel. His voice wavered, a hint of disbelief creeping in. "Begging your pardon, Sir, but in sixty seconds, we'll be dead."

Before Finlay could respond, the convict lunged forward, his movements so swift it was like he had been waiting for the perfect moment. As the man drew closer, Finlay could see his cold, piercing blue eyes, those eyes that seemed to bore straight through them, as if reading their very souls. His lips curled back, a snarl etched on his face, saliva dripping from the corners of his mouth. Long, matted strands of grey hair flapped wildly in the wind. Finlay gasped, his breath catching in his throat. Before he could react, the DCI pushed him hard, sending him crashing to the ground. The world seemed to move in slow motion as he watched the convict raise his arm, the bowie knife glinting dangerously in the pale light.

The DCI's arm shot up in an instinctual defence, but then—without warning—something flew through the air, cutting through the wind with deadly precision. The man's chest exploded in a red mist, his body jerking violently as the impact hit. Blood splattered into the air, painting the DCI in a gruesome shower of crimson. For a moment, time seemed to stop. The convict's body twisted unnaturally before he crumpled backwards, the knife still clenched in his bloodied hand. The sound of the helicopter's blades beat the air around them, growing deafening.

The DCI wiped the blood from his face, his body frozen, processing what had just happened. Finlay, still on the ground, looked up, his heart still racing, trying to understand how the situation had shifted so violently, so suddenly. "Shit," the DCI muttered. The Sargeant's feet felt like they were stuck in cement, his body frozen in place as if the world had slipped into slow motion. His eyes were locked on the scene before him, his mind struggling to catch up. The DCI stood beside him, mouth agape, one arm frozen in the air, staring at the figure before them. The convict, blood seeping from the wound in his chest, staggered toward them, clutching at the injury with one hand, the other still gripping the knife at his side.

"What the fuck was that?" Finlay muttered under his breath; the air heavy with disbelief. Slowly, he managed to pull himself upright, eyes glued to the injured man. The convict's ghillie suit, once a dull green, was now soaking in crimson, the blood streaming down his chest, staining the fabric. Finlay grabbed the DCI's arm, snapping him out of his trance. "Sir, what do we do now? Hey, can you hear me?" The DCI blinked, still processing, then wiped the blood from his eyes with the heel of his palm. "Yes… yes, I'm with you." His voice was hoarse, his brain scrambling to form a plan. His eyes flicked back to the convict, who was still standing, but barely. His breathing was ragged, but he wasn't going down without a fight.

"Prisoner Zero-Three-Zero-One," the DCI barked, his voice authoritative, the years of training kicking in. "Step away from the water. Drop your weapon and place your hands behind your back." The DCI's hand went to his belt, fingers brushing the cold steel of the cuffs. But before he could move, the convict's head dipped, blood dripping down from his chin like a twisted trail. The man gritted his teeth, his grip tightening on the knife, still clutching his chest with the other hand. The gory scene only fuelled the terror in Finlay's gut.

The convict took a step back toward the water, his gaze locked on the DCI. "Hey, where the hell do you think you're going?" the DCI shouted, a sense of urgency rising in his voice. "I'm not going to say this again—drop the knife! Now!" The convict was now knee-deep in the ocean, waves crashing around him, but still, he didn't relent. Finlay looked over his shoulder, panic creeping into his voice. "Halo Two inbound, Sir. Thirty seconds." The DCI acknowledged the update with a curt nod but didn't take his eyes off the man. His voice softened, though the threat remained. "Look, you're injured. You need medical attention. Drop the knife, and we can help you. Do it now."

The sound of the helicopter's rotors grew louder, the wind whipping up in anticipation. The convict turned his face upward, his long hair blocking his view as he squinted toward the sky. The weariness was evident in his posture, his body sagging, the knife lowering slightly, but still within reach. His breathing came in shallow gasps, and his vision blurred. Then, a shot rang out, cutting through the tension like a knife. The sound of it sent Finlay instinctively ducking, his heart racing. The bullet struck the convict square in the stomach, a violent explosion of blood sending the man flying backward, swept away by the force of a massive wave that crashed over him.

The DCI and Finlay rushed forward, hearts in their throats, but when they reached the water's edge, there was no sign of the convict. They stood, waiting, breathless, staring out at the swirling waters. "Where is he, Sir?" Finlay asked, his voice barely above a whisper, the disbelief still heavy in the air. The DCI scanned the shoreline, his gaze darting from left to right, eyes narrowing in frustration. "His bodies gone. How on earth can someone survive that?" Finlay turned to face him, still processing what had just happened. But it was the DCI's next words that sent a chill down his spine. "To be honest, I'm more concerned about who took that shot."

The wind began to pick up again, and a cloud of sand swirled around them, the fine particles stinging their skin. The sound of the helicopter overhead grew more insistent as it hovered, its shadow casting over the two men like a predator circling its prey. "This is Halo Two to DCI Craig," a voice crackled through his radio. He quickly grabbed the device, his voice tight with tension. "Copy. Are comms back up?" The pilot's voice came through, but it was laced with confusion. "Err... roger that, DCI. Comms have been reestablished." The DCI stared at the radio for a beat, then glanced up at Finlay, both men still processing the chaos unfolding around them. The convict was gone. The shot had come from nowhere. And now, they were left to figure out what the hell had just happened— and who else was out there.

Finlay scratched the back of his head, squinting against the blinding sunlight, the helicopter's rotors whipping up sand and dust, the noise almost deafening. His eyes flicked from the churning sea to the horizon, scanning for any signs of movement. "Sir," he said, his voice low and laced with exhaustion, "we really need to find this bastard. I don't think I'll be able to sleep tonight without seeing his body... if you catch my drift." The DCI's gaze shifted briefly to his Sargeant, a sharp nod acknowledging the weight of the words. The pressure was starting to take its toll on all of them.

With a sigh, the DCI hit the transmit button on his radio, his voice steady despite the tension in the air. "Halo Two, we have two missing persons. First, a civilian, female, age unknown. The second is Zero-Three-Zero-One, mortally wounded, thought to be..." He glanced at Finlay, who was watching him closely. "...we believe the convict is still at large. Please begin your search along the shoreline, within a one-mile radius. Look for any signs on the surface. Copy?" The helicopter began its shift eastward, the blades slicing through the air as it banked away from their position. The static on the radio cleared just long enough for the pilot's voice to cut through. "Roger that. Halo Two, out."

Without missing a beat, the DCI switched frequencies, fingers moving swiftly over the radio. "Tango Romeo to Sargeant Jones, copy?" The static crackled briefly before the reply came through. "Copy, Sir." The DCI's orders were precise, each word deliberate. "Sargeant, take the rest of the unit and head two hundred feet north from the rendezvous point. Secure the crime scene and relieve Officer Pheby. Over."

Finlay, still lost in the haze of exhaustion, absentmindedly picked up a small stone from the ground. He rubbed it between his fingers, feeling the smoothness, then flicked his wrist. The stone skipped effortlessly across the surface of the water, bouncing five times before disappearing into the waves. His mind briefly followed it, lost in the rhythm of the moment, but the world around him remained chaotic. In the background, the DCI's voice cut through the noise of the helicopter as he coordinated with search teams, instructing Bravo Charlie One to contact the Coast Guard, and relaying instructions to First Response Teams to head for the beach.

Checking his watch, Finlay yawned, rubbing his eyes. Eighteen hours on his feet, and it was starting to catch up to him. Every muscle in his body screamed for rest. He glanced over his shoulder at the ocean, the waves crashing relentlessly against the sand, but there was no comfort in the view—only more questions. His eyes flicked to the DCI, who was still absorbed in his task, the weight of leadership visible in his posture. Without another word, Finlay turned away, walking past the DCI, his boots crunching softly on the sand. The crash of the waves behind him was almost deafening now, but he kept moving forward, the cool breeze from the woods brushing against his face. He didn't look back, his thoughts heavy with the case, the missing woman, and the convict still out there somewhere.

The quiet of the woods ahead felt like a welcome escape, if only for a moment.

***

Flies began to gather around the lifeless body of PC Letting, their incessant buzzing filling the heavy silence. They swarmed the jagged wound in his neck like dark, mindless sentinels, marking the spot of his violent end. PC Dimmock stood nearby, stationed at the narrow, shadowy path that led deeper into the foreboding woodland. His boots felt like they were sinking into the earth, though the ground was dry. The weight of exhaustion pressed against his shoulders and blurred the edges of his vision. It was his job to keep his back to the scene, but even so, the image of Letting's lifeless stare burned behind his eyelids every time he blinked. Once was enough. The memory clawed at him, relentless, and he knew it would follow him home and haunt his nights for years to come. He shuddered involuntarily, gripping his flashlight tighter though the dying daylight rendered it useless.

Behind him, the steady sound of the Commander's pacing filled the void left by their silence. Back and forth, boots crunching dry twigs and leaves. Dimmock couldn't help but wish the man would say something—anything. A banal comment about the weather, a story about his career, a scolding for the lapse in Dimmock's concentration he hadn't yet voiced—anything would do to keep his mind from wandering to the corpse behind him. But the Commander's silence was resolute, a wall too high to scale.

A sharp crack echoed in the distance, and Dimmock stiffened, his tired mind suddenly teetering on the edge of paranoia. He strained to listen, but there was nothing now but the unnerving hum of flies and the occasional snapping of the Commander's pacing steps. The woods seemed to press in tighter, and with them came the dreadful realization, the day was just beginning.

The sunlight filtered through the canopy above, scattering shards of amber light onto the forest floor. A soft mist rose lazily from the nearby leams, curling and twisting as the last traces of cool dampness surrendered to the warmth of the day. The scene might have been serene if it weren't for the gnawing boredom. PC Dimmock flicked off his torch with a faint click, the beam disappearing into the surrounding glow. He clipped it to his belt with a practiced motion, then slipped his hand into his pocket. His fingers brushed against loose coins and crumpled fabric until they found the jagged edge of a torn wrapper. He hesitated for a moment, stealing a glance over his shoulder.

Ralph was still staring westward, his posture rigid as he scanned the trees. He looked as though he might have been carved from stone, save for the faint, tuneless hum that grated against Dimmock's nerves. A dull ache was forming at the back of his skull, one he was sure would only worsen as the day dragged on. Turning back quickly, Dimmock withdrew the wrapper and carefully unfurled it. The faint crinkle of the foil felt louder than it should, like the snap of a twig in the silence. He popped the last boiled sweet into his mouth and let the sharp burst of raspberry flavour flood his senses. It was brighter than expected, tart enough to jolt him awake for a moment. He sucked on it hard, savouring every bit of sweetness as though it could stave off the monotony.

Another glance back—Ralph hadn't moved an inch. His humming continued, a low and infuriating drone that made Dimmock grit his teeth. The man might as well have been part of the scenery. If anything, his unyielding stillness made the woods seem even emptier, as though time itself had decided to pause for them. The empty wrapper crinkled softly as he shoved it back into his pocket, a faint smirk tugging at the corners of his mouth. The sweet rolled across his tongue, and he let it linger, savouring the tangy raspberry burst. He wasn't sure how long he'd be stuck there, standing in the same spot, but he silently willed the candy to last— a small rebellion against the creeping monotony.

A dull cramp gnawed at his calf, and with a quiet grunt, he shifted his weight. Bending one leg and extending the other, he leaned forward into a stretch, his boot pressing into the dirt with a faint creak of leather. The tension in his muscles eased slightly, though the weight of the day still pressed on him, making him feel like a stone slowly sinking into the earth. Behind him, Ralph remained perfectly still, his gaze fixed westward through the latticework of trees. He looked like a man caught in the middle of a vigil, his body rigid with expectation, though of what, Dimmock couldn't guess. The silence stretched on, broken only by the faint buzz of insects and Ralph's incessant humming—a tuneless, maddening drone that grated against the fragile calm.

Dimmock shifted again, stealing a glance over his shoulder. Ralph hadn't moved, his silhouette a sentinel carved out of patience and stubborn boredom. Yet, there was a tautness in his stance, a quiet readiness, as if he expected something to emerge from the woods at any moment. Dimmock shook his head, popping the sweet to the other side of his mouth. Whatever Ralph was waiting for, he hoped it came soon—or not at all. The woods felt too alive, too watchful, for comfort.

A faint light flickered between the trees, flashing three times in quick succession, its source barely discernible in the shifting shadows. The Commander turned sharply, his eyes catching light a hundred yards away. The man was scanning his sector with precision, his posture disciplined. Satisfied, the Commander allowed himself a faint smile before turning back. From inside his jacket, he retrieved a compact torch. Clicking it on and off three times, he sent a reply: a muted green beam cutting through the dusk. The signal was subtle, just enough to be seen without drawing unwanted attention. As he slipped the device back into his pocket, the silence was broken by PC Dimmock's gravelly voice. "Sir, begging your pardon, but I need a toilet break."

The Commander turned; his expression unreadable. Before replying, he pivoted in a slow, deliberate one-eighty, his sharp eyes sweeping the surroundings for movement. The forest was quiet, save for the occasional rustle of leaves and the distant trill of birdsong. Finally, he nodded. "Alright, Officer. Make it quick, and don't wander too far." Dimmock took a step toward the path behind him, but Ralph's voice cut in, firm and precise. "Not that way," he said, gesturing westward with a gloved hand. "We need to maintain eye contact. See that tree there? The one with the split trunk. Head there. Before you, uh, get comfortable, check around the back— thoroughly. We can't take chances out here. I'll cover your six, and you keep an eye on mine. Understood?"

Dimmock nodded, his gratitude evident despite his stoic demeanour. His bladder had been protesting for the better part of an hour, and relief was finally within reach. He trudged toward the indicated tree, his boots crunching softly against the underbrush. The Commander remained rooted, his gaze steady as he watched Dimmock's movements, ensuring their watch wasn't compromised by even the briefest lapse in vigilance. As Dimmock approached the tree, he couldn't help but glance over his shoulder, reassured by the unwavering presence of Ralph in the distance. This was no ordinary piss break; even the smallest acts here were steeped in tension, the weight of the unseen pressing down like a heavy hand.

With his long stride, Dimmock easily stepped over the tangle of ferns hemming the clearing. The tree loomed ahead, its bark rough and split in places, the kind of tree that looked like it had weathered countless storms. He reached for his zipper, ready to get on with it, but the Commander's words echoed in his mind. He hesitated, huffing a small sigh, and began to circle the trunk instead, his boots crunching softly against the scattered leaves and twigs. Around the back, the tree stood as empty as the forest around it, offering no surprises except the occasional claw mark from some long-gone creature. Satisfied it was clear; he re-emerged on the other side. In the clearing, Ralph's sharp eyes tracked his every movement. Spotting Dimmock again, Ralph gave him a curt thumbs-up before returning to his silent vigil, his posture stiff with purpose. Dimmock rolled his eyes and muttered under his breath, "Right, guess this is a show now."

Positioning himself beside the tree, he unzipped his flies and let the tension finally ease, the stream hitting the earth with a quiet hiss. Despite himself, his head turned to scan the clearing. He was trained to stay alert, after all, though the sight that met him only made his blood simmer. The Commander's eyes were locked straight on him, unflinching and cold. The intensity of the stare made Dimmock's lip twitch in irritation. Under his breath, he mumbled with a mix of annoyance and disbelief, "Bloody pervert... probably just wants a good look at my bloody dick." The words hung between him and the tree, swallowed by the forest. Shaking his head, he focused back on the task at hand, his frustration adding fuel to the fire of an already long, uncomfortable day.

The warm stream of urine splashed against the tree's rough bark, ricocheting onto Dimmock's boots with an irritating splatter. "Damn it," he muttered, shuffling back awkwardly while trying to keep his balance. His annoyance simmered, but he gave a slight nod to the Commander, tilting his head upward to signal he was nearly done. Ralph remained statuesque in the clearing; his piercing gaze locked on Dimmock with unsettling focus. It was only when a faint, unnatural rustle broke the stillness behind the Officer that the true danger revealed itself.

From the shadows of the woodland floor, three figures began to rise like ghosts from the underbrush. Their gillie suits blended seamlessly with the forest, shrouding them in a predator's camouflage. Silent and deliberate, they closed in behind Dimmock, their movements almost mechanical. Before the Officer could register the shift in the air, a glint of steel appeared. One of the men darted forward, his blade flashing once before slicing deep across Dimmock's throat. The big man froze, his breath stolen mid-action. His hands instinctively shot to his neck, trying to stem the crimson torrent pouring from the gaping wound. His body staggered, a heavy, dying machine, and he crumpled forward. The bark of the tree greeted him with a dull crack as his forehead struck it, blood painting the bark in jagged streaks.

Yet somehow, Dimmock turned, his reflexes defying the inevitable. His legs buckled, but his eyes were wide with primal fury, his lips moving soundlessly. His killer stepped back, only for another man to surge forward, driving a sharp blade directly into Dimmock's chest. The strike was precise, the blade piercing his heart with surgical efficiency. The Officer collapsed to the ground in a lifeless heap, his blood pooling into the moss like ink seeping into paper.

The two-armed men fanned out in perfect synchronization, raising sleek automatic rifles to their shoulders. Their scopes scanned the woods, swivelling slowly as they swept for potential threats. The third figure stepped forward, his movements clipped and purposeful. His gillie suit shifted as he emerged from the shadows, revealing a hardened face beneath the camouflage. As he stepped into the clearing, he snapped into a rigid salute aimed at Ralph. The Commander, still as stone, raised his hand in response, returning the gesture with an air of calm authority. His voice was low and deliberate as he spoke. "Report, Captain."

"The DCI's on the beach, and Halo is in position. Comms are back online." The soldier's voice was low but steady as he delivered his report. He hesitated for a moment, then stepped forward as if weighing his next words. Ralph arched an eyebrow, his expression a silent demand for more. "And the Major?" Ralph asked, his voice sharp enough to cut through the surrounding tension. The soldier cleared his throat, his gaze flickering briefly to the ground before meeting Ralph's eyes again. "Sir, Major Strawberry has been... terminated. We can't provide visual confirmation, but he sustained two confirmed shots—one to the chest, another to the abdomen. Afterward, he went under the waves. We're hoping the local authorities recover the body, but as of now, he's presumed lost to the tide."

Ralph's jaw tightened, and he turned away, his gaze drifting toward the forest canopy as though the dappled sunlight might offer answers. His lips moved in a barely audible mutter, his thoughts clearly racing. The soldier broke the silence, his tone urgent now. "Sir, we need to move. Evac is critical. Wet gear's stashed two clicks east, and the boat's scheduled to pick us up at zero-six-hundred." Ralph stood still for a beat, his back to the soldier, before finally nodding. The tension in his shoulders seemed to ease as he exhaled, his decision made.

Ralph's gaze lingered on the lifeless Officer sprawled on the ground, his expression cold and calculating. He weighed his next move, his thoughts ticking over like the gears of a well-oiled machine. Finally, he broke the silence. "Alright," he said, his tone clipped. "Bag that one up in the clearing. He's coming with us." He jabbed a finger toward the body next to the tree—PC Dimmock, crumpled and lifeless a few feet away. "That one... we make it look like the Major's still out there. Take his head, mount it on a spike. Hide the rest of the body somewhere it won't be found anytime soon." The soldiers exchanged quick, wordless glances; their expressions unreadable behind their camouflaged gear. Ralph checked his watch, his sharp movements betraying his impatience. "Five minutes," he barked. "Let's move."

The nearest soldier snapped a salute and spun on his heel, his boots crunching softly against the undergrowth. He let out a low, piercing whistle that carried through the clearing, summoning the other two sentries. One of them immediately turned and stalked toward PC Dimmock's crumpled form, bending down to grab the Officer by the shoulders. Without ceremony, he began dragging the lifeless body toward a thick, fallen log, leaving a faint smear of blood in his wake. The first soldier pulled a heavy machete from the pack strapped to his shoulder, the blade glinting dully in the filtered sunlight. The forest seemed to hold its breath as PC Dimmock's body was hauled over the timber, his neck exposed and vulnerable. The soldier stepped forward, raising the machete high. The blade hung there for a fraction of a second, poised, before it came down in a swift, brutal arc.

The sound was wet and final, the Officer's head severed cleanly from his shoulders. The soldier worked quickly, his movements efficient, practiced. One man retrieved made a spike from a nearby branch, while the other began the grim task of concealing the remains. Ralph didn't flinch. He turned back to check his watch once more, his mind already moving ahead. Five minutes to finish this. Five minutes to disappear into the woods like shadows, leaving only a grotesque message behind.

***

Halo Two swept low over the shoreline, its rotors slicing through the salty air as the pilot and co-pilot scanned the restless waves below. From east to west and back again, the helicopter circled with methodical precision, its searchlights cutting pale streaks through the breaking surf. The co-pilot leaned forward slightly, peering out the window as the waves rolled in relentless rhythm, whitecaps breaking against the dark, shifting sand. "Tango Romeo to Halo Two, what's your status, over?" crackled a voice over the comms.

The pilot keyed the mic, his voice steady but edged with fatigue. "Halo Two here. No sign of the convict along the shoreline or the surface. We've got about thirty minutes of fuel left, then we'll need to RTB. Over." He glanced at the co-pilot, who shook his head subtly, confirming the same emptiness outside. On the beach below, the scene was a hive of activity. Officers in high-visibility vests combed the sand in staggered lines, accompanied by barking dogs. Emergency response teams huddled around clusters of equipment, radios chirping sporadically in the tense air. The sea breeze carried the tang of salt and faint whiffs of diesel from nearby vehicles.

Parked just off the dunes, Finlay sat on the open tailgate of an SUV, his gaze fixed on the horizon. Beside him, Paul sat slouched, absently stroking the head of a German Shepherd sprawled across his lap. The dog handler let out a low chuckle, shaking his head. "Came so bloody close," he muttered, his voice tinged with disbelief. "Still can't wrap my head around it. You're sure he's dead?" Finlay didn't reply immediately. His eyes stayed on the churning waves, the silver-grey surface catching glints of the late afternoon sun. Finally, he tilted his head slightly toward Paul without looking at him.

"Two shots," Finlay said evenly, his tone leaving no room for doubt. "One to the chest, one to the gut. No way he walked away from that. Even if he did, the sea would've finished him off." Paul nodded slowly, following his friend's gaze out toward the endless expanse of water. "Yeah, guess you're right. Still... wouldn't be the first time a body's gone missing. Probably wash up a few miles down the coast. Some poor family out for a nice summer holiday will find it." He chuckled darkly. "Bet that'll ruin their day." Finlay's lips pressed into a thin line, but he said nothing, his focus locked on the horizon. The ocean looked peaceful on the surface, but he knew better. It held secrets—and perhaps, one more today.

The foil blanket clung to DCI Craig's shoulders, crinkling softly as he fought to steady his trembling frame. His teeth chattered despite the relative warmth of the evening, and his body felt heavy, leaden with exhaustion and cold. A paramedic crouched before him, the sharp beam of a torch cutting into his vision. He winced, flinching slightly. "Can you not, please?" he muttered, his voice hoarse. The paramedic clicked the torch off with a practiced nod. "Sure thing," she said softly, slipping it into her pocket.

The DCI sat on the damp sand, barely noticing the way it seeped through his trousers, clinging cold and gritty to his legs. His gaze was fixed on the waves, their rhythmic crash and retreat a mockery of calm. Somewhere out there, he hoped to see the convict's lifeless body, face down and unmissable in the surf. But the water remained unyielding, offering no answers. "DCI Craig," the paramedic began gently, her tone professional but concerned. "We need to take you to the hospital as a precaution. You're showing signs of hypovolemic shock and acute trauma. This is very serious, so I recommend you're kept under observation when the ambulance arrives." The DCI didn't respond, didn't even turn to acknowledge her. The words washed over him, meaningless. His mind was elsewhere, lost in the rolling waves and the phantom shadows they created under the moonlight. Behind them, the paramedic's radio crackled suddenly, the sharp static making her jump. She stood, placing her stethoscope back into her large green bag as a voice crackled through.

"Bravo Charlie One to Romeo Tango, copy?" The sound cut through the DCI's haze like a knife. He pushed his swirling emotions aside, letting the cool discipline of his training take over.

His hand reached for the radio, steady despite his shaking body. "Romeo Tango reading, over," he said, his voice firmer now. The reply came immediately, the voice on the other end grim and familiar. "Sir, it's Sergeant Jones. Reports just came in from Tango Five and Ten. They've reached the clearing... but Commander Wardley hasn't been found." The DCI's stomach dropped, his pulse quickening. Before he could process it, Jones continued. "Sir... I'm afraid PC Letting's body is also missing." The words hit like a physical blow, stealing his breath. He swallowed hard, gripping the radio tighter. "I'm sorry," she said, her voice strained. "Repeat, over." Static crackled ominously, filling the pause as the DCI leaned forward, straining to hear. Jones's voice returned, quieter now, tinged with unease. "Apologies, Sir. We have Tangos and dogs sweeping the area for the Commander and Letting's body... but there's something else." The line buzzed again, and the DCI's heart pounded as he waited, each second dragging like an eternity. Whatever came next, he knew it wouldn't be good.

The DCI staggered to his feet, the gritty sand scraping against his palms as he pushed himself upright. A dizzying wave of light headedness washed over him, and for a moment, the world spun wildly. Stars flickered in his vision, and the horizon seemed to dip and sway, a grotesque dance that made his stomach lurch. He squeezed his eyes shut, trying to will the sensation away, focusing with all his effort on the officer's voice crackling through the static. "Continue, Sergeant, please," he forced out, the words a strain on his breath.

The radio crackled in reply, the signal weak and uneven. "Sir, we've just found PC Dimmock... well... we—" The voice faltered, hesitant, before continuing. "We found his head... it's on a..." The DCI's heart skipped a beat, his mind unable to process the horror. His vision blurred, the radio's static turning into a deafening roar, and then, nothing. His body—betraying him—collapsed forward, his legs giving way like they had turned to stone. Darkness swallowed him whole. The last thing he heard, the final sound to pierce the growing blackness, was distant shouting and the frantic pounding of feet on sand, growing fainter, then nothing at all.

Chapter 27
06:53 hours, 1ˢᵗ August 2024,
Nukeville Island, Off the Coast of Norfolk

Stepping out of the weathered boathouse nestled in the small harbour, Rich Garner paused, savouring the crisp tang of the sea air as the wind tousled his dark hair. For a moment, the world was just salt, wind, and the gentle slap of waves against the dock. "Hey! You gonna stand there communing with nature all day or actually help out?" Andrew Moss's voice broke through the moment like a splash of cold water. He strolled by with a mischievous grin, a heavy net slung over his shoulder, and gave Rich a playful shove in the arm. Rich laughed, shaking off the stillness. "Strong wind today," Andrew added, nodding toward the choppy water. "She's gonna be a rough ride."

Securing the boathouse door with a quick pull, Rich followed Andrew down the creaking dock, the boards groaning under their boots. "Hey," Rich called, "you swing by the bakery this morning?" Andrew turned, a smirk playing at the edges of his face. "Oh, don't you worry. Breakfast is five-star—sausage, egg, bacon, and a dollop of ketchup. You good with that, your majesty?" Rich chuckled, his tall frame relaxed but his tone firm. "Perfect. Now let's get our gear stowed and push off. I want us back before the sun dips." Andrew nodded; their easy camaraderie alive in the salty breeze. The day stretched ahead, full of work, waves, and the promise of stories to share when the harbour lights welcomed them home.

Fishing wasn't just a job on the island—it was the heartbeat of life, a rhythm set by the tides and the North Sea's unpredictable moods. For nearly twenty years, Rich and Andrew had plied these waters aboard their weathered trawler, pulling in hauls of cod, haddock, halibut, and mackerel when the sea was kind. The work was gruelling, but it was theirs—a testament to grit, tradition, and the bond they'd forged in countless dawns on the open water. Most days, they were up and out before the island stirred, the engine's hum fading into the early morning mist. Today, though, was different. They were running late, and the reason was slouching on the quay, rubbing his temples and cursing the sunlight. Andrew had overslept, his usual gruffness replaced with a groan of protest against the day.

"Damn migraine," he muttered for the fourth time, squinting toward the horizon. But Rich wasn't buying it. He didn't need a magnifying glass and a notebook to figure out the truth—Andrew's drinking had become a constant shadow over the past few months, and it was starting to weigh heavier than the nets they hauled aboard. Rich sighed, watching his friend with a mix of frustration and concern. The late starts and sloppy focus weren't just cutting into their profits; they were chiselling cracks into the foundation of their friendship. Out here, trust was as vital as oxygen, and Andrew's slow unravelling threatened to pull them both under.

"Come on," Rich said finally, forcing a calm he didn't feel. "Let's just get out there. We've got daylight to burn, and I'd rather it be spent working than arguing." Andrew nodded sluggishly, but the fire that had once driven him seemed dimmer. As the engine growled to life and they eased into the chop of the North Sea, Rich wondered how much longer they could keep this going—and whether he could pull Andrew back before the waves claimed more than their catch. "I'll grab the lines today; you get Daisy ready," Rich called over his shoulder, his voice calm but with an edge that Andrew couldn't quite miss.

As Rich crouched to untie the spring line from the dock cleat, Andrew stood still for a moment, hands shoved into his pockets, the weight of his own guilt hanging heavier than the nets he hauled. He knew he'd pushed it too far. Again. Snapping back to the moment, Andrew tossed the net onto the deck with a practiced swing, then climbed over the gunwale with a grunt, his boots landing on the trawler's metal floor with a sharp clang. He leaned against the railing, watching Rich work. The man was efficient, every knot and throw honed by years of practice, the kind of fluid motion that came from repetition and a steady head—something Andrew was starting to lose.

Rich had already moved to the bow, untying the starboard spring line and tossing it with precision onto the deck. "All good, mate," he said briskly, his tone making it clear he wasn't in the mood for delays. "Fire her up." Andrew nodded, stepping into the wheelhouse. The switch for the navigational lights clicked, casting a faint glow that sliced through the morning's haze. A second later, the old diesel engine grumbled to life, coughing and sputtering before settling into its usual rhythm. Beneath them, the propeller churned the water into a frothy whirl, the vibration rattling through the deck like the steady heartbeat of the ship.

Rich jumped aboard in one fluid motion, closing the gap between dock and boat without hesitation. The two men exchanged a wordless glance—Andrew's laden with unspoken apologies, Rich's tight with quiet determination. As Daisy eased away from the dock, the island shrinking behind them, Andrew couldn't help but wonder if the boat wasn't the only thing slipping out of safe harbour.

Within moments, they were cruising out of the harbour at a steady five knots, the bow slicing through the dark water like a blade. The salty breeze filled the cabin, carrying with it the distant cry of gulls and the hum of the trawler's engine. Andrew gripped the wheel, his eyes fixed ahead as the shoreline began to blur into the misty horizon. "So, where to, boss?" he asked, his voice breaking the quiet rhythm of the boat. Rich leaned toward the fogged-up window, his sharp gaze scanning the endless expanse of grey-blue. "Last few days have been a bust," he muttered, more to himself than Andrew. "Let's head west—toward the mainland. Maybe we'll find better luck out there."

At the helm, Andrew's hands tightened on the wheel, his jaw tensing. "West? Seriously?" He risked a glance at Rich, his face etched with concern. "Look, you know the Norfolkers don't take kindly to us poking around in their waters. Last time we were out that way, we damn near had a run-in." Rich turned abruptly, his expression hardening. "Yeah, well, the world's a big place," he shot back, his voice carrying an edge that cut through the cabin. "Plenty of fish for everyone." The silence that followed was thick, broken only by the low thrum of the engine. After a beat, Rich's features softened.

He slapped Andrew on the shoulder, a gesture meant to reassure but landing heavy with the tension between them. "Relax. We'll stay clear of trouble. Just keep her steady." Andrew said nothing, focusing instead on the open sea ahead. As the boat powered on, the distant mainland loomed like a ghost on the horizon, promising either salvation or strife. Both men knew the risks of straying too far from familiar waters, but out here, gambling was part of the game.

The cabin door creaked open, and a rush of cool sea air swept inside, snatching a loose piece of paper from the table and sending it fluttering to the floor. "I'll get us ready," Rich called over his shoulder, his voice half-lost to the rising wind. "Keep the boat steady, and watch out for swirls—I'm not in the mood for a swim today if it's all the same to you." He chuckled to himself, the sound dry and brief, before slamming the door shut with a sharp thud. Andrew smirked as the latch clicked into place. Maybe, just maybe, Rich had moved past last night's fiasco. With any luck, they could leave his hangover-fuelled antics behind and focus on the work ahead.

The small vessel pitched and rolled against the surf, each rise and fall so familiar it barely registered. For Rich, born and bred on the water, the ceaseless motion was second nature, his sea legs steady as he made his way down the port side. Rubber boots squeaked against the slick metal walkway, splashing through small puddles left by spray from the bow. The salt stung his nose, mingling with the rich, heady scent of fish oil and brine—an odour that would turn most stomachs but felt as ordinary to him as the scent of soap in a shower.

Approaching the hoist, Rich ran a hand over the heavy steel weights, inspecting each connection with practiced precision. The net hung heavy, damp and reeking from its last haul. To most, the smell would have been an assault—a rancid mix of fish, saltwater, and diesel. But to a fisherman like Rich, it was the perfume of a day's labour, as normal as the hiss of waves or the rumble of the engine. Satisfied the rigging was secure, he glanced up, his eyes narrowing as he scanned the horizon. The work was familiar, routine even, but out here, nothing ever stayed simple for long.

The sun climbed steadily into the sky, painting the horizon with soft hues of gold and pink. Wisps of clouds drifted lazily overhead, their shapes ever-shifting, while a handful of seagulls wheeled above the trawler, their shrill cries cutting through the hum of the engine. The birds kept close, hopeful for scraps, their sharp eyes glinting in the morning light. The boat veered smoothly, changing course from its southern heading to the west. In the distance, a faint smudge of land began to take form—the Norfolk coastline, ghostly and indistinct. Rich raised a hand to shield his eyes, squinting against the sunlight. Along the shoreline, something caught his attention, darting through the air—a dark shape moving with purpose.

Curiosity prickling, he let the net fall from his hands and turned back toward the cabin. Pulling the door open, the familiar scent of fresh coffee wafted out to greet him. Inside, Andrew leaned casually against the counter, whistling a tune, his hands wrapped around a steaming mug. "Good call," Rich said, nodding toward the coffee. "Did you make me one?" Andrew glanced over his shoulder, a sly grin spreading across his face as he gestured toward the table. "What do you think?" Rich followed his gaze and spotted his favourite mug—a worn, stained Wallace and Gromit cup—sitting on a tray. Steam spiralled from its brim, the dark liquid inside sloshing slightly as the boat rocked. Grinning, he grabbed the handle and cupped the ceramic mug in his hands, savouring the warmth that seeped into his skin.

As he took a sip, he nodded toward the horizon. "Did you see that?" Andrew raised a brow, then turned his attention outside. Squinting, he scanned the waves, the faint outline of land, and the pale blue sky. After a moment, he shrugged, his expression bemused. "Nothing out of the ordinary. What exactly am I supposed to be looking at?" Rich frowned, his gaze lingering on the coastline. "Not sure yet," he muttered, the unease crawling into his voice. "But I've got a feeling it's something worth keeping an eye on."

Rich grabbed a small pair of battered binoculars from a shelf, their lenses smudged from years of use, and handed them to Andrew.

"Not there," he said, pointing out the window. "Nine o'clock, just off port." Andrew raised the binoculars, squinting as he turned the focus dial. The faint outline in the distance slowly sharpened, and he muttered, "Uh-huh. Looks like coast guard, maybe? Could be an early morning swimmer out of their depth." His tone was casual, but there was a flicker of uncertainty in his voice.

He handed the binoculars back, adjusting the wheel slightly to keep the trawler steady on its course. Rich brought the binoculars up to his own eyes, his expression tightening. "Wish I'd gone for the next model up. These things are garbage." He squinted harder, scanning the activity near the beach. "There's something happening, but it's hard to make out. Weird thing is, I don't see any boats in the water."

His voice trailed off, the unspoken question hanging heavy between them. Moments later, the binoculars were back on the shelf, propped beside a sun-faded photo of a great white shark breaching the surface—a keepsake from better days. Rich turned toward the cabin door, his voice breaking the silence. "Better get ready. The sun's nearly up, and our little friends will be looking for breakfast soon."

The cabin door slammed shut as Andrew throttled back the engine, reducing the vessel's speed to a crawl. The boat seemed to float in place, rocking gently as the waves licked its hull. Andrew slid down the small window, leaning his head into the salty breeze. "Alright, boss," he called, his grin crooked. "She's all yours." Rich nodded, giving a quick thumbs-up before hitting the winch's ignition switch. The motor coughed and spluttered to life, a puff of smoke billowing from the exhaust as the machinery groaned into motion. Slipping on a pair of worn nylon gloves, he gripped the lever firmly, pulling it back to release the net. The heavy mesh tumbled into the sea with a resounding splash, sending ripples radiating outward.

Overhead, the seagulls cried, their wings outstretched like banners as they circled the trawler. Their sharp eyes were locked onto the boat, a flock of silent sentinels waiting for their share of the haul. Rich watched the net sink below the surface, his breath steady despite the tension in his jaw. Whatever the day held, they were committed now—nets down, lines cast, and eyes on the horizon.

Rich watched the net unravel into the depths, the water swallowing it inch by inch. His gaze flicked back toward the mainland. The helicopter was still there, hugging the shoreline, its movement deliberate. The faint thrum of its rotors reached him, muffled by the sea breeze. A sudden buzz jolted him from his thoughts. The hoist's warning light blinked angrily. He spun on his heels and quickly flipped the switch, silencing the alarm. The winch groaned to a stop, and Rich let out a slow breath. He dropped onto a weathered box labelled Emergency Raft—Inflatable in bold, peeling letters. Leaning forward, he rested his elbows on his knees, scanning the horizon as the minutes stretched. The work had its moments of action, sure, but so much of it was this—waiting. Waiting and thinking.

Inside the cabin, Andrew sat hunched on a creaky wooden stool, flipping aimlessly through a dog-eared magazine. His eyes skimmed the glossy pages, not absorbing a word. Boredom clung to him like a damp fog, seeping into his bones. What he really wanted was sleep—a good, solid rest to chase away the exhaustion still tugging at him from the night before. He glanced at the clock on the wall, doing the mental math. Another forty minutes, maybe an hour, before they'd reel in the net to check the haul. Sighing, he tossed the magazine onto the counter, its pages flopping open in defeat.

The steady sway of the boat lulled him. The rhythmic rocking, the soft slap of waves against the hull—it all worked like a lullaby, coaxing his heavy eyelids shut. As his breathing slowed, the cabin seemed to fold in around him, the dim light and soft hum of the engine a cocoon. Within minutes, Andrew's chin drooped to his chest, and his snores joined the melody of the sea.

✳✳✳

The old horse trudged along the narrow track, his hooves sinking into the damp, springy turf with each slow, deliberate step. The wooden cart behind creaked and groaned, its weight a testament to years of repairs, added boards, and layers of weathered paint. "Come on, old boy," Evie Potter coaxed, her voice warm with encouragement.

"We're nearly at the ridge."

She reached out and gave Trigger's neck a fond pat, her fingers brushing against the horse's coarse mane. Evie couldn't help but smile as she glanced around. The landscape stretched out in gentle, rolling waves of green, kissed by morning mist. Every week she walked this path, and every week it felt like stepping into a forgotten world—untouched, serene, a pocket of time where the modern age couldn't intrude.

"Tell you what," she teased, her boots crunching softly on the gravel-streaked trail. "You make it to the top, and I've got something for you." Her hand disappeared into the deep pocket of her wool coat, emerging a moment later with a gleaming red apple. The sight of it caught the horse's attention immediately, his ears swivelling forward as she let out a sharp neigh. Evie grinned, holding the apple up as if inspecting it. "What do you think, eh?" she teased, bringing it toward his mouth. "Maybe I'll have a little taste first…"

Trigger stopped in his tracks, stomping a hoof and shaking his head in protest. The loud, indignant neigh that followed made Evie laugh out loud. "Alright, calm down, sunshine!" she said, waving the apple in front of the horse's nose. "I'm just kidding. It's all yours. Just get us to the top, and we'll call it even." With a snort, Trigger pressed onward, the steady clop of his hooves resuming as Evie chuckled and tucked the apple back into her pocket. Above them, the ridge loomed like a quiet sentinel, waiting to reveal the sweeping view that never failed to take Evie's breath away.

The track was strewn with small stones, causing the cart to sway and jostle with each step of the horse. The wooden wheels groaned in protest, their creaks harmonizing with the rhythmic clatter of hooves. Evie steadied herself with a hand on the cart's edge, her gaze drifting toward the north. There, the rolling hills stretched like a sea of green waves, dotted with grazing sheep and scattered thickets of trees. In the distance, barely visible against the horizon's soft haze, she could just make out the clustered rooftops of Nukeville, nestled to the east of the island. The little town seemed to shrink and expand in her imagination depending on her mood. Its red-bricked chimneys and tiled roofs told the story of a place in transition, a sleepy haven now awakening to the world beyond its shores.

Over the past few years, Nukeville's population had crept upward, its quiet allure drawing families and retirees looking to escape the relentless grind of mainland life. The rat race was becoming a ruthless game—faster, meaner, and less rewarding by the year. For many, the idea of finding their footing in England's overcrowded towns felt like climbing quicksand. So, they came here instead, trading chaos for calm, skyscrapers for stone cottages, and the roar of traffic for the whisper of the wind across the hills.

Evie sighed as she scanned the horizon, the thought of the town's slow transformation tugging at her mind. Nukeville had always been a place where life moved at its own pace. But even here, change was creeping in like the tide—slow, inevitable, reshaping the land while still leaving its timeless beauty intact.

As they crested the ridge, Trigger came to a slow halt, his hooves scraping softly against the stone path. He stood still, waiting, as if acknowledging the moment. Evie smiled, her eyes softening with affection. "Alright, old boy," she murmured, reaching into her coat pocket. "You've earned this." She held out the red apple, the glossy skin gleaming in the morning light. Trigger's ears flicked as the horse lowered his head, sniffing the offering before nipping at the fruit with a gentle, practiced tug. Within seconds, the apple was gone, its juice sweet on the wind. The saliva-covered hand in Evie's grasp was now a testament to the horse's enjoyment. She stroked the horse's velvety nose, a quiet laugh escaping her lips. "Good boy, well done."

With the morning sun climbing higher, Evie sighed and took a step back. "Tell you what," she said, casting a glance toward the sprawling landscape below. "Let's take a moment. Enjoy the view before we head down to the docks. No need to rush—we've got time, don't we?" Trigger shifted his weight, lifting a leg before letting out a loud neigh, but as his old bones struggled to find the strength, the horse's body swayed slightly and he sank back onto his haunches. Evie's heart softened. "It's alright, sweetie. I know, I know."

She stepped directly in front of the horse, her hands gently cupping either side of its weathered face. Evie stroked the coarse black mane, her fingers gliding through the tangled strands. She stood there, the wind whispering around them, allowing herself a moment to simply breathe in the quiet. Her gaze shifted down the path they had just travelled, eyes tracing the curve where the woodland began to darken as the sun crept higher. The trees loomed in shadows, their branches twisted and gnarled, forming a darkened tunnel ahead. Years ago, she would have avoided places like that—places where the light hardly touched, where the air felt thick and still, full of secrets. But now, after all this time on the island, she had come to appreciate even those shadows. There was beauty in them, in the quiet solitude, even in the darkest corners of the world.

The island had become her home, a place where the quiet spaces held more stories than the bustling streets of the mainland ever could. And, as she stood there with Trigger, watching the first light of day break over the hills, she realized that she was no longer just living on the island. She was part of it.

A small rabbit flickered in and out of the tall grass to the north, its delicate body hopping nimbly across the meadow. It paused every few steps, nose twitching as it sniffed the morning air, then continued its journey, bounding with carefree urgency. The dandelions around it swayed gently in the breeze, their white puffs catching the sunlight like tiny stars. With a final glance around, the rabbit disappeared into a hole beneath a cluster of brambles.

"Morning."

The sudden voice broke Evie's reverie. She turned, her thoughts interrupted, to find Mr. Postlethwaite standing behind her, his frame slightly stooped with age. At his feet sat a small, wiry Jack Russell, its eyes gleaming with alert energy. "Good morning, Mr. Postlethwaite," Evie greeted with a smile. "How are you today?" With a theatrical flourish, the elderly man removed his flat cap, revealing his balding head, and beamed at her. "We're just fine and dandy, aren't we, Mr. Snorbits?" He gave his dog a fond pat on the head. The Jack Russell, tail wagging furiously, looked up at Evie with eager, trusting eyes. The little dog seemed to radiate joy, as though the mere act of sitting at his master's side was enough to make him the happiest creature on earth.

Evie stepped closer, bending down to give the dog a soft pat on the head. "You're out early today," she said with a chuckle. "I usually bump into you on my way back, not this far out." Mr. Postlethwaite shrugged with a mischievous glint in his eye. "Well, there's a first time for everything, isn't there? Thought I'd get the morning stroll in before the world wakes up. Not often I get to see this meadow in the quiet of the dawn."

The wind picked up slightly, rustling the leaves in the trees and sending a few more dandelions floating through the air. Evie watched as the tiny seeds danced on the breeze, a fleeting moment of serenity. "It's lovely out here," she said, standing back up. "Sometimes I forget how peaceful it is before the town stirs." Mr. Postlethwaite nodded thoughtfully. "Aye, that's the thing, isn't it? The world's always rushing by, but out here, it feels like time slows down. Especially with a good dog at your side." Evie smiled again, glancing down at Mr. Snorbits, whose tail was now a blur of motion. "I think you're right," she agreed. "The quiet is something special."

As Evie straightened up, a sharp twinge shot through her back. She winced but quickly masked the discomfort with a strained smile. Mr. Postlethwaite, ever observant, glanced at the horse and gave a knowing nod. "Looks like age is creeping up on all of us, eh?" he remarked, his voice carrying a hint of humour. Feeling a flush of embarrassment, Evie instinctively started massaging the small of her back with the ball of her fist. "I was hoping you hadn't noticed," she said, trying to downplay the ache. "Maybe it's time I finally go see the doc, get this looked at once and for all."

The old man offered a kind, weathered smile. "You do that, Evie. You've earned a bit of care." He looked down at his dog, who had been watching the exchange with curious eyes. "Right, young lad, you ready for another adventure?" The Jack Russell shot up with a burst of energy, his tail wagging so fast that it looked like it might spin right off. With a joyful bark, the little dog trotted happily ahead, pulling Mr. Postlethwaite down the path. Over his shoulder, he called back, "Go see the doc, young lady. Take care now, until next time!" He waved lazily, his movements carefree.

Evie chuckled softly as she watched the old man and his dog disappear down the path toward the woods. Then, with a gentle click of her tongue, she grabbed Trigger's harness, coaxing the old horse forward. The cart creaked in protest as it shifted, the wooden wheels groaning against the uneven earth. "That's it, sweetie," Evie murmured softly to her horse. "Let's go see the boys at the dock, see what we can wrangle for supper tonight." Side by side, they moved together down the winding path, their rhythm unhurried, like two old companions settling into a comfortable silence. The meadow spread out before them, and the smell of saltwater began to mingle with the scent of fresh earth as they made their way toward the harbour. The gentle sway of the cart and the steady beat of Trigger's hooves on the dirt road seemed to ease the ache in her back, if only for a moment, as the world around her settled into the familiar pace of the day.

In the distance, barely a mile from the island, a small rubber RIB sliced through the waves with ruthless precision. Its twin outboard motors roared to life, the propellers cutting through the water with a brutal efficiency, turning the sea into a churning mess. Any unfortunate aquatic creature that happened to cross its path was instantly shredded, torn to pieces by the vicious power of the engines. The boat surged forward, reaching speeds in excess of 25 knots as the 90-horsepower engine strained at its maximum capacity, carving through the surf with reckless abandon.

Four men clung to the boat's sides, their jet-black jumpsuits growing heavier with each passing moment as the spray from the waves soaked through. The wind howled as it slapped across their faces, but they were resolute, locked in a rhythm of urgency. At the stern, one of the men, his face grim and focused, slowly throttled the engines back, bringing the boat to a more controlled pace. The Commander, Ralph, glanced over his shoulder, his sharp eyes scanning the horizon before nodding curtly. He reached into the bag at his feet, pulled out a small case, and flicked open its flap. His fingers moved quickly, activating a small screen. The infrared display lit up, showing the western coastline—a barren, heatless stretch. No signs of life. It was clear.

"Proceed," Ralph signalled with a quick motion of his hand. The soldier at the helm nodded, his fingers twisting the throttle. The RIB surged forward again, skimming the water as it sped toward a narrow cove, wedged between towering chalk and carstone cliffs. The air grew dense with the scent of salt and damp rock, and as the boat approached the shore, a flock of birds nesting on the jagged shelves above took to the sky, their wings flapping in a storm of white and grey.

The RIB disappeared into the shadows of the cove, its engines cutting off abruptly as Ralph turned to face his team. "Captain," he called, his voice firm, "I want comms up in ten. The rest of you, grab the gear, hide the boat. We're moving on foot from here." He paused, his gaze sweeping over the men. "Let's get cracking." The command was simple, yet laden with urgency. There was no time to waste. The mission was only just beginning.

* * *

The door swung open, and Andrew stepped into the bar, immediately hit by the cold neon glow that cast an eerie, electric ambiance over the room. The air was thick with the hum of conversation and clinking glasses. Behind the counter, the bartender—a spitting image of Tom Cruise, with his short-sleeved Hawaiian shirt and easy smile—gave a casual wave before grabbing a glass and pouring a drink, his movements smooth and practiced. Andrew scanned the room, his eyes eventually settling on a woman sitting at the far end of the bar, sipping a cocktail with an air of quiet confidence. Her fingers were delicate around the glass, and with a slow, deliberate motion, she plucked a small red cherry from her drink. She bit down, the juice dribbling down her chin as she gave a subtle, seductive smile. Tonight, might just be his lucky night, he thought, a surge of anticipation running through him.

He approached the bar, his drink in hand, savouring the taste of it as he watched her. She was toying with a strand of long blonde hair, twirling it around her finger, her eyes meeting his for just a moment before she winked playfully. The electric charge between them was palpable, and Andrew couldn't help but feel drawn to her, his heart racing. Taking another sip of his drink, he moved closer, but as he did, the world around him seemed to fade. The buzz of the bar, the hum of the neon lights—it all became background noise. Focus, he told himself. This could be the moment. Then, suddenly, a voice cut through the tension like a knife. "ANDREW..."

It wasn't in his head. He froze, eyes darting to the bartender, who was now looking at him with a curious expression, a cocktail shaker in hand. Andrew blinked, confused, the moment shattered. The world rushed back in—voices, clinks, the sharp staccato of music— and he realized he'd been holding his breath. "Hey, you piece of shit—" another voice interrupted, louder now. The sound of it was jarring, out of place.

His heart hammered in his chest. The woman was still sitting there, but her image seemed to distort, like a mirage fading at the edges. Her features blurred, and in the split second that followed, a strange, disorienting realization crept into Andrew's mind. He glanced back at the bartender, who was now shaking his head slightly, as if in disbelief, before the world suddenly righted itself. Andrew exhaled slowly, trying to shake off the confusion. The reality of the moment—of who he was, where he was, and what was happening—crashed into him all at once. But for now, all he could do was blink and take another sip of his drink, trying to find solid ground again.

Suddenly, everything around Andrew seemed to shift. The bar, the flickering lights, and the alluring woman—his dream date— seemed to drift away, vanishing like a mirage in the distance. A sharp, stabbing pain shot through his head, and his eyes snapped open, disoriented. "Bloody hell!" he muttered under his breath, confusion swirling as he struggled to orient himself. His vision began to return, blurry at first, and as the world around him took shape, he realized with a jolt that he was no longer sitting on the barstool. His hands instinctively reached down, finding the cold, unforgiving metal of a ship's floor beneath him. "Get your head out your arse and help me, outside NOW!" Rich's voice cut through the haze, urgent and sharp.

Still groggy, his body feeling sluggish as if it were weighted down, Andrew managed to rise unsteadily to his feet. His head spun as he stumbled towards the door, which swayed gently in its frame as if the world itself was still in motion. The sharp bite of the cold air hit him like a slap to the face, jolting him fully awake. Blinking rapidly, he focused on the scene before him. The stern of the boat loomed in the distance, and there, amidst the chaos, was Rich, wrestling with the hoist. The long, metal exhaust pipe sputtered, belching dark clouds of smoke as the engine groaned in protest, straining against whatever obstacle had it in its grip.

Rich, his face drawn in frustration, slammed his hand down on the isolation switch, the engine cutting off with an angry sputter. Without hesitation, he grabbed the tangled net, yanking it with urgency. "Hurry, it's snagged on something!" he shouted, his voice tense with the weight of the situation. Andrew's mind snapped into focus. No more daze, no more confusion. Without another thought, he sprang into action, rushing to Rich's side as the boat rocked ominously beneath their feet. Something was wrong—something that wasn't just about the catch.

Adrenaline coursed through Andrew's veins as he sprinted down the port side of the trawler, his boots pounding against the cold metal deck. He grabbed the rigger gloves, pulling them on with swift determination, the rubberized palms biting into the fabric of the net as he readied himself for what lay ahead. "How far up is it?" he called over his shoulder, his voice taut with urgency. Rich didn't hesitate, his eyes scanning the situation with practiced precision. "Three-quarters of the way. We're going to have to do this manually—if we burn out the motor now, it'll take weeks to get a replacement shipped from the mainland." "Bloody hell, right, let's do this," Andrew muttered under his breath, the weight of the task ahead settling in.

The two men moved in perfect sync, each grabbing hold of the heavy net. Their muscles screamed in protest as they positioned their feet firmly against the side of the trawler, bracing themselves like two men facing a storm. The boat rocked under the strain, but neither of them faltered. "Keep the momentum going until the weights break the surface," Rich instructed, his voice steady. "I'll use the hoists to elevate the rest of the way." With that, they both heaved, their bodies straining against the weight of the catch. The net was thick and soaked, a relentless mass of waterlogged rope and twisted lines. Every muscle in Andrew's body burned as they pulled with all their might, fighting against the relentless drag of the ocean.

The net shifted, inches at a time, before finally, with a sharp jolt, the first of the heavy weights broke the surface. Water cascaded down, splashing around them as they dug in harder. "That's it," Rich grunted, a rare smile tugging at the corner of his mouth. "Looks like we've got a good catch." Andrew barely heard him, his focus locked on the task at hand. The catch was massive, heavier than any they'd pulled in for weeks.

Minutes dragged on, each second stretching as Andrew's muscles burned with fatigue. His shoulders screamed in protest, and his legs felt like they were losing the battle, slipping on the slick surface of the trawler's deck. Sweat poured down his face as he gasped for breath, the weight of the net relentless. "I ain't got much left in the tank, boss," Andrew grunted, his voice strained, his body fighting against the exhaustion that seemed to rise with every pull. Without hesitation, Rich's weathered hand shot out, gripping the side of the boat as he leaned over the edge, his eyes scanning the water below. "I can see the weights, buddy. We're close." He straightened, locking eyes with Andrew. "Alright, listen—head back to the cabin, take us forward, steady at three knots. I'll use the momentum to help lift the rest of this beast with the hoists."

Andrew barely had time to respond. With a grunt, he turned and dashed for the cabin, his feet pounding the deck. The door slammed shut behind him, the sound sharp against the backdrop of crashing waves. Rich stood alone now, sweat dripping down his brow as he braced against the weight of the net. He could feel the strain in every muscle, but he knew he had to hang on just a little longer.

He waited, watching the boat begin to move, the gentle hum of the engine filling the air. As the trawler surged forward, Rich wasted no time. His hand shot to the hoist controls, pressing the button with swift precision. The motor hummed to life, and the net began to rise, heavy and slow at first, then picking up speed as the boat's momentum helped drag it from the depths. Rich bent forward, his hands on his hips, breathing hard, feeling the years in his bones as the net creaked and groaned with the weight of its catch. He exhaled deeply, glancing out over the water. "I'm getting too old for this shit," he muttered to no one in particular, but the words carried the weight of decades spent battling the sea.

Inside the cabin, Andrew was wide awake, adrenaline still buzzing from the gruelling effort of hauling in the heavy net. He knew that kind of load could only mean one thing: a rich haul and a hefty bonus when they docked back on the island. Hopefully, Rich would be satisfied with just one full net, so they could head straight back and get to the pub before the first pint was poured. Maybe he'd treat himself to a nice malt whisky, the kind locked away behind the bar, reserved for only the most deserving. But as his thoughts drifted toward the comforts of the island, a flash of movement caught his eye. He turned quickly, his heart leaping into his throat. "Rich?"

His friend was backing away from the bow, his face ashen, mouth hanging open in disbelief. Andrew's pulse quickened. He killed the engine, stepping out of the cabin and heading toward the door. "Hey, man, what's up? You look like you've seen a ghost." Rich's eyes flickered as he slowly turned to face him, a strange, hollow laugh bubbling from his chest. "What's up? Is your catch bigger than you thought." Then, like a switch had been flipped, he broke into a sprint toward the bow, his boots slipping on the wet deck as he reached the edge.

"Bloody hell..." The words barely escaped his lips. His stomach lurched, a mix of disappointment, shock, excitement, and then pure, unfiltered fear. The net—heavy, tangled, and grotesque—was covered with fish, but there was something else caught in it. A body. A man's body. Pale skin, limp limbs, his face twisted in a silent scream, tangled in the thick, wet mess of the trawler's catch. Rich knelt down, grimacing as he assessed the situation, then stood up quickly. "Let's get him out of there. Give me a hand." Andrew didn't move at first, rooted to the spot, his mind struggling to process what he was seeing. Rich tugged at the net, the man's limbs coming free with a sickening sound. "Is he...?" Andrew stammered, swallowing hard. "Is he... dead?"

Rich didn't respond right away. He yanked harder, the net groaning under the effort. Finally, he looked up at Andrew, eyes wide with grim understanding. "I've never seen a corpse before—well, not in person. Only on TV, but this... this is real, Andrew. This is on our bloody boat." He took a deep breath, voice shaking slightly. "Shit, man, what do we do?" Andrew's hands trembled as he knelt beside Rich, pulling the tangled net free from the body. His mind raced, the weight of the situation sinking in. They were miles from land, alone in the vastness of the ocean, with a dead body tangled in their fishing net. The island suddenly felt a million miles away, and the warmth of the pub seemed like a distant dream.

They stood in uneasy silence, both men eyeing the motionless figure tangled in the net. The air between them was thick with tension as they tried to make sense of the unimaginable. Slowly, Rich turned to Andrew, who was visibly on edge, his breath quickening as panic crept up his spine. "Hey," Rich's voice was low but firm, "calm down. We haven't done anything wrong. Let's just make sure we handle this the right way, then no one can point the finger at us, alright?" His eyes locked onto Andrew's, steadying him. Andrew's eyes flickered with a mix of fear and confusion, but he nodded reluctantly, trying to regain his composure. "Yeah, right. I'll just... stay here," he muttered, wiping his clammy hands on his pants.

Rich didn't acknowledge the nervous nod. He simply took a deep breath and moved forward, his boots making quiet thuds against the wet metal of the boat. As he crouched beside the body, he examined it carefully—every detail of the man's clothes, the strange tension in his limbs. His eyes narrowed when he noticed the camouflage jacket. "Wildlife photographer, maybe," he muttered to himself, recognizing the worn fabric.

"Could explain the camo... might've been out here, trying to get a shot of something." Andrew took an instinctive step closer, leaning in with wide eyes. "Yeah, but if that's true, where the hell's his camera? It doesn't add up." His voice wavered, nerves getting the better of him again. He instinctively took a quick step back, looking around as if hoping for an answer to appear out of thin air.

Rich didn't respond immediately, his gaze scanning the body's exposed pockets and the tangle of the net, trying to make sense of what was happening. The eerie silence of the sea around them only heightened the unease gnawing at his gut. He could feel his heart thumping in his chest, but he pushed it down, focusing on the task at hand. "Let's get this right," Rich muttered under his breath, "one thing at a time." Rich let out a long sigh, refusing to let the rising tension pull him into a response. He kept his eyes fixed on the body, noting every detail with careful precision.

The man's hands were large, calloused from hard labour, his knuckles marked with tiny, faded scars. Rich's brow furrowed as he studied his face—lines of age carved deep into his features, skin weathered and leathery, still bearing the imprint of a life spent in the elements. But it was the oddities of the body that nagged at him. "Hang on," Rich muttered under his breath, his eyes narrowing as he spotted something strange.

Andrew, eager to be involved in the investigation, leaned forward, trying to peer over Rich's shoulder. "What's up? What did you find?" Ignoring him again, Rich reached forward and gently prodded the man's stomach. The fabric of his shirt shifted under his touch, revealing a deep puncture wound. "Shit," Rich murmured, his fingers brushing over the injury, feeling the jagged edges of the gash. His eyes flicked upward, and he noticed another wound—this time in the chest, a clean hole through the man's shirt. "Definitely dead," Rich said flatly, standing up and wiping his hand on his jeans. "This guy didn't just fall into the water... looks like he ran into something fierce. Maybe a wild animal."

Andrew's gaze darted over the body, his face a mix of confusion and disbelief. "Jesus, what do we do now?" Rich stood silently for a moment, scanning the dead man's features. His eyes were closed beneath long, matted hair. He looked like the kind of guy who'd spent hours in a gym, lifting heavy weights, his build solid and defined. It wasn't a face that screamed "accident." There was something darker here, something off. Turning to Andrew, Rich spoke with cold practicality. "We're heading back to the harbour. We can't fish with a body lying around, can we?"

Andrew's face twisted in frustration as he offered a suggestion that made Rich's stomach tighten. "Well, we could just, you know..." He tilted his head toward the water, giving the subtle gesture of tossing the body back overboard. Rich's eyes flashed with disbelief. "No bloody way. We found him, mate. We have a duty to report this. It's not like we can just pretend it didn't happen." Andrew folded his arms, a hint of anger in his tone. "And then what? You think the cops are gonna just let us off the hook? We get caught up in their investigation, they'll be looking at us like we're the ones who did it. Next thing we know, we're locked up for murder."

Rich couldn't help but chuckle. "You've been watching too much of that true crime crap. It's not like that, mate. We're not going to the mainland, alright? We head back to the harbour, and maybe the Doc will know what to do. But we report it to someone, not try to sweep it under the rug." Andrew scowled, but Rich was already walking to the cabin, his mind racing through the possibilities. There was more to this than just a body. And if they didn't handle it right, they might find themselves caught in something much bigger than they could've imagined.

***

The horse's gait had slowed, exhaustion settling in as they neared the small harbour. Evie could feel the rhythm of the cart's sway with each tired step, and when the trawler's engine rumbled to a stop, she gave the horse a gentle pat. "Alright, you stay right here," she said, her voice soft but firm. "No plans for a joyride, you hear me?" The horse gave a playful snort, tossing its head before lowering it to graze on the lush green tufts of grass by the quay. With a satisfied nod, Evie stepped off the cart and onto the weathered timber dock, the planks groaning beneath her weight as she walked.

The harbour was peaceful, the quiet lapping of the water against the docks the only sound that met her ears. She looked out at the boats rocking gently on the tide, the trawler now a silhouette in the distance as it idled, preparing to dock. Her eyes flicked to the left, to the old boathouse where the faded paint peeled from the wood, and then to the ferry port. The place was still, vacant—its rusty gates waiting for the ferry to return. Evie couldn't help but sigh. This time of day, the ferry was always on the mainland, ferrying supplies and a few islanders who, for reasons she would never fully understand, would venture across to Norfolk for personal errands. She had heard their stories, but no matter how often they returned, her mind always returned to one simple truth: she would never go back. Not after all these years. The island had become home, and the mainland, to her, had faded into a place of distant memories and things she'd left behind.

The sun hung high in the sky, casting a bright glow over the small trawler as it made its way toward the harbour. Evie squinted against the daylight, watching as the four cabin lights blinked out one by one. The vessel's engines slowed, and she could see Rich moving around the deck, ready to tie the line. She gave him a quick wave, but he didn't respond, his gaze fixed on the task ahead. Maybe he hadn't seen her, she thought, but her disappointment lingered as she jogged the last few meters, positioning herself by one of the dock cleats.

The engine cut with a satisfying hum, and the boat glided alongside the quay with Andrew at the helm, his hands steady on the wheel. Evie waited as Rich tossed the line toward her with a simple flick of his wrist, not even bothering to look her way. As he turned and jogged to the stern, she could feel the tension building in the air. Something wasn't right. Evie looked up to see Andrew emerged from the cabin, his face as cold as ice. "Hey, can you hear me? What's wrong, guys?" she called out, a slight edge of concern in her voice. Rich walked toward her with purpose, his footsteps heavy against the wooden dock. Without a word, he gently took her hand and guided her down the quay. Evie, now more puzzled than ever, couldn't help but feel the weight of something unsettling hanging between them. She wasn't afraid—she knew these men well enough to trust them—but she could sense their unease. "Rich, what's eating you and Andy? You…" She stopped short as they reached the stern. Rich pointed toward the deck; his face grim. "There!" he said, his voice low.

Evie followed his finger and froze. At first, all she saw was the net, tangled and wet on the floor. But then she saw the shape lying motionless beside it. A man, Aubrey. Her mind took a moment to process, confusion clouding her thoughts. She tried to break the tension, trying to lighten the mood with her usual humour. "What, no fish? Bloody hell, Rich, what am I going to have for dinner tonight now?" She placed her hands on her hips and shot him a playful look, but Rich remained silent, his jaw tight. Andrew came rushing down the port side, panic in his voice as he shouted, "No, no, no—you silly woman! Over there, next to the net—look! That man! Can you see him? That dead man!" Evie's brow furrowed, and she glanced back at Andrew. Her tone remained unchanged, though the weight of the situation was beginning to sink in. "Of course I can see him. I'm not blind. Now, it's clear to me—two boys head out to sea intent on catching fish, but instead, you find this poor chap in your net. Is that about right?" Both men nodded in unison, their faces grim and unreadable. The reality of the situation hung between them, heavier than the quiet waves slapping against the dock.

Evie planted her hand firmly on the side of the boat, swinging her leg over with the practiced ease of someone who'd spent countless hours on deck. She landed with a soft thud, then shot a quick glance back at the men. "You two stay put. Let me check him out." Without waiting for a response, she strode purposefully toward the body. Kneeling beside it, she placed two fingers gently against the side of his neck, searching for any sign of life. A minute passed in silence. Andrew began pacing the deck restlessly, the weight of the situation sinking in. Rich stood a few steps back, watching her every move, clearly anxious. The tension between them grew as Evie focused Aubrey, her brow furrowed in concentration. "Well? What's the verdict?" Rich finally asked, his voice rough with impatience.

Evie stood up suddenly, making both men take a step back. Rich, caught off guard, stumbled awkwardly and nearly lost his balance, his trailing leg almost slipping over the edge of the quay. With a quick shift of weight, he caught himself just in time, avoiding a fall into the water below. Evie, for the first time, allowed herself a small, almost teasing smile. "Congratulations," she said, her tone light and playful, "It's a boy!" The men stared at each other, utterly confused. Then, their gazes returned to Evie, who stood confidently over the body. Rich was the first to break the silence, his voice low and serious, his patience finally wearing thin. "Don't kid around, Evie. Is he dead or not?" Evie shook her head slowly, her expression serious again. "No, he's alive," she said, her voice soft but firm. "His pulse is weak—barely there. It's likely from the blood he's lost from those two wounds, but he's still hanging on." The air between them thickened with a mix of relief and dread. They had found a survivor—a man barely clinging to life in their net—but the real question now was: who was he, and what had happened to him?

✳✳✳

Rich and Andrew struggled to keep their balance as they carefully hoisted the unconscious man between them, their feet slipping on the wet quay. The shorter of the two, Andrew, puffed out his cheeks in frustration. "Bloody hell, he weighs a ton," he muttered under his breath, glancing over at Rich who was holding the man's shoulders with a vice-like grip. His arms burned with the effort, and the pressure in his head was starting to make him see spots. "You alright over there, mate?" Rich shot him a withering look, his face set in a grimace. "Fuck you, I've got the heavy end," he grunted, his muscles straining. "You're just tickling his feet."

As they continued inching forward, Aubrey's weight seemed to grow, pulling them lower with each step. Evie was visible up the path, walking Trigger down toward them. She spoke softly to the horse, soothing him as he carefully turned the cart around. "That's a good boy, well done," she murmured, her voice calm but commanding. By the time the men reached the back of the cart, it was obvious they were struggling. Aubrey's body sagged lower and lower, his backside nearly grazing the grass beneath him. Evie wasted no time. With one fluid motion, she climbed onto the cart's wooden deck, her boots clicking sharply against the planks. "Right," she said, her tone firm and commanding, "you two take his weight and lift him up. I'll guide his head down. On three."

Andrew looked at her, beads of sweat forming on his forehead. "Three?" he muttered. "You're bloody optimistic." But with no time to argue, he nodded to Rich, bracing himself for the lift. Together, they hoisted Aubrey's body, struggling to align him with the cart. Rich's hands tightened on the shoulders, Andrew bent awkwardly to support the legs, and Evie crouched down at Aubrey's head, her hands gently but firmly guiding him into position. The man's dead weight felt like a mountain, but they moved as one, struggling but determined.

"On three," Evie repeated, her voice steady as ever. "One... two... three." They lifted, and with a collective effort, Aubrey's body slid into the cart, the momentum almost too much to control. But once he was settled, they all exhaled, sweat-streaked but triumphant. Evie stepped back, eyeing the limp form in the cart, her expression unreadable. "Well," she said after a pause, "that was a damn sight easier than I thought." Rich, still breathing hard, shot her a glare but said nothing, and Andrew could only shake his head. Neither of them could shake the feeling that things were about to get a whole lot more complicated.

Evie grabbed him under the arms, her grip firm as she helped lift his massive frame onto the cart further. As they eased him down, Evie caught sight of two deep red marks on his back—one just below his shoulder blade and the other farther down, near his lower back. She paused, studying them for a moment before stepping back to give the men room. The fishermen huffed and puffed, bent over with hands on their knees, exhausted from the strain.

Andrew wiped the sweat from his brow, still gasping for air. "Christ, I didn't know someone could be that heavy, or that big," he muttered, catching his breath. Rich, ever the stoic one, straightened up slowly, his eyes flicking to Evie as she worked. He saw her placing dust sheets around Aubrey's head, stabilizing him to reduce any movement while they travelled. "You taking him to the doc? You gonna be alright?" he asked, his tone more concerned than it appeared.

Evie moved Aubrey's arm out of the way, her eyes sharp as she adjusted his position. But then something caught her eye—a small tattoo on the inside of his forearm. She frowned, but only for a moment before standing up and brushing her hands off. "Yeah, I'll be fine, don't worry," she reassured him, her voice steady. She pointed to the side of the cart, her mind already shifting gears. "Hey Andrew, pass me that rope, will ya?"

Andrew, still a little winded, walked over and grabbed the coil of rope that hung neatly on the side of the cart. As he handed it to her, his curiosity got the better of him. "What're you gonna do with that?" Without missing a beat, Evie squatted back down beside Aubrey, gently brushing his hair from his forehead before replacing it with the back of her hand. "He's got a fever. I need to get moving. Doc needs to know everything. Don't worry about it." She then flicked her gaze over to Andrew. "Now, get Daisy back out there and bring me my supper, yeah?" Andrew flashed a grin, a spark of mischief in his eyes, before turning to follow Rich back down the quay. "Aye, aye, boss." He disappeared down the dock, but Evie's focus remained locked on the man in the cart.

As she watched the men walk away, a shift in her demeanour was palpable. Her face hardened, her eyes narrowed, and she quickly untied the end of the rope, wrapping it around Aubrey's wrists with a practiced hand. She secured it tightly, then took the rest of the rope and bound his feet. There was no room for mistakes now. Hopping off the side of the cart, Evie gave Trigger a firm slap on the rear, the horse trotting forward obediently. She grabbed the harness, her movements decisive. "Come on, boy," she murmured, "double buddy, we need to get to town pronto before this ape wakes up." The urgency in her voice was clear, and she urged the horse into a quick pace, the cart creaking behind them as they sped toward their destination. The island was small, but the roads could be treacherous, and time was running out—Evie needed to get to the doctor before things escalated any further.

Chapter 28
07:20 hours, 1ˢᵗ August 2024,
Nukeville Town Centre

The noise was relentless, a shrill, mechanical scream that shattered the quiet like clockwork every morning at 7:20 a.m. The small, defiant box on the worktop rattled and bleeped like it was daring Ethan Cramner to take action. From beneath the cocoon of his duvet, he groaned, his arm slithering out like a serpent seeking prey. With a poorly aimed swipe, his fist missed the target entirely and collided with the edge of the drawer. "Ouch! Damn it!" he growled, clutching his throbbing hand. Blinking through groggy, sleep-blurred vision, Ethan squinted against the assault of daylight slicing through the curtains. The beam seemed to mock him, illuminating the hated device as it gleefully bounced away, untouched and victorious. "Alright, you little shit," he muttered, venom dripping from his words. This was war.

He lunged for the alarm clock, fingers curling around its cheap plastic frame. With a primal roar of frustration, he hurled it at the nearest wall. The bleeping stopped abruptly, the silence punctuated by the sound of the device hitting plasterboard and leaving a satisfying chip in the paint. The clock landed on the carpet with an unceremonious thud, lifeless at last. Ethan collapsed back onto the bed, exhaling a deep sigh as his legs stretched out. His toes curled and flexed against the crisp coolness lingering near the edge of the duvet. For a fleeting moment, the bliss of quite coaxed him to stay put. But reality was insistent, tugging at him like a persistent child. Without further hesitation, he flung the covers aside and swung his legs over the edge. The chill of the floor against his feet sent a shiver up his spine, but there was no going back now. Daylight was calling, and it wouldn't wait.

Listening carefully, Ethan caught the faint scuffle of tiny feet on the slate roof above, punctuated by the sharp chatter of starlings. The cheeky little intruders sounded busy, and his gaze instinctively drifted toward the ceiling. He sighed, a knot of unease twisting in his chest. Not again. Memories of his last battle with the winged squatters flitted through his mind—the two gruelling days spent knee-deep in feathers, droppings, and shredded insulation. Their mischief had forced him to toss half the loft's contents, including a few forgotten mementos from when they'd first moved to the island two years ago. The thought of them sneaking back in made his jaw tighten.

Pushing the worry aside, he moved to the dresser and yanked open a drawer, pulling out a pair of pants and some socks. His striped pyjama's clung lazily to him, rumpled and worn, a reminder of the reluctant rise from the warmth of his bed. With a quick, practiced shrug, he peeled them off, tossing them into the waiting wash bin without a second glance. The cool morning air nipped at his skin, making him shiver as he began to dress. As he tugged on his socks, his mind wandered back to the starlings. He could almost see their smug little faces, beady eyes gleaming with mischief, their talons scratching at the roof as if marking territory. "Better not be making nests in my loft again," he muttered under his breath. Fully dressed, he straightened up, his resolve hardening. If they had found a way back in, there'd be another battle—and this time, he'd make sure it was their last.

Downstairs, Harley Weber filled the kettle, the rushing water echoing softly in the kitchen as he turned back toward the counter. The hum of footsteps signalled Ethan's arrival before he appeared in the doorway, a bright smile lighting up his face. "Good morning," Ethan chimed, his voice warm despite the lateness of the hour. "Morning, sleepyhead," Harley teased, a chuckle escaping as he crossed the room. "You're cutting it fine today." He leaned in, pressing a quick kiss to Ethan's cheek. "Same story every week, like clockwork. Let's just hope there are no callouts today—would be nice to actually get home on time for a change."

The kettle began to rumble, the first wisps of steam escaping its spout. Ethan moved toward the cupboard, retrieving two small Starbucks mugs, their glossy surfaces catching the morning light. He dropped a measured teaspoon of coffee into each, the granules settling like tiny hills against the ceramic. As the kettle roared to life, he flipped the switch off with practiced speed, lifting it by the handle as the last curl of steam spiralled upward. With steady hands, he poured the boiling water over the coffee, the rich aroma filling the kitchen and mingling with the faint scent of toast left from breakfast. He glanced at Harley, who was already leaning against the counter, phone in hand, likely scrolling through work updates. Ethan smiled to himself. Even on a morning this ordinary, there was comfort in the familiar rhythm of their lives.

Ethan watched Harley with a quiet tenderness, his gaze lingering on the man who had turned his world upside down in the best way possible. They had met during the electric celebration of Brighton's Gay Pride march, a kaleidoscope of colour and music swirling around them as they locked eyes for the first time. It was as if the universe had conspired in that moment; by the end of the weekend, they were inseparable, laughing like old friends and falling harder with every passing day.

Within a month, Harley had left his cozy flat along the Brighton seafront, trading ocean breezes for the bustling streets of Croydon, where Ethan worked gruelling hours at a large NHS clinic. The job was rewarding, but the endless demands soon began to cast shadows over their new life together. Late nights turned into early mornings, missed dinners into strained conversations. Tensions crept in, subtle but persistent, threatening the foundation of what they had built.

Most couples might have let the cracks grow, either clinging to routine in quiet desperation or walking away altogether. But Ethan and Harley were different. Their bond was a rare kind of steel, forged in laughter, trust, and a mutual determination to make things work. They knew they needed a change—a fresh start, a leap of faith—and they were ready to take it together.

As fate would have it, opportunity has a way of arriving unannounced, like a sudden knock at the door. It came to them when they least expected it, a chance to reshape their lives in ways neither had imagined. And just like that first glance on the crowded streets of Brighton, they both knew this was their moment.

While flipping through a tabloid one lazy afternoon, Harley's eyes snagged on a bold advertisement nestled between gossip columns and crossword puzzles: "Wanted: Doctor for Island Practice – Adventure Awaits!" His heart skipped. Excitement bubbled up as he imagined the possibilities, and he could hardly wait for Ethan to get home. When his partner finally dragged himself through the door, exhausted from another gruelling day at the clinic, Harley practically ambushed him, newspaper in hand. "You've got to see this," he said, his voice electric with anticipation.

A month later, their decision was made. They packed their lives into neat boxes, the echoes of their two-bedroom mid-terraced house growing louder with each item removed. As they handed the keys to the estate agent, the weight of the past few years seemed to lift, leaving only the heady thrill of what lay ahead. With the car loaded to the brim and a roadmap to a new life, they hit the M11 at full speed, the hum of the engine drowned out by bursts of laughter and hopeful chatter. The familiar streets of Croydon faded in the rearview mirror, but neither of them looked back. This wasn't just a move; it was a leap into the unknown, a fresh start that promised to rekindle everything they cherished—and maybe even uncover something new.

"So, what are you up to this morning?" Ethan asked, his hands wrapped around his coffee mug as if drawing strength from its warmth. He glanced at Harley, his tone casual, though there was a flicker of hope behind his eyes. "Thought I'd run the hoover around really quick, then maybe head out for a short walk." Ethan's expression shifted, his brow knitting slightly, and Harley immediately caught it. "What's wrong? What did I say?" he asked, setting the mug down, his voice tinged with concern. Ethan looked up, meeting Harley's gaze with honesty etched across his face. "I was hoping we could head out this afternoon," he said quietly. "Maybe go a little further—explore more of the island. Together."

The words hung between them for a moment before Harley sprang to his feet, the legs of the wooden chair screeching faintly against the ceramic tiles. In a flash, he was by Ethan's side, wrapping his arms around him in a firm, reassuring hug. He pressed a gentle kiss to Ethan's ear and whispered, "Hey, that's okay. I won't wander too far—just shake off the cobwebs, maybe stroll a few streets. You're always telling me I should get to know the locals better, so I'll do that. We can save the big adventure for later." Ethan let out a small sigh of relief, his hands resting on Harley's in gratitude. "That's great. Maybe pick up a few nibbles and a decent bottle of wine while you're out. Something from Lisa Degnan." Harley tilted his head, curiosity flickering. "Who's Lisa Degnan?"

"She's the landlady at The White Hart," Ethan replied as he walked over to the coat rack. Shrugging into his jacket, he added with a grin, "Smallish, glasses, kind of looks like Velma from Scooby-Doo." Harley chuckled at the comparison, his mind painting a picture of this enigmatic island character. Ethan paused at the front door, hand on the handle. "Oh, and make sure it's a decent bottle of red. None of that cheap stuff she keeps on display by the counter." With that, he stepped outside, the door clicking shut behind him. Harley lingered a moment, finishing the last sip of his coffee, a grin tugging at his lips. "Velma," he muttered to himself with amusement. Then, with a spark of motivation, he set down the mug, grabbed the hoover, and got to work.

***

The rhythmic clatter of hooves on the cobbled street echoed through the sleepy town, a sound that stirred something deep within the older residents. For them, it was a melody of nostalgia, carrying them back to a time before progress arrived in the form of a hulking prison and smooth tarmac roads that had erased much of the island's rustic charm. For a moment, as Trigger's hooves struck the uneven stones, the island felt like its old self again.

Evie perched on the edge of the cart, her gaze fixed on Trigger's swaying head, his ears twitching in time with each step. "Keep going, boy," she murmured, her voice soft but encouraging. "We're almost there—just around the corner now." The old horse snorted, his breath visible in the crisp morning air, and plodded on. At nearly twenty-eight, Trigger was a shadow of his younger self, but he still gave his all for Evie. She'd been there for his first wobbling steps as a foal, her small hands brushing his mane, and she had cared for him as fiercely as a mother would her child. Now, as his movements grew slower and his breaths heavier, the thought of losing him clawed at her heart. She knew that day was drawing nearer, an inevitability she couldn't bear to face.

But there was no time for such thoughts now. Behind her, a groan snapped her out of her reverie. She glanced over her shoulder, her eyes narrowing as she studied the man sprawled on the wooden cart bed. His wrists and ankles were bound with thick, expertly knotted ropes, and despite his shuffling attempts to free himself, the bindings held firm. If there was one thing Evie prided herself on, it was her skill with a rope. She turned her attention back to Trigger, her fingers brushing his mane as she whispered, "Let's just get this done, boy. One more stretch." The cart creaked under the weight of its burden, the cobbles beneath giving way to dirt as they rounded the bend. Whatever lay ahead, Evie steeled herself for it, her bond with Trigger and her resolve to see this through the only things keeping her moving forward.

Evie's eyes lingered on Aubrey sprawled in the cart, her curiosity tugging at her despite the circumstances. His hair, an unruly cascade of grey, hung in tangled strands across his face, partially obscuring his features. Fragments of leaves were caught within the wiry locks, as if nature itself had claimed him during some long-forgotten night spent in the woods. Her gaze drifted to the faded tattoo on his forearm, its edges blurred by time and sun, a relic of a life lived long before this moment. His boots told another story—one tied meticulously, the other loose and undone, as though the effort to secure them both had been too much.

Trigger let out a sharp neigh, snapping her from her thoughts. The old horse came to a halt at the end of the cobbled street, his patience thin but his endurance unwavering. Evie pulled gently on the reins, her commands soft but firm, steering him onto the smooth black asphalt that gleamed in the morning light. The shift from cobbles to tarmac made the cart rattle less, but Evie barely noticed; her attention was drawn to the world coming to life around her. A child darted past, clutching a ball under his arm, his claret and blue football kit a flash of colour against the dull grey of the town. He didn't so much as glance at the horse and cart, his focus entirely on the game he was imagining as he sped around the corner and disappeared from view.

Evie's eyes snapped forward, catching sight of a man crossing the road ahead. He was tall and broad-shouldered, his dark skin catching the sunlight as he adjusted the sleeves of his faded blue shirt. His worn jeans hung low on his hips, and he moved with the casual confidence of someone who knew the streets well. "Shepherd!" she called out, waving her hand high above her head. Her voice carried across the road, catching his attention. He stopped mid-step, his gaze locking onto hers, a faint smile tugging at the corners of his mouth. Evie didn't wait for him to approach. With practiced ease, she stood, balancing herself against the cart before jumping down onto the road. The impact sent a jolt up her legs, but she ignored it, striding quickly toward him as Trigger stood patiently behind, the cart swaying slightly with the shifting weight. Shepherd waited, his expression calm but curious, as Evie approached with purpose written in every step.

Trigger ambled along, his steady steps echoing softly in the morning quiet, as Evie jogged ahead, urgency in her every movement. "Thank God you're early," she called out, her breath slightly ragged. Shepherd Akinde blinked in concern, his brow furrowing as he stepped forward to meet her, placing a firm hand on her shoulder. "Is everything alright?" he asked, his voice low but sharp with worry. His dark eyes scanned her quickly, searching for signs of injury. Evie shook her head, raising her hands as if to reassure him. "No, no, I'm fine," she said, though her words did little to ease his tension. She turned, gesturing back toward Trigger, who was patiently waiting with the cart.

Shepherd's brow lifted. "The horse?" He cocked his head, clearly confused. "Evie, you know I'm not a vet." Evie let out a short laugh despite herself. "No, you fool! Inside the cart. Rich and Andy found someone in the water." That got his attention. His concern deepened, and he started to move past her toward the cart, his long strides eating up the distance. But Evie reached out and grabbed his arm, stopping him mid-step. The urgency in her grip made him spin around, his expression now edged with alarm. "Look," she said, her voice dropping into a hushed, serious tone. "I don't know who he is, but... I think he's been shot."

Shepherd's face shifted, a mixture of surprise and adrenaline flashing in his eyes. His posture stiffened for just a moment, as though processing the weight of her words, before he broke into a sprint toward the cart. Without hesitation, he vaulted onto the back, landing nimbly on the wooden floorboards. Trigger snorted indignantly at the sudden weight, tossing his head in frustration, his ears flattening back for a moment. "Alright, alright, calm down, boy," Shepherd muttered, running a hand briefly along the cart's edge to steady himself. He crouched low, his attention now fully on the unconscious man sprawled before him. From her spot by the road, Evie watched Shepherd work with swift, practiced efficiency, his focus sharp as he began checking Aubrey for signs of life. She couldn't help but smile faintly at Trigger's irritated huff, as if the old horse were grumbling about being dragged into yet another one of their adventures.

***

Yvette Harrison stood outside the green wooden door, her arms crossed tightly across her chest as she glared at it, as if sheer willpower might make it swing open. Her father, Jim, leaned heavily on his cane beside her, his expression one of amused resignation. His leg had been giving him hell for weeks now, and yesterday's visit to the surgery had done little to help. Yvette wasn't the type to take such things lying down. No, she was here to demand answers— or at least vent her frustration at Doctor Cramner. She paced up and down in tight circles, the click of her heels sharp against the pavement. "Will you knock it off, Yve?" Jim muttered; his tone exasperated but laced with affection. "You're going to wear a bloody hole in the pavement at this rate."

Yvette stopped abruptly, spinning on her heel to face him, her hands flying to her hips. "Look here, Dad, this pavement is the last of my concerns," she shot back, her voice rising. "That doctor clearly doesn't have a clue what he's talking about! Painkillers? Really? When it's clear your leg might fall off any day now?" Jim let out a wheezy laugh that quickly turned into a cough, his frail frame shaking as he tried to catch his breath. "Ninety years," he said between gasps, his voice weathered but proud. "Ninety years I've been walking on these legs. Covered every inch of this island, rain or shine. It's just my age, sweetheart. That's all. Age catches up with all of us, eventually."

"Well, I'm not about to let it catch you without a fight," she snapped, her cheeks flushing. "I don't care how old you are—it's his job to fix this, not wave you off with a bottle of pills like you're some lost cause." Jim shook his head with a bemused smile, but Yvette wasn't done. She turned back toward the door, her patience officially run dry. "And if that bloody doctor doesn't come down here sharpish and open this door," she declared, her voice practically vibrating with indignation, "I swear, I'll kick it down myself." Her father chuckled again, shaking his head. "God help the poor man when he sees you storming in. Reminds me of your mum, rest her soul." Yvette didn't reply, but her lips twitched briefly at the corners before setting back into a thin line. She knocked loudly on the green door again, her fist thudding against the wood. "Doctor Cramner, you've got thirty seconds!" she called. "Or I'm coming in, ready or not!"

"Good morning, Mrs. Harrison! Up and about early, I see," Doctor Ethan Cramner greeted them with his trademark broad smile as he approached the green door. The warmth in his voice and the easy charm of his demeanour cut through Yvette's simmering frustration like the sun piercing storm clouds. Despite herself, she adjusted her coat with an embarrassed huff and turned to her father, whispering sharply through clenched teeth, "Stand up straight, Dad." Jim rolled his eyes, muttering something under his breath about bossy daughters, but he obediently leaned forward, making a valiant if imperfect effort to straighten his stooped back. "That's about as good as it gets," he grumbled, earning a sideways glare from Yvette.

Doctor Cramner chuckled softly at their exchange. Reaching into the pocket of his coat, he produced a key and unlocked the door with practiced ease. "Why don't you both come inside and get comfortable?" he offered, pushing the door open with a smile. "I'll pop the radio on while I get ready. Shepherd won't be far behind."

As the door creaked open, Yvette stepped forward abruptly, reaching for the doctor's arm as if to stop him. Her hand hovered for a moment before she quickly withdrew it, fidgeting awkwardly. "Sorry," she said hastily, her tone softening, though determination still underpinned her words. "If it's all the same, we'd prefer to see you today, Doctor. Not Shepherd. I mean, no offense, but—well, we came to talk to you."

Ethan paused mid-step, glancing over his shoulder at Jim, who gave him an apologetic shrug, as if to say, don't mind her; she's been like this since she was five. The doctor's smile never wavered, though his eyes briefly sparkled with amusement. "Sure thing," he said smoothly, nodding in understanding. "Not an inconvenience at all. You're always welcome to see whoever you like." Before Yvette could find a reason to apologize again, Ethan reached out and playfully touched her shoulder in a gesture of reassurance. Then, with an air of unhurried confidence, he stepped inside, leaving the door ajar behind him. Jim leaned closer to Yvette, a sly smile tugging at his lips. "You know," he teased, "you'd have better luck getting what you want if you didn't look like you were about to wrestle the poor man to the ground." Yvette shot him a withering look, though a faint blush betrayed her. "Hush, Dad," she muttered. But as she followed him inside, she couldn't help but feel a little lighter, even if she wasn't ready to admit it.

Settling into the waiting area's unforgiving plastic chairs, Jim leaned forward, his cane steadying his weight as he rummaged through the stack of dog-eared magazines on the low coffee table. He flipped past faded issues of gardening guides and celebrity gossip rags, his fingers hesitating over a brightly coloured comic book. His eyes lit up for a moment, but then he caught Yvette's sharp gaze from across the room. With a subtle sigh, he slid the comic aside, opting instead for a copy of Angler's Weekly. The cover featured a man in a green flat cap and matching jacket, grinning triumphantly through a handlebar moustache as he held up an absurdly large fish. Jim stared at the image for a moment, muttering under his breath, "Biggest catch I've seen today."

Yvette, meanwhile, sat bolt upright, her hands gripping the arms of her chair as though bracing for take-off. Her eyes darted toward the door on the far side of the room just as it clicked shut. Doctor Cramner's steady footsteps echoed on the wooden stairs as he climbed to his office, the faint creak of each step marking his progress. "This is great, Dad," Yvette said, breaking the silence, her voice bright with satisfaction. "First ones in, no queue, and nobody else here to distract Mr. Cramner. We'll finally get some proper attention." Jim lowered the magazine slightly, peering over the top with a faint smirk. "Doctor Cramner, dear," he corrected, his tone tinged with playful formality. "The man's not running a farm. Show a little respect."

Yvette rolled her eyes but couldn't help a smile tugging at the corner of her lips. "Fine, Doctor Cramner," she replied, mock-serious, before glancing at her father's reading material. "And since when have you cared about fishing?" Jim straightened slightly, tapping the cover of the magazine with his cane. "Since never," he said, grinning slyly. "But I reckon if I'm going to sit here waiting for you to give that poor man a piece of your mind, I might as well look respectable doing it."

✳✳✳

Ethan walked around his desk, switching on the computer. The familiar whir of the fan kicked in, followed by the slow crawl of the cursor blinking to life on the screen. A loading circle began its lazy spiral, mocking his impatience. Shrugging off his jacket, he hung it neatly on the small hook by the inner office door. As he reached for a folder on his desk, his gaze drifted downward, catching the thin line of light spilling through the bottom of the doorframe. He frowned, his hand pausing mid-reach. "What the hell?" he muttered. He distinctly remembered locking that door last night. His brow furrowed as he turned the handle slowly, the large white door creaking open just a sliver.

The light inside flickered faintly, casting an eerie glow. He peered through the crack, his heart skipping when a shadow shifted abruptly into view. "Bloody hell!" he yelped, stumbling back as Shepherd Akinde's face suddenly filled the gap, with Evie Potter standing just behind him. Shepherd pushed the door open the rest of the way, stepping in with an apologetic smile that did little to ease

Ethan's thudding heart. "Christ, Shepherd!" Ethan barked, gripping his chest dramatically. "I think I need to change my bloody underwear! You scared the life out of me." Neither Shepherd nor Evie replied immediately. They simply stood there, their smiles awkward, sheepish, as though caught red-handed at something. Ethan's confusion deepened. "What's this about? Why are you skulking around my treatment room?"

Evie stepped forward quickly, slipping her hand around his arm with an urgency that shut down any further protests. "Now listen, Doctor," she began, her voice low but firm. "We need to show you something. But before we do, is there anyone waiting out there?" She nodded toward the waiting area, her expression unreadable. Ethan hesitated, glancing at the partially open office door. "Uh, yeah," he said slowly, trying to look past her into the room. "The Harrisons are out there. What's—?"

Shepherd cut him off with a gentle but insistent grip on his shoulders. "Let's step inside," he said, his tone uncharacteristically serious. He guided Ethan firmly through the door, shutting it behind them. "What's going on?" Ethan demanded, his voice dropping to a wary whisper. Evie didn't answer. She moved quickly toward the examination bed, her movements precise and purposeful. She crouched slightly, inspecting something hidden from Ethan's line of sight. He heard the faint creak of rope and saw her tugging at knots, testing their strength. "Evie," Ethan began, his unease growing. "What the hell are you doing?" Straightening, Evie turned to face him, her expression now entirely serious. "Trust me, Doctor," she said quietly. "You're going to want to see this for yourself. But first, make sure that doors locked. No one else can know about this. Not yet."

Ethan muttered, rubbing the bridge of his nose, "but you know Mrs. Harrison. She's not going to take this well if she feels like she's been bumped off the list." "She'll survive," Shepherd replied dryly, "this guy might not." Evie stood by the side of the bed; her arms crossed as she watched them approach. She bit her lip, clearly uneasy, but she held her ground. Ethan's steps slowed as he reached the bed, his professional confidence faltering at the sight of Aubrey stretched out before him. The first thing he noticed was how the stranger's feet hung awkwardly over the end of the examination bed. "Bloody hell," Ethan murmured, more to himself than anyone else. "He's huge."

Shepherd and Evie exchanged a glance, but neither said a word. Evie broke the silence, pointing at the man's chest. "The Daisy's crew found him floating in the sea. Could've come from the mainland or a passing ship—we don't know. But he's injured. Look here." She gestured to two dark stains, the crimson stark against the Aubrey's soaked, tattered jacket. "Two holes, clean through." Ethan leaned closer, his expression hardening. He reached for Aubrey's wrist, pressing two fingers against the clammy skin as his eyes flicked down to his watch. His lips moved soundlessly as he counted under his breath. Seconds passed in tense silence, Evie and Shepherd watching his every movement. Finally, Ethan let the man's wrist drop with a sigh, his expression grim. "Not good," he muttered, glancing up at them. "38 beats per minute. If we don't act fast, he's not going to make it." His gaze shifted to Shepherd. "I need an IV. Now."

Without a word, Shepherd spun on his heel and headed toward the supply alcove at the far end of the room, his footsteps brisk and determined. Ethan turned his attention back to Aubrey, his brow furrowed deeply. He bent to inspect the bloodied wounds more closely, fingers twitching toward Aubrey's jacket as if to peel it back. "Don't," Evie blurted, her hand darting out to stop him. Her voice was firm, but there was a tremor beneath it. "I've already checked. Clean shots, straight through. No shrapnel." Ethan froze, his hand hovering mid-air. Slowly, he straightened and turned his gaze to her, the weight of the situation heavy in his eyes. For a moment, neither spoke. The silence between them stretched taut, charged with unspoken concern. Evie watched as his Adam's apple bobbed in his throat, his jaw tightening.

"You sure?" he asked finally, his voice low. "Yes," she said, her tone unwavering now. "But that doesn't mean he's out of danger." Ethan gave a single nod, turning his attention back to the unconscious man. As Shepherd returned with the IV, the doctor's hands moved with practiced precision, but his mind buzzed with questions. Who was this man? Where had he come from? And, most pressing of all, who had wanted him dead?

Ethan was about to turn away when something caught his eye. Pausing, he reached for Aubrey's exposed arm, lifting it carefully to study the faint markings hidden beneath the coarse black hairs. The ink was old and faded, almost blending into the mottled skin. He tilted the arm toward the light, his brow furrowing. "What do you make of this?" he asked, his voice barely above a whisper. Evie circled the bed, her curiosity piqued. She leaned in beside him, squinting at the design etched into the man's forearm. "A tattoo of some kind," she murmured, tracing its outline in the air. "Looks like a... knife, maybe?" They stared at it for a long moment, the room filled with the rhythmic hum of the IV machine. Ethan's gaze darted around the room, his thoughts racing. "There's something written here," he muttered. "Can you grab that magnifying glass?" Evie hurried to the nearby shelf, snatching up the glass and handing it to him. He positioned it over the tattoo, bringing the faded ink into sharper focus. As the image came into view, his stomach tightened. "Shit," he breathed, letting Aubrey's arm drop like it had burned him. "What?" Evie demanded, her eyes darting between Ethan and the unconscious man.

He stepped back, his face pale, his hands gripping the edge of the counter behind him for support. "He's SAS." Evie blinked, confused. "SAS? As in the Special Air Service? The military?" Ethan nodded grimly. "The winged dagger tattoo, the motto— 'Who Dares Wins.' It's the mark of the SAS. These guys are... well, they're something else." Intrigued, Evie stepped forward, grabbing the magnifying glass from the counter. She crouched by the bed, bringing the tattoo closer to the light. The black ink, faded and distorted by age, began to reveal itself. She could make out the silhouette of a sword, its hilt sprouting wings on either side. Beneath it, a barely legible inscription: Who Dares Wins.

"What does that mean?" she asked, still staring at the ink. Ethan crossed his arms, his face a mixture of respect and unease. "It's the SAS motto. These men are the best of the best—trained for missions no one else would touch. They thrive on chaos, danger, and unpredictability." He ran a hand through his hair, exhaling sharply.

"They're fearless. Or reckless. Depends on how you look at it." Evie glanced Aubrey on the bed, suddenly seeing him in a new light. "So, what's he doing here? Floating in the sea with bullet holes in his chest?" Ethan shook his head. "That's the question, isn't it? If this guy's SAS, he's no ordinary soldier. And someone clearly wanted him gone." His eyes drifted to the unconscious man's face, his mind racing with implications. "The bigger question is... why?"

Shepherd returned, the clear plastic bag of fluid swinging from his hand. His boots clicked sharply against the floor as he crossed the room, eyes focused on the task at hand. He set the bag down on the counter and grabbed the metal IV stand, moving around the side of the bed with practiced efficiency. With a quiet clink, he hung the bag on a hook near the bed, the clear liquid inside catching the light. "I'll fit the cannula now, if that's alright, Doctor?" Shepherd's voice was steady, his hands already reaching for the medical supplies. Ethan nodded, his attention flicking from Shepherd to the unconscious man on the bed. "Go ahead. Just keep it quick. We need to stabilize him before we can figure out what the hell's going on."

His gaze then turned to Evie, who hadn't moved an inch from where she stood by the bed, her arms folded and her expression unreadable. "Are those knots tight enough?" he asked, his voice a little more tense than he intended. Evie looked over at him, a smirk tugging at the corner of her lips. "Well, my horse Trigger has never escaped, so I don't think our friend over there will be giving us any trouble." She tilted her head, eyeing the unconscious man with a mixture of amusement and authority. "You don't need to worry about him." Ethan gave her a sceptical look but didn't say anything. Instead, he folded his arms, watching Shepherd's movements closely as he prepared the cannula. His colleague's hands moved with mechanical precision, the white plastic of the needle gleaming in the sterile light of the room. "I hope you're right," Ethan muttered, his eyes flicking once more to the man on the bed, who still hadn't stirred. "The last thing we need is for him to wake up and try to bolt."

Evie's smirk deepened. "Let him try." She gestured to Aubrey's bound wrists and ankles. "The knots won't be the only thing that's tight." There was something almost teasing in her voice, but Ethan couldn't help but feel a flicker of unease at the situation. Shepherd paused for a moment, glancing up at Ethan. "All set here," he said, his voice calm. "Just need to get the IV in place, and then we'll see how he responds." Ethan's focus narrowed as Shepherd prepped the cannula, the clicking of rubber gloves and the soft whoosh of the IV fluid filling the silence between them. The tension in the room thickened. They weren't just dealing with an injured man anymore—they were dealing with something bigger. Something they didn't understand yet, but would soon enough.

Shepherd carefully removed the cap from the end of the needle, his gloved fingers steady, and placed it gently against Aubrey's arm. The room was quiet except for the soft rustle of gloves and the muted sound of the IV fluid slowly dripping into its bag. With practiced precision, Shepherd searched for a vein, his eyes narrowing as he found the perfect spot. The needle slid into the skin with a quiet pop, and the faintest hiss followed as he began to insert the cannula. Ethan stood back, arms crossed, his eyes never leaving the procedure. Shepherd held the cannula in place with one hand, then quickly taped it down with two strips of medical tape, securing it tightly. The fluid began to flow, the bag above the bed swinging gently with the steady drip.

"Well done, Shepherd," Ethan said, his voice smooth but laced with tension. He turned to Evie, his brow furrowed. "Now let's get some fluids into him, and we'll see if he stabilizes. But we need to be cautious with this one. I'm not sure how he's going to react. I think we should take some extra precautions." Evie raised an eyebrow, glancing at the unconscious man on the bed, his chest rising and falling in shallow breaths. "Precautions? Like what?" She watched the steady stream of fluid enter the man's bloodstream, the weight of the situation settling over her.

Ethan hesitated, the corners of his mouth tightening as he weighed his words. "I'm going to contact Mr. Norris. We might need some extra hands—guards, if he can spare any." He paused, his gaze flickering to the door as he turned to leave. "Just in case." "Prison guards?" Evie's voice was sharp with disbelief. "You think this guy's dangerous?" The doctor didn't reply immediately, his mind already on the phone call he needed to make. "We need to prepare for any situation, Evie, and looking at those ropes, I'd say you were thinking the same" he muttered over his shoulder as he walked out of the room, his voice cutting through the stillness like a blade.

Evie stood there, her gaze shifting from Aubrey on the bed to the empty doorway. She let out a slow breath, trying to calm the unease twisting in her stomach. The air was thick with something unspoken, and she couldn't quite put her finger on it. Aubrey may be unconscious, but she couldn't shake the feeling that something wasn't right. Just as she was about to turn back to the bed, a slight movement caught her eye. One of Aubrey's fingers twitched. It was so subtle, she almost missed it. Her heart skipped a beat, and she quickly glanced up at his face. His eyes were still shut, his expression unmoving, but the finger twitched again, as if it was trying to break free from some invisible restraint. Evie's breath caught in her throat, and she took a step closer, her eyes never leaving the man. She felt a strange chill in the air, the kind that whispered of danger, of a storm on the horizon. Whatever was going on here, it wasn't over. Not by a long shot.

Shepherd was focused on adjusting the drip rate, his eyes flicking between the IV bag and the man on the bed. The rhythmic beeping of the heart monitor was the only sound in the otherwise quiet room. He glanced up, his voice steady but urgent, "Would you mind telling the Doctor the patient is ready now? We need to start dressing his wounds." Evie nodded, her expression unreadable as she turned on her heel and walked out of the room. The door creaked softly as it closed behind her, and she found herself once again in the hallway, the weight of the situation settling in.

As she stepped into the office she saw Ethan pacing near the desk, his face flushed, a furrow of concentration etched deep on his brow. He was on the phone, his hand moving in the air as though he were trying to physically map out his thoughts. His voice was low but tense, and Evie could hear the sharpness in his words as he spoke to whoever was on the other end. "Yes, that's correct, John. No, no, we need this guy locked up, pronto," Ethan's voice dropped an octave, his tone becoming more insistent, "No, we can't wait. It'll be at least an hour before anyone can get here from the mainland.

Besides, this guy…" He wiped a bead of sweat from his brow, his face tightening. There was something in his voice now, a hint of disbelief. Evie caught a glimpse of it—of a man trying to hold it together, but barely. She stopped mid-step, her eyes narrowing as she listened.

"You need to see him," Ethan continued, his voice low and strained. "I've never seen anything like it… OK, thank you, John. Please, hurry." He placed the receiver back into its cradle with a sharp click, rubbing the back of his neck as he turned, his gaze meeting Evie's. "John's coming personally," he said, his voice a little steadier now, but his eyes still haunted. "He's bringing a few guards with him." Evie studied him, sensing the shift in his demeanour. His face was pale, his jaw set tight. The urgency in his voice hadn't escaped her, and the tension between them was palpable. Something was wrong, something bigger than they had anticipated. She stepped forward, her voice quiet but firm. "What the hell's going on, Ethan?"

Ethan exhaled slowly, his hand running through his hair. He opened his mouth to speak, but the words seemed to catch in his throat. Instead, he turned toward the door to the treatment room, his hand resting on the frame. "I think we're dealing with something… I don't know, something dangerous." His voice was grim. "And I don't think the island's ready for it." Evie followed his gaze, her heart pounding as the weight of his words settled over her. The man they had brought in, the one they were trying to save, wasn't just any patient. There was something more to him, something that neither of them fully understood yet, but they both felt it—deep in their bones. As they both stood there, caught in the quiet tension of the moment, a new sense of urgency filled the air. Something was coming, and they were about to be caught right in the middle of it.

Peering through the narrow slit between his clenched eyelids, Aubrey's sharp gaze followed the Doctor's every move. He watched as Shepherd walked around the room, his footsteps slow and deliberate, as if unaware of the tension filling the small space. The doctor picked up a clipboard and began scribbling notes, his back turned to the bed. The silence was almost suffocating. Aubrey's fingers twitched, testing the ropes that bound him, feeling the fibres dig into his skin. He focused, breathing evenly, slowly working on loosening the knots. Within twenty seconds, he felt the tension in his wrists fade. The ropes fell away like brittle twine. He glanced up again—Ethan hadn't noticed. The doctor, engrossed in his writing, was now staring out the window, waving his hand to someone below.

Taking the chance, Aubrey moved silently, glancing around the room. His eyes darted, calculating his escape route. The weight of the moment hung in the air like a ticking clock. He stood carefully, testing his legs, ready to move at a moment's notice. Meanwhile, below the window, Harley was making his way down the street, his boots crunching against the gravel in his hiking gear. The sun had begun to dip low on the horizon, casting long shadows over the sleepy town. Shepherd glanced up at the road ahead, watching as Harley crossed the street and made his way down to the far end of town. A familiar sense of unease crawled over him, a quiet warning that something wasn't right.

Before he could process the feeling, something sharp flashed in his peripheral vision. Instinctively, he turned—but it was too late. A blinding pain shot into his eye, the silver object striking with a speed that left him gasping. The world spun for a moment, his vision swimming. In a daze, Shepherd felt his knees give way, but before he could crash to the ground, strong hands caught him, steadying him with practiced ease. The sharpness of the pain lingered as he was guided carefully down onto the cool vinyl flooring of the nearby shop. A groan escaped his lips as his vision blurred and the ground seemed to tilt beneath him. "Shepherd," a voice called, low and urgent. The world around him seemed to warp and flicker, the last thing he saw before darkness crept in was the glint of silver— disappearing into the air, leaving only the taste of metal in his mouth.

Aubrey's eyes flicked to the window, his fingers fumbling for the latch. He pulled, gritting his teeth as he tried to wrench it open, only to find it stubbornly locked. His frustration boiled over, and he swung his head around violently, his long grey hair whipping behind him like a wild mane, settling heavily on his shoulders. That's when he heard the door creak open. Evie's heart skipped a beat as she entered, but what she saw made her freeze—Shepherd, sprawled on the floor in a gruesome heap, his lifeless body impaled by a pair of scissors that jutted out of his eye socket. Horror surged through her, but it was quickly replaced by a cold, ruthless determination when her eyes locked onto the towering figure in front of her. Aubrey loomed like a beast in the doorway, his breath ragged and animalistic, froth forming at the corners of his mouth.

"Lock this door, Doc!" she shouted, her voice sharp, echoing off the sterile walls as she rushed inside, slamming the door shut behind her with a force that rattled the frame. She spun around, instantly positioning herself between Aubrey and the door. Every instinct screamed at her to keep it closed—he was dangerous. Behind her, she heard Ethan's voice, disoriented and calling out, "Hey, what's going on in there?" Without turning, Evie reached behind her, grabbing the door handle before it could budge, holding it firmly. "Ethan, listen to me—fucking lock the door!" Her breath came in rapid bursts, adrenaline pumping through her veins. "The beast is out of the cage." She turned her eyes back to the giant, whose movements were slow and deliberate as he stepped away from the window, his eyes locked on the bed. Evie's pulse hammered in her ears as she held her ground, watching every muscle in his body tense with some kind of twisted anticipation. Behind her, she could hear Ethan fumbling with the lock, his voice rising in confusion, but then the key turned with a satisfying click, sealing them in. The door was finally locked. Evie didn't dare relax. Not yet. The fight had only just begun.

Evie's heart pounded in her chest, but she didn't flinch. She shed her jacket in a single fluid motion, letting it fall to the floor in a heap. Her hands went to the sink, grabbing a towel and wrapping it around her palms, the fabric tight enough to give her some leverage. She locked eyes with Aubrey, her voice a cold challenge, "Wanna party, big boy?" Aubrey paused, his brow furrowing in confusion at her fearless attitude. His eyes darted around the room, calculating his options.

He was a predator, used to seeing fear, but she was different—defiant. Panic flickered in his expression for just a moment before he reached behind his back, pulling out a knife. The blade gleamed in the dim light before he flicked it in the air, catching it with ease. With a cruel smirk, he held the weapon sideways, sizing her up as he slowly advanced. Evie's gaze locked onto the six-inch blade; the blood dried along its serrated edge—a testament to its past use. Her fingers tightened around the towel, ready to strike. The room felt charged, the tension thick in the air.

Meanwhile, next door, Ethan stood frozen by the door, his hand gripping the handle so tightly his knuckles whitened. Every nerve in his body screamed at him to act, but fear held him in place. Should he unlock the door and risk his life to help her, or run? He could hear nothing from the other side, only silence—but it was the kind of silence that spoke volumes. Suddenly, a deafening thud shattered the stillness, followed by a brutal slam against the door.

Ethan stumbled backward, the force of the impact knocking him off balance. His hands reached out for something to steady himself, but only the desk met his fall. A cascade of brown patient files erupted into the air, scattering like confetti, their contents spilling across the floor, each piece a reminder of the chaos that had just erupted. Ethan's breath caught in his throat as the weight of the situation hit him—Evie was in there, facing a trained killer, and there was nothing he could do to stop it.

Evie's body coiled like a spring as she felt Aubrey's powerful hands clamp around her neck, lifting her off the floor. Her feet kicked at empty air, her vision narrowing as she met his cold blue eyes, staring back at her with an unyielding intensity. Desperation and determination surged through her as she saw the chance to strike. With a swift, brutal motion, she drove her knee upward, catching him square in the groin. To her shock, he didn't react—no flinch, no grimace. Instead, he tightened his grip, squeezing tighter, cutting off her air. Evie's vision began to blur, but she focused— zeroed in on the deep, open wound in his stomach. Pressing her thumb into the hole, she pushed forward, feeling the warmth of his flesh beneath her fingers.

Suddenly, Aubrey's hold on her neck slackened, his grip loosening. Evie dropped back to the floor, gasping for air, but before she could catch her breath, she exploded back up, her legs flying forward like a pair of pistons. Her feet slammed into his chest, sending him flying backward toward the bed. As he hit the edge of the mattress, something skidded across the floor toward the window—a knife. Both of them turned, eyes locking onto the blade lying there, still glistening with dark remnants of blood. Evie grabbed a nearby chair, her movements sharp and determined. Just as Aubrey began to push off the floor, running at her with renewed intensity, she hurled the chair with pinpoint accuracy. The metal frame smacked into him, knocking him off balance just enough to cause a stumble. Evie watched as his breath wheezed out of him, and his posture faltered, his muscles starting to twitch and spasm from exhaustion. Her own breathing was ragged, but she stood tall, her eyes fixed on the man's motionless form.

Evie's eyes flicked back and forth between Aubrey, the knife, and the distance between them. She knew he would get there first, but she wasn't going to play into his hands. Instead, she lifted her arms, palms open, adopting a defensive stance as she circled toward the bed. Aubrey's posture shifted, his hands dropping to his waist, readying himself. In that brief moment, the atmosphere thickened, tension humming in the air like a live wire. It felt like the beginning of a standoff from an old western—a showdown in the dusty streets, two gunslingers sizing each other up, waiting for the first move.

Her heart pounded in her chest as she watched him. His eyes darted—just a flicker, but it was enough. He was already calculating his next move. As he reached for the knife, the corner of her lip twitched, and without hesitation, she sprang forward. The speed of her motion was almost blinding. Her shoulder collided with his chest, driving into him like a battering ram. The impact forced the air from his lungs in a sickening wheeze as his body was sent crashing backward towards the window.

Ethan's pulse quickened as the sound of glass shattering echoed through the hall, followed by a heavy silence. He gripped the edge of his desk, knuckles white, his body tense as he listened for any movement. His gaze flickered nervously toward the stairwell door just as it slammed open with a force that made the wood groan in protest, almost tearing from its hinges. Shay Pippin, a hulking figure in a weathered jacket, shot through the gap like a bull on the charge, followed closely by Warden John Norris and two burly guards. The old man wasted no time, his voice a low growl. "Where is he?" Without a word, Ethan pointed shakily toward the treatment room door. "It's locked, you'll need the—"

Before he could finish, Shay's massive boot connected with the door, splintering the wood and ripping the bronze hinges from their frame with a sickening screech. The door crashed to the floor, sending a cloud of dust into the air. Shay didn't even glance back; his voice rumbled as he barked orders. "With me, lads." Richard Fossey and Connor Steels, both armed and ready, surged forward, stepping over the fallen door as they stormed into the room. John Norris placed a firm hand on Ethan's shoulder, his grip reassuring. "It's alright now, Doc. You're safe." But the tension in Ethan's chest didn't quite dissipate. The storm wasn't over yet.

"You better get in here, Sir." The voice was sharp, pulling John's attention toward the door, but as he stepped forward, he didn't realize Ethan was right behind him. Both of them crossed the threshold, but before either could speak, a high-pitched scream shattered the air. Ethan's face went pale, his hand instinctively coming up to his mouth in disbelief as his eyes darted over the scene. John, ever the professional, turned sharply to see what had triggered the reaction. Near the bed, Shepherd's body lay contorted, a twisted metal instrument lodged deep into his eye socket. The blood-stained tool gleamed in the dim light.

"Doc," John's voice softened, a command wrapped in concern, "you don't need to see this." Without waiting for a response, he turned to Richard. "Take the good doctor downstairs, get him some water, make sure he sits down. Calm him down if you need to." Richard nodded but didn't move immediately, his gaze fixed on the gruesome scene. John made a mental note to follow up with him later, then refocused on the room. The calm precision of his eyes never wavered, though the blood pooling beneath Shepherd's body was enough to send a chill down anyone's spine.

Shay, standing across the room, was already scanning the surroundings with a professional's eye. He crouched down to examine shards of glass scattered across the floor, each piece glinting in the light. His eyes flicked toward the window—a jagged hole in the glass, red droplets trailing down the frame like a macabre drip-feed. Carefully, Shay leaned out the window, his massive frame nearly filling the entire space. Below, in the small gated courtyard, scattered pallets and a wheelie bin lay in disarray.

Shay then stepped back, looked down and saw something slightly exposed underneath a cabinet. Richard took a cautious step forward, his curiosity piqued by the sharp edge in Shay's voice. "What have you found?" he asked, his eyes scanning the room for any sign of danger. John, meanwhile, stood by the bed, his expression grim as he carefully removed the sheet from Shepherd's lifeless body, folding it over him to shield the gruesome sight. The room was heavy with tension, the stillness broken only by the distant hum of the lights overhead.

Shay, his large frame casting a shadow across the room, rose to his feet. His hand gripped something that sent a chill through the room. He held a jagged knife, the blade gleaming ominously in the low light. The sight of it, so stark against the bloodstained floor, made Richard's stomach lurch. "Bloody hell, boss," Shay muttered, his voice low but intense. "You seeing this?" The Warden's eyes narrowed as he walked over to the guard, taking the weapon from Shay's hand with practiced care. The knife was crude, yet deadly, the kind of weapon born from desperation. It didn't belong here. John turned it over, examining the handle, the fingerprints—there was nothing distinct, nothing that could immediately identify the person who'd wielded it. But the weight of it—the danger it represented—was unmistakable.

"Sir," he said, his tone urgent, "we've got a runner. Whoever did this… they're gone. And they're not coming back." John's mind raced, the pieces of the puzzle starting to click into place. The bloodstains, the broken window, the knife—the one thing he knew for sure now was that this wasn't a simple crime of passion. It was something far bigger, something far more calculated. "We need to move, now," John ordered, his voice low but commanding. "Lock down the building. Nobody gets in or out without my say so. We're going hunting."

***

Swinging a plastic bag casually, Harley strolled down the sunlit road, the warmth of the day settling on his shoulders like a blanket. He was heading out of town, lost in thought, when a sudden recollection hit him—he still needed to see Lisa at The White Hart. Swearing under his breath, he turned on his heel, retracing his steps back toward town. The sun was high, casting long shadows as the vibrant sky stretched endlessly above. Today, he decided, was going to be a good day. With a quick motion, Harley stuffed one hand into his pocket and let his eyes wander. Above him, a formation of Canadian Geese honked their way north, their synchronized flight stirring something deep inside him. He watched in quiet envy as they glided effortlessly across the sky, a perfect symbol of freedom. No schedules. No limits. Just the open sky and endless horizons.

His thoughts drifted, and a glance to his right caught a flash of movement—a small figure with a little dog bounding joyfully through the tall grass at the base of the hill. The dog's playful energy was infectious, leaping through the air with abandon. The man trailing behind, a dark silhouette against the golden grass, seemed like the kind of person who could still find joy in the simple things. Harley couldn't help but wonder who he was, why he seemed so at ease, so untethered. Then, Ethan's voice echoed in his mind: "You need to meet people, build relationships." Harley chuckled softly to himself. It wasn't that he minded meeting people—it was more about figuring out the right ones. But today, maybe he could do something different. Take a step toward whatever this "building relationships" thing was about.

He checked his watch. Plenty of time. With a determined smile, he turned onto a narrow, overgrown path that wound through the outskirts of town. He hoped it would lead him to the base of the hill where the man and his dog were heading. Something about the peaceful, unhurried pace of their journey intrigued him. Maybe, just maybe, he could make a connection. As he walked, the sounds of the world seemed to quiet, his thoughts blending with the rhythm of his footsteps. Today might be the day everything changed.

The route ahead felt unfamiliar, an unwelcome uncertainty creeping in with each step. Harley couldn't shake the nagging feeling that he had strayed too far from the beaten path. He wasn't sure where this trail led, but he hoped it wasn't to a place he'd regret. The clock was ticking—he had just enough time to swing by Lisa's pub, grab a good bottle of red, and then head home to find Ethan, hopefully wearing those worn-in walking boots and that absurdly cute knitted hat he always insisted on. It would be a perfect end to a day that had started off uneventful. Suddenly, a voice sliced through his thoughts. He froze. Behind him, at the end of the narrow trail, a woman was waving her arms in frantic, wild gestures. He blinked, wondering if it was some sort of signal. Better be polite, he thought, reluctantly raising his hand in return. His arm was halfway up when the ground beneath him seemed to vanish. "Hey, hey! What do you think you're doing?"

The voice was barely audible as a surge of force lifted him off his feet. His body spun, head over heels, as if he'd been caught in a whirlwind. The bag in his hand seemed to lighten, the contents dropping one by one—first the cucumber, then a loaf of bread, and finally the bunch of grapes—tumbling through the air like some bizarre food chain reaction. What the hell was happening? He struggled to make sense of it, his stomach flipping as his entire world was upended. His brain registered a blur of movement—the woman in the distance now a blur of motion, running toward him like a strange spectre.

He opened his mouth to shout, to demand answers, but his voice was swallowed by the rush of air. He could feel the vertigo, the panic setting in as if he was being pulled into some invisible vortex. I'm flying—was the first thought that popped into his mind. Then, as if the sky had decided it was done with him, he began to plummet. The ground rushed up toward him with an almost sickening speed. No, no, no—his brain screamed, but there was no time for fear. With a sickening snap, his body hit something hard. The world around him went dark.

"Noooooooo!" Evie's scream tore through the air as she sprinted with everything she had, her heart pounding in her chest. She saw Aubrey—no, the monster—toss Harley's limp body aside like a ragdoll. The sickening thud as Harley's body hit the ground echoed in her ears. She barely registered the horror before her instincts kicked in, pushing her faster. Reaching Harley's side, she knelt beside him, her hands trembling as she pressed two fingers against his throat. Nothing. No pulse. Her stomach churned, but she couldn't afford to waste another second. She fought the urge to start CPR, to try and save him—not now, not like this. That killer was still out there, a relentless beast on the hunt, and she had to stop him before he claimed any more lives.

She could feel the rage boiling up inside her, but there was no time for anger. Only action. Evie sprang to her feet, her muscles screaming in protest as she took off again, her eyes locked on the shadowy figure up ahead. The bastard wasn't stopping—he moved like a machine, relentless, unstoppable, with no soul left to save. A bloody cyborg. But she wasn't going to let him get away. She couldn't. Every step felt like it might be her last, but she pushed harder, her breaths ragged, determination flooding her veins. He could run, but she would hunt him down. He wasn't the only one who could be relentless.

*** ***

Mr. Postlethwaite shuffled down the hill, his boots making soft thuds against the gravel as he adjusted his worn jacket. The crisp autumn air nipped at his face, but he barely noticed it. He had a routine, a rhythm, and he wasn't about to let anything interrupt it. As he reached the bottom of the hill, he paused and glanced over at the little dog, Mr. Snorbits, who had stopped in the middle of the road.

"Excuse me, young fella, come here. You know the rules."

The dog sniffed the air with his little nose twitching, and for a moment, he seemed to weigh his options. The world was full of interesting smells, after all. But with a determined wag of his tail, the dog turned and trotted back to his master, his paws clicking softly against the pavement. Mr. Postlethwaite clipped the lead onto the dog's collar with a practiced hand, his fingers stiff from age but still steady.

"Good lad,"

he muttered, and they both turned right, heading back toward town. The small village lay ahead, nestled in the valley like an old memory, and the only sound was the rhythmic clip-clop of their steps. Mr. Snorbits, his tail wagging enthusiastically, knew exactly what was in store. A fresh bowl of food awaited him, followed by his favourite afternoon ritual: curling up next to the coal fire while his master sat back in his old chair, puffing on his pipe, lost in some grainy black-and-white movie from years long gone.

"Sit." Mr. Snorbits immediately obeyed, his brown eyes locking with his master's with a look of quiet adoration. "There's a good boy," he murmured. The dog let out a soft whimper of contentment, closing his eyes for a moment as the man's rough, calloused hand ran through his fur. It was a simple life, but it was theirs, and in that moment, it was enough. Without even glancing to see if a car was coming—there was rarely any traffic on these streets—Mr. Postlethwaite stepped out onto the road.

The town was small, quiet, and sleepy compared to the bustling cities on the mainland. Most people here had never known the noise of an engine beyond the occasional car, and even fewer could afford one. It was a place where time moved slower, where life was about the small, everyday moments—like a quiet walk down the hill with a loyal dog by your side, a warm fire waiting at home, and the comfort of knowing that no matter how much the world outside changed, the rhythm of life here remained the same.

The dog's tiny paws pitter-pattered on the asphalt as he walked alongside Mr. Postlethwaite, the rhythm of their footsteps the only sound on the quiet road. The old man glanced down at his loyal companion and gave a gruff chuckle. "Which way, boy?" he asked, his voice low and filled with the warmth of routine. He pointed toward the long, winding road. "We could go the long way, take our time." Then, with a sly grin, he pointed toward a narrow pathway, its edges lined with dense, towering bushes. "Or we could take the shortcut, eh?"

The Jack Russell's ears twitched, his attention suddenly pulled away from the conversation. His head tilted to the side, the air thick with something unfamiliar, something unsettling. His nose twitched as a faint sound caught his attention. It was a low hum, like the quiet shuffle of a heavy footstep on gravel, but it was coming from somewhere close, too close. Before Mr. Postlethwaite could even notice the shift in the air, the world exploded in chaos. Without warning, a heavy hand shot out from the bushes, gripping the old man with terrifying strength. In an instant, he was yanked backward, his body crashing to the ground with a sickening thud. The impact sent a jolt of pain through his skull, and darkness immediately closed in on him.

The Jack Russell yelped in shock, his fur bristling as he darted in circles, trying to make sense of the attack. Confusion clouded his small, intelligent eyes, but there was no time for hesitation. Aubrey who had knocked his beloved master out cold was still looming over him—tall, menacing, and entirely unfamiliar. A growl rumbled deep in the dog's chest as he locked eyes with the intruder. His instincts kicked into overdrive. Without a second thought, the little dog lunged forward, teeth bared, and sank his jaws into Aubrey's trousers.

Aubrey stumbled, momentarily caught off guard by the unexpected attack from the scrappy dog. The Jack Russell held firm, his tiny body shaking with the effort, his paws scrabbling at the ground for purchase as he tugged with all his might. Despite the size difference, the dog was undeterred, his protective instinct flaring like a fire. Aubrey snarled and swung a heavy boot toward the dog, but the Jack Russell darted out of reach just in time, his growls growing louder and fiercer. He wasn't going to back down—no matter how big the threat looming over him. But still, it wasn't enough. Aubrey's grip on the old man's unconscious form remained unbroken.

Aubrey's breath came in shallow, calculated bursts as he watched the small dog struggle to drag him away from the old man on the ground. The dog's tiny paws scratched desperately at the gravel, barking furiously in a mix of terror and fury, its sharp eyes fixed on the larger threat. Aubrey could feel the dog's panic, its tiny body vibrating with the effort. But there was no time to waste. He could hear her—the woman—gaining on him, the rapid rhythm of her footsteps pounding closer with every second. He had maybe thirty seconds, tops, before she caught up. He could practically hear the anger in her voice, the desperate fury in the way she chased him. It was a luxury he couldn't afford.

His fingers closed around the dog's scruff with practiced precision, his hand so large it enveloped the animal's neck completely. The Jack Russell let out a sharp, frightened yelp, but it didn't stop Aubrey. His grip tightened, a warning in his touch. With a swift motion, he raised the squirming dog to his face. The animal growled in protest, its tiny chest puffed with defiance, eyes flashing with primal fury. He could feel the dog's teeth snap close to his skin, but he was unfazed. Aubrey's expression remained cold, methodical. His eyes scanned the distance, weighing the threat of the woman, and in the same instant, he brought the dog's ear close to his lips.

With a slow, deliberate breath, he whispered something inaudible, something strange, perhaps even unintelligible. His words weren't meant for anyone else—just for the dog, whose heart now raced in sync with the man's. The air between them seemed to thrum with some unspoken energy, a bond forged in desperation. The dog froze, its growl silencing as it listened, an uncanny stillness washing over its body. Aubrey's grip loosened slightly, but not out of kindness. It was more of a reminder—the dog wasn't in control here. The predator was.

His eyes flickered over his shoulder, the woman now only seconds away, her form darting around the corner, a flash of determination in her eyes. Aubrey tilted his head, eyes narrowing. Time was up. He snapped his hand away from the dog's neck with a sharp motion, letting the animal fall to the ground, stunned but unharmed. In the next instant, he turned, sprinting into the shadows, moving with an unnerving speed as the woman's shout echoed in the distance. The game was on, but he wasn't finished yet.

Evie's heart pounded in her chest as she watched the man disappear around the corner, disappearing into the narrow street. He was heading out of town, and for that, she was relieved. Every step he took away from the heart of the village reduced the chance of him running into more unsuspecting townsfolk.

Still, the weight of the situation pressed on her—this wasn't over. Not by a long shot. She pushed herself harder, her feet pounding the path as she neared the end of the alleyway, eyes scanning the horizon for any sign of movement. Suddenly, the unmistakable screech of tires sliced through the air. She instinctively pulled back, barely avoiding being clipped by a black van that swerved wildly onto the road. The heavy vehicle skidded to a halt, tires screeching as it narrowly missed the old man still lying on the road.

The van doors slammed open, and Evie's eyes locked onto the figures emerging. It was John—the Warden—and his team. Relief flooded through her in a rush. "Thank God," she muttered under her breath. John didn't waste a second. "Keep the engine running, son," he barked to the driver, Richard, whose hands were already gripping the wheel, eyes scanning the area for any threats. Evie could feel her breath slow as she focused on the task ahead. She looked down at the old man lying on the road. The small dog, frantic and whimpering, was licking the old man's face, but there was no response. The old man hadn't moved a muscle.

John's face hardened as he surveyed the scene. Without missing a beat, Evie squared her shoulders and shot him a look of determination. "This ends right now," she said, her voice low but fierce. John nodded, a silent understanding passing between them. Without waiting for further orders, she scooped the dog into her arms, cradling it protectively against her chest as she moved toward the van. Connor and Shay were already inside, the latter's massive frame filling most of the back seat.

She climbed in next to Connor, feeling the van jolt as the doors slammed shut. The engine roared to life as the van lurched forward, racing toward the next phase of the hunt. Every second counted. Evie clenched her fists, knowing that they were on the tail of a dangerous man who would stop at nothing to get what he wanted. This wasn't just about protecting the town anymore—it was about stopping a killer before he took another life.

The door slammed behind her with a force that made the van rattle. John slid into the front passenger seat, his eyes already scanning the road ahead. He glanced over his shoulder, his voice hard. "Which way did that bastard go?" Evie's mind raced as she processed the moment, the adrenaline still coursing through her veins. "I've been thinking about it," she said, her voice steady but urgent. "He can't be heading towards the coast—too exposed. The nearest route is south, but he's going north. I think he's looking for somewhere to hide, somewhere to patch himself up. He's injured, badly, so he'll need to take care of his wounds."

The four men in the van listened intently, their eyes glued to her as she laid out the facts. She could feel the weight of their attention, but her focus never wavered. "John," she continued, "this guy isn't just any criminal. He's military, former SAS at least. You're going to need more than just us. Even with this lump," she gestured towards the hulking figure of Shay, who sat still, his broad shoulders absorbing every word, "we're no match for him." There was a long silence as the men processed her words, the gravity of the situation settling in. John finally turned in his seat, his face grim, and nodded to Richard, who promptly engaged the van's gear. The engine roared to life, and the vehicle lurched forward.

Without taking his eyes off the road, John replied, his voice unwavering, "From what the Doc's said, you held your own out there, Evie. So, between you and Shay, I'm willing to put my money on us catching this bastard and locking him up by the end of the day." Evie's eyes met John's, a quiet understanding passing between them. She had no doubt that they could stop this man—but it wouldn't be easy. They weren't just chasing any man. They were hunting a ghost—a man trained to kill without hesitation. But today, they would be the ones doing the hunting.

***

With the weight of the town's pursuit pressing down on him, Aubrey vanished into the grove, the tall birch trees offering a momentary shield from the eyes that sought him. His breath was shallow, and his pulse thudded in his temples, but he couldn't afford to slow down. Not yet. Sliding a hand into the inner pocket of his jacket, he pulled out a folded, weathered piece of paper. The corners were creased from countless re-folds, its surface slightly torn from being carried in the damp confines of his jacket. He unfolded it carefully, studying the rough, hand-drawn map, its pencil lines faint but precise. He knew every curve and bend it depicted—the routes he could take, the places to avoid. It was his lifeline.

Looking back towards the town, Aubrey squinted as a vehicle appeared on the horizon, moving steadily towards him. He couldn't make out the driver's face, but the sight of the black van made his stomach tighten. His instincts screamed that it was no coincidence. Whoever was behind the wheel wasn't a friend. He scanned his surroundings quickly—there wasn't much time. His gaze shifted left, where strands of unruly hair clung to his forehead. Between the overgrown brush, barely visible under the canopy of trees, he spotted what he was looking for—a small, faded yellow sign. The words "Restricted Access – Authorised Personnel Only" were barely legible, the paint worn away from years of neglect. But the message was clear: this was the way forward.

He took a breath, his senses heightened. The black van was turning the corner. He could hear the hum of its engine now, too close for comfort. His mind raced. If he stayed hidden, the van would likely pass by, unaware of his presence. But the blood was pouring from his wound, each drop weakening him further. The longer he waited, the greater the risk that he wouldn't make it out of here alive. A dull ache throbbed in his side as he rose to his feet, his vision flickering at the edges. He pushed aside the thick underbrush and stepped out onto the road, the gravel crunching beneath his boots. He had no choice. If he was going to survive, he needed to get to the sign—and beyond it—before the van closed in. The game had changed, and the rules no longer applied.

"There! Dead ahead!" The excitement in John's voice sliced through the tension in the van, making everyone snap to attention. They all leaned forward, eyes glued to the front window. In the distance, Aubrey staggered across the road, his massive frame outlined against the fading light. Shay's voice was low but laced with awe. "Fuck me... I thought I was big. But that guy... he's colossal." The words hung in the air for a moment before Richard slammed his foot down on the accelerator, the engine roaring to life. The van lurched forward, the tires screeching as they picked up speed.

Evie and Shay scrambled to the back door, eyes scanning the surroundings, their muscles coiled, ready to leap out at the first sign of movement. "Where the hell did he go?" Richard muttered, easing off the gas as they reached the last spot where the man had been seen. But the road was empty, save for the fading echoes of their own tires. John furrowed his brow, peering out the window. "What's going on here? A guy that big... there's no way he just vanishes like that."

The back door swung open, and Evie, Shay, and Connor spilled out onto the pavement, scanning the area in every direction. The dog in Connor's arms whined, eager to explore this new vantage point, its eyes darting around as if it could sense the danger that lingered in the air. The three of them circled the van, eyes darting from one shadow to the next. But Aubrey was gone—no sign, no trail, nothing. It was as if he'd melted into the landscape. John followed them out, his boots hitting the ground with a soft thud. "Richard, take the keys out of the ignition, lock the doors when you get out." He slammed the door behind him with a finality that rang through the night.

John walked up to Evie; his gaze sharp, focused. "You see anything like this before?" Evie didn't answer right away. Her eyes were still darting around, her mind racing. Her gut was telling her they were on the edge of something far bigger than any of them realized. A small part of her admired the man's skill—his ability to blend into his surroundings with such precision. But the rest of her... the part of her that had seen too much, that had been haunted by too many scars—that part wanted to tear his throat out and watch him choke on his own arrogance. She shook her head, refusing to entertain the admiration. "No. I've never seen anything like this before." Her voice was cold, a fire simmering beneath the surface. "But I'll make sure I don't have to again."

***

Approaching the weathered brick building, Aubrey's breath quickened as he cast a quick glance over his shoulder. All clear. The quiet was almost deafening, broken only by the soft rustle of leaves in the wind. Without the map, he never would have found this place—perfectly concealed from the road, hidden behind thick undergrowth, with sharp thorns acting as natural guards against any would-be trespassers.

The path was narrow, barely noticeable to anyone who wasn't looking for it. As he neared the door, his eyes flicked up. The building was old, decrepit—forgotten by time, much like the dark secrets it held. Four-foot planks of weathered wood were nailed across the door, sealing it shut. He reached to his left, brushing aside the ivy that hung lazily down the side of the building. His pulse quickened when the faded sign finally came into view—Nukeville WTS. He'd made it. His objective was within reach.

Grabbing the first piece of timber, he yanked it from the door with surprising ease. The screws, long corroded by years of neglect, pulled free with a soft screech of metal against wood, and a cloud of brick dust drifted to the ground like forgotten history. He could almost taste the victory, but he couldn't afford to linger. Placing his hands on the next board, he froze. Something wasn't right. His senses screamed at him—danger. Peering over his shoulder, his heart skipped a beat. The low hum of an engine had stopped. Silence. The van. They'd stopped. Had they found the entrance? His mind raced as he scanned the darkened road, his pulse pounding in his ears. If they had tracked him here… no more running. It was all or nothing now.

Moving with a sense of urgency, Aubrey discarded the last of the wooden planks with a swift motion, his breath steady despite the adrenaline coursing through his veins. He reached for the doors round handle, turning it with precision. As the door creaked open, he shut it quickly behind him, then grabbed the other handle, pulling it sharply. The metal groaned, scraping against the frame, the sound grating as the plate flexed before snapping free. A rush of triumph surged through him—he was in.

Four figures and a small dog burst through the thorns, pushing their way through the thick underbrush, their rustling steps quickening as they drew closer. Connor cursed under his breath, glancing down at the large tear in his trousers above the knee. The dog, ever the optimist, gave him a playful lick on the cheek as if to say, don't worry, you'll be fine. Shay, always the first to charge ahead, was already leading the way, his eyes scanning the darkened entrance. "Looks like he's boxed himself in," he muttered, voice low but filled with certainty.

Evie, ever the sceptic, stepped forward with a measured look in her eyes. "Don't be so sure. This bastard's clever. He'll find a way out if he has to." They approached the building, each step cautious as they kept a keen eye on the surrounding bushes, ready for any nasty surprises. As they reached the door, Shay hesitated for just a moment, glancing back at his team before grabbing the handle. He twisted it with force, pulling—only for it to come off in his hands. John groaned in frustration. "Bloody hell, Shay! Do you not know your own strength?"

Shay, fuming with annoyance, tossed the heavy lump of metal to the ground. "Not funny, John." Evie stepped forward, unperturbed by the failure. Her fingers brushed the cold metal, feeling the contours, the age of it. "You guys got a crowbar in the van?" she asked, her voice calm, focused. This wasn't going to be easy, but she was determined to get inside—no matter the cost.

***

Aubrey moved silently through the dimly lit corridor, his footsteps echoing off the cold concrete floor. Fluorescent tubes flickered above him, casting harsh, intermittent light that only seemed to deepen the shadows. Every few steps, the oppressive silence was broken by the hum of machinery, but it did little to reassure him—each mechanical sound felt like a ticking clock, a reminder of how much time he had left.

He reached the end of the corridor, where the space opened up into a vast, industrial plant room. The air here was thick with the smell of rust and damp metal. Ducking beneath a maze of low-hanging pipes, Aubrey carefully navigated through the cluttered space. His fingers grazed the cold, slick surfaces of pipes and electrical units as he moved, the faint tremor of exhaustion creeping into his bones, but he pushed through.

The plant was a labyrinth of iron and concrete, and he knew he had to move quickly—there was no telling how long he could hide in here before they found him. At the far end of the room, he stopped in front of a massive, rusted pipe, which was bolted tightly into the brick wall. His hand hovered over the worn metal surface, feeling the years of use etched into its structure, before he pressed onward, trailing his fingers along a series of pipes, gauges, and electrical units.

This was the heart of the facility, where the river's contaminated water fed into the plant's systems. He knew the process—he had done his research. As the water flowed through, it entered the headworks of the plant, where the raw, polluted liquid would undergo treatment to become clean. Aubrey's eyes narrowed as he moved deeper into the heart of the operation, reaching the filtration tanks. He knew that these tanks, lined with layers of sand and anthracite coal, were designed to catch sediment and debris, trapping them between the cracks in the porous layers.

He continued, following the convoluted path of pipes until he reached the final stage of the filtration process—the disinfection chamber. Here, the water was treated with chlorine, the chemical used to kill bacteria and other pathogens. The sight of the huge, bubbling tank almost seemed to mock him; he too, in his current state, felt like he was caught in a kind of filtration process, a cleansing of sorts that he desperately needed but feared would never come.

Aubrey took a deep breath, eyes scanning the dimly lit room. His journey through this labyrinth had only just begun, and while the plant's isolation provided some cover, it also felt like a trap—a place where he might disappear forever, swallowed by the very system that was meant to clean the water… and, perhaps, him too.

The scrape of metal against metal echoed down the corridor, the sound unmistakable—the men tracking him were trying to pry open the door. They were close. But not close enough. He had time. Moving with calculated urgency, Aubrey turned his back on the entrance, his eyes scanning the room for anything useful. The air was thick with the stench of oil and damp concrete.

He stepped cautiously around the filtration tank, its enormous bulk looming like a silent sentinel in the gloom. His gaze followed a pipe running along the wall, disappearing into the brickwork. Perfect. His fingers brushed against some discarded pipe scraps, the dull sheen of metal catching the dim light as he sifted through them. But it wasn't what he needed. He needed something solid.

Something that could help him break into that pipe, pry it loose. His mind raced as his eyes flicked over every inch of the room.

Then he saw it.

A small metal cabinet tucked into the far corner of the room. The locking mechanism was old, rusted, but that didn't matter. Without hesitation, he strode over to it, testing the handle. Locked. A sharp sigh escaped him. He could waste time searching for the key, but that wasn't an option. His eyes narrowed as his fingers curled into a fist, balling tightly. In one swift motion, he slammed his knuckles into the metal door. The impact was enough to loosen it—just enough. He applied pressure again, and with a satisfying creak, a gap appeared between the door and the frame. Fingers slipping into the crack, he yanked hard, and the door flew open, scraping loudly across the concrete floor. Inside, clutter spilled out—a few dusty instruction manuals, a half-eaten apple core. His pulse quickened, but nothing useful. His stomach churned with frustration. Time was running out.

But then, his eyes snapped up. On top of one of the large distribution boards, partially hidden by a tangle of wires, gleamed a tool he hadn't seen before. A pipe wrench. His heart skipped a beat. This was it. His steps quickened as he moved toward the board, his mind already calculating the next move. Aubrey approached the clean water pipe, his steps deliberate, focused. The wrench felt heavy in his hands, a blunt instrument of destruction. Gripping it tightly, he swung it like a sledgehammer, bringing it down with a resounding clang that echoed through the room. The pipe shuddered under the impact, but it didn't yield. He swung again, harder this time, the metal groaning as it began to bend under the force. The third hit landed, and with a sickening creak, the pipe finally gave, splitting along its seam.

He stopped, the sound of water beginning to trickle through the newly formed gap filling the silence. It was happening. The plan was unfolding perfectly. Tossing the wrench aside, it clattered against the concrete floor, forgotten. He reached inside his jacket, his fingers brushing against the cool glass tube he'd carefully concealed. His heartbeat quickened as he pulled it out, cradling it with careful hands, as though it were something fragile. With a quick motion, he pulled the rubber stopper from the end, and the contents began to pour—slowly at first, then faster as the liquid flowed freely into the pipe.

It snaked its way through the metal, the fluid glistening in the faint light as it disappeared into the dark interior. He watched, entranced, as the last drops slipped away. The tube, now empty, bounced once on the floor before rolling down the walkway, its purpose fulfilled. Aubrey exhaled; his task complete. He didn't look back as he turned to leave, but his boot came down with a deliberate stomp, sending the glass tube smashing into a thousand sharp pieces. The sound rang out in the stillness, a final, chaotic punctuation to his work.

Exhaustion slammed into him like a freight train, his vision blurring as the weight of his own body threatened to collapse him. He staggered to the side, reaching out for the tank beside him, his breath coming in ragged gasps, his chest feeling like it was being crushed under a ton of bricks. The sharp smell of metal and oil filled his nostrils as he gripped the cold pipework, forcing himself to remain upright. His legs trembled with every step, but he was almost there—he had to make it to the door.

Outside, the chaos of raised voices and muffled curses seeped through the walls. A sliver of daylight cut through the narrow gap between the door and the frame. He barely registered it before the door slammed shut with a finality that left him feeling more trapped than ever. But this was it—he had no choice. His heart pounded in his chest as he gathered every last ounce of strength he had left. He planted his boot firmly on the ground, gritted his teeth, and kicked the door with everything he had.

The metal door shuddered violently under the force, but it swung open just enough for Shay to stumble backwards, the cold steel smashing into his head. The world tilted as he fell, knocking Richard to the ground with a resounding thud. Through the disorienting fog of pain, he heard the guards and Evie step back, cautious but alert. He looked up through the haze, seeing the faint glow of daylight as it illuminated the space just beyond the threshold. He was out. Barely standing, with blood pouring from the gaping wound in his abdomen, but still alive. Still dangerous. His feet faltered beneath him, but he straightened, a grimace pulling at his features as he clutched at the wound.

Shay could hear them, the tension thick in the air. They weren't backing down. "Pepper spray?" Evie's voice cut through the silence, incredulous. She glanced at Shay, who was gripping a small canister in his hand. "You gotta be kidding me. This guy needs a tranquilizer dart, not a tiny can of pepper spray." Shay looked down at it, momentarily embarrassed, then glared at the ground, muttering under his breath. "Sir," he said, his voice steady despite the nervous tremor in his hand, "nobody else needs to get hurt today. Please, kneel down, put your hands behind your head, and let my colleague put you in cuffs." Richard, still recovering from being knocked to the ground, shot Shay a look of disbelief. "You insane? I'm not going anywhere near him."

Shay gritted his teeth, his frustration mounting. "Connor's got his hands full, John's getting old—no offense, Sir—and I'm the only one who can stop this guy if he tries to run." His eyes flashed towards Evie. "What about her?" Richard glanced over at Evie, ready to protest, but she was already ahead of them. Without warning, she moved swiftly, positioning herself behind the wounded man. With a fluid motion, she grabbed his wrists, and before anyone could react, she nudged the back of his knee with a quick jab, sending him tumbling to the floor.

The men watched in stunned silence as Evie slapped the cuffs onto the prisoner's wrists with precise efficiency. She looked up, her eyes cold and determined. "Take this piece of shit out of my sight before I do something I'm gonna regret." Connor and Richard exchanged astonished glances, completely dumbfounded by what they had just witnessed. Shay stepped forward, his expression one of begrudging admiration. "Yes, of course," he said, his voice laced with respect. "Thank you for your help." Evie didn't acknowledge him, her gaze already fixed on the prisoner as she stepped aside, allowing the guards to take him into custody. The mission was complete—against all odds. And as they hauled Aubrey away, Evie couldn't shake the feeling that, just maybe, she'd taken the first step toward something far more dangerous than she'd bargained for.

***

The surgery was eerily quiet, save for the faint hum of the lights overhead. Ethan sat hunched behind his desk, elbows on the wood, his face buried in his hands. The events of the morning felt surreal, like something plucked from the pages of a crime thriller, too dark and twisted to be real. His mind felt like a maze of fog, every attempt to recall the details slipping through his fingers like smoke. Fragments of the chaos kept flashing, but they were disjointed, like pieces of a jigsaw puzzle scattered just out of reach.

The soft creak of the door breaking the silence made him look up, startled. Connor stood in the doorway, his expression grim, eyes betraying a trace of exhaustion. "Excuse me, Doctor. We need you to come downstairs. We've got two bodies down in the van. We need you to identify them." Ethan blinked, his head still spinning. "Two...?" His voice was hollow. "He's killed another two?" His gaze flickered instinctively to the surgery room where Shepherd's body was still under the white sheet, the man's fate sealed. The weight of it hit him in waves.

"Yes, sir," Connor confirmed, his tone tight, unyielding. "Please, follow me downstairs. We'll take them and your colleague to the Prison Mortuary afterward—just in case the mainland police need them for an autopsy or anything." Without waiting for another word, Connor turned and began to walk toward the stairs. Ethan pushed himself out of the chair, his legs unsteady as he stood. The fog in his mind cleared just enough for him to register the gravity of the situation. Another two lives lost, and the killer was still out there, somewhere, no closer to being caught. He followed Connor down the stairs, dread coiling in his gut as the reality of the day settled deeper, each step heavier than the last.

The doctor followed reluctantly, exhaling sharply as he blew hot air between his lips, trying to shake the dizziness that had settled in his head. The heavy weight of the morning's events pressed down on him, and he grasped the handrail for support, hoping the cold metal would steady him. He needed fresh air, something to clear the fog clouding his thoughts. As he pushed open the surgery door, the crisp air bit at his face, but it did little to ease the pressure building in his skull. Outside, Richard stood beside the van, holding the back doors open like a sentinel, his face unreadable. "Just in here," the guard said, his voice low.

Ethan nodded and walked around the van, his shoes scraping against the gravel. He studied Richard's stoic expression, but it gave nothing away. Stepping past the van's rear doors, Ethan's eyes fell on two large black bags resting side by side, their ominous presence filling the space with a cold dread. Richard moved forward, his hand hovering over the first zip, but then paused. "No, please, let me," Ethan said, his voice strained. Without a word, Richard stepped back, his face slightly lowered, as though acknowledging the doctor's need for control in the moment.

Ethan stood there for a moment, staring at the bags. His heart pounded. Which one should he open first? His hands trembled slightly as he reached for the right bag, pinching the zip between his thumb and forefinger. With a slow, deliberate motion, he pulled it down, revealing the body inside. The elderly man's face was serene, his features softened in a final moment of peace. His eyes were closed, lips slightly parted as though drifting off into an eternal sleep. The doctor's breath caught in his throat. "It's Mr. Postlethwaite," he murmured, his voice barely above a whisper. "Lives on the outskirts of town… alone, with his little dog."

Ethan stood frozen for a moment, the weight of the man's life—so quietly lived—crushing his chest. He turned quickly, his mouth opening, but Richard anticipated the question before it left his lips. "The little fella's okay," Richard said, his tone softer now. "One of the guards took him home, safe and sound. He'll be looked after until this whole thing gets sorted out." Ethan nodded gratefully, the sting of relief briefly easing his tension. He zipped the first bag back up with careful precision, taking a deep breath. But when he reached for the second zip, his hand faltered, the blood draining from his face. He pulled it down slowly, his eyes already bracing for the inevitable.

And there, staring back at him with that familiar, haunting face, was Harley. The back of the van seemed to tilt as everything in his mind went still. Harley. The man who had been an enigma, the love his life, someone caught in the web of this terrible, relentless game.

But now… now he was nothing more than another body to be catalogued. Another victim in this twisted cycle. The realization hit like a punch to the gut, and for a moment, Ethan was paralyzed, the weight of the two deaths crashing into him.

Chapter 29
16:53 hours, August 6th 2024,
HMP Nukville, Nukeville Island

The cramped cell was a fortress of concrete, its walls unyielding, its air thick with solitude. A small, reinforced steel window—a solitary eye to the outside world—stood as the only defiance against total isolation. Aubrey, Prisoner Zero-Three-Zero-One sat motionless, his back pressed against the cold, unrelenting surface of the wall. Through the narrow bars, a golden haze of sunlight poured in, casting jagged stripes of light that stretched across the room like the grasping fingers of a distant hope. The light painted the barren walls with fleeting life, breaking the monotony of grey. Particles of dust swirled in the golden glow, pirouetting to a soundless rhythm, their brilliance fleeting as they glimmered in the final rays of the setting sun. A faint draft crept beneath the heavy iron door, a whisper of freedom that teased his senses, carrying the faintest trace of a world beyond. In the oppressive silence, even the smallest details—the shifting light, the dancing dust—became mesmerizing, a quiet rebellion against the suffocating stillness.

The sharp clang of the metal panel echoed through the cell as it slid open, revealing the watchful eyes of a guard. They lingered on the prisoner, scanning him with a mix of suspicion and curiosity, before sweeping the dim room for anything out of place. Then, with a metallic snap, the panel slammed shut, leaving the prisoner alone once more. He listened as the heavy thuds of boots receded along the metal gangway, each step reverberating like a countdown to solitude.

Seated on the edge of his cot, he moved deliberately, his right hand reaching forward with measured precision to avoid jarring his bandaged left shoulder. Each movement was an exercise in restraint, pain flaring like a warning beneath the taut layers of gauze. His fingers found his knee, kneading the joint as a dull ache radiated upward, mingling with the sharper pangs in his abdomen. The memory of the prison doctor's hands flitted through his mind—deft, clinical, yet undeniably human.

She had worked methodically, cutting away ragged tissue, probing for internal damage, stitching his flesh back together with a mix of skill and urgency. The transfusion had been a gamble, but it paid off. She'd voiced her amazement at his recovery, the way strength returned to him at an almost unnatural pace. Most inmates dragged themselves from her infirmary like shadows of their former selves, but not him. His resilience was a silent rebellion, an unspoken defiance against a system designed to break him. Still, the scars remained, physical and otherwise, each one a marker of survival in a place that seemed intent on erasing every trace of humanity.

Fixing his gaze on the peeling paint flaking from the wall, he focused intently, strands of unkempt hair brushing against his vision. A small crack caught his eye—a jagged line about three inches long, snaking across the concrete like a scar on the cell's impenetrable face. It was nothing remarkable, but in the suffocating monotony of this place, even a crack seemed worthy of study.

Flexing his arm, he winced as the bones in his shoulder shifted and cracked back into place, the discomfort a familiar companion. He eased himself down onto the thin pillow, its softness barely a comfort against the unyielding cot. From somewhere beyond his cell, voices rose—muffled, unintelligible words that carried the unmistakable edge of hostility. It was a heated exchange, the kind that simmered just beneath boiling point.

Then came the loud metallic clang. Someone—Theo Boggs, Prisoner Zero-Six-Two-Nine—was kicking his cell door with wild abandon. The sound reverberated through the North Wing like a hammer on steel, setting nerves on edge. "Shut the fuck up, Boggs!" the man in the next cell barked, jolted awake by the racket. His shout carried raw irritation, the kind born from sleepless nights and frayed patience.

Another voice, gruff and laced with menace, chimed in from the left. "Hey, Boggs! Keep it up, and I'll gut you like a pig!" The noise swelled into a cacophony as prisoners across the wing joined the chorus, some hurling threats, others curses, all aimed at silencing Boggs. But the instigator only laughed, a low, mocking chuckle that rose with each stomp of his boot. He relished the chaos, feeding off the frustration of his fellow inmates like a predator toying with prey. The clangs and shouts echoed in a brutal symphony of defiance and desperation, a nightly ritual in the North Wing of this fortress of concrete and iron.

A sharp whistle pierced the air, slicing through the cacophony like a blade. Then came another, shrill and commanding, silencing all but the boldest inmates who still hurled venomous threats at Theo Boggs. The tension thickened, a tangible weight pressing down on the North Wing as the echo of the whistle faded into the concrete void. He turned his head slowly, letting it rest against the thin pillow, savouring its meagre comfort. His eyes drifted to the ceiling, its pitted surface a canvas for fleeting thoughts. Beneath the muffled din, he began to count—one, two, three... steel-toed boots thundered up the metal staircase.

Six guards, their movements synchronized and purposeful, charged past his cell. The vibrations rattled the flimsy frame of his cot, a reminder of the force behind the echoing clamour. They came to an abrupt halt twenty feet down the gangway. His ears perked up as a familiar voice barked out, sharp and authoritative, slicing through the remaining noise like a whip. "Prisoner Zero-Six-Two-Nine, step away from the door."

Recognition flared. That voice belonged to him, the big guard. The one who had pinned him to the ground outside the Water Treatment Station just after that fucking lady slapped on the cuffs, his sheer size and efficiency a brutal display of authority. The memory of that encounter played in the background of his mind, vivid and inescapable. For a moment, the air grew taut with anticipation. The prisoners held their collective breath, the quiet crackling with unspoken tension, waiting for the next move in this volatile standoff.

Keys jangled in a deliberate, metallic symphony as the lock clicked open. The voice of Prisoner Zero-Six-Two-Nine—Theo Boggs—rose in a shrill, panicked pitch. "Get away from me! Don't touch me!" His defiance cracked under the weight of fear, his words trembling as Shay, the lead guard, stepped into the cell flanked by five others. A high-pitched scream tore from Boggs's throat, sharp enough to make several inmates burst into laughter, their jeers echoing down the corridor. The guards moved with precision, cuffing him with practiced ease despite his futile resistance. His feet dragged against the floor as they hauled him from the cell, his pleas growing more frantic with every step.

The door slammed shut behind them, reverberating through the gangway. "Get your dirty hands off me!" Boggs screeched, his voice breaking. "You hear me? No… no, I'm sorry! I'll be quiet, I swear… honest… please… hang on, where are you taking me?" The guards ignored his desperate questions, their boots pounding in unison as they marched him toward the North Wing access gate. Boggs stumbled, half-carried, half-dragged, his panic snowballing into incoherent cries. The piercing buzz of the security gate sounded, and the heavy doors slid open with an ominous groan.

As they passed through, Boggs's voice reached a fever pitch, echoing back to the silent inmates like a warning from the damned. "No… not in there! Please! PLLLEEAAASSEEEE!" A loud hiss followed—the unsettling sound of pneumatic doors sealing shut. Then, nothing. Silence descended over the North Wing, heavy and oppressive. In the cells, the inmates listened to the void where Boggs's cries had been, the absence of sound more chilling than the screams that preceded it.

✳✳✳

The sharp trill of the phone shattered the quiet, making DCI Craig jolt in his chair. He had been gazing out the window, lost in the vivid replay of that fateful confrontation with Aubrey Brian Strawberry. The memory lingered like a phantom, the flash of the blade forever etched into his mind, a cruel reminder of how close he had come to death. His breath hitched, a flicker of unease tightening his chest as he reached for the receiver. "DCI Craig," he said, his voice steadier than he felt. The response was immediate, clipped, and to the point. "Stephen, it's Commander Wardley. I'll keep this brief.

The convict, Aubrey Brian Strawberry, has been apprehended and incarcerated. Life, no parole." The DCI's grip on the receiver tightened, his pulse quickening. "Where?" he interjected before the Commander could hang up. The pause that followed was long, heavy with something unsaid. The DCI knew the line hadn't disconnected—there was no dial tone. He could almost hear Wardley weighing his words. Finally, a weary sigh came through the line.

"Nukeville," Wardley said. "It's a state-of-the-art Category A prison." The DCI leaned back, the name sending a chill down his spine. Nukeville wasn't just a prison—it was a fortress. Few ever spoke of it, and even fewer truly understood the kind of people sent there. Wardley continued, his tone turning formal, almost rehearsed. "Look, Stephen, the severity and nature of Aubrey's crimes demanded this decision.

Violent, high-risk offenders like him can't be held anywhere else. Nukeville is designed to neutralize any threat to society and eliminate any risk of escape. This isn't about punishment—it's about prevention." The DCI's jaw tightened, his thoughts a tangled web of relief and unease. Aubrey was behind bars, but Nukeville wasn't a place you simply disappeared into.

The DCI paused, his thoughts racing as he considered his next words. Finally, he spoke, his tone measured but firm. "I understand, Commander, but let's not forget—he escaped from Wormwood, didn't he? What makes you so sure he won't pull it off again?" The response came swiftly, sharp as a whip. "Listen, Stephen," Wardley snapped, the irritation in his voice unmistakable. "Wormwood is over a hundred and fifty years old. Its security was outdated, riddled with blind spots and inefficiencies. Nukeville is an entirely different beast. It's state-of-the-art, built to withstand the kind of resourcefulness someone like Aubrey might throw at it. And let's face it—we don't need a man like him lingering on the doorstep of the capital. He's better off in a place with limited resources, a smaller population, and no chance to cause the kind of havoc he's capable of. Wouldn't you agree?"

The DCI opened his mouth to reply, but Wardley cut him off. "And frankly, I don't think Aubrey will be going anywhere anytime soon." The line went dead with a sharp click, the dial tone buzzing in the DCI's ear. Slowly, he set the handset back in its cradle, his hand lingering for a moment as if the connection might suddenly return. Leaning back in his worn leather chair, he exhaled deeply, the Commander's words echoing in his mind. Nukeville. The name hung in the air like a storm cloud, foreboding and unrelenting. The DCI reached for his glasses on the desk, twirling the temple between his fingers as his thoughts swirled. The logic was sound, but something gnawed at him, a quiet unease he couldn't quite shake. Aubrey Strawberry was no ordinary convict, and Nukeville…

He sighed, staring out at the gathering dusk. Even fortresses can fall.

A soft knock on the office door broke through the DCI's thoughts. He glanced up, his pen frozen mid-note. "Yes?" The door creaked open to reveal a young detective, his face pale but his tone steady. "Sir, you're needed in the briefing room. The DS wants to address the team." The DCI nodded, quickly gathering his notepad and pen. He paused as the detective started to leave. "Louis," he called, "any idea what this is about?"

The detective stopped, hesitating before turning back to glance over his shoulder. "They've found two heads." The DCI straightened, the weight of those words sinking in. He followed Louis into the hallway, his mind already racing. "Two heads? What kind of heads?" Louis kept walking; his voice low but grim. "Well, Sir… it's just that. Two female heads, thought to be in their twenties, possibly related. No torso, no limbs—just the heads, found at a Service Station off the M11."

The DCI's steps slowed for a fraction of a second as he thought about Aubrey, but then quickened his pace, catching up to the younger Officer. The corridor stretched before them, each step echoing in the oppressive quiet. "A severed head," The DCI muttered to himself, more a statement than a question. "Alright, so we're obviously looking at a double murder. Strange, though—the DS doesn't usually pull us in for something like this."

They reached the lift, and Louis pressed the button, his expression unreadable. The faint hum of the approaching elevator filled the air as they waited. "I thought the same thing, Sir," Louis admitted. "But this one… feels different. The DS didn't say much, but I reckon there's something about this case we're not seeing yet." The DCI's gaze sharpened, his instincts kicking into high gear. The lift doors opened with a sterile ding, and as they stepped inside, he couldn't shake the feeling that this wasn't just another murder. Something about the unease in Louis's voice, the peculiar assignment of the case—it all pointed to one thing: this was no ordinary crime.

The lift doors slid open with a muted chime, and both men stepped inside. The atmosphere was heavy, the kind of silence that begged to be filled. They waited for the doors to close, and as soon as they did, Louis leaned closer, his voice low and cautious. "Sir, this isn't the first case. Turns out, there've been several heads found across the country—in random locations. No bodies, no evidence left behind... nothing." The DCI frowned, the detective's words tugging at his mind like an itch he couldn't reach. "That's... strange," he said slowly, his tone edged with intrigue.

The lift chimed again, signalling their descent. As the doors began to part, Louis caught the DCI's arm, halting him mid-step. His grip was firm, his expression uncharacteristically serious. "That's not the strange part, Sir," Louis said, lowering his voice even further. "The thing is… every head has a red nose." The DCI froze, his foot hovering between the lift and the corridor. The doors started to close, but he thrust out a hand to stop them, his fingers splayed against the cold metal. "Wait. A red nose? What the hell are you talking about? Is this some kind of sick prank?" Louis's face tightened, a flush creeping up his neck as he realized how absurd it sounded. "No joke, Sir. I've seen the photos myself. I was in the briefing room while they were setting up. Each head—every single one—has a clown's nose. You know, right where the person's nose should be."

The DCI stood frozen for a moment, the image forming in his mind—a severed head, lifeless and grotesque, adorned with the kind of garish red nose you'd find in a joke shop. It was macabre, surreal, and profoundly unsettling. He let out a slow breath as the doors, once again, began to slide shut. "A clown's nose..." he muttered, half to himself. "Jesus Christ. What kind of maniac are we dealing with?" The lift continued its descent, carrying them toward a case that was spiralling into the bizarre—a grotesque puzzle of severed heads and unsettling theatrics. And somewhere out there, the DCI thought grimly, was someone who wanted them to play along.

✳✳✳

22:32 hours, 6th April 2020,
Cockfosters,
London

Entering the pitch-black kitchen, Aubrey shut his eyes tightly, his mind racing as he counted slowly to sixty, savouring the calm before the storm. The seconds ticked by, each one stretching, until finally, he peeled his eyelids apart. The transformation was immediate. His vision, once consumed by darkness, had adjusted, revealing the faint outlines of the kitchen's surfaces and equipment. Most importantly, the door on the opposite side of the room now stood clear, a beacon of his next step.

He moved with purpose, gliding past the cold gleam of the stainless-steel counters, his gloved fingers lightly brushing the edges of the work surfaces as he made his way toward the door. His heart raced as he reached for the handle, the metal cool and solid under his touch. He pulled it open, the sound of the latch clicking loud in the stillness of the room.

Crossing the threshold, he entered a vast, dimly lit space. A bar loomed at the far end, its roller shutter door drawn down tightly, a thick padlock securing it with a finality that sent a shiver down his spine. Along the outer wall, three tall cabinets stood, filled with faded trophies, and framed photographs—reminders of a bygone era, a team that had once dominated. The air seemed to hum with the weight of history, but his attention was elsewhere. His gaze

drifted toward a cabinet near the entrance, its wood a dark contrast against the sterile grey of the walls.

The floor groaned under his feet as he approached, each step echoing in the quiet room like a warning. He reached out and pulled the cabinet doors open. Inside, two shelves of carefully arranged ceramic plates gleamed softly in the dim light. But it was not the delicate plates that caught his eye. No, it was the battered old batsman's helmet, resting on the bottom shelf—its surface worn, its purpose clear. This was no ordinary relic; it was a key, a clue, something that told him he was getting closer to what he had come for.

He glanced at his watch, the seconds slipping away like sand through his fingers. The pressure was mounting, and he could feel it in his bones. Time was slipping through his grasp. Spinning on his heel, he surveyed the space, eyes locking onto three doors at the far end of the building. His instincts kicked in—he did not have the luxury of hesitation anymore. Without another thought, he dashed across the carpeted floor, the soft thud of his boots barely audible over the pounding of his heart. Reaching the nearest door, he threw it open. The damp, musty air hit him like a slap, thick and heavy with the scent of age. He stepped inside, eyes immediately scanning every inch of the room.

The space was a relic—timber beams crisscrossed the ceiling, the walls a mix of worn wood and peeling paint. The floor beneath his boots creaked under each step as he moved deeper. Along one side of the room, benches lined the walls, their surfaces covered in the dust of neglect. At the far end, two old cubicles stood, their shower heads rusty and abandoned, dripping faintly as though they too had been forgotten. But something else caught his eye—a small chest, tucked away in the corner, half-hidden in shadow. A sudden rush of hope flared within him. He strode over, urgency in every step. His hands, large and rough, worked quickly, undoing the latch with a swift flick.

The lid creaked open, revealing a jumble of dirty, crumpled clothes inside. He shoved them aside, his fingers brushing against the cold, wooden bottom of the chest. Nothing. The chest was empty—no hidden compartments, no secret stash, just the weight of disappointment settling in his chest like lead. Frustration simmered beneath his calm exterior, but there was no time to waste. He slammed the lid shut, eyes darting to the next door. There was still more to uncover, and the clock was ticking faster than ever.

He slammed the chest lid back into place, his mind already racing. The faint rumble of a car engine reached his ears, growing louder by the second. He froze, instinctively checking his watch again. A couple more minutes. That was all he had before they arrived and collected the package. His pulse quickened—this was it. The final window to make his move, to steal the briefcase and its invaluable contents. After this, it would be locked away, its secrets left to gather dust until the military decided it was time to unlock them. He could not let that happen. Without wasting a moment, he spun on his heel and bolted out of the changing room, his footsteps muffled on the carpeted floor as he ran. The seconds bled together in a blur, every instinct screaming at him to move faster. Reaching the next door in the middle, he yanked it open, his heart pounding in his chest.

Inside, the room was a forgotten archive of sporting gear—old pads, dusty cricket bats leaning haphazardly against the walls, a basket piled high with crumpled balls, and stacks of plastic chairs that looked like they had not been touched in years. The space was empty, except for the clutter, but his eyes quickly scanned every inch, searching for the briefcase. The car engine had stopped, the unmistakable sound of doors slamming shut echoing through the building. They were here. He froze, his breath shallow, his nerves taut as piano wires. The minutes had evaporated into mere seconds. His heart raced as he weighed his options—he could not afford to abandon this chance, but neither could he risk leaving empty-handed. The room seemed to close in around him, the air thick with tension. Every second felt like an eternity.

He did not have the luxury of time to explore the storeroom. It was now or never. With a quick glance over his shoulder, he closed the door softly, his eyes locking onto two dark silhouettes moving outside the entrance. His pulse quickened as they approached, their footsteps unmistakable. The clink of a key, followed by the faint creak of the door opening, echoed through the silence. The men stepped inside. And just like that, the toilet door clicked shut, sealing him in. In an instant, his trained mind went into overdrive, scanning the room with surgical precision. He could not afford a mistake. Within a few seconds, his eyes darted to an escape route. The briefcase was not in sight—his heart sank—but he could hear the two men talking, their voices muffled yet distinct.

"And this contains what?" "You don't have clearance," the second voice replied, cold and clipped. "You know the rules. Collect the package. Take it to the Commander. That's it. Simple." A tense silence followed. He held his breath. His muscles tensed, the pressure of the situation gnawing at him, but his focus never wavered.

He shifted his weight, eyes flicking up to the window above the toilet—a narrow four-foot gap, barely big enough for him to squeeze through. His frame was bulky, his movements calculated, but even for him, this was going to be a tight fit. The sound of their voices drifted closer, filling his ears with the urgency of their conversation. Without another moment's hesitation, he placed a foot on the toilet seat. His body was already moving into position, a fluid motion, the weight of the moment hanging heavy. The window beckoned, offering his only escape. He could feel the men's presence growing nearer, their footsteps closing in. Now or never. He had to move.

The silence in the room became deafening as he pulled himself up, every muscle straining against the tight confines of the window frame. His heart thudded in his chest, but he wasn't about to leave empty-handed—not this time. With one last glance at the door, he made his decision. The time to escape was now. "Where did he say he would leave it?" "Err… in the toilet, I think," Aubrey frowned, his foot kicking against the wooden ledge above the toilet. The panel creaked under his weight, shifting slightly. Instinctively, he yanked it aside. His fingers brushed the cool metal of the hidden compartment, and with a swift motion, he pulled out the briefcase from its secret resting place. "Hey, wanna grab a drink before we go?" The second man barely glanced up, distracted.

His eyes were already on the briefcase, his thoughts clearly elsewhere. He nodded, though, as Aubrey placed the case down on the floor, flipping it over. But then, a strange sensation ran through him as he noticed the four dials on the front of the briefcase, each set to zero. His brow furrowed. A combination lock? Aubrey didn't waste time. His fingers moved quickly, scrolling through the dials with practiced ease. The first dial clicked into place at eight. The next two settled on zero, then the last one also clicked to eight. A satisfying click echoed through the room as he pulled on the latches. The briefcase opened with a soft hiss. "Bring that with you," the first man said, his voice low, a grin creeping across his face. "Let's grab the package and get the hell out of here."

Meanwhile, outside, the air was thick with tension. Landing softly in the mud below, the man's boots sank into the ground. He reached up, pushing the window closed with a careful shove. Without a moment's hesitation, he turned and sprinted for the metal gate. His feet pounded against the earth, his mind already racing ahead. He needed to disappear before the storm hit. Inside the pavilion, the door to the toilet opened with a groan. One of the men, a tall figure with a thick neck, stepped forward, the sound of a smooth beer pouring into his mouth echoing in the quiet. "You grab the package, I've got my hands full," he slurred slightly, wiping his mouth with the back of his hand.

The other man, steady and focused, walked over to the toilet. He didn't pause. He lifted the wooden panel, and reached inside. His hand brushed against the cold metal of the briefcase, his grip firm as he pulled it free. He flipped it over, inspecting the lock with a sharp eye. "All good," he muttered, nodding in approval. "Let's go." And just like that, the tension hung thick in the air as the men turned to leave. But outside, everything was already changing. The game had shifted. And no one would be walking away with the prize so easily.

Aubrey sprinted through the night, the darkness swallowing him whole as he headed toward the distant bridge. A faint hum filled the air as a red and white train rumbled along the tracks, sparks crackling from the rails as it crossed the bridge. For a heartbeat, the train illuminated the world around him, a fleeting snapshot of reality before it vanished into the black mouth of a tunnel. He slowed, instinctively dropping to a crouch as he slid beneath the iron struts of the bridge, disappearing into the shadows.

The dim light from above barely touched the ground, casting long, jagged shadows across the waste ground. Graffiti-covered brickwork loomed like a silent witness to his every movement. He leaned against the wall, the grime of the old city clinging to his back. Discarded cardboard, cans, and a lone shopping trolley lay scattered around him—detritus from a world that had forgotten this corner of the city. But he didn't care. He didn't need the world to remember him; he just needed to survive the night.

A rat scurried past, weaving through the soiled clothing and under a rusted bicycle frame. He didn't flinch, his gaze never wavering as he studied the clear liquid within the small tube in his hand. He pulled it from his jacket pocket, the rubber stopper still in place, and held it up to the flickering streetlight overhead. The faint glow illuminated the liquid inside—perfectly clear, but deadly. He turned the tube over between his fingers, his eyes narrowing at the bold black text scrawled across the white label: X-75.

A smile tugged at the corner of his lips. This was it—the weapon. The thing he had fought for, bled for. He was holding power in the palm of his hand, the key to completing the rest of his plan. With a final glance toward the dark alleyway, he slid the tube into a concealed pocket inside his jacket. His heart was still racing, but now with a different kind of excitement. He pulled his hands into his pockets, his fingers curling around the cool metal of a hidden gun, then straightened up and began walking north. His path was set, and nothing would stop him. The clock continued to tick.

✳✳✳

19:01 hours, 6th August 2024,
North Nukeville Island

His eyes glazed over as a feverish warmth spread through his veins, a heat that felt as though it were tearing through his body from the inside out. His skin burned beneath the layers of sweat that soaked him through, the oppressive weight of the blanket pressing down on him like a leaden shroud. He tried to kick it off with his feet, but his strength was waning, the effort leaving him weak and trembling. The mattress beneath him seemed to absorb every drop of moisture from his body, turning soft and sponge-like under the onslaught. His chest rose and fell with shallow, laboured breaths, and his entire body felt as though it were trapped in a slow, suffocating fire.

The farmhouse was eerily still, the only sound breaking the silence being the cheerful, carefree songs of birds outside his window, oblivious to the torment inside. Tom Harris could barely remember when the women had left the house; it felt like an eternity ago, as if time itself had stretched and fractured in his delirium. His throat felt like sandpaper, dry and painful, and he craved a drink more than anything. His mind felt foggy, as if he were drifting between states of wakefulness and sleep, a haze that clouded his thoughts.

With great effort, he rolled onto his side, his body shaking as though his bones had turned to glass. He tried to push himself up onto his elbow, but the motion was too much. His muscles screamed in protest; his strength utterly depleted. His body betrayed him, slumping back onto the wet sheets, his breath coming out in an agonized rasp. "C'mon, man," he whispered hoarsely to himself, his voice barely a croak in the vast silence of the room. The words were empty, an appeal to some inner strength he no longer had.

His vision was a blur, the world around him spinning in a slow, disorienting whirl. He turned his head on the pillow, trying to make sense of the disjointed shapes around him. Through the fog, he spotted his torn shirt, draped over the back of a wooden chair near the window, its faded fabric barely clinging to the frame. His trousers were discarded on the floor, next to his shoes, a mess of discarded clothing that seemed almost foreign to him. The remnants of whatever had transpired here—the things he could not quite piece together—lay around him like a puzzle he could not solve. He closed his eyes, hoping the darkness would bring him some clarity, but it offered no relief.

Craning his neck, Tom's bleary eyes locked onto a glass resting on a small bedside cabinet. It was empty, the remnants of whatever fleeting relief it had once offered long gone. He tried to speak, to ask for help, but his throat felt like it was lined with jagged stones, raw and painful. The effort left him gasping, a sound that could barely be called a word, just a hoarse, rasping groan that escaped his dry lips. His mind, clouded by fever, struggled to focus on anything beyond the burning ache in his chest and the parched dryness in his throat.

The sound of the bedroom door creaked open, breaking the stillness. Evie entered, her presence almost like a cool breeze in the suffocating heat of the room. Tom blinked, trying to clear his blurry vision as she walked toward him, noticing a small cut on her lip and some bruising on her cheek. She froze, her expression softening with concern as she saw him attempt to move. "Hey, Tom, no… please… stay there, don't get up," she urged gently, her voice a soothing balm against the harshness of his discomfort.

He watched, barely able to move, as she approached the chair by the window. She picked up his torn shirt and placed it carefully on the bed frame, the fabric crinkling as it settled. Then, with a steady, deliberate motion, she dragged the chair gently across the carpet and positioning herself beside him on the bed. The softness of her movements seemed almost too graceful in contrast to his own disarrayed state.

Evie's warm hands, soft and steady, cupped the back of his head, and for a brief, dizzying moment, Tom felt a strange comfort in the contact. She lifted his head with surprising ease, the strength in her hands tender but unwavering. Without a word, she slipped a straw between his cracked lips, guiding it gently toward his mouth. "Here, you need to stay hydrated," she said softly, her tone unhurried, as though she were in no rush, as though time could slow down just for him.

The cool touch of the water against his parched mouth was a small but much-needed relief. He instinctively began to suck on the straw, the water trickling slowly, almost painfully, down his throat. Each sip felt like a tiny victory, but it was not enough to drown out the burn in his chest, the persistent heat that seemed to consume him from the inside. After only a few sips, the weight of his exhaustion returned, and his body slumped back onto the pillow, his eyelids fluttering with the pull of unconsciousness. Evie remained by his side, watching him with a quiet, unwavering concern. She did not speak, not needing to. Her presence was enough—calm and steady, a soothing anchor during the storm that raged within him. As he drifted in and out of awareness, he could sense her there, her soft breath and warm touch a reminder that, for whatever reason, he was not alone in this.

"I'll leave this glass here, hang on, let's get this closer... make things a little easier for you," Evie's voice broke through the haze of Tom's fevered mind. He heard the soft scrape of the bedside cabinet as she dragged it closer, the sound sending an odd shiver through him. It was not the scraping that caught his attention, though—it was the way her hands worked with purpose, as though she'd done this a thousand times before, though he was certain she hadn't. She set the full glass carefully on the cabinet top, the faint clink of the glass a signal that, in some small way, things were going to get better, at least for now. With a swift, smooth motion, she removed the empty one and placed it on the side. Then, without another word, she stood up, her presence lingering in the air, her gaze never straying too far from him.

"Look, I can try and help you," she began, her voice gentle yet firm, "but sooner or later, you're going to need to talk. I have a lot of questions. I'm going to ask a couple now. I don't expect you to answer right away, but I would like you to think about them. And when your health returns, when you're feeling better, you'll be able to tell me freely, without feeling like you're being interrogated. Is that okay?" Tom could barely keep his eyes open, the exhaustion pulling him under, but he still managed a weak nod, the faintest acknowledgment that he heard her. The words didn't quite register fully in his foggy brain, but the kindness in her tone reached him, the way she was speaking to him, not as a patient, but as a person, gave him a shred of comfort. He let his eyes slip closed, the dark softness of his eyelids inviting him into the quiet refuge of sleep.

But just as he was drifting off, a light smack on his cheek brought him back. It wasn't harsh, but firm enough to jolt him from his stupor. He blinked rapidly, trying to refocus on the room around him. Evie's face was there, close to his, her eyes bright with a strange mix of patience and resolve. "Hey, not yet, love," she said, her tone soft but teasing, like she was reminding him of something important, something he could not afford to forget. "Questions first, then you can rest."

Tom swallowed hard, the dryness in his throat making each movement feel like an effort. He wanted to close his eyes, to let the quiet lull him back to sleep, but Evie's words kept him tethered to the moment. He heard her settling in beside him, her presence a steady, grounding force, and felt the weight of her attention on him as she waited for his response. He was not sure he was ready to answer—hell, he was not sure he could—but the way she spoke, like she truly cared about the answers, made him feel like he owed her something.

Taking a slow breath, he nodded again, the motion slower this time, as if he were gathering the strength to hold on to the moment. Her hands were still warm at his side, her soft fingers brushing his arm, a reminder that he wasn't alone, not entirely. And for some reason, that thought, however fragile, gave him a small sense of security. Maybe he could answer her later, when he was stronger. Maybe the questions would help him find his way back, back to whatever had led him here, and maybe, just maybe, he would be able to piece the story together when the time was right. But for now, he stayed still, his eyes half-closed, waiting for the next question, hoping that the darkness could wait just a little longer.

She stood suddenly, her mind racing as she tried to prioritize the questions that gnawed at her. Every moment counted now. It was imperative that she understood who Tom Harris truly was—where he had come from, what kind of man he was, and, most pressing of all, why she had found him washed up on the shore, like some forgotten wreckage from a storm. Her instincts screamed at her to dig deeper, to uncover the layers of mystery surrounding him. But as she paced the room, her thoughts were interrupted by the questions that had been clawing at her since she first laid eyes on him.

The last few hours in town had unsettled her more than she cared to admit. She had tried to push it aside, to tell herself it was nothing more than coincidence, but something didn't sit right. The frantic news reports, the whispers in the streets, the rumours of a hulking, Aubrey who had gone on a violent rampage, leaving three dead in his wake… It felt like the world had shifted beneath her feet. The man they described was the same man she faced in the surgery, and her mind kept circling back to Tom. Was he somehow connected to this carnage? Was he in any way involved with the brutal spree, or had she simply stumbled upon an unfortunate soul who had become caught in the wake of someone else's madness?

She paused, her thoughts swirling like a storm. The stark possibility that Tom might have a darker past was like a cold hand wrapped around her chest, tightening with each breath. It wasn't just the physical condition he was in—feverish, broken, barely conscious—that made her uneasy. It was the way his eyes had flickered when she first spoke to him, the fleeting glint of recognition, or perhaps guilt, before he collapsed again into his dazed stupor. She couldn't ignore it. The chance that this man, the one she was now trying to save, might be connected to a senseless massacre was too great to dismiss.

Her fingers tightened into fists at her sides as she tried to ground herself in the reality of the situation. She needed answers, real answers, and she needed them fast. Tom Harris might be on the verge of death, but the truth about him—about what had happened to him, and what role he might have played—could mean the difference between saving him or condemning him. She couldn't afford to be wrong. Not when everything was hanging by a thread, and the weight of the past few hours felt like a heavy fog, pressing in from all sides.

Placing her hands on her hips, Evie took a long, steadying breath. The air in the room felt thick, heavy with the weight of unspoken questions, and she knew she had to start somewhere, even if it meant diving straight into the heart of the storm. "OK," she said, her voice firm but laced with an underlying edge of urgency. "Let's start off with the big one first. I'm aware your name is Tom Harris, but why are you on this island?" She watched him closely, studying the sharp lines of his face, the way his brow furrowed slightly, the faint flicker of recognition in his eyes as he tried to focus on her. He seemed to understand her words, even though they were sharp, even though the question hung heavy in the room. She didn't wait for him to answer—she couldn't afford to.

"Good," she continued, her gaze unwavering as she leaned forward slightly. "You know what I'm talking about. Next question:

where are you from? And I'm not asking about your place of birth—who do you work for?" His eyes flickered, a subtle movement that might have been an attempt to focus, but it didn't last. The effort left him shaking, a fresh wave of pain sweeping through him, more intense than anything he'd felt in the last twenty-four hours. A burning, foreign sensation surged through his veins, unfamiliar and almost terrifying. His chest tightened as the room spun, his vision blurring at the edges. He fought it, tried to push through the wave of darkness threatening to swallow him, but it was like trying to hold back a tide with bare hands.

Tom's body trembled, his head falling back against the pillow as the strength drained from him. His eyelids fluttered, and despite his best efforts, he could feel himself slipping away. The questions, her voice, everything around him faded into a distant, indistinct haze. He tried to cling to consciousness, but the pull of sleep was irresistible, and soon he succumbed to the darkness that engulfed him. Evie stood still for a moment, her eyes narrowing as she watched him drift off. Her heart sank. "Shit," she muttered under her breath, frustration and concern mixing in the harsh whisper. The answers she desperately needed were slipping away, just as he was, and she couldn't let that happen—not now.

Turning sharply, she headed for the door, her mind already moving ahead to the task that needed to be done. There was no time to waste. She grabbed her boots, the thick leather soles echoing in the silence of the room, and slipped them on quickly, the weight of urgency pressing against her chest. She needed to act fast—before it was too late.

She stepped outside, the warm sunlight from the setting sun immediately embracing her as the door swung open. The island was quiet, save for the gentle rustle of leaves in the breeze. She didn't pause to savour the calm; her steps were quick, purposeful, as she made her way down the hill towards the meadow below. The tall grasses swayed in the wind, but Evie's focus was razor-sharp. She had no choice but to complete the task she'd set her mind to. Time was running out, and she couldn't afford to fail now—not with so much hanging in the balance.

***

Six hours later Tom's eyelids flickered open, the dim light filtering through the edges of the room as he slowly regained consciousness. He could feel the softness of the sheets beneath him, the coolness of the air against his skin, but there was something different now—something new—coursing through his body. The pain that had once consumed him was gone, replaced by an unfamiliar energy, a sharp, pulsing strength that made his muscles hum. It was as if his body had shed its previous weakness and was now ready to embrace something far more primal.

He threw back the covers with an abrupt motion, the fabric sliding off his body as he swung his legs over the side of the bed. His feet hit the carpet with a soft thud, but the moment he stood, the change within him was undeniable. His body convulsed, a violent jolt running through him as his bones cracked and snapped into place. The muscles in his arms and legs flexed involuntarily, taut with a new, raw power. A deep, almost euphoric rush flooded his veins, like he had been reborn in some way, and he stood there for a moment, letting the sensation wash over him. For the first time in what felt like forever, Tom felt great—strong, alive, unstoppable.

He didn't hesitate. The door was ajar, and without a second thought, he strode toward it. The cottage was still shrouded in darkness, the air thick with the quiet of the night. But Tom's vision, sharp and clear, made the shadows seem as if they were nothing more than a fleeting detail. He could see everything—the faint outlines of furniture, the dust particles suspended in the air, the way the moonlight spilled softly through the window. There were no obstacles, no confusion. The world was laid out before him, and he was ready to move through it with purpose.

His stomach growled, a deep, hunger that echoed through his chest. The ache in his gut was almost painful, insistent. He needed food, now. His feet moved with urgency, carrying him across the floor and into the kitchen. The room was as still as the rest of the house, with the wooden table, the sink, and the refrigerator all in their usual places. But Tom didn't pause to look closely at the details. His focus was on the narrow hallway leading to the back of the property, a space that seemed to draw him in. There was something calling him from beyond that threshold.

As he passed the small vase on the edge of a shelf, his hand brushed against it, sending it tumbling to the floor. The sound of it crashing onto the wooden floor was deafening in the stillness, a sharp smash that reverberated through the cottage. But Tom didn't even flinch. He didn't care. His mind was locked on one thing: movement. The shards of broken porcelain scattered across the floor, but he paid them no attention as he stepped forward, his bare feet landing on the jagged pieces with a sickening crunch. A sharp pain shot through his foot, but it didn't slow him down. If anything, it only fuelled the sensation inside him—the dark hunger, the need to move, to tear through the world around him.

Each step he took left behind bloody, black footprints on the timber, the mixture of blood and the strange darkness in his veins staining the floor as he walked. The sharp shards of glass dug into his skin, but his thoughts were no longer focused on pain. His mind was consumed by something else—something darker. He couldn't explain it, but he didn't need to. All that mattered was that he was moving, moving toward whatever was at the end of this hallway, toward whatever was drawing him deeper into the house.

The hunger inside him gnawed harder. His thoughts were slipping away, replaced by an insatiable need to consume—to feed. What was happening to him? What had changed inside his body? And why did everything feel so... raw? So alive? His senses were heightened, every sound, every smell, every movement around him like an electric pulse that thrummed through his skin. But even as his body pushed forward, his mind remained a blur, the questions clouded by the dark, unrelenting need that consumed him.

The air was thick with an unfamiliar, pungent scent, one that struck Tom's senses like a hammer. It was intoxicating—fresh meat. His nostrils flared as his mind locked onto it, the hunger in his gut growing into a burning, visceral need. It was not just food that called to him; it was something deeper, something darker. A thirst that could not be quenched by anything less than raw, flesh. His body tensed as the hunger surged through him, a dark rage bubbling up from somewhere deep inside, its intensity matching the savage pulse pounding in his chest. He needed to feed. Now.

Tom's breath was ragged, his chest rising and falling in short, desperate gasps. The wheezing from his lungs was almost deafening as he inhaled through his mouth, trying to capture the scent that teased him, the scent of life that beckoned him forward. His eyes narrowed as he focused on the end of the hallway, where a room waited—a room that was filled with something alive. Something meaty. He sniffed again, his senses sharpening, every nerve in his body igniting with the hunger that now consumed him. The aroma of flesh and skin wrapped itself around his mind, driving him further into a frenzy. His blood boiled. The hunger clawed at him from the inside out, so overpowering it felt like his very bones were being consumed.

Without thinking, his feet moved faster. At first, it was a quick walk, a hurried pace, but with every step, the desire grew stronger, faster, more desperate. His heart pounded in his chest, each beat like a war drum urging him forward. He could feel the walls of the cottage closing in around him, the shadows stretching, whispering in his ears, urging him onward. The pace quickened into a jog, then a full-on sprint. His muscles rippled with unnatural strength, his limbs moving faster than they ever had before, as if driven by a force outside of himself. The wooden door at the end of the hallway loomed ahead, and Tom didn't hesitate. His body crashed into it, slamming it off its hinges with a deafening crash, splintering wood flying in every direction. The door flew across the room and hit the far wall with a sickening thud, but Tom was already inside, his eyes locked on the prize before him.

There, in the centre of the room, was the bed. And beneath the duvet, an outline of a person—still, unmoving, completely unaware of the nightmare that had just entered their world. Tom's breath caught in his throat as his instincts took over completely. He growled, a low, animalistic sound vibrating in his chest, his teeth bared in a vicious snarl. He had found it.

Without a second thought, he leapt, his body propelled by something feral, as he covered the distance between him and his target in a single bound. Six feet. He crashed onto the bed, the impact shaking the whole frame, the springs groaning under his weight as he landed. The duvet was no match for him. His hands ripped into the fabric, tearing it apart with savage ferocity, each shred falling away like the skin of a prey animal being stripped clean. His mind was a blur, a singular focus: to expose the meat beneath, to tear into it, to feed.

Saliva pooled in his mouth as his eyes locked onto his meal, his pupils dilated, fixed in an unblinking stare. Every muscle in his body tightened, a coiled spring ready to snap. The scent of flesh was overwhelming, thick and heavy in the air, making his blood run hot with hunger. His hands, shaking with the anticipation of what was to come, reached down, tearing at the duvet, pulling it away in wild, frenzied motions. The warmth of the body underneath, the softness of the skin—it was all within reach, just a few more pulls.

The world narrowed to just this moment. Nothing else existed but the flesh beneath him and the hunger that consumed him. A guttural growl escaped his throat, raw and untamed, as he hunched over the bed, ready to tear into the living, breathing feast that lay just out of his reach.

This was no longer a man in control of his thoughts. This was an animal. Driven by hunger. Driven by rage. And there would be no stopping him.

"You looking for me?"

551

The End

In The Works
The Reckoning - Nukeville Book 2
Benny - Nukeville Book 3
Retribution - Nukeville Book 4

For Updates Come Find Me on Social Media
Facebook – www.facebook.com/nukevillenovels
Instagram - www.instagram.com/nukevillenovels

About The Author

Neil Hannam grew up just outside London, where his love for storytelling took root at an early age. As a teenager, he spent countless hours crafting short stories, weaving intricate tales that sparked his imagination and set the foundation for his future as a writer. Though life led him down a different path for many years, his passion for storytelling never faded.

Over the next three decades, Neil built a diverse career, working across multiple industries throughout the United Kingdom. Yet, no matter how busy life became, he always found time to explore his creative side. In his spare moments, he pursued landscape photography, capturing the beauty of the world through his lens—a visual storytelling medium that complemented his love for the written word.

After thirty years of working and raising a family, Neil finally embraced his lifelong dream and took the plunge into the world of novel writing. His debut book, *Aubrey*, is the gripping first instalment of an all-new zombie apocalypse franchise. This intense prequel follows an escaped convict carving a bloody path across the

South East of England, his ultimate destination—Nukeville Island, a place shrouded in mystery and danger.

With the second book already completed, Neil is now fully immersed in expanding this chilling universe. He is currently working on an additional three novels, each delving deeper into the lives of the characters as they struggle to survive in a post-apocalyptic world teeming with horrors, both undead and human. His work promises to deliver relentless tension, heart-stopping action, and complex characters navigating the collapse of civilisation.

Neil's passion for creative writing has been a lifelong journey, but the courage to finally publish his work stems from the unwavering support of his family and friends. Throughout the years, they have been his greatest champions, encouraging him to take the leap and share his stories with the world. Their belief in his talent, storytelling abilities, and dedication to his craft gave him the confidence to turn his long-held dream into reality.

Now, as he embarks on this exciting new chapter as a published author, Neil remains deeply grateful for those who stood by him. Their belief in his vision fuels his determination to keep writing, crafting immersive worlds and unforgettable characters that captivate readers. His success is not just his own—it is a shared achievement, a testament to the power of encouragement, perseverance, and the people who push us to chase our dreams.